THE DRUMS OF UNREST

THE DRUMS OF UNREST

THE CYCLE OF BONES

JP CORWYN

4 Horsemen
Publications, Inc.

4 Horsemen Publications, Inc.
1497 Main St. Suite 169
Dunedin, FL 34698
4horsemenpublications.com
info@4horsemenpublications.com

Cover by Jeff Brown
Typesetting by Niki Tantillo
Edited by Joseph Mistretta

Library of Congress Control Number: 2023937849

Paperback ISBN-13: 979-8-8232-0182-7
Hardcover ISBN-13: 979-8-8232-0183-4
Audiobook ISBN-13: 979-8-8232-0185-8
Ebook ISBN-13: 979-8-8232-0184-1

DEDICATION

Simple truths are often the hardest ones to hear. They're also among the most complex things to act upon. In my experience, that makes them just about the most important, most meaningful things we ever encounter. Truth—especially simple truth—allows us to catch a glimpse of who, what, where, and why we really are in a given moment. If we're brave enough in that moment, we can find or forge something new out of ourselves.

If truth has that power, then those who *speak* the truth—without malice, arrogance, or ulterior motive—will almost certainly make an impact. That can often be felt by people and in places miles—worlds away without our ever knowing it.

This book, and indeed the entire series, is dedicated to people whom I have never met and, in some cases, never will. Never having met them, however, does nothing to diminish the influence they've had over my life.

With boundless and grateful thanks to Jocko Willink, Leif Babin, and the men of SEAL Team 3, Task Unit Bruiser.

These men were introduced to me through the proverbial lenses of both Leif and Jocko's writings and the rather more literal lenses of the cameras, which have captured their lessons and their lives for posterity. It is by no means an exaggeration to say that without these men, I would be neither who nor where I am today. Among many other important lessons, they reminded me of a truth I'd always espoused but had lost sight of—yes, that was both accurate and a blind joke.

It doesn't matter that you're off the path. What matters is that you get on it now.

~JP Corwyn
Stoke Gifford, United Kingdom
12 November 2020

Elevate your reading adventure!

Dive Into Skolf's Epic Soundscapes with "The Cycle of Bones" Original Soundtracks.

Experience the full depth of JP Corwyn's creation. Immerse yourself amidst haunting voices and the even thunder of battle rhythms. Each track is a journey through the vibrant landscapes and rich tongues of a world both vast and intimate.

From memorable melodies to choruses 'round campfires, the Original Soundtracks are a unique blend of in-world songs and symphonic scores.

Step beyond the page. Bring the world of Skolf to startling, stunning life

Start your journey now. Scan the QR code to visit JP Corwyn's Spotify artist profile, or find 'The Cycle of Bones' soundtracks (and all of your favourite #BlindIndieRock tracks) on Amazon Music Unlimited, Pandora, Google Play, or wherever you stream the music that moves you.

Remember to like, follow, and share.

TABLE OF CONTENTS

PRELUDE

-I-

Venzene Duchy of Kovalun
County Jižní Pochod
Barony of Haluzfeld - Haluz Věže
25 Gerstesykli: 3 days prior to the Red Storm at Westsong

Adelt loved the view from his balcony—the moon-painted forest some two hundred feet below. He stood naked, letting his forearms take most of his weight as he leaned against the broad stone railing. Calling the little lick of sandstone that adjoined his bedchamber *a balcony* was like dressing an Eodenth spearman in silks, but never mind. There was *just* enough room for two... so long as they were in one another's arms.

It might have been the view or the fragrant air of late autumn. *Something* nudged him toward introspection. He felt his smile growing a touch wistful as he mused over the strange path his life had taken. Neither fortune, happenstance, nor predestination had led him to this rarified existence. He'd worked his mind and body to the very rim of ruin to gain—to *earn*—all that he had, and he knew it. Even so, looking down at the pre-winter beauty of his lands made lulling himself into thoughts of serendipity a tempting thing.

"But no," he sighed. "No, luck is the common man's whipping boy. A windfall is *good luck*... a misery is *bad luck*—a *misfortune*. It's all ignorance and shadow." He allowed himself a brief smirk. "Or perhaps ignorance *of* shadow."

As if to chastise him for his dismissal of fate and destiny, the wind rushed suddenly up at him. Despite the brisk air of late autumn, it amused him to find the gust warm and clean. As it did its best to tangle his greying golden hair, he heard Vašík's movement behind him in the bed. His smile broadened.

"Aedelt?" Vašík murmured his name through a half yawn.

"Do you know I'll be fifty next sykli?" Aedelt didn't turn, opting instead to raise his tenor voice so it carried into the room behind him. He found he was in an almost playful mood now—well, as close as he ever got to such childishness. He hadn't been a child quite long enough to master whimsy. Not that that bothered him overmuch. He'd even made *that* serve him well over the years. "You'll officially be half my age, then. I suspect you'll trade me in for a much younger steed before too terribly long."

"I *may*, but I shouldn't let it worry you." Vašík's voice wore the combined finery of playful arrogance and drowsy youth. His slight features and slender frame prevented his voice from displaying any genuine authority. "Who else would keep me in such splendor, *Your Excellency?*"

"Now-now." He made a tsking sound with his tongue against the roof of his mouth. "I know you're only here for the coin, comfort, and social currency I can offer, but do at least *pretend* there's more between us."

He had once prized this youth for his excellent mind and sharp wit as much as his vigor, fine features, and supple body. Such japes had grown less witty, and far less welcome of late. His lover was only teasing, of course. But it'd still stung. He had no intention of letting that show, mind, but he felt the unmeaning cruelty all the same.

Aedelt knew he was in a far better state of health than many men of his age and station. Hells, he was more active than most men of title closer to Vašík's age. For all that, an end to youth and glory was creeping toward him, gaining ground with each passing day. His face had begun to show laugh lines of late. All too soon, those would transform into fully fledged wrinkles. *Time is man's greatest enemy. And no sage strategy or tactic can hope to best such a foe.*

He felt rather than heard Vašík rise and come up behind him. A moment later, arms slipped around his waist as the younger man pressed his cheek to Aedelt's back. "I *am* sorry," his voice sounded earnest, "but truly, if you're going to toss such absurdities into the air, even blind men will eventually crack bat to ball."

He recognized two truths. The first was that Vašík was right. Aedelt had thought he was being playful. In truth, he'd only been seeking sympathy. The second was that, in a matter of moments, his lover would attempt to make him forget such pitiful pangs.

After a delicate interval of silence, his prediction came true. It began with slow kisses along his back, then gently busy hands sliding down below where his belt would've been, were he clothed. His body still managed the old trick—a thing that many men his age could no longer claim. He was just about to turn and leave his long and self-pitying thoughts for warmer, more instinctual ones when something intruded, pawing at his mind.

"Stop." Aedelt's voice came out in a sigh. That was no good. He recognized the sudden sense of alarm scraping against his mind. He'd yet to place the cause or source, but he trusted his instincts.

Taking it for a signal, kisses rained down more rapidly and insistently. He felt hands starting to turn him away from the window, and while he wished very much to give in to those hands, he knew better.

He forced air into his lungs. "Vašík! Stop I say!" This time his voice came out sharp and sure.

"What is it?"

"I don't..." He never finished that sentence. He suddenly smelled smoke and heard what might, at first, have been mistaken for birdsong morph and shift in his ears as the wind carried the sound—the far-too-warm wind. *Not birds—screams.* Women, children, even men all screamed below him.

"My lord!" Rapid thudding on the door accompanied a frantic voice. "Baron Vagiaedelt, waken!"

He turned from the window and strode toward the door, ignoring Vašík as if his lover weren't there.

"I'm awake, Lajos, I assure you." Aedelt's voice had lost all of its recent softness, taking on a knife's edge. He threw open the door, heedless of his nudity, and looked at the young, sweaty-faced squire who stood before him. Aedelt waited a moment as the youth stared, then spoke with a sharpness made keen by what he was certain he'd heard below. "Dammit, boy, you can admire my birthright when things are not so pressing! Report! Now!"

Lajos blinked, flushed with embarrassment and perhaps a touch of rage at the insinuation, and wrenched his eyes upward to meet his lord's. "Excellency, we are attacked!"

"Yes, I can hear that. Now tell me something of use!"

"My lord, they came from nowhere."

"That's a lie." Aedelt shook his head. "Nothing comes from nowhere. You simply haven't determined where they came from yet."

Vašík snorted at this from his perch.

"I..." the squire began, then shook his head before attempting to correct himself. "We think they may have come from the woods based on what we've seen of their gear. They're ragtag and ununiformed, but..." He trailed off, uncertain how to finish.

But what, damn you, boy? They attacked without substantive gear of war. Are they looters? Is that what you mean to say? He kept these thoughts to himself, watching as the squire groped for the right words. Was that burning pitch he smelled? *Havoc's Horn, Lajos! Why did Bolek send you, of all people? You're a freehold farmer's son without so much as a wit to wield—a well-meaning, well-muscled oaf of a boy who should be back at his father's farm, not stood here making me drag a report out of you as my barony burns!*

Aedelt did his best to keep his tone cold and fearful. His anger would only serve to make the already flustered youth impossible to get anything useful out of. But enough was e-damned-nough. "Bandits? Perhaps an organized revolt of peasants? What is it you're saying to me, Lajos?"

"They're in the village, lord. There... There are too many. Too many by scores." He shook his head. "We couldn't *count* them all—there were so many! We've sealed the main gates, stationed archers on the wall-walk, and done all we can to withstand them, but..."

This was absurd. An uprising of rabble like this was put down, not hidden from behind stone and wooden walls. That showed weakness, not strength. It allowed the wretches to take their plunder and go. They needed to be punished for their transgressions, not fled from or endured.

Aedelt did his best to re-summon his oft-vaunted calm. He drew in another deep breath, battling to make himself hold it for a five-count. He managed only three beats before rage found a tiny handhold. Grabbing Lajos by his shoulders, he shook the youth. "Listen to me now." His voice was all but a growl. "You will go inform the captain of the guard to prepare a sortie. I shall attend him as soon as I am properly arrayed for battle."

"Y—Yes, Excellency!" The youth sounded breathy and distant.

Aedelt released his grip on the witless boy's shoulders, allowing a small, wolfish smile to bloom on his face. "See that my horse is saddled and barded. We shall mass in the courtyard and ride out of Haluz Věže together, rolling over them as if we were a landslide from on high. Before the hour is out, we shall drive them from our lands. Now go." The edge in his voice winked out.

Even as he turned away, Aedelt felt his blood pumping, heart racing in anticipation of the battle to come. This—*this* was why he continued. *This* was why he persisted. It was why he took increasingly younger lovers.

He refused every day to give in to the ravages of age, and thus far, he had won nearly every battle against it. Moments like this were proof that he was still on the righteous path. Opportunities to draw his blade for anything other than sparring or the tournament field were as rare as winter roses in the years since the rebellion. Even now, his sword arm begged the familiar violence of battle. Even now, his skin longed to feel the welcome weight of his hauberk, his chain skirt, his gauntlets. After casting about for a moment, he moved to dress.

"But..." Lajos was stammering now. "But, Your Excellency... my lord..."

Aedelt resisted the urge to glare at or strike the youth. He drew himself up, pulled air into the hollow of his chest to expand it, and turned to look down his nose at the squire. It was, he knew, a cold, stony stance that made others intimidated, if not outright afraid of him. He'd used it to cow many an opponent, but he used it as infrequently as he could.

"But *what*?"

"My lord," Lajos gulped rather comically, "their numbers are endless. We cannot ride out to meet them."

"*There,* you are correct. *We,*" Aedelt pointed between himself and the squire, "cannot ride out to meet them. *You* haven't the strength or stomach for it. That much is clear. Fortunately for you, Captain Bolek is made of sterner stuff. Your betters will ride out and defeat this rabble and have done. Now, obey me and inform the captain."

"Excellency..." The youth started to speak but didn't seem to know how to go on. As Aedelt drew breath to rebuke him once more, he finally found his voice. "It's the captain who sent me. He says we are surrounded and besieged."

Aedelt froze in the act of pulling his braies up. This defied reason. "Impossible. We *cannot* be besieged. Beyond the forest below is nothing save open country. We would have *seen* an army on the march toward us, and it would take an army to come anywhere near the size required to besiege this keep!" He was getting angry now. His voice was becoming steely, approaching shrillness.

To Aedelt's right, Vašík spoke from what passed for the balcony. His voice was empty... somehow vacant, as if he were dreaming and speaking in his sleep.

"...I can see them. Hundreds, maybe thousands of torches below us."

Aedelt finished yanking his braies up over his thighs, buttoning them as he strode over to see for himself. His stomach lurched. The forest of ash and pine beneath him now looked as if it were growing out of a mass of writhing earth-spew. The firelights were so numerous, so dense, that it appeared a sea of deep, tumultuous red now surrounded the collection of towers that made up his keep.

He'd almost processed this insanity when a fresh horror made its presence known. He heard drums—dozens, perhaps hundreds of them in the distance. Their break-neck rhythm was insistent but too ordered and deliberate to be accounted frenetic. The sound made it clear that they were growing closer, and at speed.

Looking past the tree line and into the expansive farmland and pasture beyond, he saw an enormous column of horses dragging multiple siege engines in its train. The night was clear, and his eyes still worked better than they had any right to at his age. He could see catapults, rams, and even what looked like a cart full of wood.

Ladders, surely. We're done, Aedelt thought. He was both awed and impressed. Fear wouldn't be long in coming, but for now, the war-wise tactician inside him was racing to confirm what his undermind had already concluded. *I don't know how it's possible, how we didn't see them coming with enough time to do something—anything other than fight and die. Even if they had conspirators to delay word getting to me, an army of that size? Siege engines? We should've seen them on the march hours ago.* He closed his eyes for a beat. A question floated across the stage of his mind's eye, cutting through the awe at how utterly unprepared they were. *Yes, they're here. The question now is how to contend with them.*

"Hells, look at them all," said Vašík. "I shall finally get to see you in your element, *Excellency.*" He was smiling—teasing.

Aedelt ignored him. At this moment, his lover was little more than a chirping bird, a pretty thing to, sadly, be forced into the background.

To hide an army of such size? Even taking sorcery into account, it seems impossible. They're prepared, no doubt provisioned, and the time to call for aid is long past. With no warning, unless peasants escaped the sword and ran for aid, there's no way to get word from here to any nearby baron nor to Edmund. We have enough food to last a month? Perhaps two? But I don't think we'll need it. Given their gear, this won't become a protracted siege. They'll breach our walls ... or the gate. And with their numbers...

"Where..." Aedelt turned to face the soon-to-be-dead boy who delivered Captain Bolek's message. He heard his own voice. It sounded brittle and small, altogether nothing like him. Taking a moment to swallow and compose himself, he tried again. "Where is Aetanis? Where is my son?"

Lajos blinked, clearly confused by the sudden change in subject. Blessedly, he managed to pick up the thread before Aedelt found the need to ask again. "He left this morning, Excellency. He took his personal guard to rendezvous with the count's men for the trek to Zlaté Pole."

Personal guard? Aetanis is sixteen. His so-called personal guard is a pair of grooms his own age. They were chosen either for the way they look, or the way they make him look stood next to them. A decade of plenty has made us—made me soft-headed. I've let my guard down, but, he sighed, *at least he's safe for now.*

His son's first actual battle as a leader might go well or might go ill. However it befell, he would almost certainly be returning to test what skills he'd learned beneath the count's gentle hand in the battle to retake what remained of Haluzfeld. He wondered idly if anything would remain of his keep, Haluz Věže, itself.

Leaving the balcony, he returned to the act of dressing. Speaking with a calm and authority he did not at this precise moment feel, he addressed Lajos again. "Tell the captain I am dressing and armoring and will be down directly. Tell him he is to do everything in his power to minimize casualties within the walls until I arrive, and we can make a plan and set a stratagem. Am I understood?"

"Yes, my lord." He straightened, clearly affected by the reassurance he must have thought he'd heard in Aedelt's voice. He bowed and charged back down the stairs.

"You don't think we're going to survive, do you?"

Aedelt slid on his right boot, completing the set, and stood to don his padded gambeson. He turned it in his hands to ensure that it was facing the correct direction before lifting it to draw down over his chest and shoulders. Finally, despite the fact that he wanted to do anything else, he spoke the truth.

"No, we won't. Not unless they take slaves. I don't know who they are, but given the drums, I suspect they're from Eoden—Eoalun, I mean."

Aedelt felt the younger man's eyes on him as he continued armoring up, attaching his chain skirt before donning his breastplate.

For a long moment, Vašík made no reply. Finally, he found his voice. "I'll kill them before I let them take you, Aedelt."

Aedelt was pleased that his back was to the man. He was touched, amused, fearful, and taken aback all at a go.

"I'm serious. No horse-humping, orc-bedding, raiding, pillaging lout will take you away from me, will take this away from us. You have my oath."

He'd never heard this tone, never seen this side of Vašík before. He was gratified, certainly, but more than a little surprised. As he tightened the last few straps of his carapace, he nodded, turning to rake his eyes over the still nude form before the balcony. Vašík had apparently turned to face the room as he'd delivered his pronouncement. Aedelt couldn't decide if the young man's nakedness undercut or underpinned the weight of his words. *There'll be time enough to think about that later.* He turned back to remove his helm from his armor stand, placing it on the bed.

When he spoke in answer, his tone was dry but warm. "Then, brave Vašík, might I recommend you find some armor? And a sword made of something other than pork?"

"*Believe* me, I intend—"

There was a sudden thump. Then two more in rapid succession from somewhere outside. Aedelt stiffened, knowing the sound for what it was—knowing there was no time to do anything about it. An instant later, the world filled with the muscular, crunching sound of a boulder as it shattered his former balcony. Its force sent the wall crumbling down, crushing the younger man where he stood.

Catapults. He managed to close his eyes just as the stone struck. He concentrated on burning the image of his now-former lover into his mind's eye.

When the dust cleared, after a brief coughing fit had subsided, he surveyed the remnants of his once lovely bed-chamber.

A few candles beside his only exit flickered in the dusty air, but it was enough light to mourn by. Nothing remained unaffected. The boulder had sent debris to all points. Its grey waste covered every surface.

His armor stand—an exquisite thing, not unlike a dressmaker's false form—wobbled as he watched. For an ephemeral moment, it spun on its round metal base, turning as if to regard him with its blank, empty gaze.

His eyes fell upon the wreck of his outer wall—of his other life. There was nothing left of his once-lover. He saw no hand, no foot, no flesh peeking out beneath the mass of rubble. No. No, there *was* something.

As the stand continued to wobble, fighting bravely to resist Skolf's pull and remain upright, he saw a red trail of blood run out from beneath the shattered stones. He steeled himself, nostrils flaring as he fought to keep control.

"No time. I have no time for the dead. The living still need me." He squared his jaw and forced his eyes away.

As if in response to his decision, the armor stand, at last, succumbed to the world's overwhelming force. It fell to the ground and rolled away from him, coming to rest with its head far too near the trickle of blood.

The first to fall, that I know of. Was he weeping? *Well, never fear, pretty boy, I shan't be long. I expect we'll all be right behind you.*

How they'd set their engines so swiftly, let alone how they'd known which room in which tower had been his, were mysteries he doubted he'd live long enough to solve, but time would tell.

"I know," he said aloud. "Still, I breathe. I live, and *while* I live..."

He found and belted on his sword, threw his gloves and gauntlets into his helm, and bolted from the room and its gruesome scene.

-II-

Venzene Duchy of Kovalun
County Jižní Pochod
Barony of Hartscross - Západní Hlídka
26 Gerstesykli: 2 days prior to the Red Storm at Westsong

Eobum gave a light cough. As his eye swept down over the valley, he leaned his hip against the weathered-looking boulder to his right. His hair had long since begun to run away from his face. Out of pure habit, he ran a hand through the rich brown crop still left to him, as if sweeping it back from his brow. The wind gusted, blowing tendrils of smoke up from the valley below as he considered.

A sudden movement to his right drew his attention. Glancing sidelong at his son, he stifled a smirk. The boy sat cross-legged atop the boulder. That same wind had done its best to knock his small hood back, forcing him to bring a hand up to keep it in place.

"Do you know their names?" The boy broke the protracted silence, no longer willing, or perhaps no longer able, to simply sit in wonder. Staring at the three settlements smoking in the twilit valley below, he made his voice respectful and soft despite the slight, scratched growl that always pervaded it. After a moment during which only the wind spoke, he amended, "Or would it be better to ask, do you know what their names *were*?"

Eobum was, as usual, content to allow the silence to play out for a few beats before he answered. The tactic gave others time to say more, if more came to mind, and gave *him* time to consider his own reply. At length, he shook his head. "Nooo..." The word was carried on a soft sigh that had more to do with the scene's innate sadness than the boy's questions. "They'll be back. All three of them will rebuild. They've been raided, not razed to the ground."

"But..." The boy shook his head, face pinched as he tried to understand. "But all three villages are on fire or at least but lately were. They're still smoking!"

Eobum was amused, as always, at the look of intense focus his son wore. That look, coupled with the coarse, dark brown—nearly black—length of his hair, pale green skin, and small lower tusks that jutted just over his upper lip, would've made him appear predatory and dangerous were he older. On a boy his age, however, this combined heritage produced a look that was more adorable mimicry than aggressive malice.

"*What?*"

"Nothing," said Eobum. He tried to keep his voice mild and fought down a grin with admirable success.

"No, *not* nothing. I see the way you mark me from the side of your eye."

The man's dark brows lifted for a moment, but he continued to say nothing.

"Well?"

"Well, what?"

"Fa-therrrr..." His voice was a study in amused frustration.

He watched his son try to maintain his look of fierce concentration—working to turn it into one of annoyance or even anger. He suspected the boy wouldn't be able to resist the fit of laughter bubbling up inside of him for much longer. He opted to help the process along.

"Laaa-kriiid..." He dragged the boy's name out, mimicking the way he'd said "Father," wrestling his normal raven's-caw tones into something more playful.

It turned the trick. A snort, followed by several bursts of laughter, escaped into the evening air. Judging by the look on his face, Lakkrid hadn't so much given *into* laughter as he'd been *ambushed* by it. It was almost as if the act were a source of embarrassment.

After each bout of giggles, he tried to regain his composure with limited success. This made each little eruption of mirth increasingly more hysterical and uncontrolled than the last.

The laughter and the accompanying look of comical self-recrimination plastered onto the boy's face forced his father's own laughter—a single, loud caw, followed by a slow, rolling baritone rumble.

When the boy's hysterics subsided at last, Eobum set about answering his questions.

"All right?"

Lakkrid was still grinning as he nodded.

"All right. The peasants and serfs here build with rough, stacked stones, not wood and thatch like Eoden or Lesalun, nor wattle and daub like Gerstealun. Raids hurt, of course, especially if there's bravery involved, as it usually means someone dies. Even so, I doubt there'll have been enough damage or burning to make them give up on their settlements altogether."

"And stone doesn't fear fire," Lakkrid mused. "So, what is it that's burning, then? What did the raiders set fire to?" He wore a transported expression. Lessons like this always seemed to draw him in.

"Stone doesn't fear fire," Eobum agreed, "but it also doesn't like heights. Once you take it out of the mountain's arms or pluck it up from the ground, it's always in a rush to find Skolf again." He caught the boy's grin at this imagery and allowed himself a small smile of his own. His son had a hungry mind, to be sure.

"So," Lakkrid sounded thoughtful, "if stone's eager to fall—roofs!" The triumph in his voice was evident. "They'd have to build their roofs out of something they could brace—something longer! They'd use timber? Fashioned into rafters and... and planks?"

"Just so."

Lakkrid seemed to draw himself up, almond eyes going to half-mast as he beamed. After a long silence, he recalled his other, still unanswered, question. "And their names? Do you know them?"

"This one's Železné Oko. There, on the left? That one's Bílá Vidlička. The farthest one, back and to the right? That's Píseň Borovic or Borovicová Hudba—I can't recall which. Iron Eye, White Fork, and Pine Song or Pine Music." He pointed to each one a second time as he translated. He saw Lakkrid stiffen slightly. He'd heard the footsteps, *too*, then. Keeping the same mild tone, he concluded, "Kovalun's mother tongue has always sounded beautiful, even when it's butchered."

"Awh, ee don' know about that." This new voice was carried on wind that sounded as if it'd gusted up from a barrel chest. "Een da mouth off-an outziderr, it sounds more like da vork off-a drunken baladeerr." He rolled his Rs on the words *outsider*, *more*, and *drunken*. The newcomer sounded jovial enough, but there was a tone of mingled greed and authority in the air.

As Eobum turned to face the owner of that voice, he put his left hand on Lakkrid's far shoulder, urging him to turn as well. "My name's Eobum, friend."

A forest of pines and yew trees loomed up as they turned, filling the world with green shadows. Four men stood along the tree line, a dozen strides of bare rock separating them from Eobum and Lakkrid.

He'd expected the speaker to have a beard just *slightly* thicker than his accent, and he wasn't disappointed. The four of them were all coal-maned and bearded, pale-skinned, and broad-shouldered. Hard times appeared to have made them lean beneath their furs and layered burlap clothing, though.

"My son and I were just going to set about making supper." He paused for a moment, as if considering, then shrugged his brows as if to say *what the hells.* "You and yours are welcome to share our fire. We haven't a vévodův feast in tow, but we do have meat—a pair of hoppers caught this morning. I can stretch that out into a stew that should feed the lot of us..."

All four men licked their lips at this offer. They clearly weren't hunters of even a *child's* skill. Small game was plentiful here, after all. That wasn't the only tale their body language told.

They held no formation to speak of—stood in a loose and untidy clump at the edge of the makeshift campsite. Their leader—or perhaps he was only their mouthpiece, time would tell—stood with his three fellows more or less surrounding him. While this proximity made their collective look like a milling pack of hunting predators, Eobum suspected it was as much for their comfort as for any such cultivated imagery. Certainly, it would intimidate the average serf or peasant, but no fighting man or woman would be cowed.

"Yindrich." This was the same voice that had originally spoken.

When he didn't bother to introduce his comrades, Eobum con-cluded that yes, he must account himself their leader, and they, his loyal servants. He expected they were the same men who'd been on a spree here in southern Kovalun, burning and looting wherever they found something worth risking their necks to take.

Four men acting even in loose concert could intimidate most vil-lages into giving up the sweat of their collective brows. *And it's possible,* he reminded himself, *that these men may be part of a larger, more well-or-ganized group.* They were awfully lean, which meant they might be under the thumb of another. *We'll hope not, but time'll tell that tale.*

"Your *son*?" Yindrich's delighted smile as Lakkrid lifted his face to gaze upon the newcomers was accompanied by a look of dark satisfaction. His voice became a rumbling croon. "Ee'll break bread and take tribute from *any* Orc raper, aye boys?" He continued to roll his Rs and broke the word *aye* into two syllables: ay-yuh.

Eobum felt Lakkrid's shoulder tense beneath his left hand but was pleased to see that the boy's face still showed a calm, not-quite-idle curiosity toward the newcomers.

"No tribute," Eobum said in a mild, thoughtful tone. "These are free lands for camping and small game, far as I've heard. Volně přístupné pozemky vévodové, není-liž pravda?" In the Trader's Tongue, this ran as *The Duke's free lands, right?* "Still..." he paused, sliding his hand down from his son's shoulder along the boy's right arm. "Our offer to share the fire, food, and fellowship holds," he paused, during which Eobum looked down at his son, then swiftly up to meet Yindrich's gaze, "even *after* you call my son a bastard and me a raper."

The bandit's eyes widened, then narrowed. Here, at last, was the danger Eobum had first sensed behind the man's false jocularity.

"You're Eodenth..." Yindrich's voice came out in a growl of mingled disgust and excitement.

Eobum knew that look—could almost read the run of the man's thoughts. Food was good, tribute and respect were better, but violence? That was best of all. Violence usually led to all of that and much, much more.

To his men, Yindrich said, "You know, lads, Gerstealun men busy demselves vith da sheep when it's cold and lonely. Eodenth men get bred by da horses, till dey learn to outrun dem." He grinned, showing a mouth full of ruined teeth—grey and chipped. As his men laughed at his witticism, he met Eobum's eye and continued, "Dey're *often* getting kicked in da head by their four-legged masters. Vhen dey finally *do* learn dat dey're meant to ride da *horses*, not da other vay 'round, dey're so addled that they can't tell Orc women from Eodenth."

At this, his men roared with the hearty tones of folk too afraid of reprisal to do anything else.

Eobum doubted his son could squint his ears tightly enough to have translated Yindrich's accent into the Trade Tongue, which was just as well. One normally didn't squint with anything other than eyes, but he couldn't think of a better word for the act required to sort through the man's words.

Hells, even *he'd* had difficulty by the end. Yindrich had replaced nearly all the TH sounds with Ds, Zs, or buzzing Ss, and had rolled his Rs with such abandon that Eobum would've had an easier time understanding him if he'd just spoken in Kovalunth and had done.

Yindrich turned his predator's eyes on Lakkrid. He adopted a near-avuncular tone as he concluded. "Anda now, boy, you knowa da truth about your father. Heeza fast on his feet, ee've no doubt, and too blind to tell tusk from tree-tart."

Eobum inwardly thanked all the gods that ever were that he hadn't taught the boy much Kovalunth yet. Still, your foes usually showed you their throats when their confidence was high, and Yindrich had been no exception.

Eobum made a show of gripping at the leather vambrace Lakkrid wore—a soft thing he'd made for him a few seasons back. As he did so, he spoke to Yindrich in a voice that began with a snort and ended with a calculated note of mockery. "Yindrich: polokrevný mluvíš." (Yindrich: a halfbreed talking.)

The chorus of derisive laughter froze before it could further pollute the air. Yindrich's henchmen looked on with faces that expected bloodshed to follow. They were right, of course.

"Vhat? Vhat do you say to me?!" Yindrich's voice was sudden thunder.

Eobum shrugged, supremely unconcerned. The effect was somewhat spoiled as he continued fiddling with the part of Lakkrid's vambrace Yindrich couldn't directly see. He would see the fidgeting, not-quite-nervous movement, of course, but not the specifics of what Eobum was actually doing. "Měli o tobě pravdu, Yindrichi, polokrevný." He nodded, face and tone seeming helpful rather than antagonistic. "Napůl hovno, napůl blázen." *(They were right about you, Yindrich, the halfbreed. Half shit, half a fool.)*

Yindrich roared his outrage and drew either a very long knife or a very short sword from somewhere on the back of his belt. He drew it inverted, in fact, so that the blade depended from the *bottom* of his clenched fist.

"Nikdo se se mnou nebaví takhle!" *(Nobody speaks to me like that!)* He half-ran, half-lumbered toward Eobum, weapon held high over his right shoulder, blade pointed forward, ready to stab.

Eobum saw Yindrich's eyes flit to where he was still fiddling with the inside of Lakkrid's right forearm. While it gave him some satisfaction to see the brigand had fallen for his baiting jibe and physical ruse, it paled in comparison to the sense of savage pride that flared up within him over

Lakkrid's reaction. He could feel the boy tense up, obviously and justifiably afraid. He was coiled, preparing to move, but that reaction wasn't on open display.

Time for pride and praise later, Eobum thought. He raised his voice and spoke a single word in a high, clear tone. "Eranoric!"

Four thuds came in rapid succession. The first three accompanied a trio of azhkasts—short spears slightly heavier than javelins—as they pierced Yindrich in his left thigh, left shoulder, and right forearm. They'd struck with such vigor that even the brigand's wild movements couldn't dislodge them from his dirty flesh. The azhkasts bounced and wobbled as he gasped and howled through a final two strides. The fourth thud came as Yindrich fell face-first to the ground. He stopped moving perhaps a yard in front of where Eobum and Lakkrid respectively still stood and sat.

"Throw down," Eobum said to the others. His voice was even and undramatic, though it held no room for further discussion.

He watched as the three remaining brigands, highwaymen, or however they styled themselves, looked about. They saw no attackers. There was the man and his boy. There was the forest of pines, oaks, and firs they, themselves, must've come through. Now that forest lay dusk-stained ... dotted with pools of shadow too innumerable to count. There was their chieftain wearing wounds full of Eodenth spears. All of this, they could see. They simply couldn't count or size up the threat.

"Run, and you'll only die tired," Eobum said. "It's no great matter to me, mind you."

They looked at one another, then at Yindrich, then did as they'd been bidden. Two daggers, a gnarled yew club, and from the leanest and shortest among them, a crude bag full of sharp stones were all tossed in the place where a fire had once been destined to burn.

"Damned shrewdies," a voice came from the tree line. A moment later saw a youngish man with a bone-deep tan and ribbons of black hair streaming back from his brow walking toward them. "I'd hoped they'd run."

Eobum grunted, cleared his throat, and crouched in front of Yindrich.

"Don't leave us just yet, Yindrich. His Excellency, Syr Edmund of Hartscross, will want the pleasure of your company ... and that of your men, at least for a little while. I'd hate to disappoint him."

Yindrich tried to spit, but couldn't manage it. Instead, he sprayed a muddy curd of spittle and dust over his own bearded chin. A few droplets landed near Eobum's feet.

Eobum pulled a thick piece of what would have served for kindling had they lit the evening's fire, holding it out parallel to Yindrich's mouth. "Bite down. I'm going to pull out the spears."

Yindrich glared but did as bidden. A moment later and he'd cracked the stick between his gritted teeth as Eobum did his work.

The black-haired newcomer quirked a brow, offering a grin to match. "Gonna let him live after what he said?"

"*You're* the one who let him live, Adric. You hit his forearm when you could have hit his neck or side." Eobum grinned up at the younger man, handing over one of the azhkasts.

"Aye, well, Eranoric insisted we wanted 'em 'live." Adric's grin widened, showing a yellow picket of teeth.

Eobum nodded, looking up briefly toward the tree line where the remaining nine members of his band had emerged from their hiding places. The grey-templed Eranoric slowed his pace to stalk in their wake. Eobum was unsurprised to see the man's head swiveling this way and that, on guard for trouble he doubted was on the come. True, it was better to be careful than to be a corpse, but Eobum was as certain as may be that these four were the sum total of Yindrich's raiding party.

The man had spoken of tribute. Normally, larger groups of raiders acted as if they were a kind of shadow-nobility. They claimed a territory and wanted all settlers and all travelers to know it. Yindrich hadn't followed that unspoken rule. He hadn't even claimed the lands as his own. He'd just demanded tribute.

All things concerned, Eobum thought things had gone off about as well as hope could hazard. Adric spoke as if reading his thoughts.

"Aye, worked a treat, I'd say. You called it right enough."

Eobum grinned as he saw Yindrich's eyes widen.

"Been tracking you for three days," he said as he removed the final spear from the prostrate man's thigh. "Your raiding's done."

Yindrich's disbelief was evident, but it didn't stay stamped on his face for very long. The blood loss as each azhkast was pulled free had finally taken its toll. Even as Eobum staunched the wound he'd just reopened, his patient lapsed into unconsciousness.

"Ahh, they look so sweet when they're asleep, don' they?" Adric's tone was that of a doting mother looking over a sleeping infant. "Makes it so you almost don't want 'em to wake up ... *ever.*"

Eobum ignored him. He produced a length of cloth from his pouch and tied it around the brigand's leg, then bound his hands behind him before rolling him onto his back.

"Bind the others," he said as he glanced back up at Adric. "Best we get them ready to move sooner rather than later."

Adric nodded, moving to see to it when a voice stopped him.

"Father?"

Eobum looked over his shoulder to where Lakkrid still sat on the boulder. Adric followed suit.

"Does this mean we won't be getting stew tonight?"

WORDS IN THE WOODS

-I-

Venzene Duchy of Kovalun
County Jižní Pochod
Barony of Hartscross - The Ash March
28 Gerstesykli: Night of the Red Storm at Westsong

The sun was almost down. A lead-colored sky hurled a persistence of raindrops with enough speed and force to sting the skin. The storm seemed to have perfected its angles of attack, scoring strikes in eyes, up noses, and in mouths and ears. The biting rain found its wintry way past clothing and armor, unerringly targeting all the most miserable places to douse.

Such weather often felt like malice. It was apt to make the lonely soul caught in it feel they'd angered some god or ancestor. That was ridiculous, of course. But knowing that did little to chase the idea away.

Eobum sat beneath an oldish pine tree, letting its needles diffuse the rain as best they could. He kept one eye on their captives, the other on his men as they went about their business.

The notion that some god or other's behind every little lament? That someone or something's been waiting for the perfect time to add that extra touch of misery to the day? He allowed himself a thin grin. *Self-import and self-pity all in one mug. Aye, that's an easy enough ale to drink.* He wasn't worried overmuch. There *was* a balm to soothe such pangs, after all. It shouldn't be much longer.

They'd been traveling for two days with their quartet of captives, and he'd thought things had gone well enough when he'd rolled beneath his hides last night. His perspective hadn't been so optimistic this morning.

The looming, grey gloom wouldn't have been such an annoyance had they not started their march beneath its threat before dawn. There'd been precious little wind, and the promise of rain had hung over them all day. It was almost a relief when the cloudburst came at last. They'd found a likely enough clearing, unpacked and unfurled their hides, and the sky had simply ... *opened.*

The prisoners had been even less helpful than expected. They'd spent much of the day dragging their feet, moving as slowly as they dared, which was no surprise. Once the storm started, their already grim moods worsened in a hurry. Skin-soaked and sullen, their unhappy condition added more weight to their collective grudge.

Makes a certain amount of sense, I suppose. We answer to Edmund, and he answers to the Emperor of Ashes. Eobum took a short pull from his waterskin to stop himself from snorting. *Even the weather must serve the crown's will, they say. If we fail to make the correct offerings to ensure that sun and storms would serve to speed us along, the fault is ours.* The idea was so much nonsense, but it was funny how often weather seemed to thwart the swift deliverance of whatever men currently considered justice.

He looked around the makeshift camp and did his best to stave off the sigh threatening to escape him. *Things aren't really as bad as all that, anyroad. We've seen worse. And there'll be hot food soon enough, with fellowship to follow.*

They'd been wise enough to pick up kindling and likely candidates for tonight's firewood throughout the day. Dry wood be damned; if not for Aldhelm, they might still be trying to coax the fire into existence, even now.

At twenty-seven, Alusc Aldhelm was older than most of them, save Eranoric and, of course, Eobum himself. He was formidable enough but lacked the natural ferocity to be a truly great combatant. The man's own work ethic had seen him through Eranoric's combat training, but he was a hunter more than a warrior. Neither his trail-craft nor his cooking ever ceased to amaze. The lads both loved and respected him for those gifts, and, for him, that seemed to be enough.

Perhaps half a bell back up the hourglass, Aldhelm had erected a small pavilion–an irenden—to shelter their modest fire. Literally translated from Eodenth as *Burning Home* or *Fire Home*, this crude construction included four spears driven into the ground, with a cover of canvas stretched tight between them and bound with twine. The irenden served two purposes. It diffused the smoke—making it difficult to spot at range—and provided a measure of shelter from the elements.

After that, starting the fire hadn't been too terribly difficult. Keeping it *going*, however, even under their irenden, had proven almost impossible for a time. No matter what direction they'd tried to block the rain from, its partner in crime—the wind—would always find a way through or else shift direction entirely.

Once the wind and rain had played their little trick for a third time, Aldhelm had stood and moved off to where his pack was. For a moment, it looked as if he'd planned on giving up supper as a bad job, but Eobum knew better.

Alusc had returned with several rolled bundles of what turned out to be linen. He handed them out to the three men stood at north, west, and south of the fire. He then reached into a pouch at his belt and withdrew several small hooks hewn of bone. They'd had eyelets carved into one end. He'd passed them out two to a man. He then produced twine and the knife, quickly cutting pieces that he measured against the length of his forearm.

Aldhelm instructed the men to unfurl the linen rectangles, place the hook ends through eyelets sewn into one of the shorter ends of the cloth, and thread the twine through the eyelet ends of the hooks. That done, the hooks were affixed above the canvas roof and tied to the spear furthest away from them. After tying off each piece at the bottom as well, the construction was complete. The net effect was that the irenden now had three walls, providing a runoff for the rain as it fell.

This preparedness was yet one more reason the men half-believed the stories about him.

For a while, they thought him a sorcerer—their Aldhelm. A wytchemand he was not, but Eobum had to admit it. The not-quite cradle tale that fancied him saving both body and soul from the crushing despair of the road because he was a wytchemand given to ensorcell both bread and beer? It was a pretty story.

Eobum expected they would all have enough to eat, and invariably someone or other would remark on how surprising it was to take such comfort from simple, humble food. They'd be honest when they said it, but it wouldn't change the fact that this was an old story, so to speak. They were always a touch more miserable before a meal. And often surprised at how much better they felt once Aldhelm had *worked his magic.*

"Bowls!" The wytchemand in question's gruff voice was a welcome counterpoint to the sound of rain on everything.

The call pulled Eobum out of his long thoughts. He watched as, one by one, his men lined up, making certain that they could see the prisoners. These latter sat huddled and sullen beneath a ragged square tent—hands bound tightly at the wrists.

Lakkrid queued up with the others. Eobum was pleased if unsurprised to see that neither the boy's hunger nor the men around him ushered him to the front of the line, nor did they relegate him to the back. He took a share like everyone else, receiving no special treatment for either his age or the position of leadership his father held.

Once he'd gotten his measure of food, Lakkrid came over to sit down at Eobum's side beneath the pine tree. He reached into a pouch at his belt and fished out a spoon. Plunging it into the stew, he picked up a chunk of meat far too big to be contained by the spoon's bowl. It balanced precariously, threatening to dive back into the broth from whence it had been so unceremoniously wrested, but Lakkrid was not to be undone. With a look of obvious relish, he moved the spoon toward his mouth, opened that mouth into the wide caricature only children are capable of, and froze in place. His eyes cut toward Eobum, and he closed his mouth, turning to face him.

"Father? Have you already eaten?" His voice was quiet, laced with dawning confusion.

Eobum shook his head a single time.

"Why not?"

"Not very hungry," said he. That might've ended the matter, but His stomach chose that moment to offer a muted rumble.

Lakkrid looked at him with obvious disbelief.

"D'you want me to get you a bowl?"

Eobum shook his head and inwardly counted his blessings. At least the boy was soft-spoken. Still, his upturned face made it clear he wasn't about to let the matter go just yet.

"Who leads here?" Eobum, too, kept his voice right-sized for a private conversation. He wasn't whispering, but unless someone was specifically trying to listen in, both the volume of his words and the omnipresent rain would make it difficult for anyone to overhear.

"You do." Lakkrid knew the answer but didn't understand the context.

"I do. That's right." Eobum took a moment to see whether his son would cut the threads of this lesson on his own but was unsurprised when he continued to look confused. His bowl of stew, hovering spoon, and its freight of meat were momentarily forgotten.

"I ... don't understand."

"I lead here. That means I'm responsible for these men. That means I eat last on nights like this. It means I make certain that all the others have gotten food in them before I take my share."

"But... But I've never seen you do that before. You always eat with the rest of us."

Eobum grinned. He said nothing for a long moment, letting the silence play out to see what else Lakkrid would uncover or remember. His patience paid off a moment later.

The boy's pale green face lit with dawning comprehension. "But we have more prisoners than usual. And... and... ahhhh! We have to march at a good pace if we're going to take them to the count before he leaves for tournament. Is that why??"

Eobum nodded. "Just so. I still have trail food in my pack, and if there isn't enough of Aldhelm's stew left for me to have a share, I'll eat that. It'll keep me going. It just won't be anywhere near as hearty or delicious."

"So that means..." Lakkrid once more wore that pinched, intense look of concentration. "That means almost everybody will have eaten well enough to be sharp—to be sure the prisoners don't escape. It means that we can deal with anything else that blocks our path tomorrow, and you won't starve." He nodded, looking thoughtful. A beat later, he seemed to relax.

With no long thoughts left between him and his prize, Lakkrid finished the chore of transporting his first bite of stew into his waiting mouth. As he was chewing, he seemed to come to a decision. His spoon dove again into the wooden bowl balanced on his lap. But instead of bringing it to his waiting mouth, he lifted it high and proffered it to his father.

"It's all right," Eobum said. "There's every chance there'll be enough left. Growing boys need to eat."

"No, Father. Take at least this bite."

"Lakkrid..." Eobum began, but the boy cut him off abruptly.

"*Father*, it's important that you eat. Now, do as I ask, please."

Eobum's brows shot up, but he leaned forward to do as requested.

"How was that?" Lakkrid's tone seemed both pleased and apprehensive.

"Delicious, as always."

"No, not *that*!"

Eobum blinked.

"I was practicing being a leader. How did I do? Did... Did I do it right?"

Eobum's grin shone out like sun after storms. He nodded, reaching his right hand over to give a gentle squeeze to the back of the boy's neck. Lakkrid might have been considered a touch too old for such behavior, but only just. Even still, it did his heart good to see the example he'd tried to set reflected back at him.

Resisting the urge to chuckle, he spoke his reply. "You did, at that."

-II-

Eobum suddenly awoke. He didn't open his eyes, nor did he move in any other appreciable way. Whatever dreams he'd been enjoying or enduring (he couldn't remember which) were replaced by the dripping, frigid, post-downpour world with the speed of a snapping finger.

He was leaning against a tree in a half-seated position. His hood was pulled down over his forehead and drawn taut, shading his eyes and nose from most of the worst this night's weather offered. He smelled the smoke of the low-burning fire. It was dry and altogether pleasant. That meant the fire's current fuel had been going for some time, and he'd been asleep for that same time. Were that not the case, the smoke would have that telltale wet smell as an undercurrent. Wet wood smoked and produced a thick, dirty steam as the fire did its work. Dry wood produced something more aromatic and less gag-inducing.

He heard a growling sigh from somewhere near the fire. It was a feral sound Eobum knew well. He noted the tiniest hitch in that exhalation, hard on the heels of another twig snap. That snap had come from outside their encampment. *That* had been what'd wakened him.

He listened for a moment longer to see if anyone else was sitting by the fire, but finally decided that his brother was alone. Rising, therefore, Eobum moved forward. His knee made an audible pop as he bent it, which, to him, sounded as loud as a pine knot shattering in a fire, and he inwardly cursed.

The flames had burned down low. Despite the wind and rain's every attempt to force it to gutter, the cheerful orange of the dinner blaze had seemed bright in the early hours of dark. Now it burned down to a pale yellow.

The irenden had been taken down at some point during the night. He could just make out the orc's silhouette, as expected, a crisp shadow back-lit by the fire's glow. The sight made him smile.

Eobum made a bit of deliberate noise as he came up to his brother's right. He sat perpendicular to him, settling himself cross-legged, hands on his knees.

"Ol nalg, Ng," the orc offered. "Aehe erld lak? Vra gak awka Feldish lash." *(The darkness is quiet, Elder. Why are your eyes open? It's the heart of the night, and the sun's light is far off.)*

Eobum grinned, looking his brother up, then down as if gauging his mood.

In the wavering glow of the yellow fire, the otherwise deep-green skin looked nearer to black. If his skin was black, however, then the orc's hair was rough-spun midnight. As Eobum's gaze lingered, the orc offered a shallow grin. As so often happened, it left the impression that his two lower tusks moved in parallel to the mildly porcine shape of his nose. This was a false sense of perspective, of course.

"Ord, Fenglem," said Eobum. He spoke the tongue with easy familiarity. "Nalgmsh, dish lash—ord." *(Hunting, Fenglem. Night's sleep or sun's gift—hunting.)*

Fenglem nodded, allowing that ghost of a grin to linger. He reached up to scratch his right temple. Before he lowered the long fingers of his hand again, he'd flicked and pulled on his right earlobe.

Eobum sighed, dropped his head as if still eager to sleep, then looked back up to meet Fenglem's eyes. The gesture had been a protracted nod of sorts. After a moment, Eobum reached across to where the firewood had been laid aside. As his body bent to the right, pulling off several top layers of wood as—if inspecting them and rejecting them one by one—he moved the fingers of his left hand against the ground, against his left knee.

Noise, if you see this.

"At least the rain stopped," Fenglem said in the Trade Tongue.

Eobum continued to move the fingers of his left hand, making rather a business of selecting a log for the fire. The ability to communicate complex ideas through sign was all but non-existent. Of course, there were those who *could* do it, but neither Eobum nor his fellows were among them. They were, however, able to communicate basic to middling concepts without speech. It was a trick they'd used when scouting or hunting almost since the beginning. It was Fenglem's people who'd developed the sign, but he wasn't proficient enough to go beyond this level of functionality. Given he'd taught his younger brother Haiga and nephew Lakkrid, neither were they.

I hear one. How many do you hear?

"Pull a second log, Ng. The night will not get warmer."

Two intruders in the woods outside of camp, then. Eobum continued his silent, signed conversation.

One to the east, the other north?

Clearing sleep from his throat, Eobum lifted a log and inspected it as he awaited Fenglem's reply.

"Not that one." Fenglem kept his voice gruff, as if he were not accustomed to the Trade Tongue.

Moving the fingers of his left hand again, Eobum selected a new log with his right.

West?

"Better. Will burn long."

Eobum pulled that particular log away from the others. So, one from the east and another near where the prisoners were now peacefully sleeping. It might've been a rescue attempt, but he didn't think so. He leaned back over to select the second log, and as he began rifling through them, he again signed with his left hand.

You or me?

"Build the fire, Ng." And with that, Fenglem stood and moved off toward the west.

-III-

Fenglem scowled at his own foolishness. They needed to catch one or both of these skulking folk decisively. Frightening them off would only invite them to be on their guard when they came back. Killing them might or might not be necessary, but if they killed only one, the other would have the same cause to be wary.

And that makes them more dangerous, he thought. No, his plan *had* been sound, walk off to attend his necessary—actually do so if he could manage it—but if not, he could make do with a slow pour from his waterskin. And therein lies the problem. He'd left his skin by the fire. If he went back for it now and the stalkers were watching, as surely they must be, it would look suspicious.

I'm getting in my own way—overthinking. He shook his head, snorting lightly. *I'm growling at my own mistake, then calling a candle a bonfire.*

He turned, planning to retrieve the skin—why in hells not?—when a voice called out to him.

"Orku! *Psst!* Heya Orku! Potřebuji srát—Cam onna—Potřebuji srát!" It was one of the prisoners.

Fenglem arched his brows and walked toward the ragged, open tent where the wretches were housed.

"What do you say?" Again, Fenglem opted to speak in a more broken form of the Trade Tongue than was anywhere close to necessary. It'd been one of Eobum's earliest lessons after Istjuk's fall—proven right again and again. It was always best to let an enemy underestimate your ability to think or understand.

"Potřebuji srát!" the man offered, voice insistent but trying to keep quiet. "Shita! I needa to shita!" The tone was more urgent than embarrassed. He clearly had no interest in waking up his fellows.

Well, Fenglem thought, *that solves my problem nicely.* He stepped into the tent, pulled a dagger with one hand, and reached down with the other to haul the bound man to his feet. He walked him to the west, into the wood line. Unbinding the fellow's dim hand, Fenglem bound the other end of the rope to his own wrist.

Angered—using that to cover his embarrassment—the man set about taking care of his necessary. He accomplished the humble act of dropping his pants with the awkward motion of someone far more used to two hands than one. Then he squatted against a tree.

Fenglem did his best to block out the grunts and sighs of relief made by the prisoner. He also did his best to block out the smell. It wasn't that it was especially bad, all things concerned, but it was a consequence of the comparatively good meal they had fed the prisoners. It had apparently been richer and more satisfying than anything they had eaten recently. Living lean for a long enough period often meant that the body forgot how to properly use food of such comparative quality. A good deal of it ended up wasted—in this case, literally.

He flipped the knife so he was holding it by the blade and turned to the South, where he thought he'd heard another twig snap. Of course, he couldn't be certain. The sound had been partially covered by that of the prisoner breaking wind.

"Dash lok, Nk." A whispered growl carried this message from almost due West. *(Stay your hand, Brother.)*

-IV-

"Pomoz," said a voice from somewhere behind Eobum. "Pomoz mi, zojáku!" The voice was insistent. Whispers rarely sounded urgent, but urgency was exactly the impression the whisper left hanging in the air.

"Come into the firelight where I can see you or flee before I rouse my men," Eobum spoke in the Trade Tongue with a deliberate and flat tone. He'd understood the voice's request perfectly well: *Help me, soldier.* In keeping with his oft-repeated idea that it was best for a foe to underestimate how much you knew or guessed, he kept his understanding to himself.

Instead, he dissected the man's choice of words. He'd been speaking Kovalunth ... and not from the north or farther west. He'd said, *"Zojáku."* It meant soldier, right enough, but wasn't the duke's speech, so to speak. That would have been *vojáku.* They sounded quite similar—only the V sound was starkly different—but still.

Where culture and language intermingled, words often did too. They meshed with one another in the markets and alehouses as if they were ingredients in a confusing, often hilarious stew of sounds. The sound of a word or phrase would absorb aspects of a similar word from one of the other languages, and folk would hardly notice unless they came from afar. The border with the duchy of Kamieńalun lay near—a day, maybe two on foot at a normal pace. Travel deeper into that duchy, and the word for soldier became żołnierzu.

So you're local, then. Fair, but what in hells are you doing all the way out here in the woods in the wee hours, I wonder? He suspected he would soon find out.

"Vill you help me?" At last, the whisper had taken on some fuller tone. It was a man's voice, albeit a young one.

"Only a fool would promise that until he knew more. I won't be the one to kill you; I can promise you that. Not unless you commit some new crime in my camp."

Silence, then a slow dragging sound. A young man wearing a thin, yellow beard and what was once fine clothing came limping out of the woods. He favored his right leg, and it was easy to see why. What might first be mistaken for mud, especially given the rains of earlier this evening, was clearly revealed as mostly dried blood when the fellow neared the fire.

Eobum vacated his seat, taking up residence on Fenglem's former perch, gesturing for the man to sit in the now empty and somewhat closer space. He guessed he'd been on the run for some time and either felt or knew he was being dogged by someone or other. His eyes were haunted things—exhausted.

The newcomer obeyed with obvious relief. Almost at once, he began warming his hands and feet, nearly shoving them directly into the fire.

"You look half-dead, friend."

The man nodded. He said nothing for a very long moment, but when he caught Eobum staring at him with undisguised interest, he seemed to realize silence would not serve his needs. Nodding once more, he spoke.

"Trade tongue?" After receiving a nod from Eobum, though even *it* was spare and singular, he continued. "I've beena running since-a just before dawn."

Eobum doubted that. Moving, perhaps, with stops for water, to catch a breath or to relieve himself. Still, he had an idea this man was attempting to speak literally as he spun the tale of his travels.

"Thisa early morning as I laya vith one of my slave girls, an escapeda slave came boorstingk into my tent."

Eobum's nod carried with it an inscrutable expression. Thus far, he thought the man was telling the truth, overall, but that truth was dressed in silks, as the saying went. It'd been prettied up to hide the less savory aspects of the man's story.

"The night vas cold, and so I vas dressed as youa see." He took his left hand and gestured down the length of his body. He wore no boots, and the yellow leather of his narrow kalhoty-style breeches hung in ribbons below his knees. He wore no shirt beneath the twin layers of his white short coat and the black expanse of his longcoat.

Rural, from the look of his trousers, but wealthy. His jacket's costly, at any rate. Eobum noted the white garment had been embroidered with black vines. He didn't recognize it as any form of heraldry. Still, he knew the trappings of nobility and privilege when he saw them—even when their owners were so down on their seemingly endless luck.

"The bastard chased me. I don't think he intended to, but he chased me."

"You obviously managed to escape him."

"No, I didn't. He'sa been tracking me, and he'sa right on my heels, I'm sure." As if for effect, the man began looking this way and that. He saw movement from the west and blanched, his already pale skin turning the color of snow under stormy skies.

Eobum looked over but knew what he'd see. As anticipated, Fenglem was returning, having just deposited the prisoner back with his fellows.

"That's," the newcomer stammered. "That's..."

"...one of mine." Eobum offered a thin smile but followed it up with a nod he tried to make at least marginally encouraging. "I can promise he wasn't chasing you, as he's been marching with I and mine all day."

Fenglem approached the fire, shooting an interested look at the newcomer and a questioning one toward Eobum. When Eobum made a nod and gestured to his left, Fenglem finished his approach and sat down across from the newcomer.

"Walked the dog," Fenglem said. His voice was even more guttural than usual. His use of the Trade Tongue was a touch more broken than their earlier ruse as well.

Eobum nodded and did his best to make his body language seem dismissive. He turned back to the newcomer, then reached behind him to where Fenglem's pack lay. Reaching into it, he removed a small sheet of bread, his eyes never having left the newcomer. It didn't take much to gauge the man's reaction. His mouth watered with such an obvious desire that he had to look down and wipe his chin clean.

"I expect that you're hungry, Lord."

"Yes," the newcomer said. If he registered how Eobum had addressed him, he was very good at hiding it.

Eobum handed him the bread, leaning to the right as he did so. As the young man took it from him, Eobum used his now empty hand to pat his new guest's shoulder in a distantly comforting gesture. If the man were honest, he needed to feel safe among them. If he were a liar, well, it was always best to calm the beast before butchering it.

The young man looked at him with obvious gratitude. He turned back, leaning over to indulge the deep and abiding hunger that'd suddenly reared up within him.

As Eobum performed these simple acts, he used his left hand, the sight of which was blocked by his knees, to sign to Fenglem.

Wealthy, perhaps a noble. Chased, wounded, hunted, afraid.

As Eobum straightened, he noted Fenglem's movement as the orc reached to find another log to put on the fire. As his left hand busied itself amid the woodpile, his right hand surreptitiously signed back.

Three of us. Killed the eldest. Was wounded and fled. Hunted.

Eobum had no idea what his brother meant by *three of us*. This was where their understanding of Hunter's Sign failed. They couldn't relay complex ideas. What he *did* know was that Feng had found the other watcher in the woods. Apparently, the pair didn't seem to be working together. He signed his response, reaching up to scratch a non-existent itch with his other hand.

Do I go to see?

Turning to the newcomer, he said, "When you've eaten, roll over. Sleep by the fire. You'll need your strength tomorrow."

"Aye," said Feng. His eyes flitted to Eobum to underscore the double meaning—yes, Eobum had given good advice to the man. Yes, Eobum should go and see the other skulker for himself.

The young man looked over, nodded, and threw the last of the bread into his mouth. "Thank you." With a decided lack of fanfare or gentility, the man nearly flopped over on his side, curled up in an awkward fetal ball, and set off for Hämärä meri–the Twilight Sea.

-V-

"Dash Kar msh awka zak erld fel dush, Ok." Eobum's voice was firm and sure. *(Stay your hunger for death and speak your long tale, Sister.)*

"Aehe erld zak ed Ok?" Her voice was rich and sweet—the sound of shallow creeks where water raced over loose stones and wind made the trees sigh. *(Why do you call me Sister?)* She made her voice polite and distant—a diplomatic tone that served to make her intriguing rather than icy.

Eobum heard a figure moving up behind him and to his left. He also heard that figure pause mid-step at the woman's last question. That—much as anything else—confirmed for him that Fenglem had indeed rousted his other brother, Haiga, to join them. It also meant that Fenglem was still seated by the fire. His eldest brother would keep a watch as the visiting wretch of a nobleman still slept.

While Eobum would've preferred the slightly older Fenglem's equilibrium for a meeting such as this, he knew the value of familiarity. When the young man woke up (whether with a start or after some restful sleep didn't much matter), seeing a familiar face would prevent him from being spooked. Even one he would undoubtedly refer to as "Orcish filth" would go far to stop him from doing something foolish.

"Ng?" Haiga's voice, behind him and to his right. *(Elder?)*

Eobum held up a hand in token of peace, then turned it so it ushered the new arrival to sit beside him. For his part, he kept his eyes on the woman sat before him.

He did his best to shake off the fascination that her countenance brought about in him and, with an effort, succeeded.

Now that his eyes had adjusted to the relative dark, the fire some thirty-odd yards behind him, she nearly glowed against the dim backdrop of the forest. Her face, throat, undersides of her forearms, and the entirety of her hands shone a deep, luminous gold. Being so far from the fire and with the night being so cold, there was nothing to give the flesh any form of sheen, so its luster came from an inner glow—an inner fire, a more poetic man might've said. The upper portion of her forearms, the sides, and, he had no doubt, the back of her neck, as well as perhaps her scalp in the uppermost portions of her forehead, were a deep blue the color of a midday sky with no clouds to mar it. Her eyes, too, held that midday blue shade. Her hair was long and uncharacteristically flowing for her kind. Its color called to mind the deep blue of dusk over the Sea of Heroes to the west.

"Ed Eobum," said he. "Ed lg, Lakkrid." He gestured back toward his left, where the boy lay curled under a cloak and layers of hide beneath the same ash tree the pair had eaten beneath earlier that night. "Lakkrid nak, ol, awka ed vra, Ok." *(I am Eobum. My son, Lakkrid. He is clever, quiet, and my heart, Sister.)*

"Erld lg Lakkrid? Gnoerk?" *(Your son Lakkrid? An Orc?)*

Eobum nodded.

"Ed lg awka Gnoerklg—Suruklg Istjuk." *(My son and an Orcish son—Suruk of Istjuk's son.)*

She turned sharply at that, looking to Eobum's right where Haiga sat. Eobum did not turn to follow her gaze to the grey-skinned youth but did gesture to him with his right hand as he spoke once more.

"Haiga... ed Nk Istjuk." *(Haiga... my brother from Istjuk.)*

"Haiga Nalgish," said Haiga. "Eobum nainak, awka mak lash el shrash awka ol shrig Istjuk. Ed, Fenglem, Lakkrid, awka Eobum. Istjuklg." *(Haiga of the Dark Beginning. Eobum was very clever, and by the moon's light, we silently escaped the conquest of Istjuk. I, Fenglem, Lakkrid, and Eobum. Sons of Istjuk.)*

"And so, you call me sister in equality ... and from a place of respect." She nodded, having spoken the Trade Tongue for the first time before them. What was more, her mastery of it was clear, suggesting she were not from an isolated area. "I will speak in this tongue out of that same respect."

Eobum bowed his head for just a moment in deferential gratitude. When he raised it again and met her eyes, his expression was one of cool neutrality. He'd left obvious deference to languish in his lap.

"You have my thanks, Sister."

"Lashjuk," said she, a name that meant either Golden Core or Center or Gift of the Center when translated from Grimdash Zaksh into the trader's tongue.

"Very well," Eobum said. "You know my name, and the kind speech of my younger brother has told you some of our tale. Is it enough that you'll tell us yours? The young noble asleep by my fire has offered a meager explanation, but the truth lies somewhere between his tale and yours."

"So, you would side with your own kind, then." Her tone suggested disappointment but no surprise.

"That isn't what I said."

"It is," said she. "You look for an excuse to justify siding with your fellow human and look to *me* to provide it." She shook her head in disgust. Her tone remained neutral, but her eyes had grown cold. "I'll be plain so we can race along to the moment you deny my request then, shall I..." Her words conveyed a question that neither her eyes nor her timbre asked.

Eobum felt rather than heard Haiga tense to his right. Beyond awareness of that fact, he paid his brother very little mind. Collecting his thoughts, he first bowed his head, then lifted it to meet her eyes.

"You mistrust me." This statement held no anger, nor did Eobum sound affronted. "You have *every* right—*every* reason—to expect mistreatment to be waiting for you behind each bend in the road. Hai Fel Lok Lo. After centuries of hearing that song? Aye, that's fair." Hai Fel Lok Lo was an old Gnoerkish spiritual song. It meant *The Far Conqueror's Hand* and was sung by the Gnoerks pressed into military service by the empire's well-heeled. Such Gnoerks hadn't been *slaves,* strictly speaking, but they were treated little better than livestock capable of speech.

She didn't respond even visually. No nod of the head, no further glare or scowl rose to the surface at his words.

"It's gone on for so long that Gnoerkish anger has become the norm. Gnoerkish anger often becomes the first thing Venzene children see when they meet someone of black blood." His tone was flat and simple.

"And so our mistrust and anger do what? Do they deepen the divide? Is that it?"

"Aye, they do."

She nodded. The once-music of her voice had now moved from the neutral-and-diplomatic. Now it called to mind a mouthful of sour fruit. As she spoke, her lips drew together around her lower tusks. This forced her words out of a space too tight to admit the polite song of easy conversation, adding to the sense of bitterness.

"Well, *master*, forgive my ignorance, and *thank* you for taking the time to teach me the truth of my mistakes. Perhaps I should lay myself down and give of my body to you, or give my sons over... Perhaps that would make amends for our unwarranted anger and frustration, our mistrust, and the ill placed blame for *our* misfortune."

"You mistake me."

"And *now* you dance away from the spot you put yourself on."

"Not at all. You asked if your anger and mistrust deepened the divide. I answered honestly. They do. That makes them no less justified."

She made her face flat, drawing it long. Her eyes bore a look of incredulity that was impossible to misread.

"Humans are unique among the peoples of the world," said Eobum. "We've never met a creature we don't seek to conquer. We enslave ourselves almost as often as we enslave others, but that isn't just cold comfort. It's no comfort at all." He paused, fighting the urge to stand up and walk away—anything to avoid making a speech.

Leading men on the field or in some task—*that* he could do ... and with ease. But this? *This* was too much like the horrors of court. He'd seen small versions of it in the command tents and camp courtyards of those who'd hired him over the years. *There's always too much talking—too much blather. Too much self-important lecturing and outright lies.* The whole affair tended to turn his stomach.

Lashjuk continued to look at him, adopting body language that made her look like a cat sizing up a bird or mouse before pouncing. Under her penetrating, predatory gaze, he spoke again in spite of himself.

"Gnoerks have been belittled, enslaved, prized, and pushed to be as warlike and brutal as their would-be masters are pleased to imagine. You cannot trust *every* person you meet, no matter their heritage, of course, but no matter my past, I'm human. You have every reason to mistrust me, and every other man you meet, or woman for that matter, if their blood's anything other than black."

"But?" Her voice had turned wary now.

"But *nothing.*"

"But nothing..." Now she'd grown distant, full of obvious disbelief.

"When you walk behind or near a horse, and the horse kicks at you, you might become wary of that particular horse. When every, or nearly every, horse you come across tries to kick you, you face injury or death, or you learn not to go near horses. After centuries of enslavement, either bought and sold on blocks or accounted *free* so long as you please your *lord* or *lady*... most Gnoerks can spot a horse, even by moonlight."

She kept a wary silence, nodding.

"I won't waste my time telling you whether to trust me. Nothing I say—nothing anyone *says* is enough on its own to justify trust. Words are just that."

He paused for a moment to see whether she would speak. When she didn't appear ready to, he offered one final word on the matter. "You may go, you may stay, you may tell us your tale, or you may keep your silence. I have no quarrel with you, nor do any of mine. The young nobleman is not one of mine. He came staggering, wounded and afraid, into my camp. We fed him, and now he sleeps. You would've received the same treatment had *you* come to us, but I understand why you didn't."

She held his gaze, letting the silence ring out before speaking, as if against her better judgment.

"And if I get up and leave your company right now...?"

"I'll ask you if you need or want any supplies before you go, but otherwise, I'll bid you a good night and wish you well."

"And you claim that you will not pursue us."

"Behind Haiga, to his right, there is a smallish, square tent. Inside, we have prisoners. Raiders that we caught two days a'gone."

"And what color is their blood, *brother*?" She emphasized this last word, stopping just shy of sarcasm or insult.

"Red?" He shrugged, then added, "Fenglem was tending to one when you met him. The others are the same." He paused for a beat, then finished, "You're welcome to go see if you like."

"The only black bloods you have in your encampment, then, are your brothers and your boy?"

He nodded, raising his right hand in a half-shrug and half-gesture toward Haiga.

Lashjuk turned her head toward the younger gnoerk, holding him in her gaze for some time. She must've seen what she wanted there, or at the least something that satisfied her, for, after a long moment of silence, she nodded once, then spoke anew.

"I will do two things, Eobum of Istjuk." She paused for a moment, as if considering, then seemed to draw herself up a bit before concluding, "I will tell you my tale, and then I will be on my way. You will do what you think is best, but you *will not* do it to me." She held up a hand, not in Eobum's, but in Haiga's direction. "Peace, young Haiga, I speak plainly, not out of disrespect."

Eobum lifted his right hand from his leg in a gesture that made it clear he'd taken no offense. Haiga would mark it, he had no doubt. Looking at the woman, he drank in the magic of her skin and eyes one final time, then closed his own, nodding. "Tell me your tale and then do as you will so long as it doesn't involve harming me or mine. As I say, if you need food or supplies, we haven't much, but what we have is yours."

After a moment of silence, Lashjuk voyaged on her tale. It didn't take long, but when it was done, Eobum found he was pleased to have heard it. It put several things into perspective for him, giving him much to think about.

A GAME OF ZVONĚNÍ V JESKYNI

-I-

Venzene Duchy of Kovalun
County Jižní Pochod
Barony of Hartscross - Jižní Lov
28 Gerstesykli: Night of the Red Storm at Westsong

The encampment was darkening with the onset of twilight. Dusk or not, it could hardly be called inactive. Men and women called to one another as the workday ended for most or admonished children to mind their siblings as they raced off in search of some post-supper play.

Three men walked toward the command tent, speaking in low tones as they moved. Their black horseman's coats fluttered in the early autumn breeze.

"Tell me what you see," their leader prompted. He was a man with hair so dark a blond it was as near as no matter to brown and the rough beginnings of a matching beard left unattended for perhaps a week.

The youngest of the three had a head full of curls—pretty as any maid—in a more recognizable shade of blond than his captain. He also had a few days' growth covering his chin and cheeks, somewhat spoiling the effect of his pretty hair. It was he who answered after a moment's consideration.

"They've stood up a wooden palisade, a sea of tents and pavilions, a semi-permanent paddock and wooden stall stable." He paused, silently calculating. "Other than those more permanent parts, it's all in accordance with military tradition."

"True enough. Those traditions date back fully five centuries and more." Their captain wound his way around several carts and a group of distracted children moving off toward the camp's center as he spoke. "The truth is, while this place was set up like a temporary military camp, except for individual tents and pavilions, it hasn't been torn down and moved in the best part of fifteen years."

Geroslaw, the third member of their party, spoke up. "It looks to me like a hunting encampment." A breeze blew his black hair across his forehead, tickling him for a beat. Without slowing his step, he brushed the hair away with an all-but unconscious movement, then tugged at the many leather thongs that bound his black beard.

Their leader sounded as if he were grinning. "It was, originally. The count's men needed a place where they could train to survive in the lowlands that make up so much of the Empire's territory. Should the need arise for military action outside of the county, the then-Baron Edmund wanted his personal forces to be well and truly prepared for it."

Geroslaw nodded, speaking up again. "A good thing, too. What was it? Just a few years later, when that ill-fated border war with the folk of Eoalun started? Mind you, I heard it had *really* been hatched here in Kovalun."

"You heard rightly. We were here." Their captain paused for a moment to let yet another group of children run past. "Edmund chose this location for the encampment because it rests nearly at the center point between both his southern and eastern borders."

"Aye," Geroslaw snorted. "Certainly served him well as a base from which to range patrols."

"You're not wrong. We did a lot of work here. Eventually started capturing enemy agents moving from point to point with dispatches." Their captain's voice made it clear he was wearing his pre-battle predator's grin. "You know your battles, Geroslaw." He sounded pleased. "We found an unlikely alliance across not one but two ducal borders. An upstart Eoalunth baron to the northeast and a greedy count to the south in Havalun were both supporting the rebellion here."

Their youngest member stopped walking for a moment, cocking his head to one side in realization.

"Was that how Černé oči happened?"

Their captain, rather than answering this, asked a question of his own. "Daian, are you planning to join us?"

Shrugging, the young man moved to catch up with his two black-clad companions. A moment later, they arrived at the commander's marquee tent. This was situated just west of camp's center and some fifty yards in from the palisade's north wall.

Count Edmund's banner wasn't on display. This meant he wasn't currently in residence but no matter. The lord left in command in Edmond's absence waited for them outside. He was flanked by a pair of guards. He wore britches of yellow leather tucked into high black riding boots, a grey shirt of wool that hung to mid-thigh, and a short, white jacket embroidered with yellow and blue. He kept his blond mop fashionably careless, completing the image of the handsome hero in a little girl's cradle tale.

As they approached, he nodded to them, then looked past them to where the camp's children were gathering. The black-clad trio turned, following his gaze.

Once the darkness had made a memory of twilight and all the light came from candles and campfires, they would begin talks with the count's seneschal. At the moment, however, the encampment was being used for something far less serious, and by extension, far more entertaining. *There'll be time enough*, Geroslaw thought, *for bloody tales of war and weapons. For now...*

-II-

Children—mostly boys with a few girls among them—were scattered all around the central courtyard. Each stood behind or beside tents, horses, and currently darkened fire pits. A lone figure—a boy by the look of him— stood in the center with his head down, a sack drawn tight over it.

A strip of a girl stood atop a wagon. Her arms were in the air, making her silhouette stand out in the shape of a *Y*. The linen dress she wore rippled in the breeze, but the wind wasn't strong enough to do much with her unbound black hair.

She looked around, nodding to herself that all the other children were in place. Pulling in a deep breath, as if she were about to yell, she drew her arms down in tandem with an urgency that suggested they'd suddenly caught fire.

The night erupted with sound.

All children, great and small, took part in the mind-numbing cacophony. The only ones not adding to this seemingly meaningless racket were the girl whose arms had signaled its onset and the boy who stood in the clearing with a sack drawn over his head.

The overwhelming majority of the children were screaming or singing "Aaahhhhhh," holding the notes for as long as their lungs would allow. Even when they were out of breath, they didn't remain silent for long. As swiftly as they could, they began drawing in great gusts of air, using it to take up the song anew.

Geroslaw smiled. He couldn't help it. The game was so absurd and so uniquely the purview of children.

As he watched, five children from different directions began to move toward the solitary boy with the sack over his head. As they did, their sounds changed, becoming distinct from the greater din.

"Cink! Cink! Cink!"

On they came, slowly, walking, screeching that solitary word as they moved toward him, arms outstretched. "Cink! Cink! Cink!"

The boy jerked his head suddenly. He turned this way, then that, until finally, he froze. With his head cocked to the side, he faced toward a new voice. A girl screamed a solitary word over and over again from somewhere behind the tents in front and to his right.

"Běh! Běh! Běh!"

The cink-shouters looked like drooling predators as they closed in. Each one glanced first beyond the boy toward the girl shouting "běh" and back to the boy again.

What is this? Geroslaw had a vague memory of a game like this. It danced gingerly out of reach and recall whenever he tried to recover it.

As the boy moved, they strove to match their pace with his. As he jogged, they jogged. As he sprinted, they sprinted.

Blindly—for he could certainly see nothing with his head covered by that heavy cloth sack—the boy stumbled in the direction of the girl screaming "běh," his arms outstretched.

He watched as the boy began sweeping his arms left and right in wide arcs. Geroslaw realized, *He must be trying to warn himself before stumbling into or over an object.*

The blinded player barked his shin on an upright before his hands recognized it for what it was. He cried out and cursed, then slid his hands along the rest of the canvas that made up the tent until he found its side. Fingers splayed across it, using his left hand to guide him, he staggered as quickly as he could alongside the tent until he'd cleared it.

"Clever," Geroslaw murmured. Jastrab, his captain, gave him a warning look, then shook his head ever so slightly. He realized that none of the other adults were making so much as a sound. What was more, they wore looks that seemed far too intense for a simple children's game.

The cink children were gaining now, but as their quarry stopped short, so did they. They stopped speaking, stopped their incessant shouting, and waited.

The *ah!* children remained a choir of undulating madness ... either singing or screaming. After the boy had remained still for perhaps thirty seconds, the girl in the cart ushered them forward with wide, sweeping hand gestures.

Still moaning that melodic "ah," they began to move in eerie, rhythmic circles, changing the direction from which their sound traveled.

The boy growled, though the sound was all but lost in the din. He dropped his head, cocking it to the left as if listening, trying to pinpoint it again.

"Běh! Běh! Běh!"

And there it was!

He erupted into action. Dropping to all fours, he performed an insane crawling sprint. While this slowed him down immensely, it temporarily hid him from the sight of the pursuing cink children. This gave him an earlier warning before he rammed himself into an object or stumbled into a pit.

The "běh" girl was positively bouncing with excitement, her voice growing both in volume and pitch as she jumped and clapped.

The crawling boy lost his balance briefly, his arm falling up to the elbow in a darkened fire pit before he yanked it back and corrected his course. As he tried to pull himself away, two hands shot up from where their owner had hidden within the pit. They grabbed the boy's wrist and tried to pull him down. He squealed with fright and frustration, throwing himself back to the left, rolling away from the fire pit, breaking the grip of his captor.

Clever and quick to react as well, Geroslaw mused. *Were I a knight, you would be a worthy candidate to serve as a page.*

"Cink! Cink! Cink!"

The voices were gaining. He was so close to the girl. But there was something in the way...

Geroslaw watched with something akin to pride as the boy leapt to his feet, turned his head left, then right, then left again before taking on a posture of triumph. He sprinted forward a few feet, pivoted to his left, and jumped. He landed in an awkward sprawl, but in fact, managed to clear the tent in his way. In order for his pursuers to catch him, they would need to jump as well or run far around other tents, sacrificing time they did not have.

He struggled to his feet, covered in dust and a tiny bit of blood where he'd scraped holes in the knees of his trousers.

Turning to listen once more, he pivoted his body toward the sound of the girl and dropped back into that crawling run which had served him so well.

A lone cink-child made the jump, a girl of perhaps twelve. She soared through the air, graceful as a faun, but landed badly. She moved to run after the boy but winced as she did so, favoring her right leg.

The children were all crowding in now, all shrieking, but none of them touched him. He was all but drowning in a sea of "ah!"

"Běh! Běh, Vlk! Běh!" The girl looked ready to explode. She was so excited.

The boy—Vlk, apparently—reached out his right arm but wasn't close enough. With a grunt of effort, he got to his feet. He reached both of his hands out and down, stumbling toward the girl.

The cink-girl pursuing him lunged forward, fingers splayed. She missed him by inches as he bent.

He had her! The "běh" girl squealed and bounced up and down, wrapping her arms around him in utter delight.

Every child suddenly shouted and cheered. Vlk had done it. He reached up and ripped off the bag, revealing an unruly mop of dark brown hair, a slightly oversized nose, and a triumphant grin.

As the cheers died down, the children could hear the laughter of more than a few adults. Looking around, they saw them clustered about the very fringe of their play area, some outside of their tents, some sitting just within them with the flaps open so they could see. All faces beamed and shared in Vlk's triumph.

The crowd of children gathered and lifted the victorious boy onto their shoulders. They carried him off.

"To the stables," their host said with a grin, "where they will find water. Then, likely, they'll reset the game with a new challenger ready to risk his bones to escape his pursuers."

-III-

The count's seneschal—Lord Alojz—returned their attention to the large marquee tent after seeing that the game was over.

Once inside, the mercenaries stood at rest in their black horseman's longcoats. More correctly called *kontusze,* Geroslaw and his fellows wore them closed, their polished wooden buttons providing an earthy accent to their otherwise dour visage. The stark and the stylish sized one another up before the two leaders smiled at one another.

Those are courtly smiles, Geroslaw's undermind told him. *They may like one another or may not, but there's respect between them and some history.*

Lord Alojz ran his fingers through his untidy blond hair as he approached the table. He filled four leather mugs from a small cask. Passing them out to each man and saving one for himself, he moved, at last, to sit in his chair.

Geroslaw noted a white woolen kontusz rested across its back. The guards outside wore similar, if less expensive, versions of the same.

Captain Jastrab offered a silent salute to their host, then drained perhaps half the contents of his mug in a single pull.

"That's a welcome thing." He spoke in a high, clear voice with a touch of gravel to give it character. "I haven't had Hartscross ale since..."

"Since the last time you came to visit the count in search of a contract?" The blond man lifted both brows. This seemed to draw the corners of his mouth up in a smile, making it fairly plain he was mostly teasing.

"Maybe?" The grin accompanying this simple response made it not just self-deprecating but charming.

"Tell me," said Alojz, "where is your Válečný Pes—your Eane?"

"Seeing to other contracts."

The lord sighed rather theatrically. "You know, Jastrab, this disturbing trend of yours—never bringing the same guardsmen more than twice when you come to visit—it really does need to stop."

"Val-itch knee..." This was Daian, the younger of the two associates Jastrab had brought with him.

"Válečný Pes, boy." Alojz turned back to Jastrab. "Another one who doesn't speak our mother-tongue?" He didn't wait for an answer. He turned back to Daian and translated. "It means war hound. Your Eane lived for warfare and was of great help during the pocket rebellion nearly a decade back."

"After the last time I visited here with him, we thought it would be best if he stayed away."

"Stayed away? Only the wives want him to stay away. No matter how much that man reveled in warfare, his true calling was stirring up trouble and finding women. The women of the court—hells, those of the entire encampment—rightly fear the crop of bastard children his antics led men to make."

"Is *that* what happened? The wives told you that you could no longer play with him and had to be home by dark for supper as well?" Jastrab snorted, although Geroslaw thought it was good-natured derision. "Did they threaten to tan your hides if you give them backtalk as well?"

The blond man laughed along with the sell-sword captain, though neither Geroslaw nor Daian joined in.

"You're damned right they did!" He drained the rest of his mug and then stood to refill it. "That man was walking temptation. No matter how cold it got and no matter what time of year, he could always find women, wine, bread, and beer for himself and anyone else who wanted them. Decorum be damned." He placed his own leather mug back on the tabletop and reached a hand across to take the captain's mostly empty one.

As he refilled it, he shrugged a shoulder. "Mind you, while that skill would have to be my favorite—one for which I will probably be everlastingly jealous—it's the man's skill with pin and quarrel that was truly astonishing. He was good with the spear, but," he shook his head before releasing the tap, "doom with a full quiver."

Jastrab nodded and grinned as he reached to take the now-full mug.

"Well, my Lord Alojz, he'll be glad to hear it. I'll remember you to him when I see him next."

An easy, artless silence fell throughout the tent as the men drank and thought.

Geroslaw took a moment to un-focus his vision, trying to drink in the whole of his surroundings rather than simply what lay before him.

The tent was fashioned from winter-weight canvas and stout wooden poles. Every inch of its inner walls was draped with heavy furs and tapestries. These combined to keep both the bitterest cold and the sharpest edge of sound at bay. Even the next round of the strange game had blended in with the general night noises outside.

Daian spoke up again. "What was that game they were playing?" He opened the tent flap, and a wave of sound hit them hard enough to force each of them to wince.

Alojz waved him to close the tent flap, and he did so dutifully enough.

"Zvonění v jeskyni," said the man as he retook his post beside his chair. "Bells in the cave."

Daian shook his head. He understood the words, but his expression made it clear he didn't remotely grasp the context.

Jastrab spoke up. "In the north of Kovalun—hells, nearly the *entire* north and most of the center beside—there are caves, caverns, and what may as well be coliseums stood within and beneath the mountains."

"Yes, that's where the mines are." Daian sounded studious as he spoke this simple truth.

"Well, *in* those caves, the people found iron, gemstones, gold, silver—*all* the things Kovalun is known for." He stretched the word "all" out as if he were falling a goodish distance or sweeping an arm toward the skyline. "They also found sweet water, mushrooms for stew and strange dreams alike, and all manner of creatures. Most are harmless, but there are a few..."

"I've heard of the Ooh-tuh? I think?"

"Oohs-tah," Jastrab corrected. "Ocelová ústa—the steel mouth. It lives in the underground rivers and, as the name suggests, has a jaw that's as strong as steel. Angry, deadly things I hear."

"Delicious things, though," Alojz put in. "Sweet and flakey, though you have to boil them before you wrap them and put them on the fire to bake or fry."

"What does that..."

Jastrab held up a hand to still the youth. "I'm coming to it. *You're* the one who brought up the fish." He grinned, taking Daian's mug to refill it. "The game is because of a different creature, the Dračí netopýr—the dragon bat."

A moment later, Geroslaw handed *his* mug over to Jastrab with a nod of thanks. He brushed a hand through his long, coal-black hair, then tightened the thongs binding his dark beard.

Why in hells am I suddenly so nervous? A moment later and he answered his own question. *Because my own Kovalunth is so basic. That's why. Well, there's no time to fix that now—Kamień jest szary* (Stone is grey).

"They're enormous things the size of a damned Eoalunth horse," Jastrab continued. "They act like bats most of the time—hang from poniards of rock and stone dripping from cavern ceilings and fly out to hunt in the late night."

"Do they breathe..." Daian's tone was a shade left of disbelief and a shade right of fear.

"Fire, aye," said Jastrab. "They sleep for years at a time... unless you find them in their halls—or holes, if you'd prefer."

"Then what?"

Here Alojz cut in. "Then, boy, they shriek and dive upon the sound they hear, carry it away, roast it, and dine on the gifts the gods have given."

"They seem to be blind." Jastrab took the tale back from their host. "That's what they say, anyway. Sound distracts them and makes their gliding, diving doom easier to duck or dodge."

"So..." Daian shook his head. "So the cink shouters..."

Geroslaw spoke in answer. He made his voice long-suffering, as if he were tired of the topic and wanted to explain it without further need of tale-telling. Daian did best with facts, he knew, not grand tales.

"They're meant to be the Dračí netopýr. The běh child is the safety of the cavern's entrance or a defensible place where, I suppose, spears could fend off the beasts, if need be."

"Zvonění is Kovalunth for bells," said Jastrab, offering Geroslaw an approving nod. "Their cries sound much like high, sweet bells."

Daian nodded his understanding but had another question. "And the singers? The 'ah' children?"

Jastrab took a moment to collect himself before answering.

"The deep delvers carry long, narrow bells with them in order to distract the creatures should they waken. The sound of other bells in the cavern tends to confuse and excite the beasts. They're looking for the source of that sound. They're looking either to mate with it or to drive it out of their territory. I know not which, though I reckon a miner could tell you."

"Exactly." Alojz nodded his approval. "Caverns are notoriously dark. If one had to run, one might well break a leg, step in an unseen pool, or crack their own skull on a low-hanging spike. The běh is the way out or at least to reinforcements. Finding it is easy enough if you can fight through the echoing madness of the bells bouncing off of every wall, and *that* is why the children sing *ah*. Their song stands in for that echoing insanity, training the hooded player to fight through that endless noise."

"Oh..." And that was all Daian could muster. He seemed lost in thought or perhaps just unwilling to go further down this road. *Oh* seemed to be all that he could manage.

After a few beats of awkward silence, Jastrab turned back to their host. "Well, I believe we have some business to discuss, Lord Alojz."

"Yes, Captain. We do, at that."

-IV-

"To begin with," Lord Alojz said, "I want to be very clear. We can discuss terms and agree in principle to those terms, but I do not have final authority to sign a contract with you. That authority..."

"...Rests firmly in the hands of the count." Jastrab nodded, making a small salute with his still mostly full leather mug. "I know that. I also know that you need to say it, so go on. Speak your piece."

"Yes, yes, I know. You've had to listen to this same speech off and on for the best part of... what, a dozen years now? It's tedious but necessary. Indulge me as I go through the dreary task of speaking plain truths in hopes that nothing gets left out or misunderstood." The man sounded the tiniest bit put upon, but whether that was due to the interruption or the task itself was less than obvious.

Jastrab gave a nod and a professional smile. This was several leagues away from the friendly smile or charming grin he usually used in conversation, no matter who the conversation was with.

No, Geroslaw thought, *that's his professional smile because now it's time to be just that... professional.*

"You'll need to have successfully vetted every single member of your company you intend to engage on the count's behalf. That task will need to be completed in advance of your signature on any official contract. If, after that, any of your men should prove to have given or sold information that we deem sensitive to literally any source whatsoever, it will be you who are personally liable. You will personally bear the punishment. That punishment may include the simple matter of public apology, the more substantive matter of coin or other payment—services owed or the like—up to the direst of punishments: death by hanging as a traitor."

Geroslaw marked how the blond man locked eyes with Captain Jastrab. Most men had a difficult time doing that. There was something unsettling in the man's gaze when he wanted there to be. Geroslaw had an idea that the look was something of an affectation, though he couldn't be certain of it.

Alojz held his gaze for perhaps a three count and then concluded, "Do you understand all that I've outlined for you thus far?"

"Understood." The response came just slow enough not to be considered swift and with just enough weight behind it to not be thought dismissive.

"Very good. Everything else is down to the details of the individual contract, but that covers the necessity of introductory falderal. Shall we move forward to the rather more interesting meat of the matter?"

Jastrab nodded and made one more salute with his leather mug but did not drink from it. There were acceptable moments to do that in contract negotiations or briefings. There were also moments that would count as either risky or utterly insulting and, thus, inappropriate.

Geroslaw had only been with the Bluemark Guard for roughly half a year, but in that time, he'd never seen Jastrab read such moments wrongly.

"Let me speak plainly to you, Jastrab. I like you most of the time. I like a good many of your men and women as well."

"Well, my lord, while the feeling is mutual, I assure you—I sense a fairly large *however* on the come."

"Your instincts have not led you astray." The lord paused for a moment, reaching up his right index finger to scratch his naked chin. "You're excellent at recruiting. Your ranks are always at the very least respectably full, and often they appear to veritably swell. You've never had a shortage of men, and many of those men are at least moderately well-trained. Therefore, we continue to hire you. Your problem hasn't ever been recruitment nor skill. It's retention."

Geroslaw winced inwardly but did his best to maintain a placid look. Jastrab, on the other hand, maintained his professional smile.

"No," he said. "That's fair."

Geroslaw could almost see the workings of his captain's mind as he held that smile. The lord's statement *was* absolutely true. Few, if any, nobles' personal forces could even claim to *rival* Jastrab's company, either numerically or in skill level, let alone surpass it. But this was the part of negotiation wherein the client listed reasons to undercut pay and to see what they could get away with in terms of intimidation.

No matter. Geroslaw trusted his captain. This was an old game and one Jastrab often won.

"One of two matters is currently on the table regarding you and your men." Lord Alojz ran his fingers through his blond hair, pushing it back from his right ear before reaching for the mug. "Count Edmund expects to attend the great annual tournament at Zlaté Pole. In roughly a week, he will pack himself, his personal retainers, and a sufficiency of men to make the trek. There must be a force left behind here in this key strategic position." He stopped to look at Jastrab, waiting for him to speak. When, after a moment, it was clear that he would not, Lord Alojz sighed and concluded, "That force will either be his own men in predominance ... or you and yours."

"I see." Jastrab did his best not to snort. "So, either you and yours will escort His Excellency to the tournament and the annual War of Counties, or you'll want the Bluemark Guard to do so. Tell me, my lord, do you, personally, have a preference?"

"I serve at the count's pleasure and perform the duties laid out to me by His Excellency's will ... or His Excellency's whim." All traces of warmth had vanished from their host's voice and face. His grip on the leather mug was strong enough to force it to creak but not strong enough to bend it utterly out of shape and overspill its contents.

Jastrab nodded. He took a moment to consider how best to respond.

"I tell you this, my lord. I've fought in my share of tournaments. I've even fought at Zlaté Pole, once upon a memory, and I wouldn't be unhappy to do so again. Nearly every man alive enjoys such competition and the gold and glory that are its fruits, should he be able to harvest them. That being said, I'm far more concerned about the contract itself than any potential winnings earned through the tournament. A contract guarantees us food and water, wine, and women through the winter. A tournament is the sort of thing that can often distract men like mine because of the potential to win that same gold and glory."

Alojz gazed at Jastrab, his look impassive and unmoved.

"Don't mistake me, my lord. I have no fear of my men rushing to leave my service because they defeated some lord or knight in single combat. I simply mean that the priority shifts when the contract involves tournament work. Fortunes and futures can be won in such a place."

"Yes, indeed." Alojz allowed a small smile as he sat back, nodding. "One victory could easily earn a bastard or nameless scion the eye of a banner knight—perhaps an even loftier patron. Of course, one could just as easily earn *ire* by that same victory."

Jastrab shrugged a shoulder. "If I'm to speak as bluntly as may be, I really don't care one way or the other. If His Excellency wants us to stay here and stand guard over his land while he wins glory, wonderful. We'll be happy to do it. If, instead, he feels that while he must make a show at tournament, the risk to his domain is too great to leave in the hands of sell-swords... If he wants to leave behind a force of people loyal to him rather than the coin he pays..." Here he trailed off deliberately, ending with a calculated insult.

Geroslaw took a moment to reflect on how deftly that had been handled. Jastrab had been careful to leave room for interpretation, but that single line hung in the air left an unanswered question dangling from its edges. Were the men here loyal to the count, as a man, or to the coin and prosperity he offered to pay them for their daily service?

"There are men here whose loyalty you could rightly question." Alojz lifted his mug in Jastrab's direction. "I suspect there are more than a few in your own company that you could say that about as well." He offered a chuckle of bitter amusement. "I know that you are loyal to your contract and always have been. It's the reason I speak so plainly with you." He offered another rueful chuckle. "As for me? I serve the count and the county. I do it gladly. Still yes. It would be a lie to say there were not men— some of them are in this camp, I'm sorry to say—who are loyal only to themselves and whatever gain they can garner."

Jastrab offered a salute and a modest pull from his mug.

"You understand why your ability to retain men is a factor here, I take it." Alojz's voice had reclaimed its cold neutrality—its business-like air.

"I do," said Jastrab. "We may be called upon to plan or execute patrol routes and schedules. Anything we touch as far as securing county lands would also involve potentially dangerous information. Those not vetted are suspect and might be tempted to sell what they know to your *good neighbors*, shall we say?"

"You agree; I take it, in principle, to these terms, then. To the nature of your duty, I suppose would be a better question." In truth, it hadn't been a question at all but a statement.

"The Bluemark Guard is at His Excellency's service, regardless of how he intends to employ us. We'll fight for him here, or we'll fight for him at tournament. I care less about where and *when*, so long as we actually *get* to fight."

Their host gave a long, approving nod.

"Very well. Think of a price. It'll be a protracted period of time, which we realize might prevent you from other work early next year. I would recommend you take that into account before settling on a number, but that's your business. His Excellency should be back in one, no more than two days. In the meantime, you're welcome to move your encampment within the walls of our palisade. Make use of our hospitality as if you were our honored guests."

"The land we'll take, and perhaps we'll share a ration of ale or two with your men ... or your good self. We brought our own provisions and wouldn't dream of demanding guest rights from the count, especially without him being here."

Alojz nodded, looking surprised but altogether pleased with that sentiment. "Well spoken, and thank you. On the count's behalf and the men's, I thank you." He made rather a business of draining the rest of his mug, then nodded. "I'm certain you've things to get back to and your own men to consult with. Call on me should you need anything before Edmund arrives. If, of course, we are, for some reason I cannot fathom, attacked whilst you are here within our walls..."

Jastrab nodded, smiling. "We'll stand by watching and lift not a single weapon, naturally. No, Lord Alojz. Of course, we'll lend the count's men any aid we can, should that happen."

After pleasant, if formal, words of farewell, the Bluemark returned to their temporary home outside of the palisade.

-V-

Geroslaw stopped Jastrab once Daian had peeled off to return to his tent. He liked Daian mostly. He simply didn't want to discuss what had been bubbling in his mind since Lord Alojz first laid out their forthcoming contract.

"Captain, a word?"

Jastrab nodded, grinning. "Tell me what's on your mind…" He paused, looking down for a moment before looking back up. "…other than our charming host, that is?"

"Is it permissible for me to leave for a time?"

Jastrab looked surprised, though not angry. "Any particular reason?"

"We're a little less than a fortnight from my home, across the border into Kamieńalun."

Jastrab's face took on a serious expression, though he didn't look alarmed. He was likely thinking about the strategies and information such a journey might unlock for him.

"Feeling sentimental?"

Geroslaw grunted, then responded with a few more well-chosen syllables. "I would like to go and recruit some men for the Bluemark under my own command. We're close enough to my birthplace that I should be able to go, spend some coin, and come back with a small company of my own. I feel that such an action…" He paused, looking thoughtful for a moment. "Not only will it help *me*, but it will add to our strength and help to influence, possibly at least, the count's decision about which way we're to jump."

Jastrab spent a long moment considering, then shook his head.

"I may change my mind when Edmund returns, but just now, I can't. If anyone notes that you've gone, they'll immediately wonder why. There are others within the company who have homes—originally, at least—across the border in any number of directions. We're near enough to the ducal borders of both Havalun and Kamieńalun, and only a few days farther from Eoalun, after all. If things change, I'll let you know, but as things stand...?" He shook his head. "I wouldn't expect to make such a journey until after this contract is over."

Geroslaw bowed his head, black hair streaming over both of his ears. His tone was resigned as he made his reply. "I see. I haven't been with you long enough to ask such a thing. That's fair."

"No," said Jastrab. He raised his left hand and placed it on Geroslaw's shoulder, giving it a light squeeze. "I know your worth. I know you're a damned good leader looking for an opportunity to prove that to everyone around you. I've seen it. Why do you think I let you stand with me in that tent? I don't need a guard, do I? I had a siege engineer with me to look at any maps and sort any numbers I couldn't sort myself. That isn't your strong suit, in any event. So, I certainly didn't need you there as a back-stop for that, did I?"

"Surely not," Geroslaw laughed.

"Surely not." Jastrab agreed with a nod and a smile. "You stood out almost from the first, Geroslaw. You're well-trained, humble, and a natural leader. Such a reputation carries a cost. It means you're one of the few folk I can lean on when the time comes. I can't be everywhere at once, can I?"

Geroslaw shook his head, braided beard swaying from side to side. He realized he was smiling. The Captain seemed to have that effect on him.

"You were there because I know I'll want you—need you in the days to come. Is *that* clear enough, Sergeant?"

"I suppose it is, Captain. And ... thank you." He paused, shaking his head again. "It's just I see an opportunity that I don't want to ignore. Or worse, simply watch as it passes me by. Three sykli—half a year a'gone since I signed on with the Bluemark. It's important to me to prove myself not only to you and the men, or even myself, but..."

Jastrab shook his head, a sad, sympathetic grin playing across his face.

"Opportunities to prove yourself to the nobility are few. Most bastards get ignored or shuffled off to one side or the other. It's the entire reason that I formed the Bluemark. When my family lost its land, they wandered and begged hospitality from hall to hall. This went on until people tired of it and offered them more or less meaningless positions in the Duke's court."

"Your father sided with the upstart against Duke Tilen, I take it."

"His Excellency, Count Csyar, yes. My father stood with him, which meant so did I. When it was over, those loyal to Csyar—those who fought for him, I mean—were stripped of land, but not title."

"To... To what end?"

Jastrab offered a light snort, though it seemed directed at the situation, not the question.

"Ah, Duke Tilen—forgive me—Vévoda Tilen was a shrewd man. Hells, he still is. It was the equivalent of gelding his enemies. They were responsible for taxes, given they had titles but had no clean source of income from which to pay those taxes. No lands to plant and plow meant that when their armor or weapons failed, they would be unable to uphold their obligations. Letting us live showed mercy. Letting us fail justified exile or execution for not fulfilling our duties."

Silence met this explanation. It persisted for perhaps thirty seconds, and when Geroslaw's next question came, it was carried on a humbled, not quite awed tone.

"Do you know how you were defeated? By all accounts, your forces outnumbered the Duke's by a goodly margin."

"Ohhhh, yes. Despite all evidence to the contrary before the war, His Grace had far more military support than anyone thought." He paused, grinning with little mirth. "Csyar was certain the Duke had *no* military outside of his house guard. The two thousands who stood against us at Eichenturm were a somewhat less than welcome surprise."

"Hells, you were there?" Geroslaw tried not to gape. "You'll have to tell me that story. As much as you'd think a count trying to up jump himself to duke would be news that ran like wildfire throughout the Empire, you'd be surprised. It was over so swiftly that there really wasn't much actual news. We only heard unsatisfyingly vague accounts."

Jastrab nodded. "Come with me." He threw his left arm over Geroslaw's shoulders and led him toward where his own table had been set before his tent. "Drink with me, and while we drink, I'll tell you what I can remember. It's been some fifteen years since the battle itself. The rebellion actually took place over a span of something like three years. It was a slow buildup as we tried to carve out the ill-fated duchy of Csyaralun. Nobody really understood what was happening on either side of the conflict until it was too late."

The two men moved deeper into the encampment, sat down, and spent the night reliving tales of Jastrab's misspent youth.

CHAPTER THREE

STORY AND STONE

-I-

Venzene Duchy of Kovalun
County Jižní Pochod
Barony of Hartscross - The Ash March
28 Gerstesykli: Night of the Red Storm at Westsong

Eobum watched in silence as Lashjuk prepared to tell her tale. She adjusted her position so that her bent knees were to her right, and her left hand maintained her balance on the ground.

She spent a long moment, longer than most would say was proper, looking at Haiga. After an uninterrupted span of perhaps ten seconds, she let her eyes move to half-mast and turned her attention to an area between where both Eobum and Haiga sat. This gave the impression she was addressing both of them, and neither of them, at the same time. It was the proper way for a Gnoerkish storyteller or singer to perform in front of a group of any size. Individual eye contact deliberately excluded others. Unless speaking directly to a specific someone, it was considered rude—sometimes outright insulting—for a performer or orator to make *any* form of eye contact.

"An uncommon tale, I know," she spoke with mirthless irony, "but I was once actually a slave. I was captured during a raid on Eoalun at the outset of my sixteenth winter. Despite their best efforts, I refused to stand meekly by and allow them to poke and prod me in the market or have their way with me along the road. Oh, they tried—but each time, they came away bloodied. The slavers decided that my youth and strength might yield enough profit to justify my continued breath and feeding ... and *their* continued bruising and bleeding."

Haiga made a brief, low growling sound in the back of his throat. Louder still, Eobum marked the cracking sound of his brother's knuckles. One look toward the woman's face showed the tiniest nod of appreciation for Haiga's reaction.

Eobum did his best to make of his face a mask, trying to absorb the entirety of her tale without passing judgment until it was over. There would be a reason she'd chosen to begin so far back up the hourglass. He simply needed to be patient enough to uncover it.

"We were in a place I would later come to know as Czarny Wodospad. I—like the rest of the unfortunates—was *prepared* before being set out, like any other line of stock, onto the auction block for our would-be masters to consider."

"How long did they make you rot there, Og?" Haiga's tenor growl came out sounding subdued as if he were speaking to a grieving loved one. His use of the word *Og*—a term for a matronly figure, an older sister, a chieftainess, or a mother—underscored this.

"I never made it onto the wider auction block, young Haiga." She offered perhaps the first genuine smile she'd managed to muster in what may have been ages. Certainly, it was the first time she'd seen fit to smile in front of them. "Guards came into the staging area. They had a brief, quiet exchange with the Sheshik slave masters. Soon, in typical merchant fashion, they began to bow and scrape. Then a well-dressed human entered."

She paused for a long moment, lost to memory, but as the wind sighed through the treetops above, she took on the aspect of *then*. She began speaking of what she was *seeing* with memory's eye—what she was *hearing* with memory's ear.

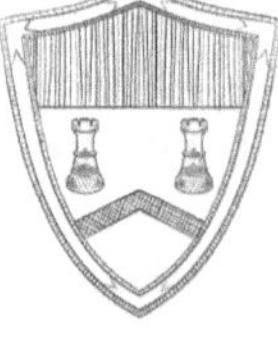

-II-

Venzene Duchy of Kamieńalun
County Czarny Wodospad
Szczyt Szymona
8 Kovsykli: 15 years prior to the Red Storm at Westsong

Lashjuk's eyes had caught swift and sudden movement near the entrance. A moment later, the tent's flap opened. The fat, Sheshik lump who ran this slave caravan escorted a severe-looking blond fellow inside. The slaver gestured extravagantly, inviting his guest to look around.

Well-dressed as he was, it did little to soften the blond man's appearance. He wore a face that might as well have been sculpted out of clay ... or perhaps ice. Tall and whip-chord thin, he moved like an animal—a predator who viewed everything around him as potential prey. His eyes moved very little, but his body language made it clear that his peripheral vision missed not a single trick.

He wore a horseman's longcoat of grey wool with buttons of what, at first glance, appeared to be silver. Upon longer inspection, they turned out to be highly polished steel.

She knew metals. Her father had been a warrior, and her mother had made his gear of war. She knew her way around hammer, fire, and steel.

Great black wings were embroidered around the broad cuffs of each sleeve. She'd noted them specifically because the speed of his right arm moving toward the curtain through which he'd entered had drawn her attention.

A beat later, the heavy cloth opened again. In came a well-armored guard wearing red leathers and an open-faced sallet helm of polished iron. He was followed almost instantly by a human boy of perhaps ten or eleven winters. The boy's hair was black, thick, and bushed out around his slightly oversized head. He, too, was well-dressed with high leather boots beneath a red horseman's coat, although the buttons on this garment were a polished bronze by the look of them.

"This is foolishness," the man in the grey coat said. His tone suggested this was a last attempt to voice an objection rather than an order from a parent speaking to a child.

"Are you going to stop me?" The boy's voice was neutral rather than accusatory. He stopped to ask this question, looking up at the man as if to read his face.

"I am not."

"Because you want to see me make my own mistakes or because you have no authority to do so?" While the cheek, if not downright arrogance, of this question was obvious, the tone with which it had been delivered was one of simple curiosity. The boy neither sounded effete nor petulant, neither triumphant nor trepidatious.

"One answer's as good as another."

"No, Uncle, it isn't." The boy began walking along the cages. He remained far out of arm's reach, though again, he didn't look afraid. He appeared merely to be cautious. He strode the length of the enormous tent within which they were all housed, clasping his hands at the small of his back. "One tells me you are counting this as a lesson. The other tells me that, lesson or not, you have reached a boundary you're unwilling to cross."

She saw the man nod to himself, though with his back to the entrance, the boy could not have seen.

"I will *not* answer you, no matter how you try to goad me into it. Whether it is your mistake or your station that will prevent me from stopping this madness will not change your insistence upon pursuing it. It will not, therefore, profit anyone for me to indulge you."

The boy stopped, bowed his head just slightly, and smiled. It was a triumphant expression that had clearly been for his own benefit. A moment later, he raised his head again, wearing the rather studious face he'd otherwise worn since his arrival.

"Thank you, Uncle."

"For?"

"...Always seeking to instruct me." Rather than sarcastic or obsequious, this response seemed altogether genuine.

He stopped at several cages that contained human women, most of whom appeared to be from northern Eoalun or perhaps from southern Shesh. He seemed enamored by several of them. Given those in this particular tent, that was unsurprising, even given his obvious youth. They *were* being presented as pleasure slaves, after all.

At length, he stopped before *her* cage. She did her best to snarl at him, even allowing a soft growl to escape her throat. The only effect this appeared to have on the boy-noble was a slight widening of his eyes—a lifting of his eyebrows.

She spent an interval considering what she might say to convince the boy to... *To what?* She didn't know. One part of her wanted him to leave—to recognize that she was not for the likes of him, soft and pampered as he was. The other wondered if going with him might mean her best chance of escape. She was in the throes of weighing out the potential of either situation when he spoke.

"This one."

"My lord?" The merchant seemed more than a touch uncertain. He looked to the back of the boy, then to her, then back to the boy's apparent uncle.

The man in the grey longcoat stood as still as stone, waiting. If he had an opinion on the matter, he apparently had no interest in offering it to the likes of this merchant.

"No fear. My uncle and my guards will ensure that I'm safe, and she's no fool. She's well aware that if she runs, death will swiftly surround her from all sides." The boy's voice was cool as he made these assessments. In point of fact, he'd been correct, at least when it came to Lashjuk. The slaver didn't seem convinced, but the young nobleman's words appeared to motivate the man.

"We must discuss price, my lord."

"No, we mustn't. A discussion suggests a back-and-forth, and we aren't entering into one of those. I'll give you twenty-seven grófok for her."

The merchant looked as if he were warring with himself inwardly. Twenty-seven silver grófok—nearly three gold vévodové—was a great deal of money for anyone not of the aristocracy. It was perhaps a week's profit, give or take, for most skilled laborers or merchants. Despite that fact, slaves were neither purchased nor sold by those who counted coin in such small amounts at day's end. Even still, this was clearly the offspring of some nobleman—the fact that he had both guards and an uncle whose dangerous, largely unmoving eyes seemed to bore into the merchant when he chanced to look his way suggested that there was more at play here than a simple exchange of coin.

"Forgive me." The merchant swallowed and tried to put on a smile. "But I fear that is a goodly bit short of the asking price for such valuable stock, my young lord."

The boy considered, or at least appeared to. In truth, he seemed to have lost almost all interest in the conversation. Instead, he was staring up at her with... *Not with puppy's eyes,* she thought. *With what? Greed? Pity? It isn't lust, whatever that look is. Given his age, that's almost surely out of the question.*

"My lord?" The merchant seemed uncomfortable with the idea of waiting for an answer. Then again, he hadn't strictly asked a question yet.

"Hmm?" The boy sounded distracted, as if being pestered by some minor annoyance or perhaps woken from an unintended afternoon nap.

"The price for the Orcish flower... it is, I fear, a good deal hi—"

"We will *not* be negotiating," the boy cut in. His voice was almost a singsong, as if chiding the merchant rather than being cross with him.

"Young man," the merchant began, then grew as pale as snow, realizing the insult in that eminently common form of address. "That is to say, good my lord…"

She saw the boy's face take on a chilly expression of muted triumph. His eyes grew crisp and small, forehead flattening into something even smoother than age had already graced him with.

"Your name is … Sareq." His voice had taken on a neutral, detached tone.

"Salem, my … lord." Something had happened between the words *my* and *lord*, for the merchant suddenly grew sickly in his aspect as if he might soon vomit. Despite the cold, his forehead was covered in a sudden sheen of sweat.

"Of course. My mistake." Again, the boy spoke in an altogether pleasant tone, which had a chilling effect for some reason. Perhaps it was because it was coming out of a voice so clear and high and a body so young. "I wonder… do you treat all buyers with such casual dismissal based on how they appear unto you?"

"Good my lord, I meant no disrespect. I beg you, please forgive me. I—"

"I will pay you eight gold vévodové from my own hand to yours. You will take all appropriate precautions and turn this woman over to Skar." He indicated his guard with a casual wave of his right hand.

"Y-yes, my lord. Of course."

"And, of course, it will be your pleasure to dress her in clothing appropriate for the weather and the house to which she will shortly be brought to live."

The merchant drew in breath to protest, looked at the back of the boy's head, then at the guardsmen who had entered the room with the nobles. His eye, at last, fell reluctantly upon the boy's uncle. Lashjuk could almost see the workings of his mind written in clear ink above his head. This concession was a minor thing that rankled his pride and did little to cut into his profits. Moreover, if he accepted the boy's rebuke and insistence, there was every chance there would be repeat business—either from the boy himself or from those with whom he interacted, to say nothing of the uncle. Nodding to himself, the merchant spoke an answer.

"Yes, of course, my lord. It will be my decided pleasure. Thank you very much for gracing my humble caravan with your presence and your custom."

The boy nodded, never having turned to face the merchant since he'd entered. He now focused all his attention on her, his face not exactly unfriendly but difficult to gauge.

"Do you speak the Trade Tongue?" His voice was a touch louder than a whisper. He made no attempt to hide the fact that he was speaking to her and didn't wish to offer his words to the world at large.

She considered lying, but the boy seemed to read this in her expression, for he spoke again with even less volume.

"You can lie and pretend, but there are others who would do me the favor of speaking to you in your native tongue. It would not buy you much in the way of time to think and plan."

She blinked, then nodded. She was too confused to be angry anymore. This—a boy his age purchasing a pleasure slave—made little sense... unless the boy was sadistic. Perhaps he sought someone upon whom to indulge his cruelty. This cheerful thought served to nearly petrify her. Was it possible that she should suddenly be more afraid of the *boy* than any of her captors or tormentors? An absurd thought, surely, but the idea wouldn't leave her mind.

"Say something to me, please." He paused for a moment, then added, "Say something in the Trade Tongue, if you please."

"I..." She was far too muddled to concentrate. She shook her head, trying to clear it. "I speak it well enough."

"Very well." He smiled, and it was a genuine thing. "I am Azhferd. Would you be good enough to tell me your name?"

"Lashjuk," she found herself saying. "I am no slave. I've committed no crime, owe no debt." She paused for a long moment, or what seemed like a long moment to her at any rate, then said again, "Lord Azhferd ... I am no slave."

"I'm sorry, Lashjuk, but you are." There was no cruelty in his speech. His words were, in fact, spoken with an almost heartbreaking kindness. Still, while there was no malice, there was a deafening note of finality in his voice.

She tried to gape at him but couldn't manage even that. She was too stunned. He was right. No matter how much she hated the prospect, no matter how monstrous and unjust it was, no matter how much rage and pain she had pent up inside her at what had been done, she was, at this moment, a slave. She was *his* slave.

She heard the cage unlock and felt herself being led out onto the ground. The world darkened for a moment as a plain but well-made dress was pulled over her head. Her feet were placed unceremoniously into wooden shoes lined with some sort of fur. A plain-looking, heavy wool coat was pulled over her numb arms before being buttoned closed across her front. All of this was accomplished with a casual cruelty, which only added to her feeling of unreality.

Strong hands clasped her wrists together, enclosing them in shackles. As if she were dreaming, she saw the chain being passed from the merchant's hands to the guard called, apparently, Skar. A rolled scroll was handed past her to someone, then she was propelled out of the enormous tent. She barely noticed as the omnipresent cold assaulted the bare flesh of her face.

She *was* a slave. While she had reason to hope that the boy would be less cruel than those whose care she had only recently been in, she was still a slave. It would be days before she would recover from that realization, and by then, a good many things in her life had changed.

-III-

Venzene Duchy of Kovalun
County Jižní Pochod
Barony of Hartscross - The Ash March
28 Gerstesykli: Night of the Red Storm at Westsong

Eobum had to fight back a smile. It wasn't a joyous one, nor one of amusement. Rather, it was one of bitter commiseration. He recalled having been a slave... recalled that very well indeed. He remembered the moment when he realized the truth of his predicament and how utterly unmanning that realization had been.

He suspected her story would contain many such familiar moments from his own life. He recognized almost immediately, however, that any attempt he made at suggesting he knew how she felt would only come across as patronizing and self-indulgent. It was not—not that he could tell, at any rate—an attempt by his undermind to express superiority or self-import, yet that would undoubtedly be how it was seen. There might come a time where it would make sense or be appropriate for him to speak of his own experiences to her, but he doubted it. Instead, he forced the muscles of his face to stay relaxed and prevented them from blooming into that bitter, knowing smile.

"He took me to his home, up many stairs, past a gate set in thick stone walls, and finally into the grand building. That building would turn out to be Wieża Szymona, the county seat of Czarny Wodospad."

Haiga spoke up. "Whose son *was* he?"

Eobum thought he knew the answer but was pleased that Haiga felt the burning need to ask the question. It allowed him to keep his mouth closed so that his eyes and ears could remain open.

For a long moment, she didn't answer. She seemed to weigh out whether it would be prudent to do so. Absently, as she thought, she toyed with a small stone using the fingers of her right hand. She rolled it to the left, then right, then left again, before, at last, picking it up and wrapping a fist around it.

"He was the son of a count." Her tone didn't suggest fondness but rather amusement, almost certainly directed at Haiga. After a protracted silence, she continued. "I was more than slightly concerned, at first, given that I was to sleep in his chambers. I thought perhaps I'd judged his age wrong. I had, as he was nearing his twelfth winter, but blessedly he hadn't crossed that all-important threshold yet."

"There was a long couch in front of the fire in his chambers. I was to sleep there for the next week."

"Is that when you made your escape?"

She thought about that before answering Haiga. "Yes ... after a fashion."

-IV-

Venzene Duchy of Kamieńalun
County Czarny Wodospad
Wieża Szymona
8 -15 Kovsykli: 15 years earlier

She'd learned much that week. The people of this place seemed to be either dour or jolly and in great quantities of either demeanor.

She'd been made responsible for the young Lord's personal chambers, albeit under guard. Still, it must be said that the guards did precious little to interfere with her and neither leered, glowered, nor became chatty with her.

By day, she would spend time in the kitchens. This meant she would often be involved with the procurement of foodstuffs from the larder, the inner market, or the village below, though in the latter case, she was never alone.

By the end of her first full day, she was exhausted and had nearly fallen asleep standing up. When the boy had dismissed her for the evening, she'd only had vague recollections of even *finding* the couch she was to sleep on, let alone curling up on it to perform that twice-blessed act.

The next morning he'd instructed her to tell the kitchen he was exceedingly hungry. He wished twice the usual amount of eggs and a second helping of bread besides.

She'd thought this was excessively greedy and privileged. Still, she did as she'd been bidden. The kitchen staff seemed to make no great matter of his gluttonous command and dutifully provided her with the requested food to bring to him.

To her surprise, as he tucked in, he'd said something about being perhaps less hungry than he'd thought, offering the extra food to her.

Not one to argue as ravenous as she was, she thanked him curtly and devoured the food. She noticed him watching her as she ate, although only in brief glances. As she finished the last of her unexpected wealth of food, he mentioned the time and that he wouldn't be able to finish his porridge. He then offered the remainder to her.

Remainder? She doubted the boy had taken two spoonfuls of porridge into himself. The bowl before her was, for all intents and purposes, still full.

Before she'd finished, he'd tugged on his red coat, buttoned it, and moved toward the door. He would see her that evening. What was more, he expected to be just as hungry as he had been this morning.

She'd gotten the message.

When he'd come home that evening, he was peppered with pale, grey dust in both his hair and on the shoulders of his coat. At first glance, she'd taken this for snow but quickly dismissed that idea. It was not melting or running, even near the fire.

Undressing, he asked her to run his clothing to the laundry and to inform them that, at the least, he wanted his coat run back up to his rooms later that evening.

After performing this chore, she went back to the kitchens to retrieve the young Lord's evening meal, double-checked the portions, and returned to serve him—and hopefully herself—dinner.

He ate with some gusto and then sat before the fire, reading. As expected, he had asked for enough food for her as well. As a servant, she'd been entitled to rations with the others. While they were sustaining, certainly, she had spent more than a month on quite meager rations with the slavers. The ability to sleep directly before the fire for the past two nights had allowed her body to not merely sleep, but rest. What was more, the extra rations today had given her boundless energy compared to yesterday's mental fog and physical fatigue.

No sooner had the coat arrived, free of dust and pleasantly warm, than the young Lord undressed and crawled into bed, bidding her good night.

Two more days passed in the same way, and she thought as far as slavery went, this was far better than she'd expected. She did not allow herself to become complacent and constantly looked at the patterns that guards and servants seemed to follow. Still, she had to admit that there were far worse conditions to be in while she looked for her chance to escape.

She knew that escape meant either luck, which had as much of a chance of getting her killed as getting her freed, or careful planning. This latter was proving slightly less difficult than anticipated, and she had almost enough information to make a genuine plan. She just needed to get a better understanding of the lay of the land on the eastern side of the village. Finding a way to do that was proving difficult. Still, an opportunity *did* present itself, which she saw as, perhaps, fate finally doing her a good turn. She'd been right, of course, but in a most unexpected way.

-V-

Venzene Duchy of Kovalun
County Jižní Pochod
Barony of Hartscross - The Ash March
28 Gerstesykli: Night of the Red Storm at Westsong

Lashjuk answered the unasked question. "The grey dust came from the young Lord's lessons."

"Lessons?" Haiga sounded genuinely curious. "In what?"

"Stonemasonry," said Lashjuk.

"That makes no sense," Haiga said. "The children of nobles learn to fight and to sniff one another's backsides. They don't learn a workman's craft!" He wasn't excited so much as incredulous. Blessedly, he kept the volume of that incredulity from carrying beyond their little circle and back to camp.

"I wondered about that too, but I came to find out that Count Hengrek knew the Mason's trade, his father had, and his father, and on—all the way back to Szymon himself." She paused, shaking her head. "I imagine all noblemen would want to know as much as they could about the thing that brings them wealth, so I suppose it makes sense."

Eobum gave a brief head shake of his own.

"You disagree?" Lashjuk arched her brows.

"Only in so far as the idea that most nobles think that way."

"I'm certain there are those who are lazy and more concerned with the wealth they have than the wealth they might lose..." She trailed off, thinking on that.

"Of course, but that isn't what I meant. There is a great gap between the information you need in order to decide the value or worth of a thing—a service or goods, I mean—and learning the how and why of a thing. If he came back covered in dust, and on more than one occasion, he was learning how to work stone himself, not merely what to look for and how long a thing takes to craft."

She shifted positions, considering his words, then nodded.

He noted that, once she'd settled back, she crossed her legs above the ankles, knees bent so they faced the two men. This was a position of counsel and was usually saved for such settings. It was likely that she'd taken this position unconsciously, but Eobum's mind marked it nonetheless.

"Do you know, I think you may be right. How strange."

Eobum took no offense, presuming she was referring to the lord's behavior as strange, not his own wisdom.

"What was the change you spoke of? What happened?" Haiga sounded a trifle impatient. He'd gotten caught up in her tale, it seemed.

"The young Lord wanted me to escort him into town," said she. There was a note of amusement in her voice at this. She let her eyes go back to that half-lidded state, allowing a small smile to play across her face. After a moment's pause, almost certainly a moment in which she was replaying events over in her mind, she continued. "He'd had the kitchens prepare some meat pies and a jug of fresh cider, crisp and sour. I was to carry these things in his wake and serve them to both he and the mason from whom he'd been taking instruction. I would be under guard, of course, as ever when out of doors or when I would otherwise have been alone in Lord Azhferd's presence."

"Still, as you say, a good opportunity." Haiga sounded altogether pleased. "What did you find?"

She nodded, then allowed that small smile to play across her lips once more.

"My Gnash," said she, "that was the day I found my Gnash. Guuvra ... was the young Lord's mason—his teacher."

Gnash: the unisex term Gnoerkish society used for spouse. The meaning was closer to mate than spouse, but that was due utterly to the lack of formal religious ceremony in such matters.

In Gnoerkish society, a couple would announce their intentions to any surviving parents, gain permission, then announce it to the extended family in private. Finally, the rest of their neighbors would hear the news in the form of a great hunt, followed by a feast. Being invited to take part in the hunt was a great honor. The success of the union was often tied to the success of that hunt.

It was a joy Eobum had been denied in Istjuk, and so he smiled to hear Lashjuk hadn't suffered that distinction with him.

"He'd been born elsewhere in Kamieńalun," said she. "His father had been a Master Mason in the baronial town of Łatka Fiodora, near the Gerstealun border to the southeast. Guuvra had performed work for the count and chosen to stay on when one of the old Masons had fallen ill and died the winter before. With permission from the Masons' Lodge, he stepped in and took over the dead man's workshop."

She paused for a moment, raking her eyes briefly over Haiga before returning to the blank area between the two men. "He stole my breath." Her features took on a daydreamer's expression. "He looked as if he had been carved out of stone himself. Well-muscled, grey skin, a broad chest, thick-limbed, with strands of pale grey or smoky black hair in braids... they hung like serpents from his proud head." She trailed off, shaking slightly with the memory, then bowed her head.

Eobum heard Haiga clear his throat uncomfortably. It wasn't that hearing a woman go on about her man discomfited him. It was the fact that the man in question looked like he did, or rather, the way he might one day grow to look. He was, after all, the human equivalent of seventeen. The colorings were the same, but Haiga was thin and lanky, not tall and proud as she had described her Gnash.

"Two days later," she pulled a handful of grass by clenching her fist along the ground, "two days later, he came home with the young Lord and asked to be my Gnash."

"So, you ran with him?"

She shook her head, looking pointedly at the ground before her.

"Did he..." Haiga trailed off, uncertain how to ask the question. Finally, he seemed to just decide it would be better to ask it and have done. "Did he haggle for a price?"

She actually laughed at this. The sound came out unexpectedly, as laughter often did, and carried with it the sure sign that she'd been weeping through her silence.

"No. You're right to ask, as slaves have no freedom for such things, but no."

That was true. Throughout the Venzene Empire, slaves were thought of in much the same way as livestock. They had no real *rights,* thus couldn't enter into any sort of legal agreement. They were *property*, not *people.* In the eyes of the crown, marriage, which was the closest thing a human would normally equate to this situation, was considered a matter of legal protection.

"As I said, he came home with the young Lord. As soon as he'd seen my shock and utter joy at being asked—followed almost immediately by the realization that I couldn't accept—Azhferd spoke up. He informed me rather shyly—now I think back on it—that he'd already signed the appropriate paperwork to free me. That whether I stayed with Guuvra or not was entirely up to me. I could go with him, remain in the castle as Azhferd's servant and be paid a proper wage, be on my way, or choose any combination thereof."

Haiga's gasp made it clear he was dumbstruck.

Eobum was once again amused. He'd thought something like this might have happened. If Lashjuk's entire experience with humans had been slavery and misery, he almost certainly wouldn't be speaking with her. She'd have moved on or tried to slaughter him and his men in their sleep.

"I didn't come to find out until much later, but the young Lord had gone to the slaver's market in hopes of finding someone who might be a match for the Mason. The pair weren't close, mind you, not *before* I arrived and not after, but Azhferd hadn't taken to the craft, or its understanding, with any great ease. Guuvra had shown him patience. He'd found a way to make him understand the things his father needed him to know. The boy considered that a personal service. He'd apparently thought long and hard about how best he could repay that service. Guuvra lived alone…"

"…And there were no Gnoerks, or at least precious few that lived in or passed through that area," Eobum hadn't intended to speak the thought aloud. He'd no idea why he'd done it, but there it was: hung in the air.

"As you say."

Even now, the truth of that strange situation left her undecided as to how she should feel. It showed plainly on her face. In one breath, she wanted to cry out her thanks for the young Lord. He'd delivered her from slavery into the arms of her Gnash. On the other, he had been clearly manipulative. He'd essentially purchased her for the sole purpose of giving an acquaintance a bride in return for some personal service. That was drawing it long, perhaps. Still, if it were boiled down to its basic truth, Eobum realized, it wasn't difficult to let the mind wander toward that darker conclusion.

"Guuvra sent word to his family. I had no way of finding my own, as nobody had heard of my home, nor was it readily found on a map."

Eobum found himself speaking up once more. "Forgive me, Sister. Have you found it since?"

She waited for a long moment before bowing her head and answering. "No."

"May I know its name?"

She had a moment of indecision, then shrugged and gave her answer. "Mi Mak."

Eobum looked up toward the sky. He wore a thin smile as moon and starlight played across his face. Haiga, he was quite sure, would recognize the expression for what it was. Adric and Eranoric had long-since taken to calling it his Face of Memory. Finally, he lowered his head so he could meet her eyes once more. He was smiling. "Eoden side of the Trpytivy mountains. Mi Mak shares a border as near as no matter with Kovalun."

Lashjuk gaped. "How…?"

"My son's grand-grand-dame… his Nai-Naiog was from Mi Mak." He paused for a moment, then added, "I've never been, mind. Istjuk lay in northwestern Gerstealun, nearly two hundred leagues from where Mi Mak is supposed to rest. I can show you whereabouts to find it on a map … or tell it to you if you like."

Lashjuk offered a slow, steady nod. She didn't mistrust him, on this matter, at least. Rather, she was uncertain how to process the information. The thought of going to Mi Mak after all the miles and leagues, all the years... it was both wondrous and daunting in equal measure. "Time for that later," she said at last.

Eobum nodded his acceptance of this and prepared to speak no more.

It took her a moment to pick up the thread of her tale, but eventually, she managed it.

"Azhferd was invited to come on the hunt with Guuvra, but he..." She grew dark of mood once more. "He didn't accept."

Her next sentence came out as if she were in an argument, although not a single new facial expression had graced Eobum's face. He doubted Haiga's had changed much, either.

"I *know*; he was just a boy and a human one at that. He almost certainly didn't understand the honor or the import." She paused, then ranted on. "Yes, and a boy of that age isn't always able to do as he pleases. And, yes, as the heir, he may have been forbidden from going off on a hunt with only a single guard to protect his soft self. I know this already!" She strangled a shout before it could escape her throat. A coarse whisper was all that she allowed to carry this last pronouncement, and it made of her voice a haunted thing.

Haiga ventured to speak once she regained control.

"What then?"

Had such a simple coupling of words ever held such a transformative effect? She looked up then. Her face suddenly appeared to be suffused with the very embodiment of joy.

"Bliss," said she. "Day became night became day again. Weeks were years. A child came swiftly into our lives. A daughter, Maklo. Five years later came our first son, Sulok. A year later, our second, Maksu."

"Are they with you now, then?" Haiga sounded happy. He'd been caught and carried along by her obvious joy.

Eobum fought back the urge to wince at this seemingly innocent question. A moment later, all joy had evaporated from their little patch of starlight, as he'd feared it would.

"My boys are..."

"Whe—" Haiga stopped himself, gasping his sudden realization. He'd likely just recalled why they were there and what they were discussing.

After a moment, she spoke on in a flat, empty tone. "Word came that the Lord Azhferd wished to hire Guuvra to affect repairs and other, newer stone works in his ancestral manor. Auburg had been passed to the heir of the ruling household of the county since time was first tallied. The coin was good, and the honor was great. We completed the work, save the final adornments."

Eobum willed Haiga not to break the silence that followed. It was clear that she had been building up to this part of the tale, and Haiga's interruption would only knock her off course. Blessedly, she began again before the silence had taunted the young Gnoerk to speak up.

"The thrice-damned lord insisted on marble! And so we took horses and cart and travelled the ten-day northwest, over rough terrain in order to select his precious marble from the quarry at Biały Klif."

-VI-

Venzene Duchy of Kamieńalun
County Czarny Wodospad
Biały Klif
27 Gerstesykli: 1 day prior to the Red Storm at Westsong

While the weather had been warm enough, the wind coming off of the lake wasn't cutting. It was downright severing. Still, they'd been successful.

The marble had been selected. The price had been so masterfully negotiated that Guuvra saved nearly a quarter of Azhferd's gold while arranging enough marble to complete the remodeling with material to spare. Even now, it was being transported at the cost of the quarry, no less, or at least included in the price they had paid, all the way back to Auburg.

The boys had helped to unload their possessions from the cart when they'd arrived. In the morning, they'd load them up again. For now, they were off exploring the town with their sister.

With the children gone, they did their best to take full advantage of the time alone, retreating to the room they'd rented for the family.

The day had been a better success than they could've hoped for.

That, in retrospect, should have set off every alarm bell her under-mind could ring. Trouble is a predator. Wasn't that what all the old women said? Trouble is a predator, and happiness has ever been its favorite prey.

The trip until this point had been stressful both mentally and emotionally. They had rarely traveled so far away from home. Still, the project looked to be completed within the allotted time, for the allotted coin, and with the expected quality. Every heir to every noble household, or member of the gentry that saw the work, would seek to hire Guuvra.

And so, now that all was over save the trek home, they had done their best to conceive a fourth child—made several valiant attempts, in fact—then fell into a soft, sweet slumber.

When they finally woke, the midnight bell was ringing.

They laughed at their foolishness, cast about the room, and realized they were still alone. They presumed the children were downstairs enjoying some alone time of their own, away from their parents' prodding, nagging eye.

They dressed quickly, then ventured downstairs in hopes of finding some pottage and perhaps a cold drink—although nearly everything was cold here—in the common room. They would allow the children to spend a little more time with them before all of them trooped up to bed. They would begin the long journey home sometime near midmorning.

The children were, however, nowhere to be found. The patrons were questioned with a quickness, but neither their fellow boarders nor the staff had seen the children since that morning.

They moved to alert the watch, but their enthusiasm for a task that was nearly the very definition of their duty was minimal at best. Despite Lashjuk's panic, the bored disdain with which the constable had treated them—and the lazy way he'd referred to her husband as "Tusk"—made things clear. They'd gain no real help in finding their children. They'd worn the wrong faces to hope for any such kindness.

First, they wandered through the town, then to its outskirts for the better part of three hours. Looking at one another at the same moment, each wore the same expression of utter panic desperately hid behind a false mask of calm confidence. Each was trying—and failing—to hide their fear.

They stopped and embraced, holding to one another, uncertain of what they could say that would offer some kind—any kind—of comfort.

The wind dropped for the first time in what seemed like hours. Everything was still. Then suddenly, there was a cry, a soft, muted weeping.

They broke apart, looking at one another, each with the same intention written upon their face. As one, they turned and bolted toward the sound.

Along the lake's shore outside of town, tucked away behind several boulders, they found a single, broad tent. It had been secured with what appeared to be enormous metal stakes sunk deep into the wet ground. A nearly dead fire glowed, huddled within the sheltering bulk of the tent's shadow. A single horse cropped grass contentedly some distance away, no saddle, bit, or bridle anywhere in sight.

Again came the sound, this time clearly from within the tent—a tired, miserable whimper with a hint of gravel.

Guuvra held up a hand for her to wait, and though she wanted to do nothing of the sort, she nodded. He laid his hand to the side of her face, cupping her left cheek gently, then turned, squared his shoulders, and barged into the tent.

There was silence for what seemed like an eternity. In truth, it was less than three heartbeats, but misery always stays the sand, they say. It stretches time, stopping it from passing until its full face at last crawls into view.

She heard a growling, snarling shriek rise from somewhere beneath the sound of the wind, overtopping it, overtaking it. It was a sound of such woeful rage that, for a moment, it froze her blood. Her Gnash roared, then sounded as if he'd sprung into motion.

There were other voices somewhere behind that shrieking sound. Voices that were screaming, weeping. Terror and horror intermingled in her mind, buoyed by that dreadful music.

Just as suddenly, the air seemed to swallow the sounds. All was quiet save the baleful, shrill whistling of the wind.

Her heart thundered in her chest, fist clenching and unclenching as she waited, listened, and offered prayers in silent fear, though she knew not to whom she prayed. Perhaps the world itself?

The wind died. In that moment, she understood exactly what that turn of phrase meant. She heard heavy breathing and soft, helpless whimpering.

Lashjuk shook, trying to prepare for what she knew she must now do. She held out a moment longer, hoping against hope that she would see or hear her Gnash, then resigned herself.

Reaching down toward the area where the fire fought to stay alive, protected by the front of the tent from winds coming off the lake, she plucked up a stout-enough looking branch. A dagger wouldn't do. She had one, but a dagger simply wouldn't do. She wanted something more visceral, something with more weight behind it.

Drawing one more breath and holding it for a two count, she strode into the tent, like the queen of vengeance given flesh and feature, tusk, and terror.

-VII-

Venzene Duchy of Kovalun
County Jižní Pochod
Barony of Hartscross - The Ash March
28 Gerstesykli: Night of the Red Storm at Westsong

Lashjuk fell silent. Her throat worked, her eyes were dry and red, and her fists were clenching and unclenching along the grass, but she could not speak.

Eobum did his best to let the silence play out, hoping she would come to herself and find what she needed to finish the tale. It was clear after a moment that she couldn't. Her mouth worked, but no words would come. She was shaking, full of such rage and misery that she couldn't... couldn't what? Think? Speak? See? All of these, and none of them. There was nothing more to commend to her at this moment. She simply ... *couldn't.*

"He'd overpowered Guuvra..." Eobum kept his voice even and neutral, doing his best to keep both rage and pity as far away as he could. She would tell him which of those things she required from him, and he would do his best to oblige, but while he could help her articulate what had happened, he could not—must not—direct her reactions. Her grief was hers alone, not a thing to be altered by the likes of him.

She nodded, mouthing, "*Yes.*"

"He had the boys?"

Again, she nodded.

Once more, he held his tongue, waiting to see if she needed more from him. When a moment later, she looked at him directly, and he saw the hollow places where her eyes had once been, he knew that she did. Never allowing his eyes to leave hers, he did his best to oblige.

"Was your daughter already gone? Had he already taken her?"

After a long moment where her breath hitched in her chest, she finally spoke. Her voice started as a whisper, but as the floodgates at last opened, it once again regained its former strength.

"He had already taken her, but he hadn't yet stolen her breath." She swallowed again, then continued. "He was..." She paused. "He was mounting her, and not... not for the first time based on the state of her raiment. My Gnash lay on the floor with red staining his shirt—red over his heart." She swallowed. "When he saw me, he gaped, brandishing a dagger still wet with blood, then tried to stand."

Eobum nodded. He stilled her with a look, stood slowly, and walked back into the encampment to where Lakkrid still slept. He returned to where Haiga and Lashjuk sat in numb, horrified silence. Wordlessly, he offered her the waterskin he had retrieved.

At first, she looked at it as if she'd never seen such a thing before. A moment later, looking up to meet Eobum's eyes once more, she reached with her bright hand and took it from him.

By the time she'd finished what she'd likely intended to be a short pull, she'd drained nearly half of the skin's contents. After a moment, she spoke on.

"I shrieked. I shrieked, cursed, and have no idea what it was that I said. It doesn't matter, I suppose, but I can't recall what I said. I have a vague memory of standing over my Gnash's body and swinging my borrowed branch at the murderer's head over and over again. At some point, he must've made it to his feet and tripped me or shoved me down. I was suddenly on my back. I'd barely gotten to my feet as he bolted. When I turned to follow, I saw my boys bound and gagged just inside the tent. I'd charged in, right past them, you see."

Eobum heard Haiga's sigh, followed immediately by his growl. Based on the sound, he knew his youngest brother had his face buried in his own hands.

"I freed them, told them to see to their sister, and bolted out after him—after the monster who had taken my Gnash from me... the beast who'd tried to take my children..." She trailed off, looked down at the skin, and decided she needed another drink. A moment later, she continued. "He'd taken the horse. The ground was wet and muddy. His trail was easy enough to follow. At first, I pursued him in earnest, then the thought of my children drew me up short. I ran back as swiftly as I could."

Eobum's eyes drifted over her shoulder. Two figures peered out of the shadows. They looked to be about Lakkrid's age. It took an effort to maintain his focus on the tale... to force his eyes back to hers. The boys had lived through it. There was no reason to shield them from its retelling. Nothing said here would haunt them more than the horror they'd already been through.

"He'd stabbed her before fleeing," said she. "The knife was... was still in..." She shook, then shook her head. "He left it behind in his haste to escape. By the time I returned..." She closed her eyes and drew in a ragged breath before speaking the words aloud for the first time. "By the time I returned, my boys were kneeling over the bodies of their sister and father, weeping."

In his haste to escape. Surely not. No, Sister. That was his way of trying to slow your pursuit. Perhaps something darker. In either case, it was almost certainly not a hasty thing.

"Ed ka," Haiga hissed, then made to stand. "Ed ka hai... Ed *hai* erld! Ed shnak erld *vra!*" He was too angry to shout, too angry to do more than speak this in a low, shuddering growl as he made to turn back toward camp. (*My sword, my sword to slaughter. I'll kill you! I'll gnaw upon your heart!*)

"De, Haiga!" Eobum's voice was a stone striking Haiga's mind. (*No, Haiga!*)

"*De?* Aehe de?!" (*No? Why not?!*)

"Because she does not need a *champion*!" He allowed his voice to move from its harsh, hushed raven's caw back to something closer to his usual, neutral one. "She needs to *defeat* him, not see him killed *for* her."

Haiga sat down. It was almost an involuntary thing, but he seemed dimly aware he'd done it.

A weighty silence fell upon them, a long, ephemeral moment wherein all three were together in body but isolated in mind, each to their own thoughts. At last, Lashjuk broke the silence.

"Will you..." She paused, looking to Eobum with hope and shock in equal measure. "Will you allow this?"

"I must hear his tale." Eobum said this with as neutral a tone as he could muster, though he found it difficult to maintain his self-possession. Fortunately, Lashjuk gave him the fuel he'd needed to regain mastery of himself. She managed it by the simplest of actions.

She glared at him.

"Turn your blue fires elsewhere, Lashjuk of Mi Mak!"

The vehemence with which this had been delivered was shocking, causing her to look as if somebody had doused her in cold water.

"If *he* had come to me claiming that *you* had done horrible things... miserable, low-bellied, murderous things like this, would you have me take *his* word? Would you have me not at least *hear* your version of events before passing judgment?"

She bore the eye contact Eobum forced upon her for as long as she could, then cut her eyes to the side, her head soon following suit. She spoke in a bitter voice, then rose.

"I will await your judgment. And I will expect it to be no more just than his." Without another word, she strode back to where her children stood after displaying a muted species of shock at seeing them stood there.

Eobum sat for a long moment, wrestling with himself. He was not *as* angry as Haiga. He was fairly certain he was *angrier*.

Everything he knew—everything he'd lived through—told him he absolutely must hear the man's side. No matter his expectations, he must listen with as open a mind as he could muster. Of course, that thought meant nothing to his heart. At this moment, the thing he wanted to do most was to stand, cross the intervening distance, and step on the man's throat. He wanted to see the light go out of his eyes. He wanted to feel the breath hitching, fighting, struggling to keep the wretch alive. But he wouldn't. He would hear his tale. Then he would pass judgement and carry out whatever sentence was necessary on whichever of the pair he deemed wasn't speaking the truth.

Here in the woods, fully a day's march from any town—Biały Klif was, indeed, the closest just across the border. With a day's march between here and Jižní Lov, might did indeed make right. The only laws that extended to the wilds were those made by the men willing to enforce them.

But no, as much as that's the accepted truth, I cannot allow I or mine to become the savage, lawless things that Venzene thinks the Eodenth are. He paused, coming to a realization. *Then again, I suppose I don't have to. I and mine are the count's own agents.*

With a winterish smile, he, at last, stood, offering a hand to Haiga. He put a hand on the Gnoerk's shoulder as he found his feet, guiding him back toward the fire.

A DRAUGHT OF THE BITTERSWEET

-I-

Venzene Duchy of Kovalun
County Jižní Pochod
Barony of Hartscross - The Ash March
28 Gerstesykli: Night of the Red Storm at Westsong

Eobum paced the perimeter of their makeshift camp, trying to find his center. He'd done so for an hour, perhaps more, and felt no less troubled in mind or sick of heart for his efforts.

His restlessness wouldn't make the march back home any easier. Marching tired ran the risk of missing the signs that trouble was on the come—bad, or reacting slowly when it did—worse. Still, they were only a day's march from their beds; sometimes rest was a luxury. Besides, most of his men still slept. He trusted them to pick up on things he missed if it came to that.

At times like this, his father, Idohelm's voice was a hard thing to hear. Yet the old goat's apparition always seemed to rise out of the murk of his frustrated mind.

It was more than Idohelm's bitterness that made recalling his voice so painful. It was the fact that the memory dragged behind it every feeling of loss and inadequacy a fourteen-year-old Eobum had carried with him from the man's early grave.

There was also all the bigotry and oppression that the Eodenth had suffered since time was first tallied. It was a thing Idohelm ranted on about ceaselessly, finding reasons to be miserable even where there were none.

If a man or woman not of Eodenth blood were to pass his father on the street and offer a simple good morning, Idohelm would be angry for the rest of the day. What was worse, he never took that anger out on its cause. Instead, he took it out on those around him ... which meant Eobum bore the brunt.

"Make no mistake," he would say. *"The Land of Duchies is corrupt, I tell you. That rot can be found nearly all the way to the feet of the right noble Emperor of Ashes himself."*

The truly wretched thing was that his father wasn't simply carrying old, mindless grudges for the sole sake of tradition and pride.

Throughout the centuries-long stand-off between the Imperial Throne and the folk of Eoden, or as the rest of Venzene insisted on thinking of it, The Duchy of Eoalun, the Eodenth had been second-class citizens at best.

The Gnoerkish and half-Gnoerkish folk who lived within Eoden's official borders, often joining Eodenth clans and tribes, were fortunate if they were considered even second-class by most of Venzene's population.

They were prized slaves, prized mercenaries, or prized pets to be treated as the whims of their masters dictated.

That tribes took in Gnoerkish blood was seen as further proof of Eoden lunacy by most. With no sense of irony, his father had been in total agreement with that sentiment. All the while, he raved about the preening, strutting nobility for their treatment of his homeland and its people.

Idohelm had been so bigoted a man that Eobum had never actually seen a Gnoerk up close. That'd held true until years later, when he'd been surrounded by them... when they'd captured him, bound him, and taken him to Istjuk... when he'd first laid eyes on Suruk... when he'd become hers.

"Where are you now, I wonder?" Only the wind replied, of course, and perhaps the crackling fire as it burned low in the near distance. He gave a gentle snort. It was a humorless thing and cold. "Did you hear her tale?" He widened his eyes as if to take in more of his surroundings—as if she might actually appear and answer. "Do you hate me for what I... no, that's nonsense. You wouldn't hate me for being who I am—who I have to be. You might *hit* me for it, but there'd be no hate in it." The thought cheered him somewhat. He pictured how she'd have responded to him and couldn't help but smile.

His voice had been low, but perhaps it was the low noises that wakened the troubled sleeper. Certainly, he'd seen the nobleman stir by the fire.

Fenglem looked over, meeting Eobum's eye with a questioning expression.

Eobum shook his head and made to pat the air with his hands.

Fenglem nodded his understanding. He would remain where he was. There was nothing to fear or to fight ... at the moment, at any rate.

The wind gusted, and he smelled the faint, somehow warm smell of horseflesh. There was at least one horse close enough to scent. That fact made him both smile and sad simultaneously. It went at least a small way toward proving the Gnoerkish woman, Lashjuk, honest. It made him sad for the same reason.

"Dish awka drak, Suruk, aye?" He kept his voice barely more than a whisper. The dead didn't need the living to shout for them to hear. "The sun and the water? Your first lesson to me, but it was that moment of ... poetry? Would you call that poetry?"

His mind's eye focused on her ruined face—or what he'd thought was her ruined face. Scarred and pitted, he'd thought her a demon-thing come to torment him at the end of his life, or what he'd expected to be its end.

-II-

**Venzene Duchy of Gerstealun
County Stromkuss
Istjuk
32 Havsykli: Twelve years prior to the Red Storm at Westsong**

Eobum had been bloodied and stripped, with no expectation of survival. She had been the one to argue with the orc—for then it had been "orc" to his understanding—that had taken him captive.

What he'd been able to see of her skin had been the shadowed green of deep forest grasses where only dappled light found its way. That face, however... that face had been monstrous.

She had ordered him carried to a deep cut in the stone face of the hillside—her quarters, as it turned out.

She'd leaned over him as he lay upon the pallet, looked him up, then down without reservation, then nodded, shrugging one languid shoulder. In a voice that called to mind honey and oats—sweet and graveled all at once—she'd spoken to him for the first time.

"Dish awka drak," she'd said, and seeing that he didn't comprehend, she'd spoken it again in the Trade Tongue. "The beautiful, the simple, these things are as steady ... as unchanging as sunlight on the water—as dish awka drak."

He'd been so struck by the imagery—the absurdity of who had painted it on the canvas of his mind's eye—that he didn't at first register the words had been spoken in the Trade Tongue. He'd been told that orc-kind weren't *people*. They were simple-minded, warlike *creatures*. At best, they were lesser-Eodenth people... Eodenth war-beasts for mercenaries or great chieftains. And he'd never actually *seen* one before their ill-fated patrol that morning.

"They're the true savages, not the Eodenth." His father had preached that gospel to anyone who'd stand and listen. And the deeper in his cups he fell, the louder and more zealous he'd become. *"Every unkindness heaped on our people? It's the damned orcs' fault. The snakes that sit on the Venzene throne? Their rot runs too deep to let 'em see the truth! The orcs are the savages. It's them what's earned the blood and bluster tales of worthless war-waking and faithless field burning. But it's we of the horse and spear who eat the ire of the Emperor of Ashes, ain't it just? Aye. As if we be responsible for tusk-minding!"*

Yet that image—that thought of life itself as a fragile light rippling with the breeze, shattering with the simplest touch to the water's surface—he had heard nothing put so perfectly, it pulled his mind, momentarily at least, away from the fear and death that surrounded him.

Then she'd removed the mask. How Eobum hadn't seen—not known it'd been a mask was beyond him. It was so damned obvious once she'd removed it. Her true face was green, fading into gold. That golden hue cradled her high cheekbones and the brilliant, burnished brown of her almond-shaped eyes, tapering as it brushed her lips and chin. Her hair was cropped close to her pate and stood a black contrast to the rest of her.

She'd smiled at him, and without the fright mask—the hunting mask, he would later learn—that smile felt far less predatory. There was still something dangerous in it, though.

She'd reached to her shoulders and slid the straps of her leather breastplate off them. Reaching next to her midriff, she pulled the entire cuirass up over her head as if it were a long shirt, then allowed it to drop onto the floor beside her.

Her breasts were on display, and he couldn't help but stare. They were colored things, deep green, just as nearly all of her seemed to be, though the gold of her face tapered down between them. They were modest in size... not simply *normal,* but *beautiful. She* was beautiful. He'd struggled to find a better word... one that did her more justice. But he was no singer or poet. Every word he knew fell short.

The orcs of his father's many stories, coupled with those of his comrades in the Venzene military, made the orc a thing of monstrous fear. Nothing had prepared him for the warm reality that stood before him.

She'd smiled once more, noting his body's reaction. He could hardly hide it, after all. With clear deliberation, her eyes never leaving his, she bent toward him again. The act nearly unmanned him. Dimly, he'd become aware of her removing her soft leather boots.

Wide-eyed, he'd looked at her, fallen into her eyes, smelled the crushed hazelnut of her breath, the sweet sweat of her skin...

-III-

Venzene Duchy of Kovalun
County Jižní Pochod
Barony of Hartscross - The Ash March
28 Gerstesykli: Night of the Red Storm at Westsong

Eobum stopped, pulling himself back from the memory. He bowed his head, turning away from the sleeping camp to face the west.

It had been nearly nine years since last he'd seen her, but some part of him still relived it. Some part of him would always dwell in Istjuk as it had been: vra, gi, awka ragkarlash *(heart, blood, and fire).*

With an effort, he forced his mind back to the task at hand. The wounded man still slept. Eobum could see him curled up before their low fire. He wanted to string him up here and now, watching until he finished his final dance at the end of one of Alusc's ropes.

I have to hear his story, have to listen with open ears, not angry ones. He had to master himself. Lashjuk might have been less than honest with him. He doubted it, and having to wait to find out and take the appropriate action was maddening!

Still, he would wait. He knew that the young nobleman needed to heal—needed some *actual* rest. He would get more out of him if the man were at least somewhat recovered and, of course, predisposed to those who had helped him get to that happy condition. *If he's honest...* Eobum doubted it, but never mind. *If he's honest, we'll wind up escorting him back to Edmund, more than likely.* The more he rested now, the easier that trek would be. If the man was false, it would be easier to get the truth from him if he believed he'd found allies.

Nothing for it. I'll give him half a bell longer, then I'll waken him and be damned to his wounds. Alusc will wind up awake near then, anyway, to prepare the morning meal. It's as good a time as any to get it over.

He would listen, then make his judgement. He would remember his Suruk. How could he not with their boy sleeping so close at hand? He would remember her, and he would remember his father, but he would also remember the truth he'd been taught many times over. It's only in stories and songs—memory and make-believe—that people are ever really the heroes or monsters we make of them.

-IV-

Venzene Duchy of Kovalun
County Jižní Pochod
Barony of Hartscross - Jižní Lov
29 Gerstesykli: 1 Day after the Red Storm at Westsong

Dawn was, perhaps, an hour off yet. The Bluemark Guard encampment was stirring. Only those men and women who truly wanted a future—who truly were willing to work for one might be a better way to frame it—were up and in the doings.

Most days, there wasn't time for individual practice with the sword, glaive, spear, or shield forms. There wasn't time to square away armor, boots, or personal effects. There wasn't really even time to personally see to mounts and tack, although the Guard had several farriers among them who were meant to make regular rounds and sort the steeds.

These fine folk even sometimes did so, but they were mostly old bastards—literally as well as figuratively. As proof of their pedigree, they seemed to operate on the same methodology that had been the sole purview of old bastards since time out of mind. To wit, if you don't care, why should they?

As with most things, the ability to see to and sort the hundred things that made a mercenary's life easier—when it was time for battle or contract negotiation—was directly proportional to the time that mercenary could carve out of the day to address them.

Days were only so long. Carving out time, therefore, meant getting up earlier. An hour, perhaps two, would be enough. One only had to rise an hour or two earlier than was strictly *necessary*. Then one would *have* that time to see to armor, boots, and tack all items repaired with leather tools.

Want more training with your horse? He recalled his Uncle Borys's voice whenever he was tempted to have a late lay-in. *Riding the beast each morning will turn the trick. Within a week, your bond will have improved noticeably. Mark me.*

It was true of most things. The kontusz—the company-issued black horseman's longcoat—for instance, often found itself in need of a stitch or three. One could try to repair it in the saddle or sort it at the end of a long shift around the fire at night.

*Another option—one far too commonly taken, I'm sorry to say—*the version of his uncle that served as his conscience never failed to remind him—*would be to leave it until that sudden, magical flash of realization hits you. Then you can rush to take care of it before someone notices how disorganized and undisciplined you—and, by extension, your fellows—have become. Or you could simply wake up early and see to that in the morning before the day gets old, and the matter gets driven out of your head.*

Rising a few hours early wasn't the solution for all stones that wound up in the boot, but it certainly made things easier when all of one's gear, training, and mind were sorted before ever mounting up or taking a shift of duty somewhere.

And so—though most of not merely the Guard's, but the count's encampment, slept and snored—Geroslaw and a handful of other men and women went about their preparations.

If owning war-trained horses was a clear mark of wealth, owning Mądra Ręka was a mark of nobility, as sure as any blue mark of birth. Rather than a breed, outside of Kamieńalun, they were considered more a size or class of steed. Going back centuries before the Empire's founding, they'd been bred for heavy cavalry and anti-infantry combat, trampling footmen before those footmen had time to soil themselves at the sight of an onrushing charge.

Even in a company that counted most of its membership as noble bastards and discarded latter-born sons, a Mądra Ręka was a rare sight. Riding atop such a beast into the Bluemark encampment for the first time had set Geroslaw well apart from the average sell-sword.

That fact hadn't escaped his notice. It was a large part of why he rose so early. Tending to the needs of his prized mount was not only of genuine importance but was an unmitigated labor of love.

And so it was that he'd just begun currying down Krwawa Zima when the first hints of hoof beats came to his ears.

He looked up in time to see a lone rider racing into the wooden palisade. Stilling himself, he listened for the sound of an alarm. In short order, the truth became apparent as banners were unfurled. They displayed heraldry he hadn't seen before but which had been described to him in great detail as they'd ridden to this place.

All heraldry was couched in Havalunth. He presumed that was because the Duchy of Havalun had begun the unification and thus founded the Empire centuries back up the hourglass, though he wasn't certain. Regardless of why it was so. The blazon—the agreed-upon terms with which heraldry could be described accurately—was in that ancient tongue, even down to the colors.

He ran the first two fingers of his left hand through the lowest portion of his black beard, smoothing it out beneath the complication of leather cord that bound it.

"So... ruter, grønne, and gyldne. En hjort, sølv... is that right? Those are ruter: gemstones—diamonds, just as they are on playing cards. I know my colors are right—green and gold... and the deer in the center is silver. Hjort, though?" He moved his left hand up to scratch the area just beneath his nose, running his other hand along Krwawa Zima's right side with the brush. "Is that the right term for a hart?"

He grinned to himself. No warning bell would be forthcoming. The device on the banners was that of Count Edmund of Hartscross. Their display could only mean one thing. The count and his party were near.

Stepping around to curry down the animal's great sorrel chest, he used his left hand to caress the area along the underside of Krwawa Zima's chin.

"What do you say? Have I gotten that right? Huh? What d'you think, Krwawa Zima?" His voice was soft, his affection for the horse obvious.

Krwawa Zima's response was equally full of clear affection. His proud red ears perked as far forward as they could go. A velvet rumble escaped his throat, and he dipped his head to first nuzzle, then push upon the man's chest, eliciting a soft, barking laugh.

"I think that's right. What do you know about heraldry anyway, eh? Syr Borys never let me bring you into the map room to study it, did he? Huh? Did he…"

He returned to his work, cheered as he thought back to his youth and the magic of make-believe.

Thunder on the come: he felt the column before he'd rightly heard it. He saw the gates to the palisade thrown wide and could just make out the stables and paddock beyond them.

The first few horses came riding in at speed. The dust clouds in their wake mingled with the smoke from the remainder of the evening's fires before rising to choke the scatter of overhanging trees. A score of assorted black, blond, and brown-haired boys and young men came running out from beneath the eaves of the wooden stable complex. In heavy, black britches and leather boots, one couldn't call what they were wearing a uniform, strictly speaking. Still, from the youngest at eight to the eldest at perhaps twenty-two, each of them bore sun-darkened flesh over a sheaf of work-hardened muscle.

They lined up four abreast, hands clasped behind their backs, and tried not to look half-asleep as they watched the horsemen slow, then come to a stop before them.

Fifty men, perhaps a few more, dismounted in reasonably ordered fashion as the stable boys came on, grabbing reins and leading mounts away as swiftly as may be.

He nodded at this scene and went back to work on his own mount.

Within thirty minutes, he had everything seen to. Krwawa Zima had been fed, watered, brushed, had his hooves inspected and cleaned, and a daub of salve applied to the area between his nostrils where a touch of rain rot had set in.

Now, he was cropping grass and occasionally stomping his forefoot contentedly some ten feet from the tent.

He seems pleased with the way his morning's gone thus far, Geroslaw thought and smiled.

He'd pulled out the pieces of an unassembled camp bench. Hands moving seemingly of their own accord, he slid the two slats of wood together, perpendicular to one another. He then slotted a wooden peg into place, locking them together. He repeated the process on the longer piece's other side. Placing his newly reconstructed seat on the ground just outside of his tent, he nodded his satisfaction.

Then he retreated into the tent and pulled out a saddlebag, a broad-bladed sword, and a heater-shaped shield of wood edged in rawhide and bound with leather cord.

Settling himself, he produced a small vial of oil, a tightly furled piece of thin leather, and a whetstone from the saddlebag.

After taking a moment to cast an eye back to his horse, he set about seeing to his weapon.

Some fifteen minutes later, the sword had been rightly sorted, and he'd started tightening the leather cords that held his shield's edging in place. Gradually, he noticed he'd been humming. The realization made him stop, look over at the horse as if in accusation, then shake his head, snorting.

It was a song from home—from his father's home, at any rate. The dissection of the count's heraldry mixed with the familiar acts of daily need had, it seemed, stirred something within him.

It'd been his little brother's favorite song. He'd taught it to the heir perhaps a year before he, himself, had lost that lofty title.

After a moment, he shrugged. Checking to see how close sunrise was—minutes by the look of the sky—he began to sing.

Oddech lasu pod niebem,
Szepcze do mnie słowa.
Mówi o ludziach którzy błagali o śmierć,
Kiedy okradli cię po raz pierwszy.

"Absolutely beautiful." Her voice came out in dark, silken alto tones. It carried a softened version of the Kovalunth accent, making the Trade Tongue sound smooth as it transitioned from word to word. "I didn't expect to find such beauty in a sell-sword's camp."

He froze in the act of drawing in breath after the last line. Hells, he'd jumped half out of his skin! She must've come from the count's encampment, a place he'd put his back toward when he sat. He turned, meaning to say ... something? He'd no idea what. At least he was smiling.

The sight of her was unexpectedly striking. She stood tall for a woman—perhaps five feet and some seven or eight inches more. She'd dressed to greet the day in riding leathers that made a dark suggestion of her figure rather than accentuating it. Her shoulder-length hair lay like satin at midnight, covering one leather spaulder. Still, it was her manner that was most striking of all perfectly calm, perfectly at ease, utterly sure of her place in the world ... which was wherever she damned well wanted it to be.

She glanced down at him, arching one thin brow at his prolonged inspection, then seemed to look past him.

"I..." He paused, collecting himself. "Thank you, Lady."

"Yours, then?"

He shook his head, grinning up and trying to meet her eyes. "Far too old to be mine, Lady."

"Nonsense," said she. "Can't be more than, what, twelve? Fifteen?"

He blinked ... hard. "No, Lady. It's been around for ages."

"It?" She bent at the waist, looking past him. "*He*, you mean, surely."

Understanding broke upon his face. He blushed, then bowed his head, issuing soft, self-recriminating laughter.

She turned her face back to him, then offered smooth laughter of her own.

"The song was pretty, too, mind. I simply know horses better than I know Kamieńalunth."

He nodded, still chuckling at his mistake.

"Aye, fair. How much Kamieńalunth do you know?"

Her answer was swift and came without the embarrassed tones one might expect when admitting the depths of one's own shortcomings.

"Including Kamieńalun, Kamieńalunth, zatrzymać, and perhaps my favorite phrase, Będę cię kastrować..." She trailed off as he laughed at full volume. As the sound died down, she finished, "None at all."

Their laughter intermingled—alto and gruff baritone. As it died away and he'd drawn his forearm across his face to wipe the tears it had summoned, he spoke again. "'Stop,' and 'I will castrate you,' eh? Useful phrases to know, I don't doubt."

"Ohhh, yes." She drew the word *oh* out long as if it were going over a gentle hill. "I've had far too many opportunities to perfect my pronunciation."

"And what am I to call you, oh Ender of Lines?"

She snorted at that title, then nodded approval.

"Ender of Lines—I liiike that." This time *like* was drawn out, though in a rising tone, being dragged up the hill rather than down.

He nodded a single time, deep and playfully respectful.

"Kastan," said she.

He stood at last, bowing a shallow, polite bow without exaggeration.

"Geroslaw." He found himself staring at her hawk-like face as he righted himself. "I can introduce you if you like."

She blinked, then grinned.

"I'd like that. First, however, I've come to deliver a message to your captain or one of his sergeants. You matched the description Lord Alojz gave me, which was what first brought me over."

Geroslaw nodded, drawing his gaze to focus on her lips as she spoke.

"What was the message, then, Kastan, Ender of Lines?"

She grinned, light dancing in her black eyes for a moment before she straightened, then clasped her hands behind her back, her feet spread to shoulder's width.

"His Excellency Syr Edmund of Hartscross wishes to meet for the morning meal an hour after sunrise. Captain Jastrab is permitted to bring a single aide as needed."

He nodded, and after waiting to confirm that there was nothing further to it, he asked a simple question.

"Do you need to return with an answer?"

"...To what question?"

That was true. There had been a polite order, not a gentle question, in the message.

"Very well. I will introduce you to Krwawa Zima, who's twenty and one, by the by."

She made a "lead on" gesture. As they walked, she tried and failed to pronounce the horse's name.

"How does it run in the Trade Tongue?"

"Krwawa zima? Bloody Winter. Odd for a stallion's name, I know, given its feminine construction. But it was the name he came with."

She beamed.

"Perfect. I shall work on pronouncing it correctly, but it helps to know what the name means. Well, it helps me, at any rate."

Krwawa Zima took to her quickly. He even went so far as to nuzzle the back of her neck into the satin cavern beneath her hair.

"I must go inform the captain. You'll be..."

"Right here where you left me," she finished for him, nodding. "If, of course, you find me a curry brush to while away the time."

He did so and left her contentedly pampering Krwawa Zima, the chore of attending to the edging of his shield quite forgotten.

-V-

Venzene Duchy of Kovalun
County Jižní Pochod
Barony of Hartscross - The Ash March
29 Gerstesykli: 1 Day after the Red Storm at Westsong

"I'm called Kuba. I'm Lord of—" He paused, allowing a disgusted chuckle to pass through his dry lips. "I vas the Lord of Cztery Wzgórza, though I vould undershtand if you had trouble believing that." *Believing* had come out *be-lie-ving*. He gestured down the length of his body, indicating his disheveled appearance and dirty state.

Eobum sat near the wounded man called Kuba in front of the newly built-up fire. Alusc Aldhelm crouched across from his commander. He'd come over to the fire a few moments before and was now frying button mushrooms in a saucepan with some salted pork that he'd cut into thick rations of bacon.

Fenglem and Haiga were off near Lakkrid, who was still comfortably curled up under a cloak and hides beneath the ash tree.

Eobum nodded, affecting an air of consideration and uncertainty. "That's," he held out the "s" before finishing, "somewhere in the northeast of Kamieńalun?"

"North-vest, though southeast of here, closer to the vestern border vith Havalun than the northern one vith Eoalun." *Than* had come out *san*.

Eobum made an "Ah" sound and nodded, looking duly corrected. He knew full well where the hamlet was. He'd raided the place as a boy, along with the rest of his clan. That this man did, too, may mean nothing more than that he knew Kamieńalun's geography. It might also mean that he was speaking the truth.

Why a noble from Kamieńalun was wearing clothing of Kovalun and speaking with a muted accent indicating he was Kovalunth, however, was a mystery—one Eobum intended to solve.

"Two veeks a'gone, during the festival, my younger brother man-age-ed some miss-shief." Kuba had pronounced *a'gone* as *ago-n* rhyming with known.

"Sigdmåne," Alusc's bright tenor voice came out soft and sympathetic as he stirred the pot both physically and diplomatically. "Aye, that's the right time for mischief. Ain't it just." While this last might have been seen as a question, his tone made it clear it was not. Rather, Aldhelm conveyed distracted commiseration, suggesting he was recalling his own Sigdmåne war stories.

The festival of Sigdmåne was a night of nearly every desire fulfilled— if one had the coin to buy or the strength to take it.

"Yuh, but only folk of Havalun take it so serious, no?" Eobum kept his tone light... well, light for him, in any event. "I mean, it's their festival... a holdover from their traditions, not the whole of the Empire's, yuh?"

Eobum had meant Aldhelm to catch the oddity—the use of "yuh" rather than his usual "aye." As he saw the cook's eyes flit toward him, he knew he'd succeeded. He shifted to sit with his legs folded beneath him, using the motion to hide his use of Hunter's Sign with his left hand.

Be wary. Be a wheel, not a stone. This was an old axiom Eobum had introduced to the unit. Stones sat by quietly and watched the world pass them by. Wheels were round and rolled. They made the occasional noise as they trundled along, helping to move a heavy thing with greater ease than simply carrying or dragging it.

When Alusc Aldhelm reached to remove a pinch of spice from his pack, Eobum caught his brief, signed response.

A wheel, not a stone.

Good enough. Alusc would help Eobum carry the deception and would make the necessary noise to keep it rolling along. *Hells...* Eobum realized with a grin that it likely wouldn't even slow down the making of the camp's breakfast.

"No," Alusc said. He shook his head, then cocked it to the side like a bird, turning the shake into a half-hearted nod. "A'mean, you're right, o'course. They celebrate it more fully in Havalun. They're all as crazed as ever. Spend all year pushing down their grudges. They wait for that sickle moon to rise each Gerstesykli so they can go mad, murder, steal, rape, raid, and wreck without reservation. Same as it ever was."

He snorted, moving the mushrooms around in the pan with a wooden camp spoon as he spoke.

"All I mean to say is this. Just because the rest of the empire doesn't spend its year holding its grudges or stifling its wants to do a mischief... you needn't think it means they don't take every chance to do such *legally* on Sigdmåne." Alusc snorted. "Hells, I nearly got killed in my sixteenth year on Sigdmåne..." He trailed off, letting that hang in the air. Alusc seemed to know his role by heart. He'd be invited to continue the tale if Eobum wanted him to tell it in front of the younger man.

Kuba made a gesture that might have served as a nod, jutting his chin forward to accomplish it. He drew his right knee toward his chest and placed his chin upon it. The result was a child-like posture, which made his youth even more pronounced. If he'd noticed Eobum's use of "yuh," he offered no sign.

"He show-ered me vith fine mead and vine, and ev-en lent me his new-bought slave for the night. He knew I'd always fancied tusks." *Slave* had come out *slav*.

Eobum caught Alusc fighting the urge to wince. He managed it well enough, but the effort had cost him a touch of focus and composure.

"'Ave you spent much time around them, then, Lord Kuba?" Alusc asked this with a hint of doubt held clearly in his voice.

"Yuh, I have had man-ee orku slaves," said he. "Have" had come out "haff," "slaves" "slavs." Most importantly, "yeah" had come out "yuh," just as Eobum had pronounced it.

"Ah." Alusc Aldhelm nodded his head as if he'd expected such an answer.

"Vhy ... do you ask?"

Kuba had elongated the word "why," though Eobum didn't ascribe any special significance to it. It was a product of the man's accent. He thought he'd almost pinned him down on that score.

Every Duchy spoke the Trade Tongue. Hells, most of the world spoke it—it was how trade between peoples and nations had been conducted since time was first tallied. Each Duchy, however, maintained its own Old Tongue—the language its people spoke amongst themselves before the unification. Serfs still spoke their duchy's old tongue, in addition to at least some broken form of the Trade Tongue. Some noble houses did, as well. The peasants and gentry—merchants, craftsmen, and bachelor knights—were all too happy to avoid learning the tongues of their fore-bears, preferring to focus on the future: the Trade Tongue.

If one were attentive and patient, one could learn a lot about someone based on how they spoke. Anyone could wear clothing if they were fortu-nate or resourceful enough to find such. Accents and language were harder things to hide or hide behind if the listener was patient.

Kuba's accent wasn't clear enough to be Kovalunth, although it was closer to that than Kamieńalunth. There was something in the way he'd spoken that last, though. It wasn't only his use of *yuh*—a pronunciation that came from the more southerly regions of the Empire. No, something about how he'd said "ask," pronouncing it as if it rhymed with "tusk."

Eobum would need to listen more—draw the man out. That suited him down to the ground. It meant he could practice his favorite social weapon—economy of speech. Better to speak last and only as much as need be. One could always learn more by listening than by speaking.

Alusc spoke in answer to Kuba's question.

"You used the word tusk."

"Yuh, I did."

There it was again—*yuh*, but *did* came out clipped, as if it were spelled *didt*.

Alusc shrugged, flipping the meat as it sizzled in his saucepan. As he did so, he made the fingers of his left hand move to scratch his beard, then his right temple.

Should I continue?

As he lowered that hand, wrapping it around the pan's long handle to steady it, Eobum saw his eyes. Alusc was looking for a signed response. In a moment, he obliged.

Yes. More.

Alusc turned back to Kuba, albeit briefly. "Well, my lord, d'you know what that word means?"

Kuba frowned, both confused and more than a trifle annoyed. "It means tusk." As if to demonstrate, Kuba moved his hands—so that his two index fingers were pressed against his chin—their first knuckles protruding just above his upper lip, mimicking the elongated lower fangs of a Gnoerk. "It de-scribesh them assa they are. They may be savages, but they are noble ones. It isn't an insult. They call one another that often enough. You must have heard this with your captain's orku, surely." He sounded defensive and, ironically, angry on behalf of the whole Gnoerkish race.

Eobum again heard a stew of accents in this rant. *Age* came out rhyming with the letter *H*, *savages* sounded more like *saff-ah-ges*, and *as* came out *ass-a*.

"Forgive me, but that's half right, at best."

Kuba threw a burning look toward Aldhelm, though it was to Eobum that he spoke. He managed a haughty, wits-end voice.

"Captain, I demand you silence your camp's cook at once. I will speak with you, who have been most kind to me, but I will not sit here and be instructed by a..." He trailed off, groping for the right insult, the insult that would avoid alienating the captain himself. Both Eobum and Aldhelm were clearly of Eoalunth stock, so a jibe of that sort—calling Alusc horse humper or mud-rutter—was out of the question.

And there it was. Eobum saw his chance, hefted his mental spear, and struck.

"Bauernsohn?" *Farmer's son?*

Eobum finally thought he'd unearthed the truth. As a result, he'd switched into Gerstealunth, the old tongue of a Duchy far to the southeast.

Kuba made a fierce "there you have it" gesture and spoke in an angry, rapid rant. The speed and vehemence with which he spoke called to mind the cloudburst they'd suffered at sunset last evening.

"Bauernsohn, du hast verdammt recht! Ich weigere mich belehrt zu werden—" Kuba froze in mid eruption. His face had gone the color of parchment, his eyes growing wide and afraid.

"Wake!" Eobum barked.

As if they'd been waiting for his word—some of them no doubt had— Eranoric, at the least, had been awake and listening from his place behind Kuba to the man's right. The camp was suddenly full of standing men with their weapons drawn. Standing men and one sleepy boy with crust in his eyes and a dagger in his hand for good measure.

Aldhelm hadn't moved. He calmly pulled meat and mushrooms onto a pair of wooden plates as if nothing had happened.

Kuba looked as if he might wet himself. The man opened his mouth to speak several times, but nothing came out.

"You have been *lying* to me, my lord. In *your* home, I *might* tolerate that. I would be a guest under your roof. The *forest*, however, is *my* roof."

Eobum found that he rather enjoyed the sickly shade of green Kuba's face had taken on at this pronouncement. He also found that for all that, he hated knowing the truth nearly as much.

Kuba's lie didn't prove out Lashjuk's tale. It only proved that he was a liar. Men weren't usually hanged for lying unless the lie was big enough.

Enough, he thought. *Time I get to the bottom and have done.*

"Let me be plain, Kuba the Liar."

Kuba bristled, eyes darting this way and that.

"I know your mind at this moment," Eobum said. "Even now, you're looking for a bolt hole, trying to work out if you can outrun my men. I'll save you time. You can."

Kuba snapped his head around to regard Eobum with frank fascination.

"Wh—what?" There was now little trace of his accent. It was all but gone.

Eobum nodded, expression helpful though not overly friendly.

"Even with your wounded knee, you could outrun them. None of them will chase you. You have my word on that score."

Kuba shook his head. He was trying and failing to get the sense of Eobum's words—which were incongruous, given the situation.

"If you run, they will not give chase." Eobum repeated this in a patient tone. After a moment, once he'd seen Kuba's shoulders slump into a relieved, relaxed posture, he continued, "If you run, I'll simply have them lob their azhkasts at you 'til you stop moving. No need to wind them. We've a long march ahead of us, after all." He grinned. It was an altogether unpleasant thing, full of white teeth and black joy. "Hear me, lads? If Lord Kuba, here, runs? Garys!" (*spears*). "The one that fells him will get my share of Aldhelm's next stew!"

This was met with arched brows, wide grins, and murmured sounds of genuine interest.

Kuba's body tensed, and the green of his face shifted to something the color of pale poison.

"What do you want from me?"

"A thing you'll likely be loath to give up..."

-VI-

Venzene Duchy of Kovalun
County Jižní Pochod
Barony of Hartscross - Jižní Lov
29 Gerstesykli: 1 Day after the Red Storm at Westsong

Geroslaw moved toward the great rectangular tent that served as Captain Jastrab's chambers. A lone guard stood outside of its entrance, looking utterly uncomfortable. A moment later and Geroslaw understood why.

A transported moan—mid-paced and rhythmic—rolled out from the tent's heavy canvas. The woman sounded as if she were enjoying herself. While she might be making a show of such, as some women were wont to do, even that seemed to be a form of enjoyment. Why do so otherwise? True, the game, then, would be more of the mind than the body, but if that made the woman happy, who was he to gainsay it?

He lifted a hand to catch the guard's attention.

His approach was met with undisguised nervousness, as if the guard had done something wrong or was somehow meant to have kept the acts within the tent silent.

"Drew the low card, did you?"

The guard made frantic shushing gestures.

"I doubt the captain is asleep."

"He is not!" Jastrab's voice came out of the tent, annoyed and amused all at once. He sounded as if he were speaking in mid-thrust.

"Well," Geroslaw raised his voice, shaping it toward the tent's opening, much to the guard's awed fear, "the captain shouldn't be entertaining anyone other than his wife in there. She won't thank you for it."

"How," he paused for a shallow, panting breath, "would she find out?"

"I'll *tell* her, of course. When she finds out anyway, her wrath will be swift and deadly." He locked eyes with the guard, grinning an imp's grin. "*You* may be willing to risk her ire, but I like my stones ... *and* my ability to speak in complete sentences."

This was met with one final thrust, two contented sighs, and a harmony of laughter.

"You give my husband too much credit, Geroslaw." She paused to draw in a deep breath and, by the sounds of it, rise from their camp bed. When she spoke next, her voice sounded nearer. "He's a wise coward, just as you are." The tent flap opened, closing swiftly to cover all but the pretty blonde head of a middle-aged beauty who likely wouldn't begin to show signs of *true* age for another few years. "I'm *so* very proud of you both."

He laughed, and so did Jastrab from somewhere behind her.

On the other hand, the guard looked as if he might pass out from fear and confusion.

"I am *always* happy to make you smile, my lady."

After a moment of genuine amusement at this byplay, she opened her mouth to speak but was cut off by Jastrab before she'd done more than draw breath.

"Well, you've failed to stop the inevitable, Sergeant. That's good, as it means you'll live to see another day."

His face appeared over his lady wife's—likewise the only part of him exposed to the outside air.

"What is it you want?"

"Not to be the man who was too timid to tell you news."

"Go on, then."

"You may not have heard it, given you were otherwise occupied..."

Jastrab grinned, though a sudden movement from behind the tent's flap made him wince, yelp, then laugh like a boy.

Geroslaw waited, snorting and shaking his head.

"I'm listening."

"His Excellency Count Edmund of Hartscross has returned. He has officially requested you join him for the morning meal in his command tent one hour after the sun rises."

Jastrab's eyes became half-lidded things. In a voice that had lost its playfulness yet avoided becoming dour, he asked a simple question.

"Did he invite aides along?"

"One."

Jastrab's face fell. Before he lifted it anew, he kissed the back of his lady wife's head.

"Come. Dress. I need you to charm his excellent head from his tall shoulders."

She paused for only a moment, her eyes mirroring his, though it seemed both unintentional and a thing she was unaware she'd done.

"All right," she managed to sing-song these two words, her face splitting into a broad grin before it withdrew into the tent.

"Edmund likes my wife." Jastrab looked down as he said this, then grinned as he met Geroslaw's eye. "He wouldn't dare offer so much as an inappropriate smile in her direction. A man's wife is sacred. Doesn't mean he won't allow himself to be charmed by her."

"She ... has that effect on people," Geroslaw said, nodding.

"She does!" He looked Geroslaw up, then down, and then looked over at the guard.

"Nikola?"

The guard turned, beginning to salute.

"Yes, Cap—"

Jastrab opened the tent wide, displaying his full nudity to the unsuspecting Nikola—who gaped, then looked away, embarrassed and utterly undone.

"Yes, Captain," said Geroslaw. "You are, indeed, the most beautiful woman ever to call himself captain. Your breasts are magnificent." He delivered this in a tone of such seriousness that poor Nikola had to turn his head to look again.

Jastrab nodded, laughing, shaking his hips from side to side a single time before entering the tent to dress.

"Damned right. Remember that, Sergeant."

Smirking, Geroslaw put a hand on Nikola's shoulder, then turned to leave, but Jastrab's voice drew him up short.

"I don't expect to be back before lunch at the soonest. I'll need you to run drill without me if I'm past the noon bell."

"Yes, Captain." He shook his head in mild surprise, then added, "I'll see it done."

"Good man."

Geroslaw moved off to rejoin the black-haired beauty who was trying to charm his horse out from under him. He was more pleased with the way this morning had gone than he'd thought possible, given last night's refusal to let him go home.

Perhaps the snow's melting at last for me. Time would tell soon enough.

-VII-

Venzene Duchy of Kovalun
County Jižní Pochod
Barony of Hartscross - The Ash March
29 Gerstesykli: 1 Day after the Red Storm at Westsong

"I have no money! I have only what you see!" Kuba's voice was high and plaintive, full of desperation and active dread.

"Truth," Eobum said.

Kuba blinked, abjectly confused.

"Truth? About what?"

Eobum reached across and took a piece of pork from Aldhelm's plate, bringing it to his mouth and chewing it in a slow, deliberate manner. It was a long, uncomfortable moment before he spoke again.

"If you tell me truth when I ask you my questions, Kuba, you have my word that—no matter your answer—neither I nor mine will be the ones to still your breath."

Kuba nodded, searching Eobum's face. He was almost certainly hunting for a lie—he would be disappointed.

As if in answer, Eobum drew his dagger from his belt. He held his left hand, palm out toward Kuba, fingers splayed. Once the man had seen both dagger and palm plainly, Eobum drew the blade sharply across his pale skin, making a jagged, red line across the heel of his left hand.

"If all you want is truth, then I shall give it you." Here, at last, his Gerstealun accent became more pronounced. *All* came out *al*, *it* came out *et*, and *truth* held a glottal T-W at its beginning.

"Good." Eobum paused for a moment, collecting his thoughts before pressing on with the interrogation. "What is your actual name?"

"Geatbern of Erstes Auftauen."

Eobum made no reply to this. None seemed necessary. Here, at last, was the truth.

"What did you do with Kuba?"

Aldhelm nearly dropped his plate into the now mostly empty pan. He'd clearly assumed that Kuba had been nothing more than a dreamt-up fancy.

Geatbern was looking at Eobum with newfound and undisguised respect.

"I killed him," said he. "Took his horse, his tent, and the rest of his belongings."

"How long ago?"

"A week? Less than ten days, to be sure." He paused, then added in a tone that suggested he'd been accused of making the story up, "What I told you was genuine enough. You'd have *liked* the part I never got to tell, by the way. He'd had a rough go of it."

Eobum ignored this.

"What were you running from? Who or what really injured you?"

"Just as I said, actually." He rubbed the light dusting of whiskers on his chin before saying more. "I'd been unable to get a room at the local inn in Biały Klif—it had been full up, or so the keeper said. I pitched my tent..."

"Lord Kuba's tent, you mean," Aldhelm said.

"Yuh, though he hadn't needed it in more than a week." He shook his head, nonplussed, then continued, "It was cold, and I was angry and, frankly, a touch lonely. I found a slaver heading out of town with his remaining stock, stopped him, and found what I wanted. A beautiful tusk girl and her two pups." He grinned a uniquely male grin, then went on. "They were expensive but worth it. I truly have always fancied orcs, you see, and here was this wonderful beauty and her two boys. They were young enough that I'd have had plenty of time to train them."

He watched Eobum as he spoke, looking for a reaction—perhaps even commiseration. When neither came, he lifted his chin to look past the man's right shoulder. When he spoke, his tone was bright and almost cheerful.

"*You* understand, Captain. I see you have a boy of your own and two young warriors to help hone his rage." He raised his voice to call over. "Hallo, boy! You'll do your master proud, won't you?"

Lakkrid's voice crossed the twenty feet between him and the fire, drifting over Eobum's shoulder.

"Yes?" He sounded uncertain and still half-asleep.

"You will not speak to him." Eobum's timbre grew dark, though he tried not to give voice to or even acknowledge the rage that had flared up in him like an eagle taking wing.

"Very well."

"You'd just bought slaves," Aldhelm prompted. Better the subject returned to this man's story. This was wise. If it didn't, Eobum was apt to kill him before they'd heard it.

"Yuh, that's right." He massaged his wounded knee, smoothing his hands down over the swollen thing in an absent sort of way.

"I've papers to prove it if it matters." He shrugged. "So, I've the boys in my tent—"

"Lord Kuba's tent," Alusc said again.

"Yuh, but by then, I was he, and it's beside the point to keep bringing that up."

Alusc snorted but said nothing more.

"I'm having my way with the girl. I suspect she was born into slavery. She had not so much as a drop of fight in her." He shook his head, smiling. "Suited me fine. I wanted a hump, not a fight."

"You raped her." Eobum's voice was flat, his words not remotely couched as a question.

"I most certainly did *not*!"

"You did. You described her as not having fought. That's a far cry from willing."

"Captain..." He paused, shaking his head in bemusement before continuing. "Captain, perhaps I vas un-cle-ar." His accent had once more become pronounced. *Was* came out *vas*, and *unclear* had been broken down into three distinct syllables, its R utterly swallowed at the end—*un-clee-ah.*

"Explain it to me…" Eobum's tone was the first hint of thunder before a summer squall.

"They were my lawful slaves."

Eobum stared not at but through the man.

"They were *mine*." He paused, then shook his head. "You cannot rape property. That would be like being accused of raping one's wife. You cannot rape your lawful wife any more than you can rape a slave … so long as they're yours, legally."

Eobum continued to stare for a moment longer, then allowed his eyes to close. He made a "go on" gesture as he opened them again. "Then what happened?"

Geatbern took a long time reading Eobum's expression, then shook his head, continuing his tale in a more reserved tone.

"Another orc—a big one, mind—entered my tent. I barely fought him off." He paused, flitting his eyes back to Eobum, then down again toward the fire. "I listened, but nothing more seemed to be moving outside my tent. I retrieved my dagger from the grey savage and found I was more ready for the girl after the kill than I had been before it." He shrugged his left shoulder. "I went back to her and tried to pick up where I'd left off."

"He wasn't alone." Eobum spoke with that same dark tone… perhaps an even darker one.

"Yuh, this one was younger and faster. I fought him off as well but had still been in the girl when he attacked. When I'd moved to stand, at last, shoving him back a pace, I planted my dagger into the ground to help push myself up… it had still been in my left hand from the fight with the brute."

Eobum bowed his head but said nothing. He didn't think the man was deliberately lying. In point of fact, he was fairly certain Geatbern believed what he was saying. In his lust and rage, his confusion and fear, he'd somehow overlooked, perhaps even buried, the truth. Ground—no matter how cold and unyielding—felt very different to flesh and bone when a blade was driven into it.

And he thought Lashjuk was a man? A young one, but still, a man? I suspect he was drunk as well, then. Her breasts may not enter a room in time to announce her, but they're hardly forget—stop that, he admonished himself. What in hells was he doing? *Worry about his throat, not her breasts.*

"I … ran. I leapt onto my poor horse, bareback, and rode hie for the hills to escape. I couldn't turn the horse, so I rode 'round the lake and headed northwest."

"Where's your horse now?" Alusc's voice had gone soft and distant.

"The damned savage followed me—on foot, somehow. An hour or so into my run, as the sun was peeking over the trees, I stopped to have a shit. I'd barely finished when he came upon me again. I ran." He looked up at Alusc, then Eobum, then the others. "I'm not proud of it, but I ran. I had no weapon. I fell into a tangle of roots and was out for some time. When I woke, I started walking."

Eobum slowly lifted his head.

"Every time I stopped, I heard movement nearby. I heard voices speaking orc-speak, as vell." *As* had come out *ass.*

"And sometime in the night, you saw our fire." Alusc nodded.

A long silence descended over the encampment. Even the prisoners, some thirty feet beyond the fire across from Geatbern, seemed wrapped in their own waiting silence.

Eobum slowly nodded his head.

Geatbern began to relax. "What more can I tell you?"

"Nothing more." Eobum's voice had grown soft and distant.

"Very well..." Geatbern trailed off, clearly uncertain as to what was next.

Eobum's eyes snapped open. "Bind him."

"Don't!" Geatbern's voice was not full of panic but authority.

Nobody moved.

Eobum blinked. When he spoke this time, his voice wasn't flat but full of force. "I said *bind* him!"

"And I said ... don't." Geatbern offered a narrow grin, pushing himself to his feet.

Again, nobody moved.

"Boy?" Geatbern sounded altogether merry.

Eobum leapt to his own feet.

"I told you not to speak to hi—"

"Put your knife to your throat."

Eobum spun, looking back at his son. Impossibly, Lakkrid was doing exactly as he'd been commanded.

"Wytchemand!" Eobum spat this with such fear and helpless rage that he shook.

"We're called *Hexer,* back in Gerstealun, but I imagine it's the same thing." Geatbern's voice was still a jolly thing, but his eyes danced with another feeling entirely: greed.

"What do you want, Hexer?" Eobum forced his fists to unclench. "Tell me." He paused as Geatbern met his gaze with a shocked expression of his own. "Tell me! Gi awka glem, tell me or so help me I'll..." *(Blood and Iron).*

"Soft-soft, Captain." He spoke in a soothing tone that seemed surprisingly genuine. "Captain is too formal, I think. What is your name?"

Eobum didn't answer. He simply stared.

"Boy? What is this man's name?"

"Eobum!" Lakkrid called.

"Leave ... him ... be, Hexer." His voice was an enunciated, feral growl.

Geatbern arched both brows. His surprise continued in his tone. "Sit, Eobum. It's time we speak about the future."

Eobum sat, albeit slowly. What more could he do?

You have no future, he thought. *I'll see to that. Mark me, Geatbern.*

"Good," Geatbern crooned that singular word with the intimacy of a lover, or a butcher calming the animal he was about to slaughter. "Good. You ask me what I want, and I shall tell you. I don't believe it will cause you much suffering." He brightened before adding, "I'll even give you a choice of paths to take."

Eobum waited. The man wasn't pacing. His knee had been wounded too greatly to make that act comfortable. As Eobum listened, therefore, he started to sign under the guise of clenching and unclenching his fists or pressing his palms into the grass and dirt around him ... to no avail. No one, not even Alusc, seemed to pay him any mind.

"I've killed Kuba, as I've told you. Well—he'd been gone for the best part of five years, now, and word had reached him of his elder brother's death at the hands of an Eoalunth raiding force."

Eobum nodded his understanding. If Geatbern looked reasonably like Kuba had...

"I was careful to learn all that I could from him before the end. I look more than a touch like him. It turns out that he was an acknowledged bastard from a tryst his father had had with a Gerstealunth girl." He chuckled and shook his head. "It amuses me how things seem just to fall into my lap, Eobum. Kuba, his inheritance of land and title... you and your men..." He trailed off, shaking his head.

Eobum continued to stare, though he was careful not to meet Geatbern's eyes directly. Wytchemandys could get into a person's head... some of them, at any rate. Geatbern seemed to have done exactly that, and Eobum wanted to avoid the same fate.

I must avoid it if I'm to overcome this prancing, preening goblin. Yet many of the others haven't met his eyes, so perhaps...

Geatbern sighed in an exaggerated, nearly theatrical manner.

"What is your plan, Geatbern? That is your part..." He grinned again, shaking his head once more. "Ah, you've no sense of humor, Eobum. So be it. I place these two choices before you. There is a third option, but I cannot imagine you would choose it. Few choose death, after all."

Eobum opened his mouth to speak, fought back the vitriol that tried to rush out between his teeth, closed it again, and simply nodded.

"I am still hunted. I need protection. You and yours will see me to the other side of the border—for I fear I've crossed into Kovalun in my haste. You will help me find and pack my gear, for I expect it's either been or shortly will be stolen. If all else fails, you will raid the town, and we will claim what gear and goods seem fitting to us. From there, we will travel north to Kuba's inheritance, and you will be my personal guard. I may even make you and, perhaps, some of your men into my House Knights. What do you think of that?" When Eobum made no reply, Geatbern sighed and added a final stave. "If you wish to continue on without me instead, I will take only a few of your men—your tusks, at the very least—and some supplies and be on my way." He made a "there you have it" gesture. "I mean you no harm, Eobum. I simply prefer to be in control of my own fate. Now I give you that same chance."

Eobum bowed his head in thought. "Have Lakkrid put the blade away in its sheath."

"...He means a great deal to you, I see."

Once more, Eobum made no reply—could not, in fact—make a reply without risking his son... his men.

"Very well." Another theatrical sigh accompanied this. "Lacquered? Boy? Sheath your knife."

Eobum heard the whisking scrape the blade made as it passed along the sheath's small whetstone and tried not to shake with relief.

"Climb that tree. That branch? The thick one? Lay with your belly across it, head and legs pointed toward the ground. Stay there—mind you don't fall without my leave."

In his mind, Eobum leapt forward, throttling the man, cutting off his wind so he could make no further command. He saw the light leave Geatbern's sparkling eyes as he groped for a final breath—a breath Eobum gladly denied him.

I cannot—must not. He's on foot and out of reach. I'm on my backside. I would have to stand and leap toward him, hoping to surprise him and get my hands over his mouth or around his throat before he gave a command to Lakkrid or the others. If I move, I risk killing them all.

"You would have some or all of us escort you over the border, find or take gear for you, and march north as your ... as Kuba's personal guard." He spoke slowly, each word strangled from fear and rage. "Have I understood your ... offer?"

"You have."

"There is ... a problem with that."

"Well, Eobum, it's those two options or death, as I've said. With a word, I can have your men kill one another ... or themselves."

"Will you hear me?" Eobum's voice was no less angry, but a desperate patience had crept into it.

Geatbern paused, trying to read the other man, then nodded in a slow, cautious manner. "Yes, I suppose..."

"I and mine serve Count Edmund of Hartscross." He was pleased to see what he'd hoped for in Geatbern's eyes: greed.

"Do you, *indeed.*"

"We were dispatched to find those raiding his lands, and we succeeded, as you see." He slowly raised his left hand to gesture to the prisoners, all of whom were watching this with expressions of wary wonder on their faces. It made them look childlike rather than foolish.

Geatbern nodded, barely glancing at them. He made a "go on" gesture.

"We are expected back. If we are late beyond a certain point, he will send out more men, thinking us lost... dead."

Geatbern shrugged. "Then I shall take the orcs and be on my way."

"No, Hexer. They belong to the count—are in his service."

Geatbern ahhh'd.

"So ... *that* is why you fear losing the boy."

"That, yes, but not that only." He looked away as if he were embarrassed. "I've grown ... *attached* to him in our time together."

Once more, Geatbern adopted a uniquely male grin, nodding. "How bold, taking such an interest in His Excellency's property. Bold, indeed, Eobum."

Eobum continued to look down, using it as a new excuse to speak without meeting Geatbern's eyes. "Perhaps you don't care a wit about I and mine beyond what we can do to defend you. Still, Hexer, surely you see the danger in making even a minor enemy of a count..."

"I do." He walked over and stood next to Eobum, reaching a hand down to him as if to help him up.

Eobum took the proffered help, albeit reluctantly. He grabbed the man's forearm, as was common in such situations, and allowed himself to be hauled to his feet.

"Look me in the eye, Captain." Geatbern's voice was cold.

Eobum could think of no way to avoid it. The bastard still held him by the forearm, and his grip was surprisingly strong. Eobum would need both hands to ensure he would come out on top of any physical contest. If Geatbern had time to draw breath and speak... he met the man's eyes and, for a moment, was lost. He saw Geatbern now, not as his own eyes had shown him, but as a mountain of a man with red waves rippling off of his body, dissipating perhaps an inch beyond his flesh. The ripple was a fascination—a distracting, devouring thing.

I'm a bird caught in a serpent's gaze. Aye. A bird, and he is a serpent, to be sure. A serpent on two legs...

"Tell me. Were you speaking truth when you said you and they serve the Count of Hartscross?" His voice was inevitable. It surrounded him... made it hard to think.

"Yes."

"And were you telling the truth when you said they expect you back?"

"Yes."

Geatbern nodded. "Excellent. We shall go to see the count, then, and I shall tell him the parts of my story and our meeting that matter to him. He will undoubtedly aid me, perhaps give me a larger number of troops to claim the land for himself, expanding his county borders." Geatbern released Eobum's hand, turning to look up at Lakkrid. "Boy? Lacquered? Climb safely back down."

Eobum's senses came ripping back into full flower. He brought his left hand up, wrapping his forearm around Geatbern's throat and squeezing.

Geatbern gasped, trying to punch at Eobum with his right hand and claw the fingers of his left hand between his neck and Eobum's grip. He connected once, twice, thrice—each blow becoming more feeble.

Eobum squeezed and squeezed, bringing his fist down in a hammer blow against Geatbern's midsection.

"Lashjuk!" His shout was an entire murder of crows taking wing.

"Eobum! Ed ragfelerld!" *(Eobum, I'm coming to you!)*

She sped toward them like the rush of a swinging sword.

Nobody moved to gainsay her.

She came up beside Eobum, eyes plaintive, voice low and full.

"Ed, Eobum. Ed raghai, deerld!" *(Mine, Eobum. He is mine to slaughter, not yours!)* There was no increase in volume in her words, but her intensity was a palpable thing. Her voice vacillated between pleading for and demanding her due.

Eobum did not release the man, whose struggles had redoubled once he'd seen her approach.

"Ed, erld, el—*dush*, Ok! Dehai wrin, *dash* wrin! Ed ka! *Shrash*!"

(Mine, yours, ours—do it, Sister! Don't butcher him; end him! My sword! Hurry!)

She blinked, then reached to his belt, where his sword rested in its sheath. She moved around in front of him, meeting his eyes.

Eobum had a moment to regret not stopping her. If Geatbern held her gaze, as he'd held Eobum's…

"Lash ed felgnash … awka ed mab." She slid the sword with agonizing slowness into the man's right side, thrusting it deep to the hilt so that its tip protruded from his left. *(A gift from my departed mate … and my daughter.)* She watched him for a moment, head tilting, then twisted the blade as she drew it out.

When Eobum felt no heartbeat through the man's neck, he lowered him gently to the ground. Without another word, Eobum dropped down, mounting the man's legs, and began hammering his face with every ounce of pent-up rage and fear he'd kept at bay.

He battered the once-handsome man until his features became an unrecognizable ruin of blood, gore, and misery.

As he slowed, still straddling the dead man's thighs, he felt a firm hand grip his right shoulder. He nodded, not looking up. He knew whose hand it would be.

After a moment, he spoke. "Eranoric."

"Eobum… I couldn't… I couldn't mo—?"

"Find rope and pliable trees. I want him pulled apart and scattered before we leave."

Eranoric managed an "Aye," then began gathering the men and tools he would need.

Eobum stood, turning to face her at last. "He was a zajh." *(a shaman.)*

She widened her eyes. "You saw him use magic?"

Eobum nodded, moving past her toward Lakkrid. "He threatened to… to have my boy…" But he couldn't finish. Hells, he almost couldn't bring himself to meet his son's eyes. He'd failed—he'd nearly lost him. He knelt, scooping the boy into his arms, holding him almost *too* tightly. Standing again, he turned to face her.

For his part, Lakkrid seemed more like a boy who'd just woken up rather than one who'd suffered a fright. He wrapped his arms around his father's neck as they rose, laying his head on the man's shoulder.

"In Eoden," Eobum said, "there are Wytchemandys like him. Men, or women for that matter, who can fascinate with a look and a word." His expression must have been enough to communicate the truth. She spoke a moment later in both understanding and, perhaps, respect.

"Then coming upon him alone would have been far more deadly than I thought." She nodded. "You could have ended him yourself. Why didn't you?"

As his eyes fell upon the magic of her face, he was nearly undone. For a moment, as he held his son, felt the boy's arms around his neck and his head on Eobum's shoulder, what he saw wasn't *her* face. It was Suruk's. She was smiling, and that smile hurt his heart.

He shook his head, half hoping to banish the image, half hoping it would still be there—she would still be there. Of course, only Lashjuk remained.

"Deed, Ok. Erld dush." *(Not mine, Sister. Your kill.)*

She nodded. She reached a slow, gentle hand out to cup Lakkrid's pale, green cheek, ran a thumb beneath his eye as if to wipe away a tear that wasn't there, and nodded.

"Erld lg." *(Your son.)*

In that moment, he realized that she hadn't quite believed him on that score. He watched in silence as she nodded, turned, and walked out of camp.

A DROP OF FIRE

-I-

Venzene Duchy of Kovalun
County Jižní Pochod
Barony of Hartscross - The Ash March
29 Gerstesykli: 1 Day after the Red Storm at Westsong

High sun found them walking with a much lighter step than they'd managed thus far. True, the prisoners were slow by design, which was no surprise. They knew what likely awaited them at journey's end. But much of the gear had been loaded onto Lashjuk's horse. Her boys, too, took turns riding when they were too tired to walk.

She'd chosen to travel with Eobum's band after the events of that morning. They'd used a combination of Alusc's ropes and Eranoric's ability to organize to draw and quarter the pile of bloody meat that had once been Geatbern. The matter was sealed for her when she saw Haiga instruct the men in how to bind and angle the trees for best effect.

She hadn't expected him to be so readily listened to, let alone so knowledgeable.

It was Fenglem who'd explained it to her, calling him their *apprentice siege engineer*—a phrase she'd heard only in passing.

She now walked behind Eobum, at Fenglem's side. What this meant for her status within this group, she neither knew nor much cared.

She didn't intend to stay with them for long.

Eobum walked with Haiga beside him, some ten feet in front of her. She saw the short-haired elder called Eranoric drop back to pass a word with one or the other of them. She had no trouble hearing their chatter. Eranoric took no pains to muffle his speech.

"We make better time than I'd expected, even *with* the horse."

Eobum grunted, nodding once.

"D'you mean to stop for a chew along the road?" Eranoric seemed more curious than hopeful.

She saw Eobum cock his head to the side, considering the idea.

As he did so, her youngest, Maksu, raced past him, chased by Eobum's boy Lakkrid. The idea that they were playing after all that'd happened… it did her heart good. Maksu, at least, would heal.

She was less certain of her eldest. She knew Sulok had been distant since his ordeal. He was sitting on Geatbern's horse atop several cloaks and packs. *Although I suppose it must be accounted my horse now.*

She saw Eobum turn his head to follow the boys' progress. Maksu tripped, but it'd been a deliberate thing. He *wanted* to be caught. Lakkrid obliged, tackling and tickling him before pulling the boy up and over one shoulder and carrying him triumphantly back to the small column of people.

Strong for his age, she thought. *They're nearly the same size.*

Eobum marked their approach, tapping Eranoric lightly on the arm. As if Eobum had given him detailed instructions, the tall man stopped walking, letting the column pass him, then came up beside the two boys.

Without warning, he plucked Maksu from Lakkrid's shoulder, then picked up Lakkrid, carrying both boys as if they were bales of hay.

"Always someone bigger, cleverer, or stronger than you, Lakkrid-boy." His voice was calm, but his face held a grin as he spoke to his quarry.

Both boys began struggling, laughing as they strained.

Utterly unconcerned, Eranoric walked toward the near end of the line to where Sulok rode, looking up to meet his eyes.

"Pardon, my lord, but does one of these two lumps belong to you?"

Sulok looked confused, then looked around as if to make certain it was to him the man spoke.

"The—the one on your bright side, sir."

"No need t'call me sir. Might wanna take better care o' yer pets, though, my lord."

Sulok smiled despite himself. Being called "my lord" was anything but normal. It was proof of play, which he clearly hadn't expected.

"Sulok!" Maksu continued to wriggle. "Sulok, get him! Help me!"

Eranoric ignored this, walking backward as the horse moved along so as to continue meeting Sulok's eye.

"I'll trade you for him…" Sulok looked as if he were only half-joking.

"No! Sulok! I'm your brother! Nnnno!" Maksu was grinning so hard that it could be heard even while he struggled.

"Hmmm." Eranoric cocked his head to the side, clearly considering.

"I know he's annoying," Sulok said, "but he's young yet. He just needs some discipline, is all."

Lashjuk rolled her eyes, smirking. If someone had asked her, even this morning, if she thought she'd smile again, she'd have told them there was a better chance of snow in Shesh. Still, here she was.

"What d'you want for 'em?"

Sulok thought about it, clearly weighing the possibilities.

"Your sword?"

Eranoric laughed.

"Sorry, but Eobum'd laugh me out of the unit if I showed up with a boy to fight instead of a sword."

Sulok looked crestfallen but nodded.

"This is your pack, isn't it?" The boy pointed to a light sling bag with the fur brim of a hat sticking out of it.

Eranoric nodded. To Lashjuk's eye, he looked surprised at that.

"You can have him for your hat in trade."

Most of the column was now listening. Each figure either smiled or laughed at the byplay.

"Can't keep my head warm with a boy, my lord, can I?"

"Sure you shouldn't, Eranoric," a younger man called.

"Mind your own, Eobald, or I'll trade *you* to the young master here."

"I'd make that trade!" Sulok said. He looked serious, which only increased the mirth of the column.

"Tell you what," Eranoric said. "I'll give you both the boy and the hat if you help me collect some firewood as we walk today."

Sulok looked thunderstruck. His bronze-colored face showed disbelief and joy warring in near-equal measure. "Really?"

Eranoric nodded. "Really, as long as I can take you at your word." He paused, once more fixing Sulok with his gaze. "I *can*, can't I? Your word's *good*, ain't it, my lord?"

Sulok nodded with a quickness. "Yessir!" He grinned. "Do I need to help you straightaway?"

Eranoric bobbed his head. "Now's as good a time as any, I s'pose."

Sulok slid from the horse after stopping it. "Sir?"

"Eranoric."

Sulok grinned. "Eranoric?"

"Yes?"

"You can keep him anyway ... if you like."

The column erupted this time.

"Nye. I don't wanna have to fight yer Og, do I?" While this was phrased as a question, it had been meant more as a statement. "'Sides, I already have to deliver this other pup to his father. May as well bring your Og her own by way of greeting, don't ya think?"

Sulok shrugged. "I tried." He grinned and ran off to collect wood.

Eobald reached forward between Lashjuk and Fenglem, causing her to draw back and glare at the offending hand. A moment later and she realized he was tapping the Gnoerk on his right shoulder.

"Feng," he said. When the Gnoerk turned his green head to look back at him, he pointed ahead and to the left. "Look. 'M I seeing clear?"

Fenglem turned and looked toward where he'd been directed. He squinted, then growled in soft annoyance. "Aye. Blodnosp." He shook his head. "Burst, too."

Lashjuk followed Fenglem's gaze. In the crook of a yew tree's lowermost branches, she saw a thin, red vine. A moment later, she realized that vine wasn't natively red but was wet and shimmering with a profusion of red juices, oily and slick. "What are they?"

"Blodnosp," said Eobum. He still walked a few feet in front of her and Fenglem. "Blood buds, in the Trade Tongue."

She nodded, though he surely couldn't have seen it with his back to her. She supposed it *did* resemble the color of mannish blood. "I see no buds of any kind." She made an "oh" sound, recalling Fenglem's words about them being burst. "What broke them?"

"It'll get cold tonight," Eobald said from behind her.

It was fairly warm at present. Warm enough for her boys to go about without cloaks or kontusze at any rate, difficult to do even on a summer's day back home.

"Plants are more sensitive to the weather. They're wiser than we." This was Alusc, their cook, who walked directly behind Fenglem.

"They burst when cold weather's on the come," Fenglem said. "It's an old hunter's truth. When you see it, you know you should find shelter before night gets too old."

Lashjuk nodded. She spoke, though she hadn't intended to do so. Her voice sounded accusatory to her own ears.

"Did your great *captain* teach you that? Another lesson in life from *wise* Eobum?"

It was too late to take it back … now that she'd said it. It'd been woefully unkind of her, and she knew it.

Lashjuk didn't deny his role in Geatbern's end. He *could* have killed the man himself. He hadn't. That was true enough. Still, a part of her felt as if his call to her had been an afterthought. Not a deliberate act of justice. She would *take* it, and gladly, but she was still not altogether warm to the man and his ways. No, that was underselling it. She was more than a trifle past tired of this human who presumed to teach Gnoerks the way of the world.

She was both surprised and ashamed of herself, then, when Eobum spoke up in answer.

"No, lady. Fenglem taught *me*. The rest of us, too." He sounded even and untroubled by her remark, which only made it harder to hear.

"Eranoric?" Eobum's voice raised in volume just enough to be heard by the entire column.

Eranoric veritably appeared at Lashjuk's side. He deposited Maksu on the ground, ruffling his hair. This elicited a wide, toothy grin from the pale blue boy.

"I hear you. I'll hunt for a few intact ones for later." Still carrying Lakkrid over his dim hand shoulder, he made as if to leave. The boy broke wind. Lashjuk saw plainly by the look on his face that he'd done so with clear deliberation.

Eranoric growled in mock anger and dropped the boy as if he were on fire.

"I yield! I yield!" he said, hands covering his mouth and nose.

Lashjuk rolled her eyes again but managed a grin just the same. Managed? No, that was drawing it short. She felt the grin fight its way onto her face, despite the prevailing darkness of her mood.

Lakkrid darted around, taunting the older man, gyrating his hips and dancing just out of reach. This—the apparent dance of the wild Lakkrid—sent Maksu into fits of uncontrollable giggling.

Eranoric chased the boy for a moment, then turned, laughing as he moved off to join Sulok in the woods to their left.

Maksu tried to follow, but Lakkrid stopped him.

"Race me!" he said.

Maksu needed no more encouragement. With a laugh of delight, the game was afoot.

"Good boy," Fenglem murmured.

"What?" She was sure she must've missed something.

"Your Sulok needs something that's *his*. Some task and some attention that's his alone," said he.

She was surprised but realized he was probably right. Turning as they walked, she watched Lakkrid and her youngest chase one another, sky blue chasing pale green. Something about that gave her pause—fear, almost, but she couldn't place why.

She shook her head and continued following Eobum as he led them west.

-II-

Venzene Duchy of Kovalun
County Jižní Pochod
Barony of Hartscross - Jižní Lov
29 Gerstesykli: 1 Day after the Red Storm at Westsong

Geroslaw's hands busied themselves, wrapping thin layers of sheepskin around one of his fellow Bluemark Guardsman's dim side forearms.

They stood off to the side of the makeshift training field while the others finished their armoring.

"Try *that*." Geroslaw did his best not to allow the frustration he felt at having to sort this with a man whose sergeant should've long since addressed the matter. It wasn't *this* man's fault. The sergeant who was meant to look after him—a man named Steffan—had sent his men to drill without him. He was more interested in whatever else he was doing than actually tending to his recruits. And so, things like this fell to Geroslaw. He could've left the recruit to his own devices, but who would that serve? No, he was a training sergeant. And he'd have an easier time training the men if they weren't fighting their own gear.

The recruit—Geroslaw had already forgotten his name—nodded and drew his bazuban up onto the forearm in question. As he slid his elbow into place within the attached hardened leather cop, Geroslaw began tightening the cannon—the forearm covering. He'd gotten the piece affixed enough that he could let go without fear that the makeshift padding of sheepskin might become too loose or unfurl altogether. Stepping back, he watched as the recruit finished the process.

The fellow fumbled his fingers on the buckles—clearly having done precious little work in or with his armor kit.

Geroslaw did his best not to look disgusted. "Better?"

The younger man flexed his arm, shaking it as if trying to flick something off his fingers or knock an insect loose. He looked up at Geroslaw, his face brightening in surprised disbelief. "Yeah-aye! It's furled tight now!" He moved his arm experimentally once more. "Doesn't slide at *all*!"

Geroslaw nodded, patting the younger man on the shoulder. "You were a smith, were you?"

The recruit looked up sharply, squinting. "Aye. How did you—"

"Right arm's more than a bit bigger'n your left."

The younger man lifted his arms to compare them. They, of course, looked to be the same size when armored. "Oh," he said. His tone suggested he'd somehow seen the difference anyway.

"That'll do for today. Once we're done here, do *not* pad down until you've gone to see the armorers. They'll take a look and, I expect, either add another layer of leather inside or get you padding of some other type." He tried on a reassuring smile that he hoped made it all the way to his eyes. "Should only cost you a few bárók." He paused, forcing himself to say what he knew he should. "If they try to take more from you, come and see me. I'll sort them."

He hated—truly hated Steffan at that moment. He seemed lazy, easily distracted by bread, beer, breasts, or bare-chested boys whenever any of them should happen by. He seemed to utterly disappear from duty if more than one should be on offer.

Still, as much as he wished to, he wouldn't be the one to bring it up to the captain... not unless Jastrab asked him directly. Geroslaw's deeds would do him more credit than his flapping, complaining mouth ever could. Better by far for the *men* to speak of the difference between the two sergeants than for those sergeants to speak ill of one another.

He noted the recruit had taken on a disappointed aspect. No, not disappointed... what was it?

Ask him, fool. Or are you trying to practice your exceptional talent for sorcery?

The sarcastic voice in his mind was his Uncle Borys's, of course, back for another lesson, prompted or not.

"Something wrong?"

"I've only got a single báró." The recruit shrugged. "Taxes and all."

Geroslaw blinked.

"Taxes?"

The recruit nodded, looking small.

"We've not been to a town in a fortnight or so."

"A dozen days," the recruit put in, sounding defensive and sulky.

Geroslaw gave a slow nod. "Fine. A dozen days. Still—we've been paid since then. Once a week, unless we're on campaign. You should have more than a single damned copper."

The recruit nodded.

"So?"

"Taxes." He shrugged, eyes flitting around as if looking for a way to escape the conversation.

"*What* taxes?"

The young man grew shifty, unwilling to meet Geroslaw's eyes.

"I asked you a question... boy." Geroslaw's voice had taken on a knife's edge.

The recruit was saved from answering as the captain called Geroslaw's name. While the nervous youth had been granted a moment of peace by Jastrab's arrival, Steffan was unlikely to be as fortunate. There was a world of difference between poor performance and outright theft. A poor performer would eventually die on the field or reveal his or her own shortcomings. Theft ran the risk of making the entire company lose reputation, translating to the loss of potential contracts.

"Wait here. Do you understand me?"

The youth nodded.

Geroslaw turned to walk a few paces off to where the captain was inspecting the rest of the men.

His lady was on his arm.

"Mistress!" Geroslaw waved a hand to get her attention. When she looked, he gestured for her to come toward him. "May I borrow your eye for a moment?"

She disentangled herself from her lord and husband with a word, then moved in Geroslaw's direction even as he walked toward Jastrab. She met him near the halfway point.

Geroslaw smiled at her approach, despite his rising frustration over Steffan's apparent antics.

"Vat can I does for yuh?" This over-exaggeration of the Gerstealunth accent carried with it a playful smile and a sparkling eye.

As she spoke, he allowed his expression to be drawn into a false but fully-fledged grin. Onlookers would see little more than the pair passing a pleasant word. But he made no effort to hide the deception from *her*.

She tilted her head to the side, trying to read his face.

"I think one of my fellow sergeants might be taxing his men." He delivered this revelation in a soft, friendly tone.

"Whom?" She, too, sounded soft and friendly. Her eyes, however, spoke of a storm to come.

"Steffan's recruit—the man I just walked away from? He has one báró to his name because of *taxes*." He wanted to glower. Instead, he made his smile broader as if she'd said something sweet or amusing. "We've been paid already since the last town we moved through. He hasn't told me what *taxes* he meant and grew shifty as I pressed him." He paused, preparing to move past her toward Jastrab. "Do I leave the matter?"

"I'll take care of it." She offered him a smile as she ushered him past, toward her husband.

"Captain?" Geroslaw came up beside the man, forcing himself to focus on the matter at hand. Steffan wasn't here. His men *were*.

"Sergeant Geroslaw..." Jastrab spoke in a playful tone, elongating both words. "Come see me once training is sorted for the afternoon. The meeting with Edmund brought some interesting things to my attention. I'll tell you my drift either before or..." He paused, then shook his head, face wearing a what-the-hells expression, "Bah! Just join my wife and I for the evening meal. We can talk about it then."

Geroslaw nodded, surprised but gratified. "All right, Captain. I can do that, and gladly." He looked at the men, then back to Jastrab, asking a silent question.

"Go on, then. Show me what you have planned."

Geroslaw nodded, stepping back and raising his voice. "Form up! Move!"

The men—most of them, at any rate—scrambled into action. They rushed into a single line, shoulder to shoulder. They were a mix of trained and green men. It showed in the lackluster status of their formation. Some were straight-backed and proud, stood at rigid attention. Others were stood with their feet wide beneath them, shoulders loose, arms swinging at their sides.

Jastrab did his best to offer no reaction to this, and Geroslaw could guess why. The captain was waiting to see how, or even if, the matter would be addressed.

Geroslaw needed no urging. In short order, he picked up a spear from a nearby rack and walked to the men's shabby line. After striding up it, then down it again, he singled three men out who were in proper stance and formation.

He pointed to a spot a few feet off, perpendicular to the existing line.

"You three—form up, facing me." He didn't raise his voice. There was no real need.

Once the men had done so, he walked toward them, setting the spear horizontally in front of his own chest. He laid the haft along the men's chests and nodded to himself. It touched all three.

"Fall out, you lot!" He looked over his shoulder. "Come see this."

They glanced at one another, then did as bidden.

"Form a column off of my left shoulder, facing me."

They suited action to command.

"You will see these men are aligned. There is space between them, and my spear haft is resting against all three of their chests evenly, yes?"

There were a few grunts from the column.

"When I give you an order or ask you a question, you *will* give an answer ... and *clearly*! Am I understood?!" His voice was sudden thunder.

They jumped. A few of them actually cried out in surprise.

"I asked you a question! Am I *understood*!?"

"Aye!"

"Aye? Aye what?"

"Aye, Sergeant!"

He nodded. "One by one, I want the column to study these men: their stance, their aspect, their distance from one another. One by one, I want each man in the column to take position along the line's dim side. The *line's* dim side. Am I understood?"

"Aye, Sergeant!"

"Where are you to line up?"

"Line's dim side, Sergeant!"

A voice came from the middle of the column, trying to hide its owner.

"Which side's the line's dim side?"

Geroslaw turned bodily, removing his spear from along the men's chest and stepping back from them to look down the line.

"Step out of line."

No response.

"Step out of line, whoever asked that question! Now!"

A man with a yellow beard and thick brows stepped—or perhaps had been pushed—out of line. He stood near dead center of the column, looking defiant. The beard made him look older than he was, based on the man's unlined face.

"Name?"

"Barneb ... Sergeant." He deliberately paused before saying that latter word. His facial expression made it clear he'd done more than consider not saying it at all.

Geroslaw nodded.

"Good. Well, lads? What did Barneb do wrong?"

One or two men murmured.

"Speak up."

"He was disrespectful!" offered one.

"He questioned orders!" This second man sounded almost gleeful as he delivered what he felt sure was the right answer.

"Anything else?"

Barneb looked as if he were about to step forward and strike someone—maybe Geroslaw or maybe his fickle comrades.

No further answers came.

Geroslaw nodded.

"Nothing."

They gaped at him, confused, looking like a collection of owls blinking in the sun.

"He did *nothing* wrong. In fact," he nodded to Barneb, "he did the best thing he could've done." He paused, then added, "He didn't know a thing, so he asked."

"We ain't a'posed to question orders, Sergeant!" This was that second, once-gleeful man. Now he seemed angry and embarrassed.

"In the midst of a fight? No. That can get us all killed. In training? That's just about the best time to ask." He grinned. "Ask, and I smile, as my uncle used to say."

Barneb looked as if someone had hit him with something heavy. He'd expected to be reprimanded for insolence, not praised for asking questions.

"Fall back into line, Barneb."

Barneb nodded, looking wary as he obeyed.

As the man moved, Geroslaw added, "And to answer your question, dim side's left for far more people than it is right. Line's dim is left. Now ... you have your orders. To it!"

"Aye, Sergeant."

Jastrab moved close and laid a hand on Geroslaw's shoulder as the column moved to inspect, then mimic and join their fellows. "Until tonight."

Geroslaw nodded. He was suddenly glad that he'd have a particularly good meal tonight. The afternoon giving Steffan's men the training they should have long since gotten was apt to be a long one. If they couldn't be trusted to stand or respond to orders properly, he had his doubts about whether they could be trusted to know which end of the spear went toward the enemy. Given *that* was in doubt—teaching them to fight with a shield or from horseback seemed laughable.

Swallowing a sigh, he set about the afternoon's work.

-III-

Venzene Duchy of Kovalun
County Jižní Pochod
Barony of Hartscross - The Ash March
29 Gerstesykli: 1 Day after the Red Storm at Westsong

Lashjuk felt the muscles of her midriff shake. A mist had rolled in just before sunset. Just as Fenglem had warned, it brought with it a sudden and blistering cold.

Their breath plumed in the growing dark, providing momentary relief to their noses. All too soon, that hint of heat fled their faces, replaced by a newly biting chill every time the wind brushed their exposed skin.

She and Fenglem shared a cloak, and she was grateful for the warmth. Pressing against him was like curling up near a campfire. Lakkrid had brought Maksu under *his* cloak. The two boys walked, huddled together and shivering a few short feet ahead of them, just behind Eobum and Haiga. While those latter two *wore* cloaks, they didn't seem to need to huddle together beneath them for warmth.

Sulok walked directly behind his mother, Eranoric at his shoulder, sharing his own cloak. She'd seen the boy wearing the man's hat, pulling the brim down tight over his ears. By the way it sat, it didn't appear to be a new state for the thing to be in.

That they were still walking, despite the cold, hinted that they were close to their destination. *How* close was another matter entirely.

As the last of the light drained away, Maksu spoke between chattering teeth. "H-how m-much l-longer?"

Eobum held up a hand and stopped the column's progress. He scented the air and sounded as if he were smiling as he spoke. Maddeningly, he also sounded as if the cold held no power over him.

"Less than half a bell. Can you wait that long to be warm again?" He turned, taking a knee before the boys. "I've something that will warm you, but it might make you feel sick. If it does, you'll be apt to start running from both north and south. Better that than to freeze, so if you can't go on, you must say. We'll be there in less than half a bell, though." He paused, placing a hand on each boy's shoulder. "Can you suffer that long if I promise you a warm bed and a hot meal if you're hungry once we get there?"

"Wh-we c-can m-make it, F-f-father." Lakkrid's shoulders were squared as he made this bold declaration.

"Don't be braver than you are smart, aye?"

"I w-w-won't. Wuh-we can make it."

Eobum nodded and stood.

"Lashjuk? Sulok?"

"F-fine," said Sulok. He was tight to Eranoric's side by the look of things.

"Go ah-on, Eobum." Lashjuk was too cold to be insistent, but not by much.

He turned and lifted his right arm high, waving them forward.

Ten minutes later, a muted thud came from the column's rear, followed by a nervous whicker from their horse.

"Adric?" Eobum's voice was bright and clear, full of concern.

"Our guest, Yindrich, wants a sleep, it seems." Adric's voice—usually crisp and full of wry good humor—seemed to hold a tight note of actual concern.

"Eranoric? Keep them moving. Adric? Get him up. If he won't move, but he lives, tie him to the horse and have him dragged." Eobum's voice was as full of warmth and cheer as the night's air.

"We'll see to it," said Adric. "Eobald? Riclov? Eyes on me. If he fights..."

"We'll cuh-crack either his s-s-skull or s-stones for 'im, right n-nuff," came the reply, though Lashjuk couldn't have said which man had spoken it.

The canvas from what Aldhelm had called his irenden was draped across their horse. This makeshift caparison swung pale and ghostly in the early dim, making the beast look like he'd ridden out of an eastern legend, the dead steeds that drew the singer's carriage. Still, she guessed the covering offered the beast at least some protection from the chill. She hoped it'd do to keep it going until they reached the walls of this fort they were heading toward.

Eobald's voice came forward in a growl of mingled discomfort and frustration.

"Not d-dead. Not awake, neither. Shallow breathin', too."

Eobum tapped Haiga and handed him something small. Nodding, the grey-skinned Gnoerk stepped aside and waited for the group to pass. She glanced back, seeing him fall in beside one of Adric's men. The fellow had been crouching over one of their prisoners but stood as Haiga drew near, leaving the wretched bandit whose name was, apparently, Yindrich laying face-down on the soil and scree.

"Here, Eobald." Like Eobum, the Gnoerk sounded mostly undaunted by the cold.

Eobald reached a hand out but stopped himself before he could take the thing the Gnoerk carried.

"No goodt," said he. His voice was clipped by the cold, adding a T sound to the end of good. "Too cold, me-self. Hands are shakin' too much."

Haiga nodded.

"Can you hold him?"

Eobald did so. He hefted the man to his feet and wrapped his arms around the brute's chest from behind.

Yindrich's head lolled back onto Eobald's left shoulder. His eyes rolled, mouth moving as if locked in some troubling dream.

Riclov and Adric stood nearby, keeping one eye on the other prisoners and the other on Eobald.

Haiga stepped forward and reached his right hand out to pry open Yindrich's mouth. He popped the thing in his other hand—a dull auburn-colored teardrop shape—into the fellow's waiting gob. That done, he snapped Yindrich's mouth closed with enough strength to force the dazed oaf to chew at least once.

Almost instantly, Yindrich was awake, eyes wide and panicky. He tried to break free, tried to splutter, but Eobald held him fast while Haiga clamped a hand over his mouth to keep it closed.

"Swallow," he said.

The man was breathing hard through his nose. Curds of snot blew out to land on his unkempt mustache and Haiga's bare hand. The bandit's eyes were watering. He gave two shallow nods and swallowed in an obvious way.

Haiga watched the man, whose eyes were becoming less frenzied and more aware of both where and who he was. When he judged the matter settled, he moved his hand away and wiped it on his own cloak. He nodded to Eobald.

"C-can you stand?" Eobald shook the man as he spoke, still bearing his weight from behind. "Can'ee walk?"

The man nodded and pulled away. He seemed unwilling to open his mouth to speak.

Eobald let him go, patting him roughly on the back as if to tell him he'd be All right. He wouldn't, of course. He and his fellows were almost certain to be hung when they faced the count's justice.

Lashjuk was just beginning to turn her face back toward their road when she saw Haiga punch Eobald in the shoulder.

Eobald looked, eyes flitting down to where Haiga's hand jutted toward him, wrapped around what was likely another of the blodnosps. He shook his head, offering a wide, flat grin.

"Nye. I'll be warm, right enough, but I'll be cleaned right out, as well." He started to walk, giving a gesture to Riclov to follow. The man was still behind him as an *in-case* measure.

"Still makes you ill?"

"Aye," Eobald said. "Manage to keep it and food down, mind, but *down* don't necessarily mean *in*, do it?" While this was technically a question, Eobald's tone made it more of a statement.

Haiga made as if to offer the blood bud to Riclov as he approached, but Adric spoke up to gainsay him.

"It's worse with that one, Haiga-lad. He'll let loose like a wet dragon." He opened his mouth wide and let rip a cone of steam to demonstrate, bending over and turning his head this way and that as if he were out of control.

Haiga snorted, shrugging before marching back to Eobum's side.

A few minutes passed in relative silence. The hazel, oak, and ash trees thinned out on their right, revealing wide fields and rolling hills beneath a cloudless, star-shot sky.

Two or three minutes more, and they were all sniffing the air. None of them remarked on it, but before long, they sounded like a troop of hogs or hunting dogs trying to follow a trail. Smoke from a long-burning fire had come to them. Eobum must've scented it earlier, albeit faintly, which explained his certainty that they were so close to journey's end.

As if this thought had prompted the man out of a daydream, he spoke up from their column's head.

"Brace yourselves." He made his voice loud enough to be heard, even at the back of their line. "The trees are falling away. When they go, the wind will grow fangs. If we've come out on target, we won't have to suffer it for too long, but still…"

Lashjuk heard general grunts of acceptance, but nothing more.

The soil crunched beneath their feet as the pines sung above them. It had been like that—must've been like that for an hour or more—but none of them had noticed the sounds until now.

"There," Fenglem said.

Sure enough, the tree line didn't simply fall away. It disappeared at the end of a stand of alders.

Beyond it were scores of twinkling lights amidst a profusion of shapes, both dark and light.

"Wh-what are they?" Maksu sounded distant and sleep-fogged.

"C-Campfires and t-t-tents," said Lakkrid.

Once they'd all cleared the trees, they felt it. The wind had indeed grown fangs. It ripped at them as if it were an angry child throwing a tantrum. Their hoods and cloaks flapped hard enough to sting as they tapped and snapped against their wearers. Dust and grit, small stones, dead leaves, and the occasional twig came battering toward them from their right. Worse still, the detritus seemed not to strike and fly on but swirl as if caught in their wake.

"Must be hundreds in that camp…" Haiga sounded awed, although it may have been as much from the wind stealing his breath as any proper shock at the scene before them.

"Two hundreds, and maybe fifty more … if the rumors are true," Eobum said. "That'll be the Bluemark."

"When'd *they* slither in, d'ya think?" Alusc's tone was uncharacteristically flat and thin.

Eranoric grunted at that. "Looks as if they've been here at least a day."

"W-what?" Sulok sounded suddenly worried. All the bluff confidence and blustering maturity he'd regained that day blew away on the miserable wind. He sounded small and uncertain … sounded like a boy his age *ought* to sound, given the situation.

"Don't much care for the Bluemark Guard," Eranoric said. "Fought again' them years back."

Lashjuk turned to regard the man, even as Sulok spoke up again. "Will..."

"Peace, my lord." Eranoric rubbed the boy's upper arm even as he tightened his own around him. "They're the count's hirelings. There won't be trouble."

She somehow doubted that but kept quiet.

They walked on.

Before long, they heard, then saw banners flapping in the wind: a black field with a blue mailed fist in a white circle.

Beyond the camp, they saw a massive wooden palisade. An enormous banner hung from atop the walls near the gate, but the wind had twisted it, so it hung more like a rope.

"Nearly there," Eobum said. "I'll run on to make certain we aren't held at the gate. We'll want it open as swiftly as may be to get in and out of the chill. Eranoric?"

"Aye, I have the command."

Sulok audibly tightened his grip around Eranoric at that, leather creaking.

Lashjuk did the same with her grip around Fenglem's waist, but in her case, it was out of angry confusion.

Why Eranoric? She had nothing against the man who had been kind to her eldest and helped him begin to heal, and certainly, she understood why Haiga hadn't been left in command. Capable as he was, he was still not quite full grown. Fenglem, however ... why hadn't he been left in charge?

The answer seemed obvious. He wasn't human. Eobum loved his brother and his son. She had seen that much and was as certain of it as of any other fact. Still, the others would surely bristle at the idea of following a Gnoerk's orders outside of particular circumstances. It was the same familiar tale. These men weren't racists, *but...*

The Bluemark Guard had their camp set to the left of the palisade, relative to Eobum's party. He'd led them to the right, so they came upon the gate in that wall's center, avoiding the Bluemark altogether.

After a brief exchange none of them could quite make out, Eobum seemed to have convinced the guards to open the gate for them.

It remained closed until they were nearly upon it, though she reckoned that was just to minimize the wind's time racing through the encampment. As they opened it, however, the air planted chill hands against their backs and nearly lifted them as they walked.

Once their drogue members were in, the gate was closed with understandable haste.

The sound of that bitter wind raked along the pointed tops of the palisade's walls, but now it was almost entirely just that—sound. The wood blocked so much wind that the air seemed daylight-warm to them.

"Adric," said Eobum. "You and yours, come with me. Let's take these brave men to meet the count."

Adric grinned and nodded.

"Aye, and gladly."

"Eranoric, Feng? Take the others home. Get everyone settled. Put Lashjuk and the boys in my tent."

Lashjuk opened her mouth to object, but before she'd done more than draw breath, Eobum finished his instructions.

"Lakkrid and I'll doze with you and Haiga."

Everyone got moving.

In short order, they arrived at an area where a ring of tents had already been set up. They formed a rough circle around a well-ordered fire pit rimmed by pale stones.

As the men moved off to their own beds, Lashjuk found herself led to a modest tent of her own. It was no bigger than the others. It was, in fact, smaller than one or two of them. Within, however, she found furs, two camp beds, and two wooden boxes at their feet. It was spare in its look and contents, but comfortable and larger than she'd expected.

She took one look at the bed and had to fight the urge to fall into it.

A moment later, she saw Lakkrid helping Maksu to crawl into what was, presumably, *his* bed under normal circumstances. Her son seemed as if he'd slept before his eyes had fully closed.

As Lakkrid moved to turn his father's bed down, he looked up, meeting her gaze.

She shook her head, then wondered why she was resisting. Nodding, she moved past him and lay her right hand to the side of his face, just as she had this morning after she'd ended Geatbern.

He gazed up at her, his color rising.

Once she'd crawled into bed, he covered her with a blanket of fur, smoothed back her hair, and smiled down at her for a single, ephemeral moment before leaving the tent.

She knew no more until morning.

-IV-

Venzene Duchy of Kovalun
County Jižní Pochod
Barony of Hartscross - Jižní Lov
29 Gerstesykli: 1 Day after the Red Storm at Westsong

The captain's wife, Sjelesanger, set a plate before him with a flourish. Before Geroslaw could lift his hand to reach for the wooden goblet to his right, she snatched it up and filled it with a fragrant apple wine with hints of yewberry.

He reached, instead, for a small triangle of *východní* cheese. This was actually less a cheese than a creamy yellow mushroom, good for spreading and baking. It had been a favorite of his since he was a boy. He hadn't realized its significance until much, much later in life. *Východní* only grew on the eastern side of hills and tree roots. In the wilds of Kovalun, where it was native, it was twice blessed as a survival tool. It was both an answer to the mystery of direction and a delicious and satisfying treat.

"Don't fill up on *them*." Her voice was musical and full of mock indignation. "Meal's near done baking."

He grinned, bowing his head as he spoke.

"I *am* sorry, Lady. I'll stop." With a last look of longing at the *východní* cheese in the table's center, he reached for his newly full goblet and raised a health to her.

Jastrab grinned at the byplay, raising his own goblet and knocking it against Geroslaw's.

"Good my wife? Can you join us at table, or should we wait to dive into things?" He offered her a warm grin. "*Orrrr* ... should I do battle with the fire and let *you* explain things to Geroslaw?"

She snorted lightly.

"No, I think I'd better finish the fight myself. You promised him supper, and I'd hate to see you turn into a liar."

Jastrab made an exaggerated as-you-wish gesture.

"Besides, you'd want to re-engineer my stove to make it hotter. I want a camp stove, not a smith's forge. *You* may like to eat metal, but some of us prefer bread and meat."

"I *only* wish to make your life easier, min kjære." To Geroslaw, he offered a shrug and a lopsided grin. "I tried."

Geroslaw didn't know that first phrase, but as the lady was from Havalun by birth, he expected it was something from that Duchy. He shrugged one shoulder and said, "Well, Captain, what is it you always say? Sergeant Obránce's saying?"

Jastrab laughed. "Best siege engineer I've ever known. You'd have liked him."

Geroslaw made a gesture of agreement. That was the man in question.

"Obránce used to say, 'You could do it that way,'" he paused, leaning his head forward as if inspecting something on Geroslaw's empty plate before finishing, "...but *I* wouldn't."

The captain and his lady-wife wore fond smiles. Their faces suggested they were remembering distinctly different moments when the departed man had said such a phrase. They looked at one another, then at different points in the middle distance for a long moment.

It was Sjelesanger who broke the spell, so to speak. "Hells—I'd better get back to it." With that, she marched back toward the wood-burning camp stove their enormous tent had housed in its center.

The entire thing was made of black iron. It had a wide belly raised up on four spindly-looking iron legs. While they might have *looked* spindly, Geroslaw had helped set the metal monster up on occasion. They were, in fact, quite stable. It rested against a large upright pole that stood in the center of the marquee. The stove's chimney rose to a round hole in the tent's roof.

"Korunasykli," Jastrab said.

"What about it?"

"It'll start before you know it."

Geroslaw nodded. He knew this already. Sigdmåne was more than a fortnight gone by now, meaning the start of Korunasykli was less than a fortnight off. That meant snows, brilliant greens for the trees he loved best, and...

"Ah. Koruni Spanek?"

Koruni Spanek—the Crown Sleep Festival was a three-day celebration. It started nearly two-thirds of the way through the year's last star sykli, on the twentieth.

It was a time for kindness and relief to the poor. Three days for families to gather "to fight off the cold with the warmth that you hold in your arms … and its charms," as the song went. Children and adults alike made—or purchased if they had the means—gifts for their families and friends. It was often said that more courtships began during Koruni Spanek than throughout the whole rest of the year. It was even a time for amnesty for all but the most heinous crimes or slights committed prior to the festival's start. No man, high or lowly, would risk cruelty or malice during the Crown Sleep.

Jastrab nodded. "You wanted to go home."

Geroslaw blinked, then gave a considering nod. "It all depends on where we are by then, I suppose. Doesn't it?"

Jastrab shrugged. "Maybe? You *do* still want to head home to recruit a lance or two, though?"

Geroslaw stared at him, trying to sus out his meaning.

"Aye, Captain. Did and do, but if we're engaged and in the field…"

"I'd give you leave, regardless at that point, if you really wanted it."

Jastrab's voice was too soft to be insincere. His eyes weren't shining, but they displayed a warmth that Geroslaw had rarely seen in them. Perhaps it was the candlelight, but Jastrab appeared unusually easy tonight in both body and mind.

"Captain," he shook his head, "I thank you. I do. I just don't have such a burning need to go home that I'll do so on no more than the dictates of the holiday. I only offered it yesternight because of our current situation."

"Because you want men to lead."

"No? Not exactly."

"Well, what is it, exactly? Tell me what you want. Perhaps I can be of some help."

Geroslaw sat back in his chair, considering.

"Listen now. I'm not trying to convince you, nor am I trying to trap you into something. We love you. That's all. You belong with us—to us. Others will come and go, but you, Daian, Blevelsket—others, like Obránce, now passed… it's different. *You're* different."

Geroslaw bowed his head in respect and gratitude.

"Thank you, Captain." It was all he could manage for a moment. The irony was not lost on him. Here was a statement of familial tie, offering to allow him to ride away from it and travel to the family that mostly didn't want him. Yet he was both grateful to Jastrab for the sentiment and anxious to make the journey at the same time.

Men want what's denied to them, Geroslaw. Find that thing, and men will gladly and willingly stand for and with you. Ignore it, and you become the leader all men eventually come to hate. You cease to be a friend and ultimately risk becoming a foe. It was his father, now, who spoke up in his mind. The memory was painful, for it had been during the early days of his life, when, bastard or not, he had been the heir—had been worthy of his father's time.

No, that wasn't fair. It wasn't his father that had wanted him to go. It was his father's wife—his half-brother's mother. It was she who had impressed upon him the idea that he should forge his own path now that he could never be the heir. She had pushed for him to serve time under Uncle Borys's ungentle hand. Eventually, even that wasn't enough surety for her. She'd given his mother a generous sum of coin—six or seven hundred gold vévodové: a fortune to most peasants, to *all* serfs. All Mother had to do was to leave Auburg and any other settlement within four days' ride of the county seat. He'd been twelve.

"Well?" Jastrab's voice brought him back to the present.

"Captain?"

"You didn't answer me. What is it you want, Geroslaw?"

He tightened the leather thongs that bound his beard and looked thoughtful.

"D'you know, Captain, I don't know that anyone's ever asked me that before."

Jastrab grinned. "Maybe they should've."

Geroslaw nodded, still considering. "I was once the heir to my father's high seat."

Jastrab's face became set and sober. "But you were a bastard."

"But I was a bastard. Father finally married. In the Kamieńsykli of my sixth year, they had a son of their own. When he lived past his *fifth* Kamieńsykli, he was officially proclaimed the heir."

Jastrab's eyes flitted off to his left.

From over Geroslaw's shoulder, Sjelesanger spoke. "So, you want to see to your half-brother and gain back the inheritance that was stolen away from you."

This was a common enough aspiration. The first-born male of any man in Venzene was the right and lawful heir of his father's wealth, no matter how meager. If the child were born out of wedlock—without the union's sanction by a local magistrate or scholar of the governing noble's bloodline—that claim could be overturned by the father and, in some counties, the mother by way of petition and tithe. With a small bag of silver and the stroke of a quill pen, a bastard's station and status could be snuffed out like a candle flame.

Children born out of wedlock to a noble father always risked a more legitimate heir coming along. Such children born to noble mothers were often drowned in the nearest river or left in the wilds to be eaten by the first predator to come along. Horrid as that was to contemplate, the prevailing philosophy seemed to be that a man could and should prove virility, and a woman should be chaste and pure. Ridiculous but pervasive, nonetheless.

"No," Geroslaw said at last. "I could see myself as a knight or a baron, but I don't have designs on my father's throne."

Sjelesanger came around to stand beside her husband. She laid a hand on his left shoulder. They looked at one another, then at him.

He bore their combined gaze for a few moments, trying to gauge it. To him, they seemed surprised, perhaps disbelieving. Finally, he'd made up his mind to speak again, but Sjelesanger beat him to it.

"You still love them."

"Some of them. Aye, Lady." He didn't plan to voyage too far out onto this uncomfortable water, but felt he needed to provide them with a touch more context. He resisted the urge to fortify himself with a swallow or two of that sweet, mouthwatering wine.

"My brother is a good man. He's not someone I'm willing to ride over on my way to glory."

Again, they looked at one another, then back at him.

"Let's leave that for now," said Jastrab. "If not your birthright, what do you want?"

It was the third time, now, that he'd been asked that question. "I want to be of use to my family—to a cause ... if nothing else. I'm like a sword who begs to be drawn but is stuck on a wall over some humble hearth. It doesn't make me somehow lesser or ignoble, but a sword seeks only to see combat. A sword seeks to serve. I needn't be ennobled or lauded in some public ceremony. It's not a matter of word fame or wealth. I'm a stallion given a field to run on, but no rider, no race, no lyst or lancer. I'm not purebred enough to be put out to stud, either—your pardon, Lady."

She smirked, then tried on a false mask of blush and indignance. It fit her face well enough, but she couldn't hold the guise for more than a few moments before dissolving into first giggles, then outright laughter.

She laughed all the way to the camp stove, where she bent and pulled out something that smelled suspiciously like venison and berries roasted together.

His stomach growled.

None of them spoke until Sjelesanger had returned to the table with her freight of food. She served them meat and fruit—his nose had been correct, it seemed—and then replaced the great ceramic pan on the makeshift hob made by the oven's opened door.

As she sat beside her husband, they tucked in.

Geroslaw began to raise his goblet meaning to salute her and thank them for the generosity of their board when she spoke up.

"You may see your chance sooner than you think. The Eoalunth have raided more aggressively into Kovalun's northernmost counties of late. Edmund is considering expanding his territory, claiming the ravaged lands for himself and those loyal to him," said she.

Jastrab grinned.

"She's quite right. If you're willing, there may be opportunity in the very near future for us to claim lands of our own."

Geroslaw sat back, eyes widening.

"How much land are we discussing?"

"Enough for Edmund to carve out a Duchy of his own, perhaps." Jastrab's tone was calm and nonchalant, but his eyes veritably danced.

"He would need those loyal to him to serve under his banner..." Geroslaw's mind was working, trying to grasp the scope of it all.

"He *would*." Jastrab was smiling now.

"Lord Alojz?"

"Would undoubtedly be the new count of Jižní Pochod."

Geroslaw nodded at his captain. "And that would mean the new county—for it takes at least two to be a Duchy, I believe..."

"It *does*..." Sjelesanger's tone was bemused satisfaction.

"...would need a stable ruler—ruling family, actually."

They nodded, grinning at him in near-perfect symmetry.

"Any county needs its barons."

Geroslaw sat in ambivalent silence for the nonce, struck by the idea.

"Such a thought does more than any drop of wine or whiskey in the belly to keep you warm, doesn't it?" Sjelesanger's smile was almost too bright to look at.

Jastrab reached for his cup, raising it toward Geroslaw as he spoke on. "If this comes to pass, I'll need someone to help keep my armies trained

and well-prepared. Who better to give such a task to—to make a member of my close court—than our favorite training sergeant?" He looked to his wife, then back across the table. "Time enough for that as and when the opportunity presents itself more fully. Just," he shrugged, "something to consider."

Geroslaw had rarely heard a statement he'd agreed with more. This was, indeed, something to consider.

SHADOWS LENGTHEN

-I-

Venzene Duchy of Kovalun
County Jižní Pochod
Barony of Haluzfeld - Haluz Věže
30 Gerstesykli: 2 Days after the Red Storm at Westsong

Aedelt stood in the wreck of his chambers as the sun set. He watched through the gaps left by the catapult's stone. It had made a ruin of both his wall *and* his lover. The liquid red of the sinking sun wasn't what he'd come to see. Consequently, it didn't hold his attention for long. He forced his eye downward, taking in the tale told by his enemy. Maddeningly, the scene stretched out below his tower still defied reason.

"That hardly matters," he said to himself. "It can defy reason all it likes. Reason seems ill-prepared to make much of a counter-argument." He spoke in a dry, low tone of disgusted resignation.

They had destroyed his outer walls and upper windows with a quickness. The oddment—the first of many—was that they had stopped aggressive action toward the keep once that had been accomplished. They had removed the structure's ability to station archers of any kind around the walls or in high windows along every tower but had left the gate utterly intact. They were still surrounded, still besieged. Yet that was all that could be said about the enemy and the keep itself.

"No," he amended. "From there, they've had a long spree with the peasants and serfs, perhaps even the slaves, unless they chose to *liberate* them. Who can say?"

He'd seen and smelled fires each night since the siege had begun. From his high vantage—loathe though he was to return to this chamber—the fever-orange glows had consistently dotted the countryside from the foot of his pinnacle, nearly to the horizon until well past dawn.

The screams and wailing had died down to an occasional burst of pain or hopeless grief. Horror and fear had been replaced by a grotesque sort of normality, a predictable outcome for such military actions.

The rabble that had surrounded him by use of some sorcery or alchemy, he believed, sounded as if they were enjoying their own festival week. Each day and each night produced new gibbering laughter, new songs sung in either Eoalunth or Orcish—which may as well be the tongue of demons or dragons for all its guttural, dark joy. This was accompanied by those occasional bursts of sorrow or terrified screams and the smell of human flesh roasting on spits over unnumbered, open flames.

He knew long pork when he smelled it. He'd never eaten it but had been forced to suffer its scent on more than one occasion while fighting beside the count during the rebellion. It had been a common tactic of the enemy to wall up those they'd once counted as comrades and roast them alive when they'd agreed to Count Edmund's terms, accepting peace.

I could respect that. It was vile beyond words, but it proved an effective inducement for a while. Few villages were willing to swear themselves to Edmund while Syr Georgi commanded the rebellion. He snorted. *I've always admired his drive and purity. One needn't be a good man to be a pure one, after all... a thing so few people understand.*

The open land between the pocket forest below and the eastern horizon had been divested of its usual grazing goats, sheep, and stone cattle. Instead, it bore the largest herd of horses he'd ever seen. True, they were all light horse—swift and suited for archers or spear and azhkast rather than the couched lance and heater shield, but if he were faced with it across a field, he would withdraw.

Against such a force, I'd want at least half as many heavy horse or an equal number of trained archers before I'd consider it a battle worth waging.

This was irrespective of long-term strategy, of course. The thought was idle—no more than Aedelt strategist's mind wandering along familiar paths carved out by time, aptitude, and the helping hand of his own secret, subtle sorcery. Barring something new entering the field—some mistake or additional force to disrupt the patterns his foes had created—there would be no victory here. He had neither the men nor the supplies needed to do more than wait here until it was over. Even his sorcery had been of no help. He'd focused too much on knowing, eschewing the sorts of magic that would directly control the battlefield or provide him the means to escape. The empire would have hunted and killed him for using such arts.

Foolish and shortsighted, but true nonetheless.

Other than the herd and the horrors of the forest, there was the dread silhouette of the town. Southeast of the keep itself, it looked like a drop of silver against the green and gold of the graze-land or the white of early winter's snows ... at least during the ordinary course of things. Now, and since the sun had risen for the first time over the beleaguered baronial seat, it had been blackened with fire and painted red with the blood of men, and by the sounds of the screams that had come floating to him on cursed winds, women and children as well. That wasn't a poetic description. The horde had taken ladders and painted red signs and symbols on the blackened stone rooftops in a shade that almost had to be blood.

He heard movement behind him. *A light step*, he thought. A *slippered foot...*

"Eliška," said he.

"Aedelt." Her voice was cool and clipped.

"What's brought you here?"

"Honestly?" She waited barely a moment before pressing on. "I needed to see you—to hear your voice." While her words carried love and desperation, her tone conveyed a bitterness that was hard to hear.

"Afraid I might do an injury to myself, my dear?"

"No," she sighed, entering in earnest. "I'm simply tired of hearing the bleating of our so-called men." Her voice had warmed, turning from cool detachment to resigned amusement. "You may be the only man *left* in this place. Ironic, really, given how many ill-conceived slings and slanders have been touted about you by the motley-minded in court."

He grinned, turning to her. The grin died on his face.

Her azure gown—a favorite worn in nearly all courtly settings—looked regal and pristine, though it couldn't diminish the haunted figure she cut standing there in the doorframe. His wife was always the picture of poise and grace. Now she had a tear-stained face, disheveled hair sticking up in thin wisps in all directions, tangling in her coronet, and the hollow, sunken cheeks of someone who hadn't eaten in days.

"Eliška?" His concern was evident as he moved to embrace her.

She fell gratefully into his arms, squeezing him tightly as she lay her head upon his chest.

"Thank you, Aedelt." Her voice quavered as she sighed through her now free-flowing tears. "Ohhhh, thank you."

He held her. For a long moment, there was nothing more he could do.

At length, he found his voice again.

"Hardly any reason to thank me. My eventual epitaph will undoubtedly be that it was my pride and perversion that led us to this misery." Rather than sounding bitter about this thought, his voice conveyed dark amusement.

"Hells haul them home," said she. She sounded angry now, and it did much to restore her oft-vaunted and oft-feared sense of personal force.

He chuckled, stroking her hair and back for a moment before releasing her to stand upright once more.

"Truly, Aedelt. They're fools—the lot of them. Nothing more than superstitious childr—"

Drums—a thousand heartbeats in eerie unison—overrode her frustrated rant.

After a moment, he raised his voice above the distant din. "Can you blame them, really?"

She shook her head.

"I suppose not." She shook her head again, but this time it seemed more of an act to refocus herself. "While we have this moment, Aedelt, I need to say—and you need to hear—something."

He nodded, eyes cutting to the crack in the stones for a moment before returning to her.

"I wasn't thanking you for your leadership or your rule. Though, truly, anyone with even a pinch of sense would see how wise and thoughtful you have been with the barony and its people." She reached a hand up to caress his left cheek. "You could have remained unmarried. You could have claimed any child as your heir and called him your own. You didn't."

He took her hand, turning it to plant a gentle kiss on her palm.

"Eliška, come now..."

"Hear me," said she. "Keep your tongue behind your teeth for once and hear me."

"Have I *ever* ignored your council?"

"Apart from just now, when you spoke after I counseled you not to?"

He smiled. "Yes."

"Often." She, too, was smiling.

He laughed. An instant later, so did she. For a magical moment, the sound drowned out the drums that now owned the night stalking toward them.

When their laughter had subsided and the drums had reasserted themselves, he made a gesture that she should go on.

"When my father was defeated, and I heard that you were coming to Kamenný Proud to take me to wife, I thought I was to be treated like chattel. I'm a war bride, I thought, and will be expected to give up all that I own and all that I know." Now it was she who sounded darkly amused. "The brilliant young strategist—Vagiaedelt of Bílá Vidlička—had outdone my father and had his eyes on adding insult to injury by taking his only child to wife. That was what they all said. Did you know that?"

"All a part of my rightly rumored brilliant strategy, of course."

She snorted. "To make me angry and afraid, or so it seemed. My hopes and dreams with poor Bolek were ended. Your arrival heralded that, surely. When you had no actual interest in me on our wedding night, it acted as *proof* that I was chattel, not even worth more than the occasional bedding."

He sat on a ruined chunk of stone forced into the room by the catapult's impact.

"I thought you or fate were exceedingly cruel when you brought Bolek into your service as my personal guard."

He laughed rather musically. It was a warm counterpoint to the chilling thud that persisted outside.

"I knew you'd long since fallen in love with him. I also knew that neither you nor I would be safe without an heir and an alliance that brought stability to our little county. Once the latter was sorted, the former seemed a fitting ever-after for you."

She nodded, smiling. After a moment had passed, and she could no longer bear the heart's pulse sound from outside, she spoke again.

"You've given me such strength, such *force*, Aedelt. You've given me a wealth of heart and inner-courage that I'd never dreamed I possessed."

"I didn't give you those things," said he.

"You did, and so very much more. Your tutelage has been the very least of it. But now..." Eliška's voice broke. "Aedelt, how? How are we to save ourselves, let alone the rest of them? I've looked and listened, written and roamed, and can see no way out. How do we..."

He held her gaze for a long moment, saying nothing.

"Am I never to see our son again?"

Once more, he merely looked at her. He was thinking, searching, trying to find any answer, any conclusion—save the one he'd come to before—that had the *slightest* hope of being true. No such answers came.

He was drawing breath to give her the miserable truth when something interrupted him: a sound from beyond the crack in the wall.

"Sdraliana thoriash rhex xro inagror nna! Sdraliana thoriash rhex xro inagror nna! Sdraliana thoriash *rhex* xro inagror nna!"

This mad chanting froze their blood, stopped their breath, and all but turned them momentarily to stone.

It took nearly a full minute before either could do more than battle their personal paralysis. The words were hard to hear. They jagged against the mind, the ears ... the heart like blasphemy.

"Aedelt?"

He managed a smile that hurt his heart to force onto his face. He stepped forward, standing at last, and took her by the shoulders.

She was shaking now. "Aedelt!?"

"Hear me."

She met his eyes, lips trembling.

"Go and be with Bolek. You should be in the arms of the man you love."

She clung to him. "Aedelt..."

He bore this for as long as he dared, then forced her away as gently as he could.

"Eliška, you are perhaps the strongest woman I have ever met, and I've been blessed to know you." He paused, fighting back—not tears, exactly. His eyes were red, dry things just now, but he fought to control his roiling emotions. This was the end. He was certain of it, though he couldn't have said precisely why. "Thank you for all you've given to me and all that you've refused to take away." He turned his back to her, facing the crack in the stone once more.

He never heard her leave. The chanting was *all* now.

"Sdraliana thoriash *rhex* xro inagror nna! Sdraliana thoriash *rhex xro* inagror nna! Sdraliana thoriash *rhex xro inagror* nna!"

Thunder cracked overhead—*directly* overhead. The room was suddenly bathed in a crimson light, charging through the gaps in the stone like questing fingers.

There was a *new* sound now. A single chord as if from a lyre or usclyd but sung rather than strummed or plucked on strings. It reminded him of a game he'd played as a child. There had always been a fear when playing Zvonění with the hood over one's face. Sound was normally a thing that simply *was*. In a game of Zvonění, however, sound was fear. Unless, of course, and until that word of sweet salvation could be heard through the din. *But who will sing běh for me, now?*

His heart sped up: a hammering, racing thing threatening to burst from his chest.

The chanting was growing louder. The source of it seemed to come from all around.

No, not from all around him—*from* him. He heard his own voice chanting the monstrous words, and while he did not himself understand them, he recognized the hells when they came to call. This was spell-work—a summons of some sort in the voice of the dark beyond Skolf's own seam.

His chest was on fire.

He'd collapsed to his hands and knees, still spewing that insane chant in great waves of rhythmic sound, the catechism of the damned if ever there was such a thing.

"Sdraliana thoriash rhex xro inagror nna! Sdraliana thoriash rhex xro inagror nna! Sdraliana thoriash rhex xro inagror nna!"

No, I'll have no part in your rite, devil-things. You may stop my breath, but you won't steal it, so help me...

As if in answer, he saw a red vapor rip its way through the wall's jagged opening and race toward him. He felt himself stop chanting, felt his lungs begging for air, felt himself reflexively drawing breath—drawing the red *in* ... and resisted.

If I am to end here, I shall end as Aedelt, not some chanting child.

He forced himself to his feet. His lungs were on fire. He turned and lumbered toward the door, still open from his wife's last leave-taking.

Passing through it, he turned to the right, moved to the edge of the landing, and paused. To his right, he saw the mist seeping toward him with one rippling tendril of vapor in the lead. He drew a deep breath and felt the chant returning to his lips. With a supreme act of will, he threw himself into a run.

As he reached the first landing, he realized he'd been hearing sword-play and shouts from below, and for some time now. He couldn't make out what they were saying through the tangle of drums and chanting ... to say nothing of the thunder of his own heart. It'd long-since started pounding out hectic fragments of frenzy in his ears.

Aedelt turned to look back up the stairs, though he knew what he would find. The mist was on him. It had somehow gained ground and was already reaching that lone tendril of fog toward him.

He felt the familiar slowness of time as his mind worked to assess—to lay tactics. *It needs me—needs to infect me—needs me to breathe it in.*

Did he know that? He did not, but he saw no reason to stand there like a lemon waiting to test the notion. He turned and bolted down the stairs. His lungs were now screaming with more force than they had whilst he'd been compelled to join in that darksome chanting.

Bursting into the entry hall, he saw his men battling foes wearing what looked like aged iron armor. Their shoulders supported high plates that served as haut guards. The style of this heavy harness would've been common among the nobility during his great-grandsire's day. But it'd been long-since unseated by lighter, more articulated steel armors. No sane person would wear such ponderous plate for combat on foot by *choice.* One well-aimed spear haft... hells, one well-seasoned *broom handle* dropped between haut guard and gorget could act as a deadly lever capable of breaking even the stoutest man's neck. No, such a corselet was only worn by the second sons of lesser Venzene lords too poor to purchase their own armor. These unfortunates were forced to wear the ill-fitting iron in order to joust at tournament, and usually spent the first purse they earned to replace it.

Aedelt heard screaming as another of his men fell. There was a time to be still and a time to act. There wasn't any *real* hope of victory, but what did that matter? He'd no intention of standing around while his men fought for their lives and his last bastion. Grinning a bitter little grin, he hurled himself down the stairs and into the fray.

His eyes fell upon a halberd on the ground beside the outstretched fingers of one of his guardsmen. He bent to scoop it up and had to jerk back as one of the armored figures turned to swing a sword at him. Looking up, he saw that its face was skeletal within its un-visored sallet helm. Its eyes were dim, white starlight.

He leaned away from the sword stroke—a hammer shot that would have sliced him nose to nethers if he'd suffered its wrath.

Reaching his right leg high at the knee, he brought it down diagonally, his foot making contact with the flat of the blade and driving it to the ground.

The once-man tried to pull the sword up, bending forward automatically for balance and leverage.

Aedelt's grin became a sour thing full of cold satisfaction. Clasping his fists together, he drove them down against the back of the thing's head, forcing it to the ground.

He took a moment to reach for the halberd once more, and this time managed it.

Driving its butt end onto the ground between the skeletal thing's haut guard and the side of its head, he used the halberd as a make-shift lever. Throwing his weight against the haft beneath the blade in a brief burst of soundless ferocity, he felt a sense of deep satisfaction. An instant later, he heard a welcome *crack,* and was momentarily surprised to see the thing's armored head tumble free.

He'd turned to find a new target when he saw the red cloud. It'd crept its way toward him and was now mere *inches* away. There were small, bruise-colored tines of lightning writhing along its surface.

He looked about, trying to find an exit—a rally point—*something,* but there were no paths he could take. He was surrounded. Bowing his head, he gave one final smile, thin and utterly without humor.

He heard himself speaking once more.

"Sdraliana-urrrrrr." He cut off the chant as he raised his head. Turning to his right, he moved his halberd into position to threaten his nearest would-be opponent. The creature did as he'd hoped. It lowered its weapon to defend itself, sword's point leveled at him.

He leapt forward, impaling himself upon the thing with all the force he could muster.

The pain was enormous — a searing sensation beneath a screaming *thud-thud-thud* that seemed all-encompassing. Turning his head as he spat blood, he faced the roiling, red fog and nodded. Summoning what remained of his once all-but *boundless* will, he forced himself to deliver a final act of defiance before he, at last, closed his eyes.

"I ... w-win."

-II-

Venzene Duchy of Kamieńalun
County Czarny Wodospad
Wieża Szymona
30 Gerstesykli: 2 Days after the Red Storm at Westsong

Azhferd sat quietly in his room, one leg propped up on his bed, the other with its foot planted firmly on the floor. He had one boot on and one off and was debating which way he should finish out this late evening. Tired and covered in sweat, he needed a bath, a meal, a full night's sleep, and to, at last, carry on the conversation he'd been putting off with his father.

The chill wind whistled outside of his arched window. The light pouring in from that open portal was its traditionally omnipresent grey. He heard in the distance the shrill and alien cry of a Zimowy Sokół as it dove. He smiled to think of the winter falcon as it plunged from some impossible height, dropping like a stone on some unsuspecting animal.

The strange beauty of these creatures had always fascinated him. Their white wings were membranous rather than feathered, and their beak had a silvery sheen to it that sometimes looked blue when caught in the right light. Slightly bigger than a traditional falcon, they resembled nothing so much as a cross between the feathered bird and the oft-spoken of but never seen—at least not by anyone he personally knew—winter dragons of old.

When he was a boy, he fancied taking the Zimowy Sokół as his chop: the device he bore as his personal coat of arms. That particular boyhood fancy, however, had long since been abandoned. He had responsibilities. Chief among them was to embrace the will of his father, Hengrek.

That worthy was old. Hengrek was still robust enough to wield the sword and sit a horse, should that become necessary. But he had spent increasingly less time simply *ruling* the county. Instead, he spent much of his time instructing his son on how that task should be accomplished. Azhferd's father hadn't given over the county coronet to him as of yet, but he was preparing for the day that would become necessary.

Besides, he thought, *such arms are more befitting for Kozioł.*

It was true. His young cousin had been fascinated by the magnificent sokół since he'd first seen one whilst they'd been hunting together. The boy had been even more enamored by the beautiful creatures when Azhferd had confided his hope and plan to bear one as his device. Such was often the way with younger relatives. They regularly seemed to attach themselves to whatever things were fancied by a beloved elder.

A knock at the door stopped his musings before they carried him away.

"It isn't locked," he said, voice raising enough to pass through the heavy wood.

The door opened. He'd rather expected one of the family's servants. Failing that, he'd thought he might see perhaps the beautiful but distant sight of his mother come to whisper advice into his ear. She often counseled him as to how best to please his father in the conversations and lessons to come. Instead, the door opened to reveal a raven-haired beauty his own age. After pulling the door wide, she stood full in its frame, offering him a coy smile.

"What brings you to me at this hour, Yeidil?" He did his best to make his voice neutral and hold his smile in abeyance, but it was a struggle.

"I cannot merely come and see you as and when I please?" She quirked a brow. Her voice drifted across the room like velvet blown by a breeze.

"You *can* not, you *must* not, and you know it well." He did his best to put a touch of reproach in his voice, attempting to hide that her presence, as always, lightened his mood. "Mother hasn't allowed you and I to be alone since you first grew your breasts. I suspect all the servants recall your weeping and shrieking as she delivered the news to you."

Her smile burst upon her face, eyebrows launching almost up to her hairline. Her laughter bubbled just beneath the surface as she stepped in, pulled the tunic which he'd set out for supper off of the waist-high dresser, and hurled it at him.

"*Me*? How quickly we forget, little Azhferd. It was you who wept for a week. I recall our uncle bloodying your face several times during sword practice because you were too busy lamenting the fact that you had lost your playmate. You hated being resigned to spending so much time with the old Griffin." She stepped forward, closed the door, and leaned against it, folding her arms. "Do *not* level slanderous accusations at *me*, little brother. I'm not *remotely* above spreading embarrassing rumors about you when you next ride to tournament."

He caught the tunic before it struck his face and laid it beside him on the bed. Pulling off the other boot, he arched his brows at his sister as she ranted and mocked him.

"Oh? And what *embarrassing truths* do you think you know and are willing to spread about me?"

"Perhaps the peasant girls that you have been spending far too much time with?"

"That's hardly new. It's presumed that at least half of the squires, knights, and lords spend time amongst the pretty peasant maids. Hells, half of them are reputed to spend as much time with the pretty peasant *boys*. And half of *them* actually *do*!" He snorted. "What else have you got hidden up your gossiper's sleeve?"

"It doesn't matter." She shrugged her shoulders, affecting's supreme unconcern. "If all else fails, I shall make something up." Her grin widened as she saw his disbelieving and disappointed look. "Come now. I'm more creative than you by half, and *I* am pure and innocent, as everyone knows. I wouldn't lie, would I?"

They both dissolved into laughter. This was an old joke between them.

"Well, you won't have too much longer to wait and think, Yeidil."

"Have you asked him yet?"

"No." He kept his voice firm, holding to his resolve.

"Not *yet*, you mean." She sounded concerned and suspicious.

"No, I mean that I don't intend to ask."

She shook her head, opening her mouth to speak, but he forestalled her.

"I *will* be count. I am a lord in my own right, with manors and income of my own. I *already* have permission to fight and take the field for the honor and glory of county and family. I do not *require* his permission."

"But you aren't riding off to fight in tournament on your own, and you know it. This is hardly the same thing as you and your young squire riding with sergeants and guards to some local *contest*, and yes, I use that word in the *loosest* sense imaginable."

"It's both different and the same." He shook his head. "I cannot and will not order them to ride with me and fight. The sons of Father's banner knights and his few barons will not be tasked to come with me and fight beside me. They will be asked to. In fact, they already have been."

She was astonished. Her mouth fell open, and it took her more than a few seconds to regain her composure and close it again. The crushed velvet of her voice had been replaced with something colder and more distant.

"He'll be wrathful. You know that."

"You're wrong."

"How can you *say* that?" She shook her head, striding forward and slamming her balled fists against her thighs. "Why do you tempt fate? You know as well as I do that he's grooming you—training you to take his place!" She bowed her head and turned away from him. "Why must you always play the game as if your life depended on winning it?" Her voice softened, full of unshed tears of intermingled love and fear.

He stood, going to her, placing his hands on her shoulders from behind. He was careful to keep his body well away from hers lest someone see them through the open door. He couldn't bear to be cold and distant while she was so upset.

"Yeidil ... hear me." His voice was soft, offering consolation without patronization. "You've spoken rightly. He *has* been grooming me. He *is* grooming me ... to lead and to rule. Over the course of the last several moons, he has been more frustrated and short-tempered with me each time I ask a question." Here he paused for a moment, considering, then shook his head. "No, that's not true. He's acted so whenever I've asked his leave for a thing, not when I've asked a question. I am, therefore, left to conclude that he wishes to see me *take* command. Not to *ask* for it."

She bowed her head, raising her hands to cover his.

"He will see this as your impatience." She said this in a bitter, downcast whisper. "Father commands ... *demands* obedience from those around him. He'll see this as you challenging his authority. Don't you *see* that?"

"You're wrong," said he. His voice was soft but certain. "He wishes to see me show initiative, not obedience. I've long since shown him obedience. He can have no doubt on that score at this late date. I'm his son, and I am—I *have* to be on his side. You know it, I know it, and I'm certain so does he."

She stepped away from him, never having turned to face him. As she strode to the window overlooking the bed, she, at last, did so.

"And if you've misread the situation?" She lowered her chin for a moment, then looked back up at him. "If you've misread the situation, what then? It will set all of your work back by months, perhaps years. You're right in that he now must surely know that you're with him. Still, in your youth, you always went your own way. You were the only one ever to tell him no." She shook her head, frustrated and obviously afraid for him. "Zlaté Pole, Černé oči... hells be hid, Azhferd, you've gone your own way so many times... Father's never thanked you for it. You've come so far. Why take such a risk? Why chance his ire?"

It was true. Azhferd had seen only twenty-five Kamieńsykli pass in his lifetime. From his ninth Kamieńsykli, when he and his sister had been forced to separate, no longer playing together by day or reading together by night—at least not alone—he had been angry and rebellious.

The year he'd turned twelve, he'd secreted himself in his father's train as coaches, wagons, mounted, and boot-bound armsmen made their way to tournament. Once there, he'd almost bluffed his way into the child's lyst, but his uncle had found him. He'd been hauled back before his father, who had looked both angry and disappointed, and then been turned over to that same uncle for discipline and more rigorous instruction.

When he was sixteen, a border war had broken out in the neighboring Duchy of Kovalun. The Count of Hartscross had taken the time to spar with young Azhferd at two separate tournaments that year, and so when the count called for aid, Azhferd saddled his horse, gathered his two armsmen, and rode North West against his father's orders.

He met her eyes. He spent a moment seeking the words to explain it to her—to give her the understanding she needed. At length, he spoke again.

"Yeidil—I know his mind. I know his mind and have learned the lessons he's seen fit to teach me. There's always more to learn. Of course there is. But you must trust me. He's waiting for me to stand up and lead." He paused, shaking his head, then added almost against his will, "And if I have somehow missed everything and you are utterly correct..."

"Then *you* should wear the gown, and I shall don your armor."

He looked at her, searching to see whether she was teasing or serious. After a moment, he decided he didn't much care. He knew his sister hated that she was expected to account the finery she wore as her armor and the social arena as a battleground. Still, as she was not just the eldest but the only daughter, she had a duty. She had risen to the occasion magnificently, as she did with everything she undertook. But there'd been several years during which he'd caught her in isolated areas, shadow sparring with a practice sword.

"I'll wear the gown, and I shall look more beautiful in it than you ever could." He offered a smirk with this, then added, "Most especially once I stop trimming my beard."

To her credit, she kept her face solemn as she appraised him openly.

"Yes, you're *quite* right. Whomsoever sets their eyes upon you will be unable to resist your charms ... Lady Blackbeard."

She held her studious countenance for perhaps a five-count, but no longer. She burst out laughing.

With a wide grin, and the music of her laughter echoing in his ears, he decided it was time to leave. He needed to wash the sweat of the day's training from his tired body.

Yes, he would speak with their father, but it would be a discussion, not a request for his leave or permission. In less than a fortnight, his fellows would come for a final round of training with him at Auburg. With that event completed, his men would be as ready as may be for the tournament at Zlaté Pole.

"Yes," he said as he entered the bath chamber. "It's nearly time. First this. I shall tell him my plans after supper this evening."

-III-

Azhferd arrived late to supper. He entered the First Hall—a chamber used for family meals, open court, and the receiving of guests in a formal setting—and took a moment to yield to the needs of custom. Just inside the door, he stood and waited.

The stone around him was a grey so dusky that it was almost black. The wide door with its arched top let in a great deal of light from the hall beyond. Directly behind him, against the wall, an enormous brazier blazed. Its positioning had the net effect of forcing someone who entered the chamber to block off the light, which would draw the eye from most places in the Hall.

He silently performed a thirty-count. While tradition insisted he do so backward, he elected to count forward instead. It made no outward difference, but it gave him the tiniest pleasure to buck tradition in this way. No one would know, after all. There were only a few exceptions—always ceremonial—where the counting was done aloud rather than inside one's head.

As ever, guards stood to either side of the door. By custom, they would also keep a count, so the chances of the entrant being woefully off and rushing through were slim to none.

As he reached thirty, rather than one, as tradition mandated, he stepped into the room in earnest. Before him sat an enormous horseshoe shape made by several long trestle tables. The red-hatted, angry man—or so he had thought of his household's arms when he was young—hung on two banners that flanked the high table.

In actuality, the arms displayed a horizontally split field—red over white. On the lower, white half rested a black Chevron in base with two black towers above it and to either side. At range, it had always looked like a frowning face with wide-set black eyes, wearing a red hat—at least when he was small. Now, at twenty-five, the thought of that childish description always made him smile.

Few people paid him more than a cursory glance as he entered. He was not the count, after all. No one was required to stand and bow to acknowledge him as he arrived.

Azhferd walked along the leftmost table, slowing his pace just long enough to lay a hand on his squire's shoulder, a brief but genuine acknowl-edgement. He continued all the way to table's end, turned right, and gave a warm, slightly longer greeting to his aunt and her husband—his knight and uncle. He again accomplished this with slowed movement, but he never stopped altogether. Courtesy seen to, he strode down to about the halfway mark of the high table and stood behind his father.

He leaned forward around the count's chair, kissing his mother's right cheek. He then stepped back, moved one seat further to the right, and sat on his father's other side.

"You'll stay when food is finished," the count said.

"I will." Azhferd kept his voice even and polite, and not only because he felt no reason to do otherwise. In semi-public places—particularly when the entire family sat together among their extended household and any guests present—it was important to wear a public face, as it were. Outsiders needed to see unity within the family even when—hells, *especially* when there was actual discord between its members. "I had thought to ask you for a few moments this evening as well... if you're willing."

Count Hengrek nodded as he sipped his wine.

"It will have to wait, but there'll be time once business is done," said he.

Azhferd began to nod when his father said something that sur-prised him.

"See that Dargory is with you. He should bear witness."

"As you wish."

They'd called the boy Kozioł since he toddled. Still, the count was notoriously firm in his belief that one called someone by the name given them by their parents, not some affectation. To Hengrek, a nickname was the same as referring to someone by the color of their hair or longcoat—absurd. He didn't insist others refrain from using such unless it were in formal settings or documents.

Azhferd could tell, looking around the room, that the evening meal was actually very close to being over. He had been later in his arrival than he'd either thought or planned.

A servant brought him a trencher of bread, added chunks of lamb and potato, and a small bowl of cabbage leaves soaked in pepper, butter, and honey: warm, yet still crisp.

By the time he'd taken his second bite, he'd noted the guests in the hall. This wasn't an official, formal feast, just the normal time of day for such fare, yet there were several men, women, and children who did not normally make their home here. They were sitting in states of either nervousness or disconsolation along what was now his left side at the lower table.

A few minutes passed in silence. Azhferd saw his squire frantically trying to gain his attention from further down to his right. He was attempting to accomplish this by the use of slightly exaggerated movements and a widening of his eyes.

Azhferd's first thought was to chastise the boy for using such tactics. No one would pick up on a widening of the eyes from so far away, would they? That thought vanished in a puff of self-recriminatory smoke when, a moment later, he realized that he had done precisely that. He chuckled at himself briefly, then reached for his goblet of wine, lifting it in the boy's direction in an acknowledging salute.

"He's smarter than his father," his own father said from beside him.

"As you say…" Azhferd didn't want to agree or disagree with that statement. The boy in question was the youngest son of Azhferd's knight and uncle. If he disagreed, he would be at odds with his father's assessment. If he agreed, he would disrespect his knight and uncle.

Count Hengrek nodded approval at his son's answer. He said nothing more for a long moment, then cut his eyes back to Azhferd's. "Are you going to put him out of his misery? Or do you want to make him sit and wait until you're ready to speak to him?"

It was a rebuke, Azhferd knew, but a gentle one.

"I had thought to have some more food and drink first while it's still remotely warm, but if I wanted hot food, I should have been swifter in the bath."

"Well, I'm certain the lamb and the cabbage appreciate your efforts to smell like springtime for them on this, their last night on Skolf."

Azhferd shook his head. He grinned as he stood. His father rarely, if ever, offered such jokes, japes, or quips. It was a mark of true affection for him to allow that side of his personality to be seen.

"Do excuse me for a moment," he said, standing. Leaving a bit more than half of his supper still on the table, he departed with his mostly full goblet of wine and walked down to where his squire sat.

He passed his Aunt Hywyn and Uncle Borys once more, catching the eye of their eldest, Bartek, as the fellow returned to the table at his father's right hand. Azhferd exchanged a warm grin with him as he neared, but that was all. Given how much time they spent training together, that was greeting enough.

Rounding the table's corner, Azhferd stopped between the next two seats. These were occupied by Bartek's brothers, Jarek—squire to the count—and Kozioł, Azhferd's squire.

Both grinned at him as he approached, each turning toward him as he crouched between their chairs.

"I told him you'd see." Kozioł's tone was triumphant. His voice was still unbroken—a fact that made the display of pride more amusing than arrogant or unseemly.

"Good," Jarek said. He didn't sound the least bit discomposed. "Then you can ask *him* your questions. He'll tell you the same thing I did." With the advantage of being all of two years his senior, he had the long-suffering voice of someone happy to pass off this chore.

Azhferd grinned. Raising his goblet, he offered a brief salute to the older of the two boys, then turned his attention to Kozioł.

"Well, go on. Ask, and I smile, right?"

Kozioł beamed. It took him a few seconds to get his thoughts in order, but once he had, the questions came out well-formed.

"There are house knights here that I don't know. Who are the three across from me?" He paused as Azhferd looked, then added, "I'm sure I've seen their children around, but I can't place them either."

It took a moment for Azhferd to figure out where the disconnect was. There *were* knights across from Kozioł, but none of them were house knights. They were banners.

"Syr Wolan and his sons, and to the right is..." Azhferd clawed through his memory. He hadn't seen the second knight often—perhaps only once. Still, there was something familiar about him. *Syr ... Wiktor—yes.* "Syr Wiktor of Skalna Marchia." His banner served a barony to the northeast that, in turn, gave its grace to the county seat.

"And the third?"

"That one you should know." He took a deliberately slow, unnecessarily long sip of his wine to give the boy time to sus it out for himself.

"Is that..." He sounded as if he were straining under an almighty weight. "Is that Syr Maks?"

Jarek winced from his perch on their left but said nothing.

"Syr Maks*ymilian*, yes. My future brother and your future cousin."

Kozioł winced himself now. He looked appropriately abashed at not recognizing the man, or at least his chop.

"You've identified *who* they are now, but you haven't identified *what* they are yet."

Kozioł blinked.

"What do you mean?"

"What manner of men are they?"

"They're house knights." The boy answered this with a speed that would have been impressive if the answer had been correct.

"They most assuredly are not."

"Don't they..." He paused as if to consider his words more carefully. "Don't they have manorial land of their own?"

Azhferd nodded. "They do, indeed."

"That means they have households, does it not?"

Once more, Azhferd nodded.

"Isn't that what a house knight is? A knight that has his own household?"

Azhferd offered a smile and did his best to ignore the elder of his two cousins. Jarek was busy trying unsuccessfully to hide his laughter in a mostly empty goblet. Rather than masking the sound, the vessel forced it to echo, making it all but impossible to miss.

"I *told* you," Jarek said.

Kozioł glared, then forced his face into a flat, plain countenance.

Azhferd resisted the urge to bask in the moment. His squire had, after all, just put one of his lessons into practice, to wit: *no emotion, no reaction should be seen by anyone else unless you want them to see it.*

"Where do most men live?" Azhferd drew the boy's attention back to the matter at hand.

Kozioł blinked, cocked his head to the side in thought, then did his best to answer.

"In cities and towns?"

Azhferd tried a different road.

"What are the two types of knights?"

"House knights and banner knights."

"Correct. Now, where do men live? Do they live inside a *banner* or a house?"

Kozioł's facial expression was priceless. He looked amused, shocked, and embarrassed all at a go.

"They live in a house, of course."

Azhferd nodded and repeated that. "They live in a house, just so. Now, when looking on a map, or when traveling on a road, do you carry houses, or do you carry banners?"

"Banners, of course."

"House knights live with the lord to whom they are sworn. That lord pays for and provides them with food and shelter, arms and armor, and horses. He does the same for their immediate families, should they have them."

Kozioł sat back and thought about that for a moment, then nodded slowly.

To Azhferd, after a moment, he turned and spoke anew. "A banner knight rules over manorial land, keeps the peace, collects taxes ... and that money and wealth pays for his family, his arms, and his armor." He paused for a beat, not asking if he was right with words but veritably screaming the question with his eyes.

"Exactly so."

"So, my father is ... a house knight, then."

Azhferd nodded, reaching forward between the chairs to place his goblet atop the table.

"He is—my father's right hand, as *well* as his brother by marriage."

Kozioł grinned at that, nodding.

"I should have known that." He frowned, looking more frustrated than embarrassed.

"You should have, but let me ask you something else. When was the last time you needed to speak about such things or think about them?" Azhferd's voice was patient.

"I can't recall."

Azhferd made a "there you go" gesture.

"Just remember, you live in a house. You *carry* a banner."

Kozioł nodded, sitting back with a smile. He repeated the saying and nodded a second time with more certainty.

Azhferd saw his father rise and heard the collective rumble as every chair was pushed back from the table, and every man, woman, and child rose and bowed.

Count Hengrek came around the side of the table with Azhferd's mother—the Countess Calpernia—on his arm. They were followed by his aunt, uncle, cousin, and several other folk formerly seated at high table. As they passed, Calpernia tapped her son on his right arm, a subtle reminder that he was expected to fall into line behind them.

Jarek had already stood and waited for Azhferd, ready to fall into line behind *him*.

For his part, Azhferd followed that same methodology and tapped Kozioł on the arm before he, too, took his place in line.

The boy blinked, nodded, and stepped into line behind his lord.

They processed down the hall, into the main corridor, and then to the right, where they entered the county throne room. This told Azhferd two things. First, it clarified that this was an exceptionally formal occasion. Secondly, it made it clear that the occasion called for both pomp and circumstance.

-IV-

The throne room was tall by design but not tremendously large when it came to floor space. The room itself would hold perhaps fifty people comfortably if they were standing and seventy if they kept quarters cramped.

Its height was fully thirty feet. Its walls shaped the room into a perfect triangle, housing the entrance in the dead center of one wall, with the thrones directly across, resting nestled within the far point.

This unique construction forced the attention of all eyes to the thrones. It also served to point and shape the sound of any word issued *from* those thrones to the rest of the chamber.

The noble couple approached the thrones, the count assisting his lady wife with all courtly manner to take up her seat before doing so himself.

Azhferd came next, his sister beside him, having appeared from somewhere. From the corner of his eye, he marked his squire's shadow on the ground—merging with his own. Ten feet from the throne, he bowed, and she curtsied before they stepped to the throne's left side.

Last came his aunt and uncle with their sons in tow. After they made their manners, all four took up residence behind the thrones.

Aunt Hywyn stood as her sister-in-law's personal advisor and retainer. Uncle Borys performed those duties for the count—adding that of personal guard to the noble couple.

Among the manorial houses, tradition dictated that first-born males would be squired by their fathers, and all who came after would be fostered out to other houses to strengthen alliances.

Among house knights, however, first-born males were traditionally squired to whomever the knight was sworn to as a further token of fealty. This was done in hopes that the child would grow up being held warmly in their benefactor's regard. It was likewise common for an especially favored house knight to be granted their lord's sons as squires, though it was hardly as common an arrangement.

This tradition had been somewhat complicated in Syr Borys's family. Their eldest, Bartek, had been ten when the decision was made to give up land and title to move into the keep. As a result, Bartek had already been squired to his father thus couldn't be fostered to his liege lord. That honor had gone to Jarek when he'd turned nine.

So it was, that this evening, like so many before it, found both Bartek and Jarek acting the dual roles of guard and page.

Kozioł had been Azhferd's to take or reject as he saw fit. Count Hengrek had made it clear that he was for the idea from the first, although he'd never given an order on the matter.

These thoughts chased themselves about in Azhferd's mind as the room filled with the overwhelming majority of those who had but lately dined with them in the first hall.

As all but the final few stragglers had taken up residence at their desired standing spots, Aunt Hywyn lifted her chin and began to speak.

"O tak, O tak!" said she—the old tongue's equivalent of oyez, a call for attention. "Pay heed, for this hereby opens the court of County Czarny Wodospad! Hear the will and word of Count Hengrek and Countess Calpernia. Nasze cienie są?"

"Długie!" In the high stone chamber, the sound of nearly fifty souls shouting this answer carried a satisfying sense of unity as it soared.

The call and response had long since become rote to them all. It was the house's, and thus the county's motto, *Our Shadows are Long,* rendered into its most ancient and authentic form.

"My lady-wife and I wish to thank you, one and all, for joining us both at table and here in this ancient chamber this evening." The count's voice held its usual velvet tone, but the shape of the chamber helped to carry his words throughout the hall. "Well," he paused for a moment, standing and spreading his arms in an expansive, inclusive gesture, "I have heard many rumors, not all of which are the stuff of gossips, or those who wish to pour honey in my ear... a practice for which I would commend their bravery in undertaking. My lady-wife has long since determined that I am allergic to all honeyed words, save her own."

This was met with general laughter. The sound seemed to buoy the count's mood.

"The rumors I have heard are the sorts of truths that any noble house can expect when they have prospered as we have." Here he turned to his wife, offering his hand to steady her as she rose, drawing her forward to stand at his side as she spoke.

"There have been a disturbing number of raids on our northern marches within the last two moons. What's more," she paused and seemed to marshal her resolve before speaking again, "the raiders have not taken livestock, food, and chattel alone. They have taken our folk as slaves as well. There are reports of hamlets, thorpes, and villages alike whose populace is all but utterly *unmade*. What few have lived to report these evils were, themselves, out in field and fen when the attackers came. They returned to find all that they knew had been broken, taken, or burned."

As she finished, the count picked up the tale before the assemblage found its emotional feet and began spouting half-formed suggestions as to what was to be done.

"There have *always* been raids from the north. Still, it must also be said that some of *us* have raided in*to* the north on occasion. This isn't a new thing." He paused, releasing his wife's hand, beginning to walk back and forth. "Yet ... no raider has ever been so bold as to attack well-peopled, well-defended places before now. Syr Wiktor comes to us from what was once his home. He had travelled to the house of his baroness, my lady wife's sister Frygga, with his own family in hopes of finalizing the marriage of his eldest—Vojciech—to Her Excellency's lovely daughter, Thyngara. When he returned to Skalna Marchia … everything was gone." He paused here long enough to weather the first bite of outrage from the assemblage. As it ebbed, he went a bit further. "Syr Viktor sent his eldest boy back to Frygga's home with guards and a warning, then rode here himself to ensure that we were given word. And for *that,* we—each of us in this room—are indebted to him, and owe him our thanks."

Azhferd felt his sister's hand creep into his and squeeze. She was afraid and angry, at least based on the grip she was employing. He could hardly blame her. The news was shocking and hard to hear. That a force would dare to organize and attack their land was unheard of, if not quite undreamt of. Peace had reigned for so long within the county—from the time of his grandsire, if not further back up the hourglass. He waited to hear how his father planned to answer this threat.

"The scorching of the earth—the slaughter and enslavement of entire settlements—this cannot go unchecked." Hengrek's voice was resigned rather than empowering.

Every eye followed his progress from left to right and back again. No voice even so much as *murmured* while he spoke.

"We have spent years honing our skills with sword, lance, steed, and shield. It must be said that we have had our share of successes. And perhaps less than our fair share of failures and defeats."

Many greeted this assessment with nods and words of agreement, though precious little humility.

"It's to no purpose, I say, to win glory at tournament if we cannot defend our own lands, our own families, and our own fortunes."

This was met with the humility that had been missing a moment before. Their failure to effect such defense thus far was just that— their failure.

"I will not ask my men to do what I, myself, am unwilling to. A ridiculous failing, I'm certain many would agree, but I am old-fashioned in my thinking. My memory is long, just as our shadows are. I remember those who have sent men forward where they themselves did not dare to tread. History may have forgotten, but I have not." Here he gestured back to Syr Borys, who raised his chin and spoke in formal tones.

"His Excellency, Count Hengrek, calls the muster. We shall make preparations over the next one, perhaps two weeks, as needed. Those banners who will muster and ride may expect consideration as we reclaim manorial land from the raiders and their influence. To those knights who remain behind as home guard, the county throne will provide extra coin for the extended duties of keeping our roads patrolled and secure."

The room was in a tumult of fear and excitement. This was more than defense. This was nearly a *crusade*! To fight for the county and gain new manorial land to till and tax? Within county borders, no less? It was the sort of event that could craft a barony—turn a simple knight into a dynastic leader.

Hengrek spoke a final word on the matter before returning his lady-wife to her throne.

"We shall ride north, drive the invaders from our lands, save those we find and are able to aid, and put an *end* to this!"

The room erupted in applause. The count whispered something to his countess, then gave a nod to Syr Borys. As the applause began, at last, to fade, he turned once more to face the chamber.

"Hear me..." His voice was no louder or more insistent than it would've been had he commented on the weather or asked for more wine. Still, the room fell deathly quiet within a very short time. "I would not have us risk our futures in order to secure our present. Those of you who have your firstborn stood as your squire... let those fine young fighting men remain behind to ensure the future of your lines should the unthinkable come to pass in the north."

There were murmurs of both approval and relief, as well as frustration and disappointment.

"There are, perhaps, those among your households who may be ready to be called to the line. *I* know of such a one, myself, but perhaps you know of others. In the days and weeks to come, I hope you will bring them to my attention so they too may stand and guard the tower."

This elicited murmurs of consideration and more than a touch of newfound excitement in the crowd. Being "called to the line" meant being called to take the knee and rise a knight. Guarding the Tower was the common term for being knighted within the county itself. All knights of Czarny Wodospad were sworn to defend and guard the count's own house, Czarnowieża—the house of the Black Tower.

"My voice." Hengrek spoke in a grave, full timbre. "It echoes from mountain to sea, from cavern to sky."

By this last pairing, fully a dozen other voices—all men—stepped into the area between Hengrek and the room's entrance, each speaking the words along with him.

"Steel must be tempered. A sword must be sharp. No steed sprints forever. All candles grow dark. As brief summer storms, ever-fleeting is time..."

Here all fell silent, save Hengrek. He paused only for a moment, sweeping the chamber with his eyes before finishing.

"Come, *Bartek*. For now, you are called to the line."

The chamber erupted with shouts and applause.

The young man who had been called looked as if he'd been thrust, unaware, into cold water. His mother moved to guide him around the thrones, handing him to the countess's waiting hands.

He was brought before Hengrek, guided to one knee—the eternal position of fealty—and bowed his head in shock and gratitude.

Azhferd noted that Bartek was weeping silent tears, though showed no signs of sobbing. He understood, or at least thought he did. He expected he would likely feel the same when *his* call to serve came at last.

Hengrek drew his sword and held it pointed down and to the side for a moment.

"Will you stand?"

"I... I will stand." Bartek's voice was a study in humility and gratitude.

Hengrek laid his sword against first Bartek's right, then left shoulders, murmuring to him each time it touched.

"What... What is he saying?" Kozioł's voice was a frustrated whisper of joy and excitement.

"Words for him alone. Only those called to the line know that secret, and to my knowledge, none have ever broken their silence on that score," said Azhferd. He was careful to keep his voice low so as to neither disrespect the ceremony nor his cousin during this, his moment of recognition.

As Bartek stood, he embraced the count firmly, then found himself turned bodily and shoved toward the waiting knights who had joined in the call.

"Soon, Azhferd," his sister said. "Soon enough. Perhaps even at Zlaté Pole... if you still mean to go."

"When I'm ready—when I'm worthy." He thought she sounded sad for him, as if she'd expected his name to be called, but that was nonsense. Bartek was far more worthy than he—far more deserving. As for the tournament, "I do. This makes the matter simpler, actually. If we truly have money to hire more armsmen to patrol the roads, then I mean to go to Zlaté Pole now, more than ever."

He waited for court to close and moved to congratulate his cousin—Syr Bartek—before, at last, speaking to his father.

SHADOW SONG

-I-

Venzene Duchy of Kamieńalun
County Czarny Wodospad
Wieża Szymona
30 Gerstesykli: 2 Days after the Red Storm at Westsong

The last of the courtiers left the throne room. Azhferd saw Hengrek stand for a moment, eyes in a half-lidded state. That meant his father was weighing some decision out within his mind's council chamber.

It'd been one of the first lessons he'd imparted to a twelve-year-old Azhferd ... and in this very chamber. It had also been one of the most useful.

Azhferd had just returned home from his failed attempt to sneak off to Zlaté Pole. Oh, he'd made it *there* without being caught. His attempted entry into the child's lyst under an assumed name—and an apparently ill-fated decision to make his hair appear pale by use of the yellowing potion his mother brewed each month, however... that'd resulted in disaster. The moment Azhferd had stepped forward to register for the child's lyst, Uncle Borys had marked him and pulled him out of the queue. He'd been made to sit alone in his father's room at the Róża i Wrona for the three remaining days of their trip. Then he'd ridden home in a state of fearful, sullen silence. His father's wordless disappointment had been worse than any punishment. The morning after their return to Wieża Szymona, when Skar—his newly assigned armsmen—had told him his lord-father wished to see him in the throne room; it'd come as a genuine relief.

"You must find or construct a quiet place inside your own mind," Hengrek had said. *"It must be furnished and comfortable for those who join you there, but never comfortable … for you."* His voice had been mild and difficult to read. Still, there'd been a sense of real import to his words—as if Hengrek *needed* Azhferd to hear and truly grasp his meaning.

"Who could join me in my own mind?" Azhferd had asked this in cold frustration.

"Anyone and everyone you ever meet, read about, or hear about."

Azhferd had merely stared at him, trying to determine whether he was being serious.

"The place of council is where you can hear what others think... gauge how they will react to a certain course of action you're considering."

"But they won't really be there. I'd just be talking to myself." He recalled sounding sulky, even to his own ears.

Conversely, there hadn't been so much as a hint of frustration in Hengrek's voice or upon his face.

"That's right, but it's also wrong. Azhferd—listen now. You've been out and about with your mother and I often enough. You've stood beside me on occasion when I've held court."

He'd waited for Azhferd to give a nod of agreement before continuing.

"Outside of the occasions where I greet someone first—someone I see in the inner or outer market before they see me, for example—who does most of the talking?"

Azhferd considered, but only for a moment.

"They do."

"They do. Just so. What is it you believe I'm doing while they speak?"

Again, Azhferd had considered this, though it took him longer to come up with an answer this time.

"Thinking?"

Hengrek had smiled, then.

"Always. But is that all I'm doing?"

"Listening. You're listening."

Hengrek had nodded.

"I am always—always listening. I try to be the last to speak and the first to listen."

"And... and when you speak because you speak last, everyone's had their say..."

It had been a revelation.

"Just so. But what do I gain from listening?"

"A better... A better understanding of what the person is saying? An idea of what they want from you?"

"Not just from me ... but from fate itself."

Azhferd's sulky tone had fallen away, utterly forgotten.

"...And then you can decide if you intend to be an agent of that fate."

"So, would you say that I gain an idea of who these people are by doing this?"

Azhferd had thought about that for a long time in silence. He recalled feeling as if reality's veil had been peeled back in a palpable, nearly physical way. It had all made such sense to him in that moment. *"You learn who they are and how they think! You can then bring them into your mind for council and see how they'd react!"*

Hengrek had been clearly delighted with that answer. He'd done something he hadn't done since Azhferd had first been allowed to wander the castle without an escort—a guard or tutor. He'd leaned over, kissed the boy on his forehead, ruffled his hair, then smoothed it back along his brow.

"It will never be perfect," he'd said. *"And you'll never stop discovering things about people you think you know. Why should you stop? They're people, after all, not statues. But,"* he'd held up a finger, *"if you keep the council chamber tidy, you can see a good many problems before they ever arise. If you can step back from yourself, you'll find you can almost see the future."*

Even now, more than a dozen years later, Azhferd considered the lesson to be foundational. He practiced its chief tenet and taught it to his squire and sergeants.

As he awaited his father's signal—the one which would indicate Hengrek was entirely ready to hear him, to focus on whatever matter his son brought before him—Azhferd took a moment to transition to his own mind's council chamber.

He saw it as he always did, as the less-than-great hall at Auburg. He stood at the foot of the table there as if he'd just entered. His Uncle Borys sat beside the fire on the right. His father stood behind the other fireside chair, his left forearm resting along its high back, looking at Azhferd, and...

Hengrek grunted a "Hmmm." The deliberate sound shook Azhferd free from the lingering memory of that lesson. It also forced him to abandon his attempt at one final foray into his own ephemeral council chamber before the start of this conversation.

He refocused his gaze, seeing his father running the fingers of his left hand over the arm of Calpernia's throne.

"You wanted to speak with me," Hengrek said.

"I did."

"But ... you needed to take council before you felt ready."

Azhferd blinked, then smiled.

"No, I didn't." As Hengrek lifted his black brows in response, Azhferd went on. "I didn't *need* to take council. I wanted to. It was a final chance to see whether I had missed a thing before we spoke."

Hengrek nodded, brows returning to their accustomed positions.

"Well," he moved to sit upon his throne, ushering Azhferd toward him, "now you've had your last council. Are you ready to ask me your questions?"

Azhferd made the short walk to stand before the throne. A coldness settled over him, warring with a sudden flood of warmth and affection for his father. It added a strange feeling to this moment, though he couldn't quite give that feeling a name.

He met Hengrek's even gaze and drew in a shallow breath through his nose, then spoke.

"I will ride to Zlaté Pole in twelve days' time."

Hengrek allowed his eyelids to once more adopt that thoughtful, considering position—half-lidded—both in the moment and in his council chamber.

"I've made it clear that I won't be in attendance this year," said the count.

Azhferd made no unnecessary movement as he spoke.

"You have. I've made no such statement, however."

Hengrek nodded slowly, head cocked to one side as if listening, although he'd only adopted this state once Azhferd had finished speaking. After a long silence, he spoke again in a calm, reasonable tone—a *just-let-me-clarify* tone.

"You intend to ride there with Dargory and your sergeants?"

Azhferd nodded.

"I do, and those who will stand and fight beside me."

Hengrek waited for a few seconds before responding.

"I've called the muster," said he. "Baron, banner, and bondsman alike will either ride in my train or remain behind to defend our homes. We mustn't *appear*, let alone prove ourselves weak and defenseless while we secure the north."

Azhferd gave a brief nod, but his face remained unchanged and expressionless.

"The sons of your banners—some of them, anyway—will ride with me. They will not leave their homes defenseless, of course, but many of them will continue as they'd initially committed and ride forth with me from Auburg in twelve days' time."

Hengrek leaned back in his throne, craning his neck to look down upon his son. The appraisal didn't last long.

"You have already gathered commitments from these young men." This was a statement rather than a question.

Azhferd nodded.

"I have. If their fathers grow wrathful, you will have no part in it. I made the decision and gained their commitments."

"You ... *commanded* them?" Hengrek's voice was its usual velvet fog. It utterly avoided accusation or ire.

"No, Father. I asked them and was clear by word and deed that they were free to reject the idea ... no favor, oath, bond, or due. I wished to go and wanted those who would train with me, to ride with me, to *fight* with me—for their own glory and that of the county. I'd pay for their expenses personally if they elected to fight beside me."

Hengrek nodded at this, head moving slowly to elongate the motion.

"It's done, then." He drew his right elbow up onto the arm of the throne, bringing his loose fingers up toward his face. After a moment, he rested his index finger along the right side of his nose, thumb beneath his chin. The rest of his fingers curled to partially cover his mouth. His eyes remained in that same half-lidded state. "Is there more?"

"No, Father. I wanted to inform you of my decision and to give you the opportunity to command me otherwise." This was a matter of respect from son to father. Azhferd had not—would not—ask leave or permission. He also would not hide his actions until it was too late for his father to gainsay him.

Both would have proven his weakness. Asking would signify that he hadn't felt confident in his right to act and decide. That would have been bad enough. Hiding until it was too late for Hengrek to deny him without incurring cost or damage to his reputation might've been the worse evil. It would signify that he feared his father's wrath and was thus willing to deceive in order to get his way. Either action would have been childish, petulant, and unworthy.

Hengrek took his time before giving his final word on the matter.

"You must send word to those who have committed to your cause," said he. "You must remind them you will bear them no ill nor account them lesser should they need to stay to defend their homes. They must know that you recognize that the state of things ... has changed."

Azhferd nodded in slow mimicry of his father, though without mimicry's rude cousin, mockery.

"I understand and agree completely," said he.

Hengrek made a "so be it" gesture with his left hand, lifting his brows for emphasis.

"You'll want to consider your route to Zlaté Pole very carefully. I doubt, as I'm sure you do, that these raiders would attack a place with so many knights and fighting men, but the road to Zlaté Pole is another matter entirely." He lowered his right arm and made to stand. "I think the town itself will be safe enough, but..." He trailed off as he stood fully.

"Zawsze bezpieczny, nigdy smutny," said Azhferd.

Hengrek nodded, smiling.

"Always safe, never sad. Just so."

The Count stood and put an arm around his son's shoulders, turning him so they could walk from the chamber together.

"I look forward to hearing of your victory. You've been training in accordance with your wine seller's words?"

Azhferd grinned. This proved beyond *any* doubt that his father had known of his plans all along. The entire affair had been allowed to play out so that Hengrek could test his son's ability ... and his resolve. It'd been an opportunity to see if he could inspire others to join his cause and to negotiate the dangers and consequences of that inspiration.

"Ohhhhh, yes."

Hengrek nodded, smiling.

"Good." He squeezed Azhferd's far shoulder and repeated, "...Good," as they exited the throne room.

-II-

Yellow robes preceded the hem of a dim red cloak gliding across the stone. The figure wearing, or perhaps being worn by these garments, walked with purpose as the floor sloped downward. The carefully laid stone gave way to an open cavern and native, unaltered rock.

No feet were visible, nor was any sound made until the basalt floor fell beneath a small subterranean pond, blocking the way.

The figure neither halted its progress nor slowed its steps. While its strides were never broken, its *silence* was. In a low, alto tone, the figure issued something between a song and a chant in slow, rolling tones, beginning just before stepping out, not into but *onto* the water.

"Szłam niepewnie w ciemności. Mówiłam nieświadomie przeciwko światłu. Moja piosenka, jak kwas, parzy pod niebem. Budzę się by przeżyć rozdartą godzinę."

(I walked, uncertain in the dark. I spoke, unknown, against the light. My song, like acid under the sky. I wake to weather the Torn Hour.)

As the woman—for such a voice surely had to belong to a woman—chanted, she strode on toward the dim shimmer of a slow waterfall on the pond's far side. The moonlight seeped through cracks and fissures high up on the cavern's walls, making moonbows in the fall's mist. Yet, for all the scene's beauty, the sound of the waterfall striking the pool beneath was muted and distorted, more a purr or the rolling velvet whicker of a horse than a traditional roar.

She reached her destination and uttered the final line of her incantation as she passed through the waterfall. No water made contact with her. Upon the far side, the dazzle of starlight and the pale glow of a full moon bathed her in its pall. It made her hooded cloak seem like the furled wings of an animal, its plumage matching its darksome crown. The yellow of her robe was turned a frosted gold.

Grasses surrounded her beneath a perfect summer night's sky. She wasted no time bathing in the beauty, however, moving off almost at once. As she did so, something slithered in the grasses—a hint of undulating, questing red amidst the soft greens. She paid it little mind as she strode on.

Some yards beyond stood a low-slung hilltop and a telltale glimmer that suggested a modest campfire.

She moved toward this with even steps, her garments and feet rustling against the grasses.

As she reached the hill's base, she lifted her hooded head upward, shaping the music of her voice toward its apex.

"Witaj, czarodziejko z wieży."

"Yes, yes. I know. *Hail, Tower Sorceress*, to you as well." This was a woman's voice and one she'd expected to hear. "Come now. Time may be our ally, but she is as fickle a bedfellow as you could ask for."

The new arrival—made dramatic by virtue of her raiment—now slumped and bowed her hooded head in comical exasperation. She strode up the hill with more haste, as instructed, and crested its top in short order.

There she saw two other figures dressed just as she was, seated before the fire she'd glimpsed earlier. The second fire-gazer struck an unmistakably masculine figure. A naked, broad-bladed sword lay beside him in easy reach of his right hand.

"Sit, girl. Sit," the older woman said. "Tell us your drift that we may begin."

She did so, crossing her legs beneath her.

"The bond persists. He has had no episodes and suspects nothing."

"How can you be so certain? He stayed behind to hold a private conversation after the throne room had been emptied." The older woman paused. "How can you know that he will not seek to ask his beloved father about such matters?"

"Because—unlike either of you, I actually know his mind."

The man snorted, though it was the woman who made a reply.

"Mind your self-import, my dear. You may believe you know his mind. You may even be correct, but you cannot be certain." She chuckled. "Hells be hid. *He* may not even know his mind."

The newcomer's response to this derision was full of a fire that burned far brighter than the one they sat around. "*Despite* the many obstacles you've put between us, I've unearthed more about him than the pair of you combined."

The elders turned their hoods toward one another, then back to hers. Again, it was the woman who spoke in a crisp, ringing voice.

"What, *precisely*, are you speaking of?"

"You've always conspired to make my work more difficult—to sepa—"

"That *isn't* what I'm asking about, girl." The whip-crack of her voice was shocking, not in its volume, which was quite low, but in its dismissive ferocity. One wouldn't normally dismiss ferociously, yet there was no more apt description. It had been sure, precise, swift, and aggressive.

"He means to ask—no, to state his intent to ride to Zlaté Pole."

The older woman huffed, then chuckled her indignance.

"The Count has already made his will known on that score. There will be no travel to Zlaté Pole this year."

"For he and his knights."

"Yes. Exactly."

"Azhferd hasn't been *called* to the line yet. Has he?" Her anger at this was evident, though she channeled it into an obvious mockery of the older woman's tone rather than abject outrage.

"Peace," the man said. "Let us move forward."

Both women bowed their heads, not in deference, but in acquiescence.

"He meant to speak with Father—"

"The count! Not *Father*, nor his full right name—nor yours nor ours, as you know full well. Have you taken leave of your senses, girl?"

"Surely, we're safe here, of all places, Mother."

"Really..." Her uncle spoke with disgust. "You'd sit here, in *this* place, and flout every rule we've given you—every rule *we* were given—and have been kept safe by for generations uncounted? Are you so arrogant that you would risk yourself, she, me, *all* those you've known and nurtured, loved and lost because you, oh maiden-fair, know best?"

Yeidil glared—an act made somewhat less effective by the all-consuming shadow of her hood.

Her uncle merely stared at her, though his face, too, was shrouded.

"I thank you for the instruction, elder. May I learn this lesson well, and may it save me from the Torn Hour when all else has failed, and fear is given form before me." She spoke the old catechism in a sigh of mingled frustration and acceptance.

"May it serve to quiet your heart when Havoc's Horn is winded once more," said he. "If you've no more to say on the matter, we shall leave the subject of your brother for now. If you have him well in hand and he suspects nothing as you surmise, then we will account ourselves fortunate."

Yeidil bowed her head in acceptance.

"Good," said he. "I'm as certain as may be that while *he* may be unsuspecting, the count is slipping away despite my best efforts." He turned to regard Calpernia. In spite of his hood, the mixture of withering contempt and abiding loyalty warred in his posture and fought to gain ground within his voice. "You must find a better solution. I am not trained as you two, not mighty enough in lore or binding magics to do more than slow the process. If your son is well and truly in hand, perhaps—"

"No!" Calpernia's voice was acid. "I will not suffer that to be entertained, let alone put into practice. We need both of them to remain ignorant for as long as possible—indefinitely, if it can be done. We will not risk one to save the other."

"Be reasonable," said Borys.

"*No.* I will *not* risk losing my son because we left the cell door unguarded. I will not race to catch one escaping soul only to wind up releasing the one we've held fast." She sighed. "I need more time."

After a protracted silence wherein the suffering, sighing wind, and the crackling fire were the only sound, Yeidil spoke. She made her voice gentle, for the words she intended to speak were harsh in their truth and bladed in their symmetry.

"Time may be our ally, but she is as fickle a bedfellow as you could ask for."

Both Borys and Calpernia laughed, first softly, then with abandon.

"You're right, of course," Calpernia said. "I am old and fear the time it takes to recover my strength between rites, but you are quite correct."

Yeidil bowed her head, offering nothing.

"I will ready the rite and marshal my strength come morning. You will need to hold for as long as you can, mind you." She looked at Borys and waggled a finger at him.

He nodded.

"I will do all that I'm able." He looked up, then around. "Is there more we need to discuss tonight?"

Calpernia shook her head.

"I think not," said she. "Help me up."

Yeidil stood, as did Borys, this latter reaching a hand down to do as Calpernia had asked.

"Keep as close a watch on my boy as you can—both of you. We cannot lose him—not least to our own incompetence."

Yeidil nodded. "No, indeed."

The trio turned, faced the fire, bowed their heads to it, and left the hilltop. They headed toward a tall tumble of stones gleaming white in the moonlight. As they approached, they repeated the rite Yeidil had used earlier, ignoring the slithering sounds amidst the grasses.

"Szłam niepewnie w ciemności. Mówiłam nieświadomie przeciwko światłu. Moja piosenka, jak kwas, parzy pod niebem. Budzę się by przeżyć rozdartą godzinę."

(I walked, uncertain in the dark. I spoke, unknown, against the light. My song, like acid under the sky. I wake to weather the Torn Hour.)

As she passed through the blank wall of stone, she awoke in her bed, eyes snapping open to cast about her darkened surroundings.

Yeidil sat up fully, allowing the bedcovers to fall from her. Almost at once, she regretted the act as the cool air struck her breasts. She instantly curled back up under her fur blanket.

All at once, she hated all of it. She hated her mother for dragging her into it, hated her uncle for accepting her mother's will on the matter, hated her father for slipping free of his bindings, hated innocent, pitiable Aunt Hywyn for being untrustworthy. Hywyn had been unable to see the larger matters at play—so much so that either her mother or Uncle Borys had put a Sagacite's rite upon her. They'd made her forget her own power...

She laughed bitterly.

"I hate my *own* role even more." Why couldn't Azhferd be a charmless, inconsiderate oaf of a man? Why was it *she* should be forced to guard and deceive someone for whom she held such love?

Almost she wished he would break loose of the binding rite. *Almost* she wished he would come to her, asking her what she thought—what she knew of these things. At least at that point, she could stop playing this dual role. He may hate her for it, but at least she wouldn't be hiding things from him any longer.

She punched the bed with her right fist, then sat up. Dressing quickly, she walked down the hall to her brother's wing. She stopped, listened ... heard soft breathing echo off of the stone and wood of the passage—a guard—good.

Turning, she walked back to her own chambers. Mother's prudent insistence had paid off. The rule of separation had seemed overprotective at the time. There were always rumors and concerns that children left alone would eventually risk discovery of more adult themes. Noble children, especially, had precious few others their own age to spend time with. Boys were common enough, but daughters were ever more limited in terms of those with whom they could spend time.

When Mother had introduced her to the truth that very week's end, Yeidil had understood. There was a duty to carry out. She needed to perform that duty and maintain its secrecy at all costs ... to value it more highly than her station, her title, worldly wealth, and personal ties. More, she needed to value it above honesty.

It had been the first secret she'd ever kept from her brother, and she strove to ensure it would be the last.

"The last..." That thought carried her down into sleep. She dreamed of castles and corpses, tears, and trampling hooves, just as she had done each night for the past sixteen years.

-III-

Venzene Duchy of Kovalun
County Jižní Pochod
Barony of Hartscross - Jižní Lov
32 Gerstesykli: 4 Days after the Red Storm at Westsong

Eobum sat in the tent with its canvas drawn and tied against prying eyes. He was mostly dressed now. Still, he was rather enjoying the momentary feel of walls—even canvas ones—between him and the rest of the world. They may well know what he was doing. Hells, he'd told Alusc about his forthcoming meeting with Edmund before he headed in to clean himself up a bit. Still, the sense that he was truly alone for just a few moments made him ... well, not smile exactly. He seemed to undergo something of a decompression, mentally speaking.

Alusc had managed some fresh fish gathered or traded from somewhere. The smell as they sizzled out beyond his canvas cloister was a thing of beauty. Mouthwatering wasn't even in it.

He hoped he'd have time to eat before the call came. The nobility ate finer food after a fashion. But he never felt quite like himself after eating it. It was somehow far less satisfying, yet it made him feel full to the point of sluggishness.

"Soporific," said he and smiled. It was a word he'd heard an alchemist use once when describing sleeping draughts. He liked the word. But how any man could use it in plain conversation was beyond him. He *was* glad he'd learned it if only to help some well-meaning fool trying to name their child after it because he or she liked the way the word fit in their mouths. Such had happened before, and since time was first tallied, he reckoned.

He'd once met an Eodenth boy named Gi, a Gnoerkish word. The lad's father had been one of those men who appeared to be in love with what he *imagined* other peoples to be rather than what they actually were. The naming of his son seemed to bear that impression out. Gi, after all, meant blood.

"Eobum, meet my boy, *Blood*." He kept his voice low, shaking his head. He could feel a species of sardonic glee beginning to bloom upon his face.

Reaching for his right boot, he dropped his hand into its opening. He drew his face into a distant, transported thing as his fingers rooted around.

"*There* you are." He smiled, pulling his hand back. Between his thumb and forefinger, he held a jagged pebble. After inspecting it briefly, he laid the troublesome thing beside him on his footlocker and pulled the boot into place.

Voices approached, and his grin turned warm. Eranoric speaking to someone. Unless he missed his guess, that someone was...

"So, what comes after the midday meal?" Sulok sounded not merely interested but positively eager.

Eranoric laughed—a soft chuffing noise that was the auditory equivalent of a cat's tongue.

"What?" Sulok sounded defensive now.

"I suspect your mother will want to at least *see* you before the day gets too much older, my lord."

"She will," Lashjuk said from somewhere off to Eobum's right.

"Og..." The boy dragged that whining, frustrated tone out just short of where it would snap the nerves of those forced to endure it. "I'm *fine*—been with Eranoric all morning, working."

"Working, is it? Is that what we're calling it?"

"Og! I work!" He sounded indignant and embarrassed.

Eranoric was wisely staying out of the exchange, Eobum noted with some small satisfaction.

"Mmmhmm."

"Eranoric, tell her!"

"Must admit he speaks truth, Lady. I had to check each and every spearhead now that we're back at camp. He was an honest help to me and to the unit."

"I'm sorry I doubted you, Sulok. I just wish you were so enthusiastic with your f-" She cut herself off, her words frozen on her tongue. She'd almost certainly been about to say the word *father*. After a moment, she spoke again, trying to finish in a more positive light. "Chores," said she, "... so enthusiastic about your chores."

Silence met this. The only sound was that of sizzling fish.

As Eobum had made his mind up to stand and head out in an effort to turn their minds away from the misery of the moment, he heard Hrothgian's tentative voice from somewhere farther back in the camp, beyond where Lashjuk's had emanated.

"Put a new head on your bledu drum for you..." He sounded uncertain, pleased with himself, and afraid all at a go.

Eobum fancied Hrothgian wasn't certain who to fear more at the moment. Eranoric was his captain, but nobody—not even Eobum— touched the man's drum without the man's word. Then there was the relative stranger in their midst, Lashjuk. Lashjuk, who was fierce, grieving, away from everything she'd known, and understandably mistrustful. Lashjuk, who was almost too beautiful to look at, when the sun, moon, or firelight hit her right.

He winced. What was he doing, thinking like that?

I'm not blind, am I? Still, I'm also not...

Not what? Not attracted to her? That was a lie. *Not interested in her?* That may be nearer the mark. He knew she'd had a rough go of it. He wanted to do right by her and her children. That wasn't the same as wanting to step into the role of gnash or Ng. Even if that were the way things wound up, thinking of such only a scant few days after she'd lost the boys' father was...

She isn't Suruk. Best I not forget that.

"Bring it to me, and take my thanks, Hroth."

"You play the drum?" Sulok sounded both interested and pleased to have a subject change.

"Aye, do and have since I was about your age." Eranoric paused. "Maybe a bit older? Can't recall which, and Gnoerkish children age differently than human ones."

This was so. Gnoerks aged quickly and, as far as Eobum had been told and shown, matured as if they were roughly three years older than their actual age compared to human children. Half-Gnoerks could age anywhere in between, it seemed, but the average for a full-blooded Gnoerk seemed to be about three years faster once they'd grown enough that they could hold their waste.

"How old are you, my lord?"

"Ten," said he. "Eleven next Lessykli."

Eranoric made a grunt of acceptance. His buckles made subtle scratching against the ceramic side of his bledu drum as he settled it onto his thigh.

"Show me—play something." Sulok sounded more engaged than demanding, although, with children, the two went hand in hand more often than not.

Eobum heard Eranoric slide his palm across the stretched hide drum head. It was a sound unique to that instrument, and one Eobum knew well.

Doom Tak doom doom-Tak doom-doom Tak doom doom-Tak.

Eobum heard him picking up speed, adding triplets with his fingers between the dooms.

He found himself bobbing his head to the rhythm, even weaving it back and forth as if he were a bird caught in a serpent's eye.

Faster and faster, Eranoric played until the rhythm was too hectic to follow, and Eobum found himself dizzy from keeping up with it through his head movements. He grinned to himself, letting his chin fall onto his chest and closing his eyes to maximize and extend the sensation.

Finally, Eranoric ceased, flourishing his end with a triplet and a final Tak.

"How!?" Sulok was astonished. "How did you move your hands so fast?"

"Just practice, my lord. You get better th' more time you put into a thing." He paused, perhaps shrugging. Certainly it was a long enough pause for such. "Same as most other things, I expect."

"Can... Can you teach me?"

Eobum smiled. He knew the answer, of course. Eranoric would like nothing *more* than to teach him.

"If you like."

The drum made little ringing sounds as it was transferred from man's thigh to boy's.

"Like this?"

"Aye."

A half-slammed, half-tentative thud sounded from the drum, followed by another and another in rapid succession. The sounds were uneven and off from one another in tone.

"Stop sto-sto-stopp, Sulok!" Eranoric sounded insistent but amused.

The boy did as told.

"You called me Sulok."

"S'yer name, ain't it?" Eranoric chuckled. "I do beg pardon, my lord."

"No. It's fine." Sulok sounded as if he were smiling.

"Right. Cup your palm like this—tighten your fingers. Right, now loosen them up a bit. No need to prove which finger's stronger 'n his fellows."

Sulok chuckled.

"Now—hit here."

"Not the center?"

"Not the dead center, no. Try it. You'll see, or rather hear, what I mean."

First came the sound of a hand striking the drum in its center, followed by a proper strike a touch closer to its edge. The first produced an uneven, thin sound. It was sharp but lacked the ringing resonance of the proper strike.

As he hit the correct mark, the sound was noticeably fuller—deeper and more resonant.

Doom ... doom ... doom.

"Huh..." Sulok sounded surprised but pleased.

"Good. Now, slide your hand out to the edge. Raise your arm and snap the wrist ... so your finger hits just inside the rim."

Tak.

"Perfect!"

"Can you teach me a song?" Sulok followed this almost instantly with a clarification. "A simple one?"

Eranoric didn't answer for a moment, then offered a neutral one.

"Let's see." He paused, then asked, "Do you think you can lift your other hand and do the same sort of thing on the rim?"

A half-hearted, uncertain sound came from the drum.

"You'll need to take your arm off the drum. Balance it on your leg." He paused, presumably for the boy to make the necessary adjustments. "Like that, just so. Now, as you bring the hand down?"

"Aye?"

Eobum smirked to hear the boy start using "Aye" instead of "Yes," but stifled his snort.

"Turn your wrist as you bring it down, then snap it with the tip of your finger."

Ka ... ka ... ka.

"Perfect, my lord. Just so."

Eranoric gave him a few more tries before bringing him back to the matter at hand.

"Right—y'have what you need, now. Listen to me and repeat it on the drum, yeah?" He paused for a long enough moment to draw breath, then began in earnest. "Tak ka doom Tak-Tak doom—tak ka doom Tak-Tak doom—just so."

It took a moment, but the boy began to put the words into the language of the drum.

Tak ka doom Tak-Tak doom, tak ka doom Tak-Tak doom.

All at once, the boy stopped.

"I... Why is that familiar?"

Eranoric was smiling. It was in his voice as he spoke.

"Play it again, my lord."

The drum began again, and after a single admonishment to slow the rhythm down a bit, Eranoric began to sing.

Aehe dash? Mak el fel! Aehe dash? Mak el fel!
Aehe dash? Mak el fel! Aehe dash? Mak el fel!
Awka dish ga mi drak, Awka dish ga mi drak,
Awka dish ga mi drak, Ng Og.
Aehe dash? Ed kar lash,
Aehe dash? Ed kar lash ed gar.

By the time he'd finished the second line, Alusc, Hrothgian, and Aderano had joined in. Eobum stood to exit his tent, but before he'd done so, he heard others singing as they neared their little patch. By the time he'd exited, nearly all of his men were there. Though none seemed to notice him at the edge of their encampment, the mountain known as Count Edmund smiled at the scene behind them.

As the song ended, nearly everyone was smiling. Only Lashjuk looked otherwise, and her face was full of shock, and the sort of pain that can only come with memory rising from the dead.

The men applauded.

"No one told us he was a drummer," said Eobald. "Better'n you, Eranoric!"

This was met with general good-natured laughter.

Sulok blushed, bowing his head, smiling broadly, and saying nothing for a time. After a moment, he found his voice, looking first at the men around him, then at Eranoric.

"I didn't know you spoke Grimdash Zaksh!" Sulok sounded impressed.

"We don't—not all of us, anyroad. I know I don't, other than a few words here and there." Eranoric shrugged, then laughed at the boy's expression. "Eobum used to sing it to Lakkrid at night when he was wee until the boy'd learned it. Then he made *him* sing it before bed each night. By the time he'd gotten it to stick in his head, most of us had learned it, too."

"Oh... my father and mother used to sing it to us when I was little, too." Sulok paused, considering. "I guess it's a lullaby."

"It is now, I think," Alusc said from the fireside. "Dun think it always was, though."

"You're right," said Fenglem. "It was a hunter's song that later became a slave's song."

"Slave's song?" Eranoric looked outraged, not at Feng, but at the concept itself.

Fenglem nodded, then recited it as a chant in the Trade Tongue.

Why stop? Moon is far. Why stop? Moon is far.
Why stop? Moon is far, Why stop? Moon is far.
And the sun's in the sky, And the sun's in the sky,
And the sun's in the sky,
Father, Mother.
Why stop? I want the gift.
Why stop? I want the gift of my home.

Eobum felt the silence descend more keenly than he heard it. Only Lashjuk looked pleased as she regarded the scene. The rest were lost in thought at this revelation.

"Excellency? What do you think?" Eobum spoke calmly enough, but everyone snapped their heads up in utter shock at the sudden realization that they were not strictly alone in camp.

"Eobum, my friend, I don't think I've heard that song since your son was..." He paused, considering. He ran a hand through his short blond hair, crouched down as if gauging height with the palm of one massive hand, then stood again to his towering six and a half feet in height. "Knee-high on most men, so that would be ... what, ankle-high on me?"

The men—those who knew him, at least—laughed. Those who had come more recently to their number managed uncertain smiles. Lashjuk stared with frank fascination and even more frank mistrust.

It was the voice from behind the mountain that was Edmund—high and unbroken—that had the final word on the matter of Edmund's gauge.

"You're taaaaallll!" Maksu said. He was in obvious awe—so much so that he hadn't realized he'd spoken aloud.

"Excellency?" Lakkrid dragged Maksu around to face the man. "This is my friend Maksu."

Edmund again crouched down, putting his right hand on the ground between his feet, fingers splayed for balance.

"A pleasure, Maksu. Any friend of Lakkrid is a man I'm pleased to know."

"He's not a man. He's a boy." Lashjuk's voice was cold and thin, though her tone stopped short of dangerous. "He's *my* boy... Excellency."

Edmund looked past the boys and nodded slowly.

"So I'm told, Lady." He stood after taking a long look at all three children. "You've my sympathies, and whatever succor I can render. Eobum's told me your tale in brief yesternight. You're welcome here until you choose otherwise." His voice was warm and earnest, stopping well short of placatory.

She bowed her head, her eyes never leaving his.

"Thank you, Excellency. We'll be fine, I've no doubt, and on our way before too long. We won't beg your hospitality any longer than necessary."

"No begging required, Lady. Count it freely given, if not gladly. I cannot see my way clear to be glad on any account, given your recent past."

He paused, then seemed to shake his head in frustration. When he spoke anew, it was clear that frustration was at his own impotence.

"A trek to Zlaté Pole is slated to begin not long from now. If you wish, you'd be welcome to ride or walk as you like along with the column. That, of course, is your business and choice." He turned back to Lakkrid, placing a hand on his head. The hand was nearly big enough to be a hat for the boy.

For his part, Lakkrid's face crumpled as he playacted being crushed by the enormous hand. The act elicited giggling from Maksu and a snort from Sulok.

Edmund beamed, his expression fond but far away. His affection was clear and genuine, but the distance in his eyes showed the weight of some great matter pressing down upon him. As he stood, he spoke to Eobum, though he kept his eyes on Lakkrid, trying in vain not to look troubled.

"If you're ready?"

Eobum nodded, then fell into step beside the man.

-IV-

The pair walked toward the command tent, Eobum keeping pace with the count's longer legs.

"I think he's grown in the month or so since I last saw him, Eobum."

Eobum grunted, and though he grinned, his position behind Edmund and to his right kept that fact hidden from him.

"Boys do that. Girls, too, I expect."

"Any mother can tell you. If you keep feeding them, they not only keep coming home, but they keep growing."

Eobum nodded—a thing his shadow obediently mirrored on the ground before him, allowing Edmund to see it.

"Have you begun teaching him trail craft yet?" He paused, shaking his head. "Of course you have. What am I saying?"

Eobum made no response. None seemed necessary.

Two guards stood up ahead, one to either side of the marquee tent to which they were headed. It was too warm this early in the day, so neither man wore a kontusz, though they were easily identified as the count's personal guard by the green and gold diamonds embroidered on the wrists of their bolero jackets. Each man had a short-bladed spear and a blunted flail tucked into his broad belt.

As the count drew to within the ten-foot mark, the guard on their right moved his spear to his left hand, reached with his right, and opened the tent in one smooth motion. His counterpart doffed his fur hat to his master and bowed his head.

Edmund gave them a very shallow nod as he entered.

Eobum followed him in after making brief eye contact with each guard in turn.

The count cast about himself for a moment, then moved to stand beside the room's only chair. He looked at the map laid out upon it and proceeded to roll it up with some haste.

Eobum waited until the man had picked up the rolled leather and moved to replace it in a long tube of wood that served as a scroll case.

"My next assignment?"

Edmund made no reply for a moment, busying himself with the tube's cork stopper.

Eobum shrugged inwardly. If the man wished to affect deafness, he would play along. Eight years in his service bought the count something, surely.

Finally popping the cork into place, Edmund spoke, affecting a hurried, distant tone not much like him.

"Jastrab will be arriving shortly. You and I will speak in earnest and more plainly once we've concluded our conversation."

Eobum took a moment to wonder why Edmund had insisted on his presence for a conversation if he'd only meant to put off having it until later, but kept silent. Instead, he nodded once Edmund had turned to look at him. He didn't care for this—didn't care for Jastrab much, truth to tell, but that was neither here nor there. He suspected he'd have liked the man a good deal were it not for their history.

"Excellency?" Jastrab's voice came from outside the tent.

Edmund spared a moment to send a confirmatory look at Eobum, then turned back toward the tent's closed door flaps.

"Come, Captain."

Eobum saw Edmund force a warm smile into being upon his face and had a moment to be jealous of his ability to do so. He couldn't have mustered so convincing a grin were his neck in the noose, and that act his only hope of reprieve.

The flap opened, and in came several black-clad men with Jastrab in the lead.

To his credit, the captain didn't stop or slow his step when his eyes fell upon Eobum. His smile never faltered.

He bowed to the count, then gave a friendly enough nod to Eobum as he spoke.

"Excellency, may I present Sergeants Daian and Geroslaw? They had the pleasure of meeting Lord Alojz the night before last." Looking back at the two men, he spoke anew. "Daian, Geroslaw, may I present His Excellency Count Edmund of Jižní Pochod, Baron of Hartscross, Knight of Kovalun, and, of course, our next employer?" Turning to Eobum, he continued. "This is Eobum, Commander of His Excellency's scouts, unless things have changed."

Eobum shook his head, meeting Jastrab's gaze.

"Ah, well, there we are, then."

Both sergeants bowed first to the count, as was proper, then turned to Eobum, performing something between a respectful nod and an uncertain bow.

For his part, Eobum gave a polite nod to all three newcomers. He was inwardly trying to parse Jastrab's choice of words while introducing the count as a Knight of Kovalun. While technically true, despite Eobum's near allergy to official courtly business, he knew that this had been an incorrect and, in the wrong company, downright insulting choice of words. The correct phrase would have been *a knight of His Grace Vévoda Harn of Vysoká Kovalun.* If that seemed too unwieldy and pompous, as it always had to Eobum, simply a *Knight of His Grace,* Vévoda Harn.

Had His Grace, Harn (or his agents) been in attendance, Jastrab would have been accounted rude to the Vévoda. At worst, he might have been hauled off for inciting insurrection—promoting Edmund as a knight loyal to the realm, not its ducal ruler. Alternatively, it might have caused Edmund to be scrutinized, thinking Jastrab a loose-lipped fool beneath Edmund's sway.

Edmund gestured to the cask of mead and the eight wooden vessels that sat beside it upon his table.

Eobum didn't move, and neither did Jastrab.

His two sergeants stood passively behind the captain.

After a moment of silence, Edmund drew in a frustrated breath, about to speak, when the tent's flap opened again.

In strode a new quartet of figures. One of Jastrab's men walked beside two young Lords—one blond in his middle teens, the other black of hair and firmly into his young manhood. Behind them strode the black-haired youth's elder sister.

"Excellency," the three young nobles offered in unintended unison.

A moment later, caught unawares, the blond-haired newcomer from Jastrab's company offered the same. He looked shocked, as if nobody had told him where he was headed.

Edmund smiled, nodding to them all but not speaking at first. He seemed to be weighing something out.

"Lord Aetanis, Lord Caros, Lady Kastan," Eobum offered by way of greeting.

He forced himself to give a touch more attention to the blond youth. His father was one of Edmund's barons—Edmund's grand strategist, in fact. Eobum hadn't seen the man personally in many years, which suited him fine. His son, however, was a more familiar presence both here and abroad. Aetanis wasn't a bad sort. He was, however, intrinsically lazy and self-important. In other words, he was a typical noble scion of the Empire.

The other two were a far more welcome sight —the children of Lord Percoy. Eobum didn't think much of their father. He was one of the county's *less illustrious* nobles. Still, the pair had been favorites of Edmund's for as long as he and his scouts had stood in the count's service.

"Eobum." Caros grinned, nodding as he spoke. He brushed a careless hand through his thick black hair. "Heard you'd returned. How was your *hunting* trip?"

Kastan silenced him with a look, then gave Eobum a smile and a nod by way of greeting.

Aetanis, on the other hand, was apparently focused on the older man with them. He seemed to take pains to make himself look taller and more imposing, which was amusing, if a bit confusing, given the setting.

Edmund spoke up at last.

"Captain Jastrab, I do not believe we need four of the Bluemark in attendance for this discussion." His tone made the statement *almost* a question but stopped just short of such a pleasantry.

Jastrab looked awkward and frustrated for a moment, then turned to the newcomer.

"I didn't summon you, Steffan. When I need you, I'll send a runner." He paused, eyeing the man before concluding, "I presume you can find your own way back to our camp?" Jastrab attempted to maintain his polite, professional tone.

"I should prefer him to remain," Aetanis said. He spoke quickly, as if to interject before Steffan could obey his captain's order.

"Forgive me, my lord, but no." Jastrab's voice was now cold and resolute.

"I beg your pardon?"

"Aetanis…" Edmund's voice was distant thunder on the come.

"I…" He paused, then bowed his head. "Very well, Excellency." He turned to leave with the blond man.

"Stop." The thunder had moved a bit closer.

Aetanis cringed at the sound, hand stopping in midair, never making its intended journey to Steffan's shoulder.

"*You* were not dismissed."

Eobum noted the Lady Kastan peering at Jastrab's man, Geroslaw.

"Steffan," Jastrab's voice was now flat. "Go. Await me at my tent."

Steffan, who had said nothing, done nothing throughout this byplay, turned back first to Jastrab, "Yes, Captain," then to the count, bowing. "Excellency." Without another word, he exited the tent.

Aetanis looked both afraid and mutinous.

"Hello," he finally said, acknowledging Eobum. "You must be Jastrab." He gave a distant nod toward the mercenary captain.

"Shall we begin, then?" Edmund's voice made this a clear and dry statement rather than a question.

All gave some sign of acceptance, a nod, a bowed head, and so on.

"Now then … Aetanis is here to, at last, undertake his first military command. He will accomplish this by securing victory at Zlaté Pole next sykli."

All eyes flitted to the blond youth. At sixteen, he was easily the youngest here and by a few years.

"When you've done so," Edmund said as he met the boy's eyes, "you will have proven worthy of battles to come."

Both lords and the Lady Kastan blinked at this enigmatic statement. Battles to come?

Edmund sighed, then seemed to decide.

"Aetanis, I know you have what you will undoubtedly consider more important matters to attend to, but there is one which I suspect you will—or at least should—find most worthy of your attention and time... the matter of your forces on the field during the War of Counties."

That got the boy's attention.

"I will send you with the guards of your household, of course, and a few of my own men with whom you've spent some time. The bulk of your force, however, will be made up of the Bluemark Guard."

Aetanis nodded, considering, then smiled.

"Excellent. I thank you, Excellency." He paused, then glanced briefly toward Jastrab. "Captain, I look forward to selecting those among your company that will fight beneath my banner."

"You will *not* be making such a selection." The thunder of Edmund's voice was growing closer yet. "Such presumption."

"Why no—" He cut himself off. A moment later, he began again. "Why, may I ask, not? If I'm to lead them, surely I should have a say in their selection—most especially if we're paying for them."

"*We,*" Edmund said, "are not paying for them. *I* am paying for them."

Aetanis nodded, bowing his head before responding.

"May I ask wh—"

"Because a leader must be able to fight regardless of the team of men he leads." Kastan's voice was even and without chastisement, though her eyes, as she turned back to the count, showed frustration.

Edmund nodded at this, reading Aetanis's expression.

"Have I overestimated your ability? Has your father not given you sufficient training for the task at hand?"

Predictably, this was enough to force the youth into a mood shift.

"He has, Excellency. I simply wished to have a say to at least some small degree." He considered, then spoke a final word. "I was under the impression that a good commander must also practice the ability to select the right person for a given task." A pause. "Perhaps I misunderstood the lesson."

Edmund sighed.

Eobum saw the look on his face and knew what would come next. The count was tired of the discussion and would yield this minor point to move things along.

Judging by his countenance, Jastrab knew it as well. He looked as if he were in the final throes of consideration on some aspect of this scene or other. Before anyone else could speak, he apparently chose his course, for he cleared his throat and addressed the count.

"Excellency? Perhaps a compromise?"

Edmund gave the man a look that said plainly that Jastrab should hurry along.

The captain turned to Aetanis.

"My lord, I have many fine men and not a few women who would serve you well and proudly. They are trained, all those whom I would show you at least, to a standard that will stand you well on the field against most, if not all, comers. I'm happy to introduce you to their commanders and help you to select those who will fight beneath your banner and in your name," he turned back to Edmund, "with the count's permission, of course."

"Fine," Edmund said.

"I will be able to make my own selection, then? From your leaders?"

Jastrab looked to Edmund, who gave a "so be it" nod.

"*Excellent*. I shall take Steffan and whomever he pleases."

"Forgive me, but no." Jastrab looked sad, though Eobum noted his eyes held a spark of anger.

"*Yes*, Captain. I am to be given leave to select my leadership, and I wish Sergeant Steffan to lead the contingent of Bluemark Guards Count Edmund has so graciously provided."

"My lord—"

"*Yes*," thundered Edmund, cutting in at last. "I want an end to this discussion. Yes, fine, take this Steffan as your subordinate—take his men. Fine!"

Jastrab snapped his mouth closed, then nodded.

"Steffan does not have enough men beneath him to accommodate your entire force. I will select another Sergeant to join you."

"Yes, fine." Aetanis smiled. "Steffan will serve as my Bluemark commander, and whichever other sergeants you think best shall join us. Will that serve?"

Jastrab nodded a single time.

"Yes, my lord. The matter is settled."

Edmund nodded.

"Go, Aetanis." His voice softened noticeably, "Kastan, Caros—one of you will remain. I care not which."

Caros eyed his sister, some silent communication passing between them, then nodded. Turning back to the count, he bowed, stepped back, and took Aetanis by the shoulder.

"Come—let's find him and give him the news."

As they left, Edmund made a gesture to the cask of wine.

Kastan nodded and went about filling goblets for the tent's remaining six occupants.

Eobum accepted his, then watched as she handed one to Geroslaw. The man gave her an almost timid look that lasted a trifle longer than it strictly needed to, then broke the contact.

With everyone watered, so to speak, Edmund took a deep breath, a shallow drink, and a modest moment to collect himself before speaking.

"Kovalun burns," said he. "Kovalun burns, and I mean to douse that fire."

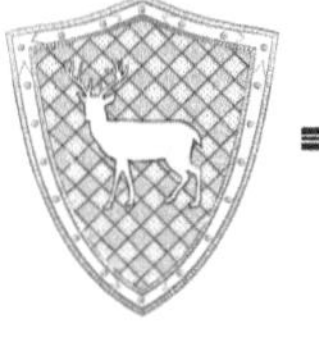

-V-

Geroslaw did his best to make his face and the language of his body as nonplussed as possible. He needed to demonstrate professionalism, not pleasure, at this so-called revelation of the count's designs.

He also had to contend with the discovery that Kastan, charmer of horses and ender of lines, was neither a pretty soldier, nor camp scribe, nor even messenger but a lady of the count's court.

Time for that later. Now, business. Edmund was speaking, and he'd already missed the first few points the mountain had made.

"...To that end, I need the right mind to help settle and sort as we move."

Jastrab's response was smooth and sure, nodding and gesturing to the curly topped head of Daian.

"One of the best siege engineers I've had the pleasure to know, Excellency. Daian's young but quite the prodigy."

Edmund nodded once, then beckoned Daian to step forward.

Daian obliged, blond curls bouncing as he did.

"Sergeant ... Daian, is it?"

"Yes ... Excellency." He didn't sound so much nervous as distracted. It was as if his mind had been suddenly called back from some sleep, only to find his body had already been up and in the doings for some time. He seemed disoriented but not overly concerned about that fact.

"Where did you learn?"

Daian blinked.

"Mostly from Captain Jastrab, Excellency." He suddenly widened his eyes, realizing the count's actual question wasn't about soldiery. "Ah," said he. "My master was Sergeant Obránce of Cervený Kámen. It's on the northwestern coast, I think."

Edmund nodded.

"It is." He paused, considering, then seemed to settle on something. "Tell me. Balista je můj oštěp. Katapult je moje...?"

Geroslaw couldn't follow the words. They'd come out too fast, and while passable, his Kovalunth would hardly be considered fluent. He saw that the room's other occupants didn't share his confusion.

"I don't ... what?" Daian looked not embarrassed but confused.

"Excellency, Daian doesn't speak much Kovalunth, I'm afraid." Jastrab laid a hand on the young engineer's shoulder.

Edmund grimaced.

"*Translate* for him, then." He seemed a touch put out of countenance. Geroslaw *thought* this was more likely *pride* than haste, given the look on the count's face.

Jastrab bowed and did as bidden.

"Balista je můj oštěp. Katapult je moje...? The Ballista is my spear. The catapult is my...?"

"Oh, hammer!" Daian's response was delighted and so rapid as to be almost comical.

Edmund's face split into a satisfied grin.

"Ah, excellent. You do know the proverb."

"Yes. Just not in Kovalunth." He paused, then added as if he'd just realized it, "Although it makes sense that it would be in Kovalunth, I suppose. You invented siegecraft, as far as I was always taught." He grinned again. "Forgive me, Excellency."

Edmund made a dismissive gesture.

Geroslaw fought the urge to breathe a sigh of relief. Daian had stumbled into victory, it seemed. Then again, he often seemed to do that.

"If I ensure you have capable scouts, can you provide them with the information you'll need to ensure swift repairs?" He paused, then elaborated. "I want to ensure we have supplies made and arranged before we arrive at a site whenever possible. I don't want to delay fortification and repair efforts any longer than strictly necessary."

Daian nodded, considering.

"I think so? It depends on the scouts, their overall intelligence, ability to understand basic mathematics, and so on." All at once, he seemed to realize that Eobum was there and was, apparently, commander of the count's scouts. "I mean no offense."

Eobum kept his face flat.

"You offered none, either. *If* is a long word. You don't know my men, and you don't know me."

Geroslaw rather liked that phrase.

I'll have to remember that one.

He wasn't certain he much cared for Eobum, though. The man was too quiet, somehow, and had a manner about him that was easy to overlook. Such men were often the very last persons one wanted to forget about. Such amnesia would end with a knife in the night, like as not.

Edmund nodded, then turned to Jastrab.

"This other—Geroslaw, was it?"

Geroslaw tried not to look surprised at his name's use.

"Yes, Excellency." Jastrab sounded a touch unhappy. "I'd meant for him to lead your advanced party when we pressed forward."

"Fine."

"But..."

Edmund raised his blond-going-grey brows.

"But?"

Jastrab cleared his throat.

"Excellency, may I speak plainly?"

Edmund nodded.

"I think you'd better."

"How important is Aetanis's victory?" He paused, then added a reluctant follow-up question. "How important is his life?"

Geroslaw noted that nobody in the tent seemed shocked at this question. This made a certain amount of sense. Tournaments were mostly safe things, but at bottom, the combatants still rode horses ... still wielded weapons of war (albeit blunted ones). People died ... and without malice or intent, most of the time. Then of course, there were the cutthroats who prowled the streets and roads, bars, and brothels in Zlaté Pole. They came out in force when a tournament was scheduled. It was a damned spree for them. While everyone seemed to know these basic truths, Geroslaw still found himself pleased to see that nobody took his captain's words as a threat or a convenient excuse to remove the boy. Likely he hadn't done more than act an ass, as far as true villainy went.

"I need him to survive intact. I would prefer him to see victory at tournament, but not if it's handed to him. There's neither instruction nor proof of lessons learned to be gained by that sort of nonsense."

Jastrab nodded.

"Then, I fear, I will need to send Geroslaw along."

"With *Aetanis*?" Edmund sounded surprised.

"Yes, Excellency. With Aetanis. I need a man whom I trust not only on the field but off of it and off the leash ... if you follow."

"Aetanis' obsession isn't a skilled enough leader, Captain?"

Jastrab bowed his head, ordering his thoughts.

"On the field, Excellency, he's a fine leader. He understands the field and the ebb and flow of combat. He has swift enough reactions, physically and mentally. What he doesn't have is my personal trust outside of supervision. I did my best to stop the young Lord from taking him, but in the interest of laying the matter to rest as you asked..."

That was bold, Jastrab, Geroslaw thought. *You've called him out on his rashness ... and in company, no less.*

Edmund sighed and nodded.

"And you trust this man to balance things and keep the boy safe?"

Jastrab nodded.

"I trust Geroslaw to do everything in his power to keep Lord Aetanis from being harmed by everyone and anyone, save Aetanis himself. I don't think it reasonable for him to be held responsible for the lord picking fights, speaking to his betters without respect, and so on. In a straight-up fight, and in matters of street and shadow, however..."

Edmund nodded.

"There, you trust him to protect the boy." He nodded once more. "Come here." He gestured Geroslaw forward.

He did as instructed, bowing formally.

"You seem familiar to me."

Geroslaw waited.

"Where are you from?"

"Auburg, Excellency."

Edmund nodded.

"That's why. I see your home hid 'hind your hair."

Geroslaw grinned, nodding.

"Been long and long since I've heard that phrase, Excellency."

"Taught me by your county's heir. He did me a service during the little rebellion we had some years ago."

Geroslaw knew this story well.

"So it's said. His father wasn't thrilled with that decision, but it certainly won him glory."

"It won him friendship and proved his own, as well as his honor." Edmund looked almost wistful. "Do you know Zlaté Pole well?"

Geroslaw thought about that—about how he would answer, then nodded a single time. Better to keep his answers direct.

"Yes, my lord. I do."

"Do you know of a reputable place for the Lord Aetanis to house himself and his men for the tournament?"

Here, Geroslaw smiled openly.

"Ohhhhh, yes, Excellency, though I'll need to ride there soon if I'm to secure it. The War of Counties always draws from far and wide."

Edmund made an inarticulate sound of consideration at this.

"You're certain, or as certain as may be, that you can arrange this?"

Geroslaw nodded but was surprised and gratified to see Kastan step forward.

"Excellency, I've spent some time with this man—it was to him I delivered your message for the captain yesterday. I won't claim I know him well, of course, but in that time, he has impressed me as a man who says what he means and means what he says." She paused, voice becoming less full— almost childlike and fearful. "I do not know how much stock or worth that assessment may carry, but I'm bound to provide it to you."

Geroslaw tried not to show his reaction to this. He was pleased, humbled, grateful, and powerfully driven to turn to her and speak to her—perhaps more—to show his gratitude. There was also a sudden desire to glare at the count. He'd managed to cow her without so much as a look or a word. This suggested a history of some sort between them that he wanted to unearth and then unmake.

"No, Kastan, you were right to speak up on his behalf. I thank you for it." Edmund smiled at her, voice and face softening in a way that seemed quite automatic and quite genuine. "Very well. On Jastrab's word and the Lady Kastan's, as well as your own comportment thus far, Geroslaw of Auburg, I agree. You will travel to Zlaté Pole, procure lodgings in your intended inn, and protect Aetanis from all that you are able."

"Very good, Excellency."

Jastrab spoke up next.

"Geroslaw? Please head back to camp and ensure you're ready to ride out in the morning. Then await me at my tent. You'll dine with us tonight, and I'll give you all the relevant information on numbers and gear traveling with Lord Aetanis."

Geroslaw bowed to the count, nodded deferentially to the captain, then to the rest of the room, and made his way out.

I might get my way after all. A trip home, a ride to tournament, a chance to serve and show beneath the count's eye as Jastrab wanted... I only have to see to Steffan and make certain he doesn't get the boy killed or maimed.

Geroslaw wondered if Kastan would see him before he left. He hoped so, but he rather doubted it. He was going home, after all. How much goodwill could one man expect from fate in a single day?

He snorted and walked back toward camp to do as Jastrab had asked.

TALES, TRUTHS, AND TUSSLES

-I-

After two hours of planning, plotting, discussing, and detailing, Eobum was more than ready for the meeting in Edmund's command tent to be over. What he'd heard had caused him more than a touch of concern for the future and his role in it, but he couldn't voice any of that until he could speak with Edmund plainly—*alone*.

Then there was the matter of the Lady Kastan. He had somewhat less concern about her by meeting's end. But her timidity didn't so much suggest that there was trouble at home as it screamed it.

He was pleased, therefore, when Edmund, at last, dismissed them.

Eobum noted that the guards appeared to have changed over while he'd been in council. The new pair were dressed as their predecessors had been, though were apparently prepared for the evening's chill. As Eobum and company exited the tent, his gaze caught their white kontusze folded on the ground, piled atop one another to the right.

Once more, Eobum made a point of making eye contact with each man in turn. Seeing nothing there that gave him cause for concern, he proceeded another yard or so beyond them before acting.

As the quartet began to separate, Eobum spoke up.

"Sergeant," he caught Daian's eye, "I'll come and see you with one or two of my men soon—tomorrow if that serves."

Jastrab wore a neutral face, though his eyes looked dubious.

Daian offered a nod, then seemed to reconsider.

"Actually, you can come by this evening. I can give you the basics then." He looked thoughtful, then brightened somewhat. "That'll make it so we're sure we understand each other. Should make other conversations go quicker."

Eobum shrugged one shoulder and nodded.

"If you like. Before supper or after?"

"I don't eat much. Before's as good as after."

Eobum nodded. He searched out Kastan's eyes, found them, and received a nod from her. If he had doubts as to if or whether she'd gotten the message he'd been trying to convey—that he wanted a word with her—her next sentence erased them.

"I'll need to find my brother once I've seen to some things here in camp. Eobum, would you be good enough to come find me when you head toward the Bluemark?"

Eobum bobbed his head.

"Aye, Lady. As you say."

Jastrab looked at the sun's position and seemed to calculate. Finally, he turned to Eobum and spoke in a voice that stayed just left of professional.

"Eobum? When you've finished with Daian, would you do me the honor of joining me for a draught of something? I won't keep you longer than that—I'm certain you have your own matters to see to." He paused for a moment, turning to face Eobum. "There are, I think, a few things we ought to discuss if you're willing."

Eobum considered him for a moment, then nodded a single time.

"I'll drink your words and your wine, and gladly." He managed a light smile, his eyelids falling to a half-closed state.

Jastrab nodded, still smiling, and turned away with Daian in tow. Kastan, too, took her leave, though in the opposite direction—toward the miniature circle set in the northwest corner of camp for emissaries and the count's guests.

Eobum waited until he could no longer see Jastrab's head through the small sea of tents, then turned on his heel and walked with a quickness back to Edmund without waiting to be announced. He made renewed eye contact with the guards, but neither seemed as if they intended to stop him.

He found Edmund seated at the tent's only chair, behind its lone table, looking at the scroll case in which he'd placed the map some two hours before. It was unopened.

Eobum walked up to the table, snatched the case up with his left hand, drawing a knife with his right point down, and stabbing it into the table's scrubbed wooden surface.

Edmund looked up, eyes flitting to the quivering knife a few inches from his massive left hand.

"... Eobum?" Edmund's voice was slow but not remotely distant. He was uncertain whether to be angered, affronted, concerned, or amused, though this last seemed altogether unlikely.

"*That*, Edmund. That is what you're courting ... only less obvious and with worse aim."

Edmund's face lit with a dry, humorless smirk.

"...A knife stabbed vaguely in my direction? Not that you couldn't have hit my hand ... had you tried."

"Exactly my drift. *I* can make a point and hit my mark. What you're proposing—what you're *planning* in the north ... you're groping in the gloom for your foe. You're apt to come away with a bloody paw that's shy a few fingers for your trouble." He paused, shaking his head before continuing, "Edmund, you're acting on an opportunity that may *not* be an opportunity at all."

Edmund met his eyes, waiting.

"We *both* know you already know this. What we *don't* both know is why you're going through with it *anyway*."

Edmund continued to stare at him.

"I see. You mean to keep me in the dark." Eobum nodded. "That *is* your right." He picked up his knife, sliding it back into its sheath at his belt. "I can and will do as you've asked. I and mine will scout, will do our best to survey, and will make as accurate a report as we can."

"...But you'll do it grudgingly."

"Not at all ... *Excellency*." He paused, deliberately returning to more formal interaction. "We simply won't do it in love. If you don't feel explaining yourself is necessary, I've no intention of pressing you. I couldn't compel you if I wanted to, regardless."

They remained in silence for a long moment, Edmund seated, Eobum stood across the table from him, still holding the scroll case. His formal stance made it clear he was waiting to be dismissed. Moreover, it was clear he intended to *make* Edmund dismiss him—to force Edmund to give him leave to depart.

At length, Edmund first chuckled, then outright laughed. Both outbursts were brief but seemed to be genuine and without rancor.

"Do you know how I know—how I always know you're wroth with me?"

Eobum straightened, looking interested, wearing a thin smile.

"Because when you're wrathful, you speak more in a moment than you usually speak in the span of a sykli." Edmund laughed again, shaking his head.

Eobum joined in, albeit briefly. He nodded. It was true. The fact that Edmund had pointed it out suggested that Eobum would get his answers after all.

"You think I'm going at this from a place of greed." This wasn't a question. "You see me carving out a ducal domain in Harn's apparent moment of weakness as the act of a greedy, power-hungry man with no thought but his age, his lack of heirs, and the burning, desperate need to make a lasting mark on the Empire—hells on Skolf, itself. Have I missed anything?"

Eobum grinned broadly now.

"You have *not*." He could use social weaponry when he had to. If this last exchange were any sign, he'd managed to keep those weapons in serviceable working order. Edmund would tell him what he wasn't seeing. He no longer needed to scratch at him about it.

The Count nodded, looking caught somewhere between fear and triumph.

"If you only see that—*you*, mind you—then I'm in a strong position."

Eobum snorted, but his grin remained.

"Much of the north burns, as I have told you. The land from Vysoká Kovalun, west to the Sea of Heroes, is still untouched."

"Aye," Eobum sounded thoughtful. "Well, the Vévoda will want to protect his capital. Easy enough to do, but still..." The Duchy's high seat was a natural fortress—a city made mostly not on but in the rock faces of the foothills of the Trpytivy mountains. The place was as unassailable as any structure could be full of balconies, tunnels, escape routes, and a veritable trove of weapons, food, and armor. It'd long been said that it could withstand a siege for more than a year before having to *think* about rationing food, water, or ammunition.

"True. He would," said Edmund. "But we know where the attacks appear to be coming from."

Eobum remained silent.

"It isn't the whole of the north that burns. The *northeast* burns, the west is unharmed—we're being pointed at everyone's favorite scapegoat."

Again, Eobum waited. He would make Edmund say it.

"Eoden is massing and has decided to raze the oppressive land of Kovalun. We must fear, and we must rally to wipe out these savages *once and for all...*" Edmund kept his voice soft, mocking the righteous import of his words.

He was pleased to hear the count use the correct term for Eobum's homeland. Eoalun was a Venzene affectation—Alun meaning *first* in Alkukieli the First Tongue, as scholars and nobles empire-wide liked to say. So far as he knew, it was the only word from that tongue that remained in popular use.

"You believe someone is setting pieces in motion so that Eodenth land can be claimed."

"I do." Edmund smiled broadly. "And whom, do you think, would benefit from such a story being put forth?"

Eobum didn't know at first. Then it hit him with a force like sudden thunder.

"Harn could demand vengeance from the emperor. He could call for aid and succor, gaining new nobles to rule the taken lands in his name—could slaughter Eodenth by the *thousands,* taking the land he butchered them on..."

Edmund nodded. His smile had become cold.

"There is a piece you don't see."

Eobum waited in silence. His face was fighting the red glare of rage that tried to suffuse it.

"If vengeance rights are claimed and accepted, there is a law Harn will employ, I've no doubt." Edmund paused for a moment, sitting back. In a voice that sounded flat and distant, he spoke again, eyes glazed over as if looking at some far-off point, moving from left to right, as if he were reading.

"Rett til svar," said he. "Be it known that when an affront or action of direct personal harm to a Peer's heritage, homeplace, or the hjertets blod of their domain is committed, and the Right of Vengeance is called, no other Peer, nor the agents of a Peer, may act or involve themselves without the leave of one or the other side, or the Venzene Throne, itself. Any who do so will have their land, title, and wealth removed from them, and, at the throne's word, such proceeds may be paid to the offended peer as recompense."

Edmund came back to himself, blinking as if he'd been awakened by the flare of a lantern.

"Do you see?"

Eobum nodded in a slow, thoughtful manner, but Edmund wasn't satisfied.

"If he uses that, all of Eoden would be his for the claiming."

"He would create a principality of his own. Hells, Eobum ... he may even challenge the Venzene Throne and either fight to claim it or break off utterly from the Venzene teat."

"Edmund..." Eobum paused, leaning forward and placing his hands, and the scroll case, upon the table.

Edmund nodded.

"I know. Which steel-clad serpent sits on which seat in which section of the empire is no matter to you."

"None at all," said he.

"Hear me now."

Eobum listened, trying to make certain his glare wasn't aimed directly at the count.

"As we've spent the last two hours discussing, I mean to take every point on the map from here to the northern marches—every tower, tract, and town I can manage before the snows set in next sykli. I mean to sweep through and come upon whomever, whatever force Harn has been using to wreck and rape his own people. We'll kill as many of them as we can and haul the rest back to either Harn or the emperor himself. Do you see *why* now?"

Eobum gave his lord a measured look. He said nothing, but his face showed dismay and doubt. He made no effort to hide his mind on the matter.

Edmund went on, undeterred.

"For Harn to slaughter and damage his own land—his own people ... that would be ample grounds for a Court of Chivalry to affect the removal of his Peerage. Either option results in my legal recognition as duke— either of Kovalun or what is currently Eastern Kovalun. If I let him, Harn will put me forward as duke to save his own name. That will put *my* ducal throne between nearly everyone and Eoden."

Eobum shook his head. "It won't be enough, Edmund."

"It will. Hear me."

Eobum quieted his mounting rage. Listening was better than speaking. It was far less useful in venting one's emotionsthan acting and reacting, but in the long run, it led to victory ... usually.

"Count Hengrek rules the county bordering our own—southeast in Kamieńalun. His lands are wide in the north, narrow in the south. He's a reasonable man, but there's no love lost between us. His son, however..."

Eobum nodded, remembering the earlier byplay between the count and Jastrab's sergeant, Geroslaw.

"When that boy ascends to his father's seat, I know—I *know* he will agree to deny others from passing through his lands to Eoden, as will I." His eyes were wide, nearly mad with an inner brilliance. "Eobum, we can finally protect them—finally do right by them!" He delivered this with a breathless zeal that made Eobum step back.

"All right," said he, "say you're right. To what end?"

"What?"

"You aren't thinking about the men of the empire—the nobility and gentry, I mean. They'll be *enraged* at losing their favorite sport."

"What do I care for that? What do *you* care for it?"

"Edmund..." Eobum shook his head. "*Think* now. There are men in this very encampment—your men, mind you—who account my boy as innocent not for being a boy but because he cannot help being *what he is*. They account Fenglem and Haiga as some of *the good ones*. Even then, I've still had to knock a man in the dirt on a time. Hells—*I've* been knocked into the dirt myself, on occasion, because some new guardsman or other wants to act on old grudges and foolish fancy about what they *think* they see."

"I don't..." Edmund shook his head, not in denial but in confusion.

"If your *common soldiery* feels that way about my kin in camp, how do you think the upper crust on the Emperor's boots—the gentry and nobility, that is—how do you think *they'll* react to being told they cannot hunt the Eodenth any longer?"

"It won't *matter*!" Edmund sounded frustrated, not angry. It was clear he felt Eobum wasn't understanding him. "Eobum, they won't be allowed to *enter*! If they wish to be miserable, what does it matter? What can they *do*?"

"Nothing."

"Exactly!"

"Nothing ... to the Eodenth who stay *in* Eoden. What of those who travel or live elsewhere in the empire? Are they to run back to, and be commanded to huddle in, the land of their fathers, never to leave it again? Are they meant to stay inland as dictated by others in the empire for fear of death and misery?"

Edmund gaped.

"Eobum, which is the worse evil?" He leaned back in his chair once more, hands folded atop his belly.

Eobum bowed his head.

Edmund went on. "As it stands now, the empire allows raid and reaving in the land of your fathers for two sykli each year. That's nearly a third of a year."

"Ninety-eight days," said Eobum.

"Ninety-eight days. We've seen it for centuries! The span from Lessykli's first sun to the end of Eosykli sees your grass-stained red, your people's works stolen or ruined. It's gone on and on, and I—*we*—can finally put a stop to it!" He stood, walking around the table to stand before Eobum.

Eobum looked up into the man's mustachioed face. He searched his eyes and found two things within them. Edmund believed what he was saying, and Edmund wanted *Eobum* to believe it, too—wanted Eobum's support and his understanding—wanted Eobum's blessing. Absurd to contemplate, yet here it was stamped plainly on the man's face. Edmund the Tall, Baron of Hartscross, Count of Jižní Pochod ... begged with his eyes for an Eodenth's blessing.

"Eobum, please... *Help* me." His voice was low and full of honest, earnest passion. "I know it *cannot* be—will *never* be perfect. There's no way to undo what's been done. We can make it better—I know we can. I know that *I* can't, but *we*... we can. Please ... help me."

Eobum bowed his head.

"What would you have me do?" He sounded defeated, resigned. Hells, he *was* both of those things. He saw Edmund's point, but he doubted—no, he *knew* it would not be as simple as the count made things out to be. Edmund was looking past the flaws in his plan. He was seeing only what he wanted to see, and while it would be better to seal Eoden away from the rest of the empire, it was a far cry from an actual solution. Edmund simply wouldn't see that or perhaps couldn't.

The count smiled, relieved.

"Prepare your men. You'll be doing more than simply scouting, as I think you know. Make for Haluzfeld. The baron will receive you. I'll have a scroll prepared for him. You'll need to deliver it into his hands and his alone. I would send a messenger, but I need the message delivered to him swiftly and silently, away from open roads."

Eobum nodded.

"And then we're to return?"

"No. From there, head on to Rosefort. I'll give you another message for the Baroness Kengar and her consort. There you will wait for the army to arrive or a message with other instructions."

Eobum nodded a single time.

"When?"

Edmund calculated.

"Not tomorrow. The morning after. Your men deserve a touch more rest, and it will give me time to ensure everything else is sorted and settled."

"I'll seek out Lord Alojz tomorrow, then."

"Alojz … is away." Edmund sounded somewhat put out by this, but it appeared to be a small matter. "I shall send a runner for you when I've drawn up the missives."

Again Eobum nodded. "Good enough."

"We will do great things together, Eobum. Your Lakkrid will know his father's long home—know it in peace, untroubled by greed and misery."

Eobum bowed his head in respect, turned, and left the tent.

He wanted to believe. He wanted to believe that Edmund was right. While he didn't doubt his intentions … his heart, he doubted Edmund's judgement.

Gi awka glem, he's the count! He's certain to know law and rights better than I…

(Blood and iron.)

If he was wrong, as Eobum feared, they would trade one centuries-old tradition of misery for a new pack of troubles.

"You believe you can save Eoden and its people. I know you *believe* that." He kept his voice soft as he walked, thinking aloud. "But the fact of your birth doesn't grant you wisdom. It places a silver shield between you and the rest of the world." He chuckled. "Or perhaps I'm just cynical. Perhaps I don't believe he's right—that this can work—because someone *I know* came upon the idea. Perhaps if some mighty mind pouring over writ and law within an empire of paper and dust…"

He shook his head, walking toward his small section of the greater encampment. For now, it was enough that he knew Edmund's mind. The rest would keep. There were other matters to attend to during what remained of this afternoon.

-II-

Geroslaw watched as the men passed him by. He judged this group just about finished with their efforts to move their portion of the Bluemark camp inside the walls of Jižní Lov.

The men had been slow to carry out this migration on Jastrab's order. He'd wanted to wait until the details of the contract had been settled and sorted. There was no point resettling if the lot of them were moving to another location within the county. Doubly so if they were splitting their forces to fight at Zlaté Pole. Jastrab, as a rule, didn't take much stock in the idea of doing a task more often than was necessary, and setting up or tearing down camp was no exception.

At first, Geroslaw wasn't certain why there would be any reason to move the short distance inside the wooden walls unless, of course, they were expecting an attack.

Now, as he stood in his open tent, selecting and inspecting his gear, the wind picked up, and the rationale became self-evident.

Inside the wooden palisade, the men and their gear would be shielded from the worst of the wind and weather. There would be a better chance of comradery, as well, if the Bluemark were in closer proximity to the count's men.

Folk feared what was *outside*. That had been one of his father's lessons. They feared what was outside, and they feared being seen as outside by those they shared their daily lives with. It often led to violence, waste, and death when those fears were at their most acute.

Fear makes men desperate. Desperation makes men fools. Fools eventually seem to wind up on one end of death or the other. That is the cycle of man. Men who are destined to command the loyalty of others... men such as your uncle or Syr Ullan—men such as you will grow into, I've no doubt—must strive to rise above that cycle, to see above the forest of fear and stand guard against the true dangers of the world.

He smiled to think of his father. It brought the reality of his situation into stark focus. If all went even *passably* well, he might soon have land and title of his own. With that in hand? His father's wife couldn't deny him then. He would be a Peer of the Empire and, as such, would have right and due owed to him when he came to call. He would be an honored guest—seen as an ally to be courted, not an obstacle to be overcome.

He heard laughter from the men as they came back for what must surely be a final load of gear. A few minutes later, they returned with a meager armload of items, and four more men in tow.

"Should be a snort to see," he heard them say as they passed.

Listening, he heard the sound of wood striking wood. Practice swords, he'd swear to it. It was a sound he thought he'd recognize anywhere. It called to mind a mixture of memories, bruised knees, arms, ribs, and of course, pride.

He shrugged as he spared one last glance around the tent, then left it to follow the men. He took time to tie the flaps that made up the tent's entrance around an upright. There wasn't much chance of rain or snow, but better not to risk any element other than wind getting into his sleeping place.

-III-

As Eobum approached their patch of land, he heard Adric's braying laughter cut through the din. The pre-supper hour always resulted in a marked increase in chatter and general noise.

You eat in the morning to fortify yourself against the day. By mid-afternoon, you'll have used up your stores. It's longing that keeps you going, then. It's knowing that in just a little while, you can take your ease, refresh yourself with the evening meal, and rest.

Who was it that had told him that? One of the soldiers at Rafe's Rest, he was certain. He could almost see the face—bearded and grizzled. The voice was clear enough, but he couldn't put a name to the man for a long moment. Quite suddenly—as such things often did—it came back to him.

"Vinter!" Eobum brightened. "That was his name, Vinterssverd." He allowed himself a small smile of self-satisfaction at that. He was pleased at being able to recall the name attached to the memory. Hells, the very act of searching for it—of pawing through such dusty places in his mind—had taken his attention from his frustrations and misgivings.

He paused some fifteen yards off from his small camp and listened. It was an old game he'd played since his first days of real training as a scout.

He bent his focus on the area to which he was headed. He tried to determine who was actually present 'round the fire.

"Alusc, obviously, and Adric. No children's laughter. If Lakkrid were there, he might be tending to one chore or another—might not be laughing along with the others, but the other boys? No. Adric makes most people laugh. Sometimes even on purpose. No children." He paused, turning his head so that his stronger ear—his left—was aimed that way. "Riclov's there. I can hear his nervous laughter."

"-eckon... time for that, I tells'm!" This voice was bright and clear—a man's voice distinct among his fellows. It had the crisp, short tones of a Gerstealunth accent.

"Aderano's there, which means Hrothgian won't be far behind. That boy follows after Aderano like a two-legg-ed *Red* Hound."

He'd heard all he cared to. He might wait longer if this were an actual scouting run, but it was enough for him for now. Adric was there, and that would do for a start.

He walked on. Once he'd rounded the few outlaying obstacles—an arming tent, a small single-axle cart, and a small pile of firewood—he raised his voice to be heard over their conversation.

"Adric?"

"Eobum?"

"A word." He rounded the final small corner and saw all the faces he'd expected to see and one he'd missed.

Adric stood near Lashjuk and Alusc, clearly speaking to the former based on his body language. Behind him, across the fire, Aderano sat with his Red Hound Hrothgian. In front of their tents, respectively, sat both Riclov—whose voice he'd heard—and brown-haired Alblod. These two had been the last to join the unit some months up the hourglass. They were, consequently, far less certain of their place within it still.

Alblod seemed to have an easier time accepting things as they came and was content to simply be counted among their number. Riclov, on the other hand, seemed perpetually nervous and uncertain. Good enough in a fight, but a goose when it came to most social matters.

Eobum eyed the pair and offered a single nod, waiting for Adric.

That worthy came over swiftly enough, bending forward at the neck and jutting his chin out slightly, as was his way when preparing to listen.

"Make certain the men enjoy an extra measure tonight."

Adric blinked, nodding slowly.

"Orders?"

"Aye, but we don't leave until the day after tomorrow."

Adric sighed through his nose but said nothing.

"Do be certain you and Eranoric are sober for supper. I don't have to remind you how much I love repeating myself."

Adric snorted.

"Favorite thing, an' no mistake."

Eobum nodded.

"Where are the others?"

Adric shrugged.

"Eranoric took some of them to see the camp's smith. Boys went with him, though I suspect they're joined in with the others."

"Others?"

Adric grinned his yellow grin.

"Aye, few'the camp's cubs were playin' wha'd'ya call it ... bells?"

Eobum blinked. He listened, heard no screaming or singing, then looked back at Adric.

"Zvonění?"

Adric brightened, nodding.

"I don't hear them singing ... or screaming..."

Adric's face split again into that yellow grin.

"Nye. N'that one. The one with the leather ball."

Eobum made a silent "Oh" and nodded his understanding.

"Zvonící míček," said he. "Bells ball."

Adric nodded, pointing.

"Off toward the east end of camp."

Eobum nodded a final time. He laid a hand on Adric's left shoulder and turned to head off north.

"Wrong way, východní head."

Eobum waved a dismissive hand, continuing on.

"Not for me."

Adric chuckled. He might have shaken his head or shrugged, but Eobum could no longer see him.

Eobum moved off toward Kastan's temporary home.

He found her sitting alone on an over-engineered camp bench before a well-tended fire. There were enough metal pins, bolts, eyelets, and hinges on the damned bench to make a goodly sized dagger, were it all melted down. Rather than frustrating him, the waste seemed to make his steps lighter. This—this was the sort of selfish, silly excess he was used to by the gentry and the nobility. Its excess served to ground him in reality, reminding him that the world wasn't so new and strange after all. His conversation with Edmund had left him unsure of his footing, uncertain of his role, and unfamiliar with his surroundings. This place, however, was familiar.

Kastan stood as he approached. She took a moment to cast about. Sure that they were alone, she ran to him and fell against his chest, embracing him as if she were a child waking from a night of fitful dreams.

He bore this patiently, enfolding her, squeezing—briefly crushing her to him.

"I have you, Lady. I have you." He repeated this several more times, combing his fingers through the satin of her hair.

He could feel her heart pounding, but as they stood holding to one another, he felt her pulse slow.

Finally, she withdrew from him, wiping a few stray tears from her face. "Better?"

She nodded, making an "mmhmm" sound through her nose.

He waited another moment, allowing her to regain herself fully, then spoke again.

"I can sit with you, or we can walk... a decision *you* must make, Lady."

She smiled, eyes over-spilling once more, causing her to laugh.

"A moment here, if you will?"

Eobum asked silently if he should sit, and when she'd nodded, he moved to a seat perpendicular to her former perch, facing the small section's only entryway.

She sighed as she spoke. "Eobum, what am I to do?"

He kept his face warm but otherwise neutral as he looked at her, waiting for her to go on.

"I'm almost out of time," said she. "If I'm not soon fitted with a suitable husband, my father will demand I withdraw from the family, legally."

Eobum nodded. It was half of what he'd feared. Now he had to ask about the other half—the one that made his heart ache and his blood boil.

"Does he know?"

She shook her head, mouthing a silent "no."

"Has he ... hurt you?"

She looked away. While she didn't outright answer with words, her physical reaction was answer enough.

"How badly?"

"No worse than were I still a child."

He grew quiet, eyes seeing a far-off place.

"Kas..."

She shook her head.

"*No*, Eobum. I know what you mean to say, but no. He's grown tired and thin after his rise to power. Caros will inherit his lands unless the Kengar boy comes stumbling out of the woods after... hells be hid. Has he been missing all of five years already?"

She wondered at the thought, then returned to the matter at hand.

"My father simply wishes to see me marry someone of appropriate rank and station. He wishes my union to secure our line for the future. Killing him..."

"Would serve him right? Would resolve all of this? Would make it so I don't find you falling into my arms in rage and grief nearly every time I lay eyes on you?" His tone was cold and matter-of-fact, though his frustration wasn't directed at her.

She blushed rather prettily, smiling.

"Who *else* would I turn to?"

He nodded.

"I'll see him in a fortnight in any case."

She blinked, looking suddenly afraid.

"Eobum, no..."

"Peace, Lady. Edmund sends me to Rosefort with a message. First, I see my way to Haluzfeld, then Rosefort."

She didn't look as if that had done much to ease her worries.

"I won't kill him," said he.

"Your word?"

"Aye, Lady. You have it. I won't kill him, nor have him killed unless he tries to do injury to I or mine." Eobum smiled, meeting her eyes. "He's no warrior, Kas. He won't challenge me—won't pick a fight."

She nodded, relieved in a palpable way.

"You *must* tell him eventually. Sooner, I think, not later." He paused. "Shall *I* tell him?"

She gaped. "Hells be hid, no! He'd kill you for even suggesting such a thing!"

Eobum laughed. "Well, then I'd have every right to kill him legally. Wouldn't I? Might solve the problem." He was teasing, but her face showed plainly she was having none of it.

"It would make so, so many new ones. Eobum, please. You gave your word."

"Kastan..." He felt the muscles of his face set in hard lines. His tone was flat, cold—full of muted anger and disappointment.

She bowed her head.

"I'm sorry. Indeed I am. I know you better. Your word was given, and nobody will hold you to it better than you. I'm sorry."

He softened visibly.

"It's a small matter, Lady. It's a maddening time. *You* can't tell him the truth. He wouldn't hear it, as you've said. I don't doubt you on it, either. *I* can't tell him. He'd try and have me killed for speaking your name in the same sentence as what he'd call an *outrageous accusation*. Then he'd be dead, and I'd be hunted until I could speak to Edmund."

She nodded glumly.

"What am I to do?"

"Might not matter much longer."

"Oh?"

"Edmund's *larger* plans require loyal persons to rule the lands we take. If you win glory, you're already seen as loyal, and you're already an effective ruler..."

She sat back, thinking.

"You're saying I might win enough renown to become a baroness in my own right?"

He nodded. Smiling, he stood. "What then could your lord father say? He would have no right to command you to marry *anyone*. You could be with anyone you wanted at that point."

She stood, eyes wide, mouth split in a brilliant smile full of white teeth.

"Eobum ... you..." She embraced him again just as fiercely as before, but for much less time. She pulled back, face still full of fire and joy.

"Thank you." It was all she could say.

He stepped back and lifted her hands to his chin. Bowing his head, he kissed the back of each hand in turn, then placed her right arm through his left.

"Shall we, my lady?"

She nodded, briefly laying her head on his shoulder, then walking beside him toward the Bluemark encampment.

-IV-

Lakkrid held back a sigh. How had it come to this? Half a bell ago, they'd been playing Zvonící míček. Now the leather ball and the freight of small bells sewn into its core lay beneath a wooden bench. It sat forgotten atop a pair of stones they'd used for bases and two rusty cowbells, looking sad and neglected.

Their bat, too, had been put by in exchange for practice swords. These were thin, carven things that were supposed to snap before they broke arms or skulls. A year of rains and snows to season the wood—and half-hearted coats of varnish applied in annoyed haste (and even *then* only after the wood had grown swollen)—made such a safe outcome seem like wishful thinking.

Maksu had seen one boy strutting around with his practice sword tucked into his belt and jogged over. It hadn't been his turn at bat. The other boy had come along to a game already in progress. A moment later, the sword was out and being swung around in a wild, showy manner Lakkrid hadn't much cared for, though he'd said nothing.

The action drew a crowd from the children not fielding or at bat, and within minutes someone had decided that Zvonící míček was done for the day. It was time for The Lyst.

He'd dutifully run back into camp and pulled his sword and shield from Feng and Haiga's tent. He usually kept them there. It was simpler, as Haiga had been teaching him how to maintain his gear for some time.

If he were being honest with himself, he'd been more than a little excited to show Maksu his shield. He'd thought seeing and getting to use it on the field might ease his mind a touch.

The boy was clearly nervous about having to fight. While he didn't strictly have to do so, being the one boy in twenty who was too afraid to take his lumps like everyone else would make him an outcast. He'd had no real trouble being accepted by the camp's other children thus far, but something like this could change that far too quickly.

Everyone's reaction to one of only half a dozen shields amongst them—jealousy and a lesser form of awe—appeared to bolster Maksu for a time. Then their audience arrived.

Lakkrid stood beside their makeshift lyst field. He'd watched as fully a dozen men in black took up positions farther down the line. They wrapped around the field, forming a semi-circle, cheering and jeering at each pair of children as they came out to fight one another.

Two of the camp's men—a stable hand and a hunter by their clothing—had also come out to watch, but they appeared to be related to two of the boys. So far as Lakkrid knew, none of the black-clad men had children in the count's camp.

Vlk pushed through the small gaggle of boys up to Lakkrid's right.

"My father says those men are hirelings." Vlk cut his eyes toward the black-clad men. His voice sounded awed—somewhere between impressed and intimidated.

Lakkrid nodded.

"Bluemark Guard. My father knows them."

Vlk's face split into a wide grin, eyes large.

"They've vorked for the count before, I think! They're not common sellsvords at all, then!"

Lakkrid didn't much care for the tone of not-quite worship Vlk's voice had taken on. He didn't know the story, however, so couldn't rightly speak against these men. Eranoric didn't care for them. Eranoric liked everyone. There had to be a reason, but Lakkrid couldn't work out how to articulate that. Besides, Maksu's turn had come, and that was more important.

"You're smaller than him," Lakkrid said.

"I *know*!" Maksu sounded just short of terrified.

"No, listen!"

Lakkrid made to tighten the boy's belt, looping its length around him and tucking it into the back. Its excess leather had hung below his knees—a trip hazard at the best of times.

"He's tall, and his arms are long. Move fast in toward him. Get close enough so you could punch him. If he runs at you, jump forward to meet him halfway. He'll fall, and you can make him yield!"

Maksu blinked and nodded.

"All right..." His eyes were glassy, lower lip quivering as if on the edge of tears. His voice made it clear that he'd had no idea what Lakkrid was talking about if he'd even registered it.

He walked numbly out onto the field, wooden sword in hand. He hefted a child-sized wooden kite shield borrowed from Lakkrid, saluted his opponent as he'd seen the others do, and readied himself to die.

"I remember feeling like that," Vlk said. His voice was sage and full of sympathy.

Lakkrid nodded.

The tall boy squared off with Maksu, focused and wary.

"That's *my* fault," Lakkrid said.

"Vhat is?"

"Look at how serious that stable boy is..."

Vlk squinted, then leaned back and placed a hand on Lakkrid's shoulder, bowing his head.

"I'm sorry. You're right. Your new friend ... probably von't make it."

Lakkrid doubted death was in Maksu's near future, but still.

The tall boy lunged forward, thrusting his wooden sword at Maksu's head.

Maksu got his shield in the way just in time, but the blow was strong enough that the shield wobbled out of position. Maksu didn't have the wrist or grip strength to weather the thrust and keep his defenses up. He staggered backward, flailing his sword arm to keep balance.

The tall boy had expected the blow to be blocked and had danced back after delivering it, preparing for a retaliatory strike. When none came, he dropped his guard, looking shocked.

The men of the Bluemark cheered and shouted encouragement at the tall boy.

"Garn! Take him! Knock the tuskling down!"

Maksu recovered his balance, then shot a glare of embarrassed frustration at his foe. He brought his shield back into position and stepped forward rather boldly.

The taller boy ran his bright forearm up to push his blond hair back from his eyes and glared in kind, though his mouth showed a delighted grin rather than an angry one.

Maksu walked to within four feet and waited.

The other boy began to circle to the right.

Maksu followed suit.

This persisted for perhaps a minute, then the other boy charged.

Maksu backed up, shield held high as he tried to duck down.

The boy smiled in triumph. He rolled out to his right and pivoted, throwing a flat snap to Maksu's exposed left side. It connected. Maksu screamed, then collapsed on the spot.

Everyone applauded, though the Bluemark men cheered as if they'd won the fight themselves.

"I'm next," said Vlk. "Can I borruh your shield?"

Lakkrid nodded, watching. He sighed and smiled as the victor reached down and helped Maksu to his feet. Placing an arm around the boy's shoulders, he walked him back to where Lakkrid stood.

"He's tough," the boy said to Lakkrid as he let Maksu go. "Needs practice, but he's tough."

Lakkrid nodded, smiling at the boy—one he didn't personally know.

"Your thrust looked strong," Lakkrid said.

"It *was*." Maksu's voice came out in a soft groan.

"I'm Andrej, the hunter's son."

"Lakkrid."

"I know. My father told me you're the son of a scout." He grinned. "I hope I get to fight you." Rather than aggressive, the boy sounded as if he were trying to flatter Lakkrid.

"This is Maksu."

Andrej nodded, saluting Maksu with his sword.

"As I say, your brother's tough. Just needs to practice more."

Lakkrid thought about correcting him, but Vlk had handily defeated his opponent. It was now Lakkrid's turn.

"You'll be all right?" He eyed Maksu, laying a hand on his shoulder.

"It hurts, but I'll be fine."

"I'll stay with him," Andrej said. "I want to see you fight, anyway." He turned to Maksu and placed a hand on the boy's shoulder. "Can I stay and watch your brother fight with you?"

Maksu grinned and nodded.

Lakkrid walked out onto the field, taking his shield from Vlk as the pair passed one another.

He was facing Pavel, the baker's son, a stocky boy who looked like he'd eaten someone Maksu's size and was ready to do so again. He was strong but slow—relying on strength more than anything else in a fight. That and overall aggression.

Lakkrid saw that the boy had no shield and relaxed his stance. He tapped his wooden sword against the rim of his kite and gave Pavel a look.

Pavel cocked his head to the side. After thinking about it for a moment, he nodded.

"To jo. Just svords," said he.

"To jo" was one of the few phrases from Kovalunth that had stuck with Lakkrid. It was a casual "yeah," at least the way the other children used it.

He nodded and walked back to Maksu, Vlk, and Andrej.

"Brave..." Andrej said with respect.

Lakkrid made a non-committal noise and handed Vlk his shield. Turning, he walked back out to face Pavel.

-V-

Fenglem stood by as Haiga and the smith's apprentice showed Eobald and Eranoric a selection of spearheads recently finished. Sulok stood at Eranoric's elbow, as had been his habit these last two days.

Haiga knew the apprentice better than the rest of them. Fenglem didn't think the pair were friends, but they'd spent plenty of time in one another's company over the years. The camp's master smith was also the count's best siege engineer. The fellow had taught Haiga most of what he knew on that score.

"You see? The heads are broad and notched. They'll rip on their way back out."

"Aye, and'll damage pelt and meat both *on the way out!*" Eobald was eyeing the spearheads with mistrust.

"To jo, to jo, but if you strike a foe vith them and he manages to slink avay..."

"Then I've failed at the mark and am out a spear with an expensive head, ain't I!"

The apprentice looked to Haiga for help but found none.

"I *did* tell you. It has its uses, but not for our fight," Haiga said. He grinned, his two lower tusks seemingly straightening in line with his nose.

Fenglem smirked as he looked between them, then cocked his head to one side, listening. Was that...

"Dash! *Dash! Stop* it!" A shrill, high voice pierced the cacophony of the late afternoon Maker's Row.

Fenglem looked back to see if Sulok had heard it. The boy seemed intent on Eranoric, who was examining a large whetstone on offer.

Good, he thought. Aloud, he said, "I'll be back." He didn't wait for a reply, moving off at a fast walk to see what had Maksu in such a state.

Feng rounded out of the narrow lane where the makers were quartered and stopped in his tracks. He saw a field of perhaps eighty feet in a rough square, as he'd expected. On most days, when work was done, the encampment's children could be found at play here. If what he saw now counted as play, Fenglem was the next Emperor of Venzene.

Lakkrid stood on a strip of bare ground where once there may have been grass. A large, round boy lay on his back on Lakkrid's dim side, unmoving, although Fenglem could see that he was breathing. Lakkrid held a wooden practice sword in the ready position, point toward a trio of black-clad men some yards away. These bold souls were moving closer in loose formation, trying to surround him. What appeared to be nearly all the encampment's children stood just across the field in front of Fenglem, to Lakkrid's left.

"Put it down, tuskling, or I'll feed it to you." This brave threat came out of the centermost of the triad of men.

Feng moved forward at a run. He leapt a bench, then a small, rude cart before at last setting foot on the barren field.

A ringing sound told him that someone had drawn a sword—a short one, by the sound of it. He spun to the right just in time to see another of the black-clad men lunge at him.

"Zurück, Biest!" The swordsman drove forward, slicing wildly at the air where Fenglem had intended to step.

He leaned backward just the right side of too late, then brought his elbow down on the man's outstretched forearm below the joint. The fellow yelped and dropped his sword at Fenglem's feet. Feng kicked it back behind him and advanced.

The other men of what he now recognized as the Bluemark Guard ran into the fray.

Feng had a moment to realize that rather than help even the odds, he'd turned one on three into two on twelve or more.

He moved to Lakkrid's dim side, near the large boy's prostrate form.

That seemed to further infuriate the men. They roared a mass negation in three languages simultaneously and rushed at him.

He drew his own short sword and leveled it at them, making his body a thin line, bright side toward them as they charged.

They stopped, kicking up dust as they skidded to a halt some two or three yards away.

"Svords!" A red-maned man spoke up. He seemed to be acting as their leader. They quickly followed this simple order.

Fenglem was dismayed to hear all dozen or so blades clear leather at nearly the same instant. They were, apparently, well-drilled, despite the rumors about mercenaries being lazy and undisciplined.

"Three grown men, to take on a single boy, a dozen when a lone man stands beside him?" Fenglem kept his tone just short of mocking.

"Orku boy, orku man," their leader said. "Ve know your kind, tusk."

"The Bluemark's afraid of a Gnoerk boy vith a vooden sword?" A human boy's shrill voice shouted this from the sidelines, holding a wooden sword of his own and what looked like Lakkrid's shield.

Fenglem saw that he was standing with another boy—a taller one who held a practice sword. Both were standing stolidly between Maksu and the field, facing the men of the Bluemark who had been ignoring them up to this point. As for Maksu? He looked terrified.

Feng had a moment to question whether he'd heard the boy say *an orc* or *a Gnoerk*. He didn't have time to dwell on it for long.

Some of the men seemed affected by this jeer, but their leader managed to cow them with a look and a growl.

The first man to attack Fenglem had retrieved his sword and now took his place on the far left of the Bluemark line.

He growled at Feng, searching for his eyes.

Fenglem obliged, locking eyes with the man. He watched as he cocked his sword back over his right shoulder. Feng saw the man's lower fingers loose upon the sword's hilt.

A man with at least some training, then. When he was in range, he had no doubt that the man would perform a flat snap or a hammer, snapping the wrist as he delivered the blow to add power and speed to the strike ... if Fenglem let him.

He saw what would happen an instant before the man leapt into motion.

"Gev vresh." Fenglem's voice was low and dull, loud enough for Lakkrid to hear... he hoped. *(On the ground)*

The man charged—sword held high.

Lakkrid crouched swiftly ... without a word.

As he did, Feng pivoted a touch to his right and looked pointedly at the man's belly.

The man realized where Fenglem was looking, his eyes flitting down for a fatal moment as he rushed forward.

Feng slid his back foot to widen his stance, leaning back on it for an instant before he allowed his sword arm to snake out. The sword seemed to be pulling Fenglem rather than being propelled by him. It leapt forward to meet the man's onrushing throat. The combination of opposing speeds drove the sword all the way through the soft, unprotected flesh, pushing meat several inches beyond the spine's natural border.

Another man had charged just behind the first. Fenglem had no time to withdraw his own sword, so he stepped forward in a lunge, picking up the dead man's weapon. As he rose, he drove the blade upward into the second man's belly.

The Bluemark brought the flat pommel of his short blade down on the back of Feng's head. While the blow lacked force and conviction, it was still hard enough to cause Feng to see brief flares of light across his vision.

He stood, releasing his borrowed blade and pulling his third weapon of the day from the new-made corpse's slackening grip.

Pulling back from his lunge, Feng recovered his stance beside a numb looking Lakkrid. Feng could see the boy still held his wooden practice sword, though he held it more like a bat than a sword.

"I'm sorry..." Lakkrid's voice was cold and small.

Feng nodded at Lakkrid's words.

"Back to back," said he.

The remaining ten men of the Bluemark held a scant few yards away in a dark knot, as if frozen in place.

As Lakkrid moved to comply, the man on the end of the Bluemark line lunged forward, flicked his wrist, and disarmed the boy.

Lakkrid yelped in pain, albeit briefly, as the action twisted his wrist.

His attacker leered at him, showing a grin that was missing more than a few teeth. Still, he righted himself and took a few rapid steps back into line with his fellows almost instantly.

Feng growled. That might have been the end of Lakkrid, and there would have been nothing he could've done about it.

He looked across at the semi-circle formed by the Bluemark. Their ends were less disciplined than their center. They were a bit farther apart from one another. Their faces showed a mixture of greedy avidity and fearful uncertainty. He thought he could take any one, maybe any two of them in a straight-up fight.

Ten men, though? No. Have to get Lakkrid out of here, but if he goes, they charge. Two Gnoerks are a threat. They're brave enough to mass against one.

"Degun tok?"

He saw Lakkrid's long shadow nod on the ground off to his left.

"Shrash."

Again, he saw the shadow nod.

(More than two? Run.)

Undaunted, Lakkrid crouched down to pick up the sword Pavel had been using and did as Feng had first instructed. Pavel had been taller by

more than a head. His sword was much longer than Lakkrid was used to. To compensate, he held the weapon in both hands, point toward the chins of his foes some eight feet away, and waited back to back with his uncle.

-VI-

Geroslaw walked behind the last few Bluemark stragglers. He saw them pick up speed, then heard the unmistakable sound of steel being drawn. That might be bad, but it might be nothing. Perhaps one of his fellows was giving a demonstration to whomever was using the practice swords a few moments ago. He picked up his pace, then heard something that caused gooseflesh to rise on his arms and the back of his neck, the telltale sound of not one but many swords being drawn in unison.

A moment later, he rounded past a small row of tall A-frame tents and saw the spectacle.

Perhaps a dozen or so of his fellows had their backs to him some fifteen yards ahead. They were faced off with some other group—he couldn't see who. A line of children stood to his right, watching the scene with grave, dark expressions on their faces.

He ran, sprinting wide and to the left, drawing his own sword. Then he heard the telltale rapid rise and fall of sound as several somethings sped toward him from somewhere in front and to his left. This was followed by a pair of screams from ahead of him. Two of his men—the Bluemark were *all* his men, on the field anyway—had fallen with short spears sticking out of their sides. If they weren't dead, they soon would be. Wounds such as that were rarely recovered from. One stuck out of a man's back, the other a man's belly beneath the ribs.

Geroslaw spun, looking for the spearmen, and saw...

"No..." His voice came out in a breathy sigh.

Two men and two orcs were racing to the Bluemark line. Behind them, from deeper in the encampment, Eobum and Kastan hurtled first toward, then past this early quartet. Judging by the looks on their faces, they were all *ready*, perhaps even *eager* to spill blood.

-VII-

"Sergeant Geroslaw!" Eobum's voice was an avalanche in full flower. "You and your men stand down or so help me—I'll kill each and every one of you myself!"

Geroslaw moved at speed, running the remaining distance to see how many of Eobum's men his own had killed.

"Retreat by step! Step-step-step-step-step! Line stop!" He gave this series of commands with barely a breath between them. Such rapid-fire orders tended to startle men into action, and this situation was no exception. As the line stopped and he was able, at last, to see, he could only gape.

Two more of his men lay dead on the ground, swords still protruding from their death wounds, their blood coloring the children's playing field. Stood beyond them, looking unharmed, were two more orcs—one man, one boy—both with weapons drawn.

He spun on his heels and looked at the men who stood shoulder to shoulder, waiting for his next order.

"Sheath your swords." He gave them barely a two count before repeating his command in a shout. "I said, '*Sheath your swords*'! *Now!*"

They complied.

"What in *hells* is this about?" He sheathed his own sword and looked at the faces of the men before him. They were Steffan's, to a man. He saw the blacksmith's apprentice—the one he'd helped to better fit his vambrace not long ago—and beckoned him forward.

"What happened here?"

The man looked defiant, which was both interesting and annoying.

"I asked you a ques—"

"That's for Sergeant Steffan to sort out... Sergeant. We don't report to you, do we?" This question had come out more like a smug statement.

The men grumbled—some of them anyway—their approval at this.

"Sergeant?" A boy's voice came from the line. He was holding a miniature kite shield protectively before an orc boy.

Geroslaw held up a hand. Speaking over his shoulder, he raised his voice so that it carried. "Commander?"

From nearly right behind him—so close that he had to fight not to leap out of his skin—Eobum's voice crawled toward his ear in a predator's growl.

"Sergeant?"

"If they belong to you, please take them and go."

"I believe we'll stay, Sergeant..."

Geroslaw shrugged a single shoulder.

"As you wish." His voice was raw and dry as if he'd been breathing smoke.

He strode forward to where the smith's apprentice still stood staring at Eobum and the orcs with undisguised hatred. As he neared, the youth turned to regard him, face still smug. A moment later, he was on his back, holding his jaw, a shocked look on his stupid sheep's face.

"Wha—?"

After his first strike knocked the smith down, Geroslaw kicked him. He kicked him hard, then stomped on him for good measure with a hobnailed heel. He heard bone crack, followed instantly by the man's gasping scream. *Good enough,* he thought. *Good enough, given what you lot've likely unleashed upon us.*

"You," said Geroslaw, pointing at random to one of the assembled Bluemark, "step forward two paces."

A red-haired man with a hatchet face did as Geroslaw had asked. He looked sullen and sulky, but intimidated just the same. He kept taking little, pecking glances down at the writhing, gasping smith's apprentice.

"What happened here?"

The hesitation didn't last long. Bowing his head, the man collected his thoughts, then stared straight ahead.

"The tusk bloodied its better. It used some trickery or magic to make the boy there on the ground headbutt the thing's sword."

Geroslaw glared, then turned to the boy with the shield, nodding to him.

"Pavel's an oaf," the boy called. "Lakkrid just outsmarted him. Then three men came in and started toward him!"

The hatchet-faced man looked defiant.

"No tusk should put a proper man's son on his back," said he.

Geroslaw wanted to scream. To be surrounded by such fools—to be sent off to rely upon men Steffan ... trained? Could it be said that he trained them?

"I think you might be hanged for this. If those orcs belong to the count, you're dead men." He paused, lifting his chin. "Hells—if they belong to the count's scouts? That might be just as bad."

"I'm fine," a small voice said from behind him. The orc child, surely. "Father, can we take Maksu home?"

Geroslaw nodded, turning. He was about to address the orc man who'd been standing with his back to the boy—his father, surely—when he saw Eobum on one knee looking the boy over.

"Maksu? Come to me," said Eobum.

Three boys came walking at speed toward Eobum's party, the orc, and his two human protectors. The latter two walked with him between them, the taller boy walking with his back to the orc, eyeing the rest of the Bluemark with obvious mistrust mingled liberally with fear.

"Are you hurt?" Eobum looked at the younger orc boy.

"No—just my side."

"From his fight on the lyst field, Father," the first orc boy put in.

Geroslaw blinked, feeling a sudden chill. *The taller orc child called Eobum ... called him* Father.

"Commander?"

Eobum stiffened and turned his head but did not stand.

"Would you be good enough to keep an eye on these brave men for a few moments?"

Eobum nodded slowly.

"I can do that."

"Back in line ... now." As the man moved to comply, Geroslaw turned his attention to the rest of the Bluemark standing there. He raised his voice to be heard by all of them.

"If you move so much as a muscle out of this line, you'd better *hope* Commander Eobum kills you." He began to walk past them, stopping beside the line to add, "It will be quicker—less *painful* for you that way." With that, he exited the palisade and marched with purpose toward Jastrab's command tent. There would be hells to pay, he was certain, but better the captain hear it from him.

WHISPERS AND WAR DRUMS

-I-

Eobum choked down a bitter smile of satisfaction. A score of Edmund's men came into view and quickly surrounded the Bluemark. Kastan and two others—one of the camp's huntsmen and what looked to be a stable hand—walked amidst another four guards surrounding an all but snarling Edmund.

When he turned back to Lakkrid, Eobum saw that the two boys who'd stood with Maksu were now shoulder to shoulder with his son, smiling. Lakkrid looked as if he were still processing all of it, but he'd managed to fish out a smile as he met their gaze.

Maksu, on the other hand, had run over to his brother and Eranoric as they approached—a thing Eranoric had held off from doing until it was certain the fighting was over. As always, he was a prudent man.

"Eobum." Edmund's voice rolled toward him while twenty feet still separated them.

Eobum stood after sparing a last look at his son. He turned to face the count and bowed his head, albeit briefly.

"Excellency."

"What in hells *happened* here?"

"These fine men sought to put Lakkrid, and then Fenglem, in their places." Eobum's tone was conversational enough, but those who knew him would recognize that tone for what it was and what it meant. Eobum had made up his mind to see blood spilled.

Edmund's face fell, his pace slowing. He took a single deep breath, then lifted his chin as he resumed his original pace. Ignoring literally every other person in the area, he pushed past his own men who were, it seemed, walking too slowly for his liking. He came up beside Eobum and crouched down to look Lakkrid in the eye.

Vlk and Andrej looked as if they might wet themselves. The count himself now stood less than a foot from them. They quickly stepped back as if he were on fire, dropping the tips of their weapons onto the dirt.

Edmund ignored them for the moment.

"Lakkrid?"

Lakkrid met the man's eyes and waited.

"Are you—"

"I'm all right, Excellency. They never touched me." He looked up at Fenglem, then back to Edmund. His voice was hollow, somehow, as if he were talking in his sleep.

"Are you certain they meant to hurt you?"

Eobum fought down the urge to clench both jaw and fists at this. He knew Edmund hadn't seen it—knew he *had* to ask. Still, he hated the subtext this question seemed to carry with it. He knew it wasn't how Edmund meant it to come across, but it felt very much as if Lakkrid were being questioned from a place of doubt and uncertainty. Absurd, but there it was.

I know better, he thought. Still, knowing a thing didn't always dictate how a person felt about that thing. It took *effort*, but he forced himself to remain relaxed.

"I can't say what they planned, Excellency, but they spoke and acted as if they meant to punish me."

"Punish you?"

"For beating Pavel."

Pavel hadn't moved, though Eobum saw his eyes were wide open and flying from figure to figure.

"Did..." Edmund stopped, then rephrased his question. "Were you two sparring?"

Lakkrid nodded.

"Looks as if you hit him hard..."

Lakkrid nodded once again.

"I feinted, then sidestepped to back cut his chest. He overextended for a hammer—head first. His neck met my sword, and he went down."

His chest hitched. "I ... tried to pull the blow, Excellency." He gulped, eyes swimming. "I *swear* to you I tried, but..."

Edmund laid his massive right hand to the side of Lakkrid's head, wiping a tear away with his thumb.

After a moment, Lakkrid finished his tale. "When he went down..." He made a sweeping gesture with his dim hand—the one nearest the Bluemark.

Edmund nodded and stood. To Pavel, he turned and spoke a question.

"Can you stand?"

Pavel nodded.

"Can you speak?"

Pavel tried. Judging by the look on his round face, he found that he could, though it seemed to hurt. The boy winced as he attempted to swallow.

"I ... can, my lord."

Edmund nodded. He reached down and took Pavel's hand, hauling him to his feet without much effort. Gesturing to one of the guards who'd come with him, he spoke to the boy.

"Pavel, is it?" When the boy nodded, too stunned to be afraid it seemed, Edmund continued. "This is my Ruční Kopí. He will take you to get looked over. If my scholar says you're all right, you're free to go home. If not, Ruční Kopí will send word to your father, mother, or whomever looks after you."

Pavel nodded, face red with embarrassment.

"Yes, Excellency."

Guardsman and boy left, and no sooner had they gone than Jastrab came round the corner with Geroslaw, Steffan, Aetanis, and Caros in tow.

Steffan looked pale and shocked when he saw the scene.

Eobum saw Jastrab's face was grim, which was exactly how it should have looked, in his opinion.

"Excellency?" Jastrab sounded as if he were struggling to keep his voice professional. "I want to apologize for my men. I'll see to it that this gets settled. It's a minor matter you shouldn't have to concern yourself with. If you'll give me half a bell, I can see to it and report to you in—"

"A *minor matter*?!" Edmund's voice was almost a physical force. "Fighting where the *children play*? Four men dead, their blood watering the ground? A boy facing down a handful of grown men after winning a *sparring match*?!"

Jastrab bore this, finishing his walk toward the end of the field where Edmund, Eobum, and the other stood.

"Are you going to hang them?" Jastrab's tone was almost light as he asked this. He was serious—his facial expression made that clear, but his tone made his true feelings on the matter uncertain.

Edmund considered. "Perhaps." His voice was somewhat less bombastic now.

"An example is in order, I should think," Eobum said. He kept his voice neutral, despite the growing desire for action—for blood rising within him.

Jastrab turned to Eobum.

"Are any of your men hurt?"

Eobum shook his head.

"Fenglem was here in time to prevent that."

Jastrab nodded and answered smoothly, right on the heels of Eobum's words, almost overriding them.

"Then you might want to take your people back to your encampment. This is a matter between His Excellency and I, at this point."

Eobum lifted his chin, eyelids moving to half-mast.

"You bring up a good point, Jastrab. Some of mine should return to camp. We're not all needed here." He spoke over his shoulder. "Eranoric?"

"Eobum?"

"Take the boys back to camp. Haiga, go with him. Eobald?"

"Aye?"

"You and Fenglem stay for now."

Jastrab looked Eobum up, then down again, then shrugged a shoulder.

"Excellency? Will you allow me to discipline my men before you pass judgment?"

Edmund grunted.

"That may not be enough to answer for their crimes, Captain, but yes. You may certainly deliver your word on the matter before I deliver the *final* one."

Jastrab bowed his head.

"Sergeant Steffan!"

Steffan jumped, walked over, and delivered a crisp salute, wrists crossed before his belly, and a brief bow before standing at attention.

"Whose men are these?"

"My men, Captain." Steffan delivered this with a bleak but steady tone that was almost admirable, given the situation.

"*Wrong...*" Jastrab's tone was short, sharp, and altogether superior.

Steffan blinked.

"These are *my* men. I have given them to you to *train,* to *lead* them on the field, but make no mistake. Those who wear *my* kontusz and fight beneath *my* banner are *my* men."

"Yes, Captain!"

"Did I ask you to speak!?"

Steffan shook his head, eyes wide.

"*Answer* me!"

"N-no, Captain!" Steffan both looked and sounded as if he might well wet himself if this kept up much longer. Either that, or he might haul off and attack Jastrab.

"Which of these men started this lunacy?"

"I d-d-don't know, Captain. I was with the Lord Aet—"

"Go find out!"

Steffan jumped, turning to move toward his men.

"Now!"

Eobum felt a presence at his elbow. Turning, he saw Lakkrid and the human boys who'd stood with Maksu beside him.

"I need to be here," Lakkrid said. "If they're to be punished for something I was a part of..."

Eobum took a moment to be both proud of Lakkrid and angry with himself. Here was a boy—*his* boy—who saw responsibility instead of reprieve... who stayed to see things through even when he'd been given leave to depart.

It was what Eobum would have done—was what Eobum *had* done, in fact, when first Sergeant Geroslaw, then Jastrab, offered for him to leave this in their hands.

I'm torn between pride at who you're growing into and misery that you're growing into it so damned fast.

He laid a hand on his son's shoulder, gave it a single squeeze, then released him. For now, that would have to be enough.

He saw Geroslaw darting looks toward Kastan and had a moment of distracted amusement.

Nothing there for you, sergeant. I fear you'll have to look elsewhere.

Steffan called two men out of line. He was berating them, based on his body language, but quietly. Eobum couldn't hear what well-chosen words he was speaking.

He noticed the children hadn't moved away—the ones who had been on the far side of the field when he'd first arrived. They stood in a lump, talking and watching the goings-on.

More than a few parents and camp denizens were gathering—inching closer. They were clearly trying to figure out what commotion had called the count himself, and what'd now swelled to some twenty-odd members of his guard, out to where the children played.

Steffan walked over.

"Captain, I have the men you requested."

"*I* don't," said Jastrab, voice flat.

Steffan blinked, then got the message. He waved the two men over.

They'd crossed the twenty-five feet or so between the line of Bluemark and the end of the field where Jastrab, Edmund, Eobum, and the rest stood. They saluted as Steffan had, then stood at rough attention.

"Do you have anything to say?" Jastrab's voice was professional, as usual, displaying notes of detached neutrality.

"We regret our actions, Captain."

"Yuh, ve vas just haifing a bet uff fun, Captain."

Jastrab brightened.

"Ah, *yuh*! A bet uff fun!"

The men nodded, smiling.

Jastrab moved with an eerie, serpent's speed. He reached forward with his left hand and pulled a dirk from Steffan's belt. Before anyone knew what was happening—any of the Bluemark, at any rate—he had stabbed master *just-haifing-a-bet-uff-fun* through his neck. He then spun the dirk and offered it back to Steffan. All the while, Jastrab kept his eyes locked on the other sacrificial lamb in black—master *we-regret-our-actions*.

Lakkrid watched this impassively. He winced just slightly at the speed of Jastrab's movements and the accompanying gout of blood, but showed no other reaction.

"Steffan?"

"Yes, Captain?"

"Kill this man."

Steffan hesitated, looking at the dirk held before him—his own weapon now covered in the blood of one of his men.

"Either *you* kill *him*, or I will ... and *then* ... I'll deal ... with *you*." Jastrab kept his voice soft and almost expressionless.

The man in question began to back away. A moment later, he turned and bolted.

"The captain's betrayed us! He's ordered our deaths!"

Steffan still hadn't taken the proffered blade.

Jastrab spun the dirk in his hand, so its bloody blade was held between thumb and forefinger. He leaned back and hurled it with an exaggerated motion. A moment later, the fleeing man fell to the ground a few feet from the remaining Bluemark line.

The men drew their swords and circled up, facing the count's guard.

"Steffan—if you had to pick *one* of them to live, just one, mind you, which one would it be?" Jastrab's voice remained even and without emotion.

"Stop..." Lakkrid's voice was soft and small.

Eobum looked down at him. He was very pale. His eyes were red, but quite dry.

Jastrab ignored him, if he'd heard the boy at all.

"I don't—" Steffan was stammering now, shaking in...

... Not fear. No, he's enraged. He's just about to break and attack Jastrab.

"Stop!" This wasn't Lakkrid, but the Lord Aetanis. "Captain, I demand that you stop this at once!"

"With respect, *Lord* Aetanis, I don't answer to you."

"But Steffan *does*."

"He answers to *me*, my lord. Were he on contract and on the road with you, that would be another matter."

"You have promised me Steffan and his men, Captain. I cannot have that promise kept if you allow them to be killed!" Aetanis sounded angry, yes, but petulant as well.

"My lord, these men broke His Excellency's *peace* and threatened His Excellency's *men* in His Excellency's *camp*."

"Yes, and Eobum's son was assaulted—I *know* that. But the men who actually attacked lay dead at our feet."

Jastrab shook his head.

"In *my* name and wearing *my* colors, they committed these acts of violence. You aren't a leader of men, my lord. You'll learn."

"How dare you!"

"Speak *truth,* my lord? Or were you asking me about something else?"

"Captain Jastrab?" Lakkrid spoke up from beside Eobum.

Jastrab waited a moment, then favored Lakkrid with a lifted brow instead of a verbal response.

"Please don't kill them."

"After what they did to you?"

"He's right." Lakkrid gestured to Aetanis as he spoke. "The ones who did more than glare or threaten me all lay dead. If you kill the rest—" He paused, eyes looking at the corpses still on the ground at his feet. He swallowed but seemed unable to blink. "If you kill the rest, it'll just mean more of your people will have reason to act and think the same way. They may even come after me for the death of their brothers."

Jastrab seemed unmoved, though he looked as if he were at least considering the boy's words.

Eobum wasn't certain how he felt. Lakkrid was correct, of course, but Eobum wanted blood, wanted to see these men who stood and frightened his son—threatened his son—to swing for it, or bleed for it, or both.

"I need them, Captain," Aetanis said at last.

"They're yours if you can afford them." Jastrab shrugged a single shoulder as he said this. "Steffan as well."

"That price was already agreed upon, Captain. The count has already—"

"You misunderstand me ... *my lord.*" Jastrab stopped short of spitting those final two words. "Steffan, you are released from my service. I grant you, and these men, your lives." He marched across the field, raising his voice. "Take off those kontusze. You're to leave anything that isn't yours by law or right in your tents. You are dismissed from my service and will be out of my encampment before dawn. Where you go and how you get there, I neither care nor want to know. If you steal from me, know that I will hunt you down and bury you in holes up to your necks, then fill them in with dirt until the animals come for you. You have that boy—the very boy you threatened—to thank for your lives." He paused for only a moment before turning back to Edmund and company, then shouted, "Go! Out of my sight!"

Steffan watched this with a stern expression. As Jastrab approached, he pulled off his black kontusze, folding it before pulling his sword and laying it atop the garment. These he offered to Jastrab as he returned.

"Sergeant!" Jastrab lifted his chin and made his voice carry beneath the lowering twilight sky.

At first, Steffan looked confused. His face showed a hint of anger a moment later as Geroslaw stepped over.

"Captain?"

"Take these back to camp and hand them to the quartermaster. Then meet me in front of my tent. I'm expanding your command."

Geroslaw nodded and took the gear from Steffan, who tried and failed not to glare.

"Satisfied, Excellency?" Jastrab spoke in his professional tones once more.

Edmund nodded slowly.

"I am, actually."

Jastrab nodded, then bowed. As he turned to leave, he met Eobum's eye.

"I'd like to hold off on our conversation, if I may."

Eobum nodded slowly. Jastrab would have enough to put in order back at his encampment. Eobum still wanted blood, but Lakkrid had the right of it. This way was, in fact, better overall.

"I don't believe we'll have time before I head out, but I'll see what I can arrange," said he.

Jastrab nodded, then looked down at the dead men—once *his* men—who littered the ground. He nodded once more, then turned and departed.

"Father?"

Eobum turned fully. Lakkrid stood with the other two boys—so silent he'd almost forgotten they were there.

"Can we go back to camp now?"

Eobum looked at Edmund, who nodded silently, then back to Lakkrid.

"We can." To the other two boys, he asked, "Would you two join us for supper?"

They looked at one another, then back to him.

"I'm expected home. I vould, but vitout varning, my mother vould be vroth vit me." Vlk looked sad and disappointed as he said this.

Andrej nodded. He, too, was expected, it seemed.

Eobum offered one final word on the matter before leading Lakkrid away.

"Tell your parents I'd like a word with them tomorrow or tonight if they'd prefer."

They nodded, and Vlk handed Lakkrid back his shield.

Eobum saw Fenglem had retrieved his sword, laying his borrowed one down beside the first man he'd killed. Eobald had already retrieved their azhkasts.

With a hand on the back of Lakkrid's neck and a look to Kastan, Eobum bowed to Edmund and led his family back to what had been home for the past few years.

He wondered how much longer that would be the case. Today had been the sort of thing that showed a community's truth to itself and

anyone who cared to look. He reckoned they would all learn this one's truth soon enough.

-II-

Lakkrid began to shake almost immediately upon starting to walk. His slightly porcine nose flared as his breathing sped up.

Eobum knew what was coming and did his best to speed the boy along without turning their movement into a full-blown run. They made it less than twenty yards.

"Stop." Lakkrid managed to blurt this out in a gummy, husky voice before breaking free of his father's hand and dropping to his knees.

He vomited.

Eobum put an arm around his chest and hauled him off of his knees, allowing the boy to stand, but put all weight onto Eobum's forearm.

The affair didn't take long.

When Lakkrid was finished, he put his hands onto his father's arm and slowly pushed himself back upright.

A moment later, Eobum saw him register that Eobald and Fenglem had moved to flank them, blocking the view of anyone still near the play yard. None of Lakkrid's friends would see him in a moment of what might be considered shameful, childish weakness.

"Better?" Haiga's voice was soft but not coddling.

Lakkrid gave a slow nod.

Eobald spoke up. His voice was kindly.

"D'you need a moment? Sure we can give y'one..."

Lakkrid shook his head. In a voice that sounded all too hollow, he spoke.

"I'm ready to head back now..."

Lakkrid still held Eobum's arm in front of his chest, gripping it with loose fingers. Now he lifted it over his head and slid to one side, placing it around his own shoulders before beginning to walk.

A few moments later, they were back at camp.

-III-

The Bluemark's sergeants sat around the small bonfire, perched on either side of their captain and his wife—Geroslaw among them.

He sat to Jastrab's right along with Daian and Blevelsket, her hair in a single war braid. To the captain's other side, he saw Waltyr, Ulrek, and Kal.

He was briefly amused to note that all six remaining sergeants had managed to sit in order from shortest to tallest on each side. Dark-haired Blevelsket sat to Jastrab's immediate right, slender, reserved Waltyr to Sjelesanger's left. Daian sat across from Ulrek's ginger-beard and the head that it wore, and Geroslaw sat opposite the massive Kal of Shesh. The firelight gleamed off of his bald pate.

"Waltyr is no friend of Steffan's," Geroslaw said under his breath. "That's sure. His son, Ulrek, drank with Steffan often enough but won't stand against his father."

Is that what you believe or what you're certain of?

His own father's voice scraped at him, as it always did in matters of social uncertainty.

"I *think* Ulrek's loyalty will be to his father. He might try to convince Jastrab to change his mind, I suppose..."

He allowed his gaze to roll over Kal's bearded face. Geroslaw looked at his muscled arms and his long limbs and came to a single conclusion.

"I hope he's not a Steffan loyalist. That is a man I would rather not fight."

"Odvážna krv!" Jastrab's voice was high and clear, rending the night, as it called the ring of men to order. This was no simple act, as there were some two hundred men and women here around the fire. Only those on guard duty, those few who were injured, and those men who had but lately been under Steffan's command were absent.

The men's collective reply was a product of having been made rote more than zeal or enthusiasm.

"Odvážna krv," came the reply.

The Bluemark motto—Brave Blood—was spoken with far more pride and fire under ordinary circumstances. Tonight, however, the company's membership bore a numb anger they hoped would be given direction at this meeting.

"I've dismissed Steffan from our number," said Jastrab. "With him, fourteen of the men that were under his command are likewise stricken from our rolls."

"Captain?" A voice from somewhere in the ring across the fire from Jastrab.

"Náčelník?" Jastrab recognized the voice, apparently.

There was a hesitation before the man spoke.

"...What happened?"

Jastrab nodded.

"It's enough, I think, to say that they disgraced our name—not only overall but before the count himself."

There was an instant uproar at this.

Jastrab held his hands up high, palms toward the crowd to quiet them. When they'd drawn down their outrage sufficiently so that he could speak, he did so.

"I'll tell you if you want to know."

They grunted and nodded at this.

Jastrab bowed his head, drew in a breath, and exhaled a plume of steam.

"Steffan's men moved to attack an orc boy who knocked down a human one in a babe's lyst."

They stared.

"An orc man joined in to defend the boy and wound up killing two of Steffan's men." He paused as the group absorbed this news. There were mumbles of anger and even rage, but the sound was decidedly soft compared to its earlier roar of protest.

"Is the orc dead?" Náčelník sounded uncertain how he felt about all of this.

"No."

"When's he to swing?" A woman's voice—this, Geroslaw didn't recognize, or at least couldn't put a name to it.

"Never, for this, at least." Jastrab's tone was matter-of-fact.

The response to this answer was a feral growl that made the Bluemark's collective sound more like wolves than men.

"Then where's he being held? Hells, *we* can take care of *that*!"

"Right now, you need to close your mouth and let my husband speak." As Sjelesanger spoke, the voices of the crowd diminished. "Before you run off half-drunk and unsheathe your swords to avenge one of your own, it might be a wise idea to remember that these men *aren't* your own anymore. They gave up that right when they attacked a child for the sin of victory."

They quieted—most of them, at any rate. Some respected her. Some feared her. Others looked upon her with disdain for feeling she was able to speak to them from a position of authority. Most managed to reign themselves in at her words, however, so that was something.

"Mistress ... if an orc boy knocked a man's son into the dirt, they were likely just putting him in his place, surely!" The same woman's voice from earlier sounded sulky and put out of countenance.

"She's right," a man said. "Our men lay dead because that orc man got involved. If he'd minded his own, nobody'd be dead now, and the boy would've been taught his place."

The absurdity of this statement was driven home more severely by how matter-of-factly it was delivered. The speaker had used a hearty, "be-reasonable" tone as if Sjelesanger had suggested something outlandish ... like marching faster in order to make town before dusk or keeping one's gear in working order.

Jastrab stepped forward toward the fire. All voices quieted.

"Do you call me Captain?"

There were a score or more murmured affirmations. When Jastrab spoke again, his voice was substantively louder, though held a decided lack of anger.

"I asked you a question. Do you call me Captain?"

"Aye!" This time the response was more genuine, though more than a few sounded as if they'd said so grudgingly.

"Let me be clear," said Jastrab. "None of you have pissed on my banner, my name, or your brothers and sisters thus far," he grinned, "...that I know of, at least. Some of you might actually enjoy that last. If so, I won't judge."

They laughed. The mood of the crowd grew lighter for it.

"What I mean to say is this. Steffan accepted responsibility for the men he commanded. It's why he still lives. It was the right decision for him—for any leader. The most aggressive men who menaced the boy are dead. Good. They died ignobly ... in the midst of an equally ignoble act. Again ... good."

The grumbling had begun again, but Geroslaw thought it was less aggressive than it had been a moment before.

"They acted in *direct* counter to our contract—to your coin purse and our collective name. They've been removed from that name as a result. They might have hung for it. The boy belongs to one of the count's men, and the count knows the boy personally."

They grew stony at this.

"If any of you don't like or accept my decision... don't accept how I handled the actions of those who stood too blind and too foolish to remember that *they* stood for something more than their own greedy joy— too selfish to remember your faces and the brotherhood they claimed to be a part of... to you, I say you're welcome to leave without question, argument, or hard feelings. Come to me or your sergeants and make your will known to us. We'll release you and send you on your way without a *single* glare or angry word."

They looked to one another—Geroslaw could see their shadowed heads turning this way and that as they murmured.

"As for those men? As for any man or woman who abandons us— who walks away without the spine or stomach to stand up and say they're going... Well? Hells haul them home."

This was met with laughter and growls of agreement.

"Questions?"

"Captain?"

Geroslaw knew that voice. He'd swear to it.

"Speak."

Jastrab didn't know this one by name, apparently.

"What about the rest of Steffan's former men?"

Jastrab grinned.

"They'll be split amongst Sergeants Ulrek, Kal, and Geroslaw."

"How?" This was the same man.

"Do you have a preference?" Jastrab offered a grin that didn't quite reach his eyes.

"...I do."

"Speak it, then."

"Sergeant Geroslaw, Captain."

"He's a training sergeant, Barneb," another man said.

"Aye, he is, and you're an oaf. The man who knows how to train you knows how to use you without throwing your life away, don't he?"

Three more men stood up.

"We're with Geroslaw, also, Captain, if we may."

Geroslaw's grin widened. That voice he knew. Aethel was one of the three men under Steffan's command who'd known how to stand in line. The other two were likely, well, the other two.

"Anyone else with a strong desire one way or the other?" Jastrab sounded amused, but only mildly so.

No other person stood or spoke.

"Very well. You four are assigned to Sergeant Geroslaw."

They saluted and sat back down, putting their heads together.

"Does anyone have anything else they want to ask or say?"

Silence.

"All right. Then we drink!"

The men cheered and broke apart to fetch their mugs.

Geroslaw stood, nodded to the captain, and turned to walk toward his new men. Before he'd gotten far, Kal called him back.

He turned to oblige, but the Sheshik giant had crossed the distance between them and now towered over him by nearly a foot. *Hells be hid* but the man was tall.

"If you need help training your men—sparring them against real opponents, I mean..." he spat to one side, "...just ask." The man's voice was a smoky tenor pitch, not quite free of its Sheshik accent. His use of the Trade Tongue was flawless, but he stammered and paused when he spoke with any animation.

Geroslaw nodded, smiling as benignly as he could manage. Kal didn't intimidate him because of his size, but because of his unreadability. He didn't know the man and found him too practiced at the Trade Tongue to fathom easily.

"Thank you, Effendi Kal." This Sheshik title was, he'd been taught, a term that offered respect to the person's wisdom or high education—a mark of honor, if not deference. He had no idea if his understanding was flawed. He *was* certain that the term was used in a positive context, making it worth the risk here.

Kal nodded, offered a bow, and a rolling flutter of his bright hand from belt to brow before righting himself.

Geroslaw moved toward his new men. Barneb offered him a small grin as he approached.

"Sergeant."

"Barneb, Aethel..." He looked to the other men, waiting.

"Borgus, Fillip." Aethel indicated each man in turn.

Geroslaw nodded, accepting a mug Barneb had procured from somewhere. He sipped it and was surprised to taste spicy apple as if it were laced with an excess of both red pepper and cinnamon. He was instantly full of warmth spreading from his core to his limbs, though this didn't feel as if it were the simple effect of alcohol.

"What is..." He took another sip, his face splitting into a smile.

"Nosp cider," Aethel offered, grinning. "Warms you up in a hurry, don't it?"

Geroslaw nodded—opened his mouth to speak—grinned—took another swallow.

"Tell me one of you brewed this," said he.

Barneb puffed out his chest a touch.

"Aye, Sergeant... less you don't care for it. Then Aethel made it."

They all laughed at that.

"Don't drain the cask or keg or whatever you have it stored in. Not tonight, at any rate."

They looked at him, waiting.

"We ride out at first light."

Barneb raised his brows, interested.

"Where are we bound?"

"Southeast. I'll tell you more when we're on the road."

In response to this, Barneb turned to the others.

"Right, you heard the man, lads. Fill your mugs now before I put the rest away."

To a man, they drained their mugs, then held them out for refills.

Geroslaw snorted.

"We won't be back here for some weeks, so pack accordingly. I'd like to be on the road by the eighth bell past midnight. If we haven't left by the tenth bell—"

"Hells haul us home. Aye, Sergeant." Barneb grinned. "We'll be ready. We'll meet in front of your tent?"

Geroslaw shook his head.

"I'll have it down and rolled before then. Much as I expect you'll do to your own."

"We're in the barracks tent—we four," Barneb said. His voice wasn't embarrassed, merely matter-of-fact.

Geroslaw raised his brows.

"Well ... we'll keep warm, I suppose."

Barneb and the others blinked.

"Won't be sleeping in my own tent while you four sleep raw beneath the stars, Barneb." Geroslaw made his voice playful rather than incredulous.

The men looked at one another, then back at him, smiling.

Barneb reached over and poured the best part of what remained in his mug into Geroslaw's.

"We'll be there to help you tear it down." When Geroslaw blinked in mild surprise, Barneb made his own voice playful. "We're not gonna sleep in your tent and not know how to pull it down or set it up, Sergeant." He made a small salute with his leather mug and drained its remaining contents in a single pull.

They'll do, Geroslaw thought, grinning. *Yes, indeed. They'll do nicely.*

-IV-

"Lashjuk," Eobum spoke softly so as not to underscore the matter at hand with unnecessary fanfare.

She looked up from her place by the fire. Her boys were on either side of her. Predictably, Sulok was between her and Eranoric. Maksu sat to her right, staring into the fire, legs out in front of him.

"El palrym ... Ed awka ed rym." *(We sit in family council ... I and my circle.)*

She nodded, looked up, and made to stand.

"Hrek erld nqas?" *(Will you stay?)*

She froze in mid-rise, then slowly sat back down, eyes widening.

"Eobum." She shook her head, trying to find her voice. "Ed de erld rym ... de erld palrym." *(I'm not of your circle ... not of your family council.)*

Eobum offered a slow nod, then reverted to the Trade Tongue.

"*That...*" he stood and moved toward his temporary home in Fenglem and Haiga's shared tent, "is *your* decision."

Eobum reached into the tent to find his cloak ... and Lakkrid's for good measure. She seemed, to his mind, to be considering his words. She hadn't gotten up or made as if to gather her children, at any rate. That was something.

"You're certain?" she said at last.

Eobum turned, crossing back around the cookfire to his low-backed wooden seat. He tossed his son's cloak over the boy's head so it covered his face, making him look as if he were a dark green ghost from a child's game of Haunted Forest. He'd hoped the act would force a smile, and at first, he thought he'd get one as the cloak remained in place. A moment later, however, Lakkrid brought his right hand out from under it and calmly pulled it off, setting it behind the small of his back.

Eobum fought back a sigh. He spoke to Lashjuk as he settled himself behind his son once more.

"You and yours live with I and mine. Until that changes, I see no need to ask you to leave. There's a saying among the high folk—no secrets on the pillow. Do you know it?"

She shook her head.

"It means family shouldn't be expected to keep secrets from one another. The saying speaks about man and wife, but it applies to kin and clan just the same, I think."

She nodded, eyeing him. She said nothing but didn't make as if to gather herself and her children to withdraw.

"Have you sat palrym before?" Eobum did his best to keep his voice light.

"Once, the night before…" She shrugged. Shortly before, she'd been taken as a slave, no doubt.

Eobum gave a sign of acceptance at that.

"I'll lay out matters I feel we need to discuss. All get a voice on them. I'll make the final decision based on that. Hold nothing back that might harm the unit." He looked into the fire, watching Alusc taste a small piece of goat haunch he'd been roasting on a spit. He seemed to be pleased with the result of his day's work. "When all matters I'm aware of have been dealt with, we'll see if anyone has anything else to bring to the rym. If so, we'll discuss it. If not, we'll end it and go to less weighty matters."

"Like Adric's Usclyd," Lakkrid said.

Inwardly, Eobum breathed a sigh of relief. Lakkrid had been silent for the three hours they'd been back at camp and had barely moved. Outwardly, Eobum nodded and made a gesture of agreement.

Lashjuk was about to speak when she froze as if she were an animal scenting prey.

Eobum followed her gaze.

"Nye-nye-nye," said Adric.

He'd stood, blocking someone's entry into camp, spreading his hands wide at the level of his midriff as if to ask, "What?" He then jerked, moving to the right, then to the left as if dancing with the newcomer. It wasn't until this last movement that Adric's dancing partner was clearly visible.

It was Kastan.

The men nearest the entrance—Aderano, Eobald, and Alblod—laughed at the byplay.

She stepped back, then right, then back again, Adric matching her stride for stride, forcing her back out of the makeshift entrance by following her. She threw up her hands, clearly frustrated, and turned to go.

Adric stood at his ease, his posture displaying more arrogance than any normal man should be able to carry. As he relaxed and turned back to those nearest his former seat, a gloat flowering on his face, Kastan spun, grabbed him by his left arm, and flung him like a bale of hay some four feet away, behind and to her right.

Adric stumbled, grumbled, and tumbled, coming to a stop in a one-legged crouch. The sole of his left boot was on the ground, as were both of his hands, but his right leg ended up kicked all the way forward, heel planted at his leg's full extension.

Lashjuk moved to stand but was stopped by the genuine laughter this little comedy had elicited from the crowd. More than a few of the men actually applauded.

Kastan bowed, then turned back to offer Adric a hand. Grinning, he took it, got to his feet, and gave Kastan a brief, "All right, well done, yes, yes," embrace, patting her on the back.

She walked toward the fire, smiling and blushing rather prettily from the activity. She stopped short when her eyes fell on Lashjuk. Kastan's color rose a notch, her expression full of surprise.

Lashjuk stopped just short of a glare in retaliation.

"Something troubles you, Lady?"

"Um." Kastan looked utterly taken aback. "N-no, Lady. I simply wasn't expecting..." She shook her head, laughing awkwardly. "Well, truth be told, I wasn't expecting *you*—or rather, for you to..." She shook her head again, unable to finish.

"Kastan Percoy?" Eobum spoke up, cutting in gently. "May I present Lashjuk of Black Falls." He looked to Lashjuk and gestured to Kastan. "Lashjuk, may I present the Lady Kastan of Sunŭv Dar."

Lashjuk looked between Eobum and Kastan, nodding slowly.

"Lady," she said by way of greeting.

"We'll eat soon, then hold council, Lady." Eobum trailed off, looking at Kastan—looking a question.

Lashjuk reached forward to smooth Maksu's hair back. As she did so, she spoke to Eobum in a flat, smooth tone.

"Wrid de erld *ok*... Aehe hrek wrid nqel? Wrid palrym?" *(She isn't your sister. Why shall she stay? Is she family?)*

"No, Lady, I am not. Not in any formal sense, at least," Kastan said as she crouched down to Lakkrid's right. "Ed..." She paused for a moment, then spoke in two rapid bursts of speech.

"Ed palrym, uhhh... ka ed vresh." She paused, looking shocked and embarrassed. "No! No, I mean ga! Ga ed vra!" She fell onto her bottom, covering her face with both hands and groaning into them.

Lakkrid giggled. It was abrupt and shocking even to the boy himself. A second, then a third eruption of mirth shook him before he could master himself. This, in turn, set Maksu off in much the same manner.

"Kastan... Ka ed vresh? You said," Lakkrid paused, succumbing to another fit of laughter, "You said *my family's sword's my dirt!*" He tried to claim his calm, distant demeanor again, but another peal of laughter burst from him without warning. "Your sword's made of dirt!" The blood rushed to his face, turning him an alarming shade of darker green, like shadowed grass. He was laughing so hard his eyes were beginning to stream. He couldn't breathe.

"I know, I *know*!" Kastan pulled her hands down, shaking her head and blushing mightily.

It had been something of a *rhyming* mistake. *Ga ed vra* meant *In my heart* and would have been an easy, warm answer to Lashjuk's question.

Eobum put a hand over his son's eyes, blocking out the light.

"Breeeeeeeathe," said he.

With no visual stimulus to perpetuate it, Lakkrid's laughing fit quieted soon enough.

"I won't be staying, in any event," Kastan said. "I only came by to check on Lakkrid and..." She trailed off, looking at Maksu, who was still grinning. "This fellow."

Eobum removed his hand, replacing it on his own knee.

"Maksu," Lakkrid said, following her gaze.

Kastan nodded, reaching over to brush a few errant hairs up off of Lakkrid's forehead.

He bore this patiently—actually smiling at her, his tiny lower tusks seeming to slide into a near-parallel with the line of his nose.

"You're all right?"

He nodded, still smiling.

"Erld vra?" *(Your heart?)*

"Aye, I'm fine." Again, he nodded, his grin widening slightly.

"*Awka erld ka?*" *(And your sword?)* "Eh? Still made of wood?" As he nodded, giggling once more, she gave his shoulder a playful shove. "*Mine's* made of dirt. *Much* better than wood." Her tone was matter-of-fact and full of dismissive pride as if he and his lackluster sword were beneath her.

Lakkrid fell over as much from the new fit of laughter that seized him as from the shove.

Maksu was beside himself, pointing at Lakkrid, rocking back and forth as he issued great braying peals of laughter.

Even Lashjuk was smiling in spite of herself.

Kastan stood.

"Well, all seems in order here, Commander." She took on a tone of mock-formality. "I shall leave these brave men in your capable hands."

Eobum arched both brows, face dominated by a broad grin, lit as much by the gleam in his eyes as the fire before him.

"*Aye*, Lady. I thank you. We'll carry on then."

She held his gaze for a long moment, then turned to Lashjuk.

"I'm pleased your boy's all right, Lady. It... It was lovely to meet you." Her tone was awkward and uncertain. She bowed once more, then turned and headed toward the exit. She stopped long enough to raise her fists to Adric in a mock-fighting stance. He raised his own in much the same manner, grinning. They bumped bright fists and exchanged a soft word or two before she exited the camp.

Eobum noted that Lashjuk seemed torn as to whether she was pleased or put out by Kastan's appearance.

"She's proof, Lashjuk," said he.

"Of?"

"The idea that gold doesn't always drown goodness."

Lashjuk offered a slow, thoughtful nod but said nothing more.

-V-

When the evening meal was all but finished, Eobum lifted his chin and spoke in a voice that was sharp enough to cut through the general chatter but not much more.

"Idor Adys," said he.

"Idor Adys," they replied—all save Lashjuk and her boys.

"It means Forest Shadows—it's our gniedlēoþ in Eoden Zhprek... The words that make us ... *us*." Lakkrid stage whispered this to Maksu and, by extension, most of the camp's other occupants.

Eobum nodded at this. He bowed his head for a moment, collecting his thoughts. Nobody spoke. After a long moment, with his thoughts ordered and the likely course of this conversation charted, he broke his silence.

"First, there's a matter that will make you smile, I should think." He reached into a leather bag at his neck, pulling it from beneath his woolen kaftan's wide collar. The bag made a suspicious jingling sound as he removed it from around his neck.

He looked to see that both Adric near the camp's entrance and Eranoric across the fire to Eobum's left were likewise pulling out their pouches, removing them from around their necks. Both men wore satisfied smiles, though Eranoric's was, predictably, slightly more subdued.

Fenglem and Haiga stood to walk toward Eobum, Lakkrid rising to stand behind them.

Alusc, Hrothgian, and Aderano stood to line up before Eranoric. Eobum waited until he saw that Adric's men—Riclov, Alblod, and Eobald—had likewise queued up before their captain.

Satisfied, Eobum reached into his money pouch and pulled out a much smaller sackcloth bag, handing it to Feng, who nodded and sat back down. He repeated this with Haiga and, with a smaller bag, Lakkrid.

"You pay your boy as well?" Lashjuk sounded somewhere between surprised and pleased.

"Half a share until he's older. He does a boy's share of the work and rarely complains over a hard pull. Eranoric, Adric, and the others watch him to make certain he isn't dragging or shirking."

Lashjuk turned to look at Eranoric, who nodded, putting his pouch back under his kaftan.

"He keeps up the help he's been, I'll start pay'n Sulok s'well," Eranoric said. As if to emphasize, he slipped his hand to the back of the boy's neck and gave a gentle squeeze.

Sulok smiled, eyes half-closing, bronze cheeks darkening before the fire at the praise.

Lashjuk was about to say something to this when Eobum's movement caught her eye. She turned back toward him, eyes falling on his outstretched hand. It held a small bag of coins toward her.

"Wh-what?"

"You and yours walked and kept an eye on the prisoners, same as the rest of us. You helped put an end to Geatbern and have been a help to Alusc here at camp," said Eobum.

She blinked, then shook her head.

"Take it," said he. "A full share is—" He was cut off by Eobald's confused excitement.

"S'more than a season's pay here. 'Ow much're the dogs worth?"

Eobum grinned.

"Oh, bout eighty-five vévodové between them," said he. "Taking out a third for Alusc and Haiga to sort provisions and gear, each purse should be five vévodové, and five grófok heavier than usual." This was two weeks of work for a maker of things, such as Lashjuk and her gnash had been. Coupled with their normal pay, it added up to a tidy sum indeed.

He continued to hold out the bag in Lashjuk's direction.

"It's like this every sykli and a half or so. You'll get used to it, Og." Lakkrid spoke as if her staying were a matter of course—a formality that she simply hadn't made official yet. To him, her joining the unit wasn't a matter worth discussing. It had already happened.

For her part, Lashjuk slowly reached out to accept the purse but paused before closing her hand around it fully.

"Eobum ... did the *others* agree to this?"

"They don't get a say as to what I do with my share of our pay." He shook his head as she drew in breath to argue. "Stay your wrath, Lashjuk. You may come and go as you like. But I won't have you penniless should you decide to go your way. You can refuse, I suppose, but you'd just find the purse in your pack a day or two after leaving our company." His voice was calm and even but full of a warmth he himself hadn't known he'd intended.

She lowered her head and nodded, taking full possession of the purse at last.

"Thank you," said she.

He nodded and said no more on the matter.

When the men had settled and their own purses had been stowed, he spoke again.

"We owe Yindrich more than thanks for lining our pockets. He and his were questioned by the count and found news that matched rumor Edmund'd been hearing." He paused, then leaned forward. "Northeastern Kovalun burns. It's suffered raids, rape, and ruin."

"Who's doing the raiding?" This was Aderano. His voice was thoughtful in its gruff baritone.

"Who d'ya think's doing it? It's us o'course." Eobald sounded angry and with good enough reason.

"Aye, Edmund and I discussed that. It's what we're all meant to see and believe. So says Edmund as well."

"Do we know who it *really* is, then?" This was Adric. "Can think of a couple of lumps in the wastes up north who'd blame us, right enough. D'we know which one's about it?"

Of *course* Adric would see it first. He was the last man you wanted to play against when coin was on the line and the first one to call when you needed to find a way out of the box you'd got yourself into.

"Aye, I'll tell you, but you'll not like the answer," said Eobum. Then he cocked his head to the side, reconsidering. "Come to that, I lie. Adric, *you*, at least, will like the answer, now I think on it."

Adric grinned, his yellowed teeth on display.

"Garn, then. Tell'oos."

"Edmund's convinced it's Harn," said Eobum. "The Vévoda himself."

He waited for them to digest this before continuing. Some were enraged. Others were shocked into silence. All understood. Harn's apparent strategy was to blame the Eodenth, then take nearly sole possession of that unwieldy land and its people. Eobum hadn't told them this latter part, but still. The Eodenth were often viewed with suspicion by the rest of the empire. But this? If left unchecked, this was apt to turn suspicion into outright retaliation against Eodenth who'd never raised a *fist*, let alone razed a thorpe. Given all of them had either grown up in or had blood ties to Eoden, *none* considered the matter minor.

When he felt the men had processed their initial reactions to this revelation, Eobum asked Adric, Eranoric, Fenglem, and Haiga to stand sentinel. He wanted their eyes focused on the area outside of their encampment. They would remain in camp and close enough to hear his words, but this would prevent others outside of camp overhearing their conversation.

That accomplished, he laid out what Edmund wanted them to do and why. When it was done, he asked them for any questions they might have. There were none. He doubted that was true, mind. They had questions a-plenty; he was certain. They simply wanted time to chew on them before asking. The men would either come to their captains or Eobum himself between tonight and when they arrived at Haluzfeld eight or nine days hence. He was patient. They'd get to their questions, eventually.

"Anything more, then? Anything else we should all hear?" Eobum looked around, making eye contact with each in turn. He was about to call their palrym to a close when Lashjuk spoke up.

"Eobum?"

He looked to her, expression expectant.

"Does the count mean to elevate you? Does he mean, do you think, to give you land and title?"

Eobum offered a thin smile, though it was Eranoric who answered.

"They'll never call Eobum to the line, Lady."

"Why not? Armed service and glory won are the usual paths, are they not?"

"Are." Eranoric nodded. "and 'ikely always will be. Changes nothing."

Adric turned to meet her eyes, nodding, before turning back to his post.

"Eobum's brave as hells's own harbinger and can knock more than a few of those so-called knights 'nto their precious blue backsides, an' no mistake." His profile grinned. "Land's no' for the likes of us, though. Open sky's hard to burn or raid. Only way to take what's ours—s'really ours—is to take our lives."

Eranoric nodded, adding his own word on the matter. "Edmund's fine n'fair. A good man, gold and all, and that's rare enough. Eobum gets called to the line, and we risk home being a place and no more an *us*. D'you see?"

Lashjuk nodded, looking thoughtful.

"I trust Edmund's heart," Eobum said at last. "I don't trust his wisdom and ability to see and hear us when we call if we live in a thorpe somewhere. If all goes ill, we can, as things stand, walk away. It hasn't done in the eight years I've served him."

"...Nine next new moon," Adric said.

Eobum nodded.

"Aye, nine then—Edmund's ruthless to his foes, kind to all others. His heart's full of poetry, story, and song, and he cannot stand to see ill done to good people." Eobum sighed, then finished his thought. He'd begun—may as well say it, and have done. "I worry he's too in love with how he wants the world to *be* to see what the world truly *is*—what it is *now*, at *this* time."

Lashjuk considered that for a long moment before speaking again.

"Thank you," said she and said no more.

"Anything else?"

"Aye," Eobald spoke up.

"Go on, then," Eobum said.

"Bluemark," said Eobald. "We'd best leave nothing of value behind. Some'll think 'bout piss'n on'r beds while we're a'field. Might well go scavengin' through camp while we're gun, just ta see if we've left 'nything worth takin'."

Eobum considered this, then nodded.

"It's a good point, Eobald." He sat back, looking thoughtful. Finally, he spoke his last word on the matter.

"We'll need a horse."

"We've got one," Lashjuk said.

"Coming along, then? You're welcome, of course, but you surely don't have to."

"El palrym, erld zak." *(We're family, you said.)*

He nodded at this.

"Aye, Lady. As you say."

"We have a horse," she said again.

Eobum nodded.

"We have a horse," said he.

"Alusc, Haiga—be certain you get a rig to haul whatever we can on the beast's back without overloading it. Leave room for a single rider, as well. Doesn't have to be comfortable, just serviceable."

Both men nodded.

"The rest of you, Eobald has the right of it. Pack, stow, or bury anything you value. No sense leaving anything behind only to be angry at finding it lost or ruined on our return."

They nodded, each in turn.

"Anything else?" Nobody spoke. After a silent ten count, Eobum called things to an end. "Idor Adys. We leave not tomorrow but the morning after."

"Will you?" Sulok's voice, head turned to look up at Eranoric.

"Fetch me soul of skin and clay, my lord? 'Course I will." He smiled down at the boy, who beamed back.

As Eranoric started to move off, Sulok asked another question.

"Can I get it?"

Eranoric snorted.

"Yer not my squire, my lord, are ya? Sit and settle. I'm back in two flaps of a wing. Then ya can play for everyone."

Sulok blanched at this but smiled just the same. He was, Eobum thought, both terrified and excited by the prospect all at a go.

Adric was fetching his Usclyd. He played with its five tuning pegs, then checked the horsehair of his bow before starting to play three long, descending notes that caused nearly everyone to smile.

Adric grinned 'round at them all, holding the third note and shaking his fingers along the neck to vibrate it.

"You lads ready, then?" His tone was full of the sort of triumphant glee that only artists and conquerors ever really seem to know.

The men gave their assent in ayes and ohhhh yes's.

"What is it?" Sulok's eyes were wide, his smile broad.

Alusc leaned forward and tapped Sulok on the knee to get his attention.

"A cradle tale 'bout fighting for a cradle-tale's king." The man's voice was full of amused rue. "It's how the Emperor'd like to think we see him, but there ain't never been a king or emperor worthy o'such. You'll see."

Eobum bowed his head at that, albeit briefly.

"Might be, Alusc. No need to piss on hope."

Alusc's nod at this bore a hint of contrition but not much more.

"Aye, Eobum. Fair. Hope's free."

Adric waited to see Eranoric arrive with his bledu drum under one arm, striking its surface with rapid, rolling taks as he sat between Sulok and Alusc.

Eobum saw him exchange a look with Adric, then raise his chin before he spoke to the group at large.

"Sulok's been learnin' ta play bledu, lads."

They nodded. A few of them smiled.

"My lord? D'you wanna show us what you've learned *first* ... or after Adric and I play a bit?"

Sulok was now so pale as to have lost nearly all the gold in his complexion.

"...Af-fter, please. I wanna hear you play first."

Eranoric gave him a dubious look, accompanied by a grin.

"Won't get you off the hook for it, my lord. You needn't think it will."

Eobum noted Sulok's color return, and all at once. His cheeks were suffused with a blush that called to mind a summer sunset.

"I know." The boy sounded pleased for the attention, though still afraid. Eobum thought that was normal enough for a boy his age.

"Ready then?" Adric's voice crossed the fire in a rising sing-song.

In answer, Eranoric gave another rapid flurry of taks. He leaned his head forward toward Adric even as he increased the volume of his strikes, moving his hands toward the not-quite-center of the drum.

At some invisible cue that both men alone sensed, Eranoric stopped his rolling and took up a new rhythm.

Doom tak-tak, doom tak-tak, doom tak-tak, doom tak-ka.

At the same moment, Adric played those three long notes once more, only now they rode on the breast of Eranoric's drumming.

As they finished the fourth *ka* in the drum pattern, Eobald began to sing. By the third word, everyone other than Lashjuk and her children was singing at the top of their lungs.

> *Beat the drum early, my brother.*
> *Beat the drum. Welcome the dawn.*
> *Raise your voice. Call to arms all of your fellows.*
> *We fight at our sovereign's call.*
> *Come lad, I see your eyes,*
> *Terror behind them.*
> *I know that you fear what's to come.*
> *I've seen it a thousand times.*
> *Call me not liar.*
> *In the hour that heralds the sun.*
> *Heretics tell you a soldier fears nothing,*
> *And poets give war her refrain,*
> *But when the war horn rings true,*
> *On the morning's first blue,*
> *Then your heart may be thunder again.*

Eobum smiled. For now, their camp was full of music and fellowship. Even as they sang, however, and sang a song he'd always loved, his mind wandered, and his heart felt heavy.

> *Time is a child running scared of its shadow.*
> *It flies though you wish it would crawl.*
> *Home lay behind you a thousand miles distant.*
> *Tomorrow you stand, or you fall.*

He looked down at his son, singing at the very top of his lungs, then at Lashjuk and her boys.

He knew Haiga and Lakkrid wanted him to take her to wife, as the Venzene referred to it. He thought he might be willing, given Lakkrid's warmth to her—one obstacle out of the way, at least. She was breathtaking to look upon and full of a fire he found all too familiar. He wasn't blind to either her beauty or his attraction to her mind and will. He was fairly certain, however, that she had no interest. She *expected* him to want her, perhaps even to suggest that she should repay his kindness by accounting herself *his*.

She's waiting to see if I want payment—if I'll hint or outright ask her to get on her back in return for what I've given her. Eobum shook his head. *She doesn't want me. She wants me to prove false. She wants me,* he grinned at this realization, *to prove that I'm human.*

An absurd thought. There were users and rapers, tyrants, and turncoats all over the Empire, hells—all over the world, as far as he knew. Humans had no claim to the office of greed. Well, perhaps the office of greediest, but they certainly weren't the only monsters that walked the world.

The Bluemark, Edmund's war, Kastan's father and his insistence on traditional marriage for his raven-haired daughter—despite what she or *anyone else* wanted for her... it all seemed suddenly on fire, or at least ready to light.

Blessedly I'm getting Feng, Haiga, and Lakkrid out of here for a few weeks. Let the remaining Bluemark carry their axes onto an empty field. Maybe with no timber, they'll chop one another down.

He smirked at this wishful thought, then his mindset itself on a familiar road of deeper reflection.

He allowed himself a moment to think, as he always did at night around the fire, that same bleak but blessed thought.

This may be the last moment we're all together—awake and aware. Eobum took a moment to memorize each and every face, just as he always did. They were his, and he would not—*would not*—forget their faces or voices so long as he was able. *We're here, now, in fellowship. If this memory is my last with them, if I or they should not wake or find that tomorrow holds our last sunrise ... at least we have this.*

BELLS BEFORE DAWN

-I-

Venzene Duchy of Kovalun
County Jižní Pochod
Barony of Hartscross - Jižní Lov
33 Gerstesykli: 5 Days after the Red Storm at Westsong

Blevelsket led a near fully laden Krwawa Zima around in a wide circle. She said nothing but smiled broadly as she walked with her left hand loosely holding to his halter. At just shy of five feet tall, she had to extend her arm a touch beyond what a person of average height would need. She'd long since learned how to accomplish this task without putting undue weight on the horse's head or dragging his velvet nose Skolfward. The sorrel steed seemed glad enough for her presence, in any case. His ears were pricked forward, and he seemed willing, if not outright anxious, to be off.

"Daian won't have too much longer, I fear. My men will be back with their horses shortly," Geroslaw said as he stood up some feet away. "Not that it matters, I suppose. I should only be gone a month."

"A lot can happen in a month, Auburg," said she, "especially given Edmund's plan for us." She clucked side-mouth at the horse, though this was merely an attempt to engage and interact with him rather than make him move any faster.

"Wellll… I'm bound to get my chance to joust, at least. That's something."

"I doubt it."

"Oh?"

"Aetanis is likely to have you on a short leash. He's still angry about the way things've turned out." Her alto tones carried a kind of amused, sing-song disdain.

Geroslaw snorted.

"He only owns us to fight for and, if it comes to that, defend him. We're retainers, not slaves."

She stopped, looking over her shoulder at him with unmistakable pity.

"Ohhhhh my. You really *do* think that way, don't you?" Her tone turned this question into more of a disappointed observation. She shook her head, laughing musically. "Auburg, you don't need to be a slave to be treated as one. A contract's just temporary slavery. Haven't you figured that out yet?"

Geroslaw grinned, bending down to tie his freshly rolled-up tent together so he could transport it. "Is *that* right?"

"Mmhmm," she snorted as if someone had taken a pratfall in front of her.

"Then why, my deadly darling, do you continue? Surely Jastrab's *living sword*—Blevelsket of Gulhav—is no slave..." His tone was playful mockery.

She turned swiftly, automatically swapping out her left hand for her right on the halter, and grinned as she now walked backward beside Geroslaw's horse.

"You've just answered your own question."

"Have I?"

"Loyalty, Auburg. I trust Jastrab. He knows what he's about, what we're about, and where we're going." All at once her grin was now full of mischief, and a clever joy that spoke well of her future—if all that Jastrab had told him played out as intended.

"So, a slave to coin for now..." He grinned, trailing off for her to pick up the tale.

"Exactly. I'm told you've already had *the talk*." This wasn't a question. "I'll do my best to pick out a pretty prize for you while you're away. Never fear... someplace you'll be able to take excellent care of this fine fellow." Her grin was enormous as she patted Krwawa Zima's neck. "I *may* even find you one whose roof can still keep out the rain, though no promises. Krwawa Zima's castle comes before yours, after all."

Geroslaw straightened, gave the Bluemark's salute—fists pointed Skolfward, wrists crossed in front of his belly and bowed formally. "I thank you..." He righted himself, hauling the tent onto his shoulder in the process, and walked to where she now held his horse. As he stopped to secure the canvas, he leaned forward to speak softly, eyes twinkling, "... your Next-ellency."

She laughed, shoving him playfully back a pace. She was easily strong enough to do it. "You just enjoy your war of counties. The rest of us will stay here and fight a war *for* a county."

As he rebalanced himself, her face grew soft. She nodded her head toward a point behind him. "Put that down and embrace me. You've company, and I don't want to be in the way."

He blinked and did as she asked. He had no idea what she was talking about but would find out in a moment. Her embrace was strong, conveying a sense of concern he hadn't previously noticed in her. Before she withdrew, she kissed him on his left cheek. "Be safe ... until swords are drawn. Then be swift."

He blushed, looking, he had no doubt, as touched and confused as he felt. "Odvážna krv," said he, lifting his right hand.

"Odvážna krv, Auburg." She turned as she said this, walking backward for a three-step, then turning back toward the inner portion of the encampment.

He turned and was, for a moment, lost. There stood Kastan, a lantern at her feet casting a warm glow. A pre-dawn breeze playing with the soft midnight of her hair.

She looked at him for a long moment, dark eyes wide with deep emotion ... or perhaps just in response to the overall gloom—he couldn't tell for certain.

"Lady Kastan..." He'd begun with ease and confidence but had absolutely no idea what else to say to her. He was angry yet had no reason or right to be. Seeing her walk beside the scout commander might mean nothing and might mean everything. Though she dressed as a woman used to sword and saddle, she was not merely a woman but a member of the lower nobility—the landed gentry. Such a station deserved the courtesy of an escort while walking from point to point, as he well knew. He hadn't actually seen them hold hands, nor—hells be hid—display some more obvious affection, had he?

And then there was the matter of her being of that class and station, to begin with. She hadn't lied to him exactly, but she'd conveniently avoided introducing herself by proper name and title when they'd first met. She was, of course, under no obligation to do such, but most women—hells, most men—flaunted their station at every turn. It hadn't been fair to have him blindsided by the news like that in the privacy of Edmund's tent... she'd have guessed they might cross paths there, surely. She had, after all, delivered the count's message to Geroslaw because he was a recognized aide of the captain.

"*Lady*, is it?" Kastan's voice was wearing a cloak of chilly surprise as it left her bow of a mouth.

"Yes," he said as he walked toward her. "Well, I wouldn't want to offend or surprise you by addressing you more commonly." He hated himself for that remark from nearly the instant it had left his mouth.

She snorted her derision in as unladylike a manner as Geroslaw thought a civilized person could muster.

"*Spare* me. Only children, or the weak-minded, find that nonsense offensive. That kontusz, on the other hand..." She made a gesture toward him.

"Why should my kontusz offend you?" He was more confused than angered. Though he felt his ears begin to burn.

She vented her apparent disgust with an audible sigh.

"You and yours marshalling your might to go after a boy? And for what? For the egregious sin of victory in a babe's lyst? Well, you're quite right. However could any *rational* person find *that* action offensive?"

He stopped in mid-stride, lifting his dim hand for dismayed emphasis and looking skyward in frustration.

"I seriously doubt those men would have actually harmed the boy. But even if they had, I wasn't *there*. I had nothing to do with it! I showed up an instant before you and Eobum started throwing spears!" He was trying to avoid shouting, given the early hour, but his hackles were up. To think she was lumping him in with those men simply because—he stopped in mid-career. His shoulders slumped.

...Because they were in this same uniform, and when one stains it, or ten, that stain stands out on everyone else who wears it. Hells haul them home ... that they should act in such a way!

"Kastan," his voice softened, "you have to know we aren't all like that. That *I'm* not like that."

"How? How could I possibly know that? I've only just met you— we've known one another for *days*, not weeks or years!"

He bowed his head. She was right, of course. In a small, soft tone, he answered as best he could.

"All of the men involved—*all* of them, mind—are either dead or dismissed from service and stricken from our rolls. We want no hint of that within our ranks."

Her voice was a frustrated rasp now, though he didn't think the anger he heard was directed at him.

"I've known that boy almost since he toddled," said she.

"And likely he's one of the good ones."

Her head snapped up. Now her glare, and the anger powering it, *was* directed at him.

"The *good* ones?"

"Yes? A well-behaved boy who doesn't start trouble?" His confusion brought another flare of heat back to his ears. "Why are you looking at me that way?"

"Because you've just suggested that he's not like the rest of his race and that his race is lesser than your own—*our* own—all in a single sentence!"

He had no response to that. His mind was swimming. "That wasn't what I meant at all!" His voice cracked with sad frustration. *This woman!* "Kastan, I meant that he was better than the common impression of his people—that he wasn't the idiot assumptions of the wider world when it comes to orc-kind."

She shook her head, closed her eyes, and drew a deep breath in through her nose, letting it out in a steady stream of steam. "Geroslaw, they're people, not horse breeds."

He opened his mouth to speak, then closed it, bowing his head.

"I know that. I'm ... sorry." He'd honestly meant the apology but found himself unsure whether she'd take his words as he'd intended.

He was relieved, therefore, when she gave a slow nod of acceptance.

Reaching back to grab Krwawa Zima's halter, he had to leap out of the way. The horse's motion toppled the as-yet unsecured tent nearly on Geroslaw's foot.

Krwawa Zima whickered his amusement at the goings-on, a low chuckle deep in his red throat.

Geroslaw glared first at his horse, then at Kastan, who was giggling.

He shook his head, laughing in spite of himself.

Krwawa Zima bent his head and shoved Geroslaw in the small of his back. This caused him to stagger a touch forward, and her unintentional mirth to reassert itself.

"Traitor," Geroslaw stage-whispered toward the horse. It was the carrot he had in his coat pocket. He knew that much. Still, the sense of minor magic in the pre-dawn air was genuine, for him at least.

Like most of the Empire, he feared and mistrusted magic, and he had no real sense of its scope. He certainly had no particular talent to sense its presence beyond feelings of intuition, and all men could claim that. Hells, every story seemed full of blessings or curses of sudden awareness. It had always added a sense of horror to those tales for him. The idea of seeing or knowing often dark truths denied to most of the world haunted his dreams even now.

He knew he'd always had a strain of the dramatic in him—one he kept to himself like a secret candle. He'd kept one of those as a boy, too, lighting it only after all had gone to sleep. Then he would block the crack beneath the door, so he could read or imagine in peace, without being bullied into going back to bed.

"You never did tell me," her voice shook him loose from those old memories, "about that song you were singing when we met."

"What of it?" He was amused and confused all at a go. "As I recall, you were far more interested in Krwawa Zima than my singing." He was teasing ... mostly.

"What was it called?"

"Oddech lasu," said he. He was happy to have a subject change. He saw Kastan open her mouth, knew what she would ask, and translated for her. "Forest's Breath."

She nodded, closing her mouth for a moment. After they'd looked at one another awkwardly for what felt like an unfathomable amount of time, she opened it again to speak.

"Does it translate well into the Trade Tongue?"

He considered that for a moment. Finally, he gave a half-hearted nod.

"It won't be exact, mind, but near enough, I suppose."

Before he could speak further, she spoke in a rush that seemed urgent, at least to his ears.

"Will you sing it for me? Before you ride out of my story for who-knows-how-long?"

He winced, bowed his head, and nodded.

The forest's breath beneath the sky, it whispers words to me.
It speaks of men who begged to die when first they stole from thee.
No silent stones beneath the trees, no cave will shelter be.
No guile or guard could stay my hand, when once they stole from thee.

From Sheshik sand to Skolf's own seam,
From Winter's Maw to Singing Sea,
Eyes keen, mind free,
With shadows long beneath the sky, I swear my oath to keep,
...That forest's breath shall claim their dreams and haunt them in
their sleep.

When he'd finished, he looked at her. He couldn't have done so while he sang—wasn't capable of doing both, somehow, though he couldn't have said precisely why. He'd certainly taken his turn at bardic circles, and even in his father's and uncle's halls, respectively, before he'd left home. Hells, he'd even sung in his mother's house on occasion. Why, then, could he not sing for her and meet her eyes?

She was staring at him with an utterly unreadable expression on her face. Shock, awe, fear, disbelief, disdain, polite neutrality—he couldn't decide how to read that face. Rather than annoying him, this only served to further confuse him. Once again, he found himself lost and staring at her.

"A song of revenge wrapped in such a slow and deliberate melody..." She sounded distant but not strictly detached. "It had a haunted feeling, I thought—perhaps even that of a lost love ... how strange."

"I'm ... sorry, my lady," said he.

"Whatever for?"

Now that she'd asked, he realized he had no idea what he'd just apologized for. He was spared answering when he heard a high, clear bell ring, tolling the hour.

He looked away sheepishly and was bemused to see his horse defecating directly upon the spot his eyes had fallen.

A new sound took the place of the bell as it faded. A cart and several horses rode around the bend in the camp's main lane. On the cart sat Barneb, with Daian beside him. Aethel, Borgus, and Fillip rode three abreast behind the cart.

"Would you call yourself my friend, Geroslaw?" Her voice drew him up short, forcing his eye to focus on her again.

"Of course, Lady." He spoke this on instinct. He'd meant it, he realized a moment later, but it had been pure reaction.

"Then bring my brother back to me in one piece. He rides with you in Aetanis' van. That's why I came—to ask you to look after my brother."

He tried not to show how much this statement hurt him. That she came not to see him, but to ask him a favor—that she came out of fear, not for his life, but to ask him to risk that life for another's... he felt that sense of magic—of predestination—shatter like crystal against stone.

"I'll do all that I can, Lady Kastan." He kept his voice professional, adopted a more rigid, formal posture, and saluted her in the Bluemark fashion. "He isn't my contract, but I'll do my best to do as you ask."

She grew pale. When she spoke, her voice was confused and more than a touch hurt. "Geroslaw, I didn't mean..."

He turned away as the men approached, smiling broadly at them. "Daian! I was afraid I wouldn't see you before we were off."

Daian grinned, hopping down from the wagon's seat, his golden curls bouncing as he moved. "Aye, well, thought you might like a useful surprise for the road." His voice was halting, but his face was all smiles. He gestured back to the cart. "Figure this'll make the trip a touch easier on the five of you."

Geroslaw nodded, walking over to take the younger man's hand. As he did, he heard Kastan's footfalls crunch on the grass and gravel that led back toward the palisade.

He looked back in that direction, seeing her lantern fade into a bright suggestion in the early morning dim. He wasn't, at that moment, entirely certain how he felt about her, Aetanis, the Bluemark, or anything else. Uncertainty was something he rarely tolerated for long, however. And so he made up his mind to focus on the aspects of doubt he could do something about the Bluemark, or at least his small section of it.

"Daian, thank you. Truly, the cart will be of more than minor use." He saw the younger man drawing breath to speak. He spoke on, hoping to forestall him. "I hate having to take that gift and swing into the saddle in mid thanks, but we've a long road ahead if we're to reach Zlaté Pole with time enough to arrange everything for the contract."

Daian nodded, that earnest grin still in full flower on his face. "I understand." He extended his hand again. When Geroslaw took it, Daian drew him in for an embrace. "Well ... stay safe ... until swords are drawn."

Geroslaw withdrew from the embrace, quirking a smile. He liked Daian ... mostly. He was honest and good-natured, if a touch socially awkward. The fellow came across like a grown version of a slightly tedious younger brother—earnest, helpful, and occasionally downright annoying. Geroslaw was surprised to realize that he'd very likely miss him, and the thought softened his manner. "I know, I know—then be swift." He patted Daian's shoulder. "Odvážna krv."

"Odvážna krv, Geroslaw, Barneb, Aethel, Fillip, Borgus." He nodded to each in turn as he spoke their names.

They responded in kind, each offering a smile and a nod.

Borgus had already moved Geroslaw's fallen tent into the back of the wagon. Next, he reached a hand up to untie the ropes holding the rest of the gear in place on the back of his horse.

"Leave it, Borgus. We're minutes from leaving later than I'd like. I'll reshuffle gear when we stop later."

Borgus gave a nod and walked to his horse, swinging smoothly back into the saddle.

A man comfortable on horseback, Geroslaw thought. *That's worth remembering.*

Taking just a moment to scratch Krwawa Zima's chin where he liked best—eliciting both the warm tones of the horse's voice and the movement of his ears to about as far forward as they could go—Geroslaw swung himself up into the saddle. With a nod to Daian's cheerful, slightly distracted self, he got their little column moving out of camp and toward the road Southeast.

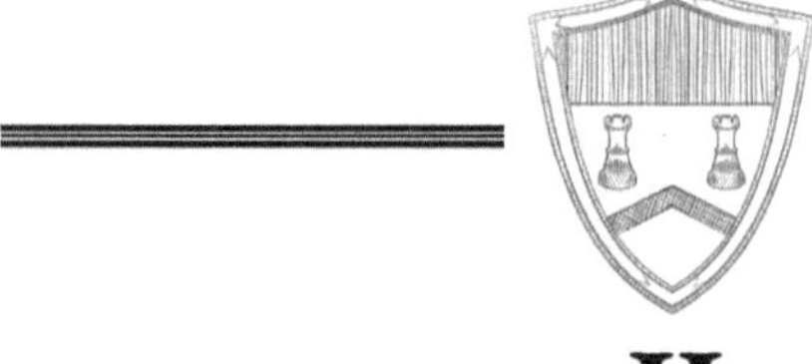

-II-

Venzene Duchy of Kamieńalun
County Czarny Wodospad
Wieża Szymona
33 Gerstesykli: 5 Days after the Red Storm at Westsong

Azhferd stood waiting in the courtyard of his father's castle, red kontusz rippling in the pre-dawn breeze, sword hung at his side.

Horses for him and his sergeant would shortly be brought up from the rear where the stone stable complex was housed. The sergeant expected to make this ride with him would have been Skar, in the ordinary course, his senior-most. He somehow doubted that would be the way things turned out, given what he'd just caught sight of, but time would tell.

Kozioł would be along, likely with another stable boy in tow, but in the meantime, there was this.

He looked as the three men approached him. He knew them all, of course. The yellow oak that was Deiter, his pale blond waves streaming out behind him, would have been easy to recognize even at twice the distance. To Deiter's far left walked small, dark-maned Iwo, son of Rietan. His father was one of the count's personal sergeants and had served the family since before Iwo's birth. Between them, however, walked an old man with a beard the color of snow after a day's tread had discolored it. He was wrapped in enough layers to make him appear fat, though his limbs and the way he walked suggested otherwise. He was taking wide, sweeping, long-legged strides that seemed to roll him forward. His head was bowed, shoulders lowered as if he struggled under a moderate weight. Behind him, at the entrance from the inner market not yet open for business, a young girl stood near a brazier, warming her hands.

Azhferd felt his hand beginning to move, rise, and adjust his hat, but he willed it to remain at his side. The hat was new and felt as if it didn't quite fit his head yet. In a moment, once the old man had been escorted to him, he could remove it. It would seem a gesture of kindness, a sign of somewhat lessened formality for the man to see the heir doff his hat to speak with him. Sometimes kindness and courtesy truly were their own rewards.

Skar seemed to materialize to his right. He'd come up from the stables ahead of Kozioł, Azhferd knew. He'd just moved so quietly that he hadn't heard the man's approach.

"My lord," said he, "do you know the man?" His voice was the auditory equivalent of a taut silk rope: delicate, smooth, and potentially dangerous.

Azhferd fought back a wince. Skar's black hair had lashed out to tickle and slash at his ear in the shifting wind.

"By face, but not by name," Azhferd said.

"Jozef, newly of Auburg." Skar's voice was as neutral as may be, but there was a tightness to it that spoke plainly of more at play here than first glance suggested.

"I recall him now. Yes. He was one of the craftsmen who wanted to take up residence there after completing work on my manor." Azhferd paused, then shook his head almost imperceptibly. "If he'd waited, we'd have been there to speak to him this evening. We might have saved the poor man a ride."

"Everyone in Auburg knew you were to arrive today, my lord. We made certain of it."

That boded ill.

Azhferd waited. A moment later and the men arrived before him. Jozef moved to kneel in the snow.

"My," he grunted. "Lord Azhferd..." He began to slip, but before he could fall entirely, Deiter took one arm, Iwo the other.

Unseen by the man, Azhferd nodded at the guards, who gently hauled Jozef to his feet.

"You needn't kneel in the snow, Jozef. While I appreciate the respect you show me, let me return it in kind. Surely a grandfather has earned the right to keep his feet and save his knees."

Jozef looked shocked, though whether this was for the kindness offered to his old knees or the fact that his lord knew him by name was anyone's guess.

"Th-thank you, my lord. Thank you." He simply stood there for a moment, staring at Azhferd's face with an almost impudent fascination.

Deiter cleared his throat softly, causing Jozef to start, then blush. He, too, cleared his throat, then began to speak anew.

"My lord, uh, forgive me. Your orcs..." He trailed off, then cleared his throat before coming at the conversation again. "That is to say, your mason and his ... um, brood."

Azhferd's even smile faded, though it wasn't instantly replaced by a scowl.

"You mean *Master* Guuvra, the mason I selected to finish my manor? What about him?" He kept his voice reasonable, neutral, and soft-spoken. He felt Skar tense just a bit on his right, however, and smiled inwardly.

"Um, yes, my lord."

Azhferd waited.

"Well ... that is to say, my lord..." He looked between Azhferd and Skar, then drew himself up.

"He left with his brood and, by all rights, should have been back days ago, my lord. He left, and with your gold, my lord, and his entire family packed on that cart with him, my lord. I think ... that is, I fear..."

"Spit it out, man!" Skar sounded as if he were just about out of patience with this entire conversation.

"Yes, well, I'm *coming* to it!" Jozef's anger was like a line drawn taut before it snapped back, striking him in the face. He seemed altogether shocked at his own bravado. "Forgive me, my lord—I fear he has taken your money and fled your service with it. I can find no other explanation."

Azhferd allowed a bland smile to cross his face, making a point not to let it reach his eyes. In a voice that was calm, polite, almost sweet despite its low gravel, he asked an innocent question.

"Jozef, did he give you any sign or anyone else that you're aware of that he was hiding something?"

"My lord?"

"Did he, perhaps, seem nervous or agitated? Did he seem as if he were anxious or fretful, perhaps?"

"I ... well, no, my lord, but..."

"Was he acting like a man afraid, or in some way aggressive?"

"Well, my lord ... how would I know?"

Azhferd blinked. Of all answers, that one had been quite outside of his expectations.

"I don't understand, Jozef. You did see the man, did you not?"

"The orc, you mean? Yes, my lord. Saw him plain. Saw his brood, too."

Azhferd let that pass. Such slurs were common enough, and as far as slurs went, this one was minor. Hells be hid, he'd heard many humans with larger families refer to themselves as a brood. He continued to maintain that calm, rational voice.

"Jozef, I consider you a clever fellow. You're possessed of great skill and a keen eye. What's more, you thought highly enough of me to make the day's journey to tell me of your suspicions. I appreciate that curtesy. What I'm asking is, what specifically leads you to suspect Master Guuvra of stealing from me?"

Jozef basked in the glow of this praise, smiling a grey-toothed smile ... right up until Azhferd had asked that seemingly incongruous question.

"I ... don't understand, my lord. He had a large leather satchel full of your own vévodové, a pair of horses, a cart full of children and supplies."

"Yes? I know all of this."

"Well ... he's an orc, my lord."

"That also hadn't escaped my notice." Azhferd allowed his smile to droop slightly.

"I mean to say, begging your pardon, my lord, but he's an orc! He's gone days overdue, and with your hard-earned gold and your horses, my lord! Can't trust a beast-like—"

Azhferd dropped his smile utterly, as if stones weighted his lips.

"*Man*, Jozef. A man like that." He kept his voice even, but the warmth had gone from it as if it'd been carried away on the early winter wind.

"An orc *male*, I suppose. But after all, we're not speaking of the Naushath, or the Traeadish, are we? Not even speaking of the Eodenth, Lord Azhferd. We're speaking of orcs! They aren't *men*, my lord. Begging your pardon, but they just aren't. We've civilized a good many of them, and they're a dab hand with most anything laborsome, but they're not, well, *us*, sire."

Azhferd bowed his head briefly. He wondered that Jozef had said Eodenth, not Eoalunth. He had, in effect, spoken as if he were sympathetic to that duchy's rebel cause and mindset. He doubted if the man had even realized he'd done it. Likely it was just a matter of Eodenth being easier to pronounce.

Abruptly, he turned to walk toward the stables. Kozioł was about halfway to their little gaggle of men. He appeared to be taking deliberate slowness in his approach. Azhferd made a mental note to praise the boy for that. It showed not merely courtesy, but perception and wisdom as well. He spoke to Skar before walking off, but kept his voice loud enough to be heard by all four men.

"There is no *speaking* to this man. He cannot see past his beard. Skar, take Iwo, and leave me Deiter. Go ride Guuvra's back trail. Return with what you find, and let us hope he was delayed for a good reason. Escort he and his family back to Auburg. "

Before Azhferd had taken his second step away, Skar spoke up.

"If it takes longer than it should?"

"Ride to meet me at Zlaté Pole."

"My lord," Jozef spoke with a mixture of greedy obsequiousness, "I've travelled long to do right by you, my lord."

"...And so you have," Azhferd said as he walked toward Kozioł. He kept his pace slow and measured.

"Might... Might my trouble be worth some small consideration, my lord?"

"It might." Azhferd now raised his voice to be heard clearly as he withdrew. "If your fears turn out valid, I will reward you in ways you cannot imagine, for you'll have taught me to reshape my judge of character. If your warning turns out to be false, however ... I may let you rot in some remote dungeon cell for slandering a good man's name and reputation."

Jozef spluttered, but whatever he was spouting in response, Azhferd had no interest in hearing it. He heard a footstep behind him and to his left. Deiter had fallen into step.

Ten minutes later found the pair riding side by side down the hill. Azhferd was too angry to speak. He refused to believe that Guuvra would betray his trust in such a flagrant way. They weren't close, of course, but there was trust there. He'd known the man for more than half his life at this point.

No, his fear wasn't betrayal. He didn't want to name it, even in the hollow places of his mind where nightmares were supposed to sleep. Thinking or giving voice to them risked making them real. An absurd thought, he knew, but a pervasive one nonetheless.

"Skar'll get to the bottom of it, my lord. No fear." Deiter's voice was a crisp, bright tenor. It carried with it a brief warmth and reassurance that Azhferd hated to admit he'd needed.

"I'll look forward to seeing him at Auburg. Hopefully, he and Iwo will meet Guuvra's family on the road, and we'll hear that they were delayed by a day or two. Something simple like that seems likely enough."

Deiter nodded and offered a thin grin. Given how rarely his face showed any sign of joy or jocularity, this may as well have been a wide smile full of white teeth.

Azhferd grinned at this thought and urged the horse into a faster pace. "Let's see if we can make it before dark."

Deiter silently matched Azhferd's speed.

By the time the first rays of sunlight painted the left side of their faces, turning the snow eye wateringly bright, Azhferd had turned his thoughts toward what was to come. He hadn't forgotten the Guuvra matter, but for now, he'd done all that he could. He needed to leave it to Skar and focus on the run up to Zlaté Pole.

It's actually best that he's not with me. Skar's too easy to rely upon. What is it you always say, Uncle? If you only fight from horseback, you're apt to forget how to throw a punch. He smiled to himself. *Aye, Skar's presence'll be missed for the next few days. Good. It'll give me a chance to remember what my fists are for.*

Hadwald and Vonrik—the only two men at court he accounted as actual friends, would meet him either tonight or tomorrow. They would spend some time training and planning. Soon enough, the other lords and gentry's sons would arrive in Auburg—those who had pledged to fight with him, at least. They would train, live together for a short while, and then be off to Zlaté Pole.

They'd soon find out just how long their shadows truly were, and he could ... not ... wait.

-III-

Venzene Duchy of Kovalun
County Jižní Pochod
Barony of Hartscross - Jižní Lov
33 Gerstesykli: 5 Days after the Red Storm at Westsong

Eobum sat around the smoldering embers of last night's ir fire with Lashjuk, Eranoric, and Adric as the sun hauled itself up over the horizon.

He felt rather than saw the other men tense as Lashjuk spoke. They were *used* to this silent moment—a tradition wherein they would watch the living world waken itself. The rite had its origins in old Eodenth practices of … perhaps not *divination*, but certainly of portenture. It was an Eodenth man's first chance to see what the world meant to show him on a given day. While mystic sign was rare, the natural world certainly had its share of early warning systems and lately left stories of oddity in the night to make the *not-quite-rite* worth the effort.

"What is this place we're headed toward tomorrow? I take it you—some of you, at least—have been there before?" Her voice was soft in deference to those who still slept. Set against the soundscape of sighing breezes, insects, birds, and the more peopled portions of camp, however, she sounded harsh and almost grating.

Eobum met the other men's eyes to gauge their true reaction—the one that came on the heels of their shock at the sudden intrusion of sound. Eranoric was amused, judging by the twinkle in his eye. Adric seemed annoyed but tolerant. Both reactions made sense.

Eobum held the silence for another moment or two. In fact, he waited until she was about to ask again before speaking.

"I think we've seen and heard all there is to see and hear, aye?"

Lashjuk blinked, then widened her eyes in surprise, blushing slightly. When the other two men had nodded agreement, she opened her mouth to speak.

"Forgive me, I thought the silence was because of the early hour and slow-waking minds." Her face still held a burnished blush high on her cheekbones.

Eobum did his best not to stare.

"First half's right, Lady," Eranoric offered. "S'an old Eodenth morning rite."

"Mourning rite? For the fools Fenglem killed?" She sounded annoyed now, if not utterly disgusted.

Eranoric blinked, not understanding.

"What?"

Adric actually snorted, then laughed.

"Nye, Lashjuk." He laughed again. "Wrong kind of morning. S'an Eodenth *daybreak* rite's what it is."

Her blush redoubled, and she bowed her head.

"...Oh." She paused, then added, "I didn't know." Her voice made her embarrassment almost painfully clear.

"S'allright, Lady. I didn't know 'til a year agone," Eranoric said.

She looked up, surprised.

"Aren't you Eodenth?"

He nodded, grinning.

"Am, but ain't been there since... oh, I'd guess I was younger than your Maksu at the time. Maybe five or six?"

She nodded.

"You grew up in Kovalun, then?"

"Aye, mostly. Havalun for a time, but, aye."

Lashjuk gave a nod of acceptance, smiling in a distracted sort of way.

"Well, at least you've seen fully half the Empire. That's something."

"Aye, after a fashion. Anyroad, Adric and Eobum taught it to me after I joined them last Gerstealunth—right before sickle moon."

"Sickle... oh! Sigdemåne, you mean." She shook her head, mostly at herself, Eobum suspected.

Eranoric nodded.

A noise drew Eobum's attention. He looked across at what was once his tent. Sulok was pulling on his boots. He could just make him out through an opening in the tent's flap as the breeze played with it.

"In answer to your question about where we're bound?" Eobum spoke up again, looking to Lashjuk at last, "we know it, as you guessed. It's a badly named place, but it's quiet enough."

"Badly named?"

"Aye," said Adric. "About, oh, a few *thousand* years a'gone?" He made his face a caricature. "This young knight won a tourney somewhere or other—wasn't Zlaté Pole, but something like it further south. Anyroad, the prize was land in Kovalun—unpeopled, but rich enough in timber and soil, or so the story goes. Was meant to be a full forest of ash and oak, pine and poplar. Turned out that the duke at the time hadn't been aware, but folk had been stealing timber from that lot of land since time was first tallied. There s'hardly any forest a'tall by the time he arrived."

Eobum smirked as he took up the tale. "Our knight took one look at what was left—a pocket forest below a tall jut of rocky hill, and he named his new acreage Haluzfeld. Haluz is twig in Kovalunth, feld is field in both Gerstealunth and Eodenth."

Adric smirked. "He built tall towers 'top that hill. Called 'is keep Haluz Věže—the Twig Towers."

Eobum nodded. "Which is backward. Should have been Věže Haluz, or really Věže Kamenných Větviček—the Towers of Stone Twigs. Something like that."

"Aye, well, pretty'n one tongue's often poison in 'nother," Eranoric said.

The men all chuckled at this, though Eobum saw Lashjuk had long since lost interest in the topic.

Sulok emerged, sleep-staggered to his left to a point just outside of camp, and let his water go against a nearby hazel tree. They remained silent while this went on, chiefly because none of them had anything important to say. Sometimes, after all, silence was best. Sulok had other plans, however. Over his shoulder, in a voice that sounded sulky and half-dazed, he spoke up.

"You don't have to stop talking just so I can make water."

They looked at one another and smirked.

"Aye, well as sleepy as you seemed, my lord, we was afeared you'd need t'concentrate." Eranoric sounded both serious and rather studious, though he worked his face to suppress the grin that threatened to flower.

Sulok snorted, then laughed. He finished and moved back toward the low fire. He looked between Lashjuk and Eranoric, both of whom were watching him with mild interest, then seemed to come to a decision.

With a look of purpose on his pale bronze face, he crossed the short distance between them. He removed Eranoric's right elbow from the man's thigh and lifted it to the height of his own shoulder. He promptly sat in its place, facing his mother before bringing the arm down over his own chest.

Eobum saw Eranoric's eyes widen, then flit to Lashjuk. He wasn't bothered by the boy's decision to use him as furniture, but waited to see his mother's reaction before offering his own.

For her part, Eobum saw Lashjuk's eyes widen a touch as this tableau unfolded.

Sulok reached his right hand out to take his mother's left one. She allowed this, and he drew it toward his chest. As it neared, he brought his left hand to bear, placing hers between both of his, atop Eranoric's forearm.

"Og?" He sounded very small but very serious. His voice was an alto-ranged growl, almost a purr.

"Lg?" She elongated this, the word for son, so it came out *ulllg*.

"Thank you."

"For what, Sulok?" Her face and voice made her confusion clear. She was pleased to see this side of him. That much was obvious. She also bordered on actual fear at this interaction.

"For staying... for saying that we'll stay here, with the unit." His face was far too serious for a boy his age, but he'd been through a great deal. Their entire family had come to that, and in far too short a time. "You've made the man pay for what he did to father." He paused, swallowing hard. "For what he did to us, and... and for what he did to Maklo." Tears came now, but his voice was quite steady. "You make them proud... you make *me* proud." He drew her hand up and planted a kiss on her knuckles. "I was afraid you'd make us leave—that we'd be alone, now—just we three." He leaned to his right, laying his head in the crook of the silent Eranoric's arm. "I don't—I didn't want to go."

Eobum saw that Lashjuk's eyes swam. Eranoric stared down at their tiny once-blaze, body frozen even as his throat worked. Adric, too, was staring into the former fire, trying to be as unobtrusive as he could. Nodding to himself, Eobum followed suit. It was something to look at other than the grief—the healing these two were undergoing. It was happening in front of them, true enough, but it was a private thing, and he didn't trust himself not to interfere.

He recalled young Fenglem's grief when they'd finally stopped running from Istjuk, then Haiga's... Haiga, who had been Sulok's age, then. Finally, he thought of Lakkrid's howling, miserable grief at the loss of his mother, his home, his world. Eobum hadn't had time to process his own grief until much later.

From the corner of his left eye, he saw Lashjuk's hand move to cup her son's face, her thumb wiping away his tears.

"Erld ed vra, Sulok ... Erld awka Maksu," said she. Her voice was a rough whisper. *(You are my heart, Sulok ... You and Maksu.)*

Eranoric gently tried to extricate his arm, but Sulok stiffened, pressing his own down to keep Eranoric in place. The man stopped, smiling and bowing his head.

Eobum saw Lakkrid crouched just inside Fenglem and Haiga's tent, watching this and smiling. The boy met his father's eye. Then, as quiet as a field mouse, Lakkrid crouch-walked to what would ordinarily be his own tent. Slipping inside, he moved to where Maksu slept, sitting on the canvas floor between the two beds, facing the entrance.

He had no time to consider this, as he heard movement to his right. Glad for the distraction, he stood and walked toward the camp's entrance in one swift motion.

-IV-

Eobum stood a few yards beyond the ring of tents that formed his personal camp, speaking to two men that were somewhere near his own age. One was bald save a natural ring of brown hair above his ears. The other was dark blond of both hair and beard and was perhaps the very definition of Kovalunth citizenry. If one were to paint the every-man of Kovalun, this man would come to life on the canvas tall but not giant, well-muscled but not large, sleek but not underfed.

"I'm Rákos," said the bald man. "Andrej ess me boy."

Eobum nodded, looking a question to the other man.

"Liška," said he. "Vlk ess mine."

"Liška—you work the stables, yes? I've seen you there trying to do something with the no-necks new recruits ride in on, haven't I?"

Liška grunted at this, nodding a single time. Rather than pleased at being recognized, he seemed altogether annoyed by it.

"You vanted to see us?"

Eobum chose to say his piece and let these men get on with their respective days. It was clear that Liška, at least, had better things to do this morning.

"Your boys did a service for one of my folk. They had no reason to, no debt or call, nor even someone to ask it of them. They did it anyway."

The bald man's smile was plain and honest. He'd heard some of this story from his son, Eobum had no doubt, and he was altogether pleased at what he'd heard. That much seemed clear.

"I've heard," said the every-man. "My vife ess none too heppy."

Eobum nodded his understanding.

"For a boy to stand against grown men and risk more than their bones? That's not a thing to cause a mother joy. Still, I owe them and their parents for teaching them to stand up like that."

"Vas foolish. My vife beat him 'til he couldn't sit easy, then sent him to bed vithout supper for hess foolishness." Liška delivered this grim report in the same gruff tones he'd used throughout. "Vlk von't be so dim again. Not soon."

Eobum fought back an urge to speak his mind. This Liška might be exaggerating, might be overselling the beating Vlk had gotten. He also might be telling the literal truth. Eobum had no authority to do much about it. A man's child was just that—that man's child. Still, the idea of punishing the boy without supper for defending a smaller boy from the Bluemark's former folk... it was enough to summon the beginnings of true anger in him.

"How can I thank you for the *good* your son did, Liška?"

Liška shook his head.

"I owe a debt and mean to see it paid," Eobum said. He'd decided to press the man in an effort to drive the point home, and of course, because he did indeed feel indebted.

"I vant nothing from you, Eodenth."

Eobum blinked, nodded, and allowed his voice to become flat and detached.

"I can ask Vlk when next I see him if you'd prefer."

"You von't ask my boy any such thing."

"Have I ... done something to you that I'm not recalling, Liška?"

Liška shook his head. "Stay clear uff my Vlk, Eodenth. I vant no trouble vith you." He paused. "If you vant to pay a debt you feel you owe me, then stay avay from my boy." With that, he turned and walked off, back straight, eyes forward.

Eobum clenched his right fist—the one farthest from his other guest. That worthy had thus far remained silent. He bowed his head, as well.

He heard Liška some yards off.

"My lady."

Looking up, he saw Kastan nod to the man, who was bowing formally, before she continued on toward Eobum and his remaining guest, Rákos.

At Kastan's approach, Rákos ran a hand through his beard, looking nervous.

"Eobum," said she.

"Lady Kastan. This is Rákos—father of Andrej, the taller boy who helped Maksu yesterday."

Kastan's face lit up as she regarded the man.

"Your son showed the very bent of honor ... Rákos, was it?"

"Yes, Lady. Thank you!"

Eobum turned to make of the three a triangle, so he could face them both. "To Rákos, then." He again made his offer.

"Your son had even less a reason to stand yesterday. He wasn't someone my Lakkrid knew, and certainly *Maksu* didn't know him."

"My Andrej ess a good boy, as you say. I'm very proud of him." He rolled his R on "proud."

"I owe him a service, and you for teaching him to stand as a man... to be true even in the face of danger."

Rákos grinned, blushing and nearly bouncing with excitement. Rather than making him appear childish, the action made him somehow endearing.

Eobum grinned. He couldn't help it. He liked Rákos. It wasn't only because of the comparison to Vlk's father, though such a chilly fellow would make most men likable by contrast. No, Rákos had the look of a good man not long out of hard times: clever, determined, and still able to find something to smile about.

"Tell me, Rákos, what service—what favor can I do for you?"

"I'm a hunter, Commander. I vant to be more. I vant to join vith you and your men—my boy and I both."

Eobum blinked, looking at Kastan in frank surprise.

"Eobum?" Kastan lifted her brows as she spoke. "Ed wrinsh..." *(I'll take him...)*

Eobum nodded slowly, thinking about this. A hunter never wanted for meat but had to barter for all else. They earned protection, but no wage to speak of. In Kastan's employ, he and his boy would eat without having to hunt, as she and her retainers were Edmund's guests. This meant that anything he hunted would be his to sell back to the encampment or its denizens. That'd change once Eobum returned to claim the pair... if they still wished to join the unit by then.

"Rákos, I cannot take you on just now."

Rákos dropped his head rather comically.

"Oh," said he.

Eobum grinned.

"I leave come morning to do His Excellency's bidding. I can, however, take you and your boy on upon our return. In the meantime, the Lady Kastan has room for you both in her retinue, if that will serve."

Rákos's eyes grew wide, his face nearly erupting into a delighted grin.

"Truly? My lady, truly?"

She smiled, nodding.

"Pravdiva jako zítřek," said she. This was a commoner's expression—true as tomorrow.

He jumped and pumped both fists in a show of obvious joy. As he landed, he blushed once more and dropped to a knee between the pair.

"My lady, Commander, I and my boy vill do all ve can to serve you vell. I cannot," he shook his head, "*cannot* thank you enough for vat you've done for my Andrej and I."

Eobum took this for as long as he thought he could stand, then reached a hand down to help the man to his feet.

"That will be the first and last time you ever kneel to me, Rákos—you or your Andrej. I'm no lord, no noble, no knight."

Rákos went snow white, jaw hanging limply open, fear etched on his kindly face.

"*Peace*, Rákos. You were right to kneel before the Lady Kastan."

"Just not to you?"

Eobum nodded.

"Very vell, Commander. They'll call you to the line soon enough, I expect."

Kastan exchanged a knowing look with Eobum. He knew she thought the same. Blessedly, she also knew *his* mind on the matter and kept prudently silent.

"Come, Rákos. I shall show you where you and your son will be sleeping."

Rákos beamed, nodded his thanks, and turned to bow his head toward Eobum.

"Commander," said he, and then turned to leave.

"I leave at dawn, Kastan."

"I'll be there to see you off. Lakkrid would never forgive me otherwise." She headed out with her new, albeit temporary, retainer.

-V-

34 Gerstesykli: 6 Days after the Red Storm at Westsong

Come dawn, they gathered at the northern gate, and after Kastan, Rákos, and Andrej had made their farewells, eleven men, one woman, three boys, and one horse trooped out in a loose double column.

Eobum took a moment to check the pack hung from his shoulder for perhaps the tenth time this morning. Two sealed scroll tubes rested securely near the bottom of his haversack in a pocket sewn into the wall of the leather.

Edmund thought they were the first steps toward Eoden's liberation... the beginning of the end for the centuries-long tradition of raids from the so-called Venzene nobility. While Eobum had his misgivings, he didn't doubt the weight this mission carried.

"A week," he said under his breath. "A week and the first move in Edmund's game is made... unless you count I and mine as that first move." He smirked to himself, shaking his head, and after repositioning the way his pack sat over his shoulder, set his mind to the task at hand.

They'd have a week of mostly cross-country to manage. That meant living raw—fine for he and his, but the new additions might find it more difficult than they wanted or expected. Their presence had been the main reason he'd refused to bring Rákos and his son. While he expected the pair would have done well enough—Rákos was a hunter, after all—he didn't want to add any further pressure to Lashjuk and the boys. He didn't want to introduce a pair of newcomers before they'd gotten used to how their lives would be if they remained with the unit.

"Sulok, Maksu—you haven't walked as long and as far as the rest of us. That won't slow us down. No fear. It's part of why we've brought your horse along. You *will* slow us down if you try to tough it out when your legs and feet are screaming at you. Take turns on the horse as and when you need to. By the time we get where we're going, you'll be much stronger for it, aye?"

"Bru, Ng," they said in sleepy unison.

"Brewing?" Riclov sounded confused and amused, but stayed prudently short of coming across as insulting.

"Brew ung-ga," Fenglem said, taking pains to focus on each syllable, truncating the *ga* at the end. "*Yes, Elder.* Ng is our word for elder male, father, or chieftain."

"Oh," Riclov said and said no more.

Eobum had a moment to wonder which meaning of the word the boys had meant to convey. For Sulok, he expected it was either elder or chieftain. For Maksu... he didn't know. More than that, he didn't know what he wanted the truth to be.

He put the matter out of his mind for now. They had a long road ahead, and his mind would be better focused on that. The rest would take care of itself.

He heard the bells in the distance marking the turn of the hour back at Edmund's camp. It tolled seven times.

One, hopefully, for each day ahead of us, he thought and smiled.

Things felt right, somehow—a feeling he barely registered, but it was there. None of his had been wounded or killed, despite the Bluemark incident. He'd met yet another in a long line of fools who saw tusks and presumed trouble. He'd also gained a new member, for now at least, for the unit—and another boy roughly Lakkrid's age. Edmund's plan might or might not work, but it would have to go so far awry as to be the stuff of legend in order to make things actually worse for the Eodenth people, at least in the short term.

Long thoughts later. He nodded to himself and led them northwest. *On to the field of twigs.*

SHADOWS SHARED

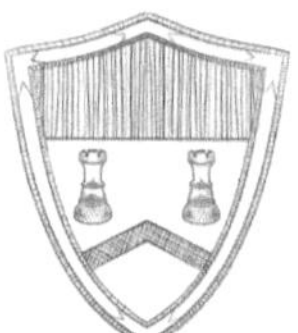

-I-

Venzene Duchy of Kamieńalun
County Czarny Wodospad
Village of Auburg
38 Gerstesykli: 10 Days after the Red Storm at Westsong

Azhferd watched Vonrik exit the manor house. His friend's hair hung in a fashionable braid over one shoulder, its coal-colored length sharp against the chain shirt he wore.

The man turned his rather wolfish looking face this way and that as he pulled on his leather gauntlets. These were demis—half gauntlets that covered the back of the hand and a portion of the thumb. While they were pretty things, they wouldn't get much use in this early part of the day. They offered protection enough if one held a shield and a weapon with a basket hilt attached. This morning, however, wasn't about hilts and heaters. It was about the spear.

"Stables!" Azhferd raised his voice so that it carried.

Vonrik turned, his black brows shooting up comically as a smile graced his face. He nodded and stepped down onto the cracked cold of the ground, walking toward where Azhferd and the others stood.

"Morning, my lord," he said once he'd gotten close enough to make shouting unnecessary. "Didn't think I'd be the first one out here, but I surely didn't expect to be the last."

The assorted armsmen—two grooms each for Hadwald and Vonrik, and Deiter, Azhferd's lone attendant—all bowed at his arrival.

"You're in plenty of time. I wouldn't let it worry you." Azhferd's voice was easy, almost complacent.

"Good." Vonrik grinned. "What's first today, then?"

Azhferd continued with that same tone as he spoke.

"You won't be needing those demis, I can tell you that much."

Vonrik pulled a comical frown.

"Forget your fulls?" Azhferd lifted his brows in mild surprise. "Well, no matter. You can borrow mine."

"Won't you need them?"

"The only thing I'll be fighting today is the urge to mock you." Azhferd quirked a smile. "You won't have time to run back or send someone once we hit the field at Zlaté Pole. Best sort—"

"I know, I-know. They're upstairs, buried in my chest. I never use the damned things outside of tourney. I shall sort them before I sleep tonight, my lord. No fear." He pulled his gauntlets off and lay them atop a mounting block that was stood near at hand. "Besides, I'm not giving you an excuse to stand there looking pretty."

Azhferd bowed in mock formality, then leaned against the stable wall.

"Well, Vonrik , if my beauty distracts you so, all I can do is apologize and swear not to bat my eyes at you at a crucial moment."

Vonrik's infamously infectious laugh made an appearance at that. It was the sort of thing that somehow managed to unhorse anger even when it was about to strike.

"It must be said, my lord. I'd rather hit you in your pretty face than be made to stare at it. Drool has never been a comely sight, even on *my* fine-featured face." His teeth shone out in a wide, snow-white grin.

"Well, I'll pull my demis out later, and we can put that *rather-ance* of yours to the test with sword and board … Von-*wreck*." Azhferd pushed off of the wall to his left, standing fully upright and patting Vonrik on the shoulder. "Come on. I'll get them for you."

A few moments later found them all standing in as near as no matter to the heart of the stone stable building. Its roof peaked at some fifteen feet over the central aisle.

Lying propped up against the outer wall of an empty stone stall were six spears with wide, leaf-shaped wooden heads, ten heater shields, and ten wooden swords—some with metal baskets and some with standard quillon cross-guards.

A rope hung stretched taut some nine feet off of the ground, across the aisle. From its center, another rope descended. This second cord was perhaps two feet long and ended in a large leather ball, suspending it to about the height of a man's helmeted head.

Hadwald—stoic as ever—stood beside the weapons, spear in hand. He had long limbs and a thick sheaf of muscle. In the torchlight, his hair looked to be a preternatural red. Beneath the ordinary magic of the sun, however, his short waves would look a more natural mussed auburn.

He gave Vonrik a nod and the suggestion of a smile by way of greeting. To the uninitiated, this might have seemed terse, perhaps even disrespectful. But Azhferd knew better. Hadwald certainly *had* emotions, but he considered them private things. A nod and a recognizable smile? *He may as well have tackled Vonrik and swung him around like a long-lost lover,* Azhferd thought, grinning to himself.

Azhferd reached down behind one of the shields and pulled a pair of leather gloves from where they'd waited. These had a modest bell that stretched over their wearer's wrists and lower forearms. Their true magnificence, however, was in the meticulous workmanship of the metal that covered their backs from wrist to tip of finger. They were fully articulated at each point where a man's fingers bent, allowing for unheard of manual dexterity without their wearer having to sacrifice protection. They weren't, so far as he knew, enchanted in any way, but one could be forgiven for thinking otherwise.

Vonrik sighed, smiling as Azhferd handed them over. Slipping them into place, he flexed his hands and admired the gleaming steel backs of the miraculous metalwork, laughing softly.

"Every time I see these things, I wish I'd gone with you back then—wish I could've mustered up the mettle," said he. "Might have earned such a gift, myself."

Azhferd shrugged, giving the answer he knew he needed to as the heir, let alone as Vonrik's friend.

"You did the right thing, staying behind with your father."

"Easy for you to say! You rode off to glory, came back with your reputation increased, a lifelong friend in Count Edmund, and these pretty things. Not the stuff of legends, maybe, but a worthy start, given you'd just seen your sixteenth Kamieńsykli."

"That early glory earned me my father's disappointed silence." Azhferd's smile faded somewhat at this.

"Bah." Vonrik waved a dismissive, newly gauntleted hand in his direction. "Fathers forgive, Kamień jest szary." This was a favorite expression among the gentry. Literally rendered in the Trade Tongue as *stone is grey*, it bore the diminutive connotation of either, *so be it*, or if conveyed with disdain, *it doesn't matter*.

Hadwald picked up a spear from against the wall and tossed it to Vonrik. He then handed one to Azhferd's man, Deiter, before he looked to Azhferd with a question in his eyes.

"Vonrik, step to the right against the stall there. I want you to see the exercise in action first."

Vonrik obliged, then turned and watched with an interested expression. All humor seemed to have left him as he narrowed his eyes in concentration.

One of Vonrik's armsmen followed suit across the aisle. His other groom, however, and Hadwald's men, pulled on helmets, picked up shields and basket-hilted swords, and made ready.

"Hadwald's been out here for half a bell or more. His blood's well and truly awake. You'll need to hit a hundred." He lifted his chin toward the ball. "...cleanly, mind you, before you begin in earnest."

Vonrik nodded, but said nothing.

Hadwald and Deiter took their places with a few feet between them, facing the leather ball and its defenders.

The three armsmen locked their heaters left over right. Their gauntleted bright hands were held high, baskets beside their foreheads. They pointed their blade tips downward at a diagonal just in front of their shields on their dim sides.

The long angle this made was called a *tent block*. It served to defend face and head alike when in a default guard.

With a nod from Azhferd, the drill began.

"One..." Hadwald's voice was little more than a grunt. As he said this, he poked his spearhead between the center man's blade and the top of his shield.

He got the wooden spear tip beyond the shield's lip, but the shield man dropped his basket hilt double-quick. Bright hand, basket hilt, and blade trapped the spear between them before it could strike the helmet beyond.

Hadwald grinned—the only outward sign of his satisfaction. He spun his spear in place so its head was vertical, and yanked back toward himself.

The shield was pulled out of formation, opening wide as its owner tried to recover both his balance and his place in line; all while he struggled to defend himself with the sword held in his bright hand.

"Two!" Deiter's crisp tenor came out just as clipped as Hadwald's grunt had a breath before. He drove his spear into the gap made by the open bulwark, but rather than aiming at the shield man, he shot over the man's shoulder and struck the leather ball. He connected with enough force to make the rope it hung on stretch out parallel to the ground. It hung for a moment, ball straining against the rope before returning to strike another shield-bearer in the back of his helmeted head.

"Good!" Azhferd's voice came sharply over the clatter of moving weapons and armor. "Reset!"

Hadwald and Deiter stepped back as the three shieldmen shifted their positions. From the spearman's perspective, the shield on the far left stepped out of line, then walked to the far left. The other two men had taken a single step to their right. The man Hadwald had opened up was on the far left, looking for all the world as if he wanted to crawl into a hole for how that last exchange had gone.

"Hold," said Azhferd. He turned to Vonrik, brows raised in silent question. Did Vonrik see? Did he understand?

"Pull the shield, but leave the shieldman alive?" Vonrik's question bounced off of the stone walls in the stillness. It was a sensible enough thing to ask, but even as he asked it, his face lit with understanding. "...Ah, because the spears will be the knights and must be taken out of play first."

Azhferd grinned, nodding.

"Can you tell me *why*?"

"Range?"

Azhferd's face fought hard to fall at this, but with an effort, he kept that urge at bay. *Vonrik isn't seeing it.* He thought for a moment, then tried a different line of questioning.

"Tell me, Lord Von-*wreck*, who's likely to see themselves as most important on the field?"

"The nobility," said he.

"The nobility," Azhferd nodded. "Why is *that*?"

"Well... they're more well-trained, aren't they?" Vonrik drew himself up and back, leaning more heavily upon the stone stall wall as he considered.

Azhferd doubted that, but that topic was a matter for another discussion. Meeting Vonrik's eyes, he pressed a bit harder.

"What is it they *do* on the field?"

Vonrik's face lit up. His smile was bright, teeth so tightly together it was a wonder they weren't starting to show stress fractures, as stone eventually did.

"They're *spearmen*! They're spearmen who rely on their armsmen to defend them. Take out the nobles, and there's nobody left to command their forces!"

Here Azhferd allowed a smile but felt the need to correct that last part.

"Well, no. Nobles do command. But the armsmen do, actually, know how to fight without a noble there to tell them how to do it." He looked around as if hoping nobody else had heard him make such an absurd and dangerous claim.

Deiter snorted. Hadwald offered a thin smirk at that, elbowing him good-naturedly. The other armsmen looked uncertain as to how to feel, or rather, what reaction to show.

All of this Azhferd noticed, but he kept his focus on Vonrik to gauge his reaction to this rather unorthodox view.

"My Lord Azhferd!" said Vonrik. "How could you say such a thing aloud?" He leaned forward off of the stone wall, wearing an expression of disbelief. "If you say that sort of thing where they can overhear it, they'll know!" His eyes danced. "What's worse, my lord, they'll know that we know!"

Hadwald chuckled. Deiter kept his expression neutral, as did Hadwald's two grooms. Vonrik's men, however, actually laughed at their lord's antics.

This was an old game. Vonrik's grandfather had been called to the line before his handfasting had concluded. While he could have married a wealthier prospect—given his then-new status—he'd chosen to thumb his nose at the idea and married the miller's short daughter as he'd originally intended.

Azhferd made a gesture of shock and contrition, covering his mouth as if to recall his dangerous words. He looked around furtively as if to check to make certain no upstart commoners had overheard him.

After a moment, he made a gesture for the men to make ready, then began the exercise again.

They trained and fought until dusk, then returned to the manor, knowing they would be pleasantly sore come morning. They would rise and repeat their efforts until the training became rote.

Their dinner was humble but filling, and before the tenth bell had struck, they were all in their beds dreaming of Zlaté Pole. All, that was, save Azhferd. As usual, his was the sleep of the dead. If he dreamed, he never seemed to remember it.

He woke with a start at midnight, as the bell struck, and found himself in a curious position. He was halfway between wide awake and exhausted. In one breath, it was as if a sudden thunderbolt had roused him ... or a heavy knock had pounded on his chamber door. In the next, he felt he'd run an impossible distance.

He checked outside his door, then outside his window to the rolling rocks below. All seemed well, though his heart wouldn't stop beating as if he'd just ended a footrace.

He resigned himself to go back to bed and made it his focus to calm his hammering heart. Before long, he began to doze once more.

-II-

Venzene Duchy of Kamieńalun
County Czarny Wodospad
Wieża Szymona
38 Gerstesykli: 10 Days after the Red Storm at Westsong

Kozioł slept, but it was fitful. His dreams were twisted things wherein he tried to fight but couldn't. Where his cousin tried to fight but couldn't, and where graveyards stood waiting for fresh corpses—long narrow pits laid out neatly before blank, grey headstones.

At thirteen, and a seemingly endless time from his first manly growth, he should have been past childish, senseless nightmares. He should have been dreaming of glory, of tournaments and races, of women—in short, all the things he was given to expect a boy his age should find dominating his thoughts. Yet, here he was, stood in the misted air, in a place of sadness and terror, beneath a storm-laden sky that looked ready to burst.

He hadn't had the same dream nightly, but he'd had it before; he was almost certain. With each visit to this ominous dreamscape, that unhappy condition was a fear that never seemed willing to leave his mind for very long.

The grey dreamscape shifted, and he found himself stood naked in a field of golden wheat or long grass with a sky too blue to look at. The sun, normally a benign thing, seemed altogether watchful. He cast about him for a weapon but found none save the one he'd been born with. That wouldn't be much good if it came to a fight, as his dreams often seemed to.

He heard voices but couldn't find their source. There weren't even *trees* to hide behind here. So, where in hells were they coming from?

In a slow circle, he turned about himself in an effort to find anything to either walk toward or hide behind. There was nothing.

He stood near the top of a hill, which rose in a gentle slope. As far as the eye could see was an impossible sea of green and gold. Even Gerstealun didn't boast fields like this. He had been there once, at harvest time no less, and had been astonished by the waves upon waves of flowing grass and wheat. This, though... This was something else entirely.

Distantly, he heard the sound of swords clashing against one another. There were screams, growls of effort, and pitiful, wet sounds as iron or steel entered flesh.

He wasn't certain whether to run to or run from the sounds. He had a vague understanding that people he knew were fighting, but he couldn't determine whether he should run one way or the other. It didn't much matter; he supposed. He couldn't really determine direction, either ... save up and down. The sound hadn't come from a clear point. There was nothing for it to be hidden behind. This *should* have meant he was able to see its source. Should, however, was about as far as the matter went.

I'm safe here, but not for long, he thought. He had no idea why that thought should occur to him, but it did.

Movement behind him... he turned and saw an enormous horse crest the hill. It was the very definition of the word stallion, its dark beauty stark against the dazzling blue above and vibrant green and gold below.

It stomped the ground, tossed its noble head, then pawed at the sky, rearing up on its hind legs. As it came back down, he noted it was bleeding. Heedless of the danger, ignoring his confusion, he ran toward the creature.

Its sides had been scored with what he at first took for strokes with daggers or swords. Slowing his steps as he neared, it was obvious to him, though he couldn't place why that would be so, that they were actually tooth and claw marks.

They're human, he thought. That made no sense either, but what really *ever* made sense in dreams?

The horse nuzzled his neck. He felt the velvet touch with a sense of reality that went far beyond any simple dream. For a moment, this was almost utterly real to him ... almost. The horse nuzzled his ear, and he felt a shiver race up his bare spine.

All at once, he was weeping. He didn't know why. He heard only the dusky murmur of the horse's voice, low in the back of its ravaged neck. The creature didn't sound wounded, nor did it sound afraid. His eyes fell upon their mingled shadows stood close upon the ground. He saw its ears were pricked all the way forward, which he'd always been told meant the horse was in a happy mood.

All at once, he found himself weeping again. He threw his arms around the beast's neck and shuddered.

The horse bore this with a level of patience that shamed him. He leaned back and looked at the creature. It met his eyes and made another of those low, whickering sounds.

"How?" He heard himself—felt himself say this, yet he had no conscious understanding of having done so. It was as if he were outside himself, or perhaps so far *inside* himself, that he was no longer in control. "Tell me how!"

The horse dipped its head, nuzzling him from navel to neck. No, that wasn't right. It wasn't a nuzzle. The force behind it ushered him backward, down the hill, and away.

He did his best to hold on—he was still embracing the magnificent beast—but it once more moved to push him back. At first, the gesture was gentle, but in short order, it became insistent. The horse reared up on its hind legs, albeit briefly, dislodging his arms from around its neck. He stood there looking up at the creature and again heard himself speak without ever having meant to.

"No, I won't! You *cannot* make me do that! I cannot stand by while you—"

The horse pawed at the ground again, as if in answer, and tried to shove him back once more.

He found himself resisting, standing his ground with his feet spread apart for balance.

The horse shook violently, reared up one final time, then lowered its head and charged.

He felt the impact on his chest. Next he knew, he was flying backward through the howling air.

And then ... he wasn't. He stood atop a parapet, a familiar one at that. He couldn't place it, but he'd been here before.

All around, there was rain and fog, sleet, and misery. Guards rushed this way and that along the parapet, and below, he heard a sliding, shoving, undulating sound that he couldn't place.

As if he dreamed, which he supposed was exactly what he was doing, his head slowly turned to look down over the lip of the wall. Below was a near-literal sea of people. Arms and heads, torsos wrapped in armor, torn clothing or ribbons of ragged flesh stretched from the wall and the great gate, quite literally, to the horizon beyond.

"You need not fight," a voice said. Kozioł looked around but couldn't find its source. "Your line need not end here. It's not too late, even now. Even now, I will forgive all past sins against me—against the world. *You* are not the sins of your fathers. *You* did not betray my faith or trust in you. *You* did not abandon me. *You* did not fall from the path—did not become drunk on the lies of the enemy. Speak the words. Swear to me—renew your line's shattered oath, and I shall gladly open my arms to you again."

He tried to speak—to make some sort of reply. Nothing came out. He had no words. There was no malice, no rancor, merely a sadness that he could almost touch. The voice was soothing... reasonable... yet there was a trace of hope even in that sadness. "Come back to me." The voice spoke with a tired sorrow. "Speak the words, renew your line's sundered oath. All is forgiven, child. Come back to me..."

He couldn't bear it anymore. He would go mad. Was he shaking? Sobbing? The voice was *everywhere...*

-III-

Kozioł's eyes snapped open. He was in his bed, in his chambers, at home in his Uncle Hengrek's castle.

At first, he took the moisture on his face for sweat. He felt as if he had been working in the hot sun or perhaps just running. On further inspection, however, he realized he'd been crying. No, that was pride talking. The truth was that he was *still* crying. It was the dream—the voice's final sad plea.

He pulled himself from his bed, stripped off the long linen nightshirt he wore, and crawled back atop the coverlet.

For a far-too-brief span, it was good. He felt cool, and that seemed to soothe his confused mind. It didn't take long for his bare skin to sprout gooseflesh. He tried crawling under the fur blanket for warmth, but that was no good. While his body was now warmer than it had been, it wasn't warm enough.

With an effort, he made up his mind and forced himself to move. He crawled out of bed, shuddered, and dressed as quickly as he could. A walk, night air, perhaps a mulled wine if he could find some still resting on a hob.

He left his boots off, though he couldn't have said why. On some level, he felt perhaps it was too much effort to lace them again, though that would've been unnecessary. It wasn't as if he was planning on dangling his feet over the edge of the outer wall. As long as he didn't do that, his boots weren't going anywhere. Hells, they were damned near in need of replacement as it was. His feet had grown this last year, one of the few things about him that had, it seemed—much to his consternation. Whatever the real reason, he left them behind as he padded out of his bedchamber and down the hall.

There were no servants or guards walking about, but as it was the middle of the night, this didn't really surprise him. The few guards who remained on watch would be standing sentry near the count's chamber, not out patrolling every corridor.

He went down toward the second hall, which was where his father and his uncle liked to spend the latter portion of most evenings. They usually spoke of strategy, of Azhferd, of politics within the Duchy, or of the general goings-on both here and abroad. None of that mattered, however. What mattered was that they did this while drinking. This late in the year, he was certain, that would mean either mulled mead or mulled wine. It was rare he got to drink such things, at least in quantity, but he thought right now it would be just about the perfect thing to ease his troubled mind. Even now, he felt the dream's lingering effects. He walked the halls of the castle, almost as if he still dreamed.

Coming to the hall doors, he stopped just before his hand reached them—voices coming from inside? That wasn't right. It was too late, by hours no less, for anyone to be awake unless some great matter was afoot.

Yet there had been no great matters afoot, (other than the skirmishes to the north, he supposed), since he was very small. Beyond that, unless they'd arrived after he'd gone to take his sleep, no riders had come from afar to deliver dispatches from the northern border or to stand a few days as the Count's guest.

Though he knew better, he listened. All right. So listening at doors was the act of the spy or servant. They were often one and the same. But by the same token, he knew full well that this was out of the ordinary, and things that were out of the ordinary ran the risk of being dangerous. He would listen for a moment, and so long as the thing he heard did not immediately cause him alarm, he would withdraw and leave those within to their business. He wasn't interested in things that didn't concern him, and that included information. If this didn't pertain to him or his family, he would happily ignore it. The kitchens would have wine; if he were truly desperate, he could always go there.

"It's getting stronger. You know that." That was his uncle's voice.

"Is it getting stronger, or is your fear simply building up the fire?" And that voice, which was no surprise, really, was his father's.

"Do *not* mock me. I did not bring you into my councils so you could mock me." The count's voice was even and not more than a few steps away from playful, but there was an undertone of frustration in it.

"Then do not act or speak as if you are old and frail, jumping at the first clap of thunder as if you'd never heard its like before."

"I've considered the thought that this might all be for nothing. Of course, I have, but that doesn't make sense, either. I cannot fathom why I should be afraid of a thing like this, nor why such fear should call it into being that much faster." He paused and sipped at something. "Still, here am I stood in the middle night, ranting at you about a dream as if I were a child."

Kozioł froze. He'd been about to leave, despite his curiosity, but those final words stopped him in his tracks.

"You're talking as if you were certain of its origin ... certain of its truth. You speak in doom-ish tongue as if you were sure of what, or even *if* these dreams mean for you ... for your line. The truth ... the *only* truth here is that they repeat. While that's certainly enough to warrant attention, hells be hid, don't jump at every shadow, Hengrek..." He spoke in a hearty tone, clearly trying to wrest his lord—his wife's brother from these darksome thoughts.

"I'm well aware, and it's probably as you say." He paused, and when he spoke again, it was clear he'd been fighting to hold back the words that followed. "Borys, I know it sounds like madness. Still, the images, the *voice*—I can*not* shake the sense of foreboding that accompanies this lunacy."

Kozioł had to fight back the urge to rip open the door and charge in. He wanted to ask a million questions, to tell his uncle that he wasn't alone. That he, too, had had the dreams. But it could be nothing. His uncle could be talking about something entirely different. The count had the lives of many people on his mind, didn't he? The dream he spoke of could easily have been the pressures of the border conflict bubbling up just before he rode out to take personal command in the field.

Of *course* that was it. Why would it be anything else? After all, he, himself, had only had this one night's dream that he could remember ... or was that right? He knew he dreamed, and dreams were sometimes dangerous things. He often woke up as if he'd either been fighting or fleeing at least half-a-dozen times each month. Even still, he had no memory of this particular dream coming prior to tonight... did he? Something scratched at the back of his mind, but it was gone before he could seize upon it.

"You don't fight with the spear outside of the war of counties... well, at Zlaté Pole, and the rare occasion you ride down to Sommerregen for the Schild des Grafen, Hengrek. Why should the dream of the spear seem so real to you?"

"I wish I knew. But the voice is always the same. It's always sad. It always speaks as a father trying to forgive a wayward child. The speaker shames me more with each and every overture. I hear it, and I want to weep. I hear it, and I want to fall on my knees and beg forgiveness."

"When have you ever fallen on your knees a'purpose?"

The count gave a light snort at this.

"I'm serious," his father said. "I cannot think of anyone, living or dead, who could raise such strong feelings of uncertainty or guilt in you. Your father couldn't, the Duke certainly can't, nor the Emperor himself. You are someone who is nearly always certain of the path he should take—that his household should take. Why then would this voice?" He stopped, murmured a negation, then changed tactics. "Why would you ever feel guilt over a thing you could not possibly have done, have no memory of doing, and which hasn't even properly been laid out before you as an accusation?" Kozioł heard his father's voice drop in volume yet gain in intensity. "Hengrek, where is your center?"

After a long moment, the count replied.

"It stays behind to guard me as I sleep, I suppose." He snorted again, though with no real zeal for the task. "There is no magic to speak of anywhere in Venzene... certainly none that would account for this sort of... I don't even know... What would I call such a thing? An invasion of my dreams? I'm compelled to do nothing in them. I'm merely spoken to in a manner that seeks to convince me."

"If there is no proper explanation, and there is no enemy to attack or to defend against..." His father trailed off.

"Very true, Borys. If we cannot see an enemy, then we have no target. If we cannot find a target, we must bide our time, look, and listen."

"Exactly."

"Thank you. With luck or fate, or the sorts of luck or fate we make for ourselves, we will find a way to put a stop to this. So long as it doesn't spread like some sleeping sickness, for want of a better term, then all may yet be well."

Kozioł thought they were preparing to either change the subject or withdraw. He'd just about made up his mind to do the same when he nearly wet himself. A chilling hand covered his mouth and nose from behind, and a strong arm gripped him about his upper body, pulling him backward, pinning him to its owner.

-IV-

Venzene Duchy of Kamieńalun
County Czarny Wodospad
Village of Auburg
38 Gerstesykli: 10 Days after the Red Storm at Westsong

Azhferd wasn't overly worried as he made his way down the stairs. The hour was late. No, hang that. The hour was so late that it was early. But he knew full well that his work tomorrow would predominantly be observation and instruction, at least until the afternoon. The physical exertion required to teach successfully was minimal, and the physical requirement to observe was less than nothing.

There was every chance it would only be himself, Hadwald, and Vonrik again tomorrow. The others weren't due for a few more days, although one or two might come early, he supposed.

If he needed it—he didn't expect he would; after all, he was only twenty-five—he had already planned out a way he might recover himself.

His staff would provide a noon meal to the visiting sons of his father's banner knights and their armsmen. As they ate and blathered with one another, he could retire to his chambers. So long as he ensured that someone came to retrieve him after the appropriate hour had passed, he could, if necessary, put his back on the ground, bend his knees, and lay his lower legs atop his bed or chair while he rested. This was a trick taught him by his uncle, Syr Borys, and it worked a treat.

So, despite the fact that it was only a few hours until dawn, Azhferd walked quietly down the stairs to try to quiet his mind.

Had he held a formal feast last night with wine-soaked entertainment, and if he were to uphold the presumption of what a younger heir should play host to ... equally wine-soaked debauchery, he would've expected to see listless figures who'd passed out where they'd been sitting—and now snored where they'd passed out. Given the occasion, however, he had held no such feast.

Azhferd was surprised, therefore, to find the lone figure of Hadwald sat in front of the fire, boots off, feet toasting at a safe distance from the meager blaze. He looked as if he'd been there for about an age.

"Hadwald?" He offered a nod as he walked over. The subtext behind this decidedly benign greeting was clear, mild confusion without displeasure, concern, and a gentle rebuke. The hour was either late or exceptionally early. They would begin the day's activity in a scant few hours.

"My Lord Azhferd..." Hadwald's voice carried a slurred softness—a tone quite unlike him. In conversation, just as in fighting, once Hadwald had decided upon an action, he committed with a full heart. To hear him speak softly now, therefore, was, at the very least, something worthy of note and, at the very worst, boded ill for the man's current state of mind.

It's lack of sleep, Azhferd judged, *not an overindulgence of drink.*

Azhferd moved to sit in the chair opposite Hadwald before the fire. He deliberately held silent for a space of perhaps five minutes. He thought Hadwald was trying to build up the will to speak and wanted to give him the time and space he needed for that effort to run its course.

After a moment's consideration, he recognized the anguish on his friend's face. *No, it's not just his face. He's wearing it like a damned cloak.*

It's in his posture, his eyes—even the way his fingers and hair hang off of him. Hells... Whatever this was, it'd robbed Hadwald of not only sleep but also his very center. Azhferd made up his mind to speak, if only to remove the stress of having to start the conversation.

"Hadwald, my friend." He paused for a moment, looking into the fire rather than at the young man across to his left. After a brief interval, he turned back to regard the Heir to the House of Ullan. "You needn't answer, of course, but I would be remiss if I didn't ask. What troubles you? What can I do?"

Hadwald stiffened, then all of his muscles seemed to give way at once. He slumped, head down. In that same soft voice, perhaps tinged with a touch of impotent frustration, he answered this deceptively simple question.

"I've given everything," said he. "I've put not only my trust but my future in your hands, my lord."

Inwardly, Azhferd winced. This seemed woefully dramatic given the situation, but he took pains to remind himself that he did not, personally, have the perspective or life experiences that Hadwald did.

Hadwald Ullan was the heir to his father's knightly manor and, by extension, his household. That would have been a rarefied position to be in—in most cases. Syr Ullan, however, had but one manor and four sons.

Hadwald's three younger brothers, triplets, in fact, were often perceived as stones around their father's neck and impediments to Hadwald's perceived worth. To those outside of their household, the future prospects of that long loyal line looked grim indeed.

The boys still haven't managed, as of yet, to catch the eye of any knight. None seem willing to take them on as pages or squires, at any rate. This meant that Syr Ullan still needed to train them and pay for their daily upkeep, making things both financially and socially more involved, which, in turn, made them more difficult.

Daughters could be married off to form alliances, both political and social. They were, in many senses, a commodity for a noble intent on growing their political reach.

Sons only required coin and influence to propel them into the world. When such wealth wasn't easily at hand, the hope was that one or more of those additional sons might be taken in as a squire.

If the boy fared well, he would likely be offered a position as a house knight. If things went ill for him, at *worst*, he would be released from service rather than being called to the line. He'd be forced to find some other path to earn his daily bread. This usually led to life as either a mercenary or a common raider. The two were often much the same.

Your father still has yet to make a wedding match for you, either. If he did, he might manage an alliance that would strengthen your standing at court.

Such matches were often made by the mothers and merely formalized by the children's fathers. Here, too, Syr Ullan had been unlucky. His wife had died giving birth to what was quietly thought of as Ullan's litter.

All of this, Azhferd knew. He did his best to roll it around in his mind before answering, though if he were honest, he hoped that Hadwald would elaborate. No such luck.

"Hadwald … for you to be awake at this hour? If there's something that I can do, some help that I can render … you must tell me."

"No…" Hadwald shook his head. He sounded not so much frustrated now, as miserable. "I do *not* mean to…" He trailed off, shaking his head and hissing through his teeth in frustration. "I know…" He paused here again, trying to collect his thoughts.

Azhferd reached across the distance between them and laid a hand on his friend's right shoulder. He squeezed it, then patted it before letting go and leaning back.

Hadwald allowed a mirthless chuckle to escape his lips at the touch, first shaking his head, then nodding it.

"My lord," he began again, albeit with more confidence this time, "you've done absolutely everything I could've hoped … and more. By all accounts, I should be the least in your regard when it comes to the sons of the banners, and yet I'm among the *first* you call upon." He shook his head. "Your friendship has meant more to me than you can possibly know, and I'm grateful for it, and for you."

Hadwald had always been like a stone. He was immovable, unflappable, and, once he'd finally made a decision, resolute. As Azhferd reckoned it, for Hadwald to bear himself in this manner wasn't so much a frightening or even unmanly thing. It was simply so utterly out of character for him that it was unnerving.

The man wasn't shuddering in the corner, weeping into his non-existent ale, or the like. Still, it was clear something had shaken him, and Azhferd needed to uncover what that something was.

Outwardly, Azhferd allowed his face to bloom into a benign smile. Inwardly, however, he was both humbled and a bit afraid. He liked Hadwald—liked him from the first. He hadn't, however, understood the effect he, himself, had had on Syr Ullan's heir.

"Hadwald, both your friendship and loyalty have always meant a great deal to me. I trust you to stand at my back—to stand beside me now and for many years to come. You have my *every* confidence."

"Azhferd, I know it! Don't you think I know it?" Hadwald's outburst came carried on that soft, wretched near-whisper again.

Azhferd presumed that the tone was mostly an act of courtesy, given the hour and those sleeping upstairs. Still, the raw emotion stamped on Hadwald's face—the language of his body did nothing to ease the discomfiture Azhferd was inwardly combating.

"Azhferd... I'm *afraid*," he said at last.

"Of what?"

"Failure?"

"No one wins every fight, Hadwald. There's no shame in a loss."

Hadwald shook his head with surprising vehemence. He clenched his right fist, unclenched it, then clenched it once more.

"No, my lord, no! I'm afraid of failing *you* ... you, and all the faith and trust you've put in me, all the time you've put into training with me..." Silent tears rolled down his face. He wasn't sobbing, but he could no longer hold back whatever storm this evening had brought to the forefront of his mind. "I'm afraid of being the one man who cannot remember or do the things that you need done on the field when we reach Zlaté Pole! I'm afraid that I'll prove my house is already dead, already ignoble and buried. I'm afraid that the only way, the *only* way we'll gain footing to pull ourselves out of that miserable state is by currying favor with the count ... with you, once you ascend to your father's high seat."

Azhferd sat back, allowing his eyes to drop to a half-lidded state. He knew he couldn't remain silent for long, lest it make matters worse. He hadn't realized how important this tournament truly was in his friend's reckoning.

"Hadwald, listen to me now. Will you listen?"

Hadwald nodded but didn't turn his head or look up.

"Will you accept what I tell you as truth?"

Once more, Hadwald nodded.

"You have never lied to me, my lord. Not that I'm aware of, at least."

Azhferd nodded, considered his next words very carefully, and then pressed on.

"We have a few days before we gather here, then not quite a week of daily training with those who prove willing to fight beside us, then five days' travel, provided the weather gives us good, clear roads."

"Then Zlaté Pole," said Hadwald.

"Then, Zlaté Pole." Azhferd paused, then pressed on again. "A fortnight, and then we stand and fight."

Hadwald looked uncomfortable, as if speaking the words aloud gave them some new power over him.

He'd been driven, largely by the pressures of his house's current situation, to excellence. He was so focused on the journey that he hadn't stopped to recognize literally any of his accomplishments thus far. Hadwald didn't revel in or recall his own successes. Azhferd would have to take pains to point them out to him with more active purpose. Victory needed to be celebrated, if only for a moment. He realized that, with Hadwald, he had left that truth out of his lessons.

Azhferd chose his next words with a training axiom of his uncle's firmly fixed in his mind. Repetition builds memory, and memory can overcome uncertainty.

"There is every chance you'll be able to place highly, if not outright claim victory in the Squire's Tournament. There is every chance that you will place highly, if not outright claim victory in the Heir's Tournament." Azhferd held up a hand to forestall the man, who was already drawing breath to speak in protest. "You said you would listen." He waited until Hadwald nodded and settled himself, then spoke on. "When it comes to single combat, you're a much better warrior than I am. I'm a shieldman, but my skill with sword, or on horseback for that matter, is noticeably lacking by comparison to your own."

Rather than taking encouragement from this, Hadwald's shoulders slumped. He took on a miserable aspect, becoming a hunched and battered thing, as if Azhferd's every word had been a blow.

"That glory, should you indeed win through... That glory is your own, and I look forward to celebrating that with you. As for the War of Counties..." He sat back in his chair, letting his eyes slip to a nearly closed state. "The rest of the Duchy—and those across the border, by all accounts—consider infantry work to be beneath them. They train for tournaments, but not as groups. There, we have the advantage. If all that I have seen and learned regarding our friendly foes, as the saying goes, is true, there is every likelihood that we will take the purse and win the prize this year."

Hadwald straightened his shoulders at this, seeming to grow slightly more heartened. He kept his eyes downcast, however, looking at some point between his bare feet.

"You're that certain?"

"Nothing is certain, but I'm as sure as may be, given the information I've received."

"How did you gain this knowledge? I..." This was followed up by a near-instantaneous addendum. "I know it's rude of me to ask, and I *do* beg forgiveness, but..."

"Not at all. We are in private at this very moment, and as I've told you more times than I care to count, I believe in the old engineers' proverb."

To this, Hadwald's profile grinned.

"Ask, and I smile." Hadwald recited the old catechism with a nod of understanding even as he wiped his eyes.

"Exactly. Better you ask before building your understanding on unsteady ground. Better I explain in case you have a better idea than I."

Hadwald snorted at this but shook his head and made a "go on" gesture with his right hand.

"There's a wine merchant whom I assisted after his caravan had been sacked along the road. He'd meant to bring a large shipment of casks from his travels straight to my father's house."

"...I remember that." Hadwald looked up, smiling. "It was last Kamieńsykli—the last days of it, actually, just as the snows had really begun to melt." He paused, allowing his grin to widen. "You sent word to Vonrik and I that we were to hunt for the bandits, kill or capture them all, and hide whatever had been in their possession until you could make arrangements to sell it. My share of that turned out to be enough to replace my shields, repair my armor, and have coats of leather scale made for my brothers."

"Just so." Azhferd wore a smile he hadn't expected. He hadn't known exactly what Hadwald had done with his share of the spoils from that particular endeavor. It made him happy to know that not only had he handled the needs of his own kit, but he'd managed to outfit his younger brothers as well. "While you and Vonrik went off to catch the thieves, I saw to aiding the merchant. I arranged to give him a sum of money and send him off with Skar and Dieter just over the border to Hartscross. They returned with a fresh shipment of wine. The merchant sold that wine to my father's head of household, and my father was none the wiser ... or wouldn't have been if I hadn't told him."

Hadwald snapped his head around.

"You told him? Whatever for? Why would you do that?"

"I wanted to make certain I hadn't made any missteps. As it turns out, my father agreed with me."

Hadwald gaped.

"That particular wine merchant travels all throughout our Duchy, regularly making treks to neighboring ones at *least* once a year..." Azhferd said nothing more. He wanted to see if Hadwald could work it out on his own. A moment later, he was pleased to see he'd done so.

"The merchant owes you. Rather than lightening his purse, you've had him *spying*..." Hadwald sounded shocked, shaken, and more than a little impressed.

"I have. Only on benign matters, overall, but yes. I couldn't risk doing something of that nature in a way that affected any of our quarry masters or stonemasons, of course. There is no profit, no benefit to risking our chief industry and export just to win a tournament."

"But a wine merchant must go everywhere. They must visit common inns and noble households alike." He shook his head. "My lord, the scope of it..."

Azhferd grinned.

"My reports tell me that none of the other counties have any sort of consistent training or concentrated effort when it comes to melee. Sword and shield are focused weapons for tournament field of single combat. Armsmen are tossed into the front lines, and the gentry play spearman during rare tournaments that focus upon it ... and during the War of Counties. They see Zlaté Pole as nothing more than a chance to settle grudges in tournaments, to boast, and to prove that the knights and nobility are willing to get down in the mud with their sergeants and men at arms should the need arise... Of course, it likely never will."

"We really *can* win." Hadwald's voice was awestruck as he began to hope, to believe again.

"We can. That doesn't mean we will, of course, but we have a better chance than I suspect anyone else would imagine."

Hadwald looked as if a stone was beginning to roll off of his chest. "... And so, we'll be seen, should we be victorious, covered in glory, gain word fame, and more than a bit of coin."

Azhferd nodded. Each year at Zlaté Pole, Duke Harn of Kovalun offered up coin for each of the individual tournaments, as well as some finely crafted piece of armor, weapon, or steed. For the overall prize, he also put forward the income from at least one settlement for the year, all the way through the harvest. Sometimes it was a city, sometimes a village, sometimes several thorpes. Regardless, there was always at least one settlement whose earnings would fall to the winning county.

This year, his father had decreed that neither he nor the overwhelming majority of his knights would attend the festivities. While he'd made this decision prior to announcing the muster to sort the trouble along the northern border, Azhferd thought it more than possible that Hengrek had heard earlier rumors as to what was going on there. True or not, the northern crusade, as some were foolishly calling it, all but guaranteed few, if any, knights would attend this year.

As the heir, Azhferd would both assume command of what forces they brought to bear during the War of Counties and have sole discretion as to how to delineate the winnings, should they win. No portion of those winnings would be required to be passed along to his father, as his father would have no part in the battle, nor would he be there to witness or guide the actions of his army on or off of the field.

"Time will tell the tally, of course, but yes. We will be seen, and should we win through, we will be covered in glory, and will return with at least more wealth than we arrived with."

"Thank you, my lord. Thank you for telling me, for entrusting me with this."

Azhferd was pleased to hear that Hadwald was starting to sound more like his old self.

"Of course," said he. "As always, ask, and I smile."

They spent perhaps ten minutes in companionable silence, during which Hadwald's grin kept resurfacing. He was clearly mulling over all that Azhferd had said, seeming to find himself more and more pleased with what it portended.

Eventually, Hadwald stood, picking up his boots from beside the fire. With a brief bow of his head and a murmured good night, he turned and walked back up the stairs to the guestroom he'd been given.

Azhferd looked around the empty hall, nodded, and decided that perhaps that wasn't the worst idea anyone had had today. He could at least get three or four good hours before dawn. He had an idea that sleep wouldn't be long in coming. That was just as well.

Tomorrow, he, Hadwald, Vonrik, and their men would continue their training. No amount of intelligence would win a battle unless that intelligence were acted upon. For his part, he was more than ready to act.

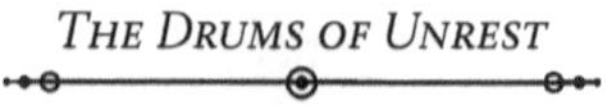

-V-

**Venzene Duchy of Kamieńalun
County Czarny Wodospad
Wieża Szymona
38 Gerstesykli: 10 Days after the Red Storm at Westsong**

She was careful to maintain her grip over the boy's mouth and nose with her right hand; her left arm around his own and upper chest. She bent her chin low so that it was level with his right ear. Her voice came out in a soft, deliberate whisper directly into that ear.

"Be still," said she. "With me now, before they catch you."

The words seemed to get through to him. She dragged his mostly willing form backward and around the corner into a blessedly unpeopled corridor. As he moved with her, she loosened her grip so that his nose was clear, allowing him to breathe. Five steps along, and she stopped, turning him to face her.

"Yeidil?" Kozioł mouthed this in obvious surprise. He was both shocked and visibly relieved.

She made a shushing gesture and beckoned him to follow her as she turned to walk further down the hall. She hoped he'd follow and was relieved when she heard his padding footfalls behind her.

Another thirty feet and the hall ran into a T intersection. She turned right and, a few paces farther along the hall, found her turning left toward a room she doubted the boy had ever been in the castelan's office.

As she put her hand to the door's iron handle, she did her best to murmur under her breath. The words made her smile, albeit briefly, and took her back, as they always did, to a time when she was small and almost carefree, save the monsters that she had been certain lurked in every shadow.

"Boję się ciemności," said she. *(I'm afraid of the dark.)*

Kozioł crowded into her, body pressed against her left hip. He was shaking more than a touch. She somehow doubted that this was due only to the omnipresent chill in the stone corridor. He'd been caught eavesdropping on both his father and hers. He undoubtedly expected her to demand some service or promise from him in order to keep his secret, but that would be preferable to the wrath of either of their fathers.

She opened the door and was pleased to see the candles along the wall to her left, and upon the room's lone desk were, indeed, lit as she'd meant them to be.

She bustled him in with a hand to the small of his back. He obediently moved, looking up at her in both gratitude and fear.

Shutting the door behind them, she gestured him to a seat in front of the desk and promptly walked to sit in the castelan's rather more imperious chair behind it.

He obliged, shoulders hunched, and bent his knees so that his feet were beneath his chair. He folded his hands in his lap and bowed his head, waiting.

She kept her voice low as she spoke, hoping he would have the sense to do the same.

"Dargory," said she, "what *were* you doing listening in on them?"

The use of his given name made him lower his head even further. When he spoke, it was in a small voice that sounded on the verge of tears.

"I... I don't—"

"Please do not tell me that you don't know. We both know that would be a lie, and you aren't a liar, are you?"

He looked up, eyes swimming, mouthing his negation, then drew a ragged breath down his throat. He held it for a long moment, then let it out slowly. When he'd finished, he looked much calmer.

"Azhferd taught you that, I expect."

He nodded, blinking to clear the tears from his eyes. This wasn't a matter of fear or sorrow—not anymore. Now it was a holdover from those once-vibrant emotions.

"I think I know what Uncle Hengrek was talking about," said he.

She did her best to hide her amusement.

"He won't thank you for thumping your chest about that fact, Kozioł."

He'd gone by Kozioł since he'd toddled. He smiled, pleased to hear the nickname once more, but it was a distracted thing.

"I'm *not* thumping my chest, Yeidil. It is thumping, mind you, but it's coming from inside, not out—my heart, not my fist."

She blinked at this, offered a reassuring smile, and made a gesture that said he should go on.

"Yeidil... I swear to you... I swear that I haven't done anything."

"Other than eavesdrop, you mean."

He shook his head, throwing up his hands in frustration.

"Yeidil, *please*!" He kept his voice low, but the intensity with which he spoke was enough to give her pause, at the very least.

"All right, go on."

"They were talking about your father's dreams—dreams he's had for some time, now—dreams that repeat."

Hells, how do I settle this now? she thought even as the gooseflesh began to rise on her blessedly covered arms.

"Keep your voice *down*, Kozioł. They shouldn't have to walk this way, but you may not be the only one on a midnight walk-about."

He nodded, drew and held another breath, then released it, steadying himself before pressing on with his tale.

"It's a dream that comes again and again. There's a sa voice that speaks of past sins..." He shook his head at her. "I'm serious, Yeidil. That's what they were discussing!"

"Perhaps you heard them—" She'd done her best to keep her voice even and calm, but he cut her off rather defensively.

"No, Yeidil! I know what I heard!"

How could she calm him or direct him elsewhere? It was dangerous, him discovering this—but if it stayed with him only, all might yet be well. If he began telling others about it—if he told Azhferd, things would be unrecoverable. She didn't like it, but she was fairly certain that her mother would either break his mind and leave him a gibbering idiot or outright kill him. Such a threat, no matter where the threat came from, or how innocently the truth had been stumbled upon, must be swiftly settled before it could undo their work.

Calpernia would make either situation look like an accident or the machination of some external source. An Eodenth assassin seemed the most likely scapegoat, given the state of things just now—but the end result would be the same. Bright, sweet Kozioł would be no more.

She thought she could kill him if she absolutely had to. She would weep and add yet more reason to hate her beloved mother for dragging her into this, but she thought that she had it in her to commit the actual act if it came to it.

Please, please, please, Kozioł, be dim this one time. Please be a normal boy, and not my brother's little mirror. Please...

"Even so, Kozioł—even if you're right about what you heard, what of it? My father has dreams, and sometimes they seem to repeat? We've all had that, or something like it before, haven't we?"

He gulped, looked at her, sniffed.

"Yeidil," his voice came out in a whimper, "I swear to you, I've done nothing... but..." His face was plaintive. "I've had the same dream..." This last came out in a ragged whisper, and with it, his tears began to flow.

"Come here—now." Her voice was suddenly cold and hard.

He bowed his head once more, stood, and shuffled around to stand before her.

She placed her hands upon his hips, guiding him so that he was in front of the desk's edge. She then raised her right hand to his belly and pushed him gently backward. He lifted himself, sitting on the desk with wide, miserable eyes marking her every expression.

She tried to force down her reaction to the news that he, too, was having the dreams. She needed more information to see exactly what this development might mean.

Taking his right hand between both of hers, she squeezed. The act made him smile, but the expression was brief.

"Yeidil, I swear on my mother's life, my father's name, a stack of lineage texts—anything you like. I did nothing. I've practiced nothing save the skills I'll need to one day be called to the line. I'm no czarodziej. Please ... I'm not."

"I know you aren't," said she. "You're a boy—not far from being a man. You're clever, kind, and quick. You're also clumsy and occasionally outright obnoxious. You are not, however, a czarodziej."

His relief was so obvious that she actually laughed, albeit softly.

"Still," said she, "wizard or not, we have to keep our voices down." She paused, summoning her will as she added, "Chcę, żeby nikt nas nie słyszał." *(I want nobody to hear us.)*

He nodded but otherwise showed no reaction to her words.

Good enough, she thought. *Now at least we won't be overheard.*

"Tell me everything. Let me see if I can help you."

He did so, allowing his eyes to glaze over as he recounted his dream. His face showed surprise that he remembered it so vividly. He recalled every word the sad voice had said to him—recalled the sound of the swords, the lines of shuffling men that stretched to the horizon. There was only one thing he couldn't recall.

"The horse *did* speak to me, as I say. I know that sounds impossible, but it did!" He struggled to keep his voice low, his frustration obvious. "I just... I don't know what he said. My dream-self did, but I couldn't hear the horse's response. Is that strange? It feels strange."

Yeidil knew the dream in question far too well—could have given it back to him sentence by sentence in nearly the same detail as he'd recalled it, in fact. She found this part of the tale anything but strange.

"Kozioł, that's the one part of your dream that sounds like a dream. It wasn't, of course, no more than your visit to the old keep at Adaldburg."

He nodded, then did a rather comical double-take.

"Wait! I never named it! Hells, it wasn't ever named in the dream, either! It looked like here, this castle, almost, but different somehow. Adaldburg? How do... How can... Yeidil? You've had the dreams too?"

She grinned, nodding.

"Clever boy," said she. "I've had them since I was nine." What in hells was she doing? She didn't know, truth be told. All she knew was that speaking openly of this with Kozioł made her feel a weight had been rolled off of her heart.

"What... What does it mean?"

"You feared I would think you a wizard in secret," said she.

He nodded.

"You feared being discovered as a wizard? Or did you fear discovering that you, yourself, were a wizard?"

"I don't... I don't understand."

She thought he did, for all that. His mind was working. She could see it in his pale eyes.

"Did you fear that you were a czarodziej—a wizard, or that people would discover or accuse you of being one?"

"...The latter."

"It isn't magic that you fear, then. It's the thought of disgrace."

He grinned weakly.

"I don't want to be driven away, Yeidil. I don't want to make my mother and father, your parents, anyone—ashamed of me."

She paused, squeezing his hand warmly again, though still not releasing it.

"You would never be driven away, Kozioł—not for that."

He smiled at her, face sad—almost pitying.

"Of course, I would. The Emperor's law is quite clear."

She drew in a breath and held it for a three count, then spoke words she had been commanded never to speak to anyone.

"The dream is real. Its call is real. Your blood—our blood—is marked by it, calls to it, draws it on."

He blinked, eyes widening, mouth slack.

"No..." He shook his head—met her eyes—dropped his gaze. "You are not the sins of your fathers. You did not betray my faith or trust in you..." He shook suddenly—shuddered as if chilled from within.

She stood and took him in her arms, careful never to break contact with him lest the spell that kept them silent to the outside world be broken.

"I have you, Kozioł. I have you."

He rocked with her, allowing himself to be soothed.

After a moment, he spoke in a cracked, hoarse voice that didn't sound much like him.

"He sounded so sad... We betrayed him—I betrayed him, somehow. Yeidil... how? What did I do? What did we do?"

"I will tell you. I will teach you. There is so much you need to know, Kozioł—so much that will be hard to hear, and so much of it involves Father and Azhferd."

He leaned back, hands on her shoulders, looking her in the eye.

"Does he have the dreams?"

"No," said she. "I protect him from them."

"How?" His eyes grew enormous. His hands gripped her shoulders tightly. "You're a czarownica?"

"Not a witch, Kozioł. They're something else entirely."

He met her eyes, brows knitting together, not in anger but in an obvious expression of irritation at her mincing of words.

She took one final deep breath, then said it aloud for the first time within these walls.

"Czarodziejka—a sorceress." She paused, then amended, "A Czarodziejka z wieży."

"A ... tower sorceress?" His face registered the connection instantly. Her family's surname, when rendered into the Trade Tongue, was, after all, Black Tower.

She nodded.

"Yes, and you..."

"I'm not a sorceress," he said, then blushed as he realized the gender of that particular word.

"No, not a sorceress. You are, however, a caster. You're either a Tarcza Clariona or a Miecz Clariona—a Clarion's shield or sword. We'll need to figure out which."

He blinked, shook his head, and tried to pull back from her, but she held him fast.

"Listen to me, Kozioł. I have been hiding Azhferd from these dreams since I was about your age. I've done my best, and thus far, it's been enough, but you're his squire. You'll ride off with him wherever he goes. If you'll let me train you, you can protect him when I cannot." She shook her head, still amazed at her own boldness. Was she truly going to take him on as an apprentice in secret? Without her mother's leave, or Kozioł's father's?

"If anyone found out—if my father found out... Yeidil, I love you—I love Azhferd, but..." He shook his head. "I'll keep your secret. Of course, I will. But I'm not what you think I am—if I were, my father would skin me and hang me out for the crows!"

"Your father might hang *me* out for them, but not you. Your father knows. He's my father's Tarcza Clariona."

Kozioł froze.

He searched her eyes, tried to lift both hands to her cheeks. She allowed his left to do as he wanted, but refused to release his right until his left had made contact with her flesh. Now, more than ever, the spell must not be broken.

"Swear it to me. Swear it on your mother's name, Yeidil ... swear you're true! *Swear* it!" His voice was full of desperate intensity.

She took his wrists in her hands, smiling. She had won, and she knew it.

"Kozioł, I swear it on Azhferd's life."

He held her eyes, then brought his forehead forward to press against hers.

"...All right." It was all he could say. Then again, to her mind, it was all the affirmation that was needed.

"Will you?" she asked. "Will you be both Azhferd's squire and my apprentice?"

He nodded, forehead still pressed to hers.

"Say it—swear it to me, Kozioł. Swear you will keep the secrets—mine and ours. Swear you will help me protect him from the voice."

Kozioł swallowed.

"I, Dargory Syn Borysa, swear to keep your secrets and our secrets, to be both Azhferd's man and Yeidil's apprentice, and to protect my lord from…" He trailed off, cocking his head to one side as he leaned back. "Who is he, Yeidil?"

She paused for a long moment before answering.

I have to tell him something, and he'll learn it soon enough. What name can I use? What words are safe? She thought about all she knew of their old foe—their once-master, and settled on a descriptive term, rather than a name.

"The King of the Dead," said she. "He and his retinue, his army, and his avarice."

His eyes first widened, then narrowed as he rolled that title around in his head. Finally, he gave a single nod of acceptance, finishing his oath.

"…To protect my lord from the King of the Dead, until the sky falls, my life is lost, or my mistress proves false in her love of that lord."

She smiled with a warmth that seemed to surprise him.

"Cleverly spoken, Kozioł." She embraced him briefly but fiercely. "I will find you come tomorrow. I'll have you attend me in the inner, then lower markets, which will give us time to begin. An hour or so is all we need worry about for now." Still smiling, she leaned forward to kiss his forehead. "You cannot know how good it feels to have you with me— someone who I know I can rely upon."

He smiled at her. He was uncertain, clearly, but he was with her.

What is it you always say, Father? The loyalty of men is yours to lose?

Ten minutes later found her back in her bed. She couldn't stop smiling. If she handled this correctly, her mother's mewling would be of no great matter. Her overconfidence would, perhaps, be Hengrek's undoing, but Azhferd would not see the same fate. She would keep him hidden from all of this until the time was right, which may well be never. His dreams would belong to her and her alone.

Kozioł, be true. Please, be true…

With that final thought, she drifted off to a sleep more restful than any she'd had in recent memory.

THE BURDEN OF MEMORY

-I-

Venzene Duchy of Kamieńalun
County Czarny Wodospad
Wieża Szymona
41 Gerstesykli: 13 Days after the Red Storm at Westsong

The room was dark. The dark was … *there.* It wasn't a presence, exactly, but a sense of anticipation as anxious as any child on Koruni Spanek waiting for someone to either give or open a gift.

Kozioł lay atop his bed, fighting against his own impatience. His fingers pinched and combed through a thick lock of hair the color of winter's blackest night.

As his thoughts began to spiral off into random incoherence, he unconsciously twisted the lock around his right index finger, then unraveled it, re-wrapping it around his left. Spinning its other end around his thumb, he pulled the strands taut in his left hand.

He slid his right thumb and forefinger up, then back down along its silken length several times before realizing what he was doing–what the motion emulated. Blushing, though nobody could see it … he hoped. He pulled his right hand away as if the hair had bitten him.

Where was she? Kozioł thought he might have been lying there for ten minutes, perhaps as long as an hour. Who could tell in this purgatorial blackness?

He resisted the urge to call to her. She wouldn't have fallen asleep, surely.

Kozioł whispered to himself, running over what he had learned while he still had time. Tonight, she would ask, and tonight he would answer ... he hoped.

"Wayfarers bridge where they are and where they want to go. Walkers travel to other worlds and places of concept—whatever that means."

He rolled his eyes beneath their closed lids. What in hells were *other worlds*? Come to that, what in the hells were *places of concept*? She'd spoken of the realm of fire and the realm of order, but all such words conjured in his mind were enormous columns of fire, and an endless row of shelves, respectively.

He stopped trying to chew on that and continued his recitation in that same soft whisper.

"Prol ... prom ... prolagents?"

"Promulgant," Yeidil's voice came from his own belly, where he held the lock of her hair.

He jumped, giving a small "Meep!" sound and nearly flinging the hair away.

She laughed warmly, though only for a moment. When she'd stopped, she spoke again, her smile evident in her tone.

"I *am* sorry, Kozioł. I didn't mean to startle you."

"You... You can hear me?"

"I can, and I would keep my voice down, were I you—or the rest of the *keep* will hear you as well—but yes. I can hear you plainly."

"And you're ... on the other side of the castle," said he. He didn't sound as if he didn't believe her, but rather as if he wanted confirmation.

"I am, as we speak, seated on my bed with the door closed and locked."

He smiled, sitting up and looking down at where he was fairly certain his hands were.

"Don't sit up, Dargory. You'll need to sleep soon."

His eyes went wide. It wasn't the use of his given name, though he'd registered that as well. "You can see me?" His mind went back to where it had been when he'd realized what he'd been doing with the lock of her hair, and his entire face felt as if it were burning bright enough to set fire to the bedding.

"Noooo. The rustling on the fur blanket and the batting being crushed as you moved more weight onto your pillow were fairly good indicators ... little Kozioł." Her voice was playful, but only just. Another step to one side or the other, and she'd have sounded genuinely patronizing.

He obeyed, making himself comfortable.

"Say it." Her voice was cool, formal sounding.

"What?"

"Prom-ul-gation," said she.

He repeated the word, taking care to pronounce it correctly.

"Good. And those who practice promulgation?"

"Promulgants," he said and smiled.

"Good. What is their province of power?"

He scrunched up his face, then sighed out his answer. He'd gotten hold of it, now. Saying the word—hearing it pronounced correctly brought him back to the lesson she'd taught him over the last few days.

"Promulgants bend the will of others, charming, convincing, or commanding them to act, or stay their actions."

"Excellent. Next?"

"Fabricants make magic—"

"The Weave..." Her voice wasn't cruel, but she overrode him with force.

He winced.

"The Weave—Fabricants forge the weave into items of power." He didn't wait for her next question before plunging ahead. He was finally on track, as he saw it, and wanted this part of the night's training over with. "Callers conjure and summon creatures and sometimes items from where the Walkers... um... walk." He blushed at this, uncertain if he'd made the right connection between the two forms of power.

"Kozioł ... *very* good!" She sounded pleased and genuinely surprised. "It isn't a great leap, certainly, but that you've made such a leap at all is a very good sign."

He grinned, then pressed on to the end, fighting the urge to wrap and unwrap the lock of hair from his index fingers again and again.

"Wakers work what most people see as battle magic. They draw on fire, ice, and the like, creating them from seemingly nothing. They can also offer protection from such things."

"And the final two?"

"Sag... sagissss..." he trailed off, willing her not to speak as he hunted for the word. "Sagacite and Author!"

"Shhh!" Her hiss came through from atop his belly, making him think of air escaping through his navel. He laughed and snorted into his own forearm for a moment, then became more serious.

"I'm sorry, Yeidil. I am." Before she could ask, he finished his litany. "Sagacites deal in augury and communication. It's what we're using right now. The Author deals in false things. Allusions."

"Illusions, Kozioł. Illusions. Allusions are hints to things. Illusions are pretty lies."

He nodded, face growing serious in the dark.

"Illusions, then."

Silence met this. He was about to call her name when he realized why she'd stopped speaking—the catechism.

"I thank you for the instruction, Elder," said he. "May I learn this lesson well, and," he paused, screwing up his face as he groped for the words, "...Ah! May it save me from the Torn Hour, when all else has failed, and fear is given form before me. I should have said it sooner. Forgive me."

"May it serve to quiet your heart when Havoc's Horn is winded once more," Yeidil said. Her tone was measured, but she sounded altogether pleased with his answer.

"Will we..."

"Yes, Kozioł, we will move onto the next lesson." She paused for a moment, then spoke in a voice that was small and steely. "I will teach you words to carry you down into sleep. You will repeat them until sleep stops your mouth. Do you understand?"

"Yes, Yeidil."

"You will sleep, and when you next see, you will be somewhere else. Speak the words there again, and the fog will lift from your mind. Do not leave that place until I am there. I will be wearing a yellow robe with a red hood and mantled cloak. Do you understand?"

"Yes, Yeidil."

"Tell me what you understand."

"You'll teach me words. I'll speak them until I sleep. When I look around, I will be somewhere..." He paused, shaking his head in rueful self-admonishment. For a moment, he hadn't believed her. Then he realized that he was disbelieving the woman who was speaking to him—by means of a lock of *hair,* mind—from across the castle and through multiple stone walls. "...Someplace else. I will speak the words again to lift the fog. And look for you to appear in yellow robes and a red-hooded cloak."

"Good," said she. "There's one more matter to discuss before we begin. You've already shown me that you understand the risks of being caught wielding sorcery. Women—even noblewomen—have challenges of their own, should they be caught practicing such arts. But men and boys are at *much* greater risk. Do you know why?"

He paused for a beat to consider his answer, then spoke up. "Death."

"Bad enough, I grant you. But no. That risk exists for us all. It's something else—something with much farther reach. Something with a broader impact."

Kozioł spent a few more moments trying to come up with an answer, but nothing felt quite right. His mind kept returning to thoughts of Azhferd, who would one day be called to the line. Hells, his cousin wouldn't just be knighted, he'd be called upon to serve as Count, once Uncle Hengrek stepped down. Yeidil was trying to teach him how to better protect Azhferd. The notion that he was already missing something ... But that was absurd. Of *course* he was missing something. All right. So he didn't know what Yeidil was driving at. Why should that surprise him? This was his first real day of training, wasn't it?

So I don't know the answer. So? Kamień jest szary, he thought. (Stone is Grey.) Azhferd, Uncle Hengrek, even his eldest brother Bartek all said the same thing whenever he didn't know a thing. *Ask, and I smile...* Now *he* was smiling.

"I don't actually know, Yeidil."

There was a pause before she replied, but not a long one. "Who is it that's most likely to own or inherit land and wealth, assuming there's any to be had?"

His eyes shot open in the dark. "Men, of course. And... and if a man is found guilty of sorcery, his family..." Kozioł's voice came out in a tone of breathy awe.

"That's it *exactly*, Kozioł. Men are more likely to be drunk, gambling, or both in a tavern. They're more apt to find themselves in conflicts that end in bloodshed even if they don't end in their deaths. Be it out of anger or desperation, in a fit of drunkenness or fear of death; men *already* hold more than their own lives in their hands. One careless or weak-willed moment..."

A silence fell. When he could no longer stand it, Kozioł spoke up again.

"Hells, Yeidil…" His voice was thin and frightened even to his own ears. "I can give you my *oath*, and I do so. But I can't be on guard forever. *Nobody* can. I'm *bound* to make a mistake!"

"You are. Everyone does, eventually. That goes for men *and* women. So what are we to do?" Yeidil paused for a beat. "We must stack the deck in our favor before we sit down to play our deadly game of trefning."

"How?" He felt his heart beginning to slow. When had it started thundering? "Am I never to drink anything stronger than milk or breakfast ale again?"

"While you could do worse than resist drinking yourself into a stupor, no. The incantations are things you'll avoid saying in public at all costs."

"But what if I'm drunk? If I'm angry enough in a brawl or a tournament? What if I—"

"All incantations are rodzaj żeński, Kozioł … rodzaj żeński, or rodzaj nijaki." *(Feminine, or neuter.)* Yeidil paused, as if to let him absorb the idea.

"You … want me to speak spells like a girl? Using girl's words?" His first instinct was to refuse out of hand. All right, he wasn't a man yet, but he certainly wasn't a *woman*. "Is there no other way?"

"There are risks and prices we pay for anything we want. If we stay up late to listen to a bard, or talk round the fire, either we wake near our usual time anyway and lose sleep, or we have a late lay in, and chores and duties don't get seen to. This is the price men pay to learn and wield such power. Other places in the world may do things differently, but this is how things are done here."

"My father would *never* speak in women's words, Yeidil. He'd never put his damned *sword* down for all of the challenges to his honor or your father's."

"Which is exactly why the rule exists. You're quite right. Your father *would* never speak such words in public for those very reasons. Men would mock him for being unmanly and mock my father for letting such a man stand as his knight and bodyguard. And so he is forced to be careful with his sorcery. He's forced to be more aware of his surroundings and forced to have to truly take a beat to create the incantations he speaks so that they're constructed rightly. Do you see?"

Kozioł sighed. It made sense. He hated it, but it *would* force him to actually think before he acted in any way involving sorcery. No matter how drunk he got, he couldn't imagine spouting something off using rodzaj żeński construction. If word got round, he'd be mortified.

"All right, Yeidil. I hate it. But I understand. Just ... not *too* feminine, all right?"

"Agreed," said she. "Now... lay back and be as easy as your mind will allow."

He rolled his eyes as he moved to obey. Was he blushing? Well, so be it. He settled himself into a comfortable position, then nodded.

"I'm ready, Yeidil."

"Good. Repeat after me." She paused for perhaps a four count, then spoke in a clear, flat tone. "Szłam niepewnie w ciemności. Mówiłam nieświadomie przeciwko światłu. Moja piosenka, jak kwas, parzy pod niebem. Budzę się by przeżyć rozdartą godzinę."

(I walked, uncertain in the dark. I spoke, unknown, against the light. My song, like acid under the sky. I wake to weather the Torn Hour.)

He'd been worried that he might have difficulty committing the words to memory, especially given their feminine construction. As it turned out, he needn't have concerned himself. The words had a rhythm to them. It had the cadence of certain old walking songs.

That realization caused three things to happen at nearly the same moment. Kozioł had always loved song of almost any kind. And while sometimes he forgot other things as the day rolled by, he rarely forgot a verse. He wondered how much of that Yeidil had considered when coming up with this ... song? Could one rightly call this a song? He didn't know, but that felt right to him.

Directly on the heels of that thought came another.

It's like the old walking songs—is this a Weave Walker rite? Someplace else! Yes! Surely it must be! She said I would be someplace else!

No sooner had he come to that conclusion than his own voice became distant to him. He felt his head grow heavy. His mind was floating, filling, full ... of fog.

An interval of warm silence passed. When next Kozioł knew, he was lying in tall grass, surrounded by overgrown trees. These giant things had trunks as thick as silos and branches that strove to steal the light before it could spill more than a few drops through to the ground.

His limbs were heavy. He tried to move but found it was like trying to walk after being struck in the head.

"I... The s-say..." He tried to speak, to instruct himself, remind himself of what to do, but his voice sounded foreign to his own ears. It was so hard to focus. He tried to move his right hand up and over to paw at his own cheek.

At first, nothing happened. His body simply would not, or perhaps could not, obey him. With an almighty act of will, he tried once more. This time, the arm obeyed and ended with him punching himself squarely in the right eye.

He yelled, though the voice that came out was slow and far away.

He felt the grass beginning to grow insubstantial, the trees starting to fade from view as if swallowed by the fog that lived inside of him.

"No!" In his mind, his voice was strong and clear. While the punch had done something to knock him a pace toward his right mind, he was still leagues away from that happy condition.

He began to murmur. He saw the trees grow, or perhaps he was sinking through the unreality of this place.

"Złam łem niepewnie w ciemności..." He couldn't find the rest. What was it? What were the words? "The Torn... The Torn Ho—"

The world shook. No, the forest moved! He saw red vines slithering along the gargantuan surfaces of the trees, slowly spinning down toward him.

His mind rejected what he saw. This was a dream! A dream! Things in a dream weren't real! They couldn't hurt... couldn't...

"Szłam niepewnie w ciemności. Mówiłam nieświadomie przeciwko światłu. Moja piosenka, jak kwas, parzy pod niebem. Budzę się by przeżyć rozdartą godzinę... Say! Speak the words!" Yeidil's voice ... and growing closer.

With an effort, he fought against the horrid chill that seemed to grip his every numbed nerve, simultaneously wakening and weakening them.

"Szłam... Szłam niepewnie w ciemności... Mówiłam nieświadomie przeciwko światłu... Moja piosenka, jak kwas, parzy pod niebem. Budzę się by przeżyć rozdartą godzinę!" As he found the words—as he spoke them aloud, he felt warmth returning to his limbs. More importantly, he felt clarity returning to his mind. "Budzę się, by przeżyć rozdartą godzinę!"

He repeated the words again and again. By the end of the third recitation, he smelled the forest, the scents of strange blooms he did not recognize, and the lower, darker scent of animals. He felt the grass around him, felt the influx of bright sights, smells, and sounds like a slap.

Yeidil was there, at last. She moved to him with confidence and deliberation, but not, he noted, with haste.

"You went faster than I expected," said she, reaching a hand down to him. "You've an aptitude for Weave Walking, it seems." She sounded as if this fact held only mild interest to her. If she was impressed by this discovery, she gave no sign.

He took her hand and found it quite solid. A moment later found him on his feet, her hand prudently on his bright side shoulder.

"Where are we?"

"Well, *Apprentice*, we are in a near place."

"Near?"

She guided him away from the massive trees. Looking back, he saw the red vines undulate once more, retracting into the trees' upper branches.

"It's a place outside of Skolf. It touches Skolf—nearly mirrors it, in fact—but lay apart from it and its rules."

He shook his head, trying to grasp it.

"The Shesh call it Akhdir la Yantahi—the Endless Green. The Eodenth name for it is Taghido, which means nearly the same thing."

He shook his head once more, then tried to laugh through his discomfort. He hated the falseness in that laughter.

"So, it's the Green Land, then?"

"I suppose that's as good a name as any."

"What *is* it? What're we doing here?"

"You need to meet someone—or rather, you need to visit someone."

"Who?"

"We're nearly there. Patience, apprentice."

"Yei—Yes ... Mistress." He'd nearly said her name—a thing he'd been told not to do when they were anywhere save the keep when the Weave was being discussed.

She smiled, moving through a thinning forest before, at last, shifting a low-hanging branch aside.

When she'd led him through, he froze on the spot. A gasp escaped his lips. He looked up and fought the strong urge to actually cry out.

She moved behind him, placing both hands on his shoulders.

"If you feel dizzy, Apprentice, speak the words again..."

"N-no. I'm ... fine." The sky, the hill, the grasses—it was the place from his dreams, down to the last detail. He found himself looking to confirm he was still dressed. In the dreams, he had always been naked. He was relieved to find that he was, in fact, still in the same clothing he'd worn to bed.

"Are you calm? Do you have mastery of yourself?"

He nodded. He didn't trust himself to speak.

She walked around him and sat on the golden grass, pulling at his hand for him to join her.

Kozioł did so readily enough, pleased not to have to balance any longer. He wasn't dizzy, exactly, but there was something safer about being seated.

"Can you speak? Think?"

He nodded.

"What does it mean to wield the Weave?"

He took a moment to draw a steadying breath. He exhaled before making his reply. His heart had slowed, at last. He hadn't noticed before that moment, but it had begun to race when he first entered this tranquil place.

"Wielding the Weave is the act of bending reality to match the will of the weaver," he said at last.

She nodded.

"What aspect of power concerns itself with coercion: command and charm?"

"Prom... Promulgation." His voice held a note of triumph as he answered.

She nodded her approval.

"Excellent." She took a moment to consider, then nodded as if making up her mind. She reached forward and took both of his hands in hers.

He tried to read her intent by searching out her eyes but discovered that he couldn't precisely *find* them amidst the shadows of her red hood.

"This place is as safe a place as any here. This is where you should come to meet me for training." She paused for a moment, then smiled, shrugging her left shoulder and looking down to her right as she added, "While you're away with Azhferd, that is."

"How will I do that?" He paused. "Without him noticing, I mean."

She blinked. "How would he notice?"

"Well, I mean, if I'm not in my room when he calls me, or if I'm late or get lost returning..."

She laughed.

Kozioł blushed and glowered at her.

"I'm serious!"

"I know." Her voice was high and breathy as she spoke through the last of her laughter. "We aren't *here*. Well, not in the way you think we are, at any rate."

"I don't..."

"You are, as we speak, lying on your bed back at the castle."

"I... Wait, what?"

"Focus on me now. Listen."

He drew his focus to the movement of her mouth and waited.

"There are a few ways to enter this place. All are dangerous, after a fashion." Once he'd nodded, she then continued her lesson. "There are some natural places where the boundaries between this place and Skolf are thin. They're usually hidden and often guarded by some great power—a champion, great beast or monster, or the like. That's the first way, and how the uninitiated occasionally make their way here."

"All right. There *are* cradle tales that talk about entering the underworld, or the hallowed halls..." he trailed off, eyes growing wide. "Hells be hid! That? *That's* what you meant by other worlds?"

She beamed at him.

"You really are catching on quickly."

He smiled weakly, pleased at the compliment, but still staggered by the realization. He could go to the Hallowed Halls, where his grandfather now rested? Could visit children he'd played with when he was small, and a pox had ravaged the lower town? The Hallowed Halls held a place for children taken by fate rather than their own foolishness, after all—and he could go there? Madness!

"Look at me." Her voice was firm, though not cold or cruel.

"I... I'm sorry, Yei... Mistress."

She smiled, squeezing his hands.

"Are you ready for more?" When he nodded, she continued. "The second way into this place is through potent use of Weave Walking mixed with a grounding in Wayfaring. The Caster opens a way between this world and Skolf and physically walks through or leads others through. You and I didn't walk here, however, did we?"

"We walked into this *specific* place, but no. I lay on my bed and sang your song."

Her face softened at that.

"...Sang my song. I rather like that turn of phrase."

He squeezed her hands gently in response.

"The third way is dreams, then," said he. "Dreams take us here on their own, but the place *feels* like a dream then because it *is* a dream. Is that right?"

Her face displayed her pride at his conclusion.

"Just so. The chant—the song, as you put it, acts as your center—your tether to keep your mind, your *will* here."

This made sense. He fought down the sudden urge to laugh.

So—magic is dangerous, horrid, monstrous, and evil. We're taught to fear it because of the evils it did to the empire centuries ago when we invaded Nausha... or tried to, anyway. Not only am I here learning it from my cousin—a woman I've known since I first learned how to speak—but it makes sense to me... sense. Magic ... makes ... sense? I'm mad. I must be. Shaking his head, he found that he had a question.

"How did you know about this place? This specific place, I mean. Was it from the dream I told you about?"

"It was." She nodded. "That, and the fact that I've been here before. So has your father."

"Wh-what?"

"Your father's sword came from this place. My..." She paused, clearly rethinking what she was about to say. "My teacher brought me here, too. We didn't stay here for very long, but long enough for me to gain and learn what I needed to."

His mind was racing. A sword? His father's sword? And Yeidil's teacher? Why didn't she say the name? It must be his own mother. Who else could it be?

"You'll have your own choice to make soon enough."

"I will?"

"Do you remember what I said to you a few nights back? The castelan's office, do you remember?"

He didn't. That night had been a whirlwind of emotions. Much of the detail had been lost to him in the days that followed.

"Tarcza Clariona..." She trailed off, hoping to jog his memory.

"...Or a Miecz Clariona," said he. "Shield or sword, you said. But is it *my* choice?"

"In a manner of speaking, yes. The choice you make here, either tonight or in the not-far-off future, will close one door and open another."

He sat back, pulling his hands gently out of her grip and leaning back on them.

"How will I know which to choose?"

"That's exactly why we're here. Best we take what time we can before you ride out to Auburg."

He considered, then leaned forward again, forearms on his thighs.

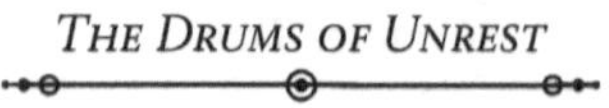

"All right, *Mistress*," he smiled at this, teasing her a bit, "tell me what I need to know."

-II-

County Thorion
Eastshadow
41 Gerstesykli: 13 Days after the Red Storm at Westsong

Gordan ran a hand across the empty space where his hair had been fully five years before. About two-thirds of the way back along his bald pate, he reached the fringe of flyaway blond that remained. He combed through it with ungentle fingers before bringing his hand back down to rest on the lip of the parapet's wooden wall.

This whole thing was ridiculous. After having survived at Westsong, the idea that life would change for all of them had been an easy wine to get drunk upon. He supposed the prediction hadn't been untrue, strictly speaking, but the reality fell far short of his initial expectations and heady dreams.

That Barnic had received Eastshadow had been a surprise, certainly, but nobody questioned that he had earned a prize of such magnitude.

The truth was they had each earned such a place. Apart from Alnik and Jaron, most of them had received a holding of their own. It was only the boys from Knell's Stone that had been forced to stay banded together for some machination he himself did not yet understand.

Gordan (Sir Gordan, he reminded himself—and not with undue pride) should not be stood at a guard's perch along the tall wall-walk of Sir Barnic's new holding. He should, by his own reckoning at least, be currently in his own chambers, within his own manor house on his newly granted lands. At this very moment, he should be thrusting deeply into some peasant girl, glad for the safety and security brought by being his mistress. Failing that, he should be asleep, dreaming of the noble daughters of the court, one or another of whom he could now reasonably expect to marry.

Barnic had asked him and the others to take up shifts on night-watch, two per night. He'd wanted them to show solidarity—that they took the safety of the villagers seriously. Gordan had agreed, as had the others, but he was sure they'd all done so as grudgingly as he had. The work was long, dull, and trivial.

The horrors of Westsong wouldn't reach this far east, surely. Even if such a thing did come to pass, they knew the signs to look for. They knew how to best the monsters that brought such misery to bear.

Eastshadow is important, I suppose. No, he amended, *suppose isn't the right word. Admit... Admit is the right word.* He admitted to himself that Eastshadow was a place of import. It *did* deserve more than one knight living within its pristine palisades and well-ordered thoroughfares. Especially given what was going on to the North, or rather what they presumed was going on to the North, the idea that Eastshadow had but one lord protector did leave it vulnerable.

"But dammit all," he murmured to himself. "There should be a hard limit on how long we're meant to stay here, shouldn't there?"

"Sir Gordan?"

This was one of the guards he was in charge of on this shift. Damned if he could remember his name. Of course, he was likely having trouble recalling it chiefly because he didn't think his name much mattered.

"Nothing. Thinking out loud. Trying to figure out exactly what we're supposed to be looking for."

The guard made a grunt of acceptance, nodding his head but saying no more.

That was fine by Gordan. There was enough conversation going on in his own head.

What was he *doing*? Was he really laying contumely on the people whom he not long ago counted himself numbered among? He'd been an armsman. He'd been Sir Valad's armsman. Even now, the thought of his liege lord dead caused his eyes to begin welling up, his fists to clench, and his jaw to set. He mastered these things with only mild effort, but he still had to make an actual, conscious effort to claim control over his wounded heart and mind.

Valad had been a friend, a mentor, and something of a father to the boys. The boys? None of them had been boys for years. Gordan, himself, was twenty-eight now. This made him two years older than Barnic, three years older than Jastar, and one year younger than Raegus and Aethan. He was, he realized, and not for the first time, the middle child, so he'd been stuck accepting Barnic's will.

What would you have told me, Valad? It only took him a moment to work that puzzle out, and when he did, he snorted lightly, allowing a wry smirk to lift the left side of his mouth. *You would've told me to pay more attention to the guards beneath my command, and at the very least, to learn their damned names.*

The voice of that good old man came back to him now, replacing the inner voice of his own mind. It made his smile broaden.

If you have no respect for them, how can you expect them to show any respect to you? Fear? Perhaps, but that will only hold while you're there to enforce it. Fear and intimidation, much like intelligences, decay rapidly, away from their sources. If you want them to respect you when you aren't around, as well as when you're in their presence, you must respect the men you command.

He sighed, ignoring the quirked look of curiosity the guard threw at him from the corner of his eye. *Didn't you ever get bored with being right, Valad?* With a shake of his head, he found that he had an answer for that, too. *No, of course not—just with the rest of us being wrong.*

With another soft snort at his own expense, Sir Gordan refocused on the task at hand, resolving to go on better than he'd begun.

Eastshadow stood as the settlement closest to the county's northern edge. The river, some three leagues and a bit more to the north, created a natural barrier, marking their practical borders—those which they could control and maintain. While the Thorion Throne officially claimed ownership over an additional seven leagues beyond the river, no enforcement or patrol roamed so far.

Because Her Ladyship's coach and coterie—her ramble and retinue—claim dominion over that patch. Nobody really wanted to try their hand at wrestling it away from death's own bride.

The Shivering Song even now, thinking about the horror she represented, was enough to send a chill up his spine. For centuries—since time first told, or so they said, the area north of the river had been the stuff of cradle tales for indolent children, dares for idiot youths, and boasts for intoxicated fools. It was green and wonderful, lush and wild, save the bleak marshland that slowly fed the river as it ran westward. The lands were ruled from the only construction north of the river for days of travel.

The Shivering Song reigned over a court of Hamara Fe—dusk fae: terrible and unending monsters of wicked, deadly repute.

Her Ladyship would ride within her courtly carriage, the Coach Devour. It was said to be drawn by eight magnificent stallions, their death wounds on display, ghostly blood, and viscera trailing behind, dripping off of them in the moonlight. That light pervaded, somehow—whether the sky was blank and grey or bright and clear.

Her soldiery came with her. They escorted the Coach Devour, ensuring that the lonely lady could tour the countryside, lamenting in peace, looking for some lost love, singing for her sundered kin.

It had long since been said—was sworn to by many of the county's older residents—that on nights of the new, half, or full moon, all and sundry were to beware the mist and stay indoors. Were mortal man, woman, or child to be found out upon the road, in field, or near fen, the bright lady and her outriders would find the unlucky soul, take them into the Coach Devour, lull them to sleep, and carry them back across the river to the Hamara Fe lands beyond.

Never would such an unfortunate be seen again unless it were as one of the Shivering Song's coterie of soldiers, on the lookout for the next prize found wandering the world when all the air grew cold.

He'd marveled at the men of this place ... and the women, indeed, even the children, once upon a dreaming day. That they could live in the very shadow of the Shivering Song and work and toil—that they had the fearlessness to carve out normal-seeming lives with her so very close at hand—had always filled him with a quiet awe.

That, however, was before he'd arrived here with his brothers-in-arms—before he'd survived Westsong.

Now that he was here, Eastshadow seemed more or less a place like any other. The village was more structured than most, but that had been due to Sir Cedric's well-ordered mind, and he was now gone.

Gordan paced along the parapet, trying to gauge the hour. It was frustratingly early yet. He looked at his fellows, stood along the wall, and was annoyed to see an utter lack of fatigue and discontent.

His first thought was that these men would never be worthy of knighthood. They were too content with their lot in life. The thought made him smile. A moment later, his face fell. He bowed his head in silent recrimination.

That was unworthy. They act with diligence. I act in pride at my station—a station I was granted due to extraordinary events, not my extraordinary self.

He fetched a sigh and turned to look out over the village, or township, or whatever one called such a place.

Eastshadow was a collection of palisades. Each section held its own small silo for grain, its own small herd of livestock—cows and sheep, mostly, turned out most nights, and its own well. It gave the impression of a military camp that had been taken over by the descendants of its original soldiers. A lovely tale, but the truth was far less romantic.

It was common knowledge that Sir Cedric's father had been killed and his holdings raided by a pack of bandits and sell-swords. Cedric had been expected to give chase, to make vows to hunt them to Skolf's own seam. Instead, he set about borrowing the Throne's craftsmen and paying nearby manors for timber and iron.

The result was a single, long lane bordered on either side and at one end by these wooden fortifications.

If anyone should breach one such palisade, they would be sealed into that area and either filled with arrows or burned alive along with that section of the township.

One man's practicality is another man's romance, I suppose.

He'd been out here under a mostly moonless sky for the best part of two hours. They hadn't seen anything more interesting than a vixen leading her children through the tall grasses southeast of town.

The sound had stiffened his spine with a quickness, to be sure. He'd heard the rustling and immediately thought back to Westsong. He saw the movement in the grass and began trembling with fear, drawing in breath to shout alarm before one of the guardsmen—the one who'd spoken a moment ago, he was sure of it—pointed out the vixen.

Falxes fall, Gordan, have your nerves really been shot full of that many holes or stretched to that much incredulity? The appearance of a vixen and her cubs running through the grass at night sets your teeth itching, chills down your spine, and a need to feel your sword in your hand? It's all just ... wrong!

His world had been turned upside down, and he had no idea how to right it. Giving Eastshadow to Barnic made sense. That, he admitted once more, was true enough. Barnic was their leader, had been the senior squire, was more levelheaded, and consistently outclassed them all in terms of skill at arms on a near-constant basis. Of course, he would get the earliest harvest. That made sense, bitter as it was to choke down, and Gordan had done his best not to begrudge it.

Won't be long before you and the others are given your due. You can rely on that, and you know it. So why are you seething about the state of things?

"Sir Gordan?" This was the same guardsman, but he was speaking quietly as if trying to maintain confidentiality.

Gordan looked at him, raising his eyebrows by way of both acknowledgement and question.

"Movement from the south and east... mainly the east." There was a softness to the man's voice as if he were uncertain of what he was saying ... or perhaps of his permission to say it.

"What of it? Probably just another fox."

"Nay, sir." The guard sounded ominous, somehow.

"What do you mean, no? How can you possibly tell? And if not a fox, what?" Gordan hoped he sounded more annoyed than afraid, given he wasn't certain which one of those two currently held chief position in his mind or heart. Something in the guard's tone and body language chilled him, though he couldn't place what.

"Sniff the air. Tell me what ee'smell, sir."

Gordan complied with this strange request. He drew first a shallow, then a deeper draft of sweet night air. That had been his intent, at any rate. The scent which assaulted his nose was anything but sweet. There was a smell like carrion and rot. It was distant enough not to make his gorge rise, but not by much. He could smell it, and smelling it made his skin crawl as if he'd been touching its source.

"Storms be swift!" This ancient farmers' stave escaped him in a sighing rush. He was too stunned and sickened to be afraid and too afraid to be authoritative. "What in hells is it? What vile thing could—*would* choose to be heralded by such a stench?"

"Goblins, sir," the guard's voice was hollow, though it sounded steady enough. "Goblins, or I'm the countess's long-lost heir. That stench comes out of the mountains this time of year, although 'ey rarely move this close to town. Every now and again, 'ey'll get 'ungry enough no' to fear if we kill one or two of 'em, but that's all."

Then why the hells do you sound and seem so damned worried?

A moment later and Gordan answered his own question.

"How much movement did you see? Can you pinpoint and quietly pass the word to any archers we have on the wall?" Gordan's voice was steadier than he felt it had any business being. His lips were numb, and he was sure he'd broken out in a cold sweat.

"Aye, mi'lord. I make eight. A thing to note, though." The guard did his best to deliver this next sentence with as plain and unemotional a tone as he could muster. "'Ey usually travel in triads." This meant that the eight separate movements spotted in the tall grasses *might* mean as many as a score or more goblins waiting to pounce.

Gordan nodded, made a dismissive gesture with the altogether numb fingers of his left hand, and watched with some small satisfaction as the guard moved off as instructed. With slow deliberation, he passed the word.

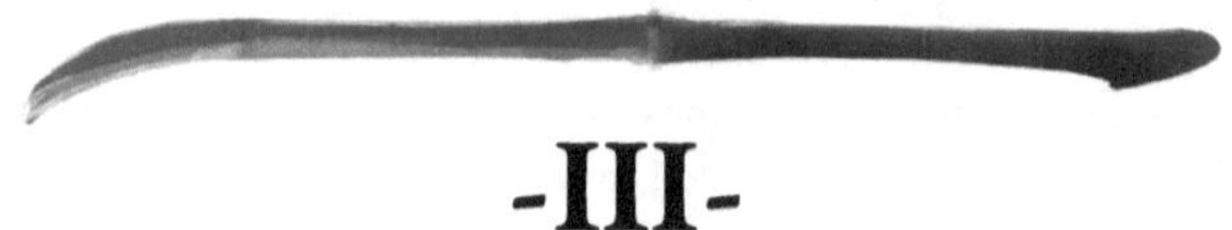

-III-

Barnic sat in the great chair of Eastshadow. The long stone trough which held the low fire provided the only light in the room. It'd burned down enough that Jastar had installed himself on its edge, seated with his forearms on his knees facing Barnic. They'd been like this for the best part of an hour now. It was often their way to sit up late into the night and talk about events. It had been for as long as they could remember. Still, in the dozen or so years they had known one another, there had never been quite so much to talk about as there was now.

"Barnic, you're allowed to feel guilt. You know that, surely..."

"It isn't... isn't guilt, exactly, it's just—"

"...Guilt wearing something of a party cloak." Jastar didn't wait for him to finish before speaking. In other company, that would've been considered rude... would have almost necessitated a loss of face and status for whichever one backed down. When it was just the two of them, however, those pleasantries were regularly tossed aside by one or the other of them.

Barnic glared briefly but then shook his head, allowing the sudden flare of frustration to dissipate harmlessly.

"You're right, of course. It just seems mad to me that the others..." He trailed off, lifting the splayed fingers of his hand and then the hand itself to the air in the universal gesture of inarticulate frustration.

"Just because they're older, and were here before either of us, doesn't mean they should automatically gain the spoils. You know that. Sir Valad always believed in merit and always dismissed the marks of age." He allowed a grin to play across his pale face and looked up. "How many times did he say it?" He adopted an air of very gentle mockery as his voice took on an exaggerated mimicry of their fallen master. "The marks of age..."

"...Do not always equate to the marks of wisdom," Barnic finished with him in unison.

They both grinned, though each saw plainly that the expression the other wore was bittersweet.

After a protracted period of silence, wherein each man was left alone with his thoughts, Jastar finally spoke anew, returning them to the point at hand.

"It never occurred to you that because we were the youngest, we were the ones most likely to distinguish ourselves?"

"That seems absurd to me." Barnic ran the palm of his right hand up the side of his face, brushing along the stubble there. He hadn't shaved in days and wasn't certain whether he wanted to.

"Look at you!" Jastar made his voice amused and incredulous rather than angry. "You haven't shaved—since the announcement, in fact. Trying to grow a beard just to prove that you are, in fact, old enough to sit in Father's chair?" This was pure mockery. That chair hadn't belonged to any of their fathers. Barnic's father, Jastar knew, had died on a bandit hunt perhaps a month after the boys' first meeting on Valad's estate.

"That's," Barnic chuckled once and bowed his head for a moment before looking back up to meet his old friend's eyes, "the plain truth of it. You've caught me, which is good because I hadn't yet caught myself. It just makes no sense to me. Every one of them fought just as well as I, and I have no doubt just as well as you. We all did right by Valad's teachings and his memory—all of us. Why, then, am *I* rewarded with Eastshadow of all places? Why are the rest of our brothers knighted but given no lands to call their own?"

Jastar nodded at this. It was true. Added to the essential strangeness of the situation was the fact that his old friend—his taken brother—had never been comfortable with praise or reward. Even as boys, it had been so.

"Why must you *always* sour your own joy? Even when you stand victorious at day's end—even when you leave the tournament field covered in glory. Defeating all opponents fairly and cleanly, you question yourself and seek to eschew the reward you're due."

"Jastar." He shook his head. "Can you not see how this is different? I have Eastshadow! I am the new Lord of *Eastshadow*!" Barnic wasn't shouting but rather emphatic as he ranted. "Add to that the fact that you are preparing to undertake a commission like none other. Meanwhile, Aethan, Raegus, and Gordan are meant to... what? Drink the bitter potion of service without station? They are banner knights, true and sure, or so their patent claims. Yet, they've been granted no land of their own! Why?" He thumped his fists on the arms of his great chair and issued a growl of muted frustration.

For a long moment, Jastar didn't answer. It was a reasonable enough question. Finally, after perhaps a minute had passed, he stood and, meeting Barnic's eyes, crossed the intervening distance between them.

Barnic put his hands up as if to ward off Jastar.

"Jast, hear me. They see change in their fortune—well earned, to be sure, yet are expected to serve and remain here under my banner. Where is the sense—where is the justice in this? How am I to reconcile it? Hells, all three of them had been learning under Sir Valad's hand for years before I'd ever set foot in Knell's Stone! How can I look them in the eye?"

"Are you my brother?"

Barnic's frustration gave way to a reluctant grin. He couldn't help it. This was an old game. They'd been together nearly at all times from almost the minute they'd been introduced.

The sons of lesser noble houses which possessed no lands of their own, the boys had been given over to Sir Valad's care in hopes that such an association would improve their future prospects. Both had been relatively new to any form of combat, let alone any form of direct attention prior to that.

They'd liked one another from the first. Being forced into the rigors of knightly service at nearly the same tender age had only served to strengthen that bond. They'd sworn their brotherhood to each other long before the rest of them began referring to one another as squire brother.

"Aye, I am. You know I am."

"And am I yours?"

Barnic nodded. "Always."

"Good," Jastar nodded. "Then listen to me now. After a certain point, age no longer matters. Not until such time as the age of dotage is threatening. You kept us together, fought as well as any champion, and have been the first among equals-amongst us at any rate—for half a decade now. You are still young enough to have taken risks and still resilient enough of mind and heart to have stood your ground, even in the midst of that horror. More, you had the wit and spine to bark orders when orders needed barking. Is anything I have said untrue?" He knew the answer, of course, but he needed Barnic to speak the words aloud and acknowledge them as truth.

Barnic looked away, looked up at him again, then finally decided he needed to stare at the fire in order to truly think about this. After a few moments of reflection, he nodded.

"What you say is entirely true. I can't speak to why I was able to do it, but yes. I stayed the course—stayed the line, fought, survived. And I barked orders as you so gently framed it."

"Oh, forgive me, mi'lord Eastshadow. I should have spoken in more genteel tones, should I not? When I'm addressing someone of your great stature, how-*ever* could I *not* be awed into gentle speech?" Jastar made his voice almost a child's mockery, adding to it an exaggerated bow, deliberately allowing his hair to whip forward and nearly smack Barnic in the face. Given he wore it in a long war braid at present, it would've stung if only for the intricate metal star it was threaded through near its end.

Barnic snorted, pulled his head away, stood up, and shoved Jastar back, almost knocking him to the ground. Both men laughed, and just like that, the mood lightened.

Jastar watched Barnic turn and walk toward a side table. A carafe of wine, a quartet of wooden goblets, some horse bread, and a fruit preserve Jastar'd never had before were set out upon it. Barnic filled two goblets, turned, and strode a few paces, offering one vessel toward Jastar, accompanied by a warm grin.

"How long before you leave?"

Jastar shrugged. He didn't know.

"It won't be tomorrow, I can tell you that much. Perhaps the day after, perhaps the day after that. I need Eastshadow to feel comfortable and familiar before I go."

"Why is that? I should've thought it would've made more sense to leave while everything was unfamiliar still, lest you get too attached..." Barnic didn't sound as if he were trying to push his old friend out the door but was genuinely confused.

Jastar allowed a few pinches of frustrated disdain to enter his mind, making themselves known through the bitter tones of his voice.

"Now that the Lord of Eastshadow has been replaced... It's time I'm on the move. There's no place for me in the new lord's court, so it's time for me to find a place where loyalty is rewarded."

Barnic looked thunderstruck.

Jastar grinned, saluted him with his goblet, and took a very long pull. Smacking his lips a bit (the wine here seemed to have a spiced, almost peppery aftertaste), he laid his dim hand on Barnic's bright shoulder. The gesture—shield hand on sword shoulder—conveyed the simplest sentiment: *I have you.*

"It's all right," he said. "There needs to be a reason for me to go, and this is as good a reason as any."

Barnic nodded slowly. After a moment's consideration, he spoke with a level of seriousness that the situation didn't quite call for.

"You know you'll always have a place in my court and a room here... clothing, food... whatever you need." He paused, looking down between his feet, before adding, "You're the only family I have."

Jastar was touched. He knew full well that Barnic didn't have anything against the rest of their brothers, nor did he view them with any disdain, but he'd never been close with them.

In a flash, Jastar realized that Barnic knew that the story regarding his lost place in this court was pure fabrication—meant only to inform his behavior as he undertook Sir Greggor's commission. Still, some part of Barnic needed to spell his mind and mood out clearly. Sometimes speaking a burden aloud was enough to lighten it. Sometimes it was enough just to know that a thing hadn't been left unsaid.

"I know it well," Jastar said. "And there will come a time that Sir Jastar's with you again. Make no mistake." He smirked a bit, then allowed that smirk to bloom into a full-blown smile. "If nothing else, I have to come back when you finally get married. It won't be too long. Either Marcza will agree, securing her family's tie to Eastshadow, or the countess will make a selection for you." He moved back toward the table, laying his goblet down upon it. "The Lord of Eastshadow cannot be without an heir for long."

Barnic shook his head. "I can't marry her."

"Who?"

"Marcza's half-sister ... the one Sir Lamwreigh was going to marry."

"Alysuun of Southwall? Why in hells not? She's beautiful, willful, and will run your life as you need and as she should do. You don't need a meek flower. You need a lioness."

"Jast, the woman is *sixteen*. She's barely a woman at all."

Jastar shook his head, a rueful smile on his face.

"Have you *seen* her? She's an entire conflagration in a tiny package. And I promise you, Barnic, she's—at least according to my eyes—most assuredly not a girl. That woman, should she consent, will ensure that you stay trim, fit, fed, and fairly drained on a regular basis, I've no doubt."

Barnic's face flushed. He was notoriously strait-laced when it came to things like this, and the age difference between he, at twenty-six, and any suitable match, almost certainly to be years and years younger than him, made him absolutely uncomfortable. It wasn't that he had no lust, merely that he found the idea of any grown man wedding and bedding a half-grown woman to be absurd, if not downright evil.

"Barnic…"

Barnic shook his head, held up a hand, then shook his head again.

Jastar walked back over and set himself to stand directly in front of his old friend.

"Wed yourself to her anyway, assuming the match is made by either the countess or Dame Marcza. No matter who the woman is, marry her. Do so unless you have active reason to dislike her, either physically or, and I suspect this will be more important for you, as you speak with her."

Barnic opened his mouth, but Jastar forestalled him.

"No, hear me."

Barnic closed his mouth and nodded, resigned.

"Get a thimbleful of blood, or have your bride-to-be find a thimbleful of blood. Explain to her your concern, and be sure that the thimbleful of blood finds its way into your marriage bed, spread appropriately on the sheets. When the bedding goes to be laundered, word will spread that you have, in fact, consummated your marriage and that the new Lady of Eastshadow was indeed virginal. When she's old enough by your reckoning and hers, then sleep with her, as a man and woman should do. Not every couple has children within the first year or three, although it is relatively common."

Barnic looked stunned.

"You're suggesting I lie? That I drag her into a lie?"

Jastar sighed.

"Well, your choices are limited. You can tell a small lie and then later make it true. You can go against your better judgment and bed the girl, anyway. Failing that, you can have questions at court from every quarter. Let them all talk about the strange, solitary Lord of Eastshadow who cannot, or will not, secure a household in that crucial fastness for one peculiar reason or another." He allowed himself to grin again. "You must drink poison. There's no choice there. What I'm offering you is an opportunity to choose which poison you drink."

Barnic nodded. He didn't like it, but he understood it. After a moment's silence, he nodded again.

"I hate the advice, but it's good advice. Thank you."

The door burst open. A guardsman came rushing into the chamber, skidding to a halt before the pair and bowing as he spilled both blood and his words out before them.

"My lords! My lords! Goblins! We are attacked!"

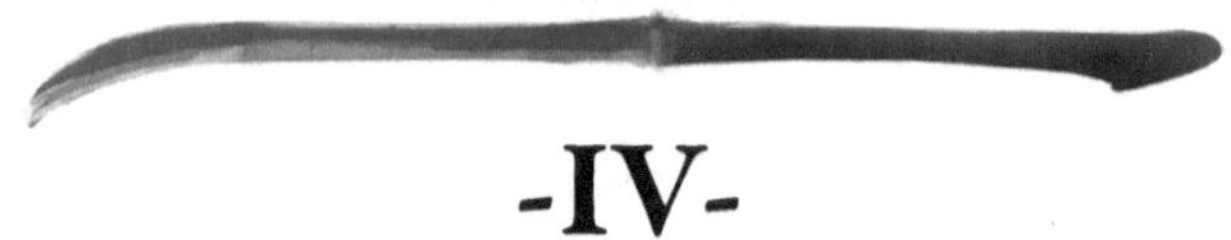

-IV-

Arrows rent the air, sounding like giant dragonflies buzzing angrily as they dove Skolfward. They were aimed down toward the grasses below at any movements that bent the tall stalks away from their fellows.

Gordan had heard at least two hits score on something other than the cold earth beneath, but there'd been no sound of pain, no cry of outrage or fear.

The memory of Westsong still whispered in his mind. The unnatural appearance of men whose faces he'd known, fought against, and occasionally beside had been miserable enough. Their monstrous strength and haunted hatred of Gordan and the rest of the newly dubbed *Nineteen* had almost been too much. They hadn't talked much about it since that day, although he imagined that Barnic and Jastar had done so when in private. It still gnawed at him in the watches of the night, when he pulled himself from red dreams where he and his fellows were outnumbered and overtaken. He suspected the same was true of the others.

Westsong had been a horror of the heart, and some part of him still dwelt there, fought there, and would not return. Tonight, by contrast, Eastshadow was a horror of the mind... the movement of a foe he couldn't see, couldn't hear, and could only trace by virtue of the stench of putrefaction that hung about the area below... yet he knew that they were there. His flesh crawled, eyes and mind raced, but he remained locked in a state of inaction. What could he do?

He looked toward the mountains to the east, from whence the attack had apparently come. Their feet and, indeed, their peaks were shrouded in frosted mists. No, that wasn't quite right. The peaks were wrapped in an icy fog, but the mountain's feet were covered in pale clouds of browns and greens.

It's like... like being able to see the smell, he thought. The idea made his stomach perform several feats of acrobatics before it settled itself.

As he tore his gaze away, his eyes fell upon movement just to the east of the next palisade. He watched in horror as a pale green arm, long and well-muscled, reached up from the concealing grass, and groped for a handhold between the planks. A second arm joined the first, where it stopped and began to pull backward and down.

"There! There!" Gordan drew his sword, pointing it down at the thing, his dim hand grabbing the nearest guard's shoulder. "Bring him down! Now!"

Gordan's fear broke out along his brow in a thin layer of clammy sweat. He wanted it dead before he had to see the horrid body that bore such limbs—the alien head that directed them.

The guard whose shoulder he'd grabbed shook the hand free, aimed, and fired. He'd loosed a second arrow before Gordan had registered the first one'd hit its mark.

The arms withdrew. They didn't fall or slink away. They withdrew. A moment later, that particular patch of grass erupted.

Gordan felt the desire to look away, to run, to vomit, to scream... He did none of these. Instead, he merely stood, sword lowering to point toward his feet, mouth agape.

Three goblins rose from their hiding places, standing well beneath the six-foot mark—the height of most human women. Each was naked to the waist, despite the cold, revealing sickly green flesh hung on narrow shoulders. Their arms were long, their bellies slightly distended. Their faces, however, were wrinkled, wide-mouthed things, housing wet, glistening fangs. Two slits served as nostrils. This nightmarish image was rendered complete by virtue of short, sharply pointed ears beneath silver clumps of coarse-looking hair ... or perhaps fur.

The one nearest the palisade—surely the one who'd been about to climb up or rip down the board—raised his arm, pointing at Gordan with a digit that bore far too many knuckles. It widened its mouth as if it were shouting, though no sound came out.

Silent or not, the goblins began moving with an eerie, unearthly speed. One goblin dove forward into the grass and disappeared beneath it as if diving into water.

Another pulled a bow from somewhere in the grass below his knees. He made an arrow appear from his dim side inner forearm as if by some trick. He drew back, aimed, and fired ... directly at Gordan.

Time seemed to slow for him as the arrow flew. He saw the starlight glint off of its surface as if the shaft were lashed with metal. He had an instant to wonder at that, then realized that it didn't much matter ... not anymore, at least.

I'm dead, he thought. *All of Valad's teaching, all the fights both won and lost, even Westsong, where I earned my spurs... and here is where I die.*

Something crashed against him. The world was movement and freefall, then sudden, searing pain as his back hit the wooden stair that led down from the wall-walk.

His vision blurred. He lay there, alive but dazed, staring up at the night sky and a face—a familiar one. It took him a moment to register it as the senior guardsman he'd spoken to before the attack—the same man who had carried his orders to the others and had shot twice at the goblin leader... the man whose name he hadn't bothered to learn.

He saw an arrow sticking out of the man's left side. It protruded from beneath his upper arm, sunk to just above the fletching. The expression he wore was one of determination fading to shock. Even now, Gordan saw the man's jaw shake, then go slack.

Gordan doubted he'd meant to take the arrow for him. Surely the fellow had simply reacted to push him out of the way and gotten caught, hadn't he? With a jolt, Gordan realized he'd just seen the light go out of the man's eyes.

Trying to close his own, he found he couldn't look away. Instead, he pushed himself to a sitting position, then tried to stand.

Arrows were still buzzing through the air. Men still called out targets to one another, and Gordan—Sir Gordan merely stood there, for a moment, lost.

That moment was shattered as he saw a pale green hand come up over the lip of the palisade. Two arrows sprouted from its forearm, but it was doggedly heaving itself up onto the wall, reaching for the arrow that had been meant for Gordan.

He reacted.

His eyes fell upon his sword, dropped as he'd been pushed to safety. He reached for it, pulling it from beneath the fallen guardsman, and took two steps backward, climbing the stair without turning his back on the goblin.

It glared at him, making a face that should have had an accompanying hiss or screech as its herald, though none came. The creature seemed to be mute.

Gordan took a single step backward, then leapt upon the thing, bashing its left ear, then slashing down as it staggered away.

It offered no resistance but glared at him as if he had affronted it somehow. It reached for the arrow once again.

With a cry of mingled rage and disgust, Gordan brought his blade down against the thing's outstretched arm, then its neck. It survived the first blow, but he felt bone give way under his second.

He breathed heavily as the thing twitched and, at last, ceased.

"They're retreating!" He heard a man cry from some distance.

Gordon walked past the guardsman's limp form, fist shaking around the hilt of his sword, and came upon the goblin-thing's body. He kicked it, then kicked it again, thinking that would be enough to get the rage and fear out of his system. But a moment later, he found himself striking its face with the pommel of his sword.

The next thing he knew, strong arms were pulling him back away from the ruined thing.

Someone had sent for Barnic. *Good. Leave it to the new lord to sort. Let him see what awaits him.*

Gordan knew what they were. They weren't goblins or demons out of cradle tales. They weren't people to be treated with or beasts to be hunted and culled. They were heralds. He had seen that face, had heard their muted cry. They were death—a punishment, a lesson for some sin they did not recall.

He had no idea why or how he knew this, but he was certain it was true—had to be true. Such a face... such walking wrongness surely must be a harbinger of the end.

"And I killed one of them. What brave punishment awaits me for such arrogance?"

He slumped against the man who walked with him and led him toward his own quarters.

"I have killed death," he said under his breath. "I have killed death and must..." Must what? He didn't know. He didn't know anything, least of all where this sudden onset of darksome thoughts had come from. It wasn't like him to think, to speak so dramatically.

He had a vague sense of being put to bed, an equally vague memory of being embarrassed by being treated as a child, or an invalid, then knew no more.

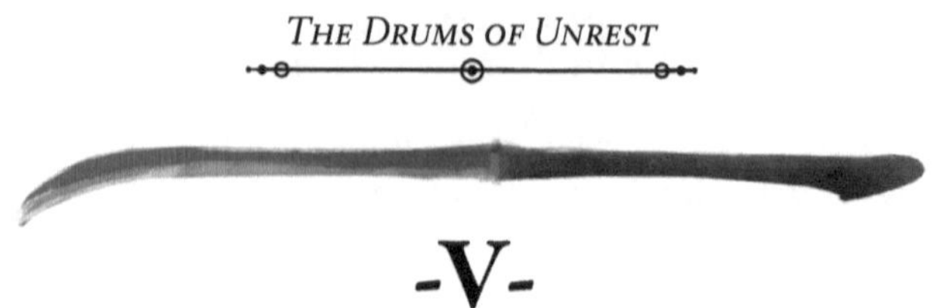

-V-

The Guardsman's tone was emphatic. His words sped across the chamber in a dry, cracked voice.

"'Ey weren't satisfied with th'cattle outside th'walls; they came hunting f'people!"

Jastar and Barnic looked at one another, then both turned to the guardsman's wounds. He had three arrows sticking out of him, although based on the way he moved, most of what held them in place was the thick padded leather gambeson the man wore. It didn't look as if they'd sunk deeply into his flesh, although they might've done. There was some blood, at the very least.

"Are they *still* attacking, man?"

Jastar turned as Barnic began to question the man, strode over to the table, and reached down to pull the sword and its belt, which lay against the seat at table's head.

"No, mi'lord, though th'may still be some out 'mong th'grasses that we cannot see, we drove thm'off. Sir Gordan drove thm'off with our help."

Jastar started at that. It sounded very plainly as if this man were afraid of making Gordan seem like anything less than a knight. That would have to be dealt with. It was Barnic who'd need to deal with it, but it would need to be dealt with, and soon if he wished to stave off the discontent such impressions could cause.

"All right," Barnic said. "I want you to get a detachment of guardsmen together, ideally one equal to the number of goblins you saw. I want them to patrol between the palisades and out to where the herds are. I want everyone on the wall armed with bows watching the area and tracking the party of guardsmen moving on foot to make certain they have support should they need it. Am I understood? Are there questions?"

Jastar doubted there would be, and although he hadn't been asked, he utterly agreed. This was why he knew Barnic would do well. He had learned all of Sir Valad's lessons and taken them to heart. He rather thought Valad would be proud.

"No, mi'lord. I sh'll see it done." The Guardsman sounded eager to work, perhaps eager to get back into the fray.

Barnic nodded and dismissed the man, who turned and jogged out with a quickness.

Jastar approached, took the half-empty goblet from Barnic's hand, slapped the sword and its belt in its place, and grinned as he turned to carry his freight of wine back to the table.

"What makes you think I'm going out there?"

"Because I've met you?"

Barnic snorted but nodded as he strapped his sword on.

"Are you coming with me?"

"I am *not*."

"What, then, is it you intend to do, Sir Jastar?" Barnic's tone was dripping with false formality.

"Take the time to retrieve both sword and armor, and ensure that the relevant people here, within your own palisade, are correctly alerted and prepared. I also want to inspect your walls and make certain there aren't any chinks or ditches that can be exploited should the goblins decide *this* is the place they want to invade." There was also the fact that he wanted Barnic to be seen walking, talking, and leading utterly on his own, *without* the shadow of Jastar's presence. Barnic would, he knew, rule well and wisely on his own. He wouldn't get there any faster, however, if he had Jastar to lean upon. It was in that very moment that he made up his mind. He would leave the day after tomorrow.

"Very well, as you say." Barnic nodded his head in mock deference. "I trust to your wisdom and cunning."

Jastar snorted. He made a dismissive gesture before the two grinned at one another and went their separate ways.

-VI-

Within ten minutes, all of Eastshadow was secure. No cattle had been taken, although the goblins had definitely come near to where the herd grazed. All of them were nervous, making the sorts of sounds that cattle only ever make when there's something new or dangerous in the area. Moreover, there was a smell around them—one which they did their best to try to slink away from. One wouldn't normally think a cow could slink away from anything, but beef on the hoof still managed to do so, galumphing this way and that, nostrils flaring as they shoved against one another.

Twenty minutes later, Jastar found Barnic outside the guard's barracks speaking with his men.

Gone are the days when you and I can hide, I think. No more slipping away, not for you, and soon enough, not for me. Jastar allowed himself a small smile at this thought, but it felt heavy on his face. There was too much else on his mind to think fondly on days long-gone, at least for any length of time.

He approached, moving slowly through the crowd of two-dozen men until he reached a space where he could meet Barnic's eyes.

If there're this many men here, where in the hells are all the wall guards? Looking up, he answered his own question. They were on the wall, where they should be. The men Barnic was speaking with weren't *this* palisade's guards, then. They must be sergeants and captains from the other districts, along with, perhaps, some of their own senior men.

"Sir Jastar?" Barnic's greeting carried a question.

"My lord." Jastar bowed his head in brief but genuine deference. It was the right thing to do in front of these men. It showed solidarity, even if between them, the idea seemed silly and unnecessary. "I have reports coming in from the men I've spoken to which interest me and might, therefore, interest you."

Barnic nodded. After a brief pause, he made the universal gesture that Jastar should continue.

"We have only one corpse from the goblins," said Jastar.

"Aye," an older man in a worn chain hauberk cut in. "Th' goblins tend ta take their dead. Sh' count ee'r, that is ta say we sh' count our blessings that we 'ave any, though my nos'd count it a blessing if we'd none."

This was met with general laughter from the men but not from either of the knights.

"It isn't the fact that we have a body that's worth noting. It's the *reason* we *have* a body."

"Forgive me, my lord, b' I weren't 'ware eer time at Westsong taught ee ta read th' minds a' goblins, or divine th' plans of foes fro' battles ee 'aven't ta'en part in."

Barnic met Jastar's eyes and asked the silent question. *Shall I deal with him, or will you?*

"Yes, well, Sergeant, if you had been there a fortnight up the hourglass, you would know that *everyone* who survived Westsong can read minds, and the duller the mind, the easier it is to read. Now, if I might be allowed to continue?"

The sergeant allowed a predominantly toothless smile to crawl across his face, though it made no attempt to reach his eyes.

"Well, 'course mi'lord, far be it f' me to int'rrupt." To the others, lifting his chin slightly and unnecessarily, he brayed, "Come lads, lis'n up! Sir Jastar, Lord of..." He looked down and squinted as if he were suppressing wind. "S'right, ee're n' Lord of any'ere. Ah well. Sir Jastar, hero of Westsong's going ta 'light'n us as ta th' great secrets ee'nearth-ed from th' goblins!"

Jastar spun on his heels, delivering him a swift right cross. His aim was good. He struck the hinge beneath the man's ear, where the jaw met, and the sergeant fell in a heap.

As the lout's face came into view, once his head had stopped rolling, he fluttered eyes that were shocked zeros.

Turning back to regard the new Lord of Eastshadow and the rest of the men, Jastar spoke as if nothing had happened. He didn't even sound winded.

"As I was saying, my Lord Eastshadow, we found one goblin corpse. Sir Gordan managed to fell him and prevented his mates dragging him off into the grasses. Apparently, the creature refused to give up his prize—an arrow made of bone. It had been shot into one of our other guardsmen, and this particular goblin raider had his heart and mind set on recovering that tool."

Barnic looked thoughtful.

"Where is Sir Gordan, now?"

Jastar did his best to keep his answer short. Far easier that way.

"Recovering from his wounds. Sir Aethan is with him."

Barnic made a face of sympathy and nodded, gesturing for Jastar to go on.

"Judging by the look of the pin, it'd been used before. There seems to be a reasonable amount of dried blood on it farther up the shaft."

Barnic arched his brows, nodding back in silence.

"What... Sir Jastar, what does it mean?" This was another guardsman. Judging by the tone of hesitation in his voice, Jastar's message had been heard, and clearly—at least by this man.

Another of your old lessons, Valad. When you must act in violence, do what's required and nothing more, then turn back and move on with your day. Do that, and you will unman those who are considering you an easy mark.

"It suggests a ritual of some sort, at the very least. Wary hunters and warriors have always held to such rituals since time was first tolled."

"Aye, sir," said the same guardsman. "They copy wh' they see, just as 'ey thieve'r tools..." It was clear he was struggling to grasp, or perhaps struggling to accept what his undermind *already* understood.

Barnic nodded to the man but didn't wait for Jastar to respond.

He was unsurprised to see that Barnic understood the run of his thoughts. Unfortunately, based on the blank and fearful expressions on the men's faces, Barnic seemed to be nearly the only one who did. It was time to employ one of Valad's old lessons.

Barnic was, apparently, thinking the same thing, for a moment later, he turned to Jastar and allowed his voice to take on a questioning, uncertain tone.

"That goes counter to everyone else's understanding, at least as it's been explained to me, as to who and what these things truly are."

Jastar shot the new Lord of Eastshadow a brief, burning look of mingled triumph and gratitude.

"Aye, my lord. Knock on every door and unless you're speaking to children, and perhaps even then, what you're going to be told about the goblins is that they're beasts. They're monster things out of cradle tales with no soul, no mind, and no wit. They're nothing more than tool using monsters. True?" Jastar looked about the assembled men and saw slow, not-quite-fearful nods. "Well, if they have rituals like this, it at least makes an argument for the idea that there's an actual mind behind them." He paused, then grinned a hangman's grin. "Something without wit or will, mind or malice wouldn't need or value, let alone know how to craft tools like these, now would they?"

The men all seemed to be surprised into sobriety by the sum total of Jastar's pronouncement. These weren't thinking men, as a rule. They preferred, as did most folk, it must be said, for things to fit neatly into even rows and square-sided boxes.

"But." This was a different guardsman. "What does th' mean we're ta do with them? They're filthy creatures, n' they come ta steal from us. 'F ee say they 'ave a mind 'n aren' simply beasts..."

Barnic spoke up. There was a coldness to his voice that Jastar approved of.

"You just answered your own question."

"My lord?"

"They steal from us or try to. That means they're punished, and as they will undoubtedly run rather than submit themselves to our justice, you shoot them. You shoot them, stab them, run them through, run them over if you're mounted. I don't care if their skin is bright blue, green, brown, red, or orange. Doesn't matter to me what the shape of their heads is. The only thing that matters is that they do not leave having hold of anything of ours. Am I clear?"

"Yes, my lord," the guardsman said, bowing.

"What about the rest of you?" Jastar lifted his left eyebrow and cast about himself, looking to the other guardsmen. "Is the Lord Barnic of Eastshadow clear? Has he been understood?"

"Yes, sir." They answered in unison—voices not thunderous, so much as stone-firm.

Jastar nodded once, then added one more instruction.

"Well, don't tell *me* that. *I* ... am not your master."

They looked confused, but only for a moment. Within that moment, the torches began igniting over their heads, or so the look in their eyes suggested. They were, at last, starting to understand.

"Yes, Lord Eastshadow," they said nearly as one, turning to face Barnic.

Barnic nodded a single time, then offered simple words in a simple tone. " I don't expect we'll see more trouble tonight, but keep your eyes peeled and your weapons ready. We'll double the guard as planned and see how the song spins out for the next few nights. Dismissed."

With a final "Yes, mi'lord," the men left, carrying their now groggy sergeant between two of them.

"Was that necessary?" Barnic offered this with an air of disapproval in his voice, but any child would've been able to see it for what it was: little more than sarcasm.

"*I* thought so," Jastar said. "Someone needed to hit him, and it couldn't be you."

"True. Either that or kill him." He paused, then allowed his smirk to grow into a dour smile. "Kill him or promote him, I suppose. Either way, he couldn't be permitted to undermine things in such a blatant way."

"I'm for bed," Jastar said, smirking. "I need to get used to daylight hours again, which means I actually need to sleep by night."

Barnic nodded.

"I'll likely see you before noon, I should think."

Jastar stepped back a pace, straightened, and bowed formally without irony or mockery.

"Enjoy the rest of your evening, my lord."

Barnic rolled his eyes and grinned.

Yes, Jastar thought, *Barnic will do all right.* The idea to keep the rest of Valad's former squires here with him for a time would prove to be not only wise but far-reaching and full of forethought.

Now I understand why the countess gave Knell's Stone to you, rather than one of us, Greggor. You see much more of the board than we do, even when we put our heads together.

Tomorrow he would arrange all the final preparations required for his journey, ensure that he didn't drink overmuch that night, and leave at first light the following morning. He hoped he would be back here—hoped he would see Barnic happily married and settled into his new role. He hoped it, but in his heart, he doubted it.

There's a part of me that thinks I'll never see you again, or if I do, it won't be a feast or celebration. I hope I'm wrong. Given that I have no reason to believe that I'm right, that should be enough, but... He let his thoughts trail off, choosing to focus on what he knew rather than what he feared.

He found his room right where he'd left it and was asleep nearly before his head hit the pillow.

-VII-

Venzene Duchy of Kovalun
Baronial City of Zlaté Pole
42 Gerstesykli: 14 Days after the Red Storm at Westsong

The first light of dawn burned welcome color onto the hard canvas of the sky. It left a diffused mixture of spring grass and raw honey hues in place of the dingy, wet linen of last night's fog.

It hadn't been all bad. The fog had been damp, of course, but the omnipresent cloud-cover had been a lucky thing. It'd kept the temperature warm enough to make the overnight almost comfortable.

Still, the weather this time of year was rarely predictable. None of Geroslaw's little band had really been surprised at the sight of their own breath when they woke to make the final league's trek this morning.

The men hadn't been to the city before. Geroslaw was amused to see them react with hopeful awe as the nominal gate came into view over the brow of the hill. The portcullis was capped by a dramatic stone barbican. To add to the imposing sight, the entire structure rested between twin tower spikes as narrow as any field tent.

As strange and impressive as this bulwark seemed, Geroslaw did his best to keep his face neutral, if not outright bored-looking, so as not to spoil the effect.

As they crested the hill—one of several that surrounded the town to the north, east, and south—the rest of the north wall came into view, and beyond it, the hilltop town itself.

The city's wall, or what passed for it—was a squat, ugly line of grey stone that most children would be able to see over by their tenth year on Skolf. In its center, its entrance capped by the nominal gate, lay a broad stone way. It stood nearly twenty feet in height at its roof's peak. While the town was an impressive example of urban planning, the design of this mean outer wall went a long way toward devaluing its overall impression.

The mild urban sprawl of Zlaté Pole was dominated by a tidy collection of peaked, slant-roofed houses and broad, curved-topped buildings. These latter served as larger businesses or more expansive personal estates. The streets were cobbled, slanting in toward their centers where thick iron grates were lodged. In the distance, at the far southern edge of town, high walls surrounded the broad mass of the baronial estate. The baron's manor veritably loomed against the painted morning sky.

Even at this early hour, the streets were bustling with warmly dressed men, women, and children going about their daily lives.

"*Drown* the *fish*," Barneb said. "A garden wall surrounding a city? Why bother with the damned gate?"

Geroslaw grinned at last, looking to the other men to find the same confused expression shared between them.

"Wait until we've passed the gate," said he, and said no more.

"Look at the munging manor house!" Barneb was on a tear, it seemed. "May as well be a damned palace. The Vévoda's home can't be half as grand!"

Geroslaw continued saying nothing. Three of his men had come from small thorpes or hamlets—only Aethel had come from a proper village. None of them had come from towns, let alone spent any time in or around castles and keeps. If he told them that the baronial residence was actually mild and undramatic by comparison, they would think he was bragging or belittling them. Neither would do.

They passed through the gate without incident. The guards saw the uniform kontusze and only asked if they were here for the tournament. Once that was sorted, the five of them trundled down the main road at a fully fledged amble. Before they'd gotten too far, Geroslaw asked them a question.

"Can you tell me why?"

"The wall?" Barneb sounded doubtful. "Not really?" His tone turned his answer into something of a question.

Geroslaw resisted the urge to chuckle. Instead, he looked back at the other three men. He'd expected vacant looks of good-natured uncertainty. He was surprised, therefore, when Borgus sought to catch his eyes.

"Gus?"

"Only short from the outside. The rain runoff drops into pockets of stone on the inside of the wall."

The others looked first to Borgus, clearly confused, then to Geroslaw, who nodded and finally back over their shoulders toward the inner walls. From this vantage, they could see things more clearly. Small metal railings stood on the town's side of what must be twenty- or thirty-foot pits to either side of the covered stone way—in actuality, a bridge. These stretched nearly to the outer wall and were essentially invisible until one was on the town's side.

Geroslaw took a moment to be impressed, if only mildly. *I didn't notice that 'til the fourth or fifth time I'd been here.*

"Well spotted, Borgus. Those stone pockets lead down to the city's sewers. Did you note the walkways?"

Gus nodded, grinning.

"Archers," Geroslaw said with a nod. "There's a wall-walk just inside. You can set dozens of archers there in time of need. Very few folk would survive getting that many pins in them on the charge. If a few horses get through, thinking to leap the low walls..."

Fillip, who was driving the wagon this morning, made a falling whistle and mimed something dropping down in an arc.

Barneb and Aethel grinned at this and nodded their understanding. Borgus wore a thoughtful expression but was otherwise impassive.

Geroslaw led them on, picking up the pace just slightly. They moved along the main thoroughfare for some ten minutes, passing market stalls setting out fresh goods and a few storefronts putting out their painted shingles.

Finally, he turned their course to the west along a packed dirt road. This new lane was lined with slender homes capped by the town's requisite peaked roofs, each with a Sediace oak, their white trunks stretching up fully twice as tall as the houses they stood sentinel before.

"Is that the inn?" Barneb's voice was a sigh of satisfaction, clearly pushed out past a broad smile.

Geroslaw nodded, smiling to himself, though as his men rode behind him, none of them saw it.

"Welcome to the Róża i Wrona," said he.

"If you're right and you can arrange the necessary rooms for the count's party here, they'll have no complaints—even that puffed up priss-of-a-lordling will have a hard time finding fault." Aethel sounded almost giddy.

Geroslaw merely continued on, absorbing the familiar sights, sounds, and smells. Even Krwawa Zima seemed pleased. His ears flicked forward, twitched at the occasional sound or hint of breeze, then jutted forward again.

At the end of this shady lane stood a large building of smooth, stacked grey stones crowned by a rounded roof. Behind it stretched a small wooden paddock surrounded by a chest-high log fence. A pocket orchard of olive, pear, and cherry trees rose over the building's brow. Individually, each of these elements was mundane and simple. When the mind was allowed to grasp the scope of the lane, they combined to turn this sense of modest means into a kind of mortal magic. From the first sentinel oak to the warmth of the paddock, from the peaked roofs of the houses to the inviting shade of the orchard, a feeling of order, warmth, and plenty was impossible to overlook.

Geroslaw rode up to the log fence that surrounded the paddock and stopped. Dismounting, he moved in long strides and was at the inn's door before his men's boots had collectively hit the ground. No sooner had he opened it than he was greeted by a cry of utter shock before a blond blur nearly knocked him over.

He bore the embrace for a single heartbeat. He then lifted the woman—who had fallen against him—spinning her around once before placing her back on her feet and embracing her again.

"Hello, Mother," said he. "I have a lot to tell you."

CHAPTER THIRTEEN

SHADOWED STONE

-I-

The Green Lands
42 Gerstesykli: 14 Days after the Red Storm at Westsong

Yeidil stood behind Kozioł, her hands on his shoulders as they looked up at the hilltop. They wouldn't have much more time before the seventh bell rang back at the castle. When that happened, they would waken and begin their respective days or be forced to answer for their absences. She would survive such interrogation, but Kozioł was still a boy with responsibilities, albeit limited ones. He would have a harder time avoiding trouble if he were overly late to begin his day.

"I just ... what, call him? Like any other?" Kozioł's voice veritably dripped with uncertainty.

Yeidil resisted the urge to sigh. Had *she* been so unsure of herself? She supposed she had, but she couldn't remember it. Then again, Calpernia hadn't been one to tolerate what she called *foolish megrims.*

"He's already yours. If you want him here, he'll come ... at least as swiftly as he can."

"How do I call him?" He shook his head. "I mean—*what* do I call him?"

Yeidil did her best not to allow her frustration at this question to seep into her voice.

"Close your eyes, Apprentice." She peeked around to see that he'd done it, then continued her instruction. "There is a boy standing near a hill in a grassy field."

He chuckled a single time, albeit softly. His chest hitched once, and he shook his head, then spoke in response.

"I wonder who *that* could be."

"Certainly not you, Apprentice. Not if you don't find your center. We're almost out of time."

That stiffened his spine a touch.

"Good. Yes, the boy is you or is meant to be. You are looking at him from overhead. There is a shimmering cord bound about his bright side wrist. Its length trails to the ground where an iron ball is tethered. Do you see it?"

After an interval of silence wherein she tried not to shake him in frustration, he finally nodded, shoulders lowering as relief washed over him.

"I do. Yes, Mistress."

"That is the song I taught you," said she. She felt him relax further at the use of the turn of phrase he had, himself, coined.

"There is another cord—this one made of shining steel. It's coming from the boy's chest—his heart." She paused, then asked in as gentle a voice as she could conjure, "Do you see it?"

After an excruciating length of time, he finally shook his head.

"I... I don't." He sighed in frustration, balling up his fists and striking his own thighs. "I *want* to, but ... I don't."

She cocked her head to one side, thinking. This was strange. It might be that he simply wasn't seeing it, but... She tried to force the thought out of her head, but it was persistent.

What if... Mother, no... You didn't. Uncle Borys would never have allowed that, surely.

"Tell me, Apprentice. In your dreams of this place, was there ever a time you were here with anyone else?"

"Anyone... no? I don't... no." This second negation was delivered with slightly more confidence.

"Are you certain?"

"Mostly?"

She sighed aloud this time. She couldn't help herself.

"This is important, so you must answer swiftly—the first answer that comes into your mind, not one you deliberate over and consider, do you understand?"

"...Yes?"

"On a scale of one: I'm guessing and have no surety whatsoever, to ten: I'm as certain of it as I am of snow being cold, how certain are you that before tonight, you've never stood here with anyone else?"

"I..."

"Answer!"

"Seven!"

She'd have sighed with relief, but for the fact that a distant bell was ringing.

"We shall have to table this until tonight. We'll be missed otherwise."

"But..."

She turned him to face her, lifting his chin with her right forefinger. "You go first. I'll follow."

"How!?" He sounded afraid, which made sense. He *looked* afraid, as well.

She saw him tremble as the bell tolled, far and wee.

She squeezed his shoulders. He winced but refocused his eyes on hers.

"Sing my song again. Do so, and close your eyes here. Walk forward toward the hilltop as you sing. Do you understand?"

He nodded, eyes shimmering.

"I'm afraid, Yei... Mistress. I don't know why, but ... something in that bell fills me with dread."

"That'll be your father's wrath if he thinks you're having a lay-in because Azhferd's away. Go." She turned him, loosening her grip on his shoulders as she did.

"Szłam niepewnie w ciemności. Mówiłam nieświadomie przeciwko światłu. Moja piosenka, jak kwas, parzy pod niebem. Budzę się by przeżyć rozdartą godzinę."

By the time he'd finished the final two words, the *Torn Hour*, he had disappeared from her view. She waited for a moment to be certain he wouldn't reappear in a moment of panic, but when he didn't, she did just as he had.

-II-

Venzene Duchy of Kamieńalun
County Czarny Wodospad
Wieża Szymona
42 Gerstesykli: 14 Days after the Red Storm at Westsong

She awoke in her own bed, as expected. The disorientation passed almost instantly, as it had for years now. She swung her legs out from the bed and stood.

Reaching for her own hair, she murmured once more to it, calling down the power.

Singing the song, she thought, smiling.

"Musimy porozmawiać..." *(We need to talk...)*

She felt the tingling along her scalp as her power grew dim, fleeing from her, off to work her will. She stood still so as to make the process less taxing. Working the Weave was like training or playing with an enthusiastic and faithful hound. It was happy to return to her once it had completed its task, but if she moved or strayed, it would have to work that much harder, hunting for her in order to do so.

The trick was to maintain as much power throughout the day as possible. Overuse could have effects ranging from overall fatigue to downright exhaustion, which in turn could lead to sickness or, worse, poor decision-making.

The wise caster always works the mind more than the muscle whenever possible, her mother had said, and she'd been right. To that end, incantations were as simple as the work's complexity allowed. This was also true for any physical components that were necessary.

She'd borne that in mind when creating her eavesdropping rote using her own hair as the component—usually from her brush. It was innocuous as far as substances went, and as it was once a part of her, she had a natural affinity with it, which made the physical cost of power a nearly non-existent hardship. It had been a simple leap to add the ability to speak through it as well.

"Kozioł," she whispered. "Wake—"

"I'm awake and putting my boots on," he hissed back. "What is it?"

She smirked to herself. He'd managed to sound petulant, whingy, embarrassed, and dutiful all at the same time.

"I shall see you at table shortly, then. Just making certain you were well and truly awake."

She heard the leather creak as he, apparently, pulled his boots on.

"Wide awake, actually. I can't think of a time I've been so... so... awake this early?"

She chuckled lightly.

"Your mind was away, so your dreams didn't much trouble your body. It slept more soundly for your absence." She realized where this would lead him and spoke up before he'd gotten there. "You cannot do it every night, or you'll risk trouble getting back. You can go for a little while each day, and you and I shall, but to spend the entire night in the Green Lands too many nights in a row will weaken your ability to return to your body. You'll become addicted, like the men our fathers speak of as *fond of strong drink.*"

"Oh," said he. After a few moments of silence, he spoke up again. "I'm hungry."

She laughed.

"Go then. Take the lock with you. If the chambermaids find it, they may toss it in the rubbish bin."

"I will. See you at table."

She allowed the connection to fade and went about dressing herself for the day.

Ten minutes later found her walking toward the banquet hall.

She found herself wondering again if someone—*likely Calpernia*, she thought—had actually severed Kozioł's connection to his *cień*. Could that really be?

Mother, surely even you wouldn't stoop so low... hells.

She paused just before she rounded the corner into the banquet hall's corridor and clenched her fists. Her eyes were wide with shock and horror.

"Hells!" This time she hissed it aloud through gritted teeth.

Uncle Borys pressured her into finding a way—uncovering some way to power the rite to settle things for father. If she took Kozioł's cień... duch Simona! (Simon's ghost!) *It'd be like gelding him!*

Yeidil took a moment to compose herself, making of her face a mask of neutral good-humor, and turned to enter the banquet hall.

She found it sparsely populated. Only a few servants, her father, his squire—Kozioł's brother Jarek, and, of course, Kozioł were present.

She waited the requisite thirty count, then moved past her father, kissing him on his cheek before taking up her seat two chairs to his left.

Hengrek smiled at her, then sat back in his heavy wooden chair and looked around.

She could see an idea take hold of him. He wore an impish, "who can stop me" look in his eyes. She was pleased to see it. It was a look she'd seen often enough when she was a girl. Still, as time and responsibility brought their weight to bear upon him, Hengrek had been less and less inclined to allow it to flower.

"Jarek, take your father's seat. Dargory? Sit in Azhferd's." He turned to Yeidil and met her eyes, then cut his own to the lone seat between them: Calpernia's.

She nodded and moved, smiling broadly.

"My son is away. Both my wife and Borys are attending to other matters and won't be joining us for the morning meal." He allowed his smile to broaden, his eyebrows arching just above the bridge of his nose. In others, those brows might have left an impression of sadness or longing. On Hengrek's face, however, the expression made him look younger and far more light of mood. His tone seemed to underscore that idea, for without prompting of either word or deed, he said, "Why should I not gather the once-children of my family around me to enjoy the meal?"

Both Jarek and Kozioł shot confused glances toward Yeidil, looking for confirmation as to how to react.

She leaned her head briefly against her father's left arm, then smiled sweetly up at him.

"If they dare to question you, Father, I'm certain Jarek and Kozioł will defend your noble's rights."

Hengrek smiled at this, nodding briefly, then turned to his right to catch their respective reactions.

"Is it so, my squire?" He leaned forward to look past Kozioł, meeting Jarek's eye. "Will you stand and defend my right to ... rearrange who sits on which furniture at mealtimes?" Leaning back, he next sought Kozioł's eye. "Dargory? Can I rely upon you, should the need arise?"

The boys grinned, nodding. They seemed unable to stop themselves. After a moment, during which Hengrek merely looked at them, the grins burst into outright giggles. The spate was swift but genuine.

Satisfied, Hengrek returned his attention to his meal.

What are you playing at, Father?

All at once, she didn't think this little comedy had much to do with a doting father and uncle.

"Dargory," Hengrek said, "when do you ride out to Auburg?"

Kozioł blinked, bowed his head to compose himself, and looked up again with a pleasant but otherwise detached expression. Azhferd would have been proud to see his lessons in action, she had no doubt.

"The last morning in Gerstesykli, Uncle... although I might leave a day sooner if everything's seen to."

"Three more days, then." Hengrek nodded at this.

He speared a rather large chunk of pork on the end of his knife and, after looking about with a conspirator's eye, popped the entire piece into his mouth.

This elicited more unintentional giggles from both boys, as, she suspected, her father had intended it to. While the nobility—at least the male portion thereof—weren't known for dainty gentility, such boorishly uncouth behavior at table wasn't acceptable in most Venzene courts.

Hengrek allowed a thin grin as he chewed and swallowed. It made him look like a boy after a fashion. Whatever this was, Yeidil decided she was pleased to be seeing it.

"Dargory, you need new boots," Hengrek said suddenly. "Get that sorted this morning. Then you'll have them for when you ride out on the forty-fifth."

Kozioł blinked, blushed, and bowed his head.

"I ... don't believe the cobbler will have time, Excellency," said he. His voice was full of embarrassed misery.

"Nonsense," Yeidil said. "I'll take you to the bootmaker I used last Koruni Spanek. You liked the boots I had made for my brother."

"Everyone liked them," Hengrek cut in. "I thought they looked the same as his old ones."

Yeidil ignored his dry, mocking humor.

Kozioł sent her a pleading look that, at first, she couldn't make sense of. Then, all at once, she could. Azhferd hadn't left him money to arrange new boots, or he had, and Kozioł had lost it—something to that effect, at any rate.

"We'll go after we've finished here if that will serve, Father."

Hengrek nodded his approval, then reached his right hand across to place it on Jarek's shoulder.

"Be certain the horses are well-exercised these next few days, good my squire." He released his grip and moved his hand to pick up his wooden mug. "Did you know, Dargory, we mean to leave on the forty-fifth as well?"

Yeidil felt a jolt of surprise, then delight. As her father drained a portion of qahua—the Sheshik drink he so loved—she tried to meet his eyes. When he avoided them, offering a small smile instead, she thought she'd been right.

How will he take the news? Will he feel honored or horrified?

The rest of breakfast was a quiet affair. While the conversation was warm enough, it was, she thought, rather carefully choreographed by her father to avoid any topic that strayed close to travel, Azhferd, the War of Counties, or the like.

She played the game, doting on him just a touch, trying gently to steer the conversation to any of those things, but it was only for show. He wanted her to guess at his plans to ride south, without confirming them, at least in front of the boys.

Finally, she stood, bent to kiss his cheek once more, and ushered Kozioł out with her. They went back to their rooms to gather warmer clothing, then met just inside the entry hall.

She would purchase the boots for him, and that was that. If she was right, he would want them for what was to come. Even if she wasn't, he would want better fitting boots for his time on the field at Zlaté Pole.

This year looked to be far more interesting at its end than it had been at its beginning.

-III-

Venzene Duchy of Kovalun
Baronial City of Zlaté Pole
42 Gerstesykli: 14 Days after the Red Storm at Westsong

Geroslaw turned as the men approached—Barneb in the lead. He was amused to see all four men's faces wearing a mixture of dawning comprehension and uncertain wonder.

"Barneb, Aethel, Fillip, Borgus—may I present my mother, Mari z Auburg. Mother? These are my men."

She slid an arm around his waist as she looked at them. While she was tall for a woman, perhaps eight or nine inches above five feet, she was still half a head shorter than her son. Her once-blonde hair was streaked with delicate silver lines that became apparent as the men drew near. Her eyes were merry, and she had a ready, sweet smile as she regarded them.

"Mari Radość, boys. I welcome you to my house." She looked up at Geroslaw, a dreamy, delighted expression playing across her face. "Especially if you come with my Geri."

Geroslaw smirked at the old endearment, leaning down to kiss the top of her brow.

"Well, mistress, your *Geh-ree* told our captain he knew of the finest inn in Zlaté Pole, and that was that."

She grinned, squeezing Geroslaw's arm.

"Welllll, he just might. You'll have to be the judge yourselves, I expect." She began to drag him by his arm, turning her back to the inn yard even as she led them toward the door. "One of the boys will see to your mounts and your wagon. There's breakfast for those 'can eat it, and breakfast *ale* for those can drink it."

Geroslaw allowed himself to be dragged without so much as a moit of protest. He saw Aethel's face grow distant and wistful.

"Breakfast ale and a hot meal... Mistress, bless you."

"Mari Radość at your service... Aethel, was it?"

Aethel grinned, nodding.

"Yes, Mistress. I don't..."

"Radość means Joy in Kamieńalunth," Geroslaw said as he disappeared past the front door.

A moment later, he saw the others enter and stop to stare.

"Drown the munging fish..." Barneb breathed. "Drown it and fry it in ice."

Geroslaw did his best not to beam with pride for his mother's not-quite-public house.

"As I said, lads. Welcome to the Róża i Wrona."

Most inns were dirty, ill-lit places with dung and food mixed with, if not beaten into, the straw rushes on the floor. Old, scarred trestle tables with tallow candles upon them and splintery benches beneath them were apt to be the rule rather than the exception.

The Róża i Wrona's massive great room, however, was a wonder. Its floors were polished flagstones of an altogether pleasing shade of pale brown. The light from the open front door, the low fire, and the great bay windows behind the bar and along the rear wall seemed to dance along the stone as if it were wet.

While there were, indeed, trestle tables, they were clearly well-made and well-tended things, as were the small benches set beneath them. A modest balcony overlooked the main room, accessed by a stair along the right wall.

The entire place had a feeling of warmth and reality to it that was almost disorienting.

Geroslaw saw Fillip's nostrils flare as the mingled scents of food and fellowship made their welcome assaults.

"Boys—horses. Girls? Fetch me eggs, apples, bread, butter, and bacon for five." Mari Radość issued her commands in an easy, half-requesting tone that wrapped her confidence in honest good nature.

Geroslaw was pleased to see things hadn't much changed. There was little doubt that his mother ruled this roost, but she apparently still ruled it with warmth rather than whips and warnings.

He walked to a table near the low fire. After shooting a confirmatory look to his mother, he pulled out one of the small, one to two-person benches and sat. The men joined him in short order.

His mother disappeared into a door in the rear wall behind the stairs. It led to the kitchen, he knew, and he could hear the sounds of rapid activity as the door opened and closed.

Two boys of Sheshik origin ran down the stairs at speed apt to result in broken bones one day. As they saw the quintet of like-attired men, they skidded to a halt, all dark-eyed wonder, and bowed. A moment later saw a blur of dark olive skin as they bolted through the front door without so much as a word, presumably to attend to the horses, as bidden.

"Sergeant?" Barneb's voice.

"Hmm?"

"You ... all right?"

Geroslaw had been staring after the boys, lost in thought. He didn't know them, of course. His mother often cycled her staff as they grew, married, or otherwise found ways to take their futures into their own hands. No, the boys had forcibly reminded him of Steffan's pack of fools and the boys who had stood up to them. To Barneb and the others—for now all four were eyeing him with what seemed to be genuine concern—he offered a smile and a nod.

"Fine, just lost in thought."

"Good to be home, I expect." Barneb grinned at him.

"Aye," Fillip said. "This's my home I don't know as I'd leaff et." His Gerstealunth accent was unmistakable but wasn't difficult to parse.

Geroslaw made a noncommittal nod, but saw that his men wouldn't be satisfied with that. He knew he could leave it there, but it would be an act that shut them out at a time when he needed them to draw and rally around him. Inwardly, he sighed. Outwardly, and in spite of himself, he forced his face into a small smile.

"My home wasn't ever really here. I was born in Auburg and spent much of my time in that part of the Duchy. When my father was matched with a noblewoman, however, and their son lived long enough to be thought safe from Złodziej Kołyski, my mother and I were ... encouraged to move along."

"...Złodziej? That's ... that's thief, isn't it?" Barneb sounded almost as confused as he looked.

Geroslaw nodded, bowing his head for a moment in deference to the weight of his words.

"Złodziej Kołyski—the Cradle Thief," said he. "She appears as an old, lonely woman with age's failing eyes. It's said she lost her husband, sons, and grandchildren to Piosenka Burzy in a snowstorm. She ventured out to seek them during a lull in the weather's wrath." He paused here, meeting their eyes to ensure they hadn't grown bored of the tale.

"Piosen..." Fillip shook his head, clearly knowing nothing of Kamieńalun's legends or lore.

"That one I know," said Barneb. "He's the storm."

Geroslaw made a gesture that suggested he was impressed but made the necessary correction.

He did his best to make his voice easy so as not to seem as if he were chastising Barneb. "He sends them. Piosenka Burzy sounds something like Storm Song in the Trade Tongue. Traders and scouts commonly make an offering to him before they begin their day's journey. Should you die from, or perhaps even simply *in* a storm, your light is shredded, leaving you without it. You're doomed to wander or fade, never to find your way to the Hallowed Halls."

Borgus was nodding and looking solemn but said nothing.

Geroslaw once more read the faces of his fellows. Satisfied with what he saw there, he continued.

"Her body failed her, as it would anyone out in the cold for so long. It's said they found her once the storms passed, but she was long dead. They say she comes looking for her lost kin. When she happens upon children, especially drawn to them when they sicken and cough, she comes to claim them. She thinks they must be her own lost ones, and seeks to lead them up to the Hallowed Halls before Piosenka Burzy can catch them and rob them of their lights." He sat back, smiling at them in a knowing way, before adding the final touch. "It's why so many smalls die in the colder months, so they say."

They all bowed their heads at that, following his earlier example. After a respectful moment, Aethel spoke up.

"So, your half-brother lived long enough for them to feel safe, and you and your mother were sent west?"

"No." Mari appeared with half-a-dozen full mugs held three to a hand. She placed them all on the table, then slid in next to her son. "We were given a generous sum of vévodové if we removed ourselves more than three days' easy ride away, and agreed not to press a claim for Geroslaw's birthright over the heir's. Such a claim had no legal force behind it in most cases, and so here we are."

They nodded slowly, eyeing the mugs but not daring to reach for them without her leave.

Geroslaw took a long look at his mother, laying his palm on the tabletop.

For a moment, she was lost in her own thoughts, then seemed to realize what he was doing. To begin eating or drinking without a host's sign that "the remove"—the *meal's course*—had begun was the act of either an animal or an uncultured lout. Smiling, she nodded.

"I expect you're all thirsty." She gestured to the mugs, clearly offering her permission to take them.

The men didn't wait. A moment later and their mugs were half empty.

"After you've eaten your fill, we'll talk about why you're here." Before anyone could do more than draw breath to reply, she spoke again. "Don't bother flattering me. I know you didn't come here because you missed my cooking. You're not here just to see *me*." Rather than sounding put out of countenance, she sounded as if she were altogether pleased. "I expect it has something to do with the tournament. Regardless, whether you're looking for a contract or currently on one—it can wait until you've eaten."

She stood, bending down to kiss Geroslaw on his right cheek before pulling his beard down in a single quick motion.

He yelped.

"...Is that a hint, Mother?"

"That your beard's overgrown and needs a trim? Of course not. When have you ever known me to have an opinion on the way you present yourself?"

The men snorted into their beers.

Mari turned on them at once.

"And why, exactly, are you four laughing? Aethel's beard looks as if it were trying to sneak onto his face. Fillip's isn't much better. Barneb, was it? Yours is more of a b*eer*-d than a beard." She tipped her mug from side to side for emphasis. "Borgus is about the only one who's got better than a hog's chance at a butcher shop to find a wife who still has all her teeth." She delivered this assessment with a broad grin and a twinkle in her eye so bright that it nearly glowed.

The men roared at this. Each one looked at their fellows, jeering one another with little copies of her playful and rather literal japes at their expense.

She curtsied to them, holding her mug high in her right hand, and—grinning like a fiend—turned to walk back toward the kitchen.

As the men stopped their mockery of one another, they turned to observe a stony-faced Geroslaw looking down at the table, hand on the wooden mug's handle.

He let them stew for a moment, noticing their deflating, fearful body language.

"My mother's not as clever or wise as she thinks she is," he said in a small, cold voice.

"...Sergeant," Barneb said. His tone was one of contrition and honest concern. He clearly thought he'd crossed a line, somehow, by supporting Mari's wit over Geroslaw's air of respect.

Geroslaw made his knuckles whiten on the mug's handle, drawing out the tension. When he was certain all of their eyes were upon him, he looked up suddenly, meeting their collective gaze.

"I *did* make the trip mostly for her cooking."

They roared again, pounding the table and raising their mugs to clatter against one another's over its center.

-IV-

Venzene Duchy of Kovalun
County Jižní Pochod
Barony of Haluzfeld - Southern March
42 Gerstesykli: 14 Days after the Red Storm at Westsong

Eobum knelt on the dewy grass. He was re-tying the knots on the hides he'd slept beneath, making certain they were as compact as he could make them. There were times a loose roll was useful—padding for something fragile, for instance—but this wasn't one of those times. They would reach Haluz Věže sometime after mid-day. The more well-balanced his pack was on his shoulders, the longer it would take him to begin feeling fatigued.

They'd already lost half a day's progress due to the weather and the relative inexperience of the boys—specifically Maksu. He seemed to be regressing. Eobum wasn't so worried about the time or minor frustration this had caused. He wasn't worried about the men's overall morale, either. His concern was the effect it might be having on Lashjuk and Sulok and what that might mean for Maksu.

Eobum didn't think he was doing it for attention, as some children did. He thought it more likely that it was simply his way of protecting himself returning to a time in his life when others took care of him in a more active way... a time when things for him and his family were simpler... when things were familiar and safe.

Aye, likely he's just defending himself against the memory of seeing his father and sister murdered ... and the rest.

He tried, at first, to leave the matter there—to leave the thought unflowered, but after a moment ceased the effort. Best to acknowledge it.

The rape of his sister, he forced his mind to say. *She isn't simply dead. They were taken, bound, and made to watch as their sister was raped. Then they saw their father—the very image of strength in a child's eyes—fail to protect them. Then they saw their sister killed by their tormentor—by Geatbern.*

He spat in disgust, then found himself shaking with the memory of his own encounter with the wytchemand.

With an effort, he forced his rage and the memory of his fear back into their respective cages. There were more important things to focus on at the moment... like Maksu.

Everyone reacted to horror a little differently. Some grew aggressive, some afraid, some closed off and swallowed or buried their reactions, while others became nearly feral with panic or, well ... horror.

Maksu had begun to slur his speech by their second night out from Edmund's encampment. By the fourth night, he'd started pissing himself in his sleep. Most Gnoerk children had outgrown that by their third year of life—fourth on the outside. That seemed to fit the way Maksu was speaking.

Best to let him work through it for a bit longer. He'll come out of it on his own, I expect, so long as nobody harasses him over it. I'll need to watch, though. In fact...

He looked up and sought out Eranoric, finding him brushing dust from his hands as he stood from where their low fire had been.

"Eranoric?"

"Eobum?"

"Ge hla." *(Come here)*

Eobum didn't often speak in Eodenth these days. More than half of his men didn't know their own mother tongue. Every now and again, however, he worked short phrases into camp chatter or otherwise low-stakes situations.

By ensuring Lakkrid knew his mother's tongue—his people's heritage, and that Fenglem and Haiga retained the same, he'd made a misstep. He'd managed to teach the rest of the unit more about Gnoerk-kind than their own Eodenth culture and history.

Eranoric walked over, joints still a touch stiff from the chill. He crouched down in front of Eobum, their knees a hand-span apart.

"Hla." Eranoric grinned a thin morning's grin. *(Here.)*

Eobum nodded.

"Sulok," Eobum said, pausing to order his thoughts. "You'll need to keep a closer eye on him."

Eranoric made a slow gesture of confused acceptance, waiting for the explanation.

"Maksu pissing himself might be an especially easy target."

Eranoric made an "ah" sound, nodding.

"You're asking me to ... keep Sulok's nose—"

Eobum cut Eranoric off with a look, then arched his brows as if to ask, *Really?*

Both men snorted at one another. An instant later, the snorting had been replaced by good-natured laughter.

Eobum shoved him in his right shoulder, causing Eranoric to fling that arm out wildly in a vain attempt to keep his balance. His palm struck a small scree of stones and slid as he tried not to drive them into his flesh. The dewy grass helped him slip even farther, forcing the man to drop onto his backside with an unceremonious "oof" sound.

Still chuckling, Eobum got to his feet, reaching his right hand down to haul Eranoric to his own. He froze as the older man's hand made contact. His smile winked out, his eyes first widening, then narrowing. He was suddenly on full alert.

He saw Eranoric's face show first confusion, then understanding, and finally alert fear.

There were no birds, no insects… no sounds of any kind save the wind making the pines sing.

Eobum finished the act of hauling the man up without a word, releasing the hand as soon as he was certain of Eranoric's balance.

He cast about, performing a silent headcount. All of his men were there, but Lashjuk and all three boys were nowhere in sight.

"Up—now!" Eobum didn't shout but rather projected, making his voice hard and cold.

As the men complied, they looked at one another, then to Adric, then back to him and Eranoric.

"Adric," Eobum said. "Circle up. Haiga, you're with Adric and his men."

"Aye." Adric nodded and motioned his men into position.

Eobum didn't wait. He tapped Eranoric once on his left arm, then gestured to the rest of their men who even now were approaching or slinging their azhkast quivers into position. As Eranoric nodded, Eobum turned and disappeared into the trees.

He suspected the four of them were off attending to their necessary. When he first stopped, he drew a bright brand of concentration across his senses. Listening and sniffing, trying to find some sign to direct his search, he felt rather than saw someone behind him, coming up on his right. The figure stopped some ten feet back, his shadow stretching out thin on the ground beside Eobum.

The shadow waved its right hand, then began to move its fingers in deliberate and familiar sign.

All's well. I'm with you.

Eobum nodded, making a hand gesture to signify he'd seen. It would be Fenglem. He didn't have to look, though his paranoia strengthened the urge.

With me, Eobum signed, then moved off through the underbrush, sniffing, listening, looking. He allowed his eyes to dart back, keeping track of the shadow beside him. They couldn't have gone too terribly far, but the silence of all creatures great and small—and not merely at their camp, but within hearing range—meant one thing: trouble on the come.

-V-

Lakkrid stared at a nearby tree as the last of his bladder let go. Sulok was a few feet away, still mid-stream by the sounds of it. He was also still muttering rather unsubtly, and Lakkrid couldn't help overhearing. It wasn't that he was trying to listen. In point of fact, he was trying as hard as he could *not* to listen; the words seemed aimed at his ears.

"He's acting like a baby. I *know* it's embarrassing, but he's not *your* little brother. He's not *your* responsibility."

Lakkrid finished and made the necessary adjustments to his clothing. He waited for a moment before turning, trying to get his own reactions under control.

Lashjuk had taken Maksu off to a stream nearby, wanting to bathe him after he'd either pissed or shit himself—Lakkrid didn't know which, nor did he much care. He'd offered to take Maksu himself, citing that he could do with a bath, too.

Something was wrong with the boy—had been for the last three or four days now. Maksu was obviously upset—maybe about his father and sister, maybe about something else. Lakkrid didn't know, but he wanted to do something if he could. He'd thought perhaps if he'd gone with Maksu to clean up, it would make the boy feel a bit less like a baby.

I'm not trying to take him away from you, Sulok. I just wanted to help him, and your Og, and you...

He turned and froze. There was movement both high and low amid the undergrowth. He drew in a calming breath that did far too little to deserve that name, really, and stalked toward Sulok, who was just finishing up.

"Turn around, slowly," Lakkrid said in as flat a tone as he could muster.

"In a minute."

"Now, Sulok. Tie a knot in it and turn around."

Sulok ignored him, rearranging himself with deliberate and maddening slowness.

Lakkrid grabbed him by the back of his kaftan, pulling him backward, walking as he did so.

Sulok's voice became cold, suddenly, and carried with it the authority that came from being the eldest of the camp's children. "If you don't let go of me, Lakkrid, I swear to you I'll—"

Lakkrid stopped walking and yanked, throwing all of his weight into the pull, sending Sulok stumbling back behind the younger boy.

Sulok sputtered but froze in mid-rant as his eyes saw what Lakkrid had feared—an enormous grey wolf unlimbered itself from beneath the undergrowth and stalked toward them.

The lines of color in its fur were jagged, giving the impression of shadowed stone. It made no noise but bore sharp, gleaming teeth at the boys as it came on, snarling.

"Sulok, do exactly as I say, exactly when I say it. Do you understand?" Lakkrid's voice sounded eerily calm, even to his own ears. It was a calm he did not remotely feel, but if he lost control of himself—if Sulok did, one, maybe both of them, were dead.

Sulok's voice came out in a whimpering hiss. "What... What do we do?"

"Turn your anger at me toward the wolf."

"What?" Sulok still spoke in a whimpering hiss.

It was stalking closer. Now only ten or eleven feet separated them. It continued growling its silent, accusatory growl. It would pounce soon if it thought it could take them. That or it would call for aid from its pack mates.

"When I shout, you shout, if you can. Get to your feet and walk backward—backward, mind—to the tree behind us. No matter what happens, you don't turn and run. If you turn your back, we die. Understand?"

He swore he could almost *hear* the boy gulp.

"I—"

"Do you *under-stand!*?"

"Yes!"

Lakkrid brought his hands down to grab the hem of his cloak on either side. He waited, looking for the animal's eyes, before he sprang into action.

Lakkrid lifted the cloak, making it fan out like giant wings, holding his hands high above his shoulders, up past the top of his head. The result was that he had almost tripled the amount of space he appeared to take up. As he did this, he stepped forward, shouting at the top of his lungs.

"Wolf!" He made it a battle cry, dragging the sound out long and full.

He heard Sulok scrambling in the thin winter grass behind him, but no accompanying yell. He was alone in this fight, then. It would have to do.

The wolf dropped its belly to the ground for a moment, skittered back, then stood again, pacing around him in a half-moon.

Lakkrid drew in a breath again, stepping a single pace back as he did—a minor one which he covered by leaning forward for his next shout.

"Wolf!"

As his voice fell away, he heard the shaky sound of weeping behind him, followed by a barely audible, "No..."

In a voice that was drowning in terror, Sulok managed three words that froze Lakkrid's heart for several beats.

"There are more..."

He saw them—he almost hadn't, but he did now. Two more had joined the first, slowly coming out of the underbrush to widen their net around the boys.

Lakkrid had but one thought. His mind was stuck on a loop. *We're dead unless someone comes. We're dead. If I draw them off... no.* There were three of them. Both boys would die. If he attacked, both boys would die. If they ran, both boys would die.

He was suddenly aware of the blood crashing through his veins, washing away his resolve—leaving him with a lone, crystalized truth.

I don't want to die...

-VI-

Eobum heard Lakkrid's shouts, and his heart nearly burst from his chest, first in relief at having found him, then in fear at what the boy was shouting.

"Feng!" he said ... and said no more. He bolted through the underbrush as if it weren't there, leaping felled logs, sharp stones, and tangles of weed, root, and vine without so much as a pause to gauge the best pathway. That act of navigation was far away, happening in a part of his mind that was a close cousin to instinct.

He came upon the scene and forced himself to stop some ten yards out. The wolves weren't attacking ... yet. He needed to get as much information as he could before crashing through the trees and into the open space beyond.

If I charge in and there are more hidden in the brush, I won't save anyone.

He reached back and checked to be certain his azhkasts were secure and all still there. Feng appeared at his elbow, no longer keeping his distance.

Blessedly, the wind's in my favor.

"I make three," Eobum murmured as the third wolf came into view.

Feng sniffed, then nodded, holding up three fingers. Then his face fell. "Ariculf," said he.

Eobum blanched, then nodded. Stone wolves—silent, swift, and supremely cunning. He was about to move when Eranoric appeared across from him. He shook his head once, then turned to Fenglem, eyes bright.

"Time for a game," said he.

Fenglem looked at him, clearly confused.

"...A version of Zvonění v jeskyni," said he. "I'll be the bell—draw them off. Ready?"

Feng's eyes widened, and he nodded. "Ra shrash, Ng." his voice was full of real fear but no argument. "Ariculf rana awka shrash. Dedash." *(Be swift, Brother. Ariculf are powerful and fast. Don't stop to rest.)*

Eobum grinned a hunter's grin and nodded, drawing an azhkast and mentally marking Eranoric's path forward.

It was now or never. The wind was, for the moment, blowing their collective scents away from the wolves, not toward them. If he waited, the wind might shift, turning against them, or—and this was just as bad—Eranoric would enter the clearing in an effort to save the boys. Either of these would change the way the Ariculf saw their chances and might lead them to press the attack on the boys or raise an eerie, soundless howl to call any of their fellows that might be close at hand.

"Cink-cink! Cink! Ha-ha-ha! Cink! Come on, Cink!"

Eobum bolted into the clearing, skidding to a halt, then bolting off toward the space between two of the wolves—to his own eleven o'clock.

The ploy worked. The wolves, two of them at least, leapt back, bellies to the ground, hind-quarters high, tails wagging with furious excitement. This lasted only for a moment before they jumped up to give chase.

Eobum could hear the sound of their massive paws as they gained ground. *Gi awka glem, they are fast!*

"Cink-cink-cink!" he shouted, curving to his right to jump over a stump. "Come on! Cink!"

He heard them closing in. The utter lack of any normal animal sound was just about the most terrifying thing he'd encountered, Geatbern notwithstanding. Horrifying though that lack of feral sound was, it almost didn't matter. The thunder of their paws beat a war drum that was more than enough to keep his heart racing.

As he ran, he looked about, hunting for something—anything he could use.

He heard a sound that caused his hunter's heart to smile—the sound of distant, tumultuous applause—the sound of water rushing over rocks. He arced his course toward it, putting on a terrific burst of speed. Even as he ran, he did his best to make the chase hard on his pursuers by virtue of every obstacle along the way.

-VII-

Lakkrid had avoided crying out when his father burst into the clearing. This wasn't due to any act of will, but rather out of plain shock.

He'd promised to always come to find him, and Lakkrid had believed him—had believed Fenglem and Haiga when they'd said much the same thing. Hells, he even had an idea that Eranoric—maybe even Adric would come for him if he were in need, but that had never really been tested before... not like this.

As his father shouted and ran, a part of Lakkrid's mind knew what he was doing, but all he could think about was the fact that this might be the last time he saw his father alive.

If that happens, it'll be my fault, he thought distantly. *I should have been able—been strong or clever enough to save us from them. They're only wolves...*

Now only a single wolf remained. Lakkrid met its eyes and was about to tell Sulok to run—that he would lead the thing away—when two figures burst out of the trees, one to either side.

Lakkrid looked to the right, as did the wolf, and saw Eranoric jumping forward, short sword in hand. He ran behind Lakkrid, standing between him and Sulok, facing the wolf.

Fenglem snarled as he ran from the left, racing to a point between Lakkrid and the wolf, short sword in one hand, azhkast in the other.

"Back up to the tree!" he barked, then advanced toward the wolf with a single stride.

"Now, Lakkrid!" That was Eranoric's voice.

He lowered his arms and did as he'd been bidden.

Eranoric's voice was warm with encouragement. "That's it. Your father's led the other two on a chase. We need to sort this'n, n'fast."

Sulok, he could see, was clutching at Eranoric's left side, hid under his dim arm.

"Take him back," Lakkrid said. His stomach was full of angry bees, but his voice was steady. "Feng and I—"

"Notta chance, Lakkrid-boy. Draw your dirk and stand beside me now. Might need ya 'fore this's over."

Lakkrid nodded and did as the man asked. He held his dirk inverted, point down, and took up position with Sulok between them. Widening his stance, he made ready, drawing his arms up to make a triangle shape in front of and below his nose, a hand-span between his two fists. Lakkrid no longer thought they would die here, but if there was blood to be spilled, he would not—would *not* allow his father's gamble to result in him standing aside while the other men fought on his behalf.

He saw Fenglem balking the circle, following the wolf as it tried to get around him. As the beast rolled out to one side or the other, Feng followed it, shouting inarticulate death knells and thrusting or swinging his hunting sword at it whenever it grew too bold.

"Jung ed hai—shrash! Eranoric? Bruu?" Fenglem's voice came out in a low growl, even as he widened his stance before the solitary wolf. *(When I attack—run. Agreed?)*

Eranoric cocked his head to the side as he mentally translated, then nodded. "Aye. Lakkrid?"

"Aye—Bruu!" He didn't want to accept this and had made up his mind to double back as soon as he was certain Eranoric and Sulok were clear. Lashjuk and Maksu were still out here, and he wouldn't leave them unguarded.

Fenglem nodded without turning. He once more balked the circle made by the wolf, still focusing his feints and thrusts through his short hunting sword, until...

"Idor Adys!" Fenglem leapt to the creature's right, as if to deliver a dim-handed flat snap to its jawline, even as he pivoted.

Lakkrid thought the wolf had only a few options. It could leap backward, could rear up on its hind legs to dodge the stroke, or could drop to its belly and hope the blow swung cleanly over its head. A skilled swordsman might well have come up with other tactics. Still, though wolves were reputed to be unnervingly clever, they were *not* swordsmen—skilled or otherwise.

The wolf stepped backward, rearing briefly to allow the sword to pass before it. The blade missed cleanly, slicing through the air inches away from the creature's nose... and Fenglem smiled.

Having already pivoted, so he faced the ariculf's left side, he drove forward with the speed of a striking serpent. He thrust the azhkast in his right hand—his bright hand—forward with all the strength he could muster.

Lakkrid saw the spear disappear into the thing's flank, just behind its left foreleg. The force of the blow drove the spear far enough to put Feng's fist no more than a finger's span away from its stony fur.

It tried to pull back, and while it managed to shake Fenglem's hand free, the spear stayed buried within its grey-shadowed bulk.

It turned to face him, hackles raised, then staggered, then ... froze. There was a sudden absence of sound, as if a hornet that had been buzzing right beside Lakkrid's ear had suddenly been silenced.

Eranoric and Sulok stopped, the former giving an inarticulate cheer.

Lakkrid approached Feng, who tried unsuccessfully to remove his azhkast.

The wolf was no longer a wolf—it was an exquisitely carven stone statue—its snarling mouth and wild eyes rendered in perfect splendor.

"Fenglem..." Lakkrid hardly knew where to begin. "Fenglem, jash ral-rgan?" (What happened?)

"It sleeps."

"It's not dead? Gi awka glem..." Lakkrid stood next to him, Eranoric and Sulok making their way over at a slower pace. "It sleeps? For how long?"

"Until it heals from the wound." He looked troubled. "They don't usually attack folk unless they feel threatened." He looked over at Lakkrid and Sulok, each in turn, then shook his head.

"Come," Eranoric said, forcing Sulok to lay his hand on the once-wolf. By the way he was shaking, Sulok wasn't willing. Eranoric, however, refused to let the matter go.

Lakkrid recalled his own father forcing him to touch game they'd hunted so as to rob the death of its power over him. All at once, he felt sad for Sulok. Sad that his father hadn't done the same, but happy that Eranoric was willing to. It was a father's task to teach...

"Father!" He turned and started to bolt off, but Fenglem grabbed him by the shoulder, hauling him back.

"I'll go. You head back to camp."

"No! Lashjuk and Maksu are out there, and Father may have led the wolves right toward them. Come! I know where they went, but I only have a dirk!"

Fenglem blinked, letting him go. He passed a hasty word with Eranoric, taking an azhkast to replace the one he'd lost, then took off in Lakkrid's wake.

Well, the boy thought, *I only had a dirk. Now I have a Fenglem.*

-VIII-

Eobum slowed his pace twice, doubling back to make certain they were still with him. He'd run through two small creeks and managed to temporarily confuse his pursuers. Ordinarily, this would have been a welcome thing, but not now. Now he needed them to follow him.

He heard the water ahead at last, no more than a few hundred feet.

Cresting the low hill before him, he saw it—a narrow river, wide and deep enough to swim in, too fast to take lightly. He scanned the shoreline even as he ran down the hillock. Several grey stones stood near the water's edge, like malformed steps. The highest was perhaps ten feet from the ground, but the lowest was only three.

That might do, but they can follow me easily enough. I need... There!

A wide tree limb overtopped a stone that stood perhaps six feet tall. More importantly, the limb jutted out over a point several feet into the river's body.

Eobum changed his course, moving as fast as he could toward the lowest stone, leaping across to it before he'd gone more than two-thirds of the way down the hill.

Hearing them drawing closer, breathing heavily, he had a moment to be pleased that he wasn't the only one winded by this insane chase.

He made a long jump forward, landing on the next stone, then turned to hurl his azhkast at one of the oncoming beasts.

The wolf skidded to a halt—the spear pinning itself into the ground where the thing had been about to step.

"...Hells."

He reached back for another, aiming at them each, in turn, forcing them to slow their pursuit. They began to circle toward him, probing. As their half-moon pattern grew closer, he turned and fled toward the nearest stone, taking leaping, lunging strides from one to the next, and finally the last.

He heard the scratching of their claws on the stone behind him, swore he could feel the breath from one of them, and leapt out over the water, twisting and reaching up to grab the branch, even as he aimed at his would-be killer.

He felt his hand connect with something—a vine, he thought. He grabbed onto it as if it were a dream from which he didn't want to wake. An instant later, he had it, but it wouldn't hold. He'd barely had time to draw that conclusion before a miserable rain of insects and grit fell down upon him from the partially dislodged vine. He felt a thousand legs crawling over his arm, hand ... fingers, then the first sparks of fire as the owners of those legs began to bite at him.

The pain was instant and maddening, threatening to overwhelm his senses. In a haze, he sought out the face of the wolf who had come so close to catching him and threw. Blessedly, the violence of his throw sent a good many of the crawling things flying off into the void. How his handhold hadn't come free of its moorings, he neither knew nor cared.

He thought of a thousand things he wished he'd shouted as he watched the spear fly through the misty air toward its target. *A cradle tale hero would have found something to shout, surely.* The best he could manage was a moment of hope that he would survive to tell the tale at all.

The azhkast struck home, entering the ariculf's broad chest just below its pale throat. It fell backward, skidding with the force of the blow, then struggled to get back to its feet once more.

Eobum saw it harden, freeze, then stagger. Finally, it tossed its head to the sky, and a great shadow passed out of its open maw before it collapsed onto the stone.

Eobum saw its fellow dance one way, then the other, then turn to flee back into the tree line.

He laughed. He didn't know what else to do. Reaching up with his bright hand to brush the remaining crawlers off of him, he moved to steady himself on the branch and simply laughed.

The branch snapped.

-IX-

The water was deep. It was also crisp and cold, which temporarily drove all thoughts of the fire on Eobum's dim hand out of mind.

He clawed upward, lungs burning, cursing every time his scabbard slapped against his thigh, feeling like it was somehow fighting his progress up toward the morning sun.

For a terrifying instant, he thought he wouldn't make it—that he would drown here, for black clouds seemed to race above him, blotting out his vision. A moment later, he realized that they were fish and had to fight the urge to laugh at his own idiocy.

His lungs were screaming, near to bursting, but his mind hadn't yet begun to let go, nor did his limbs feel heavy, although his feet were sliding within his boots on each desperate kick. He burst out from beneath the waves and sucked down a draft of sweet morning air.

Looking about, he saw no new wolves and did actually begin to laugh. After a moment of this, he ceased treading water and made for the shore.

He'd crossed about half the distance when he felt something brush against his leg. An eye-blink later, he felt something wrap *around* that leg.

He kicked at it with his free foot and struck something hard. It let go of him, but the foot he'd attacked with felt as if he'd kicked a stone wall.

He drove forward, pulling at the water with each powerful stroke, desperate to reach the shore before it grabbed him again.

He sensed rather than felt the creature gaining on him, but it didn't matter. He could see the stones beneath the water up ahead. A scant few heartbeats passed, and he was pushing himself to his feet. He glared, then swooned. His legs were numb. The pain at scraping his shins against the rough stones of the shoreline was a distant echo, at best—a message delivered from a far-off duchy.

He tightened his grip on his sword and tried to focus his attention on the water—on what lay beneath.

All was still, which, of course, meant either everything or nothing. Either whatever he had kicked had fallen away and given up or was preparing to strike.

His vision blurred suddenly, then faded back into focus. What *was* this?

His right arm sprouted goose flesh. The hair on the back of his neck had begun to rise. Eobum tried to turn his head but found it difficult. He slammed his hand on the rocky ground—the sword making a harsh, clattering sound.

Pain shot through his hand and the sound shot through his head like a bolt of green lightning ... and something else. To his right, he heard a hiss of surprise.

Green? And no, not just my right. Up ... the stone above!

Eobum leapt to his feet, only to first stagger, then fall heavily back to Skolf, landing on his rump. His teeth came together in a hard, cracking click. He'd only made it a foot, maybe two, but it was far enough to see, at last, what was hunting him.

The nearest stone stood some five feet in height. Atop it sat a slender, wet-looking man. His hair and beard hung long, limp, and the palest green. His clothing was an eclectic mixture of rain-colored leather breeches, a patchwork woolen shirt, and a short-coat that seemed to be dyed in every shade of green at once.

He sat with one leg bent beneath him, the other up so that his knee was near his chin, his arm balanced upon it. A serpent with what looked like a human's face hung around his neck, lifting itself to watch Eobum. Beside him was, of all things, a cracked ceramic teapot.

Eobum dropped his sword arm, too stunned to do more than stare.

The man gave a two-fingered salute, then spoke in a light, rolling tone.

"You won your battle, but not without cost."

Eobum blinked, trying to make his mind work. Who was this man, and why did he fill Eobum with dread?

"You don't speak?"

Eobum lifted his dim hand, palm out in token of parlay, and closed his eyes. It was hard to think, but he did his best to plow through the mud that was his mind.

Green hair... green lightning, and green hair... Why does that tug at my memory? Why does the teapot fill me with sadness? Why can I not... Why can I not concentrate on the... on the... the serpent-thing?

He opened his eyes, facing his interlocutor again. "Your ... companion is as slippery on my memory's stage as any serpent in the sea, friend."

The man smiled a moss-colored or perhaps simply leaf-stained smile.

"Servant, you mean. He ... isn't meant for men to 'member, but you see he's ad-jit-at-ed." The green-maned man emphasized each syllable in a slow, descending pattern of notes before he chuckled. The latter sound was too sane to be accounted unhinged, but not by much of a margin.

Eobum's head spun again, but he forced himself to focus on the man.

"I feel I know you, friend, but cannot place where or why."

The green-haired man nodded slowly—barely more than the jutting of his chin twice over. He seemed to grow thoughtful as he spoke.

"You ... do not know why I sit here before you." This wasn't a question. "You see me and face me with honest eyes. It will be a pity to remove them, I think. Perhaps some other agreement can be reached to settle our debt, Eodenth."

Eobum's eyes widened, but for a moment, he found he could not speak.

Green hair... Gi awka glem! Why do I know this man? It was so hard to concentrate.

"You have taken a thing from me with your careless flailing about in my water. You have robbed me of a thing I worked to harvest by the sweat of my brow, Eodenth. I would have repayment from you, so says I..." His voice was carried on several gusts of air which began as rapid—nearly manic—pacing and ended in the slow enunciation of each fusillade's final syllables.

...So says I? That's from the northeast of Kovalun, near the Eodenth border, isn't it? He cannot be Eodenth, else he wouldn't have thrown that term at me... Gi awka glem, why do I know him?

"Tell me what I've done and how I may repay you for it," said Eobum. "Careless damage is still damage."

The serpent had been spiraling around the man's neck and upper body, disappearing behind his head, under one arm, and around to pop out from the other side of his narrow shoulders. At Eobum's words, however, the thing stopped in mid-career, then slowly turned that all-too-human head toward him.

"You have robbed me of a servant, Eodenth. You must take that servant's place, or find me one to do so."

"I'm ... on an errand for a man of some import."

"Who?"

"Count Edmund of Hartscross," Eobum said. This much of his mission, he could certainly divulge without fear of reprisal.

The green-haired man smirked. When he spoke, his voice was full of undisguised disdain.

"What do I care for your Count Ed-moond? He has no power over me, no thing that grants him more import than my own wounding, so says I?" His lilting tone made of this last a question.

"He's the master of all of these lands, friend. I owe him service and must follow through with his errand. What can I do? I cannot serve two masters who call me to do two things at one time."

"He is not *my* master," the man said.

"Forgive me, but he is. He is master of—"

"All of these lands, yes, so says you, but I do not live upon the land, nor do my servants..." There was a sinister and almost gloating gleam in the man's eyes, which were, of course, green.

Understanding crashed over Eobum's waking mind as if a great winter wave had rolled over him, threatening to drag him out into the sea as it retreated.

"Vodník!" he breathed. "You are a Vodník?" Eobum said it aloud simply to hear it hung in the air. He knew it was true even before the creature's smile returned. He'd begun to stand, but the realization arrested that movement before it had rightly begun. Instead, he shifted to rest on one knee, not in fealty, but in wary deference.

"A Waterman," the Vodník said. "He sees at last." These final words came out in a tone of chilly yet somehow charming good humor.

Gi awka glem—a pocket-pack of Ariculf, now a Vodnik? Not merely on the same day, but in the same damned wood? And if he's not playing me false, I cracked his prison and freed a captive soul... hells! "Vodník, I have a—" Eobum choked back what he'd nearly said. He had been about to speak of how he needed to get back to his son but suddenly thought better of the idea. He didn't want to reveal anything to this water fae, spirit-demon, or whatever its nature truly was—accounts were unclear on that score.

His eyes fell on the all-too-human face of the otherwise black serpent. It slithered and coiled about the Vodnik's upper body, but its tiny, wise eyes seemed to be seeking out his own.

The Vodnik's voice urged him back to the matter at hand. "You have a ... *what*?"

Eobum felt his mouth work. He'd wanted to avoid answering but couldn't have said precisely why. The Vodnik was a friendly enough fellow, wasn't he?

The serpent briefly locked eyes with him, jolting him back to himself. Had it been giving him a warning look? Perhaps a look of sad sympathy?

He was seized with a certainty that he'd been *right* to try to keep his silence. The Vodnik would surely use such information for his own purposes.

Vodnik were known to be ruthless when they felt slighted in even a minor fashion. Ransoming Eobum's debt and freedom by taking one of his loved ones instead was more than possible.

He slammed his hand down onto the stones, palm up so that its back was dragged against them. The pain was instant, sharp, and—he realized a moment later—bloody. While his hurts were honest and bright against his nerves, his mind began to clear rapidly, as if a wind had blown smoke away from a wet fire.

"Ahhhh. Eodenth ... you know a thing! You know Sympatetická magie—the sympathy in magic! How ex-celent you are!"

Eobum, who had known no such thing, merely gazed up at the creature. As he watched, the Vodnik's eyes widened in anticipation and, perhaps, amusement.

To Eobum, he said, "You will need that sword, Eodenth, if you mean to escape this place, so says I."

Eobum wrapped his hand around the blade's hilt and was about to get to his feet at last when he was tackled from behind and to his left. A large, grey boulder appeared to have rolled against him, knocking him forward. His face missed a sharp stone outcrop by inches, and he had a moment to realize that if he'd struck it, it would have been the end of his journey.

He felt arms as thick as young tree-trunks to either side of him and struggled to roll onto his back. He threw his left elbow up and behind him, feeling warmth coming from that quarter, and felt himself connect with a veritable wall of firm, unyielding heat.

The Ariculf—it must be. Hells ... hells!

He forced himself onto his back, cracking the thing in its lower jaw with his elbow as he thrashed. He brought his hunting sword up to bear, seeking the thing's open jaw with the weapon's length, pressing into the soft flesh where its lips met.

Blood began to pool in the shelf of flesh and bone beneath the beast's tongue, dripping down from its front fangs in long, thin tendrils of carmine above Eobum's face.

The creature's breath was somehow gritty, calling to mind the altogether earthy scent of freshly turned graves.

He heard a high-pitched screaming coming from somewhere, but the sound was bouncing off of the stones near his head before being drowned by the river. It ripped across his senses: an inarticulate, keening shriek, long and shrill in the middle distance. The part of his mind that kept track of the battlefield could neither intuit its location nor identify its source.

The ariculf bit and snapped, but not with enough force to break its own teeth. It tried to pry his arms apart with its massive front paws.

He strove to sit up as he pressed the edge of his blade forward, deepening the cuts in the flesh of the animal's mouth, forcing it back. It glared at him, retreating with an angry, loping gait.

He dragged his feet beneath him, pulling himself into a crouch, then standing, the blade between him and the beast.

As Eobum got to his feet in earnest, it cocked its head to the side, trailing thin rivulets of blood as it moved. He saw it briefly stagger before dropping its muzzle as if to look down its nose at him.

Will it flee, or must I turn it to stone like its mate? Killing it will mean timing as it leaps in to strike or back out again. Better if I can frighten it.

He stepped forward, widening both his stance and the spread of his arms. He held the sword high in his bright hand, splaying the fingers of his left, making it into a wide, spanning claw.

He shouted at the wolf—shouted "cink," in fact, and leaned forward.

The ariculf took a single step back, circling with its head cocked once more. Its tail was wagging in a slow, hopeful way.

Eobum thought to re-center his balance, but he was struck with a sudden wave of confusion. He bit down on his lower lip, forcing his mind to clear once more, and yelled again, leaning forward.

"Cink!"

No sooner had he done this then the ariculf charged. He had a moment to see it lower its head a touch farther, then felt its massive paws shoving him backward, its weight bearing him down, its skull colliding with the underside of his jaw with the strength of a boksers final, purse-winning uppercut.

The sword slipped from his hand as his back struck the ground. He felt the wind rip its way out of his lungs, the ariculf's bulk atop him, belly to belly.

He drove his chin down toward his chest in an effort to keep the thing from his throat, bringing his left arm up to cover his eyes.

He saw its tongue, now painted the rough red of ruin between its stained teeth. It sounded as if it were coughing. A moment later, he realized what the sound meant. The beast was positively shaking with excitement. It pressed down on him, bodily, pinning him, even as it began to drive its nose beneath his forearm, searching for his soft throat to at last end the contest. It had won, and it knew it.

Again he heard that scream, but it was far and wee—too small to process. A part of his mind tried to grab onto the sound, to understand something about it, but that part was far from the dancing point of *now*.

He fought to hold the position of his forearm, leaning forward to headbutt the thing's long snout before returning his chin to his chest. That was a mistake. It had been like getting cracked on the head by a spear haft!

He shook his head to clear it and saw the ariculf was doing the same. It snarled, snapping forward once again, aimed at the exposed top of his head.

Eobum didn't think. He reacted. He drove his forearm into the open maw, jamming it as far back as he could, further ripping the flesh that joined the beast's lips, causing it to bite down even as it tried to withdraw. It had a hold of his vambrace and was cracking the hardened leather. All at once, he felt several tiny stabs of pain in the meat of his forearm.

The ariculf did not growl—could not growl, according to both rumor and legend, but that was fine. Eobum growled for both of them. He let out a cry of mingled pain and desperate rage as he felt the thing's teeth puncture his flesh.

He groped with his right hand, trying to find the hunting sword he'd lost—it had to be there. Ah! His fingertips brushed against the pommel! He stretched toward it...

The thing began to press down on him, shaking the forearm in its jaws from side to side, just as it would any other prey animal once it had been cornered and caught.

The violence yanked Eobum out of position, nearly dislocating his dim side shoulder in the process. He cursed and tried again. He couldn't reach his dirk, so the sword would have to do.

A new sound pulled his mind up short—this one far closer at hand, almost on top of him.

"Msh ol-ord!" *(Die, silent hunter!)*

"Lashjuk?" His mind was reeling. She couldn't be here. The ariculf, the Vodnik—gi awka glem! Had he led these dangers to where she and Maksu were?

He saw the wolf turn away from him, releasing his forearm to snap to its right—his own left.

Eobum saw Lashjuk stood there in nothing save her small clothes, stabbing over and over into the ariculf's flank with an azhkast she'd found somewhere.

The one I missed with, his undermind told him. Yes, that was almost surely right, but it didn't matter. The thing would leave him to kill her—currently the biggest threat. He had to get her to flee.

"Shrash!" *(Run!)*

"De!" *(No!)*

Their witty repartee ended there. He had neither the time nor the wind to argue with her. Instead, he focused his mind on giving her at least some chance of victory.

He brought his other arm to bear—never mind the sword. Grabbing the thing by its left ear, he tried to force his dim side forearm further back into its mouth. Once its head had come lower to relieve the pull on its ear, he threw his right arm around the back of its neck, pulling it down toward his own chest.

At the same time, he pressed his legs outward with all the strength he could muster. What seemed like roughly a year later, his bright side leg popped out from beneath the wolf, even as the grey nightmare tried to pull away and attack Lashjuk. Eobum brought the newly freed leg up, curling it around the beast's bulk to entrap it.

He felt it struggle, saw its eyes—its focused, intelligent eyes. He saw two things that he doubted he would forget as long as he lived—even if that were only another few minutes. There was hatred in those eyes, and there was recognition. It had him marked, somehow, and not by scent or taste. He felt himself falling into those eyes: vast gulfs of dusky gold.

He felt his grip starting to weaken, his sense of the moment beginning to fade. He tried to close his eyes but found he couldn't, nor could he look away.

He heard, as if distantly, the wet sound of the azhkast's steelhead being driven into flesh again and again. He heard a voice calling his name—Lashjuk, he thought. She was screaming.

He had no breath left. He fought to remain conscious, tried to bite his lower lip again, but even that effort was distant, as if in a dream.

His eyes, at last, began to close.

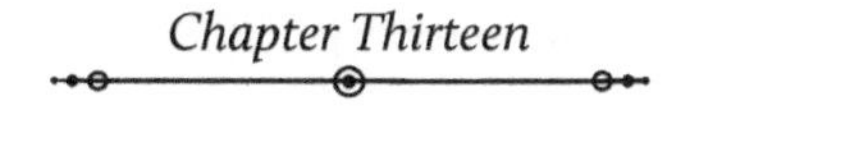

-X-

Lashjuk stabbed the creature thrice, four times... five... more. She'd stopped counting.

Eobum was being crushed by the massive wolf. Was it a wolf? He held it tight against his own body. She saw him grow pale, grow still, though his muscles continued to hold the thing pinned atop him. The sight of it hurt her heart.

She heard a loud scraping sound, the echo of some giant trying to spark a fire with its flint and steel. She also felt the deep, reverberant slap along her palms and up into her forearms, travelling along the javelin's haft. It left a dull ache, as if she'd slammed both hands down on the cold ground in a fit of pique.

The wolf-thing had become a statue, somehow. She suddenly knew what the creature was, and her fear redoubled. The ariculf were the emblem of the mason's lodge throughout Kamieńalun, for they were said to be the stone rite's ally and guide... and she had just killed one.

She stepped forward, reaching to touch the creature's stone side with trembling fingers, full of wonder and fear. She looked to Eobum, whose limbs were relaxing yet were still held in place. Was he breathing?

She bent down, searching for breath, a heartbeat, anything to show he still lived.

"Eobum?" she crooned. "Eobum wake... Eobum?" There was no response. His pulse was slowing, so much so that at first, she couldn't find a trace of it.

Her voice broke, coming out in a hoarse whisper. "Eobum? Nqas ... zak ed, Ng—zak... jagrl erld prak vra!? Eobum! De... de msh-sh-sh!" She sobbed this last, rolling the Sh sound out on diminishing waves of grief. *(Stay... Speak to me, elder—speak... Where is the thunder of your heart?! Eobum! No ... do not die!)*

Lashjuk shuddered, laying her forehead atop his as she wept. She would stay with him until his heart stopped. She owed him that. She hadn't thought about him dying—hadn't even considered the possibility.

"You didn't try to save me or change me," said she. "You stood ready to do as much or as little as I needed. I was never a thing to be tamed nor to be bargained within your eyes." She laughed bitterly. "I kept thinking you meant to exact payment, to lay claim to me. That was unworthy. If you can still hear me, I—"

A scream cut her off before it, too, was cut off. She leapt back onto her haunches, reaching for the azhkast, raking her eyes around for Maksu, whom she'd left hid beneath a thick overhang of stones where the river was shallow. He was nowhere to be found, but she was certain it had been his voice.

"Here, orku!" It was a man's voice, full of wry, good humor tinged with a species of gentle regret.

The voice was coming from above her to her right. Looking up, she saw the Vodnik stood atop a tall stone. In his arms was a naked Maksu. The creature (for certainly it was no mortal man, any fool could see that) had Maksu perched in the crook of its left arm. Its right hand was held over the boy's mouth. Above that hand, Lashjuk could see Maksu's eyes. They were wild, terrified things that were a step away from feral.

She tried to think, but found herself speaking before any appreciable thought could form.

"*That* is my son."

"A handsome thing," the Vodnik said. "You knew that one, did you?" He nodded toward Eobum.

"Aye." She hadn't realized she'd picked up that particular word from the unit's members until that moment. Her mind tried to seize upon that fact, to explore it and prise it apart. She found Maksu's eyes and was rewarded with a clearing of her mind. "He helped me take vengeance upon the demon who wronged I and mine." There was yet another phrase she'd taken from her time with them. Again, she had to resist the urge to explore just how and when that had happened. Again, it was Maksu's eyes that held her back—*drew* her back.

The creature smiled—a green, moss-colored smile. "A good man, then. It is a pity to watch him fade, given how valiantly he fought, so says I."

She nodded but found she couldn't speak. She walked around to face him in earnest, putting Eobum and the statue atop him behind her for the moment.

"You never *did* repay him for his kindness, I think."

She shook her head, eyes brimming with unshed tears. "I did not— *could* not, though I tried." She gestured toward where his body lay, bowing her head before looking back up at the Vodnik. "I would have, and gladly. He was a better man than most."

"You can still repay him—and will, I think." There was a light in his eye and a note in his voice that froze her heart.

"How?"

The Vodnik turned his head to the left and kissed Maksu's tiny, pointed ear. He then turned back to regard her, smiling his evergreen smile.

"No!"

He laughed discordantly. "Yes!"

"He is mine and has done nothing—I have done nothing to earn your wrath, demon! You will return him to me, or so help me I—"

"You what? What will you do, orku? Will you offer me a better thing to repay the debt your good man owes me? He took a thing from me... took a thing that I can never, *ever* get back. He was no *thief*, but he broke and wrecked what was mine." He nodded toward the teapot before him on the stone where, indeed, a large crack marred its surface. "I must—I *shall* be repaid." He delivered this rant amidst shaking, delighted laughter as if he were speaking to a child who deserved punishment yet was cleverly trying to wheedle out of any consequence.

She backed up, glaring up at him, trying hard not to weep. How could she safely get Maksu back? She didn't trust herself to hurl the weapon she held. Even now, she felt her fingers slacken along its haft.

She heard movement somewhere off behind her. Looking at the creature who held her son prisoner, she saw he had heard it as well.

"Lashjuk!" Fenglem's voice.

"Og!"...And Lakkrid's.

All at once, there was a crashing, rolling sound, as if the angry sea had risen in wrath to drown the land. Before her eyes, a spout of water erupted into the sky behind the creature, then dove down toward the stone upon which he stood. It spiraled around him like a whirlpool given parole to walk upon the land. Engulfing the Vodnik's lower legs, it coalesced, forming a storm cloud as black as sin's first secret.

The Vodnik rose into the air, hovering over the river some feet behind its former perch, and glared green hatred toward Lashjuk and the others.

"So-so-sooooo many orku!" He made a tsking sound. "Well, I need but one, so says I, and I *have* but one, so all is well!"

"Maksu!" Lakkrid was in terror.

She was fairly certain he hadn't yet seen his father. She dreaded the boy's grief and resigned to help him—to take him for her own. She was soon to be short one son, after all. Lakkrid would need her and would be good for her to concentrate upon. There was nothing she could do.

"De! Ed deagrib, nalg han!" The thing had somehow put the sense of resignation in her mind, and she would not—would *not* have it. She hefted the azhkast over her right shoulder, bright hand tight upon its haft, and leveled her gaze upon the thing, seeking its eyes. "Erld *hrek* lash ed lg, keb erld hrek msh!" Her scream of rage and fear tore its way out of her. *(No! I am not so weak, dark spirit! You will give me my son, or you will die!)*

Fenglem was beside her, off to her right. He began circling, trying to flank the thing.

It levelled its right hand toward them, removing it from Maksu's mouth. Great tendrils of wet, ichorous green fanned out, spreading across the distance, searching for them with groping, questing deliberation. They were like alien hunting-animals, sniffing the air between them as they hurtled on.

Fenglem hurled the azhkast he held at the outstretched hand, then drew and threw another. The first one flew low, disappearing into the roiling storm cloud the Vodnik rode upon. The second, however, struck true, burying itself in the demon's palm. While the Vodnik growled at the wounding, he seemed to be otherwise unaffected.

The creature rose higher, laughing in a way that called to mind the last scream of a drowning man. He released Maksu for a moment, grabbing him by the wrist as the boy fell, screaming. He now dangled, naked, thirty feet above the surface of the river, mere feet out from the nearest standing stone. The Vodnik swung him to and fro. The boy's arc turned him into a living pendulum, blocking Fenglem's angle of attack lest he strike Maksu.

Lashjuk stepped back, eyes wide, nearly transfixed by the horror show before her—all around her.

A lone tendril drew close—was a foot from her now, and she stood there paralyzed, unable to do more than stare at the green serpent... serpent... her eyes shot upward as she stepped back. Hadn't she seen a serpent around the demon-thing's neck? Where was that serpent now?

Lakkrid shrieked and wrapped his arms around the vicious thing, stabbing it with his dirk, or trying to, even as it thrashed in an effort to dislodge him.

She snapped—no thought as she calmly stepped to her left, away from Lakkrid's desperate flailing. She felt time slow, as most warriors said it did in battle. Focusing, she found an opening—a path her azhkast could and would travel if her arm and nerve did not fail her. She drew a breath, held it for a heartbeat she did not feel, and threw.

She saw everything in vivid, surreal detail. The azhkast's shadow passed inches above the upward snap of the tendril that served as Lakkrid's sparring partner. Fenglem shouted, trying to get the Vodnik's attention, though she couldn't make sense of his words. The creature turned to him, however, swinging Maksu as if daring him to throw the azhkast he'd recovered from somewhere. She saw movement from the corner of her left eye, running along the surface of the standing stones. The Vodnik slowly turned toward the movement, and the azhkast she'd hurled struck him in his open, snarling mouth as he drew breath to shout.

She saw him shudder, then a creeping grey seemed to suffuse him, rushing along his flesh like the shadow of a swiftly moving cloud as it obscures the sun. He tried to scream, but couldn't—his face was a study in terror.

The vine-like green limbs winked out of existence, leaving only a pungent, rotting smell in their wake. No sooner had the tendrils disappeared than the storm cloud tattered and was no more. As the Vodnik fell, taking Maksu with it, she saw that the creature was frozen in place, unmoving even to rebalance for its impending swim.

Maksu screamed—had never really *stopped* screaming. As he disappeared from sight, falling behind the tall grey stone, she saw a figure—the movement she'd caught, surely—leap in after him.

The sound they made when they struck the water was far too loud and low.

She ran to the left, making for the bank nearest where Eobum—had been?

The ariculf was on its side, a leather vambrace in its open jaws, and bits of fabric along its flank, but Eobum was nowhere to be found.

"Fenglem! Do you see them?" Panic and hope warred within her chest, affecting her voice as she waded into the drink.

If Feng answered, she never heard it. The Vodnik's right side surfaced, Maksu sprawled atop it, his arm held in its gripping hand. He wept and spluttered, which she accounted a good sign. Dead boys didn't, as a rule, cry or cough. As for the boy's tormentor, he had been turned utterly to stone, even as the ariculf behind her had.

She swam out the few feet to meet the statue that was serving as a raft. It bobbed, nearly sinking twice before she could get to it. She grabbed the thing's arm and pulled it toward her, hauling it backward to the shore.

An enormous bubble came up from beneath it, followed by two more, then all was quiet save the ripples her freight was causing.

Feng was suddenly beside her, adding his own strength to hers. With an effort, they dragged the thing into the shallows and lay back, panting.

A tense moment passed before Fenglem shouted, pointing, then dove into the water.

She was beside Maksu, eyes searching for wounds that, blessedly, weren't there. She could not, however, pry the boy's wrist loose.

Fenglem resurfaced, Eobum vomiting a great gout of water beside him, his arm over Feng's neck and shoulders. He looked—small wonder—exhausted, nearly used up.

The pair moved into the shallows and toward where Maksu lay.

"Huh-huh-hold him, Lash-juk," Eobum managed. "Feng?" He pulled his heavy dirk from his boot, eyeing Fenglem.

Feng nodded and produced a metal hand axe from somewhere out of sight. She'd seen them before. All of Eobum's men seemed to have them somewhere in their gear. The blades were used to make quick kindling. Opposite the blade, there was a small, blunted spike that served as a pry bar. Protruding from the axe's top was a short, wide shovel the men called an entrenching tool. It was this last that Fenglem set against the Vodnik's wrist, beneath Maksu's arm. He set the edge of the short shovel at an angle, then gave Eobum a nod.

Eobum, in turn, looked at Lashjuk, then met Maksu's eyes. He laid his dim hand along the boy's cheek and spoke in a voice that still seemed out of breath, "Be easy. We're going to get you free, but it won't be a quiet affair. Can you be brave a little longer?"

Maksu nodded, shuddering.

She saw Eobum nod to Fenglem, who braced the axe into position. Eobum brought the pommel of his dirk down against its base with a loud crack.

It took them far longer than they'd hoped. Eobum and Lashjuk kept up a steady stream of soft, encouraging words to Maksu in an effort to keep him calm. He met their eyes and nodded, but never spoke so much as a word in response.

Nearly ten minutes passed before they managed to break the stone wrist. No sooner did the hand come loose than the entire thing crumbled into dust.

Maksu leapt away, clinging to his mother as if he feared being turned to dust along with his tormenter. Eobum and Feng stepped back to either side, watching the thing crumble away, its particles picked up by a sudden wind and carried off west.

Eobum nodded, spat where the thing had been, gave Lashjuk a look of pure and unguarded fatigue, and walked onto shore. Lakkrid waited for him, looking tired but happy.

Eobum scooped him up, held him briefly, then turned back to the others.

A moment later and Lakkrid was on the ground once more, walking over toward Lashjuk.

She met him halfway, and he fell into step beside her.

"Maksu?"

The boy turned in her arms to look down at Lakkrid. He seemed to be fighting the urge to drag his thumb into his mouth. It hovered at the halfway point, parallel to his shoulder.

"You were very brave." Lakkrid didn't sound placatory, nor did he sound awed or full of exaggerated praise.

Lashjuk smiled as she walked to where Eobum stood, nearly out on his feet. "So were you, Lakkrid," said she. She thought to say more, but her mind was elsewhere.

Eobum cast about, eyes clear, though that clarity was costing him. She could see it in his posture.

"Fenglem—are you well enough to find the others?"

Fenglem nodded. "The last ariculf is stone. They'll be back where we slept."

"Go—tell them we'll be along."

Lashjuk stepped closer to him. Maksu, who hadn't spoken since the Vodnik took him, reached both arms out toward the man.

She moved closer, and Maksu put his arms around Eobum, briefly burying his face in the man's neck. Eobum bore this, sliding his fingers through the boy's wet locks but not pulling him out of Lashjuk's arms.

She smiled at him, full of a tired, unexpected joy. After a moment, she spoke.

"I thought... I thought you dead, crushed by the ariculf. Your heart was... had almost stopped."

He nodded as he stroked Maksu's hair. "I thought so, too." He laughed lightly—barely more than a puff of air and a lifting of his brows. "It was a near thing—nearer than I'd have liked, at any rate."

"I'm glad."

He arched his brows again, a playful smile creasing his lips.

"No, I mean." She smiled, shaking her head. "I'm glad it was only a near thing."

He'd known what she'd meant.

They stood there for a moment, Fenglem walking toward the wood line.

Maksu leaned away from Eobum, keeping his left hand on the back of the man's neck. He looked to his mother, laying his other arm behind her for balance.

They both looked at him and smiled, then at one another. He met both of their eyes, each in turn, then pressed them toward one another.

Their eyes widened. Each resisted the literal push.

Maksu looked annoyed, though still he didn't speak. Instead, he reached around to first Eobum's, then his mother's far ear, and pinched.

Each winced, and at the moment they shifted focus, he shoved their heads toward one another.

Their noses collided.

Maksu laughed wildly, pulling himself out of his mother's grasp and running over to Lakkrid, giggling and dancing like a fool.

Lashjuk laughed. She tried to glare at her youngest but couldn't stop laughing.

Eobum was doing the same—a series of short raven's caws, followed by a peal of breathy snickers.

She laid her palm on his chest, bent forward slightly until their laughter had subsided. She looked up into his face and saw two things: desire and fear. She slid her hand to his right cheek, sliding the pad of her thumb along its stubbled surface.

The moment stretched out, becoming ephemeral.

He leaned forward but stopped himself. He had, it seemed, gone as far as he was willing to.

That suited her fine. He had met her halfway. Lashjuk felt that she could do the same. She might well feel guilt later when thoughts of her Guuvra came to court her in her dreams, but for now, this was enough. This was the road before her—the one that had crossed the path she'd been on for as long as she could remember. She took a final draft of indecisive air and stepped out onto that road.

Their lips met, and for a moment, the world grew brighter.

-XI-

Lakkrid looked on, his bright arm around Maksu's shoulders, and smiled.

ORDERS, OATHS, AND OFFERINGS

-I-

County Thorion
Thorionden Castle
42 Gerstesykli: 14 days after the Red Storm at Westsong

The air within the castle had arrived this morning dressed in a bright autumn chill ... or perhaps an early winter's one. Kaith couldn't decide which. He supposed it didn't much matter, but he'd been waiting in the antechamber for the best part of two hours as, at the countess's summons, its occupants had been slowly winnowed down. Any line of thought—even one as pointless as trying to label the sense of cold hung in the air—was preferable to sitting glassy-eyed, staring at the same four-paneled walls.

He wanted to be out and in the doings. Better to be mucking out stalls beside Ryko than sitting here being idle.

Kaith snorted as he realized he was whingeing a child's frustration at being forced to sit still for so long. Absurd, really, but there it was. He resolved to adjust his thinking.

I'm a knight now. 'Haps, I'd best start acting like one... whatever that means.

He cocked his head to one side, realizing for the first time that he hadn't really given the idea much thought as of yet. He'd sworn his oath and meant every word of it. It was true that the oath was at the heart of knighthood, but it didn't speak to the mental and emotional trappings of the office.

"And it most certainly *is* an office." He kept his voice low but felt he needed to speak—to give voice to the idea. It was somehow too big for him to keep it rolling around in his head. How to qualify, to quantify what a Knight of Thorion should be... how such a one should act. It was a daunting thing to contemplate. He laughed suddenly. It was a rueful thing, made up entirely of self-derision.

"If you'd asked me what made a *lackluster* knight—that I could have said. I've seen my share of them, as has every armsman in the county... thick-necked, dull-witted, puffed up, power-drunken children whom life has seen fit to reward with dominion." He snorted again, though this time it was accompanied by a shake of his head and a clenching of his fists. "Anden, in other words, he and his knightly mongrels, Giles and Dorean."

He thought back to the last time he'd seen them—the last time he saw Anden, moments after the lout had felled Sir Valad with a blow that would've been more appropriate coming from a damnable hedge blade than an oath-bound Knight of Thorion.

He tried to think of him—of them—as a pack of yellow-backed harriers. It was easy to do, which made him think twice.

"Sometimes a bird in flight's just that. On the other hand, sometimes, it's the world warning you of trouble ahead." Greggor had taught him that—had begun drumming it into his head perhaps a month into his service and had never really stopped. It had made him shrewd, forcing him to think darkly, bending his mind in a way that always made him uncomfortable, if not outright sick. Kaith hated the person he became when he practiced this skill—the person who thought of those around him, friend or foe, ally or adversary, as pieces on a game board to be manipulated or even sacrificed to serve his own designs and desires.

Still, there was no denying the usefulness of such training. Difficult as it was to live in someone else's head like that, even for a moment, it let him see traps both physical and social, let him find weak points, even brought a person's motivation to light when applied correctly.

"It all comes back to building—*being* the bridge, doesn't it?" Still, that training hadn't warned any of them of Anden's cowardice or treachery. Certainly not in time to save Valad. "Because he *wasn't* being cowardly." He hung his head. The realization struck him so suddenly, anger directed inward, coming right on its heels. The notion was almost a physical weight. Anden wasn't a coward. He was a calculating opportunist! How had he missed it?

Kaith sighed. "Anden saw a trap that Ylspeth was leading us all into. He didn't believe—not in her wisdom, nor her commitment. He was a fool. Of course, he was utterly wrong. He should've stood before the countess and counseled her. Failing that, if he'd had genuine conviction, then to *save us all,* he should've tried to take her captive." He shook his head, trying to detach his own sensibilities from those of the hated man. "But no. Best to save those who were willing to follow him, better to let the rest fend for themselves. The fight that you can win—the path of familiar strength. Anden was afraid, like the rest of us, but had no control over even the fight we would eventually have—the one thing he knew how to do well. Hells! Of *course,* he chose to ride away."

Kaith sat back in a daze. The tag ends of a memory tumbled past his mind's eye. As he seized upon it, he felt the wind that carried it. It was bitterly cold, colder than the air in the chamber. It brought everything into sudden and sharp focus.

"He said..." He struggled to recall the man's exact words before he'd faced off with Sir Valad. "He said reinforcements. He wanted to flee before the *countess's madness* undid them all, and he demanded he be allowed to ride for reinforcements. Something like that, at any rate. He'll not have ridden for his holdings as it would have meant riding into the dead, but if he didn't fall to the once-men on the road, then he'll be back. He'll return with armed men at his back... and when he learns that we survived—that the countess lives? Then there will be war."

He stood, planning to enter the throne room—to barge in, if necessary—to tell the countess and the assembled knights therein of his realization. He stopped short. Greggor was standing in the hall just beyond the chamber's open door, watching him. How long had he been there?

"Worked it out, then, Sir Kaith?" His voice was a study in sad, wistful pride. "I thought you'd get there on your own."

Kaith turned fully to face him. He wore a look of confusion, but it quickly faded into a wan smile. Of course, Greggor had worked it out already.

"S'pose so," Kaith said. "He'll go for new hireling men, then run back to win glory and renown in the name of cleansing the blight and avenging the countess."

Greggor grinned as he made his reply. His voice was like rough spun wool dragged against bare skin. "Aye... but the blight was defeated. Many of us survived—too many to dismiss or counter when they speak against he and his. As for the countess—well, she does need to be revenged upon

Sirs Anden, Giles, and Dorean. What d'you suppose he'll make of that, Sir Kaith?"

Kaith offered a thin smile. "Seems like an easy question to answer, Sir Greggor."

Greggor quirked a brow. "Oh?"

"Trouble, Greggor. Sir Anden will make *trouble* of that."

Greggor offered a slow, thoughtful nod. "I suppose he will, at that." He let the silence play out for a moment before shifting the subject to the one which had, presumably, brought him here. "The countess is ready for you now." Before Kaith could move toward the door, however, Greggor spoke again. "Stay a moment, Kaith."

Kaith arched his brows and nodded, making a gesture of acceptance with his dim hand. It hadn't been Greggor's words that had drawn him up short, but rather something in his tone—perhaps in the way he stood. He looked as if he were struggling beneath some weighty subject. In Kaith's experience, when Greggor was worried, it was wise to be wary.

Greggor stepped into the room, coming quite close. The falling waves of his reddish-brown hair drew shadows across his features, reminding Kaith forcibly of the once-men at Westsong. He banished the image, forcing himself to lean in as his second father spoke.

"You'll be brought before the throne and Dame Marcza. You'll be presented with your device, your official title, and the task or tasks. Her Excellency and the dame have set for you. At some point, you will be asked about one other matter. What you will require from the Thorion Throne in order to complete these tasks."

Kaith nodded his understanding and was drawing in a breath to ask a question when Greggor pressed on.

"Horses, coin, gear, and men-at-arms are the usual requests. Once you've been established with a manor of your own, you'll be expected to sort most if not all of those things for yourself, but given the situation..." He trailed off.

Kaith picked up the thread, nodding. "Given the situation, Her Excellency will likely make accommodation for me."

"You can leave out the likely, Kaith. But hear me now. You can ask for any of those in the countess's employ. She isn't required to turn them over to you, and certainly, the men or women in question will have the right to refuse, so long as they're not slaves. You're free to request anyone of lesser station than a bachelor knight."

Kaith's eyes widened, then narrowed. He hadn't considered the idea of armsmen, though he instantly realized he should've done.

Be it scullery maid, stable hand, guard, groom, sergeant, or squire, service in the castle was a thing most on the outside would be proud of. It was stable and secure, so long as a body did his or her duty. It provided a place to live, food to eat, and the necessary tools to ply the trade in question. There were, however, limits to how far one could advance in such a place. Service with a knight was perhaps the only path for the common man or woman to earn his or her way to a higher tier of society. Once in service, anything was possible. Time and effort, loyalty, and skill could lead to the office of squire. If that should happen, it might lead to knighthood.

Kaith had lived and worked within the castle since his eleventh year when Greggor had taken him on. What was more, he knew most of the other folk who worked here and had a good rapport with many of them. He reckoned more than a few would jump at the chance to earn a better future.

"Kaith? Kaith—come back from Hämärä meri." Greggor took him by his dim side shoulder and gave a soft shake.

Kaith blinked, grinning. "Not dreaming, day or otherwise, Greggor. Was just cobbling a list, is all. Trying to be ready for the moment."

Greggor nodded, releasing him. "Aye, well, don't get too set on a name or face. Most of those I expect you'd have wanted were already offered service with our brothers."

Kaith's face fell, but he nodded. It wasn't much of a surprise, really.

"I have a solution and a favor to ask of you on that score. Would you hear it?"

"'Course," said he.

"I've a man—an old friend. He's a worthy man and a good soldier... and I've done him a disservice." He paused, looking down as if trying to swallow his shame. "In order to place him in a position to gain reputation and renown, I assigned him to a post away from the castle. I thought it his best chance to earn... well, to earn a better life than the one we both came from."

Kaith was almost alarmed at this. Greggor never spoke of his time before his service to the countess. Kaith hadn't thought much about it, but on some level, he hadn't imagined the man had lived anywhere else.

"He'd have been with us at Westsong had I not taken that step, and we could well have used him there." Greggor shook his head. "If I take him on myself, it will seem... it might feel as if I'm just rewarding him based on our friendship. He deserves better than that."

Kaith nodded, considering. "You want me... you want me to take him on as one of my armsmen. I've not seen his worth—hells, I don't even know the man's name yet, but you feel all three of us would gain a thing from the match." This wasn't a question. "He'll gain a path to improve his lot. You'll be robbed of your guilt, and I'll have a skilled man at my back and in my service. Have I got that right?"

Greggor tried to remain silent as he nodded, but found after a moment that he couldn't do it. He spoke in an uncharacteristic rush—the words tumbling out of his mouth in a torrent of justification.

"He's a good man, a man I'd have kept here—and gladly—if I'd had even an inkling we'd be facing real trouble in Ylspeth's service. Hells, Kaith, he's better suited to the work than anyone else you might select from the castle's guardsmen and no mistake." Before Kaith could speak, he blurted, "I'd consider it a personal favor..."

Now it was Kaith's turn to lend a steadying hand. "Peace, Greggor. You speak as if I've argued with you on the matter!" He offered a small smile. "I was just going to say that I'd be looking to you for suggestions as to who was a fair fit for my needs, anyway. Make your suggestion, and I'll gladly accept it."

Greggor's face split into a wide, relieved smile. When he spoke, his voice came out carried on a sigh of such obvious relief that Kaith had to hold back a laugh. "Thank you, Kaith. You've no idea how much this means to me." He shook his head and chuckled. His expression suggested he hadn't meant to do so. The sound had apparently slipped past his teeth when he wasn't paying attention. "You'll not be sorry. You've my warrant on it."

"You've never steered me wrong, Greggor. Can't imagine you'd start now."

Greggor turned his body to the side, grinning as he ushered Kaith from the room. "Never in life, boy. Now come. Her Excellency waits, and I've held us up for far too long already."

Kaith allowed himself to be led from the chamber toward the right and through the carved cedarwood door. It was time to learn his lady's will.

-II-

Venzene Duchy of Kovalun
County Jižní Pochod
Barony of Haluzfeld - Southern Stride
42 Gerstesykli: 14 Days after the Red Storm at Westsong

Eobum walked at the head of their little column. Lashjuk was beside him. He marveled at that but was wise enough not to question his good fortune... aloud, at any rate. Inwardly his mind wouldn't stop leaping from point to point, trying to make sense of it ... of how it would change things, not merely for himself or for Lakkrid but for the unit as a whole.

He tried to tell himself that it didn't matter—that there would be time enough for such long thoughts later, when he was seated around the fire, perhaps.

That idea proved foolish. Thoughts of a fire before him led to thoughts of Lashjuk sitting beside him in the half-light. That led naturally enough to thoughts of the pair of them not *seated* beside one another but rather *laying* that way—which drew him back to the unexpected, breath-stealing kiss they'd shared.

He chuckled. It was a soft sound he hadn't intended to make, but there it was.

She looked at him from the corner of her eye, trying and failing to be surreptitious about it. When he shook his head, she bowed hers, smiling in spite of herself.

"What is it, then?" Her voice was uncharacteristically soft and sweet.

His small smile turned into a full-fledged grin. "I'm just..." He trailed off, looking up at the sky.

"Just what?" She snaked her dim hand into his bright one, lacing their fingers together.

Eobum squeezed, happy for the contact, but that act of warmth was there—on Skolf. His focus was far above, dragged toward the horizon. He bent his gaze to the sudden storm clouds moving toward them at a stallion's pace. Had they been there a moment ago? He'd have sworn not, though he'd been distracted by his newfound fortune.

He looked back over his shoulder with the intent to catch Eranoric's eye but was brought up short as his eyes met Sulok's. The boy wasn't glaring daggers. He was glaring ballista bolts.

He's chosen Eranoric, and his mother's chosen me. We'll need to talk about that when there's time... and there needs to be time sooner, not later.

Eobum forced himself back to the task at hand. "Eran—caves? Storm's on the come ... and fast."

Eranoric looked complacent as he shook his head. He was smiling, despite all, though—which Eobum thought a good sign.

"No caves, but there's a farmstead northwest of here—can see the barn just through the trees."

Eobum looked, inwardly marked the barn, and nodded. "Barn... get them moving. I'm for the others." Turning to Lashjuk, he released her hand as gently as time allowed. "Go with the others. I'll be along."

She nodded but pulled him back before he could depart utterly. She took his face in her hands, leaned forward, and tilting her head upward, drew him in for another kiss—their second if he were keeping count, which he was. It was all he could do not to crush her to him right there along the cracked and rutted road.

Eobum suffered sweetly. He knew time was running out—that the storm wall would arrive before they knew it. He had to force himself to break the kiss, and for a moment, found he couldn't. He heard Eranoric barking orders at the others, getting them moving as he'd asked, but even this wasn't enough to motivate him.

Maksu's voice came into his ears. His speech was still slurred, as if full sentences were somehow new to him. "But ... what if storms come a'we not there yet?"

Eranoric pulled Maksu from the horse's pack-laden back, slinging the boy up into position across his own, even as he answered, grinning. "Well, then... we'll get wet!"

Maksu laughed, which at last broke the spell. Eobum managed, with an effort, to withdraw, smiling at her. He was helpless not to. He backed off some five paces, then turned to run ahead to find the others.

Eobum caught up to them nearly a furlong ahead of the column. Under a dense canopy of firs, Feng, Lakkrid, and Aderano were busy gathering firewood and kindling as swiftly as they could.

"No time!" Eobum shouted as he saw them. The wind was suddenly fierce, the air dropping from autumn's chill to winter's claw in the span it took him to issue those two short words. "Farmstead! With me!"

He saw Fenglem drop into a crouch in front of Lakkrid, who wordlessly leapt onto his uncle's back. As the boy settled into position, the men began sprinting.

He bolted westward, veering his steps only slightly to the south. His men followed. There were those who accounted trail-craft a form of sorcery. Eobum knew it, though he'd never understood why. These folk would find the seemingly perfect sense of direction he'd employed a thing to either be in awe of or to fear outright. The truth was, he'd spotted the barn when Eranoric had pointed him toward it, put a marker over it on the map he kept in his mind, and looked for moss or mushrooms to point true east or north.

The world's full of ordinary magic, he thought, then shook his head as if to clear it.

In short order, they broke through the scant tree line. Eobum was more or less on target. Just over a hundred yards of harvested land stood between them and the tall and weathered barn. A stone lower wall, redwood above... he was no proper carpenter, but he thought it would serve well enough to keep them for the duration. *Apt to be a long one, too.*

The sky chose that moment to loose an enormous boom of thunder as near as no matter to directly overhead. There was nothing quite like a sudden startle to refocus a wandering mind.

No sooner had the sound rolled away than the wind picked up... *Aderano.* Eobum saw the slender youth actually lose contact with Skolf for a terrifying heartbeat before the gust died.

He had a moment to look over his shoulder at Feng and Lakkrid, who were stumbling toward him. Fenglem was using one of his azhkasts as a walking stick, point-down to spike the ground before each step.

Eobum made his bark loud enough to be heard even over the chorus of wind singing through the fir trees. "Aderano! To me!" He reached his hand toward the man, willing him to be swift. They needed to make it to the relative safety of the barn ... and double-quick. Even now, he heard the rain racing toward them. It sounded like a damned waterfall.

With an effort, Aderano reached Eobum, clasping the offered hand in his own. Eobum pulled the hand toward his belt, forcing Aderano's fingers into the space between it and Eobum's side.

For a moment, Aderano's knuckles caught on Eobum's vápntreyja, slamming against one of the leather plates within the Eoden-style gambeson. With an effort and a death grip, Aderano secured himself and nodded to Eobum.

"Ready?" Eobum kept his voice a sharp shout to be heard over the wind.

"Nye, but I'm gripped! Go!"

Eobum nodded, looked back at Feng, then at his son. Both seemed more than a touch nervous, which only made sense. Blessedly, they looked to be courting fear's kind cousin, keeping them focused and alert rather than wild and wary.

Eobum took up his own azhkast, inverting its point in his bright hand. With his left, he grabbed Fenglem's belt just as Aderano had grabbed his own.

Nodding to Fenglem, he gave the only command necessary in such a situation. "Go!"

Their triad moved at a wide walk, looking like performers in a tandem dance troupe. As Feng swung his dim leg, Eobum stepped with his bright one, and Aderano stepped with his own dim side boot. They rolled forward toward the barn as fast as this odd comedy would allow—far faster than the uninitiated would have guessed.

The wind leapt up as if to challenge them. The storm's fury still hadn't crashed down over them, but it was close. Eobum could feel the bitter bite as the temperature shifted. What was worse, he heard the trees responding to it. A creaking, guttural ripping sound was followed by a series of tumultuous cracking noises as heavy things were hurled against one another. In his mind's eye, he kept seeing trees ripped out at the root and flying through the air, only to slam into those who had survived the wind.

He was spared from thinking about this and what sort of damage a flying tree might do to the barn they were loping toward by a trio of shrieking voices. He knew them for what they were at once—sheep ... and their shepherd boy.

An instant later, he saw them fly past him some fifteen strides to his left. They rode high, tumbling through the air like dead autumn leaves. The boy was perhaps ten or eleven.

Eobum saw him reaching for the nearest sheep as if the weight would somehow save him. His fingers danced with the great black wool but couldn't quite reach. The boy was facing Eobum, toward the wind. They locked eyes, and Eobum found he couldn't look away. He wished he could.

With sick fascination, he watched as the boy screamed and stretched for what could not possibly be his salvation. He was still reaching when he splattered against the great girth of first one, then two more giant redwood trees. The blood left behind on the first heralded the boy's silence as he was bounced between them and out of sight.

Nearly there. Nearly there. A few dozen strides. Nearly. Lakkrid... don't let go of Fenglem's harness—not for an instant. Just a few more...

He saw the barn door slide open—it was on a track, not hinges. Haiga and Lashjuk were there, and others behind—far more of them than he'd expected.

"Give a gap!"

They did as Eobum commanded, Haiga ushering Lashjuk behind him, pushing the door open a bit farther.

Eobum saw the fear in Haiga's eye, and that was when he heard it... a screaming, tearing sound as the storm wall finally neared them.

"Triple timmmmmme!"

They moved.

Eobum felt spikes of pain along the back of his neck and head, as the first flaying fingers of rain struck. He heard a brief whimper from Lakkrid as it lashed him. Then he heard the sudden swell of the storm wall's final approach.

He let go of Feng's belt, then barked a single word.

"Charge!" He switched his azhkast to his dim hand, then helped Aderano along with a shove in the small of his back. "Go!"

Eobum slowed his step by a single stride. The others were just closing on the barn's open door, and there was too great a risk of a clog if they'd arrived in a three-man clump. As Aderano crossed the threshold, Eobum put on a burst of speed and managed to get inside just as the rain and—hail? Hells, was that hail?—began to hammer the barn.

As he passed them, the knot of bodies stood just inside the door, heaved the massive thing to its left, then ran the heavy iron bolt to brace it closed.

The men dropped to their knees, panting, sucking great gusts of air into their lungs. Lakkrid, rather comically, let go of Feng's vápntreyja and literally rolled off of his back and onto the ground. Eobum saw he was silently weeping. Seeing the poor shepherd had been a shock to *him*. It was only natural that it would be a shock to Lakkrid, too.

He looked around as he got to his feet again. There were, indeed, a job lot of people here. He was about to say something to that effect when a familiar voice caught him utterly by surprise.

"Commander... I'm glad you made it."

"Lord... Lord Alojz?"

The blond man strode through the gathered crowd toward him, white kontusz open, its hem buffeted by the movement of his footfalls. He laid a hand on Eobum's dim side shoulder and nodded, smiling. "Truly... I *am* glad."

-III-

Venzene Duchy of Kovalun
Baronial City of Zlaté Pole
42 Gerstesykli: 14 Days after the Red Storm at Westsong

Geroslaw and his band spent the morning truly at their ease for the first time in weeks. Even in the Bluemark encampment, as familiar as it had become for them, there was a sense of rigor and focus that made relaxation an act measured in minutes, not hours. Perhaps it was due to the obvious difference between sleeping raw and sitting indoors, but he didn't think so. No, it likely had more to do with the sense of warmth and, well, joy his mother cultivated in this place. Looking at the men, he could see that they were growing drunk not on the deliberately weak breakfast ale but on the rather more heady taste of not-quite-rustic luxury the inn provided. Each of them—even dour Borgus—seemed to take every opportunity to smile or laugh, no matter how minor the cause.

Well, let them laugh. We take our joy where we can find it. He looked to his right, where his mother sat, smiling as she watched their collective antics. Watched? Hardly. She was doing everything in her power to encourage those antics. Mari was a charming hostess, to be sure, pouring as many healths of laughter as she did of ale or mead.

As he looked at her, she turned to him, her face softening into a smile... a smile that could make a miser sign over his fortune without so much as a *hint* of regret.

He heard the distant sound of a bell tolling the hour.

"Is that noon already?" She glanced around, then got to her feet. "Rrright..." Turning to his men, fists planted against her hips, she was suddenly all business. "Barneb, I can have one of the boys show you where you and the lack-beards are sleeping, or you can wait. So, say it swift. Now or after?"

Barneb, shocked by the sudden shift, struggled for a moment to find his mental footing. Looking at the others, seeing no clear desire on any of their faces, he turned back and answered in a half-questioning tone. "...After, Mistress."

Mari nodded, then turned to walk toward the kitchen, but not before swatting her son on his arm. "Geroslaw? Collect your thoughts. I'll be back in a beat or two. Then you can tell me your drift." Her voice wasn't angry, but there was a sternness in it nobody seemed to much be at ease with. Each of them bore a transported expression, displaying clearly the inescapable feeling that they were children again, chastened for inappropriate behavior none of them had actually engaged in.

They sat together in silence for perhaps ten minutes, each man to his own thoughts. Fillip tried his hand at telling what he'd no doubt intended to be a funny story about a drunken Sheshik monk, an Eodenth brigand, and a horse, but it garnered little more than courtesy laughter.

When Mari reappeared, at last, walking toward their table, Geroslaw marked the anxious looks in the eyes of his men. They were *still* children before her, anticipating her wrath. He would have laughed—hells, most folk would laugh at such a strange comedy—right up until she turned her dreamer's lamps on them. Those eyes could be the warm gleam of a candle in the window or the killing light of the hells reaching out to devour you from beyond Skolf's own seam.

She carried two large pitchers in her bright hand and a plate of fruits and cheeses in her dim one.

Setting the plate down with a flourish, she transferred one pitcher to her dim hand and refilled a mug from each simultaneously. She did this with an expression of mingled boredom and distraction that only served to make the strength, balance, and coordination this act required all the more impressive... which was, Geroslaw knew, the very reason she did so. He'd seen the trick before, of course. Still, he saw no need to spoil its effect by making comment or offering sign that he was surprised or impressed.

...And is that a tiny tremor I see in your bright hand, Mother? He drained his mug and slid it over with a forefinger and a nod of thanks. *Better to lighten her load and accept her hospitality than start that discussion in front of others.*

Once all drinks had been poured and the pitchers had been set at table's center, she sat down with a soft sigh.

"All right, Geri, tell me. You've made me wait in suspense for long enough." Her smile was back again. It lightened her voice as well as the mood of those around her.

The men descended on the offered food (once she'd gestured them toward it) as if they'd never *seen* such before.

"There isn't much to tell, Mother." He took a short pull from his mug before continuing. "I joined the Bluemark after running their back trail for half a year. The captain—Jastrab of Červená Päsť—accepted me into the company as a Sergeant."

"Thank you, Uncle *Borys*," said she.

"Partially? I think Krwawa Zima had nearly as much to do with it, honestly." He grinned. "There's a kind of magic that happens when people lay eyes on him. When I'm in the saddle, some of it rubs off." He saluted toward the door with his mug as if toasting the steed's health.

She grinned at that. "Well, then it's your father you must thank." She leaned forward to pluck the second-to-last pear slice from the plate, popping it into her mouth.

"He was a mighty gift, to be sure."

She reached for her mug but spoke before drinking from it. "Stay for the tournament, and you might get to see him."

"Might?"

"Well… there's rumor of trouble along the Eoalun borders. I've kept rooms available, of course. They're bought and paid for just as any other year. I don't know if he'll be caught up in the troubles or not—if they're even true."

Geroslaw nodded, looking thoughtful. After a moment, he met the eyes of each of his men in turn, then continued the conversation with his mother.

"I'll find out for you. I'm headed there, come morning."

The men looked at one another, then at him. His mother nodded acceptance. She wasn't surprised, he saw.

"My men will stay here. They'll be needed. The Bluemark has been contracted to guard and fight beside Lord Aetanis of Haluzfeld to, during, and home again *from* the War of Counties. He'll be carrying the county banner into battle, as well. So…"

Mari laughed, a low, bemused giggle. "*So*, you thought I might provide, and you'd simply ride up and gain my goodwill on the matter? Is that it?"

Geroslaw allowed a slow grin to play across his face as he nodded.

"How many do I need to feed and house?"

"As many as fifty when we're done, though likely less."

She nodded. "The count's banner, aye? Well, I suppose that makes sense. And..." She looked up, calculating, then turned to face him again. "If your father comes, I should have enough to cover it all."

Fillip spoke up. "Forgive me... Where? How?"

Geroslaw exchanged a look with his mother, then turned back to the men. "You mean to ask about where to house us all?" When Fillip nodded, he pressed on. "The entire block is Mother's. There are very few rooms in the inn itself. The houses serve as guest quarters."

Geroslaw was pleased to see the looks of dawning comprehension on their faces. Turning back to his mother, he forced himself to choke down his delight at what was to come next. "I can help with the cost, Mother."

She made a dismissive gesture. "No, Geri. It's fine. It'll be tight, but I can manage it."

He dipped his hand beneath the collar of his shirt, pulling out his money pouch. As his mother protested anew, albeit with more zeal this time, he reached in again and removed a second pouch. This he opened before gently grabbing her dim side wrist and depositing the pouch in her hand.

She frowned at him but looked inside... and gasped. It was a momentary slip, and she recovered almost instantly. For a single, shining moment, however, he had delighted and surprised her. It made him glad.

She closed her mouth, and the bag with its wealth of rubies and Blackstar sapphires, then placed its cord around her neck. "I'd better get things started, then." She began to stand but stopped as Geroslaw caught her eye.

"I'm headed back to see Gurin. I mean to recruit him and some of the others into the Bluemark, under my command."

She cocked her head to the side, clucking her tongue against the roof of her mouth, clearly debating on whether to speak. After a moment, she sighed and opted to say what was on her mind.

"Geri, Gurin's gone—no, not dead. I didn't say that. He's gone."

Geroslaw blinked, feeling the blood first drain from, then rush into his face.

"A recruiter came through—a hedge blade for some baron or other far to the east. The fellow was looking for people to work the baron's land, set up freeholds on it, and defend it. Our Gurin was here when the man came through and didn't feel he could pass up the chance at something better... I'm sorry."

Geroslaw bowed his head for a long moment. When he looked up, he caught the eyes of his men. They were on fire with curiosity but unwilling to pry. He put them out of their misery ... and his.

"Gurin Vek grew up with me, and would have been one of my sergeants, had I ascended to my father's high seat. I was nearly four years his senior, but still. We were fast friends. In my last few years there, I taught him—practiced each lesson my uncle gave me with him. When my brother was recognized as the heir, and we moved, I made him a promise. When I could—when I'd made a place for myself, I would find him and bring him along."

The men bore looks of mingled surprise and respect. A moment later, they looked to Mari as she spoke up.

"His mother passed more than a year a'gone, now. There wasn't anything left to hold him. I suspect he felt like he had to take the chance for a better life."

Geroslaw bowed his head again, this time in memory of the woman who'd passed. After a moment, he asked a final question. "Do you know the name?"

"The place he went?" She leaned back, thinking. "It wasn't Venzene, I can say that for certain. Dairy something." She shook her head. "Sounded... sounded almost Sheshik. The Dairy of... oooh, what do they call their horsemen?" She sounded more than a touch frustrated as she sifted through the untidy storehouse of her memory.

"Karns?" Barneb's voice was uncertain both of his answer and his right to offer it.

Aethel shook his head. "Nah, Coins! Like money coins, I think..."

Geroslaw grinned at them both. To the room, at large, however, he gave the necessary correction. "Khans... such are called Khans."

Mari slammed her bright hand down on the tabletop, making a loud, reverberant *slap*. "*That* was it!" She beamed at him. "The Dairy of Khans, somewhere off toward the Mroźne Kły." Seeing the nearly identical looks of nonrecognition on the men's faces, she exchanged a grin with her son, then translated. "The Frost Fangs, boys—the spine of mountains to the east, along the Singing Sea."

They made a collective sigh of understanding and nodded almost in unison.

Geroslaw sat back, thinking. "The Dairy of Khans out east is looking for defenders and steaders. Good to know. Thank you, Mother." He leaned in and kissed her cheek, causing her to blush delightedly. "I'll head out, come morning. Barneb and the lads will stay behind and man the gate each day. Take it in shifts until they arrive. I should be no more than a day or two behind them unless they're very early, or I'm very late."

They all nodded at that.

"If you know anyone here who might be a fit, Mother, send them to these men, and no other. I don't care who rides in with the Lord Aetanis. I don't care if they're Bluemark or blue-*skinned*. I don't want to find they've been given orders by anyone else. I'll vet them personally when I get back. Clear?"

They all nodded.

Mari looked dubious, but she said nothing.

He was pleased she'd kept silent. He didn't want to delve into Steffan just now.

"Lads, I'll want you doing what you can to get the other Bluemark on side. Do it softly, and away from prying eyes or ears, but do what you can."

He would need coin. The gemstones had belonged to the count, and it wouldn't do to use any of it for his own gain. But he would need to outfit those who called themselves *his* men. The others needed to see that loyalty had its rewards. He didn't believe in outright purchasing loyalty, but removing the obstacle of Aetanis' wealth—at least on a practical level—when it came to the men would have to be a priority.

He didn't relish the idea of arriving home with his hand out, but he thought it might be his best course of action. Hells, it might be his only course of action. He'd think on it more. With five days in the saddle, he'd have nothing but time on his hands.

He smiled at the others. "Mother, before I forget, there's one more thing." He met her eyes, reading the question within them. "Thank you."

There was that smile again. She leaned in and kissed his bearded cheek.

"You might owe me extra for the quiet one." She lifted her chin toward 'Gus. "He doesn't say much, which gives him more time to eat and drink." She leaned over and patted Borgus's belly, making him jump and laugh.

"I'll consider it," Geroslaw said. "Barneb might have a little something to trade in exchange for your goodwill, though. He's a brewer."

Barneb both flushed and grinned, looking down.

Mari looked the man over as if seeing him for the first time. "Is he now..."

-IV-

Venzene Duchy of Kamieńalun
County Czarny Wodospad
Szczyt Szymona
42 Gerstesykli: 14 Days after the Red Storm at Westsong

A new pair of beaked yellow boots exited the cordwainer's cramped shop, striding out onto the mid-day high street. The boy they wore looked absolutely delighted.

Yeidil exited behind him, their armed escort in tow.

Smiling, she asked her question in as gentle a tone as she could in an effort not to burst the happy little bubble in his chest. "How badly are your feet sliding?"

Kozioł waved a dismissive hand, grinning as he spoke. "Nothing an extra pair of woolen socks won't set to rights."

"Good. Well, let's head back then. I should like a bite to eat before the day gets too terribly much older." She shoved him playfully as they began to walk. "Watching you spend my money is hungry work."

With good grace, he allowed himself to be pushed. "Thank you. Truly Mi-cousin. Thank you."

She slid her arm into his, forcing him to escort her properly. "It's a small matter. If my father felt it important enough to bring up, then it was best we had it seen to."

He spoke softly to her as they made their way, taking furtive looks around to ensure they weren't likely to be overheard. "A pity boots won't help me in the green lands."

She squeezed his arm, smiling down at him. "They might, actually."

He stopped short, looking up at her for a moment in wide-eyed incomprehension.

"You needn't look so surprised. When a thing weighs on your heart or mind, it can stifle your ability to focus and progress. Your fear of embarrassing Azhferd by asking him for coin, or showing up in ill-fitting boots that made it hard to walk steadily, let alone fight... yes, that could certainly be a heavy enough burden to distract a boy, I think."

She tugged at his arm. Dutifully, he fell back into step.

"Truly?" He sounded as if he didn't dare to hope.

"I've seen less important things cause delays. I once mooned over one of my father's banners for a fortnight. He had recently lost his wife in childbirth. The cunning baby was healthy enough, but the knight seemed so sad and lonely at the loss of his lady. He'd always been kind to me, and I'd hoped—I'd known that my destiny was to wed him, raise his son, and rule over his lands while he rode off to win glory." She grinned at the drama of her words. "This was long and long ago, mind you. It kept me from... progressing for weeks while I pined and schemed over how to convince both he and my father to propose the union."

Kozioł looked thunderstruck. "Hells be hid." He breathed. "Who was it? What happened to the knight?"

She chuckled. "Haven't you guessed?"

He cocked his head to the side, then shook it. "No idea. Tell me!"

"Syr Kamil Gazlee." She grinned.

Kozioł stopped once more, though this time, he recovered more swiftly. "But he's so... so old!"

Yeidil laughed.

"You'd have been Eldred's mother." He realized with a start. "Hells, Yeidil! Why in the world did you fancy ... *him*?"

Again, she laughed. They were almost to the top of the hill. The gateway into the upper market loomed a dozen yards ahead. "He was fair, Kozioł. Back then, he was fair and strong, and full of a brooding sadness that made me..." She trailed off, realizing what she'd been about to say.

"Made you what?"

"... Made me think *kindly* upon him." She hated to lie, but some things were best not said aloud, especially to a boy his age. "We shall see tonight, regardless."

He tried on a slow, sly smile, which made him look younger than he was by at least two years. "That was before you met Syr Makssssss..." He would've ended his teasing there but suddenly recalled the last time he'd discussed the man. He hastened to speak the rest of the man's name in a supremely ineffective attempt to hide his misstep. "... symilian... Syr Maksymilian, right? Now you'll marry *him* ... eventually?"

She eyed him, fighting the urge to grin at his discomfort. "It was, and I will marry him ... eventually." She did her best not to show her feelings on the matter.

She liked the man well enough. Maks was fair and brave, but so utterly dull and slow-witted when it came to the world outside of the tournament field. A normal woman in her position might've been pleased at the match. She could run and rule over his household, find in him a kind and devoted husband... she would have more freedom and power than most over her fate and fortune. What was more, he'd come from a proper bloodline along the county's northern marches. He'd give her children who would carry on the family's legacy both politically and magically... If only those things were enough to hold her interest in him.

Kozioł blinked, momentarily confused. It took him a moment to recall how the topic of her girlhood hopes of wedding Eldred Gazlee's aged father had come up in the first place. He got there eventually, however. He was just drawing in breath to speak when his brother's voice rang out clearly.

"There you are! I've been doing your work for you while you were off trying to look lord-ly!" Jarek jogged over, his tone and face clearly annoyed, though neither suggested too terribly much genuine resentment for Kozioł's absence.

"Why've you been doing my work? Nothing needs doing so swiftly for you to have to step in."

Jarek bowed his head to Yeidil, a mark of deference, but not a dramatic one. They *were* cousins, and this was the courtyard, not court.

To Kozioł, he said, "That's where you're wrong. Father returned with a message from the north. It's sped everything up. We ride for Auburg in the morning—at dawn, I think. If you need to eat, do it swiftly. I've my own chores to get to and don't want to be about them till dark if I can help it."

Kozioł gaped, nodded, and turned to Yeidil. His expression was suddenly full of utter terror.

"We'll speak tonight, Kozioł. I've some last-minute things I wish you to deliver to my brother—news, mostly. For now, you'd best get to it."

He nodded, then turned back to Jarek. "I can eat later. Thank you for your help. Will you show me what you've done already?"

Jarek nodded, smiling with obvious relief. "Come. I'll help you get finished if you'll help me after. We may both make it in in time for supper that way."

Kozioł nodded. As he stepped forward, he turned to face his cousin. Walking backward, he again nodded and offered his thanks.

As he turned to go, Jarek beside him, she found herself more than a touch worried.

Had things in the north truly gotten so bad that the count himself was needed to command? That boded ill ... and odd.

Still, if her father was rushing to Auburg, perhaps it wasn't as bad as all that. He felt he had time to see his son before heading off to battle. Surely that was a good sign... wasn't it?

She didn't know. She would ask her mother either this afternoon or at table this evening. Calpernia would know, certainly.

With a final glance around the courtyard, she nodded to her escort, dismissing him before heading into the keep's grand building.

-V-

Venzene Duchy of Kovalun
County Jižní Pochod
Barony of Haluzfeld - Southern Stride
42 Gerstesykli: 14 Days after the Red Storm at Westsong

The barn had a wide loft to either side and a narrow walkway along the far wall across from the building's only door. Eobum marked the rich and heady scents of newish-mown Lucerne, red clover, and orchard grass.

The unit sat in a rough ring in the western loft, as they'd been directed. Lord Alojz was with them, listening to their tale.

Alusc had pulled out a thin stone bowl from somewhere amongst their gear. When, where, or how he'd come by, it was a mystery, but not a shocking one. Alusc Aldhelm always seemed to have some here-to-fore unknown domestic treasure lying about, and this was just another instance of that not-quite-magic in action. He'd set the bowl on the loft's floor, inside a shallow pan usually used for cooking in the field. With a few strokes of flint against a steel file, the wood and kindling Fenglem's party had collected were blazing cheerily in the makeshift brazier.

The light served to drive back the witchy glow that clawed its way in between the old wooden boards, and while the wind shrieked and called about the eaves, and the rain and hail pelted down outside, they'd managed a little warmth.

When Eobum and Lashjuk had finished recounting their tale, Alojz leaned forward, looking thoughtful.

Eobum felt the press of Lashjuk's right leg against his left, and fought the urge to look at her, take her hand—anything for more meaningful contact. There would be time. Besides, they weren't children in the first throes of discovering desire.

Alojz made a thoughtful humming sound, then turned to meet Eobum's eye for a protracted breath—an acknowledgement of Eobum's authority before he, at last, turned to Lashjuk.

"How did you manage to turn the thing to stone? Vodnik are fae creatures. All the old wisdom says it's cold-forged iron that undoes them, but nothing about them turning to stone."

She met his eyes for a moment, then looked down, shaking her head. "Ask me how to turn stone into swords, snow into supper, or wind into wine, my lord. The answer's the same."

Alojz blinked in momentary confusion at this answer, but Eobum spoke up to unknot his mind.

"She doesn't know, my lord."

Alojz nodded slowly, and the group fell silent for a time.

"Ng? Og?" Haiga spoke up.

"Haiga?" Eobum turned, as did everyone else, to look at him.

"Did the azhkast that felled him also fell the ariculf?"

Lashjuk nodded slowly.

"Was its blood, then." Everyone stared at Haiga, Eobum included, and after a moment, he elaborated. "Ariculf turn to stone to heal from deep wounds. It's something like a bear's winter sleep." He looked to Feng to confirm he'd gotten creature and habit to match up. When he saw his brother nod, he continued. "Shulnak bodies have some of their power left in the meat and muscle, blood and bone... at least if harvested soon after death."

"Shawl..." Alojz looked between Haiga and Eobum.

"Shulnak: monsters of the mind. It's a term for all the thinking creatures spoken of in legend, cradle tale, and old wisdom."

Alojz nodded, looking thoughtful. "I like that: *shoool*-nack." He nodded again, smiling wanly as he looked back to first Eobum, then Lashjuk, then Haiga. "The *magic of monsters,* my grand-dame used to say, but I rather like the orc word for it." He gave another surprisingly warm smile to Haiga before turning back to Eobum. "So, how did you get out from under the mason's maw?"

"The ariculf, you mean." Not a question. Eobum shrugged a single shoulder before answering. "Before I dropped into the twilight sea, I'd gotten both arms and my bright leg out from under its bulk. After I swam back up from Hämärä meri's depths," he shrugged again, "I pushed. I managed enough leverage and rolled free. Its once-fur held onto my bright side limbs when it became stone... enough to fight Skolf's pull, but not so tight I couldn't break free."

The assemblage was looking at him with a mixture of understanding and surprise, but no confusion.

Eobum widened his gaze, trying to take in as much as he could without staring at anything in particular—especially the Lord Alojz. The man seemed to dwell on the tale longer than he thought the story warranted. Then again, Eobum didn't know him well.

After an interval of thoughtful silence, the lord swept a hand through his blond hair and changed the subject.

"And Edmund sends you to the baronial seat, then onward to gather the other banners he feels he can trust."

Eobum hadn't told him anything about his mission thus far, but did his best to hide his surprise. "Aye, well, it isn't my place to tell you Edmund's plans. If you know them, then I wish you joy of it. If you don't, no doubt he'll tell you when he feels he should."

Rather than being put out of countenance by this reply, Alojz seemed both amused and pleased. "Not down to you to confirm or deny them either way." He laughed. "Commander... this—this *very* attitude—is what separates you from the others."

Eobum shrugged both shoulders this time. "I serve at the *count's* pleasure, my lord."

Still smiling, Alojz concluded, "And not mine, nor anyone else's in His Excellency's employ. Exactly my point. You are, near as I can tell, the only man in that encampment whose loyalty to Edmund I do not question... Jediný, kdo je věrný." (*The only one who is faithful.*)

Eobum blinked at this last. He nodded, but that act was reaction more than any agreement with the man's mercurial words. Why had he switched to Kovalunth for just that phrase? Was it a mark of... what, respect? Eobum had always found Alojz distant and forgettable. He was a functionary, and in that role for Edmund, he was certainly efficient, but there had been nothing to bring him to Eobum's attention beyond that. Their interactions had always been brief and to the point. Hells, the only healths they'd shared were in the command tent as they discussed scouting reports or other such official business. Perhaps he'd misjudged the man. He—Eobum—knew that there were more than a moit of folk in the encampment that were there purely for pay and a chance at currying Edmund's favor. They were just as apt to turn on him for a few grófok if the act served to better their lots.

Before the silence could grow fangs, Alojz seemed to come to a decision. Looking into their brave little fire's yellowish depths, he spoke once more in Kovalunth. "Veliteli, slovo... vy a vaši nejdražší poradci." *(Commander, a word... you and your closest counselors.)*

Eobum stood. "Walk with me, my lord." Without waiting for a response, he turned to the others. "Haiga, Lashjuk, look over the wood and stone. See what can be done to strengthen it against the storm. If I'm right, the day's done for traveling. Might clear, but I expect we'll be here overnight. Alusc? May as well start on supper. The rest of you—help who and where you can."

Lashjuk looked more than a touch surprised at being given a task.

Eobum reached his bright hand down to help her up. Taking it, she rose. As their eyes met, he offered a grin. "Not going to tell me I'm wrong, are you? You know more than a touch about stability and foundations, aye?"

Her face split into a wide smile. She squeezed his hand. "*Aye*, I do." The word was still new to her, but her expression suggested she liked the way it felt on her tongue.

He squeezed back and found he had to fight the strong urge to pull her close, to touch her, to kiss her once again. He thought she might be fighting the same impulse. With an effort, he released her hand, stepped back a pace—nearly bumping into Haiga who'd walked toward them— and turned to leave.

Alojz looked around as the others stood and set to work, then stood to walk beside Eobum. As they moved to the part of the loft that overlooked the door, he spoke again.

"I wish half of Edmund's men were so well trained. His personal guard are the only ones I trust to take their roles seriously. The rest..."

Eobum offered a small smile at that. "Aye, well, Edmunds men live waiting for work, not walking the wilds. Need drives men to work more than desire, my lord."

Alojz grinned, nodding as they reached the loft's front wall. He gestured Eobum to a bale of hay. For his part, he leaned against a wall, so they faced one another.

"Edmund has no idea you're here, does he, my lord?"

Alojz gave Eobum an appraising look, then shook his head. "He … does not."

For a long moment, nothing was said. The lord appeared to be undergoing some final process of either decision or the ordering of his thoughts. Eobum was content to keep silent. As was so often the case, silence was best. He reached down and plucked a strand from the twine-bound pile. He stuck its end between his teeth and instantly smiled as he recognized the flavor: orchard grass.

"Commander," Alojz paused, forcing his voice into a slightly less formal tone. "Eobum … I must ask you an odd question, and I beg you take no offense to it."

Eobum's brows rose slightly. "If you plan to offer no offense, my lord, I shouldn't worry. I'm not likely to go hunting for any."

Alojz bowed his head and smirked at that. "Fair," said he. "How loyal to Edmund, are you? We both love him, I know. He's an easy man to follow. How far would you go to serve and save him?"

Eobum blinked at the question, then bowed his head both in respect and in an effort to give himself time to think.

What are you asking me, Alojz? Are you trying to catch me out in some lie, a disloyal word? Or are you trying to recruit me into some intrigue or other? He quickly concluded that he had absolutely no idea one way or the other. So, he did the only thing that made sense. He asked.

"My lord, I take no offense, but I have no answer. You've given me nothing to measure such an answer against."

Alojz looked surprised but not displeased. "Pretty. Well-spoken, indeed." He considered, bright forefinger scratching his chin absently. "Would you lie for him?"

"He'd never ask."

"Ha! Quite right. Very well. Would you… yes, of course, you'd kill for him and shed blood for him—even yours, if necessary." He closed his eyes as if groping for a way to ask what he wanted without upending the mug. "There is a force on the move, Eobum. It will either join with Edmund, or it will undo him. It is, I've no doubt, the very force you've been sent to warn the barons about."

Eobum snapped his head up to meet the man's eyes. They were steady and, as far as Eobum could tell, held no lie within them.

Alojz shook his head in obvious frustration. "I'd hoped it wouldn't come to that, but it's gone too far now."

Eobum had to bite down hard on the orchard grass, grinding it between his teeth to keep from breaking his silence.

"I..." Alojz sighed. "I want Edmund to live... at least as long as the rest of us do. I don't know that I can convince him on my own. If he fights... If he fights, he will die, Eobum, and neither of us want that."

Eobum finally spoke. When he did, his voice was flat and low—a shade left of the dangerous tone he used to speak with Geroslaw upon the children's field not long before. "Tell me ... what ... you know."

If Alojz took offense to either tone or phrasing, he didn't show it. "Eobum..." He trailed off, fighting back—hells, were those tears standing in his eyes?

"Alojz, we agree as far as wanting Edmund to live. Of course, we do, but I cannot help you if you don't first help *me* understand the risk and threat to him."

Alojz nodded. His voice was steady, though his eyes still shone with unmistakable emotion. "I serve in the ranks of the Kongens Trofaste."

Eobum blinked ... and hard. "That's... I'm sorry, my Havalunth is—"

"The King's Faithful."

Eobum nodded slowly. "...All right. Go on."

"Eobum, the army—*our* army marches across Kovalun to unseat all kings, all emperors, all rulers. It means to unite as much of the world as it can, while the world lasts, in order to birth a new and better one."

Eobum's sudden laughter was a crow's caw.

Alojz looked at him for a long moment, as if trying to gauge the meaning of the laughter. Finally, he shook his head and asked directly.

"Where, Commander, is the humor in what I have said?"

Eobum quirked his brows. "Truly?" When Alojz nodded, he sighed. "You call yourself the Emperor's faithful, yet you've raised an army to attack and unseat him?"

Alojz's smile had returned, though it was painted bitter beneath his aquiline nose. "Those who have sat upon the Venzene Throne are broken and greedy people, Eobum. There hasn't been a worthy ruler in centuries." He shrugged a single shoulder and looked away briefly before returning his gaze to Eobum's. "I'll admit Einar Daggryspyd is a better ruler than we've seen in generations, but he's still a weak and petty emperor. He's unworthy by any measure."

Eobum looked dubious. That was fitting. Eobum *was* dubious, to say the very least.

"Alojz, worthy or worthless, your Empire will fall apart without him. I have no love for the throne or its master, but you aren't speaking of a plot to overthrow some weak-minded noble. Even if you managed to win through and usurp the throne, what then?"

Alojz's eyes lit with an inner fire that was too focused to be simple madness. "I want... They want... *We* want Edmund to sit upon the Venzene Throne, but if he refuses... if he sees the army and turns down the offer to lead—to take control, bringing the empire together under a single banner..."

He trailed off. After a moment, Eobum picked up the thread. "They'll kill him."

Alojz nodded miserably.

"They'll kill him with no more malice or thought than any clever conqueror kills those who could grow tall enough to challenge them or pose a threat."

Again, Lord Alojz nodded.

"And if I refuse to help you... you'll kill me."

Alojz looked up in surprise, but then nodded. "I'd have to. If you refuse to help and you stand against me—I can't risk you getting in the way. But..." He looked away, biting his lower lip. "I don't want that, Eobum. So help me, I don't. You are the only man—the only man who loves and respects him, as I do. You're the only man alive who has true loyalty to Edmund, the man, not Edmund the Count, or Edmund the wealthy." He sighed through his clenched teeth, bowing his head.

The pair sat in silence for a time. At length, Alojz spoke again, his voice little more than a ragged sigh. "Help me, Eobum. Please... help me to save him. If he sees them and opts to fight, he'll fall. His light will be extinguished, and the world will be so, so much darker for it!"

Now it was Eobum who bowed his head in thought. After a moment, he asked a question. "Does anyone else know that you and I are speaking about this?"

Alojz considered him, then shook his head. "No."

"Then I have time to think ... while this storm lasts."

Alojz nodded again. "I suppose you do."

"I won't be telling my men. Not until I've made up my mind one way or the other. I'll avoid that on a single condition, my lord—that your wrath falls only upon me, should I decide not to aid you."

Alojz thought for a long moment, then sighed, nodding. "My word, Eobum. You and I are the only matter here. I won't use them against you, so long as you don't speak of what I've told you. My men would kill them, man, woman, and child. Neither of us want that, I think."

Eobum considered that, then nodded. He didn't think Alojz was threatening violence as much as he was stating facts.

"Souhlas?" Eobum's flat tone only suggested at a question.

"Souhlas."

For now, at least, they were agreed.

-VI-

County Thorion
Thorionden Castle
42 Gerstesykli: 14 Days after the Red Storm at Westsong

Kaith followed Greggor into the county's high chamber. It was the first time he'd been here since returning from Westsong, and he found the experience passing strange.

Physically, the room was no different from when he'd last seen it, save perhaps the presence of a trestle table sat just below the dais at the throne's right hand.

But no, he thought. *There's a heaviness—a sense of weight to the room now.*

The countess sat in state upon her throne. Dame Marcza stood at her left, nodding to him as he approached. Both faces were unreadable, yet he had the unmistakable feeling that they'd stopped speaking only a moment before, and quite abruptly.

He approached the throne and bowed, hand on heart. As he righted himself, he dropped to one knee before the throne.

"Sir Kaith," Ylspeth offered by way of greeting. "Rise and be welcome before the Thorion Throne. We have things we must discuss."

Kaith felt a wave of … not dizziness, but stability … overtake him. He could scarcely credit it, but as he stood, he felt crisp and fresh, as if he'd woken from a deeply restful sleep.

He bowed once more as he stood. Righting himself, his eyes fell upon the tabletop. A map of Thorion County was carved and painted onto its surface. He could see settlements marked by various painted dots: blue for thorpes, green for hamlets, white for villages, and yellow for towns. Each of these had their names calligraphed delicately beside them, making it easy to tie color to code.

Ylspeth's voice pulled his mind back to the matter at hand. "Before we can discuss the commission, I mean to send you on. We've some business to conduct."

Kaith blinked, then nodded. "As you say, Excellency." He clasped his hands at the small of his back and widened his stance before adding, "How may I serve you?"

The countess smiled at that. It was a genuine thing, that smile, though it remained for only a moment.

"Sir Kaith, you were named as a Knight of Thorion County. The tale of the nineteen souls who stood and stayed at Westsong not only *will* spread but *has* spread throughout the county."

Kaith bowed his head in deference, then looked up to meet Ylspeth's mountain-top blue eyes once again. Response was unnecessary.

"The official rolls reflect your station as a Knight of Thorion. The common folk will refer to you as *one of the nineteen* if things continue to spread at this pace. This leaves all matters of public recognition settled and sorted, and now we must discuss ... the *truth* of your order."

Kaith blinked. He felt foolish, but he wasn't certain what else to do. He did his best to look merely interested, as opposed to showing how he truly felt, like a man in a runaway cart. At bottom, he wasn't comfortable with all of this. No, that was underselling it. Speak the truth and spurn the treasure. He was damn near undone by it all. The idea that his name and deeds were being spread about as if he were a subject fit for a song was absurd. He'd done his share, of course. He wasn't so churlish as to pretend he hadn't made an impact that black night, but...

"Sir Kaith?" Ylspeth's voice suggested polite inquiry and nothing more.

Once again, he felt that wave of clarity and focus—of strength—overtake him.

"Forgive me, Excellency. It's..." He chuckled, feeling his cheeks beginning to burn. "It's still all a bit much to take in."

She nodded, her smile indulgent. Her voice remained soft and sure as she pressed on. "Quite understandable, given the situation. Yet you'll have to get used to people seeing you for what you are."

"What I..."

"You are a Knight of Thorion County, Sir Kaith."

He felt his spine stiffen. Once more, that sense of strength, of will, overcame him, clearing his mind of the dreamer's dust that tried to assure him it was all false... that Westsong had been a nightmare, and that every-thing after was just a lingering lie.

"Yes, Excellency," said he.

"Sir Greggor?" She gestured with her long-fingered right hand to where the man stood to Kaith's left. "If you please." She paused, lifting her slender brows,

Greggor bowed his head as he stepped forward, arranging himself perpendicular to both Kaith and the throne. He removed a tightly furled roll of vellum from the small satchel he so often wore. Unrolling it, he spoke in formal tones.

"In accordance with rite and tradition, the Thorion Throne does hereby forge a new chivalric order. Its robe and office: to protect the lives of Thorion's people and their allies from any and all forces that threaten to extinguish their light." Here he paused for a beat as the gentle echo of his voice faded. "Hear now the tenets of the order: to teach and to train, to listen and to learn, to speak and to sponsor, to fight and to forgive, to dream and to die in service to this worthy charge."

Kaith's mind raced. He knew those words—*knew* them. Where had he heard them before? As Greggor drew breath to read what must surely be the last words writ upon that scroll, the answer came to him. Nor, he realized, was he surprised once he'd worked it out.

With these words, The Thorion Throne does hereby ordain and establish The Order of The Valadin, and names Dame Mareza of Southwall as its commander.

Done this day, 38 Gerstesykli, Thorionin vuosi 481.

"Will you accept this charge, Sir Kaith?" Ylspeth's voice made it clear that while she anticipated that he would accept the offer, she in no way considered the matter a mere formality.

The Venzene calendar was used, he knew, for all official writs and decrees. Kaith had no idea how to reconcile it with or against the measure of moons, which was the way all sensible people measured the passage of seasons. Still, that didn't stop him.

Once more, Kaith knelt before the throne. Bowing his head, he smiled as he spoke. He was growing used to hearing that honorific *Sir Kaith* ...was beginning to derive strength from it rather than trepidation. He cast about in his memory until he found the moment he was looking for, then spoke his answer.

"I will watch and warn, act and accept on the will and word of the keeper of my oath—Ylspeth of Thorion until death take me, the sky falls ... or the stars refuse to shine."

He felt a change in the air—a shift he couldn't identify. Ylspeth made no reply for a long moment. So long a moment, in fact, that he nearly dared to raise his eyes to her—a breach of decorum and circumstance that was almost too disrespectful to contemplate. Blessedly, however, she broke her silence before his concern overrode good form.

Rising, she stepped to the edge of her dais. A moment later and he felt the light touch of her fingertips spread wide across his scalp. "The Thorion Throne hears your words, accepts your oath, and offers you its own fealty with love, valor with honor, oath-breaking with deadly vengeance."

She held the touch for a long moment. He didn't mind. To feel her touch was accounted a blessing by most. At this moment, he understood why. Her presence—a thing he had taken for granted in the time before Westsong—had been revealed as the inestimable force it had likely always been. How Anden and his mates had stood against that force was something he simply couldn't reconcile.

"Rise, Sir Kaith, Companion of the Valadin." She withdrew first her hand, then her immediate presence as she retook her seat. "I have consulted with Sir Greggor and Dame Marcza." She gestured to the latter as Kaith stood, indicating that she should speak.

"Kaith, we must prepare for what's to come," said Marcza. Her voice was calm, but it was clear that she was impatient to get on with matters here as swiftly as she could. "None of us believe that Westsong was isolated or that it will remain so for long. To that end, the countess has awarded manors in accordance with our strategic goals—our long-term ones." She paused, searching his face for understanding.

When he spoke, he thought he'd assuaged whatever concerns she may have had on that score.

"You've set them like stones in a pond, making certain the rest of our brothers are given land where they can influence the other knights of the county ... or at least keep an eye on them."

Greggor's smile was brief but full of an unmistakable pride. Marcza looked relieved. The countess remained poised and seemingly impassive.

"Aye, that's it exactly." Marcza moved toward the map table, pointing to each place in turn as she spoke. "Edran has Ashacre where he'll found a training camp. Hemmet is the new Lord of Greenfork, controlling trade from the west. Valgar has Birchorg."

Kaith snorted lightly. "That should please him. He was born there."

Marcza grinned and nodded, but pressed on. "The south is secured, more or less. Raun is the new Lord of Oakwind to the southwest. Greggor is the new Lord of Knell's Stone to the southeast, and I've long since ruled over Southwall in the uttermost south."

Kaith nodded, looking over the map. "The east and north?"

Marcza pointed. "Barnic has Eastshadow. Gordan, Raegus, and Aethen are there with him for the nonce."

That made a certain amount of sense. It was nearest the ford and nearest the pass into the Frost Fang Mountains that bordered Thorion to the east. It needed a strong leader. Barnic wasn't local to that town, nor was he a well-known figure in the county as of yet. A cadre of knights would ease the fears of Eastshadow's people. Valad's former armsmen had lived and trained together for years, making them a logical choice.... *But wait. You only mentioned four of them.*

"What about Jastar? Where have you sent him? Wick? Rockvale?"

Once more, Kaith noted Greggor's brief, burning look of pride. His former master then held up a hand to forestall whatever reply Marcza was about to make. He then spoke his request in a gentle baritone.

"Commander, if I may?"

Marcza nodded, looking both relieved and annoyed.

"Kaith, The Throne has dispatched Sir Jastar on a delicate mission of his own. We must hope for his success and his safe return to us. For now, however, that must suffice."

Kaith cocked his head to the side, nodding. He had been about to speak his acceptance of Greggor's final word on the matter when his eyes again fell upon the map.

Barnic and the rest of Valad's retinue are all at Eastshadow. The countess spoke with Sir Valad, when last I stood in this chamber, about the Shivering Song ... about the Dairy of Khans that had stood up in the lands north of the river where she used to rule. The turn of phrase had amused him once he'd heard the truth. He paused, then met Ylspeth's eyes. He found she was looking at him intently, as if studying him.

"Sir Kaith?"

Ylspeth's voice was a potent thing in his ears—in his head. Seeing her at Westsong had clearly changed his view of her.

"Thinking about the Sheshik dairy, Excellency. Forgive me." Turning to Greggor, he saw the man looked utterly confused and none too happy about it. "Aye, Sir Greggor, Dame Commander. I'll speak no more about Jastar's commission."

Ylspeth's eyes grew briefly wide, a bright and unguarded smile flowering on her lips. "I *Khan't* tell you how pleased we are to hear you speak with such wisdom, Sir Kaith."

He grinned at her, even as he bowed in answer. There was no more denying it. His fear was, for now, at least, nowhere to be found.

Marcza drew him back to the topic at hand. "We would have been pleased to grant you Wick. There is precedent for removing an underperforming manorial lord, but—"

"*Underperforming*?" Kaith grew angry. It came out of nowhere—asleep above the stables one moment—armed, armored, and ready for battle the next. "Lord Ricgerd has had no chance to underperform. He's been lord there for barely more than a week, and then only if word's reached him!"

"Sir Kaith!" Ylspeth's voice was a whip-crack.

He bowed his head. "Forgive me, Excellency."

"We agree—all three of us." Marcza's voice was just left of defensive. "To that end, we are sending you to aid and support the new lord until you and the Throne itself deem him worthy."

Kaith's eyes grew wide for a moment. He drew a last deep breath to ready himself before speaking. "You wish me to make of the Lord Ricgerd a puppet."

"No!" Marcza's voice was shocked, almost as if she'd been slapped.

"Yes," said Ylspeth. "Sir Kaith has the right of it. We needn't dress the matter in silks, Commander."

"Excellency, I—"

Ylspeth was having none of it, it seemed. She drew her left hand up in a gesture of peace, palm out toward Marcza.

For her part, Marcza bowed her head, nodding, then looked at the countess's unreadable face before looking back at Kaith.

She's an outsider, here. For all her poise and skill, her grit, and her cleverness, she's still an outsider in these halls. What's more, she knows it.

Ylspeth spoke anew, her voice somehow regal in its neutrality. "Sir Kaith... Ricgerd is, by all accounts, loyal to the Thorion Throne. Moreover, he is reputed to be possessed of skill at arms. Both of these are welcome things—things we shall have need of in the days to come. Unfortunately, Lord Ricgerd is also possessed of a fierce temperament. Wick must be ready for what is to come."

Kaith nodded, not daring to speak or even to agree with the countess. He kept prudently silent, awaiting her invitation to comment.

"He has suffered two terrible losses in a single blow. I cannot summon him to court, for he would see no comfort, no ally here. I cannot send him a simple writ of condolence and support. He would see it as an insult to the memory of his kin, and he would be right to do so. I must, therefore, send an embassage to offer condolence, support, and guidance. That embassage must wear a face he knows." She paused, lifting her chin slightly to look down upon him. "You do know the man, and he you. Is that not so?"

"We aren't boon companions, Excellency, but, aye. We've spent a few nights talking and drinking to the health of his father and yourself." Kaith knew he sounded as if he were making excuses, and perhaps he was. He could tell Ricgerd of the loss. Who better to do so, really? None of Robis's closies survived the Red Storm, after all.

"This puts you in a better position than most to deliver unto him the truth of Westsong. Further, you will, perhaps, be able to guide him toward the tomorrow we strive for. Lastly... Wick must both be prepared to support the northern marches and have troops to call upon if and when the Dame Commander requires. If he should prove unwilling or unable, of course, then you will need to be prepared to assume the lordship. We must hope that it does not come to that, of course. Yet it does us no good to rely on hope alone." She paused for a beat, then spoke the five words that would entrap him. "Will you accept this charge?"

He bowed his head, taking several breaths to focus his mind, though this was a formality. Of course, he would take the commission. How could he refuse? Questions of the countess and his duty be damned. Even ignoring all of that, he owed Robis this much, at the very least.

"Yes, Your Excellency. It will be my honor to bear the swords of Sir Robis and Sir Reginald back to Wick and to do my best to guide Lord Ricgerd along the path."

Ylspeth smiled, though the others kept their faces blank.

"Very good. On to the next matter, then. You are not a bachelor knight, Sir Kaith, which means you must be supported by the incomes of a manorial estate. Given you will need to spend a protracted period away from any such holding, the Thorion Throne is of a mind to grant you the lands of Westsong."

The room fell into shocked silence.

"It will earn you no new income until it is cleansed and re-peopled, of course, yet the coin it has earned over the decades has mostly been put by until it was needed. You shall have coin and to spare in order to support yourself and your household, as well as to rebuild Westsong when the time comes, yet that coin will not grow or renew. You must spend it with care and deliberation."

"Th... Thank you, Excellency. I..." He shook his head. He was at a loss for words. It wasn't a matter of the proposed wealth or the understanding that he was now a lord responsible to rebuild the place where he had been called to service. It was the fact that he now bore the honor and burden of being the living symbol of what he'd come to think of as *that red symphony*.

The countess had gestured to Greggor, who walked to the eastern door of the chamber—that which led to the living quarters and what had been Greggor's office. A moment later and Kaith saw two figures enter. He recognized both, though for very different reasons.

The first was a much cleaner version of the boy who'd awakened him as they rode toward Ashacre. He was dressed in the uniform of one of the countess's pages. Kaith presumed he'd been orphaned by the battle. It was good that the countess, or more likely Greggor, had seen fit to give him a home and purpose. What profit was it to be free when there was no place to go?

The boy walked with a measured, deliberate stride toward the throne's dais. He carried a heater shield covered in black cloth to hide its heraldry.

Behind the boy was a youth Kaith knew well. Huron had been brought to the keep a few short months after Kaith had arrived. They had often found themselves sharing the same duties in those early days and had struck up a friendship with a speed and ease that only children seem capable of. When Kaith had been informed that his new friend was a slave, Kaith had only asked one question—was he forbidden from spending time with him? When Greggor and Valgar had assured him that he was not, Kaith had simply nodded and continued on as he'd been.

Nearly eleven years had gone by since. Now the slave boy had grown into a slender man of twenty. His skin was the color of dark mahogany.

His eyes were a liquid brown, and both the short hair on his crown and the shortened spearhead growing beneath the center of his lower lip were the color of smoked honey ... and, naturally, he remained a slave.

Kaith watched as Huron processed into the chamber behind the shield-bearer. He carried a banner pole, its cloth furled tightly against the horizontal bar.

As the pair stopped their progress and stood beside the throne, Greggor spoke up.

"Sir Kaith, Lord of Westsong, in recognition of your service, the Thorion Throne does hereby grant you the right to bear these arms as your personal banner and the symbol of your household. Blå, sølv øye I toppen, hammer ved foten."

Kaith hadn't the slightest idea what that heraldic description meant, but he didn't have long to wait before he found out.

The boy uncovered the heater's face, presenting the shield to him. It bore a blue field, upon which rode a silver eye above a silver hammer. Greggor had come to him perhaps an hour before they'd arrived in the capital and asked him if he'd had the foggiest notion of what he might want as heraldry. He'd been careful to make no promises, but he'd apparently got the design past the countess's scribes and heralds, somehow.

He took the shield and slipped it onto his dim arm. Huron had unfurled the banner as well. It, too, bore his newly granted device upon it.

He opened his mouth to offer his thanks when something struck him.

"Forgive me... no."

The room's collective population looked at him. The two newcomers were slack-jawed and gawking.

"No... *what*, exactly, Sir Kaith?" Ylspeth alone seemed comfortable with this new development.

"I shouldn't be accounted Lord of Westsong, Excellency. Westsong isn't a living place just now. Besides, Westsong belongs to you. I thank you for the trust of it, but I'm only its caretaker... for now, at least. When all of this is ended, and I've restored it for you, and in your name, I'll return it to your keeping."

Marcza stood in stunned silence. She opened her mouth several times as if to speak, then seemed to give that idea up as a bad job, bowing her head and smiling as if to say *so be it*.

"Very well, Sir Kaith. We shall amend your official title to Keeper of Westsong if that will serve."

Kaith couldn't tell if the countess were pleased, humbled, or annoyed. Her face and voice were difficult to fathom.

He bowed his head. "Thank you, Excellency."

"Then let us move to the final matter. What is it you will require in order to carry out the commission I have granted you?"

He considered for a moment, then asked a question of his own. "Forgive me, but what is it appropriate to speak of in this context? Gear? Men? Beasts? Coin?"

Ylspeth nodded thoughtfully, considering. "Dame Commander, Sir Greggor? Perhaps you could guide your brother-in-arms?"

Marcza nodded, exchanged a glance with Greggor, then turned back to Kaith.

"I would recommend you recruit at least three armsmen into your service, one of which should be able to assume the role of sergeant for you. Outfitting them with gear and horses, provisioning yourselves for the road, and so on. If you can think of anything else you might need for either the journey or its end, that should be added as well. I speak generally, mind. In this instance, I should focus on building the foundation of my retinue, were I you."

Kaith nodded, then turned to Greggor. "Sir Greggor has more knowledge of those capable and fitting to serve as a Sergeant, I should think. I would welcome any suggestions."

Greggor kept his face even, looking thoughtful. At length, he said. "There's a man called Terrek—a good man who's served for many years now among the wardens of the Shivering March."

Kaith blinked, and hard. Greggor hadn't said his old friend had served in the north! The Wardens of the Shivering March patrolled the lands nearest the river and the court of the Shivering Song. They were feared because they were fear-less. Standing a bitter watch when the Coach Devour was said to ride. They alone were tasked with defending pilgrims or the wayward, should they be caught out of doors when the moon was right.

"Will he suffice, Sir Kaith?" Greggor did his best to pull Kaith back to the moment.

"Yes... Yes, of course. Thank you." Kaith felt that wave of stability overtake and ground his wandering mind once more.

Greggor nodded, considering. "I can find you one or two others, I'm certain..."

Kaith looked to Marcza, then the countess ... then a thought occurred to him.

"Excellency?"

"Yes, Sir Kaith?"

"I have leave to take and offer service to any who owe allegiance to the Thorion Throne and that are below the rank of Bachelor Knight. Is that right?"

The countess nodded slowly. "It is."

Kaith fought back the urge to grin. If he was right...

"Then I wish to take Huron into my service."

All seemed surprised by this, and none more than the man in question.

"You wish to take and recruit one of the castle's slaves." Ylspeth wasn't questioning so much as confirming her understanding. "There are many slaves for sale in the lower market, Sir Kaith. You needn't select one as an armsman."

Kaith nodded his understanding. Still, he held his ground. "True enough, Excellency, yet it is this *particular* slave that I wish to obtain." He paused, meeting her eyes. "I would be willing to pay for him out of the coin at my disposal if that would be of use to the Throne, for he cuts a fine figure stood there bearing my banner."

All eyes turned to Huron, then back to Kaith.

"The Thorion Throne grants you this boon, Sir Kaith. He now belongs to you."

Kaith nodded his thanks, then turned to Greggor. "Sir Greggor? Please arrange the necessary paperwork to free Huron of Thorionden, formally. If he or any man is to stand and serve in my retinue, they must enter into it willingly. No slave has the freedom to make such a decision, as I understand it."

Greggor offered a slow nod. "I shall see it sorted. No fear, Kaith."

Kaith nodded at this, then turned to Huron. "Well, Huron of Thorionden... will you stand?"

Huron's eyes shimmered, though when he spoke, his voice was full of utter surety. He spoke in a musical, lilting voice. "Yes, Sir Kaith." It was all the affirmation needed in such a moment.

Kaith's smile was jewel-bright in the torch-light. Greggor would find him a third man, he had no doubt. Here, however—in this moment, he, at last, began to see what kind of knight he wished to be.

He had been trained to be the bridge. That bridge, he found, could be moved to cross different rivers and valleys. He thought back to Westsong.

He and his fellow Valadin had been the bridge there, as well. On their backs, the survivors had crossed out of death and ruin and into new lives beyond the Red Storm.

... And so it was, and so it is... and so it shall be. I'm still the bridge. My reach and my shadow are longer now... but, aye. I'm still the bridge.

CHAPTER FIFTEEN

SHADOWS SHAKEN

-I-

Venzene Duchy of Kamieńalun
County Czarny Wodospad
Wieża Szymona
42 Gerstesykli: 14 Days after the Red Storm at Westsong

The banquet hall sounded appropriately animated, given it was the dinner hour... or did it? Something seemed off. As Yeidil walked toward the murmur and clink that pervaded nearly every evening meal, she thought she sensed an undercurrent of subdued solemnity.

Her eyes fell upon the brazier at hall's end. Its light flickered as the fire held within danced.

It's like a child singing in the fields and forests... so lost in its own joy that the rest of the world hardly matters.

Hells, was she *truly* feeling so melancholy? So jealous ... of fire? She laughed at herself, keeping her voice soft so as not to draw undue attention. One did not enter the banquet hall lightly, especially when one observed the traditions at the door.

Thirty seconds may as well be a lifetime when all eyes are upon you, reacting to some breach of decorum. The daughter of the Black Tower does not act in such a way.

The daughter of the Countess *Calpernia* did not act in such a way. That's what her mother had truly been saying.

Yeidil turned to her left, placing the brazier at her back, and strode into the chamber. Two steps in, she stopped and stood beside the two guards, each of whom bowed their heads to her in greeting. A thirty-count later saw her moving down the left side of the horse-shoe-shape made by the tables, past her cousins, aunt, and uncle, whom she greeted courteously, and down to her seat at high table.

She bent to kiss her father's left cheek, then her mother's right one before taking her position to Calpernia's left.

"You're in time for the second remove. You've missed only the bread's warmth." Calpernia nodded her approval. "I expect you've already heard that your father rides come dawn." This wasn't a question.

"Yes, mother. Do you…"

"… Know why? Don't be foolish. Of course, I know why." Calpernia's face remained warm and smiling—her Courtly Face as Yeidil thought of it—but her tone was dismissive, bordering on outright pique.

Yeidil kept her voice soft, her expression nonplussed. "You always do, mother." She left the next question unasked. A moment later, she was pleased she'd done it, for Calpernia's aspect eased slightly. After she'd sipped from her goblet in the dainty, pecking way she had, she answered her without further prompting.

"A messenger came through mid-morning. He was wounded— nothing horrid, but he'll need a few days' care to ensure he remains on the mend." She searched Yeidil's face for understanding, then smiled past her to the far left of the table where one of Father's banners—Syr Austorn— sat with his wife and eldest son. Calpernia lifted her glass toward them in a token gesture to their health.

"Ambush, I take it?" Yeidil reached for her own goblet, then turned to follow her mother's gaze and mirror her action.

"That's right. They'd driven off or killed the cozening beasts. But they found something strange about them. They wore the raiment of our own common folk. While not the most cunning deception ever dreamt of, it certainly warranted dispatching a messenger back to warn your father."

Yeidil nodded and sighed her relief. "Wretched, but not as horrid as I'd feared."

"Horrid enough, my girl. Horrid enough."

Yeidil saw Calpernia smile as servants brought the next remove small ceramic bowls containing mizeria—the thick slices of cucumber drizzled in spiced sour cream and vinegar. It was her father's favorite—light on the sugar, heavy on the pepper and dill. She could smell pork as well, certain to be swimming in a mushroom sauce.

Her mouth watered as her serving was set before her. With an effort, she resisted the urge to indulge herself as her mother spoke anew.

"We never seem to have enough time. I fear this hastened departure sounds the very knell. I simply haven't had the time needed to recover and refresh myself adequately. Unless I am very much mistaken, the door will soon be open, and your father will be lost to us." She delivered this with such a sweet, soft tone that *almost* she sounded relieved... perhaps even happy for the outcome.

An instant later and Yeidil saw the tears standing in her mother's eyes and knew better.

"Another cień must surely be enough, Mother... surely." She kept her voice light and soft, her face the picture of the dutiful daughter locked in conversation with her wise and gentle mother. An absurd picture, really... leagues from the stark reality.

"Hardly. It would take more than the addition of a new apprentice now. We would be hard-pressed even were we blessed with an *enclave* of noviciates at this late date. I've ignored the hourglass for far too long, I fear. Even if we had another supplicant or sacrifice, there wouldn't be nearly enough time to prepare the rites."

Calpernia shook her head, brought her bowl close to her face as if to sniff its contents, then leaned back, blinking and dabbing at her eyes with the napkin that had languished in her lap. It had been cleverly done. The strong smells of pepper and vinegar could be eye-watering, most especially when it came to father's preferred mixture of spices.

Yeidil sat in thought. Calpernia wasn't given to exaggerated doom-saying. She'd never seen her in such an obvious state of... of what? It took her a moment to unpack the complication of emotions her mother both was and was not showing.

Defeat, she thought. *This is Calpernia in defeat.* It had been the first time she'd ever encountered such a thing. Calpernia was always, always in control of herself and nearly everyone and everything around her. To see her bravely facing defeat was humbling and frightening all at a go. Beyond the initial shock, and—she'd do better to admit it—the petty, childish delight in seeing the mask of her mother's perfection finally crack. The realization forced Yeidil to think of Kozioł's plight.

If Mother hadn't taken Kozioł's cień, then why was he having so much trouble calling it? Could it truly have been the weight of worry he'd held over embarrassing Azhferd? She'd said it was possible. It *was*, of course, but she'd said it mainly to help bolster his lack of confidence. She'd *thought* her mother had been the real culprit...

Her thoughts were cut off abruptly as a grubby-looking man was held up at the hall's entrance. She knew him, she thought—had seen him in and about town.

"What... is the woodcutter doing here?" she heard Calpernia ask. The question had been loud enough for her father to overhear but soft enough to avoid disturbing the table at large.

The man looked impatient but accepted the guards' order to stand fast at the entrance. Finally, they allowed him through, but it was Uncle Borys who walked to meet him.

The pair spoke briefly; the woodcutter clearly agitated, though not, she thought, at having to speak to her uncle. A moment later and Borys walked the man to where the count waited, two seats to Yeidil's right.

"Your Excellency," Borys began. "This is Marek, a woodcutter who serves in the county's militia as well."

Hengrek nodded, speaking in his soft, understated way. "Marek, I welcome you to Wieża Szymona." He reached a hand toward a servant who, without a word, set about pouring a fresh goblet of mulled wine. "Tell to me what I may do for you."

The servant moved forward to proffer the fresh drink to the new-comer, but Hengrek stopped her with a gesture. He took the goblet him-self, then stood and offered it to the dumbstruck woodcutter, who took it gratefully.

"Thank you, Lord." The man simply stood there, holding the goblet for a moment.

Hengrek sat back down and made a gesture that seemed to encourage the man.

"My lord... my boy—my Cezary... he is gone." He gripped the wooden cup as if he were trying to shatter it. "Nor, my lord, is he the only one. Several other children are now missing. One or two might wander off into the snows and forests—can be lost, or eaten by animals, or be taken by slavers or unworthy men, but not so many in so short a time. More go each night!" He was becoming desperate now, not shouting so much as showing a raw emotion that hurt to hear or see in so strong a man. "We have lost five in the last three nights, my lord!" He swallowed audibly, face haunted. "There has been song on the wind, Lord. There has been laughter in the storms and snows... me, I don't say—not for true and sure—but it seems as if she walks among us... Lord. It seems that..." His voice was a husky whisper now. "... That Złodziej Kołyski's walked each night this last week."

Marek, at last, seemed aware of the goblet in his hand. He looked at it as if he'd no idea how it'd gotten there but drained it in a single draft, clearly glad for the comfort.

Hengrek waited for the man to take a few breaths, looking thoughtful. At length, he made reply. "Piosenka Burzy has been mild these last few nights. We haven't had a proper storm in the last fortnight. True?" He held Marek's gaze. That worthy worked his jaw but nodded. "I do not say that this changes what has befallen. Only that we may be seeking the wrong cause." Again, Marek nodded. "You have lost your boy, and *that... that* is a misfortune I would not wish on an *enemy*, let alone one of my people. And you say there are others—your neighbors and friends—who have likewise suffered this misfortune."

"Yes, Lord." Marek's voice was a mixture of misery and hope.

"I will not promise you they will be found. I will not promise you that if they *are* found, they will yet live. I would not lie to you nor give you false hope as if you were yourself a fool. I do not take you for such a man, Marek. But..." Hengrek held up the first finger of his bright hand, "*this* much I will promise you. I ride out tomorrow with many of my men. Our borders are threatened, and I am needed to command the force we have arrayed to defend them. Yet I will leave men here to defend our homes. My lady-wife will rule in my absence and will see that the monster that has taken some and threatened all of our children is uncovered and unmade."

Calpernia nodded, reaching her hand to her right to place on Hengrek's dim one.

Marek looked between them, then at his goblet, then down. "Th-thank you, my lord... twój cień jest długi!" He bowed from the waist in an awkward, unpracticed motion, nearly overbalancing. *(Your shadow is long)*.

"Nasze cienie są długie , Marek." Hengrek gave a nod to Borys, squeezing Calpernia's hand before releasing it. *(Our shadows are long)*.

Borys began to escort the man named Marek to the door. Calpernia rose to follow.

Yeidil blinked, shook her head, then looked at her father. She inwardly said a prayer to no deity in particular that her mother was wrong—that her father was not doomed to be lost to them. In her heart, she feared it was a hollow hope, but hollow hope was better than none at all.

She met Kozioł's eye and offered a small salute with her goblet, which he returned in kind. She would have to hope tonight was the night they unearthed at least *that* mystery. All of her plans to ensure Azhferd did not suffer the same fate as her father appeared destined for... they all required Kozioł to find his cień. If Calpernia hadn't cut it from him, there was hope there as well.

"We will see soon enough," she murmured before at last beginning to eat the mizeria before her.

-II-

County Thorion
Thorionden Castle
42 Gerstesykli: 14 days after the Red Storm at Westsong

Kaith sat in the room he'd once shared with Valgar—the second story of a narrow guard tower in the southwest corner of the castle's outer wall.

It was among the gentry's many privileges to be permitted to call upon the County Throne, or indeed, at any lord or lady's residence, to request hospitality. Thorionden's castle maintained fully a dozen such rooms to accommodate these requests, as well as the housing of visiting nobility and other dignitaries. These were either above the stables or on the castle's second floor.

Valgar had moved into such a room the very day they'd arrived from Westsong, leaving Kaith with the chamber all to himself.

The countess had seen fit, given his situation, to grant him effective ownership of the chamber—lock, key, and cupboard, as his father used to say—until such time as he had a manor or family of his own. While he was grateful, of course, the decision left him with essentially nothing to do to prepare himself for departure. All that he owned was already in the place where he would, officially at least, live.

He looked at his armor upon its stand, a shortened chain hauberk, vambraces splinted with bands of steel, a padded steel gorget, and an open-faced sallet helm.

"I should have cuisses made and knee cops," he said to no one in particular. "Come to that, I should get elbow cops and pauldrons as well if they can be arranged before I ride out."

He marveled at himself. *Spending coin I haven't earned on armor I clearly don't need...* but no. He might not need the armor for its protection, not that the extra defense would be a bad thing. No, indeed, but it was. He'd do better to admit it, a necessary mark of his station to be so well-armed and armored. A knight—especially a member of the landed gentry—must be recognizable *as* a knight. It was the same lesson he'd been taught as a boy about cleanliness.

You needn't smell sweet or flowery, Kaith, Greggor used to say. *But if your reek hangs about you like witch-fog and buzzards circle overhead wherever you walk, you'll not make many friends.*

His eyes fell upon the tower shield propped against the wall. It was dented and scratched ... and plain. He would need to get his new arms painted upon its surface, as well ... now they were accounted legally his.

A knock at the door drew his mind away from such thoughts. That would be Greggor's recommendation for the role of sergeant, a man called Terrek.

"It's open!"

The door swung in toward him. A lone figure stood silhouetted in the hall's torchlight. With his dark blond hair meticulously trimmed and parted, his face shaved bare, and his empty yet somehow knowing brown eyes, Terrek was a study in equilibrium. He managed to appear both unassuming and commanding simultaneously, which was no easy task.

Kaith gestured him into the chamber. When he'd entered in earnest, Kaith stood, looking the man over.

"Aye, blue mantled cloak and all—you're certainly a match for Greggor's description. It's good to meet you at last."

Terrek bowed, hand on heart. His posture was a bit stiff, his movements practiced and intentionally rigid. When he spoke, his voice was a rather more formalized version of Greggor's in cadence and accent. He'd come from the south of the county, obviously.

"Sir Kaith," said he, "I'm honored to stand before you. Sir Greggor's spoken highly of you." He paused for a moment, then added in a more genuine, less rehearsed tone, "I hope that I prove to be a good fit for your needs, sir."

Kaith allowed a smile to play across his face, unfettered by thought or plan. He was pleased to see the man had a side *other* than tightly wound.

"I'll be surprised if you somehow fail to. Greggor is, as you must know, an excellent judge of character." He gestured for the man to sit on one of the room's two chairs. He, himself, returned to his bed, sitting on it to face him. "I'd offer you a drink, but all I have is water at present."

Terrek held up a hand to indicate that it was no matter to him.

"Greggor tells me you come from duty among the wardens of the shivering march. How long did you suffer that chilly duty?" Kaith was careful to keep his voice easy. He neither wanted to insult the man nor be seen as obsequious. He must have struck a fair balance, for when Terrek answered, his voice seemed unaffected by the question.

"Five years. I served as a guardsman under Sir Aldo Trallot of Rockvale for four years prior to that, and his father Sir Anzo Trallot for two, before he passed."

Kaith nodded slowly, considering. "And how many Harvests have you seen on Skolf?"

"Harvests, my lord—funnily enough, I was born during Harvest—the eleventh. Just saw my twenty-ninth."

Kaith nodded, trying not to comment on the date. It was the night before the so-called Red Storm.

"What more can I tell, my lord?"

Kaith considered the question. What did he want to know about the man? After a moment, he spoke up. "Can you tell me what *exactly* Greggor told you about my commission?"

Terrek bowed his head, considering, before giving an answer.

"You're bound for Wick, initially, at least. You're to deliver the grim news to the new lord—that'll be Ricgerd—and to stay for at least as long as it takes to shore up the defenses there in advance of some conflict to come. I ken that what's coming has to do with what you faced at Westsong. There are rumors, but I honestly don't have a clear picture of what you and the lads—your fellow knights, I mean—actually fought there."

Kaith nodded, but left the unasked question equally unanswered.

"That's fair enough. I confess I was a bit surprised when Greggor said you were here, in the capital. I'd have expected you to still be afield."

Terrek's face wore a thin smile. "Aye, my lord, well, my cadre was at the end of the season. We—the wardens, that is—cycle out once per season. It gives time to replenish the ranks, train, and refresh ourselves for the task we're charged with. It gives folk the chance to end their service honorably if they're of a mind—many are, or used to be after hearing Her Ladyship's song—even at a distance. It also gives time to spend with their families as well, for those that have them. And so, as Harvest now draws to an end, we've returned to the motherhouse. It's just inside the southern gate."

Kaith made a gesture of acceptance. He thought he liked Terrek—that Greggor had, indeed, chosen wisely for him.

"Well, as you know, my knighthood came as an unexpected gift. I'd never intended nor striven for the accolade, and so am not as familiar with the office's... oh, what's the word Greggor used for it? Nuances! That was it. I'm not as familiar with the office's nuances as I should like to be."

Terrek again offered that thin smile, nodding his understanding.

"Your time under the Trallot family would certainly have given you more regular interaction with the gentry than I've had." Kaith chuckled. The juxtaposition was a rueful joke. "I expect I'll pick up the bits I don't know along the way, but I think it important to be as clear as I can with you. You're not entering the service of a storied soldier with high blood and noble lineage to commend to him, nor one who knew when he woke up on the twelfth that he'd end the day with an honorific attached to his name. I *will* make mistakes. That I can promise you."

Terrek again nodded his head. "May I speak, my lord?"

Kaith gestured him on. "Aye—always and freely when we're alone like this."

Terrek lifted his chin, looking down his rather hawkish nose toward Kaith. Rather than making him appear arrogant, Terrek merely looked thoughtful. At length, he nodded and spoke his peace.

"My lord, if you thought to frighten me off with such, I fear you'll be disappointed. Quite the contrary, in fact. When Greg—forgive me. When Sir Greggor first broached the idea with me this afternoon, I feared your age. I feared you might be callow and full of talking... that he'd some hope of, perhaps, me serving to ground and temper you and your impulses." His thin smile turned into a toothy grin. He shook his head, actually chuckling. "I misjudged you and Sir Greggor's intent, and for that, I owe an apology."

Kaith sat back, considering the man, then nodded. "Everyone has some bias, I suppose. No harm in it ... once you've spotted it, aye? A large part of what I have to do is to open eyes—to draw those I can under one banner, make them see past their own small hills and small minds so we can fight together when the time comes."

Terrek's eyes widened slightly, his smile winking out. "Yes, my lord. As you say."

Kaith let the silence play out for a moment before asking his next question. "I still need one more armsman. Before he selected one for me, Greggor thought it wise to ask if you had someone to recommend. Do you?"

Terrek considered, then gave a slow nod. "I know of one, my lord."

Something in his voice gave Kaith pause. "Well-suited?"

"Aye, my lord. He's a fair hand with a blade, good in a tight spot, and follows orders."

"... But?"

"My lord?"

"You're holding a thing back, Terrek."

"My personal opinion or impression of the man, that's all. He's sure to perform the duty for which you're considering him admirably."

Kaith stood, walking toward the wall where his tower shield lay. He crouched down, turning his back on the man. Running his bright hand's fingers along the scarred wooden surface, he was forcibly reminded of Valgar's early training with the enormous thing.

Kaith had had a difficult time, at first, with the bulk. It hadn't been its weight but the lack of visibility it left him with when wielded in certain stances and guards. Valgar's lessons on that score—like *most* things he'd discovered—always seemed to carry much broader truths... *when the mind's allowed to connect them, at least,* Greggor would say.

"You have to listen to your shield, I think—have to trust it to weather the blows it blocks for you. The wood will creak and groan when weight's against it, telling you the time you have left before it buckles and you're to be left vulnerable." He slid his forefinger into a groove that had undoubtedly been made by the claw of a certain white wolf, repeating once more, "You *must* be able to trust your shield..."

Terrek must've gotten the message, for he cleared his throat before speaking up again.

"Vilmocz is his name, my lord. His father and he were caravan guards to and from Venzene. Two years ago, they made Thorion their home, settling in Eastshadow. He took up arms in Sir Cedric's guard but found he didn't care for town defense. A year later, he entered service with the wardens. He's a lout with too much of Venzene in him for my liking, but as I say, he's a good man to have at your side or back when trouble comes."

Kaith nodded, turning as he stood. "Thank you. Huron, my groom, is off in the lower town. I'll want you to meet him in the morning—to fetch him, actually, from the Dove and Falcon."

"The brothel—yes, my lord."

Kaith gave a smirk. "First time he's had coin and to spare in his pockets. When I asked him what he planned to do with such newfound freedom, his first thought was the Dove."

"When shall I fetch him, my lord?"

"I want you both here by the ninth bell. If you see him this evening, tell your Vilmocz to be in front of the tower, here, by the time the tenth bell tolls. I'll want to get you lot fitted for armor, assess your collective gear, and so on. We ride out either in two or three days, depending on how quickly we can get everyone kitted out."

Terrek nodded, standing and bowing. "Yes, my lord. Will there be anything else?"

Kaith looked the man up and down briefly, then shook his head. "No, Sergeant. I think that's enough to be going on with for now."

Terrek started at that. Apparently, he hadn't realized he'd gotten the job, officially. "Yes, Sir Kaith. Thank you, sir." He bowed once more, backed away, then exited the chamber.

He's not remotely intimidated by me, nor my station. That's something.

Kaith began to undress for bed. Tomorrow would be the beginning of a new path for him—one with new responsibilities, new perils, and a new household under his banner... *his* banner. He couldn't imagine what his father would've made of such madness. The thought made him smile, and he took that smile down into sleep with him.

-III-

Venzene Duchy of Kamieńalun
County Czarny Wodospad
Wieża Szymona
42 Gerstesykli: 14 Days after the Red Storm at Westsong

She knows that she dreams. Even now, she slumbers beneath an old and seasoned barn roof, wooden floor beneath her, hides and cloak covering her... but none of that matters. What does matter is the familiar high street that she walks upon.

The sun casts a strange, overexposed grey light through the laden clouds that hover above. The snow pushed to either side of the street looks almost as if it were made of crumpled vellum—although who would waste such treasure in quantity like that is beyond her reckoning. It isn't real, in any event. This is a dream, and dreams stretch and bend the mind's eye, ear, nose, and sense of touch in ways too fantastical to explain easily in the light of day.

"Pale copies," she hears herself say as she walks. "Pale copies of whatever magic makes them so..." So what? She doesn't know. It doesn't seem to matter too terribly much to her. What matters is what lay before her only a few strides away.

Three buildings down on her right is the carpenter—Oleg and his wife. "Wife," she snorts. "She's young enough to be his granddaughter, the old goat."

The building after that belongs to Zofia and her daughter Amelie, the bakers. The daughter is pleasant enough. Her mother finds reasons to be deaf or simply busy when Lashjuk happens to come into contact with her. No matter. This building, too, holds no allure for her.

Past the baker's is their well—one of two along the high street. Both the eastern and western districts have their own water source—a stroke of luck, perhaps even a blessing from on high, for few places she's been to have more than a single well within the town's limits. Most towns are set near a river, instead. This place—her home for so many years now—has that as well. The falls from which the county derives its name feed a slow-moving river with sweet, clean water. She fights to bring her focus back to the well. Across from it, yes. The left side of the high street... yes. Yes, there—the thing, the place she's come to see.

"Home..."

She wants to run, but fears that doing so will take her out of this dream that much faster. Calm controls the dream world, not conflict, or so her grandmother liked to say.

No, she would remain at peace, riding her joy like a slow-moving horse over uneven ground.

She was at her door now. Should she knock? No, of course not. This was her home, after all. "Was? Was, or is?" She hesitates, unsure.

After a moment, she reaches, touching the door's handle. She intends to pull it open. Instead, she abruptly finds herself stood in the entry room. She sees and smells the familiarity of this place, where they took orders, collected coin, and undertook the thousands of other small acts required to run a business.

The air is full of the mingled scents of ink and parchment, as well as a fainter undertone of iron and stone dust.

She sees not a soul, yet she hears the tink-tink-tink of a chisel being tapped from further in … from the workshop.

Her heart flutters. She knows, knows, knows this is a dream, but the chance to see, to touch her Guuvra once more, is such a powerful draw.

"I cannot stay long, my gnash. If you'd see and say, then come. Keep me company while I finish." His voice is full and rolling—not booming, but distracting, engaging.

It can only be him, only truly him, she thinks and moves toward him. He would insist on utter quiet when first he began a project, so he could hear the stone, as he liked to say. However, as the day passed and work had progressed, he would invite her or perhaps one of the boys if their chores were sorted to keep him company while he finished.

Once more, she finds herself suddenly *in* the place where she'd meant to go, without having actually moved there under her own power. She sees the familiar stone walls, the carvings along them of horses and winter falcons, elk and snow leopards, and, of course, the massive ariculf heads over the room's two doors—calm and lifelike. Like the others, these were only carvings—yet after her recent encounter with the ariculf by the river, she finds herself fearful to look upon them.

Blessedly, there's something far more interesting to look upon—Guuvra. He stands naked to the waist, his back to her, head down as his hands busy themselves with their work.

She marvels, and not for the first time, that such enormous hands could work the tiny point and tooth chisels used to carve such delicate lines into the unforgiving stones. Yet, she knows or perhaps knew the truth. She'd often seen the light in her gnash's eyes. Whenever he had the time or better still—the commission to do more than create structures... to create true art with his hands—*he came truly to life in those moments*, she thinks.

As if in answer—as if he'd heard her thoughts, he speaks without turning. "No longer, my gnash. My time to create beauty is done, save only this." He moves his head to gesture his chin toward his current piece. "It isn't ready for your eyes just yet. *Almost*, but not yet. Keep me company while I finish."

"Can you lay it by?" She knows the answer even as she asks the question, but she has to ask. "If you put it by, we can stop the hourglass—turn it on its side..."

His laughter is warm. "You breathe, and our children need you yet." He shakes his head, still not looking at her. "My time is over. I can inspire beauty but can no longer create it. Tell me—is he a good man, your human?"

His voice holds no bitterness, yet she feels as if he's slapped her. She tries to speak but can think of nothing to say.

"Lashjuk... my time is over. Yours is not." He continues tapping on the chisel's end, then puts it by, grabbing one with a finer point. "I think it a fair question."

She finds her voice, though it comes out in a whisper. "Yes."

Guuvra nods. "Will you take a new name for your new life?"

"Should I?"

He laughs again. "Only you can answer that, Lashjuk. Some take a new name each year or decade, some once only, some never." He pauses to reach for a small whisking brush. As he employs it, clearing away the stone dust from his most recent foray with the chisel, he adds, "Stages of growth, oaths sworn or achieved, the having of children, or their loss... It all amounts to the same thing—change. You've gone through—you *go* through change enough to at least consider such. You're becoming a new thing even now."

She nods, knowing he's right. First, she thinks about it, then she speaks it aloud. "I hadn't given it thought, gnash. I think I feared yet more change for our sons."

He freezes, then. "Our ... sons, you say. Not our children, but... but our... sons. So he killed... he killed my..." He trails off, leaning forward onto his hands, chest shaking as he sobs.

She moves toward him, laying her hands on his shoulders, pressing her cheek to his muscular back. "Yes," she whispers, and for a moment, it's all she can say. She can feel the tears first burning, then chilling on her face. "He took you from us, then Maklo... but he will poison the world with his miserable breath no more. Not two days later I... I took him—I watched as the light left his eyes, then bore witness as he was torn apart by rope and trees. He was torn limb from limb, the pieces flung into the woods, or buried." Her voice is black and low as she speaks these words. Her huntress's heart is evident even to her own ears.

"I will search for her," Guuvra says, voice still hinting at the tears of rage and misery he has yet to shed. "I will search for what time is left to me, before Felruu Ahnsiblund, or her children, come to claim and devour me."

"... If the pact still holds." She sounds both hopeful and doubtful in equal measure, even to her own ears. "If she can find you, or even cares to—Guuvra, let me see your face... please."

She moves to turn him, but he resists. "You must let me finish, gnash. If I turn now and your living eyes see me as I am, you will waken before I've finished."

"What does it matter?" Her voice is full of unshed tears. "The work of your hands is a thing of great beauty, but it's nothing to my heart—to my eyes when set against gazing upon your face again!"

"Lashjuk, hear me. I speak because I alone *can* speak here. I am brought here before you as a gift in repayment for making you see—for making an introduction. You must let me finish my work and be content to speak with me while I do. It's all that's left to me now and all I'm able to give you—it's all that's given ... to *me*."

She opens her mouth to speak when her eye falls upon their mingled shadow along the wall. She sees there what Guuvra wants her not to see— the shadow of not merely their bodies but of the dagger that juts from his chest, just above the breastbone—his death-wound.

She slides her arms around his waist, feeling the smooth flesh drawn taut over his belly. Her cheek is once more pressed against his back. She wants to close her eyes, to drink in his scent, but she doesn't dare. No, closing her eyes may mean he fades. She doesn't know how she knows this, but she does.

"I'm out of time," he says at last. "I'm out of time. I pray that I've done enough."

She begins to move—to release her grip on him, but he forestalls her.

"I will step away now, just to the side. Look upon the stone, then turn to me and close your eyes. With luck and his goodwill, perhaps we can share one final moment before the hourglass empties."

"No."

"Yes," says he. "This isn't the time for you to plant your feet and argue! Time's short enough. Please..." His voice is a harsh whisper—the first fleeting sound of shifting gravel before the avalanche begins. He slides to the left, turning his back even as she steps forward.

She gazes down, and for a moment, she's utterly lost. The beauty is far, far beyond any work Guuvra created in life. She's sure of that much. On his workbench sits a flagstone sized piece of cordierite. Its dichroic shifts between blue and grey are nearly enough to take her breath. A piece of this size is nearly an impossibility. Cordierite was prized for the accenting of other work. A pure deposit, which she was certain this had to be, of such prodigious size was akin to finding a diamond or ruby the size of a man's head!

Carved upon the stone is something that, at first, she can't fully grasp. It looks like a face made black by shadows she cannot find a source for. The face is familiar to her, but its connection to time or place in her mind is fleeting.

"Yes, but I don't know from where..." She hears herself speaking and knows it's in response to a question, but she's *heard* no question. "My... my shadow? My cień?"

All at once, the carven face moves, drawing back away from the surface of the stone as if it weren't stone at all but a frozen pond.

"I... No, I cannot. I can't go with you—I cannot leave now!" Her heart begins to hammer in her chest, breath shortening as if she's just run up the high street. She feels a warm, familiar hand on her shoulder—Guuvra's.

"It's time, Lashjuk," says he, and his words are a knell of dread and misery. "Close your eyes, and let me taste your breath a final time."

She turns to him, though she doesn't mean to. Her eyes close, though she doesn't want them to. She feels his finger beneath her chin, as it always was whenever he saw that she was angry or sad. It was a thing that he alone had ever done—such a silly thing to hold on to a memory of his finger lifting her face to his.

"I can't," she mouths, but no air, no sound escapes her.

"*I* can," Guuvra says, and then he is kissing her, breathing her in, breathing into her, his fingers sliding through her hair, cupping the back of her neck.

She pretends not to feel his dim hand sliding down her bright arm. She pretends not to notice as he lifts her wrist and places her hand atop the stone.

-IV-

Venzene Duchy of Kamieńalun
County Czarny Wodospad
Wieża Szymona
42 Gerstesykli: 14 Days after the Red Storm at Westsong

Szłam niepewnie w ciemności. Mówiłam nieświadomie przeciwko światłu. Moja piosenka, jak kwas, parzy pod niebem. Budzę się by przeżyć rozdartą godzinę.

The words rolled through Kozioł's head like a whirlwind. He'd mentally chanted them all through the evening meal, only stopping after the third remove, when he'd felt the room begin to fade, becoming itself dreamlike.

He'd been shocked by the sudden realization that even *mentally* reciting the words, he might have actually found himself in the Green Lands.

He'd also been hit with a wave of abject tiredness, yawning in an animated fashion all the way through pudding. This had elicited elbows to his ribs, and even a firm heel to his dim side shin from his brother, along with grumbled rebukes such as "Stop that," and "Cover your damned mouth, you mongrel!" His brother Jarek was so, so *very* loving at times.

As swiftly as he was able to politely excuse himself for the night, he did so. Before he'd known it, he was back in his room and laying atop his bed.

"Yeidil, please hurry," he whispered. "I don't know why I'm so tired, but I don't think I'll—" He was interrupted by a great and shuddering yawn that demanded his attention. "... be awake for much longer."

Once more, he began to review the words she had taught him. He wanted to be prepared this time. This was the last night they'd be able to train before he rode out. Come dawn, he'd be mounted and headding south out of town.

Szłam niepewnie w ciemności. Mówiłam nieświadomie przeciwko światłu. Moja piosenka, jak kwas, parzy pod niebem. Budzę się by przeżyć rozdartą godzinę.

He had to be ready for her.

Szłam ... szłam niepewnie w ciemności...

She was counting on him to help her protect... protect ... Azhferd. She was counting on him to help her protect Azhferd. He had to be ready—had to be strong and prepared.

złam niepewnie w ciemności. Mówiłam nieświadomie przeciwko światłu. Moja piosenka, jak kwas, parzy pod niebem. Budzę się by przeżyć...

-V-

The Green Lands
42 Gerstesykli: 14 Days after the Red Storm at Westsong

His eyes opened slowly. They were meant to snap open, but they refused to obey. Kozioł lay on the grass with vines and tree limbs swaying against the grey clouds, and the star shot firmament beyond.

He managed to achieve a sitting position, but at first, it was all he could do. He was so tired. His limbs, his mind... everything was so very heavy.

The song—I should speak the words—should sing the... the song...

With an effort, he began to do just that.

"Szłam niepewnie w ciemności. Mówiłam nieświadomie przeciwko światłu. Moja piosenka, jak kwas, parzy pod niebem. Budzę się by przeżyć rozdartą godzinę."

As before, he was rewarded with a sense of clarity—a sense of being drawn up out of deep sleep or deep water. He repeated it twice more and felt, at first, delighted with himself. Yeidil hadn't had to help or guide him! He'd somehow made it to the Green Lands on his own!

As he began to walk forward, the full weight of his situation struck him. He had no idea where in the Green Lands he was, nor how exactly he'd gotten there. The realization nearly overwhelmed him.

"I must have... but surely not. Am I not to think of the words to the rites I learn until it's time to use them? That makes no sense at all! How would anyone ever memorize anything?"

Movement ... in the trees. Looking up, his eyes fell upon an impossibility. The overhanging tree limbs appeared to be bending lower, as if reaching for him. The vines, too, were swaying pendulously toward him. Everything seemed tinged in fresh, red sap and scarlet blooms. Even the oak leaves on the tree nearest him were outlined in a shining red that made his stomach clench.

He turned and walked quickly from the spot where he woke. Movement... behind him. He spun around with a quickness, meaning to catch whatever was stalking him. *It'll be a small beast*, he thought. *Whatever stands in for the rabbit here, perhaps.* Nothing stirred.

He turned again to walk from the clearing. Once more, he heard a rustling, first inching, then racing toward him.

Kozioł spun on his heels again, hand reaching for a dagger that wasn't there. He drew in a breath, then roared—a high growl that, given his age, was more endearing than intimidating. Once again, there was nothing save the vines swaying in the non-existent breeze, and trees whose limbs seemed to have bent closer to him, somehow.

He walked backward for a few feet. He was terrified but didn't think it wise to show it to ... to ... to whatever was out there. Finally, he turned to *walk* once more—*walk, damnit*—from the clearing. The sound came again, loud enough to make his eyes water! It, or perhaps it was *they*, were almost on top of him nearly the instant he'd turned his back.

He ran. "There's bravery, and there's lunacy," he said aloud. "A wise warrior knows ... the ... difference!" He burst through a wall of roots and slender limbs. He could see a clearing ahead—a path in the forest he now found himself in. Rushing forward, he heard a tumult of rustling noises all around him.

"No! Get off me! No! No!!!"

The vines and tree limbs, weeds, and wildflowers paid his miserable struggling no heed.

He drew in breath—tried to call out. The words! He needed to recite the words! But his throat was wrapped tightly by something wet and darkly fragrant. Black flowers followed, blooming across his vision.

"Blood in the soil..." A voice he didn't recognize. A man's voice, though young, speaking the Trade Tongue. "So much bounty—so much temptation—to stay and harvest..." The voice had drawn closer. Kozioł could hear a horse whickering not far away. "Such hungry landscape." The voice seemed to drop down, as if kneeling. "The sap is freshly run... a yellow boot?"

Again, Kozioł heard the horse's velvet rumble—closer this time, he'd swear to it.

"I have easier meat for you," said the man. "Release my kind, and I will give it to you."

The vines that held Kozioł tightened their grip, shaking him from side to side.

The man's voice suddenly grew flat ... darksome. "Do as I ask and be sated. Do it not, and be seared. Make your choice."

Kozioł felt himself spun around, over and over again before he struck against a figure that surely had to be the man who'd been speaking.

He tried to right himself but was too dizzy. Strong arms caught him about the shoulders. "Easy, easy, eeeeasy. I have you. Can you hear me?"

Kozioł couldn't open his eyes. His head was still spinning, though his body had long since stopped. He nodded briefly, but it only made his sense of vertigo stronger.

"Good. And you understand me?"

"I... yes."

"Good. Are you alone? Are there others?"

"No, sir. I think just me." Hells, it was hard to think.

The man gave a sound of acceptance and began to move away with him. Kozioł heard an angry rush from behind him and froze, arms going around the man's torso. It was an instinctual reaction—a child's fear. He was instantly angry at himself, though he didn't rush to pull away. The man's twilight colored cloak swirled around him for a moment as he pressed himself in tighter. He felt the familiar sensation of chain mail beneath the man's clothes.

"I haven't forgotten. Patience, hollow. Patience."

The man gave Kozioł's shoulders a reassuring squeeze, then began to walk on toward the sound of a horse pawing at the grasses.

Kozioł felt the man lean him against the steed's flank.

"Can you stand if I leave you with him for a moment?"

He, at last, opened his eyes and nodded. "I think so, yes, Lord." His head had stopped trying to fly from his shoulders, at least.

"Good. I won't be a moment."

Kozioł looked on as the man returned to the tree line. He saw a helm—a barbute? He wasn't certain—atop the man's head. The cloak caught the wind as he walked, flying out behind him, back toward where Kozioł stood.

He saw the man approach the angry, red tree line, which seemed to reach out toward him. He stopped some five feet from its edge, ignoring the tendrils of vine and root that pawed at him. From beneath his cloak, he pulled something and tossed it underhanded into the forest.

To Kozioł's revulsion, every inch of vegetation retracted as if a rope had been cut. He heard yet more rustling and the sound of something tearing.

He forced himself to look away. The sound was wet and somehow predatory. He thought he had himself under control until he came to the realization that had this stranger not come along, he would have met the same fate as the man's offering.

He vomited.

The horse danced back from him to avoid the sudden rush of liquid but remained close enough for Kozioł to lay his bright hand against for support.

When his stomach had finally stopped its spasming, he felt a hand on his shoulder.

"Better?" The voice was kindly, but not placating.

Kozioł nodded, wiping his mouth with the back of his dim hand sleeve.

"Water?"

Again, Kozioł nodded. A moment later and a skin had been handed over his bright shoulder.

He drained a deep draft from it, took a few breaths, then rinsed his mouth with another swallow's worth before spitting it onto the ground.

"Thank you, my lord." He started to turn, intending to hand the skin back, but he never made it. Instead, he felt himself lifted, then placed atop the horse's military-style saddle. When he realized what the man was doing, he moved his legs accordingly so as not to make the task any more difficult. "I can walk, sir—truly. You needn't—"

"Hush."

Kozioł hushed. He leaned against the saddle's high back and felt himself deflate in absurd, child-like relief. A moment later, he felt the horse begin to walk and saw the man walking to his left, alongside it.

He tried several questions in his mind, but they all sounded foolish to him. He was relieved, therefore, when after a few moments of silent travel, the man spoke at last.

"You're from Venzene." Not a question. "What cave did you wander into, boy? The Trpytivy can be treacherous, not least because of how little they've been explored."

Kozioł blinked, then smiled, though the man couldn't have seen it from his angle. "I'm not from Kovalun, my lord. Our hills are the Zmierzch."

The man lifted his face as if in thought, then nodded. "The Obserwatorzy Zmierzchu, you mean? The Dusk Watcher mountains?" He paused, then added, "You're from Kamieńalun?"

Kozioł laughed in spite of himself. He was pleased this man knew at least something of his home. "Yes, my lord. I am."

The man nodded. "I suppose I shouldn't be surprised. Natural portals can occur almost anywhere." He paused. "Well, I can get you home, but it'll be the long way, I fear."

Kozioł blinked, finally realizing what the man was driving at. "Oh, no, my lord. I didn't come through a portal. I brought myself. I just don't know how in the hells I did it. I wasn't speaking the rite aloud, you see. I didn't think *thinking* about it would actually bring the power into being."

The man stopped. Without so much as a gesture, so did the horse.

"You're an apprentice, then? Fair enough. Are you certain you weren't muttering aloud?" He turned, looking up at Kozioł.

The helm, he saw, was indeed a barbute. The man's eyes, the lower portion of his nose, and his mouth were visible. The rest of his face was covered by a full bevor, and his chin was cradled in what looked like a hardened leather strap. His eyes were hazel, or perhaps green, flecked with gold. The light made it hard to be certain.

"Boy?"

Kozioł blinked, looking, he had no doubt, as embarrassed as he felt. "Forgive me, Lord. Yes, I'm certain. I wasn't speaking aloud. It happened at supper as well, almost. I stopped myself, though, and kept the lines of the rite separate."

"And ... did you feel any different once you'd done that?"

Kozioł blinked, then nodded. "Aye, I felt as if I could sleep for a week."

"Hecnvel," the man murmured. Then, as if answering a person who wasn't, as far as Kozioł could tell, anywhere in sight, he spoke again. "Yes, obviously. As much as I'd like to..." He trailed off, then snorted. "No. That would likely start a conflict I truly, *truly* don't need just now. It's tempting, but it would be a mistake—a greedy one, at that."

"... My lord?"

The man looked up, read something in Kozioł's face, then grinned. "Why here, boy? Why were you practicing a rite to bring yourself here specifically?"

"I train here, Lord." Kozioł was starting to grow annoyed with being called *boy*. He wasn't certain he should give his name, however.

"...I see." He paused, then added, "The wilds are a vast place, Apprentice. Do you know where you were trying to go?" A pause, then, "Do you know how to travel in this place when you know the spot you seek?"

"I... I think so?" Kozioł considered the question. He was pleased to find his mind was working once more. He found he had a question of his own. "Do I need to tell you where I'm bound in order for you to help me?"

The man actually laughed. "An excellent question. No. Others might insist, but I ... have my own business to attend to here."

Kozioł nodded, smiling. "From the other times I've come here to train, I walked out of my waking place, moved forward to a ... less red ... place?"

"Coming here is always a danger. The slow-coaches risk being snagged by the hollow ones—the red-sap runs when they smell meat. If you don't dawdle, you'll be free of them before they fully wake up and start to reach for you."

Kozioł gave a wide-eyed nod at that. He did his best to file that bit of knowledge away for later consideration. "As you say, my lord. I stand, move out of the red, er... the hollow one's grove, I suppose?" When the man nodded his approval, Kozioł continued. "Then I walk toward the greener vines and limbs, thinking of where I'm bound, and my mistress, and move the green aside. When I step beneath it..."

"You're there." He nodded. "That's the way of this place, and it will work from any point, so long as you know where, exactly, you're going."

Kozioł's face split into a wide and relieved smile. That smile turned to confusion, however, in an instant. He heard a door knock, then creak open somewhere.

"Kozioł... Kozioł, wake up!" A whisper—a harsh and insistent one.

"I think... I think my mistress calls me, my lord..."

The man laid his hand on Kozioł's forearm. "Are you certain it's her?"

"I'm there ... and here," he said. "I can go back—I know the rite."

"*Don't!*" His voice wasn't loud, merely insistent. "Ask her a thing that only she knows. I cannot hear her, but you can. If she's *actually* who you think she is, she'll answer true, and you can either meet her in your training place or return back to the place you spend your waking hours." His eyes held Kozioł's fast. "Safe beats sorry, Apprentice."

Kozioł nodded. "Aloud, then?"

The man nodded back. "Aloud, to be sure you don't miss anything."

"I'm here, and I'm there. Where do we meet?"

"Kozioł, what have you done? You're fading! Wake—I cannot find you!" Yeidil's voice was a harsh whisper, still. He could hear the worry in her.

"I can find *you*, mistress. Tell me where. Tell me the place you want to see me again... *please.*"

For a long moment, there was silence. His companion merely looked at him, face unreadable. The magnificent black charger Kozioł rode upon seemed utterly relaxed at the goings-on.

"Kozioł—can you make it back to the hill? To the place we wait for the bells together? Can you make it back on your own?"

"I can." He tasted iron—a mark of his instincts returning to a calmer state. He hadn't realized how on edge he'd still been until that powerful wave of relief struck him.

"If you can, then go now. I'll stay in your chambers until you're there. Then I'll come find you. If we don't manage to call your cień tonight, we're bound to wait until after Zlaté Pole. Do you understand?"

Kozioł sighed in happy relief. "I do, Mistress. I'll go there straight away."

The man nodded, smiling. "It's her, then? Good. There's green just ahead. Shall we go?"

Kozioł nodded. "Thank you. Truly, thank you. I... I suppose it's best we not share names."

"Safest, to be sure. I'll tell you this, however—something to keep under the hat I suspect you usually wear."

Kozioł smirked, nodding even as they began to move. One didn't leave the house in Kamieńalun—wasn't properly dressed without a hat.

"There's a war coming—returning, actually. Dreams are less safe than they were. The dead are stirring, their master returning from his exile. I don't say this to frighten you or to gain your trust. I say it because you deserve to know."

Kozioł did his best to hide the shock on his face. Blessedly, his bene-factor walked with his back to the boy once more.

"If not to frighten me, then why tell me?"

"To make you cautious, I suppose."

The horse came to a stop. Up ahead and to the right, Kozioł could see a stand of green trees and bushes.

"Do you want help getting down?"

Kozioł slid easily from the saddle and onto the ground beside the man, shaking his head. "You've been kind to me. I thank you, my lord." Kozioł bowed formally, as he'd been taught to do when meeting or departing from a nobleman. He thought a caster was close enough, though he'd never say such a thing to those he knew in his waking life.

"I bid you as safe an evening and as uneventful a life as you're able to find." The man bowed in return, then righted himself. "Keep careful watch over your power when you're memorizing rites, or they'll call you the sleeping sorcerer."

Kozioł grinned, nodded, and ran off toward the green. A moment later and he was through to the other side—looking up at their hill.

"I'm here, Mistress. Come and find me."

Five minutes later, Yeidil walked up behind him, spun him around with enough force nearly to dislocate his shoulder, and drew him into a tight embrace.

"Never, never, *ever* again! When you weren't here, I feared the worst."

He allowed the embrace but spoke in answer when she, at last, let him go.

"I know more about the Green Lands, now. It won't happen again. I was slow, and the hollow ones nearly got me, but it won't happen again."

She nodded, then blinked. "Who told you about the hollow ones?"

He grinned. "I have things to teach *you, too*, Mistress."

-VI-

Venzene Duchy of Kovalun
County Jižní Pochod
Barony of Haluzfeld–Southern Stride
42 Gerstesykli: 14 Days after the Red Storm at Westsong

Lashjuk woke all at once, heart racing. Her senses came alive with so sharp a focus that, at first, she couldn't think. Gradually, as her heart slowed to its more normal pace, her mind asserted itself, allowing her to categorize what was going on around her.

It's late, she thought. Perhaps midnight, perhaps a bit earlier. The boys were sleeping in a row to her right, followed by Eranoric and, she thought, Alusc. All breathing was steady and deep. The rain had mostly stopped, she realized. A thin, chilly breeze played across her exposed face from somewhere near the front of the barn.

Eobum isn't beside me. He'd been asleep after taking only a few bites of food ... curled up under his hides without any fanfare, and never mind the gentle noise of the unit's conversation. *That would've been four, perhaps five hours ago...*

She looked to her right, past the sleeping boys. A thin ribbon of moonlight slipped in from an opened door at the far end of the loft. She recalled there being a terrace out there but hadn't expected to find it still intact, given the storm.

She sat up, then climbed to her feet before picking her way over the slumbering bodies of her fellows. *My fellows*, she thought. How strange that thought was. Yet for all that, it felt fitting enough.

Like the barn's main door, this one slid on a metal track. It'd been left open only a hand's width, but that was enough for a cool wind to come softly into the barn. As she padded silently along the western loft, she began to hear soft singing. Far from delightful, it was perhaps somewhere in the same township as a musical key, but not much closer than that.

It was most assuredly Eobum. She could see him seated against the terrace's railing beyond the door's narrow opening. She froze, listening—trying not to laugh.

Re shrash mak. Re shrash mak. Re shrash mak. Re shrash.
Re shrash. Ra ed lash. Re shrash. Ra ed lash. Re shrash.
Ra ed lash mak su.
Su lash ed gnash, Su lash ed gnash, mak su ed vra.

Her heart skipped a beat as the words came to her. Suddenly his singing—key-adjacent at best only a moment before—held a warmth and honesty that catapulted it far beyond such surface reactions.

Come swiftly, moon. Come swiftly, moon. Come swiftly, moon.
Come swiftly.
Be swift. Become my gift. Be swift. Become my gift. Be swift.
Become my gift, moonstone.
A gift of stone for my love. A gift of stone for my love, a moonstone
from my heart.

He stopped, though whether it was because the song was at its natural end or because he'd heard her, she didn't know. With no particular reason she should wait to find out, she finished her journey to the door and slipped through it after widening the opening slightly.

She was in his arms instantly. They did not, however, kiss. For untold minutes, they merely cleaved to one another, her head against his chest, content to listen to his heart's drum.

After some time, she withdrew, turning within his embrace to place her back against him, pulling his arms about her middle, beneath her own.

They sighed together, then laughed. Neither had meant to do so—it had been the sort of happenstance children take for a sign.

"You sing," said she.

"You stalk." His reply came back almost instantly, accompanied by a gentle squeeze.

"Stalk?" She made her voice playfully indignant. "I haven't any idea what you're driving at, *count's man*. I'm but an ordinary woman trying to make my way..."

He snorted. "You can playact if you like, *ordinary woman*, but your huntress's heart will always catch you out."

She melted against him, smiling. After a moment, she lifted her chin, raising her bright hand to draw his face toward hers.

They kissed for a long time, growing increasingly more heated. She turned in his arms once more, feeling the moment rushing toward them. Her nails marked the back of his neck, and the sensitive place behind his ear, drawing a hungry moan from him.

At length, he broke the kiss, holding her—crushing her against him— as if she would fly out of his grasp if he did any less.

She bore this, then kissed his neck, moving down, hands fumbling at his belt.

He grabbed her wrists, forcing them away with gentle yet firm pressure.

"Wh—what?" Her eyes searched his, fearing some new horror from without, or worse, that she'd done something to make him reject her. "What is it? Aehe dash?" *(Why stop?)*

The look on his face hurt to see. He was obviously in pain, but at first, all he did was shake his head at her.

She put her hands to either side of his face, becoming afraid now. "Tell me..."

"We mustn't." His voice wasn't cold but held a finality in it that made it somehow hateful.

"Why not?" She paused, forcing the words out, hating the weakness— the need in her voice, quiet as it was. "Do you not... Do you not desire me?"

He bowed his head. "More than you'd guess."

She blinked, pulling back from him utterly. "Then, why?"

"It's too soon, Lashjuk."

She slapped him. She hadn't meant to do it, but once it was done, she found she was bitterly glad she had.

He bore the strike, saying nothing.

"Too *soon, is it*?" Her derision was a sharpened sword. "Too soon, yet not too soon to taste my breath! Not too soon to paw at me, to wrap your arms about me, to hold me as if you fear the wind will take me!" She kept her voice soft enough not to wake those within, but it was a struggle.

"You speak the truth. That's near enough what I fear."

"But it's too *soon* to join our flesh? To be as one? Erld vra sed, Eobum." *(Your heart is hidden from me, Eobum.)*

He looked at her for a long moment before he gave his answer. His voice was still that matter-of-fact tone—the note of finality she'd heard before now tuning up to be an entire song.

"We cannot, Lashjuk... not while someone still lies between us."

"Someone..." Her eyes narrowed. "You're right. I see that now." Her voice was nearly a growl, black and predatory. "Kastan's raven hair and full lips stand between us. I'd thought better of you than that—more open. I was mistaken."

He blinked, then snorted in miserable surprise. "I suppose you don't know me as well as I thought, then. Nor I you, clearly. Still, that should please her."

"Aye, well, if it's only a dalliance you wanted, I wish you'd said so sooner."

He blinked. "What? That's the very *last* thing I want!"

She threw up her hands, then grabbed him by the throat. "If you believed for even an instant that I would be your broodmare or your harlot... if you believed I would share you with her, or anyone else, Eobum, then you aren't half the soul you pretend to be. I'll be gone ere the sun rises. Mark me."

His eyes widened rather comically. He had done nothing to defend himself from her, physically, but now he brought his hands up and pressed his thumbs and forefingers against the flesh between her own.

She tried to maintain her grip, but the pressure forced her thumbs to release. She stepped away, drawing back to slap him again.

"You thought she and I? That I wanted..?" He laughed, shaking his head.

The act defused the sharpest edge of her rage.

"You do... You do *not* desire her?"

He shook his head, smiling weakly. "I feared *you* did." Her shock must have shown on her face, for he smiled and shook his head again. "Well? It was you who mentioned her, not I."

That was true, but still.

"Lashjuk, the Maklash pact doesn't hold for humankind. Even in Eoden, such things are seen as strange and, at the least, worthy of gossip. She hasn't either of the two things that could grant her peace. She's too powerful to be ignored or left alone, and too powerless to ignore the slings and opinions of others without peril."

She began to draw in breath, meaning to ask if that meant that Kastan... the idea of asking him how he knew about the Maklash pact— the ancient charter of Gnoerk kind—never occurred to her. Later she would think on that fact, but for now, her mind went in a more pressing direction.

"If not her, then who? Who is it that you see between us, Eobum? Who?!"

"Your gnash," said he.

She felt the color drain from her face.

"You still see him—he still visits you in your sleep, and I shouldn't wonder." His face was once again full of sad acceptance. "Don't think that I turn you away lightly. Never think that I... that I somehow don't desire you!" He grabbed her hand, dragging it below his belt.

She felt the stone hardness there and was torn between ripping her hand away and pressing closer to him, kissing him again. He made the decision for her, gently withdrawing her hand and releasing her wrist.

"Why your mind or heart have changed—why you've chosen me at all, I cannot guess. It almost doesn't matter, save that I want to do more of whatever I did to deserve you. Lashjuk... I would gladly, gladly keep you beside me—would happily walk beside *you* until my road ends... but I won't tempt you to turn away from your grief just because of how I feel."

She gaped at him, then bowed her head, nodding. "My Guuvra won't return to me. He's off to find our Maklo and seek the moon warden with her at his side."

She saw Eobum's shadow nod on the terrace floor before he bowed his head.

"I dreamt of him tonight. He asked about you." She nodded, fighting the urge to crumple. "It's too soon. You're right. They've been gone a fortnight." She looked up suddenly, eyes streaming. "It doesn't *feel* that way..." She stepped toward him, stopping only when he took her by the shoulders—gently, but firmly. His hands were shaking slightly, though it may have been the chill. "I feel as if I've lived whole sykli with you and the others! The boys seem to feel the same! I know, I see it. It's been barely a fortnight, but it feels... My heart feels..."

"Different," he finished. "I know. I feel it too."

"Thank you," said she.

"Hells, for what?"

"For seeing me and for not taking what you could have."

He nodded. "I would rather have you with me still come next year than for one night."

She nodded, wrapping her fingers about his wrists, gently withdrawing his hands from her shoulders. "Give me some time to dream—to know that I've honored Guuvra and our daughter. Then I'll return to you and walk the road beside you."

"... And for now?"

"Water, not wine," said she. For all the pain this night had caused, her voice was somehow lighter. "I'm not leaving you, Eobum. I *will* be putting the boys between us when we sleep ... for a time, at least. But no, I'm not leaving you." She turned to go back into the barn. "You'll need that time, anyway."

"Oh?" He grinned, sad but relieved.

"Aye—time to find me that moonstone."

CHAPTER SIXTEEN

TRUST, TUNNELS, AND TOWERS

-I-

The Green Lands
43 Gerstesykli: 15 Days after the Red Storm at Westsong

Yeidil had sat with him for what felt like hours. Hells, it might have actually been hours. Looking up, she saw the dawn hadn't yet begun to kiss the horizon, so that was something.

Kozioł had asked her nearly every question she could imagine, and a few she'd been surprised by.

How did I wind up so far afield, Mistress? Is it true that we always enter in a Hollow's grove? Does it really not matter where we enter, then? Why can we not simply appear here, on the hill? On and on, and on yet more, the questions came.

She'd answered them as swiftly and completely as she could. You were so far afield because you lost concentration. You must balance the song's cadence and rhythm, even as you balance the image of where you wish it to take you. Yes, we always enter in a Hollow's grove. No, that's incorrect. It does, indeed, matter where we enter, in that the farther you must travel in the Green Lands to reach your destination, the more power you risk that travel exacting from you. We cannot appear here because this place is protected by the hollow ones, and the hollow ones protect the Green Lands from those who would damage it.

Her hope was not simply to educate, but to tire his mind enough that they could focus on the matter at hand. Time was short, after all, and this unexpected jaunt had not only delayed their start but had clearly absconded with her apprentice's fire for the lessons he so desperately needed to learn.

His encounter with the hollow ones left him exhilarated rather than intimidated—a dangerous quality, though it certainly served to inform his future as either sword or shield. And there was more beyond even that. What of his rescue by the strange caster? He may only be accounted as strange for his convenient timing and placement—their chance meeting in that exact spot within the vastness of the Green Lands, and at that precise time. What of that? It was coincidence enough to make her wary, at the very least... something her apprentice seemed incapable of doing just now.

"Mistress? What is..." He screwed up his face as he tried to recall. "What is ass and vel?"

She blinked. "What is... what?"

"Ass in vel? Passing bell? No... no, it was a V sound, to be sure. Vel."

"Give me the context in which you heard him say it." She refused to ask if he knew the word *context*. Azhferd would have seen to that much of his education, surely. It was the way Borys taught everything—her father, too, for that matter. Think deeply, see far, understand context, listen for subtext, thus will the world unwind its secrets for you.

"I was speaking to the man in the barbute about how I'd come to the Green Lands. He said... whatever the word or phrase is—it sounded like ass and bell or vel, though I don't think he was saying it to me specifically."

"Did you..." She paused, choosing her words carefully, all the while, trying to mask the sudden fear in her heart. Had he unwittingly revealed clues to this stranger? The wrong words, even thrown out unintentionally, might lead a wise caster to uncover who they were and where they made their home.

Kozioł looked at her, trying to gauge her mind.

She shook her head, forcing a calm she didn't feel as she spoke again. "Did you speak any part of the song to this man? Did you mention the Torn Hour?"

He blinked, smiling uncertainly. "No, of course not. Those are secret things, Mistress." He sounded almost hurt, as if she'd accused him rather than asked.

She nodded, doing her best to make her expression as warm as she could. "Good. Even if you had, the fault would be mine, not yours. I'm pleased that you understand how important our secrecy is." She reached forward, patting his forearm before continuing. "Go on, then. You told him what—that you spoke the rite you were learning and found your way here earlier than usual?"

He shook his head. "No, Mistress. I told him the truth."

Yeidil blinked, then made a go on gesture. "And what is the truth, then?"

"That I've no idea—had no idea that it could happen."

"What could happen, exactly?"

He shrugged, looking down. "That... That my speaking—that singing the song in my head could affect the rite."

"In your..."

"In my head," he supplied. "I was trying to commit it to memory all through supper, but I felt dizzy—began to see the hall as if it weren't truly there." He met her eye and became instantly defensive. "I stopped myself straight away! I swear, I did. By then, I was so damned tired it was all I could do to concentrate on individual lines. I did manage it, though. I said other things, spoke to Jarek, drank, looked around—anything to put time and other thoughts between the lines of the song, and it worked. No more fading."

She stared at him. This was impossible, surely.

"What then?" She tried to keep her voice conversational but wasn't sure she'd managed it.

"I went to my room shortly after the woodsman left. I tried to wait up for you, but I was so tired..."

She opened her mouth to speak, then shut it again, nodding. It was perhaps ten seconds before she trusted herself enough to continue. "And then?"

He began to grow pale, as if he were suddenly afraid. "I ran the lines in my head again, lying there and waiting for you to speak to me. I kept them spaced out. Of course, I did. I didn't get through all of them, I don't think. Next I knew, I was in the grass." He shrugged, eyes widening. His next words came out high and breathy. "Tell me! Yeid—Mistress, why do you *look* so?"

"Hecnvel," said she.

"What? Yes! That! That was it! Ass on vel!"

"Hess-en-vell," said she. She took pains to enunciate each syllable, meeting his eye and holding it.

"Hess-en-vell." Kozioł rolled the sounds around in his mouth for a moment, then made a gesture of acceptance. "What is it? What's it mean?"

"Blood magic."

"What!?"

"Hecn means red or blood. Vel means magic, or a near enough equivalent. They don't use that word on Nausha, as a rule—magic, I mean."

Kozioł moved from a sitting position up to his knees, then stopped himself. With an obvious effort, he forced himself to sit back down—forced the muscles of his jaw and his brow to loosen and unbind.

Yeidil was impressed. Most adults weren't capable of calming themselves in a time of stress, let alone in extraordinary circumstances. That Kozioł had done so at a time like this spoke well of both him and the training he'd received thus far.

"Please explain, Mistress. Please..." His voice was low, for him at any rate. He wore an expression of utter, focused solemnity.

"I will. It's simply more than I'd intended to teach you tonight. Need must drive us, however. A moment to clear and order my thoughts."

He drew back, seeming to settle into himself, and waited.

"You've learned the wrap, yes? My brother's taught it to you?"

Kozioł nodded, the ghost of a grin playing across his pale lips. "This past Lessykli."

"It's the hardest blow to master, isn't it?" Her tone made it less a question, more a commiseration. "You throw it around the pell's flank, snap your wrist and forearm as you pull the sword back toward you, hunting for the magic combination of timing, speed, power, and aim to make the blow a telling one."

Kozioł couldn't nod. He was too busy gaping at her.

She grinned at him. "And all the while, as you deliver poor, misshapen shots, the vibrations do their best to force your hand to release your weapon, adding embarrassment to frustration."

"How... how do you...?" He couldn't get the question out.

She snorted. "Did you think only men and boys paid attention to that sort of thing?" She fought back a powerful urge to wear derisive triumph on her face and won the contest—work to do and all that. "The point is, you had to work at it, yes? At first, and for some time, you had no idea how in the hells anyone could manage it ... until you'd done it."

He nodded slowly. "Practice is the only way to get better—either practice at home, or putting your training *into* practice against others... sparring and the like."

She beamed at him. "Azhferd would be so proud to hear you speak like that." She saw him beginning to smile, but pressed forward before he could bask in the compliment for too terribly long. "When you first started practicing, your arm would grow tired quickly. Until you began to run regularly, your breath would run out swiftly."

Kozioł made a gesture of understanding. "The more you practice and train, the longer you can hold the shield or sword—the longer you have 'till you're out of breath."

"Exactly so." She waited for a moment, searching his eyes to see if he'd interrupt her with questions or further conclusions, then pressed on. "Magic's the same. We all begin with talents—your weave walking talent, for instance, but we also begin with a limit to our ability to *use* magic in a given day."

"So... you're saying it's like a muscle?"

She grinned widely. "Exactly. And like the sword and shield, you have to do more than hit the pell in order to improve."

"I... yes. Yes, I see. You find a person or creature to use the magic on, even yourself, I suppose, to see if what you've used on the... well, there's no pell, but something like that. Have I got that right?"

"You have. Books and someone teaching you rotes and rites they, themselves, have mastered... *That* serves as the pell."

"Working on my own—that's a match in tournament or brigands on the road..." His eyes were wide again, but he looked awed rather than afraid.

"Just so."

"All right, and Hecnvel?"

"You'll strengthen the muscle of your power with practice. Like hoisting sword and shield, or better control over your wind, things will get easier for you with time and work. What drains you now will seem a trifle, eventually." She saw him nod his understanding and pressed on. "Blood magic literally draws on your blood—your actual blood, mind— and converts it to raw magic to accomplish the rite or rote you're trying to use or cast."

"But... but how?!" He was too stunned to be afraid, and it showed in his voice. "Wouldn't it make you ill?" His eyes were suddenly large enough that they looked about to fall from his skull. "I was so tired suddenly—not because of the extra work in preparation for our leave-taking, but because I gave my blood to create magic!? Hells! How!? I didn't do it a-purpose, so how do I stop it from happening again?"

"*Peace*, Apprentice. It isn't as daunting as all that." She waited for him to calm himself before continuing. It didn't take him long, and once more, she was pleased at how much self-possession he seemed to have. "Blood magic is most specific. It augments existing work in very particular ways, and each such augmentation is its own form, with its own cost. One can be taught its use, but on rare occasions, the tie and affinity to magic is strong enough that such an augmentation comes as an inheritance, as it seems to have with you."

"An inheritance? Blood magic can be ... passed down in..." He trailed off, unwilling to complete the turn of phrase.

She had no such reservations. "... in and by the blood, yes." She chuckled as he rolled his eyes. "You felt this wave of tiredness when reciting the song's lines in your head. That suggests to me that you've somehow inherited the Stilled Tongue Hecnvel. It's supposedly a comparatively minor augmentation allowing the caster to work a given rite without having to speak the words aloud."

Kozioł frowned. When he spoke, his voice was dark and a touch disparaging. "That sounds like a tool for a thief or an assassin."

"Well, Apprentice, if you'd spurn the gift, then simply don't use it."

He nodded at that, aspects of the sheepish and the resolute warring on his young face.

"It could be put to good use, certainly, if only to protect my brother without anyone knowing you were the one providing that protection."

His brows lifted ... a hopeful smile beginning to form. "I hadn't thought of that. I'll consider it. Thank you, Mistress."

She stood, smiling at him. "If you're finished with your questions on that score, we should consider the hour and try to press forward with the *actual* reason we're here tonight."

He stood as well, brushing grass from his knees and shins. Rather than nervous, as he had been previously, he looked calm and focused.

She considered commenting on this but thought better of it. Instead, she began to rekindle their previous lesson.

"What are you here to seek?"

"I'm here seeking my Cień Duszy. I'm here to call him to hand, to bring him here, to me."

Yeidil nodded. "Quite correct. He is exactly as the name suggests, Apprentice. Already you have given it an aspect—a gender. Already he is yours, for your mind is what gives him form. He is the shadow of your soul—your agent and aid, your intimate and familiar." She saw his spine stiffen, his hands splaying their fingers. She raised her voice, not in volume, but in intensity. "He is as bound to you as the shadow beneath your feet, the dark you see when you close your eyes. He is *your* Cień Duszy, and he *must* come when you call him!"

Kozioł nodded once, swiftly, fingers bending into claws.

"Reach for him—call to him... *now.*"

Kozioł's bright arm rose toward the top of the hill, hand reaching up and outward, shaking. His head was lowered between shoulders hunched with effort, though his gaze remained locked to the place where his hand—his power reached.

"Twój czas na walkę *o* mnie dobiegł końca. Czas wreszcie walczyć obok mnie. Przyjdź do mnie, cieniu mojej duszy..." *(Your time to fight for me is over. It's time to finally fight alongside me. Come to me, shadow of my soul...)*

She smiled at his use of the old tongue. That he was already creating pathways—methods to couch his own rites and rotes—was an excellent sign for his future.

She hoped with her whole heart. If he failed this summons, it was likely someone had, indeed, severed the connection between him and his shadow. The ramifications of such an act were horrid to contemplate. As each second passed, however, she found that her mind kept coming back to that miserable idea.

"Ah! Mistress! I..." His voice was near to weeping.

She took a single step toward him, then stopped.

The sigh of the wild wind through the long grass was the most perfect of heralds as, at last, his shadow came.

The hilltop was suddenly home to the embodiment of the word stallion. His aspect was muscular and impossibly tall, yet there was an amorphousness to him. His color seemed to swirl through the darker shades: now brown, now red roan, now brindled, now deep blue, now as black as sin.

It tossed its head, rearing like a delighted colt as it saw Kozioł. It stepped down toward him as if to bow before him.

She heard his laughter mingled with soft sobs. He stepped forward to meet the creature and embraced him, murmuring too quietly for her to understand. So be it. His words weren't for the likes of her. Not just now, at any rate.

Her own relief was so very great that almost *she* began to weep. They would need to discuss all that this meant for him, and he would have a choice to make. For now, however—for tonight, at least—this was enough. She would stand, perhaps sit by for his questions, should he have any, but for now... it was enough.

Mother... forgive me. I feared the worst. That in a mad race to save your sense of control—your ownership of Father's dreams, as I own Azhferd's—you severed and subsumed Kozioł's shadow. I was wrong, and I've never—never been happier about discovering that. She smiled once more, and as she did, her eyes over-spilled. *You'll never know it, but that doesn't matter. It's right—it is meet that I acknowledge it.* She took a deep breath, bowed her head briefly, then looked up to gaze upon Kozioł and his shadow stallion once more. *And so, I thank you for the instruction, elder. May I learn this lesson well, and may it save me from the Torn Hour when all else has failed, and fear is given form before me.*

-II-

Venzene Duchy of Kovalun
Baronial City of Zlaté Pole
43 Gerstesykli: 15 Days after the Red Storm at Westsong

Geroslaw woke without fanfare in the wee hours of the morning. The bell wasn't currently tolling, but his internal sense of time told him it was likely near the fifth bell past midnight.

It had been good to sleep under his mother's roof again—had been good even to hear the music of two-dozen voices laughing and singing below as he drifted off to sleep. It'd been quite early—perhaps three hours from midnight, but that had been by design. He wanted an early start this morning, and as always ... there were things to do.

As he sat up, a strange thought came to him. *That was it. I've slept my last peaceful night—dreamt my last untroubled dream.* It made him sad and a little melancholy. Absurd, surely. Still, it was a powerful notion he found difficult to shake.

He did his best to banish it as he dressed, but it was persistent. It seemed only to be thwarted by the image of his beloved Krwawa Zima. The stallion walked onto the stage of his mind's eye as he mentally ticked off tasks he needed to accomplish before he headed out.

Pulling his boots on, then standing to strap his sword belt into place across his hips, he took in the sounds of the inn around him. Nothing stirred in the common room. He did hear the soft breathing of the first and the thin, flute-like snores of the second boy somewhere on the other side of the wall. Mother's Sheshik boys asleep in the loft. He didn't know whether she'd taken them in as orphans or purchased them as slaves, though with her, there was little difference.

They were children. They would pull their weight with chores and lessons, regardless, or there would be wounded pride, grumbling bellies, extra work, or in rare cases, difficulty sitting without pain. Such were the stages of penance for keeping Mari from what she saw as her duty to the boys or girls who happened into her care. Children were children—in her eyes, at least. They deserved what chance she could afford to give them.

He took a single step toward the room's door, then stopped. He'd just heard the morning's true music. There had been a shuffling sound, a dull knock as something pliant struck either a table or perhaps, the stair's banister, and then—as if the rest of the percussion had been little more than a prelude for it—a single hissed word.

"Shit..."

Up and in the doings already, I see. He grinned but now wished he hadn't put his boots on quite so swiftly. Stealth in the thick heels would be almost impossible when set against her near-supernatural sense of hearing. Ah well. At least he knew the time now. It was before the fifth bell, not after it.

He knew something else as well. There would shortly be a fresh pot of qahua for the drinking. He hadn't tasted it in so, so long... if things hadn't changed, she'd have a goodly store of summer harvest beans from the Last Grass put by to take her through winter and beyond.

I've slept my last peaceful night. May as well break my fast with a last peaceful mug to mark the occasion.

He frowned as his mind again wandered back to this joyful thought. Shaking his head, he exited and made his way downstairs as quickly and quietly as he could. Whatever was troubling his undermind, standing in his old room would do nothing to get him past it.

Before he'd reached the common room's floor, the smell he'd anticipated had grown strong enough to walk on. It drew him on like the promise of a warm bed after a hard week's ride. He veritably floated toward the kitchen door, face caught in a childlike smile of utter bliss.

He'd been reaching to pull it open, but Mari beat him to it, pushing it toward him with a sleepy look of amused recrimination. She pointed back the way he'd come, mouthing a single directive. "Sit."

He obeyed.

Ten minutes later found them seated together—their faces lit by a single candle's brave flame. They'd been silent save the occasional grunt, sigh of contentment, or scrape as clay mug either left or returned to the tabletop.

Finally, she met his eyes, brightened the room with her smile, and reached across the table to squeeze his hand with a warmth that needed no words to cheapen it.

He turned his palm, linking their fingers, albeit briefly, then withdrew.

It was safe, at last, for him to speak to her. One did not risk the wrath of Mari before her morning mug without hells' own hounds close behind. Even then, it might be wiser to face the hounds.

"I hate having to rush away so soon, Mother. I *am* sorry."

She shook her head, still smiling. "You've things to do, Geri. You're on the edge of something great. It's just over the hill—just beyond the horizon. It makes me happy to see and to be a part of it."

He shook his head, smiling in spite of himself.

"Don't shake your head at me, boy." Her voice was a soft breeze. "You fear what, to leave me with the lack-beards?" She made a rather unladylike snort. Her eyes danced. "If they give me trouble, I'll either put them to work, send them to bed without supper, or stripe them with my ladle."

He chuckled, taking pains to keep his voice low.

"No fear, sweet boy. If they fail you, they'll have fine futures as pot boys or stable hands under my gentle glare." She delivered this with a smile, but her voice held such an honest tone that it was difficult to tell if she were making sport or a genuine offer.

"Fair enough, Mother. Shall I bring you anything back from Auburg?"

She considered, lifting her chin as she did so. "See if they've managed a crop of jagody zimowe yet. If she's still with us, Oliwia should have some put by."

He nodded slowly. "Winterberries, eh? You truly are glad to see me."

She smacked him with the back of her hand to his forearm, grinning widely. "They're not for you, Geri."

"Oh, no? You aren't asking for fresh winterberries in order to bake my favorite pie while you have me here?"

She made her face flat, but her eyes were nearly glowing with amused delight. "Not at all. They're for me. I hang them in my kitchen." She didn't meet his incredulous gaze, instead opting to top off her mug with more of the steaming brew. "I just enjoy the smell. It reminds me of a boy I once knew."

He bowed his head at that, nodding. "I'll ask Oliwia when I see her."

The bells tolled the sixth hour past midnight as he rode toward the nominal gate. He was half daydreaming, half making a final tally of all that he'd packed and anything he might have left behind at his mother's inn when he saw them. All four of his men were up, dressed, and standing on the town's side of the gate's causeway.

He did his best to hide his concern. All four stood along the right side of the road in positions of ease. As he came near, he heard Barneb mutter something to the others. They smartened up their line, then executed a near-perfect *wheel left* maneuver, stopping at the point where they stood across his path spaced, not *quite* shoulder to shoulder.

Geroslaw rode close enough to them to speak in conversational tones, then stopped. He looked at them, meeting each eye in turn, coming to Barneb last. Each looked tired but awake and ready to face the day.

"Sergeant," said Barneb. "Good morning."

"Morning…" Geroslaw focused on the facts. It was, in fact, morning. For now, that was all he was prepared to comment on.

"You look surprised," Barneb smirked.

"There's a perfectly good reason for that, Barneb. I *am* surprised—to see you lot, at any rate."

"Well … did you really think we'd let you slip out the munging gate without us seeing you off, Sergeant?"

Geroslaw saw all four men were fighting the urge to grin.

"I did, actually." He fought to keep his face and voice firm and detached—devoid of any clear indication of his mood. "I expected you to be in your beds or squaring away your kits."

The smirks faltered.

"I... well, we've already—that is to say..."

"Given how loud you lot were last night while I was trying to sleep..."

They began to bow their heads.

"And not one of you had the discipline or common decency to drink enough to be properly sun-sick this morning? I'm disappointed. I expected you to make much, *much* bigger asses of yourselves."

Four heads snapped up to meet his eyes. Their own were wide with shock, their mouths agape.

"I... that is..." Barneb was grinning but couldn't seem to get hold of his own tongue.

Aethel, on the other hand, lifted his chin and fired right back. "Aye, Sergeant. We'll do our best Steffan impressions next time if that'll serve better."

Geroslaw managed to avoid laughing aloud, but it was a near thing. He wanted to agree—hells, he actually *did* agree with the comparison, but they'd be working together soon enough, his men and Steffan's. With an inward sigh, he dropped the air of displeasure and dismounted, walking toward them.

"Fall out, men." As they did, he let his face adopt a genuine smile. "Truly, thank you for seeing me off. All else aside, I'm grateful for the gesture." He let them respond with their own kind words before stepping back to ensure all four were facing him. "I know your former commander wasn't ideal."

"That's for damned sure," Aethel said. General laughter met this.

"But..."

Their laughter stopped.

"But," Geroslaw said again. "We'll be seeing him in a week or so and working with he and his men until the tournament ends, and we escort the count's war leader back to the encampment. We won't win over any of the other Bluemark by deriding him in front of them."

They nodded, Aethel looking shame-faced.

"Think what you like, and when it's just you four—say what you like. Just know that what you say matters to those who're listening."

"...And there's *always* someone listening," Borgus put in. "The sergeant's right."

The others nodded their heads. No more needed to be said.

"Right—I'm for the road. I'll be back in less than a fortnight."

"We'll look after the place whilst you're gone," Barneb said. The others agreed, grinning once more.

Geroslaw mounted after a final farewell and rode southeast. He'd stay in Kovalun for the next two days, then dip into Havalun for a few hours before, at last, seeing Kamieńalun once more. To breathe familiar air—to smell the cold and ride beneath the soft blues and greys of an early winter's sky would make his heart sing. Whatever came after would wait its turn. For now... for now, he was going home, and that was enough.

-III-

Venzene Duchy of Kovalun
County Jižní Pochod
Barony of Haluzfeld - Southern Stride
43 Gerstesykli: 15 Days after the Red Storm at Westsong

Eobum sat on the edge of the loft's floor. His back was propped against one of the uprights, his dim side foot dangling down over the ladder. He looked at his... men? He couldn't say that any longer. Lashjuk was many things, but a man wasn't one of them. Most of them slept as peacefully as may be, given their location.

He saw Lakkrid stir, then sit up, casting about in the dim light of not-quite-dawn. The boy rose, staggered under the weight of his half-dozing mind, then turned to walk toward the terrace door. As he passed Eobum, he made no sign that he'd registered his presence. Instead, he padded down to where the door remained cracked, slipped out, and, more than likely, took care of nature's call.

Eobum returned his attention to the rest of his sleeping folk, then across to the eastern loft where Alojz, his men, and the few refugees slept. No sign of life there.

His mind wasn't so much restless as it was anxious. He wanted Alojz to wake so he could get things rolling along.

He heard Lakkrid padding back toward him and was only mildly surprised when the boy stopped beside him.

Placing a hand on Eobum's bright side shoulder for balance, he sat himself down, back against his father's arm. Eobum shifted his own balance, then slid the arm from under the boy's weight, wrapping it around his belly instead.

After a moment, Lakkrid spoke in a sluggish fricative. "You're wearing that face."

Eobum made an inarticulate noise that sounded like a question. "Mmm?"

"That face," Lakkrid said again, as if repeating it would make his point somehow less vague.

"What face?"

"Your—what does Adric call it—your *planning costume.*"

Eobum snorted. "Aye? I suppose I am."

"What're you—" He was cut off by a great, shuddering yawn, which he tried nonetheless to talk through, "What are you planning?" He nuzzled closer, stretching his legs out perpendicular to Eobum's side. And the loft's edge. "Is it to do with the Lord Alojz?"

Eobum grinned. "Aye. He's wanting help with something."

"For the count?"

"Aye, for the count."

The silence that followed this made Eobum wonder if Lakkrid had fallen back to sleep—but when his next question came, it was clear he'd been thinking, not dozing.

"Will we help him?"

Eobum considered how to answer this, but ultimately thought it best to be direct.

"I think so, yes. Alojz is loyal to the count and fears he needs us to help him keep Edmund safe."

Lakkrid again fell silent for an interval, chewing on that.

"How do you know whether to do what the count says or what the lord says?"

Eobum tried not to laugh. He'd weighed out that very question.

"There's no easy answer. Each situation is different from the last."

"So, you have to think which one's more pressing…"

"Aye, more pressing in time, and more dangerous in outcome."

Lakkrid nodded slowly, opening his eyes fully for the first time this morning. He met Eobum's own and grinned. "The count doesn't know about the trouble—Lord Alojz's trouble does he." This was more a statement than a question. "That means we *have* to go."

Eobum arched his brows as he met his son's gaze. "Oh?"

Lakkrid nodded. "Aye. We're scouts. We're supposed to see trouble first, then report back, right?"

"You're not wrong."

Without a word or warning, Lakkrid pushed himself up to a sitting position, got to his feet, and turned to face his father. "I'm hungry," he announced and walked back toward where Alusc was beginning to sort through his pack for breakfast makings.

Eobum watched him go, amused by the sudden shift. He caught movement across the gap. Turning his head, he saw Alojz looking at him with an expression of tired hope. Eobum gave him a slow nod, then lifted his hand to gesture toward the ground below.

Alojz nodded agreement, moving toward the ladder on his side.

They met near the great barn door, and after simple greetings, they pulled it open and stepped out into the grey morning.

"I'll not spar with you, my lord. I've a bit to ask, but I expect my mind's made up unless I've misread things."

Alojz made a gesture of acceptance. "Good enough. Ask."

"I'm bound for the twigs, as you know. How dear is our time? Is the hourglass so empty that I have to choose between your duty and Edmund's?"

Alojz considered. "It's only a few hours' walk to the twigs. We can make that trek first—would be best to, in fact."

Eobum gave a curt nod at that. "Will we make it to him in time?"

Alojz again considered, then nodded. "Perhaps only barely, but yes. If we head north first, then head back to the hunting camp together, we'll be to him before the offer's made. We're a small party. They're an army. We'll have speed on our side, which should make enough difference."

"All right. One final thing, then." He fixed Alojz with a flat, almost insolent gaze as he spoke. This would be the difficult part. "I trust you. No, that's not true. I trust you *in this*. I believe you when you say you want Edmund to live. I believe that you love him and want him kept safe."

"...But?"

"But if my instincts are wrong—if I find you've pulled me away from his commission in order to work against him—if I find you've put him in danger or put his life at risk..."

"*You'll* kill *me*." Alojz grinned, nodding. "Is that it?"

Eobum answered, unsmiling. "If I have to. I'd take you alive, if I could—bind you and bring you before Edmund dressed like a hog for the fire—let him see to the man that betrayed his trust. If I can't, though, yes. I'll hunt you, track you, stalk you, and eventually kill you."

Alojz's grin widened, then softened. He shook his head, then nodded it. "I can ask for no more than that, Commander. I can tell you, and do so, that you needn't worry about my breaking faith. Saying it does little by way of proving it, but time will bear me out." He reached up, running his fingers through the sleep-scattered mop of blond atop his head. "Are we agreed, then?"

Eobum continued to hold the man's gaze for an uncomfortable moment of silence, then nodded twice. "Aye, my lord. We make for Haluz Věže itself as soon as we've fed everyone and loaded up."

Twenty minutes later, and Eobum had explained things to his folk as they broke their fast. There were many questioning looks, but no actual questions raised. Half a bell later, and they were on the march.

-IV-

Venzene Duchy of Kamieńalun
County Czarny Wodospad
Village of Auburg
43 Gerstesykli: 15 Days after the Red Storm at Westsong

"All right, all right!" Azhferd laughed as his head rocked back. The blow had been a stout one. "You..." He tapped the shield man in front and to his right on the shoulder. "You're... Aer?"

"Yuss, Lord." The answer came out clipped tolled in a higher register than most of the others here.

"You're Lord Jesion's groom?"

"Yuss, Lord."

Azhferd nodded. "I'll want you in the wall." He laid his dim hand on the shoulder of Aer's shieldmate. "Tomorrow, I want you to work with Deiter and your master." He lifted his bevor and raised his chin, shaping his voice to where Vonrik stood watching from a few yards off. "Did you see?"

Azhferd was altogether pleased to see Vonrik's focused expression as he nodded and walked over. It had been clear from the first that he was applying himself to their training with genuine zeal. That, in turn, was infectious to the other lords and landed heirs.

He met Azhferd's eyes, asking wordlessly for leave to speak. When he'd gotten it by way of a slight nod and an encouraging smile, he spoke to Aer's shield companion.

"Jakub, you're strong and sure-footed. You always have been. There's nobody I'd rather have guarding my back." The man bowed his head, but before he could speak a word of thanks for the compliment, Vonrik pressed on. "You're used to sparring and tournaments, like the rest of us. Lord Azhferd's training is uncomfortable because it's new, but it'll serve us well on the field. I've seen you wrinkle your nose each time the spearman sneaks past you or pulls your shield out of position. You're fighting the training more than you're fighting the foemen."

Azhferd kept his hand on Jakub's shoulder. If he'd removed it before Vonrik spoke, it'd have been fine, but to do so now would deepen the man's sense of being singled out. He caught Vonrik's eye and mouthed a single word. "Soft..."

Vonrik gave a barely perceptible nod. He'd gotten the message. To his sergeant, then, he offered a smile, placing his own hand on the frustrated armsman's other shoulder. As he did so, beginning to speak again, Azhferd let his own hand slip off.

"No fear, Jakub. Now that you're here, at last, we can spend some time working with the rope and ball Lord Azhferd's had rigged up in the stables. It's the same way I learned it a few days ago."

Jakub looked up. Azhferd couldn't see his face, but his body language suggested surprise. "This ain't a thing you've cracked on at for more than a few *days*, Lord?"

Vonrik's smile shone dazzlingly white. "Got here on the thirty-seventh, the heir taught it to me on the thirty-eighth, and here we are."

Jakub's chest expanded, his spine straightening visibly. "Right then. That's a task worth toiling over, *ain't* it?" His hopeful smile was evident in his tone.

At that, Azhferd lifted his chin again, shouting to be heard over the individual skirmishes and conversations the other lords were having with one another, their younger brothers, and their armsmen. "We're done for today. Time to get out of armor and into an early supper ... and spirits!"

More than a few of the men threw up a cheer at this. Some kept at it for a bit longer, but most were out of their helms and gauntlets double sharp and were starting to uncouple the rigid collars they wore for neck protection.

Vonrik gave Azhferd a final grin, then turned to usher Jakub away, nodding to Hadwald as he passed him. "C'mon, Sergeant," said he. "Let's go see how the lads have fared."

Jakub bowed his head slightly to both the suggestion and the approaching Hadwald and allowed himself to be led away.

Hadwald looked Aer up and down as he approached. It'd been he who'd gotten his spear around Jakub's shield to score on Azhferd's bevored face.

"You're just about the toughest shield we've got. You're hard to move or get round," said he. "Lord Azhferd's right to keep you in the wall from the first."

"You're kind. Thank you, my lord." Aer's high register came out a touch brittle. It suggested compliments were a rare thing for the young groom.

"I'm not." Hadwald's voice was honest and without fanfare, as usual. "If a dozen more picked it up as readily as you've done, the enemy would charge our line and get bounced onto their backsides."

Aer had no idea what to say. Another thank you—this one quieter than the last—was all the poor groom could manage.

"Go on," Azhferd said, patting the shield man's back. "Food won't be long in coming."

Aer stepped forward, turned to both Azhferd and Hadwald, bowed, then jogged off.

The pair stood there, side by side, watching the few remaining men on the makeshift training field. They remained that way for perhaps ten minutes in companionable silence, mentally critiquing the individual matches. As the last three were pulling off their helms and preparing to join the others by the ale barrel, Hadwald turned to his lord and offered a lopsided grin. He was drawing breath to speak when the color drained from his face.

Azhferd was about to ask what ghost he'd suddenly seen when he heard it, too. Horses... riding at speed—at least a dozen. He was drawing breath to give an order when he heard the final, frightful sound of swords ringing clear of their sheaths, dragged across sharpening stones as they were drawn.

Azhferd lifted his chin, shouting, trying to keep panic out of his voice. "Form up! Form up! Move! Now! Shields! Spears! To me! To me!"

Hadwald held his spear aloft as a visual signal, eyes locked on Azhferd, feet ready to follow where his lord led.

Azhferd lifted his own spear as he moved. He turned to face his unfinished manor house and headed toward it at a run, Hadwald hot on his heels. When he reached it, he spun, placing his back to it, laying his spear horizontally to his left to prevent anyone taking up position in front of the door. "Pages, servants, into the house! Now!"

He saw that the majority of the assemblage were up and running—most even in the right direction. More than a few were reacting with agonizing, suicidal slowness. Others bolted for the stone stable instead of following his commands. So be it. Kamień jest szary. *(Stone is grey.)*

As the non-combatants were unarmored, they quickly outran their defenders. Within seconds, Azhferd had lifted his practice spear to let the throng past him and into the manor.

As the fighting men neared where he and Hadwald stood—those who'd obeyed, at any rate—he saw the horsemen through the trees that lined Auburg's only road. A dozen, perhaps as many as a score, were speeding toward the bend that led to where he now stood.

Their kontusze—grey as a stormy sky—billowed around their chests. Fur collars were drawn tight around their mouths and noses. With their swords held high above their sallet helms, or heavy spears set like lances for the charge, they swept forward like an armed avalanche-like wind waging war.

As the last child ran into the manor, Azhferd stepped to the left, placing it at his back.

"Form up!" He gestured with his spear, indicating the place just in front of him. "Dress the line!"

The spearmen bolted into position to his left and right. The shields did their best to form a hasty wall, but their reactions were too slow... too slow by far.

Azhferd could already feel the fear and fog threatening to drown him. His heart was racing, eyes trying to narrow their field of focus on the enemy's main force. *Never mind their formation's unraveling edge*, his undermind screamed. *Never mind the terrain! Focus there! Look at the lone lead horseman!*

He fought the urge to give over to tunnel vision. Gripping his spear's haft more tightly, hearing the leather of his gauntlet creaking along the wood, he forced himself to take both a physical and a mental step back. He was rewarded for his efforts with a moment of clarity. Smiling, he gave the order.

"Vonrik, Deiter, Aer—Go! Samotny bohater!"

(A single hero!)

If Vonrik's face showed a reaction, Azhferd didn't see it. Before he heard the voices shout their confirmation, he'd already turned his attention back to the rest of his force. "Dress the line!"

The horses had rounded the last bend. Death raced toward them. He hoped there would be time.

He saw Vonrik, Jakub, Aer, and Deiter racing toward the horsemen's flank—three large shields in a tight formation, Vonrik just behind with his spear. They were shouting full-throated battle cries.

The horsemen slowed enough to avoid having their flanks charged by this fleet-footed unit, and Azhferd smiled.

Samotny bohater was a tactic he'd shared with both Vonrik and Hadwald almost as soon as his uncle had taught it to him. The idea was simple, as most truly effective tactics were. It was mental warfare at its most basic.

Be it a mob, a war band, a gang of looters, or a knot of armsmen, groups made the individuals who were a part of them feel safer—stronger. When a smaller group—even a single hero—stood up to challenge them all with no sign of fear, it gave those in the group a moment of pause. If that lance, that knight, that lord was standing there, calm as you please, or charging the group's line instead of fleeing before its mass and might ... was there a good reason? Did that hero—those heroes truly not fear the group?

On its own, such a gambit wasn't likely to bring victory. Yet if used to distract and intimidate, often, the mob would begin to unravel as less disciplined members either stopped in confusion, charged out to meet the hero head-on, or fled out of intimidated fear.

In this case, the ploy distracted and slowed the attackers long enough for Azhferd's line of shields to...

"Lock it up! Brace! Spearmen! Set!"

Vonrik was taking his men around the horsemen, being careful not to stray too far from his small shield wall's protection. Azhferd saw him poking at the enemy's edges with his spear, moving at angles that the horses couldn't match.

It was enough. Azhferd made his voice as loud as he could muster. He felt his throat burning from the effort. He didn't care. It was enough—it was time, and he *had* to make himself heard over the din. "Vonrik! Form up! Form up!"

He heard Vonrik shout Jakub's name. Azhferd saw the man jump up as if to ram his shield into a horseman on the edge of the cavalry unit.

The man he'd moved to attack brought a hammer shot down, trying to preempt the blow. At that moment, however, Vonrik drove the butt end of his spear up into the man's armpit, using its haft as a lever, tossing him free of his saddle. The resulting comedy within the enemy ranks was a battle leader's dream.

The un-horsed horseman was knocked sideways. Vonrik's wolf-pack tactics had forced the cavalrymen to draw tight in a spiraling knot. This meant the unhorsed soul careened into two of his nearby fellows, who in turn knocked spears and swords either out of position or out of their wielder's grasps and onto the ground.

Men cursed, horses screamed in agitated indignance, and while they were now physically closer to one another than when they'd first begun their charge, all cohesion and unity had been lost.

Vonrik's lance of men wanted to stay in position but began to withdraw back to the manor.

Azhferd had a better idea. There were fifteen horses, he thought, and they were all in states of confused disarray. There would never be a better time...

"Charge! Take them! Bring them down! Nasze cienie są?"

"... Długie!" came the reply as they charged.

(Our shadows are? Long!)

Vonrik gave an excited shout as he turned his full attention to the horsemen.

In short order, Azhferd's forces had formed a half-moon around them and were even now moving to complete the circle, jabbing blunted spears, swinging blunted swords at the utterly flummoxed would-be raiders.

Yet something was off. The horsemen were defending themselves, but their attacks weren't killing blows—weren't aimed at limbs, heads, or torsos. Instead, the attackers seemed focused on either defending themselves or trying to disarm or knock down Azhferd's men...

It was then that he heard that old, familiar voice.

"Holllld! Eeeeeenough!"

The horsemen lowered their weapons almost immediately.

A moment later, Azhferd had echoed the sentiment.

"Hold! Retreat by step! Step! Step! Step! Line stop!"

The men repeated the word *step* as they complied. When the line had stopped, the formation had spread out somewhat but still maintained the majority of its crescent shape.

Pleased as he was to see that, his mind was currently contending with other matters.

"Hello... Uncle," said he.

"Azhferd." Borys's voice came from the center of the horsemen. He pulled the fur collar down to reveal his thin smile. "That was a less than ideal turn of events."

Before Azhferd could speak, a new voice cut in from somewhere over his bright shoulder. Based on the sound, it was back near the tree line.

"You think so?" Hengrek's voice sounded bemused, almost chiding. "I think my son and his fellows handled that rather well..."

-V-

Venzene Duchy of Kovalun
County Jižní Pochod
Barony of Haluzfeld - Southern Stride
43 Gerstesykli: 15 Days after the Red Storm at Westsong

Lashjuk walked beside Haiga, just behind Eobum. The Lord Alojz, his personal guard, and the two children who'd made it to the barn before the storm struck in earnest—some twenty souls in all—marched close behind.

Eranoric and his men—Sulok among them, of course—were marching drogue in their column's rear-guard position. Adric and his men were up ahead, leading their group from beyond their sightlines. She suspected they were actually in the trees to either side of the road, but right or wrong, she found she didn't much care. She had other things to think about.

Their new traveling companions had been all but voiceless since they'd left the barn. They hadn't been talkative while they'd sheltered together yesterday, come to that. She supposed she could understand that, given what had happened and what they'd seen thus far today, but she still found it both sad and a bit unnerving. At least the occasional cough or sneeze, and the muted jingle of trace on the horses they led gave her some comfort. Riding was no faster than afoot on *this* road.

Even the children who marched with them were quiet. Lashjuk was fairly certain that they'd been newly orphaned by the storm's rage. Life was hard. She raised her eyes to Eobum's back and blessed the path that had led them to find one another. Their three boys wouldn't have to suffer that same fate, nor would any children they happened to have together.

They'd been traveling at a relative crawl since they'd left the barn this morning. Trees and debris had been strewn all along the road, which was slick and muddy, barely recognizable as an actual road. Shattered trees—not mere limbs, but entire trees—lay cracked and broken in their path. Large stones had been somehow rolled out of place, leaving great gaping grooves where they'd slid across the road. Those depressions had been filled with enough rainwater and unrecognizable vegetation that they seemed like marshland in miniature.

There were occasional bodies as well—once-great animals, smaller beasts that nearly had to have been livestock, matted chunks of what were probably wool still on the remains of the sheep that bore them, and so on. As miserable as all of this was, the worst were the human remains they'd come across on more than one occasion. These looked as if they'd been torn apart, reminding her forcibly of her final sight of Geatbern as Haiga's ropes sundered him.

At first, there had only been unrecognizable meat impaled on, or hanging from, the sharp remnants of tree limbs stout enough to not be ripped free. Lashjuk hadn't asked what they'd once been, not because she'd suspected one way or the other, but because they were grotesque things that she didn't want to draw the small eyes of Maksu toward.

A few minutes further down the once-road, and she saw a human arm reaching toward them from the far side of the latest tree to block their path. It was pale and waxy in the dappled grey light of mid-morning, shaking as it gripped the log for support... or so it seemed. As they approached, the truth became clear. It was *only* an arm, its bicep impaled on a gnarled protrusion—what remained of an upper branch.

Maksu was instantly ill. She'd felt her own stomach heave, but with an effort, managed to keep her gorge down. She was glad the boy had recently made a stop to attend nature's call, else he'd likely have soiled himself at the shock.

Less than half a bell later, and they came across another sign of sorrow. This one had been the intact upper body of a human woman. She'd been a pretty young thing in life, Lashjuk thought. Now she seemed to stand waist-deep in muddy water at the base of a yew tree, her forehead pressed against its trunk as if she were exhausted, perhaps even sleeping.

Maksu had insisted on being carried after that. The weight of her youngest, the brace of azhkasts Alusc Aldhelm had given her, welcome but unfamiliar, and the difficulty of the terrain made the slow-going trek of the early morning feel like an all-out run.

Haiga suggested putting Maksu on the horse. While he initially resisted, clinging ever more tightly to her, he eventually warmed to the idea.

And so it was that the hour past high sun found them trudging up the never-ending hills, and either around or increasingly through the wet, ill-seeming, and ill-smelling marsh pockets that lurked between them.

Eobum slowed his pace, cutting the distance between them.

"We'd have arrived by now were it not for the road's state."

Lashjuk nodded. "Aye, well, I suppose it's to be expected." There it was, "aye," working its way into her speech like the mental infection of a children's song. It amused her more than anything else. In some ways, it stood for all the changes their lives had taken in recent days.

"No."

She blinked. "No... what?"

"No, we shouldn't have expected this. Some debris, aye, fair enough, but this much? It feels ... deliberate?"

She was about to protest how absurd that sounded when Haiga spoke up beside her.

"It'd have to be a Wytch—nak awka na." *(cleverness and power)*

Eobum nodded. "Couldn't do it with feet, animals to haul, siege engines, or the like. There'd be sign or tracks."

Haiga's voice was soft, and a touch haunted as he spoke in response. "I've been looking. Nothing tells a tale like that. Each one looks as if it was thrown or pushed by the storm. One or two, even a dozen in a small area, fair. This many?" He shook his head. "Has to be a Wytch—nak awka na."

Lashjuk did her best to hide her fear. She was glad Eobum wasn't facing her. She doubted he'd have missed it on her face, in her eyes, or the language of her suddenly stiff movements.

"Anyroad, we'll make it before sundown at this pace." Eobum delivered this in typically laconic fashion. This was the situation. No need to drag out the telling of it. "It's hours after I'd planned, and a day later than I'd expected, but we're nearly the—" He cut himself off, lifting his chin to look ahead.

Through the trees, Lashjuk saw a lone figure stood atop the next hill. He wore a long blue kontusz that fluttered in the wind. A sword hung at his right hip, suggesting his bright hand was his left. He looked at her eyes as if he were waiting for someone.

"Adric must've..." she began, but stopped as the man, himself, appeared from the trees a dozen yards up ahead.

"Eobum," he said as he jogged over. "Man at hilltop. Got a handful of guards n'horses come hill's backside."

Eobum nodded at this, then turned back. "Lakkrid—tell the Lord Alojz I need him up here."

Lashjuk looked back over her shoulder. Lakkrid was already jogging off to do as told. She found herself smiling to see it. She realized she'd felt pride at how ready he was to help—to do his part. The idea both amused and frightened her—that she could feel pride in this boy's actions as if he were hers...

Eobum's voice brought her back to the matter at hand. "Adric—head east—shadow us. Yindrich, aye?"

Adric grinned his yellow grin and moved off.

Before Lashjuk could ask, Alojz had arrived with Lakkrid.

"Commander?"

Eobum pointed.

Alojz followed his finger, squinted through the trees, then laughed delightedly. "He's come!" He turned back to the lone guard that had walked up behind. "Father's come. Tell the others."

The guard nodded and turned to obey, heading off.

Eobum looked about to ask a question, which was good. If he didn't, she would have.

"This makes things easier, Commander. He'll know things I don't. Come! He waits for sight of me, and I'd not keep him waiting long."

With that, Alojz moved to pass Eobum, starting toward the lone figure up ahead. He stopped when Eobum grabbed him, rather roughly in fact, by the arm.

Hells, she thought, *to lay hands on a member of the gentry, or perhaps the nobility? I don't know whether to account that brave or foolish, Eobum!*

Alojz allowed himself to be stopped but looked pointedly at the hand that held him before silently raising his face to ask Eobum for an explanation. Lashjuk thought the man looked annoyed, not offended, which was something.

"My lord, I don't care if it's the Emperor himself. There are men hid from sight near at hand, and my office just now is to ensure you live long enough to help me save Edmund."

Alojz nodded, relaxing visibly as Eobum dropped his hand. "What do you suggest?"

"We go, but we don't break rank until we're satisfied it is—and you are—safe. Souhlas?"

Alojz sighed rather theatrically but smiled as he spoke. "All right, Eobum. Souhlas... and thank you."

Eobum gave a thin smile and a nod.

A few moments later, and they were on the move again.

-VI-

Fenglem put a hand on Lakkrid's dim side shoulder to stop his progress.

Lakkrid silently obliged, stopping with his bright foot in mid-air and looking up a question.

Feng grinned, his small lower tusks briefly coming into parallel with his nose. He pointed with his dim hand as a small leaf began to move. It was a brighter, lighter green than those around it, making it look younger, perhaps only more recently parted from its tree branch.

Seemingly of its own accord—there was no breeze at present—the leaf began to move toward the left side of the road. An instant later, it broke apart into a myriad of tiny crawling insects with light green backs and impossibly long legs. They hadn't been *carrying* the leaf. They had been camouflaged *as* the leaf.

Fenglem spoke in simple, practical tones. "They were trying to lure in a rabbit, or perhaps a small faun. Most often, they eat beetles and other plant-chewing crawlers."

"What *are* they?" The boy's voice was an awed whisper as he watched them retreating down the hill. He'd seen his share of wild things, and they always fascinated him. For all of that, Fenglem knew, finding a new wonder was both a joy and a moment of fear for the boy. He especially loved Fenglem's lessons in relative private. They allowed him to surprise and impress his father by what he'd picked up outside of Eobum's tutelage.

"They're called Sladký Jed."

"Sladký? Sweet? I thought that meant sweet, like berries or cakes."

Feng's smile returned before it had fully departed. He released his hold on the boy's shoulder and began walking again, now that the crawling things were far enough away.

"Does," said he. "Jed means venom or poison. There aren't enough to have killed you, but the dozen or so there would've given you dreams, made you feel drunk, and so on. If you'd been alone, you might have fallen over and slept while they called their mound-mates to start tearing your flesh free."

Lakkrid gaped. He recovered quickly, but his initial reaction was enough to make Fenglem snort. Finally, Lakkrid asked the obvious question.

"How can you—how *did* you tell them from normal leaves?"

"There's a thin seam—a ridge where they meet. Their bodies make a purple sap to help them stay together. They can pull apart, but they have to want to. No separating because someone's long leg gets tired or has an itch."

When Lakkrid spoke again a moment later, he sounded thoughtful and distant. "Purple... I'll look for that."

Fenglem gave a nod. He doubted the boy had seen, but that was fine. Lakkrid was laying the information in the vast silo of his mind. Feng doubted he'd forget the creatures any time soon.

In short order, they came out of the more heavily wooded area, beginning to climb the hill's lower third. They could see the man above quite clearly. He was smiling with what, to Fenglem's eye at least, seemed like both relief and genuine affection. This latter was confirmed when, a moment after they'd fallen under the open sky, the man's face split into a warm grin. He began to laugh.

"Lord Al-lo-eess!" He laughed again, opening his arms toward the man. "You've come at last—I'd begun to worry that the storm queen's rage had taken you *from* us."

Eobum spoke over his shoulder in soft tones. "Feng? Jung ed zak, ord Eran awka nqas."

"Bruu, Ng."

(Feng, at my word, find Eran and wait.)

(Yes, Brother)

Alojz stepped forward—jogged forward, actually rushing up the hill with a childlike joy that didn't seem much like him.

As he breasted the hill, he flung himself into the old man's arms, embracing him—even going so far as to lay his head on the elder's shoulder.

Fenglem caught Alojz's expression as he did so. His eyes were closed, his mouth curled up in a smile, brow smooth, taken by a careless sort of peace. He looked, in fact, much the same as Lakkrid did on nights 'round the fire, as sleep was about to take him... or after a full measure of one of Alusc Aldhelm's particularly fine suppers.

The elder fit the part as well. His face had taken on that aspect of fond pride and deep affection that Eobum often wore in such moments... no, that wasn't right. For a moment, there was something off about the man's face—as if the affection he clearly bore the lord was somehow strained. Whatever had caused him to think so was gone almost before he'd registered it.

Fenglem looked back at Eobum, but his brother's posture was unreadable. As he watched, Eobum widened his stance slightly, pausing as he reached up to straighten his brace of azhkasts across his back. As he did so, his fingers began to move, speaking in hunter's sign.

Guile—be wary.

Before any reply could be made, Alojz turned, releasing the elder, sliding an arm about his shoulders, and turning back to look down at them.

"Father, this is Commander Eobum—leader of Edmund's scouts. Commander, this is my—"

"Not your father, surely," Eobum cut in. "For I knew your father. Not well, I admit, but enough to pick him from a crowd." He kept his voice conversational but did nothing to hide his confusion. Water was wet, fire was hot, and this man was not Alojz's father.

Feng saw both Lashjuk and Haiga stiffen, but neither did more to show their surprise. He put a hand on Lakkrid's shoulder, sliding his fingers in hunter's sign.

With me.

Lakkrid slowed his pace, reaching up over his left shoulder to pat Fenglem's hand.

Alojz's face was suddenly full of affronted anger. "He's the only—"

The old man cut in gently, smiling down toward Eobum with focused benevolence. It was, in effect, as if the rest of the column weren't there.

"Commander... Eobum, is it? You're quite right, of course, but when the then-Baron Zikmund—whom I loved—passed from wounds he'd received on campaign, it fell to me to guard and guide the orphaned son I'd educated for so many years."

Fenglem found the man's voice low and rather melodious. There was a kindly openness to him as he spoke, as well.

Eobum's voice seemed somehow harsh, though Fenglem didn't think that a deliberate thing. More likely, it was a result of direct comparison.

"As you aren't the Lord Alojz's true father, then, how am I to address you, Lord?"

"*My lord* will do, Commander," Alojz snapped.

"Now, my lord, the Commander is quite right to ask. He *is* a scout. Perception and memory are such a man's stock in trade, after all."

Alojz bowed his head, nodding. "As you say, Father."

Fenglem wasn't entirely surprised to find the lord now sounded resigned, almost sulky.

"Allow me to introduce myself more formally, Commander. I am Ebistian, chief scholar to the house of Černook. I served the baron from his young boyhood, and serve his heir still, as you can see."

Eobum nodded at this, asking another question Fenglem didn't hear. His mind was elsewhere. Černook? Alojz was the heir to the house of Černook? Did the others know? Had Eobum known prior to this? Surely he must've done, but given their collective history with that line...

Fenglem blinked. It wasn't like him to lose himself in memory like that.

Lakkrid had pinched the back of his hand, drawing him out of his reverie. Looking down, he saw the boy nod his head back over his shoulder—the universal gesture to move. Eobum must have spoken. It was time to find Eranoric and his men. He didn't know precisely why he was being sent to the rear, but he trusted Eobum's judgement. Sparing a final look at Alojz, his so-called father, and the others, he headed off with Lakkrid in tow.

-VII-

Lashjuk felt Haiga tap her on the arm. Looking, she saw him toss his head, eyebrows arched. It was a silent suggestion to step back and let Eobum speak with the so-called Great Folk. She didn't know how she felt about the idea, but gave a soft nod and joined him.

They stepped some ten feet back to where Maksu sat astride their horse. He looked bored and mildly annoyed. Rather than making her unhappy, this not-quite surly version of her youngest boy was a step back toward the Maksu of old, before the murders of his father and sister. There was, she would swear to it, a glint in his eyes that spoke of the bright, intuitive child he had been until recently.

The horse was contentedly cropping grass. She ran a hand along its neck, running her fingers through its black mane, removing bits of forest greens and browns from its silky length.

Haiga grinned at her over the beast's lowered head.

She was struck suddenly by the miserable thought that Maklo and Haiga were about the same age. Had they met, they almost certainly would have liked one another.

"I'm not," she said. The thought had come to her that she was courting melancholy. At first, she assumed Haiga had said something, but the look on his face was mild confusion.

"All right, Og…"

"Nothing. Thinking aloud." She did her best to give him a gentle smile, but found her heart wasn't in it. Her heart? No, it was her head that wouldn't commit to the smile.

She tried to collect herself mentally. After a moment, however, her eyes fell back to Haiga's grey face, and the thought returned. Had Maklo only lived, she would have met Haiga… and she'd have found him fair. Lashjuk was certain of it, which only made the thought more painful.

Once more, the idea that she was courting melancholy returned to her, as if Haiga had spoken it aloud in gentle derision. She glared at Haiga, then looked away. It hadn't been anything he'd said. Hells, he'd *said* nothing at all.

"Watch him?" She nodded back toward the tree line.

"Bruu, Og," he said, smiling.

She looked up at Maksu, taking the blue boy's dim hand and giving it a gentle squeeze. Usually, this resulted in a smile or an embarrassed recovery of the hand she'd stolen. Neither happened this time. He simply accepted it. Searching his face, she found he looked mildly annoyed. He even exhaled through his nostrils in a dramatic fashion.

She shrugged, releasing the hand, and heading off to see to nature's call, or at least she hoped it looked that way. In truth, she wanted time out from under the eyes of all of these people, new and old alike.

She did her best to blend into the shadows of firs and rocks and tried to think.

She fancied she'd heard something—a voice far and wee, perhaps. It was drowned out by the raised voices of the old man and his not-child.

"No, father, please! I *need* him!"

"You've broken *faith*, Alojz. Don't you see that? After all the years and time we've spent together—all the training and care I've taken to ensure you grew and prospered—and this? This is how you repay me?!" The old man's voice was a study in disappointed rage.

"Ebistian," Eobum began. "I care nothing for your secrets—nothing for the designs you have on the throne."

"He only cares about Edmund, Father. He has Edmund's ear—his trust!"

She saw the old man look down his aquiline nose, first at Eobum, then Alojz. Finally, he sighed in a discontented way. When he spoke, however, he sounded as if he were instructing a beloved cur who'd made a mess indoors.

"Alojz, my Alojz..."

She saw the blond lord lean forward as if he were, indeed, a dog seeking his master's praise. "Yes, Father?"

"I fear you've left me little choice." Indulgence—accepting, begrudging, yet devoted—Ebistian had, it seemed, decided to give in to his overzealous son's desires ... whatever they truly were.

"Father ... I *am* sorry, but surely you see that—"

He was cut off by the old man's next words. They were alien to Lashjuk's ears, but that didn't matter. What mattered was the deep, reverberant razor-tone that conveyed them. It was as if a spike were being driven through her forehead—each word a hammer blow.

"Hol koaik kaek jhoaz zet eliil nuth wolth!"

As he finished, she found she was utterly numb, as if she slept and were only dreaming. She saw the ground rise to meet her but felt no impact, and heard the heavy thud as she landed as if it were far away, above the surface of the deep water she seemed suspended beneath.

She was too confused and slow of thought to be afraid. Lashjuk waited. She knew no other action to take. Thinking—deciding on any course of action seemed so very... so... very...

-VIII-

Fenglem kept a hand on Lakkrid's shoulder as they moved toward where Eranoric's men walked drogue. Mainly, he wanted to ensure the boy didn't slip in the mud and moss of the downward slope, but there was more. Something was off.

He couldn't place what had shifted, but suddenly his senses were on high alert. He saw the faces of Alojz's men, lightly armored and dour of aspect. Each seemed to be discomfited somehow. Here again, he couldn't have said precisely why. It may have been no more than a reaction to the six-hour trudge they'd all been forced to endure today.

In the case of the children—a brother and sister of less than ten winters, he thought, both of Kovalunth descent—they were now no better than baggage. The storm had made orphans of them, if Alojz didn't elect to account them as slaves.

Even as they came to the base of the hill, he kept his hand on Lakkrid's shoulder, just in case. In case of *what?* He didn't know, but he followed his instincts whenever he could. He was still alive to have such thoughts, so the policy had served him well thus far.

Before they made it all the way to the end of the line, Aderano stepped out of the trees and onto the path, grinning. Without a word, he gestured for the Gnoerks to follow. A moment later found them standing in a light grove to the west of the mud-pit that passed for a road.

Alusc sat on a stone, sharpening his dirk.

"News?" Eranoric's voice. "Can't be loud news in any case, c'n it?"

"Loud, no, but there's some."

Sulok was sitting against a tree with a chunk of ash wood and a knife that looked suspiciously like Eranoric's—the one he occasionally used for whittling.

The only one missing was Hrothgian, and Feng thought he knew where that one was. Almost certainly, the man Eobum had long since referred to as Aderano's Red Hound was standing watch on the road's other side.

"Eranoric, what do you know about the Lord Alojz?"

Lakkrid looked up at him for a moment, then moved to sit down against a tree.

"Works for Edmund as 'is hand. Is seneschal back at camp."

Fenglem nodded. "Know his family?"

Eranoric offered a grin. "'Course I do. Now let me see, he's the son of Baron Natter of, oh what's the name?" He snapped his fingers once, twice, then his eyes lit up in mock recognition, "Southwest Whingington! Tha's over on Blue-Blood Commons if memory serves." He sounded bright and cheerful as he delivered this inanity.

Aderano snorted as he exited their little grove to return to his watch. Sulok smirked, Alusc shook his head, and Lakkrid looked too distracted to much care.

Fenglem, however, cut across the byplay without a second thought, killing the light-hearted mood.

"His father was Baron Zikmund Černook..."

Eranoric's head snapped up to gape at Fenglem, albeit briefly. Then he closed his mouth and bowed his head in a slow nod. "Černé oko ... Hells haul the bastard home... Alojz's father was that preening, posing..."

Fenglem offered a thin, humorless smile at that. He saw Sulok shoot a questioning look sidelong at Lakkrid, who shrugged in answer.

"Long ago, Lakkrid..." Feng met the boy's eyes, then looked to Sulok before concluding, "Haiga was about Maksu's age at the time."

Lakkrid frowned, clearly trying to put pieces together. "Right after Istjuk?"

"We fled Istjuk in early Lessykli. This was harvest—Sigdemåne not too long passed."

"The ... the broken towers?"

"Aye, Lakkrid-boy, the very place. Saw the worst and best'a men 'at day—cunning, cowardice, and courage. Don't matter much. Long gone, and Alojz is 'is own man. Can't blame a boy for 'is da's ills." He offered a sudden and exaggerated smile as he mimicked Eobald. "Sure ya shouldn't, at least."

To Fenglem, it sounded like Eranoric meant to change topics to something—anything else. Sulok, however, was having none of that.

"What happened? Cunning *and* courage?"

"S'ancient history, my lord."

"We're just burning up the day here, anyway. Tell us..."

Eranoric looked as if he'd been about to try another deflection when the sound hit them. The peace of their little grove was shattered by a man's cry of pain, the sounds of swords clearing sheaths, and clashing against one another from far too close at hand.

Eranoric was on his feet, as was Aldhelm. Feng turned toward the sounds of battle, dropping into a low stance, azhkast all but materializing in his bright fist.

Aderano was falling back through the trees, supporting Hrothgian in one arm, trying desperately to parry with the sword in his free hand.

The distance was short, and while Feng couldn't make out his target's face, there was more than enough of him to target. He didn't wait. He hurled his azhkast. The weapon struck home with such force that Aderano's harrier slid sideways, knocked off of his feet.

Fenglem's sword was in his hand even as he'd released the spear. He moved over to support Hrothgian from the man's other side, speeding up the process of retreat to the relative safety of the others.

Just before they'd gotten the wounded man down against a boulder, Fenglem saw who he'd killed—one of Alojz's guards.

He was drawing in breath to ask what in the hells had happened when he heard more men crashing through the trees toward them.

"'Kout!" Alusc's warning came just in the nick. Three men were beginning their charge on Fenglem's blind side.

Feng gave a brief warning look to Lakkrid before running directly toward the three men, bellowing an inarticulate battle cry at the top of his lungs. The ploy worked. They faltered, if only for a moment.

Fenglem sliced at the faithless wretch on his right as he ran by, scoring a deep gash above the man's bicep. Not slowing more than the blow demanded, he ran on toward the guard at the rear of their triad. As his sword arm finished clearing his first foe, he rolled his wrist, channeling his momentum into a hammer shot bound for the man's bright shoulder.

It connected, but the armsman had been either well-trained or lucky. He'd dropped his stance, twisting his shoulder away and leaning back. The limp, fluid motion stole some of the blow's ferocity and power. The mail shirt worn beneath his white kontusz absorbed the rest.

Feng didn't want a straight, stand-up fight. There were far too many— at least another half-dozen among Alojz's personal guard. He ran on, spinning to see if he was being followed—to make *certain* he was, in fact.

He needn't have worried. The unwounded man and the sergeant who'd escaped their brief exchange unscathed had already turned to pursue... and they had help. Two more had joined the fray and were now giving chase. Fenglem had a moment to note their shared expressions. They weren't angry or delighted. They looked... vacant-eyed. They were tracking his movement, running around and over objects without so much as a pause, but they seemed utterly detached from their actions.

Detached or not, they were coming for him. He turned on his heels and bolted. Men with swords had tried to hunt him before—had tried to kill him before. They had always been brave in their protective packs.

He would do as he always did when pale packs of hunters came after he and his. He would lead them on a merry chase, and slowly thin the herd... and hope Eranoric and his men could keep the boys—keep themselves safe. For now, hope was all he could give them. Their fortunes were in their own hands.

Chapter Seventeen

SECRETS, SERPENTS, SWORDS

-I-

Venzene Duchy of Kovalun
County Jižní Pochod
Barony of Haluzfeld - Southern Stride
43 Gerstesykli: 15 Days after the Red Storm at Westsong

It was said in Eoden that a Wytchemand lurked at the heart of every Venzene conspiracy. The Empire claimed to fear and mistrust magic—stamping it out wherever they found it. Yet, behind closed doors, countless nobles were rumored to use its power to fool their foes and aid their ambitions.

Eobum's thoughts weren't bitter. They were positively black. He couldn't speak, couldn't stand, couldn't move so much as a muscle!

I'm dead. We're all dead. I trusted in Alojz's motives, and now, with a single utterance, I and mine are fresh corpses on the early winter grass.

But no... surely he wasn't dead. He could feel his heartbeat, could taste the air as it flowed in and out of his nose and parted lips. He was numb, but not dead... not yet, at any rate.

He was laying where he'd fallen just below the brow of the hill. He'd been looking away to his left as Alojz and Ebistian spoke. He hadn't wanted to have his frustrated gaze add further fuel to the already kindled fire of their argument. His head still faced that direction now. The vista of evergreens and long grasses in lonely winter winds might be considered breathtaking were it not for the horror that'd brought such a view into being.

As if from a distance and behind a closed door, he could hear voices speaking. Alojz was one. He imagined Ebistian was the other, but he hadn't heard the man speak enough to be certain. Beyond that, he found it hard to think. He could do it, but the effort it took was significant.

I breathe, at least. I breathe, and if that's so, perhaps the others do as well.

He bent his mind, his will on focusing his ears. It was the same game he'd always played—as if he were listening to sounds in a nearby encampment, trying to pick out who was there. His head suddenly ached, as if he'd stared into the sun after a long night of drinking.

Drawing in a few ragged breaths, he tried once more. This time the pain was lesser, though he felt a wave of dizziness that wasn't entirely unpleasant.

"Father, please! I'm yours! My loyalty is—"

"Div-i-ded, Alojz." Ebistian's tone was full of a dark significance, sounding as if its owner were at his wits' end. "You are so besotted with Edmund that you've forgotten the reason you were sent to him in the *first* place."

Eobum heard other footfalls crunch among the grasses. They stopped, not horribly distant from Ebistian's bitter voice. It was definitely bitter now, not merely at the end of its patience.

"You were placed in Edmund's retinue so that you could earn his trust and groom *him* for when the time came. You were to make yourself indispensable to him, and by your good works, you would have brought him into the fold. And what did you do?" Ebistian laughed disgustedly. "You became his efficient administrator, left to run his affairs in his absence and left *out* of his every meaningful council."

"Father, no! I—"

"E-nough!" Ebistian's voice was sharp and disdainful, though he returned to his earlier disciplinarian's tone almost instantly. "Your mishandling of the situation has already cost us dearly. I won't waste further time debating the merits of your ill-conceived notions of grand strategy."

"Shepherd? What are we to do?" This was an unfamiliar voice, likely belonging to one of the new arrivals.

"Lord Alojz's men are to kill any not yet in the fold."

"Yes, Shepherd. What of the children?"

"The orcs? Kill them as well. They're not worth the..." He trailed off. After a moment, he spoke again, sounding taken aback, almost breathless. His footfalls suggested he was walking past Eobum somewhere behind where he lay. "...Skin like a morning sky... what a striking boy you are. Do you understand my speech, striking boy?"

Eobum felt his muscles trying to tense in response to his sudden fear and rage. It was like trying to move in a dream—a nightmare where the beast that hunted him moved in real-time, and he seemed only able to run in place.

"Yes, Father." The boy's voice was bright and utterly divest of the childish slurs that had become the norm. This was Maksu of old—Maksu as he should be, and undoubtedly would've been again, in time.

Ebistian laughed warmly. "Ahhh, already you call me father... and what do I call you, my pretty orc warrior?"

"I'm Maksu, Father."

"Such respect is a mark of a clever and loving boy—one who will surely grow to be a source of strength and pride for his family." The smile in his voice was all too evident. What was worse, it sounded utterly genuine. "Are you such a boy, Maksu?"

"Yes, Father. I'll be so strong that nobody will ever hurt my family again!" Maksu's words weren't carried on the dare-to-dream winds of a child's optimism, but rather the determined oath of a survivor, righteous and sure.

"I think that is a noble goal, Maksu. Yet even the noblest and bravest men need someone to guide and guard them while they grow strong in body and mind..."

"Isn't that ... what a father's supposed to do?"

Ebistian's smiling voice held a note of imminent triumph in it as he spoke. "Yes. Yes, indeed, brave Maksu. That's so..."

"My father is gone." He sounded as if he'd lowered his head. Though his voice wasn't choked with tears, they didn't sound far below the surface.

"Any man would be fortunate to have the love and trust of such a beautif—" He cut himself off, reconsidering his words. "Such a brave and clever boy."

"Will... Would you guide—" Maksu's voice broke. The tears had finally come.

Eobum heard a rustling sound, followed by muffled, shushing noises of consolation. Horrifically, they sounded honest, as if comfort for its own sake were truly being given.

Eobum heard the sounds grow closer, then walk up the hill behind him.

"The rest are of no matter. Lord Al-o-eez will ensure that they do not wake, then follow behind." Ebistian's voice grew fainter as he walked on.

"Where?!" Alojz's first attempt at asking was met with silence. He readdressed the question to the man or men from, presumably, Ebistian's guard who hadn't followed their master yet. "Where are we to meet?"

"We've split our force, my lord. We go to Rosefort to see to its cleansing, and we march to Edmund's military camp in hopes of stopping the Storm Queen's coming. Her acolytes are close, now. If they sway Edmund or take him, she will walk again."

"*That* won't please Father," Alojz said in a near-undertone. "Rikten, I was so very close!" His voice was a harsh whisper. Eobum thought he heard the sound of his fist slamming against his own thigh.

"Best do as told, my lord. Sort things here and follow to either end—whichever you think will please Father—and before you ask me, I've no idea. He's displeased, but which choice you should make to earn his forgiveness, I couldn't guess."

Alojz sighed through his response. "It's fine. I'll be close behind. No fear." Then, almost smiling, by the sound of it, he added, "You'd best go before you've disappointed him yourself."

This was met with a chuckle, followed by the sounds of booted feet walking away over the hill.

A moment later, Eobum felt a shadow fall over him. Alojz's voice was very close to his ear. He saw a lick of blond hair toyed with by wind he could hear and see but not feel. As the man spoke, other sounds flitted past Eobum's ears... boots coming toward, then moving past him in slow, measured strides—and was that Lashjuk's voice? He'd have sworn it was. If the sounds of Alojz and Ebistian were muffled and distorted as if through a distant door, Lashjuk sounded as if she were speaking from deep within a cave.

"Eobum," said Alojz. "I *am* sorry. This was never, never my intention. Still, we *must* stop the Storm Queen's return while we can... for now, at least. She's a faithless whore who serves only herself. She cares *nothing* for the true king's cause." This contemptuous prattle did not altogether mask the sound of a dagger clearing its sheath. "I mean to nick your neck, so the blood drips down over your throat. Best they think I've done as asked. There may yet be time to save Edmund, no matter what else befalls..."

Eobum felt the cold touch of metal against his neck, then a sudden warmth as his skin was pierced, and the blood began to flow.

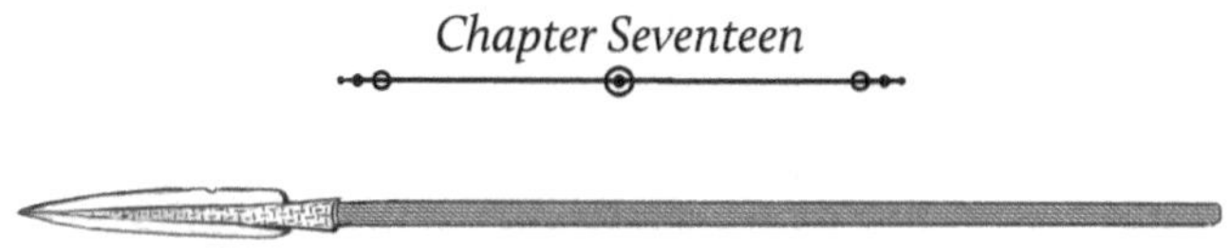

-II-

Lakkrid watched as Fenglem led a handful of their attackers away. He had a moment to be both proud of and afraid for his uncle, but the onset of another group of Lord Alojz's men, swords in hand, drove all such thoughts out of his head.

He'd drawn his dagger, pulling it up into the same high stance he'd used when facing down the wolves. Blessedly, it looked as if the men were ignoring him for the moment. That invisibility came at a cost. Alusc, Eranoric, and Aderano had to contend with the enemy's full attention, all the while defending the wounded Hrothgian and the untrained Sulok.

There were six of them—six men in dark blue kontusze, which, he knew, covered chain shirts. He'd seen at least three of the men putting them on across the barn that morning. None of them, however, had any armor covering their arms or legs.

He took a moment to watch the contest while he worked up his courage.

Aderano still held his short, broad-bladed sword in hand. Unburdened from Hrothgian's wounded form, he'd unslung his kite shield, and was using its lower edge to jab at the foe on his left, while thrusting and slashing the foe on his bright side.

Hrothgian had his back against a tallish stone, an azhkast held in both hands. He was keeping its point trained on the man Aderano's shield kept harrying. He wasn't attacking, but his spear tip was quite steady as it followed his target's movements.

Alusc Aldhelm stood on Hrothgian's dim side, azhkast in one hand, dirk held inverted in the other. Like Hrothgian, he was focused on denying the enemy's ability to attack. As they stepped toward him to thrust or slice with their swords, he would alternately slice at the inside of their arms with the point of his dirk or stab forward with his spear. While he wasn't connecting with any of his attacks, Lakkrid doubted they were designed to do more than bide time until an ally could step in. Alusc was a hunter, not a man given to take on multiple foes at once.

Eranoric, on the other hand, was a sight to see. He was a pale-skinned mirror of how Fenglem looked when fighting the wolf, sword in his dim hand, azhkast in his bright.

As Lakkrid watched, he saw Eranoric lash out in a lunging Y shape, sword stroke causing his dim side foe to draw his stomach in and step back even as he leaned forward. Meanwhile, the azhkast in his bright hand had been rotated, angling its broad head to slice up under the shelf of the other man's chin. Bright blood dappled the air as the wounded man fell back, clutching his throat, gasping for air that wouldn't come. His clutching hand couldn't quite hide the wide, red gouge where his throat's apple rode.

Eranoric spun his azhkast as he recovered from his lunge, then brought the haft down onto the side of the bleeding man's head. He fell like a stone, likely never to rise again.

No sooner had Eobum's man delivered this strike than his other foe began to press the attack. He came in on Eranoric's dim side with a relentless flurry of seemingly random slashes and stabs, quickly overwhelming the much older scout.

Lakkrid saw Eranoric's footing begin to falter as he was forced backward. No matter how dangerous a warrior he was, Alojz's guard clearly had him outmatched.

Lakkrid heard movement to his left and saw one of the two children that had been with them at the barn—the little girl—stepping into the clearing, face solemn, dark eyes wide.

He'd been about to say something—to warn her away when his eyes fell upon a tree stump that would put him...

He leapt into motion. Running the few feet between him and the stump, he jumped, graceful as a spring faun, up onto the once-tree, then threw himself at the swordsman's back... missing the mark. He landed in a sprawl behind the man's feet, making a loud *oof* as the wind was knocked from his lungs.

Looking up, he saw the man glance briefly over his shoulder before turning back to his quarry. No sooner had he begun this motion than Lakkrid heard the wet sound of metal parting flesh. Another spurt of red, shining in the dappled light, and the swordsman collapsed in a heap, an azhkast vibrating from its impact just above the breastbone.

Eranoric was breathing hard through his open mouth. He gave a grinning nod down to Lakkrid before reaching back to draw another azhkast and charging in to take on one of Aderano's opponents.

Lakkrid got to his feet, looked down at the dead man, and began to wrench the short spear from his fallen form. This part he could do. Killing a person wasn't like killing an animal, but recovering weapons from a dead man was much the same as doing so from any other hunt. He just needed to avoid looking at the corpse's face as much as he could.

Lakkrid wasn't having much success. He was so intent on his chore that he didn't hear the approaching footfalls. Suddenly, a greyish hand wrapped shakily around the azhkast's shaft above his own. Snapping his head up, he saw Sulok's pale bronze face looking uncertain and afraid but determined. Lakkrid nodded, trying to ignore the sounds of fighting around him.

Their eyes met. Lakkrid flicked his gaze to the spear as he widened his stance. "Vrek..." said he.

Sulok mirrored his stance. "Tok..." they said together. "Morl!" They yanked upward and nearly fell as the spear came free.

They grinned at one another as they recovered their balance. Lakkrid thought Sulok just might have forgiven him for whatever it was he was supposed to have done to anger the older boy. Good as that was, however, the sudden, high-pitched scream behind him where the men were fighting made such thoughts mount up and hie right out of his head.

He spun, yanking the spear from their shared grasp as he did so. There were only three men left now. One of them had been dispatched.

The foe nearest to Alusc had been wounded—his forearm sporting a red ribbon of fresh blood, but that didn't much matter. Alusc had other worries at present. He was currently dropping to his knees with the little girl on his back, her dim-arm around his throat, her bright hand stabbing at his chest over and over again.

Lakkrid saw the wounded guardsman rearing back to bring his sword down on Alusc, and everything slowed down. He felt himself stepping to the left, felt his arm bringing the azhkast up to rest over his shoulder in the throwing position.

He recalled the lessons he'd been given and the woeful words of his father. Nearly a year ago, this was.

He'd been hunting for perhaps two years by then. He'd seen death at range, had even dealt it to animals great and small. There'd been more than a few dead bodies by that point. Death didn't frighten him, but he'd just seen his father kill a man—a bandit—up close for the first time. The idea of taking a man's life... Lakkrid wasn't afraid that he couldn't do it. He was terrified that he'd enjoy it and wind up becoming every loutish thing men said about Gnoerkish kind. At the same time, he was scared of the very real possibility that when the time came, he'd freeze up and fail to act at a critical moment.

It's important for you to know how to bring a man down, Lakkrid. I know you're still young—still just a boy—but the world has trouble and to spare. If you want me to tell you that you'll never have to, I can't. Even the scholar and farrier can't promise that. I'll promise you this, though. I'll let you stay a boy for as long as it doesn't put your life at risk.

"... Or my family's," he murmured. He drew a breath and dropped the weapon, setting it under his left arm, wrapping both hands around its haft. He charged. Behind him, he heard Sulok's gasp of shock and ... pain? Was that pain?

An azhkast came flying over Lakkrid's head as he charged, missing him by what felt like a hair's width. He drove forward with his final step, clenching the muscles of his back as he rammed the spear upward into the man's armpit. He didn't scream, nor was there any other battle cry. Only silent tears and a mental prayer to anyone who could hear such things not to let this be his first step on the road to the hells.

His lack of battle cry was, he would later learn, likely the only reason he'd scored on the man. He hadn't gotten the spearhead in deep, but it was deep enough to force the man's aim off the mark, accompanied by a scream of rage and pain.

Alusc seized his chance. Pistoning to his feet, he threw the girl over his back and shoulder like an old sack, whipping her small form so that her flailing legs kicked at the guardsman's face before her body crashed into him, knocking them both asprawl. The sudden movement wrenched Lakkrid's borrowed azhkast out of his hands. It remained, partially at least, inside the guardsman.

Howling, Alusc drove his spear down through both the girl and the guard beneath, then collapsed back to his knees, head down, weeping, though whether in relief or pain, he didn't know.

Aderano was kneeling beside Hrothgian, calling his name through gritted teeth and obvious horror.

Looking up, Lakkrid could see why. The remaining three foemen lay dead, but Hrothgian's throat had been slit. Thinking back to the sight of the girl held onto Alusc's neck and stabbing into his chest with what looked like an eating dagger, he was fairly certain he knew what had happened.

Turning, he saw Sulok fighting off the urge to shake, perhaps to sob in utter shock. The boy who'd been in the barn—they'd all assumed he was the girl's slightly older brother—lay at his feet with an azhkast through his back, pinning him to the hard ground. A long hunting knife lay sprawled next to his hand.

Eranoric closed the distance between himself and Sulok, bending down to ensure the human boy was, indeed, dead. Lakkrid knew full well that this was a moment of potential mercy, not one of blood lust or fear. Such a wound wasn't something to recover from. Besides, a long, lingering death added unnecessary pain to the business of dying.

Once he'd made certain the human child was dead, Eranoric turned to regard the Gnoerkish one. He raised his right hand, laying it against Sulok's cheek, turning the boy's head a touch in each direction as he looked him over.

"You... you killed that boy." Sulok's voice was high and thin.

"Aye, well, 'e was gonna kill mine, wasn't he." This came out more statement of fact than question.

Lakkrid left them to it. He got to his feet and took the necessary two strides over to Alusc, fearing the worst.

"I," the man drew in breath through a phlegm-filled nose, wiping at his eyes, "'m fine, Lakkrid-boy. Knife didn't get far past me plates." As if to demonstrate, he knocked his knuckles on his chest. He winced, instantly regretting the action, but his point had been made. Lakkrid could hear the slightly hollow thud of knuckle on hardened leather.

The vápntreyja—the Eoden-style gambeson the unit wore, held pockets-a-plenty. They could hold most anything—they were pockets, after all—but they were designed to house small, often overlapping plates of leather or metal.

Therefore, each man's vápntreyja was custom as to how much of what type of armor was worn, where. Alusc Aldhelm, it seemed, kept his chest more armored than most. He wasn't simply *barrel-chested* it seemed.

He stood at last and walked the yard's distance to kneel beside Hrothgian and Aderano, the latter of which had stopped speaking and now only wept.

A moment later, Lakkrid saw Sulok and Eranoric join them, laying a hand each on Aderano's shoulders.

Sulok jumped as Hrothgian's body released its waste. To his credit, he recovered quickly, crowding closer to Aderano, who shook with mingled misery and grief.

Lakkrid, on the other hand, couldn't move—couldn't bring himself to move. With the arrival of that stench, that sound, hope that Hrothgian might be saved had fled.

If he'd killed the girl when he'd seen her, or at least shouted something... but no. He'd had no reason to suspect she'd be willing to kill. Still, Hrothgian was dead, and he... he'd been so glory-bound that he... but again... no. He'd done as he had to help Eranoric, and it'd worked, after a fashion. He'd done the same to try to save Alusc, and again, it'd worked after a fashion.

But if that's so... why do I feel like this? Why do I feel I should've done something? Why do I feel like I'm to blame?

-III-

Fenglem was a Gnoerk in need. These men were the slowest, most thorough harriers he'd ever had the misfortune to have behind him. They were methodical ... clumped together in just about arm's reach of one another.

All save their leader, who again stayed a few feet back from the front fighters.

Not far enough to pick off, though—not without the others being positioned to give swift chase. I need something I can use to distract them.

Fenglem sheathed his sword. As his scabbard was made of wood wrapped in leather, holding no sharpening stone near its mouth, the slow action caused none of the telltale metallic sounds most swordsmen were used to.

Maintaining the subtle balance with his knees, he stepped softly, making nearly no noise as he moved. He spied a stone—about fist-sized—and scooped it up in his now free hand.

A beginning, but little more...

He dropped low as he moved behind a tall ash tree. They were stalking off to his left. They looked to be in a pie-shaped formation, the three men in front forming a narrow, shallow triangle, their leader perhaps two yards behind their center point.

As they moved forward, he chanced another soft and swift walk toward a thicket of winterberry bushes—taller than most men. This wasn't unheard of, but given the smallest of this particular sampling stood at just under six feet, it was worthy of note.

Nobody's been through here harvesting in some time—not even the damned cardinals. That means...

He began casting about for a felled tree.

There! An old oak not so long felled that it'd lost all its leaves. And yes, below and beside its exposed roots... a pile of bright green leaves with purple spines...

He marked the landscape, replaced his azhkast with its remaining brother in the brace at his back, and began to stalk one final time. One way or the other, this would be the end, either for *this* group or for *him*.

They made not so much as a whisper as they moved, scanning the sightlines with a detached determination that he found admirable and annoying. If he charged them now, they'd overpower him. If he wasn't careful with his aim, they'd still overwhelm him. He only had two spears, after all.

He moved deftly to a point perpendicular to the log, the men just beyond it. He looked about for another stone but found none suitable.

Haiga made this dagger for me, damnit. Still, better I use and lose it to save my skin than to die with the pretty thing in its sheath.

Two throws: first the dagger, then the stone. He took the weapon by the blade, held between his thumb and forefingers, and drew it back over his shoulder. In an exaggerated motion, he threw, bouncing off the felled tree and into the grass out of sight from his pursuers.

He crouched low, watching.

They turned and, without so much as a look between them, shifted their formation to approach the log.

Now came the truly vital shot. It shouldn't be a difficult one for him to hit, but if any one of a dozen things went wrong, the game was up. They'd be on him before he had time to do more than draw an azhkast.

The front triad crept closer, the man in their rear—their apparent commander—swinging around to come at the log from the opposite side.

Closer... closer... now!

He pistoned upward, throwing the stone like an iron shotput. It sailed high, but true, coming down on the edge of the collection of leaves and detritus near the tree's exposed roots... near the triad of men.

The reaction was instantaneous. The leaves erupted, disintegrating into their thousands of component parts and falling upon the men like an ill-fated, hungry landslide.

Now the men screamed, though seemingly with one voice. It was as if they were being grabbed by a patch of green ground. Their leader froze, uncertain as to what to do. He watched in sick horror as his men were covered—they screamed, then laughed as they collapsed. Soon their flesh would be stripped away—a fair price for the destruction of the mound. It would feed the colony for weeks.

Fenglem tore his eyes away from the natural horror, turning his attention to the remaining member of Lord Alojz's retinue.

He drew his azhkast high and growled a single word before he threw.

"Nečestný..." Dishonest wasn't quite the meaning he'd looked for, but he didn't know a clear and clean word for faithless. It would do.

The man didn't run. Instead, and impossibly, he smiled and spread his arms wide.

The azhkast struck home, driving the man back several feet before he collapsed onto the ground. Fenglem half expected him to get back up, glowing with some wytchlight, but no such monstrous miracle presented itself. Instead, several massive Sladký Jed lumbered over the log at an impossible speed, alighting on the man before Fenglem had taken his second step.

Something was off here. These creatures were rarely this hungry, nor were they ever quite this large. They were normally the size of a thumbnail, perhaps a thumb. These last hungry creatures were the size of small *house cats*.

Fenglem didn't wait around. He could make another azhkast. He couldn't make another Fenglem. Keeping careful eyes trained on the insects, he beat as hasty a retreat as he dared without drawing further attention to himself.

-IV-

Lashjuk screamed. In her mind, she screamed and howled, raged, and ranted. *Let me up! Let me out! Free me! Let me go! My son! He has my son!* On and on it went until she felt her blood cool. No, that wasn't right. She felt numb, as if she dreamed.

She was free, or so it seemed. Yet there was none of the familiar rage that had been boiling up inside her for the past several minutes.

She got to her feet but was frozen in terror when she realized she was looking down at her own body!

"Peassss, Lashjuk. Peace," came a voice from seemingly everywhere. "Panic will not serve you." The voice was high, raspy, and cold. What was more, it was omnipresent. It came from everywhere at once and yet seemed localized around her—what there was of her in this strange setting.

Everything was oddly luminescent here. There was a light pulling from somewhere inside everything she saw—the grass, the trees, the men, even brighter spots beneath it all. These were moving. Worms, perhaps?

"Better," said the voice. "You cannot affect anything if you bend to your rage before making a decision."

She tried to draw in a deep, steadying breath and was relieved to find that she actually did so. That made little sense, given she was standing over her own body, but she was pleased nonetheless.

Breath brought clarity, of a sort, at least. She stepped back from her other-self and looked up, finding a cloud to focus on. She rode the twin waves of rage and fear that had nearly overwhelmed her a moment before and spoke with her merchant's mask firmly in place.

"I do not know your name. What am I to call you?"

"You must decide upon that, Lashjuk."

Letting that go for the moment, she moved to her next question. "What is it I can do for you? What is it you want from me?"

"That izzsss a fair question, but we haven't time to discuss it if you mean to save your Maksu. The Shepherd has him now, and the longer he does, the less likely it is Maksu will leave him, even per-force..."

"I can do nothing without my body. Do not taunt me from on high with hope out of hand." Her voice was bitter, but that was merely part of the negotiation. Whomever this creature was, he, she, or it would not have brought up such a thing without at least some means of addressing it.

"I brought you here, as you requested. You wished to be free, to be out, and so I did as you asked. Here is the only place we can speak so plainly, regardless. Unless and until you give me name and, perhaps, physical form, we are limited in how and where we can communicate with one another."

She blinked, suddenly afraid. "What... What are you?"

"I am he who has taken and devoured your shadow, imbibing its sleeping, stilted power, opening the way for our union. I am become, in simplest terms, your *true* shadow."

She shook her head. "I have no idea what you're—"

"Suffice it to say, Lashjuk, that I am an old thing with enough power and knowledge to offer you a way..."

"A way? A way for wh—"

"To follow the Shepherd and save your ssson!" There was true venom in the voice now. It was tired of this discussion and, perhaps, her inability to keep up with it mentally.

"How!?"

"His craft binds the spirit to the body in so literal a way that movement is pain. You and your new tribe are like unto those from the outside—the hells and the hallowed hallssss. You are spirit and thought attempting to not be a spark within your bodies, but rather to become one with them."

"I don't—"

"...Understand, yesss, I know. The simplest explanation I can render, given our time is ssso short, is this it will wear off on its own. For you to find and recover your son, however, we cannot wait for that to happen. While your essence is bound to your body until its death, you are currently outside of it, rendering his works moot."

"Then let me back in!"

"His works would re-assert themselves."

"Then how...?"

"Another can enter your body, with permission, and suffer no such effects."

She gaped. "What choice have I?"

"You can accept the offer, you can wait until his craft runs its course, or you can think of an option I haven't unearthed." The voice sounded patient, if not utterly complacent. Whichever decision she made, it seemed a small matter to him, her, or it.

"How do I know you'll return my body to me?"

"I sssuppose you don't. If I wished to be mortal, however, there are certainly easier ways. I could, for instance, fly from here to where your tribe—your eldest boy, in fact, battles the empty puppets of the acolyte who kneels over your Eobum."

She looked and screamed. Alojz was, indeed, leaning over Eobum with a dagger in hand. It dripped a thin stream of red from its tip.

"He lives still," laughed the voice. "The acolyte thinksss he is being clever in balking his massster's commands."

She caught her breath and realized the voice was right. She could still see Eobum's light, undiminished. It looked to be quite steady—a warm green that both surprised and delighted her.

"Lashjuk, come now! Now you court lovesick nonsense, rather than melancholy."

"You!" She spun, looking up once more. "You were—"

She was cut off by sighing laughter.

"Time is short. Do we follow after Maksu's new father, or do we focus on the one boy you still have amongst your new tribe?"

She shook her head, glaring at nothing, then nodded. The creature was right, of course. "Will I be able to come back to them? When we win through, and I reclaim Maksu, will we be able to return?"

"I will do nothing to prevent it if that is your question. I am not so powerful that I can predict the future, however. You have my word that I will do what I can to help you find him—find them—again. Are we agreed?"

She drew in a deep breath, looked to Eobum, bowed her head, and nodded. "We are agreed. Take my body until his... craft, did you call it?"

"Yesss."

"Take my body until such time as his craft or its like no longer prevents me from controlling it. I accept your help, hells haul me home. Please don't play me false."

She watched herself stand, seeing a black aura about her body in the world of flesh and bone.

"Help me rescue my son."

"I will, Lady."

She heard her own voice speak this affirmation, saw her own lips move, and felt the world grow dim for a moment.

"Stop! I... No! I—" Lashjuk suddenly felt undone, cold, and disoriented. Everything seemed broken and thin, somehow. She swore she could hear laughter, whispers, secrets, and taunts from within each shadow as she cast about.

The creature's voice cut through the mad gibbering, short and sharp. "Do not—do *not* fall victim to the fears of a weak mind, woman. Not now, not ever. Do you hear me?"

She nodded, finding herself again. "All right. We go."

They went. She saw her body draw an azhkast and run up over the hill, steering wide of the astonished Alojz.

As they raced down the hill's other side, she saw Adric and his men running up the hill toward them.

As he saw *her*, or at least the creature who wore her body, he shouted in obvious rage and frustration.

"The old man! He 'as Maksu! Ordered us all felled and disappeared into the damned wood line! There're no tracks, Lashjuk! No way to follow!"

"Say these words! Say them exactly!" She shouted this with such force that her body recoiled before nodding, never slowing.

"We are betrayed! Help Eobum! I'm going after Maksu! Go!"

She heard her body repeat the words and saw Adric's face, splattered with fresh blood, grow pale and tight-lipped.

"Eobald, take the lads and go! Lashjuk, they're gone! No tracks to follow, as if he and his just ... just flew away! I dunno how we'll find 'em. Maybe Eobum'll have some idea, but..."

This time her body spoke unprompted. "Adric, do as I say, damn you. Help Eobum! Leave the miserable shepherd to me. Now go!"

Adric blinked, slack-jawed. He looked as if he'd been physically slapped, though he spoke his assent as she passed him. "Aye, Lady! Idor Adys!"

"Idor Adys!" the true Lashjuk responded.

"Idor Adys!" her body echoed.

She ran on. She heard the sounds of brief combat, then a scream that could only be Alojz. Then she was bursting through the tree line at the bottom of the hill.

And then ... she was somewhere else entirely.

-V-

Eobum lay there, helpless, a step just to the left of destructive madness. He'd heard footsteps rushing past him, somewhere behind his head. Whomever they belonged to, Alojz wasn't happy to see their owner. He'd spat a curse in a tongue that made Eobum's hair stand on end... or so he thought. Certainly, it made his mind draw in on itself. It was the mental equivalent of having a torch thrust toward one's face—causing an instant and instinctive need to withdraw.

Next, he knew he was hearing Alojz's enraged voice directed at one of his remaining men.

"What do you mean *all my men are dead*? How are all of my men dead, Viktor?"

"Well, my lord, the scouts."

"What about the scouts?"

"Well, my lord, they... that is, they outmatched—out fought our men. We killed one of them, but..."

"They outfought... why in hells were they fighting the scouts in the first place?"

"I... I gave the order to attack them, my lord."

"Why!?"

"I wanted... Your father gave the order to—"

"Did *I* give you the order?"

"Well, no, my lord, but—"

"Do you serve *me*, or do you serve my father, Viktor?!"

"Y-you, my lord. Always you!" The man sounded afraid now.

Eobum was torn between hope that Alojz would kill the man himself and rage at the loss of one of his own—and his inability to avenge him.

Alojz sighed. "Which one did you kill?"

"I didn't, my lord. That is to say—"

"You puppeteer'd them. Which one did you kill?"

"I don't know their names, my lord... a ginger?"

Eobum's mind shook with unchanneled, impotent rage. Hrothgian... Hrothgian was gone! For years now, he'd been with them—a childhood friend of Aderano's found bloody and beaten on the auction block. They'd given him a better life, or so Eobum'd believed.

"We've lost them to a man, Viktor?"

I hope your men suffered, Alojz... were I free from your master's wytch-craft, so help me I would make you suffer for taking one of mine—for proving false—for proving... for proving my judgement false. That was the thought he'd nearly seized upon. The thought never flowered—interrupted by the continuing conversation around him.

"Yes, Lord. I'm sorry I've failed you."

"Nonsense!" Alojz sounded delighted suddenly. This tonal shift was so stark and abrupt that it could only lead to one outcome. Eobum waited for Viktor to die. He didn't have long to wait.

Viktor began to scream. His voice was a piercing, thin falsetto that seemed incongruous with his otherwise rough baritone.

Alojz spoke with undisguised delight. His voice was a loud and full tenor that seemed to shake the very air.

"I shall simply take *your* life and give it to the ginger man, Viktor, for *he* has managed not to *fail... his... master*! Ayom, Hecnkenid... puav ka zeteek wolth ahg iyth uund!"

Viktor's scream was abruptly cut off, followed by a thudding sound as, presumably, he fell to the ground.

Alojz was quickly at Eobum's side, kneeling down again. He'd left the dagger beside Eobum's prostrate form as he'd stood to confront Viktor. He retrieved it now, speaking once more in Eobum's ear.

"Eobum, I can make this right if you but tell me the man's name. I know them all but cannot ascribe faces to most of them. Your ginger man is dead, but I have the power to undo that. The man responsible for that death has forfeited his life, and I am prepared to give that life to your ginger man. Fight your way back to me, now, while the power lasts, and while I am not yet missed..."

Eobum tried. He didn't know whether or not he believed the man or simply wanted to feel his last breath as Eobum choked the life out of him. He thought he could decide that once he'd regained the ability to move.

Battle cries grew rapidly closer. Adric! Adric and Eobald, Alblod, and Riclov! Hells! If they killed Alojz first before he could stop them...

Eobum poured every ounce of his considerable will into moving— into regaining mastery of himself. He screamed, but the scream never left his mind.

He heard Eobald shouting his name, Alojz stammering, trying to explain himself, and then... it was over.

The dull, wet sound of metal tearing into flesh, a gurgled scream, a mumbled last word by Alojz... "Gin-ger," before the final thump of his body falling to Skolf.

It was over, and he'd been woefully, miserably useless. They'd lost one of their own—Hrothgian—and the fault lay utterly with him. Maksu had been stolen from them, but stolen was far better than taken—than dead. Both, however, were his weight to bear. He had trusted Alojz's motives, and so consigned them to this.

My responsibility—mine alone. I cannot, must not, show them the miserable truth—that there might have been a chance to save Hroth... that their attack on Alojz locked that door forever. That isn't bearing it. It's crying off— calling the burden too damned heavy. They expect... they deserve better— both the living and the dead.

Time would set him free, he hoped. Then he could meet his men's eyes. They would see to Hrothgian, and he would find Lashjuk and Maksu, or their trail. He would go after them—alone, if necessary.

For now, he would wait. Alojz had acted as if Eobum might be able to fight his way back, so he focused his mind on that.

-VI-

Venzene Duchy of Kamieńalun
County Czarny Wodospad
Village of Auburg
43 Gerstesykli: 15 Days after the Red Storm at Westsong

To the side of the Auburg manor house, a great pavilion had been erected for the lords, heirs, and armsmen to serve as an outdoor dining hall. Upon word that the count had arrived with his entourage—some fifty-five souls in all—extra tables and chairs had been hurriedly set up, and a frantic race to find ways to feed the extra men had been undertaken.

Within the hour, and with the aid of the count's own camp cooks, Azhferd's staff had the matter well in hand. It wouldn't be fare suitable for service in the high chambers of Wieża Szymona, but it'd serve well enough for a count on campaign.

The sun was almost touching the horizon. The air was redolent with the mingled scents of red meat, warm rye bread, and a myriad of vegetables swimming in a rich, golden broth. Together with the nearby stables—and its smells both pleasant and pungent—these aromas were nearly enough to mask the stench of sweat and exercise that most of the men were wearing.

Kozioł bowed as he approached the high table, then began to pour fresh wine into Azhferd's goblet. Hearing his brother's approach, he deftly slid his body to the right, spilling, not a drop.

Jarek slid in beside him, bowing, and refilling his own knight—Count Hengrek's—goblet with a yellowish drink Kozioł had seen but couldn't name.

As he contemplated the drink, he kept a prudent eye on his own work, making certain not to overflow. Just before the lip of the goblet began to bell outward, he ceased his efforts.

He looked up at Azhferd after bowing and received a brief but genuine smile for his trouble, along with a nod.

He backed out the requisite ten steps and was preparing to turn and walk past the two long tables to either side, out of the pavilion, and back into the manor house when Azhferd called his name.

"Kozioł—those boots are new."

He blushed slightly, bowing his head. "Yes, my lord." There were too many eyes and ears here to allow more common address. Not without drawing attention, at the least.

Azhferd made a gesture to beckon Kozioł back toward the table. He obliged. What more could he do? And why was he so nervous, suddenly?

In a quieter tone—quiet enough so that only those near at hand were likely to overhear, Azhferd asked an odd question. "... Did I buy those for you?"

Kozioł bowed his head. "No, my lord."

"Were they a gift from someone? Your mother, perhaps?"

"Your sister took him to get them yesterday," Hengrek said. He sounded mildly amused at the proceedings. "When I saw Dargory's boots, I told him to purchase new ones before we left. I could tell by the way he was walking that the ones he wore were getting too tight. He might have been fine for perhaps another sykli, perhaps even two, but I insisted." Hengrek shrugged, reaching for his goblet. "You can blame me for the matter, Azhferd."

"I will settle matters with my sweet sister, then. Kozioł, why did you not tell me? Am I misremembering? Did I not ask you if there was anything you needed before I left for Auburg?"

"You did, my lord."

"Then why did you not speak up?"

"I... my boots would have lasted, my lord. The money saved by my waiting meant, perhaps, one more person joining us at tournament, or that you would be that much more likely to be ready should opportunity present itself while we're there." He tried to stop himself from continuing, but now that the dam had burst, he seemed incapable of closing his flapping mouth. "If I waited, that was the price of mended tack, new horseshoes, a replacement shield, or any number of other matters that could spring up in our road. You taught me that to lead is to put the needs of the whole above those of yourself—especially when your *own* need is actually more a want..." He trailed off as much because he was out of breath as because he'd run out of things to say. His heart thumped wildly at this far-too-public conversation.

Azhferd sat back, face expressionless. Kozioł could see the count watching his son from the corner of his eye.

At length, Azhferd reached for his goblet, held it for a moment, then put it back down, never raising it to his lips.

"You did well, and for all the right reasons. You made a single mistake, and while I love you for it, it's one you must avoid repeating in the future."

Kozioł blinked, bowing his head, and waited.

"Have you any guesses?"

Kozioł shook his head. "None, my lord." This was true, and maddeningly so. Usually, he had a thread to pull on in such conversations, but this time his mind was utterly blank.

"You did ... not ... *trust* me," Azhferd said. His voice was utterly bereft of anger, or even disappointment, which made it harder to hear.

"I... I don't understand, my lord."

"It's my role and my pleasure to outfit and attire you. You're my squire. A part of my duties as your lord involves me doing so, as well as ensuring you're rightly trained. You meant well, I've no doubt, but your well-intentioned decision robs me of that portion of my responsibility. If you fear I've made a misstep or cannot attend to a duty for which I am bound and promised unless the matter is delicate and time-sensitive, why would you not bring it to my attention?"

He felt his face burning. Forcing his voice to retain a calm he did not remotely feel, he made what reply he could.

"You seemed so intent. I didn't want to burden you with something I could easily suffer through."

"You made the decision to suffer in silence without coming to me." He paused, then allowed his face to soften into a warm smile. "Kozioł ... did it never occur to you I'd already made provision to ensure you were taken care of? Did you think that in my race to the War of Counties, I had forgotten you, and the pleasure of my responsibility to you?"

Kozioł bowed his head once more. "Forgive me. I thank you for the instruction," he said automatically. Realizing what he'd begun—the formal words of repentance, he placed a hasty hand on the table before Azhferd, bowing his head. "Truly, I'm sorry. I just wanted to find a useful way to contribute—to make the path broader, smoother. I'm ... I'm sorry."

Azhferd put a hand over his. "I'll make you this bargain, cousin." His voice was suddenly playful. "I shall forgive you if you will forgive me ... for not noticing the state of your old boots myself."

The men in earshot laughed at this. It wasn't uproarious, but rather good-natured mirth.

Kozioł looked up, meeting his cousin's eye, and nodded, fighting back a smile. "Souhlas, my lord."

Azhferd removed his hand and gave a *that's-settled* nod.

Hengrek adopted a broad grin, then leaned back in his chair, turning to Kozioł's father.

"Have you anything to add, my friend? Anything you wish to say or ask?"

He'd known Borys was there, of course. But he'd made such a practice of focusing on Azhferd, as was his duty as a squire, that Kozioł had done little more than bow his head and greet his lord father, thus far.

Regarding him now, the man he loved (albeit in a distant sort of way) was staring at Azhferd, then Kozioł, and finally Hengrek. His expression, as always, was unreadable, save for the fact that he was in obvious contemplation.

Finally, Borys spoke in answer. "Excellency, I would beg a boon, formally."

Hengrek nodded, eyebrows raised in mild surprise. As always, it made him look somewhat boyish. Turning to Jarek, who had stood off to one side, nearly invisible for the duration of this conversation, he spoke.

"Good my squire? Would you do me the small service of opening my court?"

Jarek grinned, then bowed his head. "Yes, Excellency." He placed the half-empty decanter of whatever it was that the count had been drinking onto a side board before stepping to the center of the pavilion.

Most people ignored Jarek's presence, right up until he opened his mouth. He'd always had a fair singing voice. He'd practiced and honed that gift for as long as Kozioł could recall. Now, he employed that skill to undeniable effect. His chin was lifted so that it angled upward. His voice rose to the high canvas roof and seemed to catch there.

"O taaaaaaaaaaaaak!" Jarek let the latter of these two notes—the higher one—vibrate long and loudly until the entire pavilion had grown otherwise silent. "This hereby opens the court of His Excellency Hengrek Czarnowieża, Count of Czarny Wodospad. Nasze cienie s ?ą"

"Długie!" came their answer.

With that, Jarek stepped back into the not-quite shadows, waiting.

"Thank you, my squire." Hengrek stood, looking around the make-shift room with a neutral expression as he moved to stand in front of the high table. "I've been asked formally for an audience." He nodded to Jarek, adding, "If you will, please?"

Once more, Jarek took center stage, so to speak. Again he made his voice carry in the fading light. "His Excellency would see before him Syr Borys, Knight of the Black Griffin!"

Kozioł saw his father stand, walk to his right all the way down the long trestle table, and far out of his way before entering the pavilion anew from its mouth. He walked up to the count, bowed with some ten feet between them, then took to one knee, head lowered.

"Rise, my friend." As Borys complied, Hengrek spoke on. "You have served the county and shown me true friendship—true kinship these many years. In all that time, you have asked for nothing in return. I look forward to at last being able to show such friendship and loyalty to you in kind."

"Thank you, Your Excellency. Your words do me great honor."

"Please, speak your piece. Ask of me anything. If it is in my power to grant and does not do harm to my people, my family, or myself, I shall see it done."

Borys bowed his head for a long moment of silence before at last responding.

"We ride to war, Excellency. We ride to battle as we have not done, nor had to do in forty years. Even then, we rode more to make our presence known than to do actual battle."

Hengrek nodded, wearing an expression of warm interest.

"Yet while our *shadows* are long..." He paused to cast about, receiving smiles and words of agreement. "So too are our *teeth*!"

All laughed in delighted surprise. Older men mocked their own age often enough. But for the ever-dour Syr Borys to have done so? Once the noise died away, he spoke again.

"While I have no doubt that you and I still have more than our share of glory yet to be won, and wisdom yet to be imparted, I would be an ill counselor were I not to advise you to think of the future—beyond the battles that lay directly before us."

Hengrek gave a solemn nod at this. "Yet, you are not such a one, to shy away from such advice."

"I am not, Excellency."

"And what, then, is your counsel for the future? What would you advise me to consider beyond the battles directly ahead of us?"

"May I speak both plain and freely, as an honest man should do?"

Kozioł stood beside Jarek, utterly caught up in the moment. His father was reckoned to be a leader of men—a term Kozioł had heard all throughout his life but had never truly understood. Borys was as tough as stone and about as prone to emotion, yet here was he speaking loudly before the assembled nobles with a charisma that seemed utterly unlike the man he'd grown up knowing.

"You have never lied to me, my friend," said Hengrek. "...Never worn a false face. Not in all these long years. I wouldn't ask you to do so now."

Borys held Hengrek's gaze for a pregnant moment, then bowed his head, smiling.

"My voice, it echoes from mountain to sea ... from cavern to sky."

Kozioł couldn't breathe. His eyes were so wide that his face was beginning to hurt.

He heard the sound of chairs and benches being dragged back along the grass and stone as men stood along either side, speaking the words that followed in grave unison.

"Steel must be tempered. A sword must be sharp. No steed sprints forever. All candles grow dark. As brief summer storms, ever-fleeting is time..."

Here all fell silent, save Borys. They held their breaths, waiting on his final words.

"Come, Azhferd, for now, you are called to the line."

The eruption of cheers and shouts was nearly a physical force. Kozioł felt his face grow wet. Was he weeping? Looking to his left, he saw that his brother made no bones about his own tears. Jarek's eyes were streaming, yet he smiled as if he, himself, had been so-honored.

Kozioł saw his lord stand, looking pale and full of barely masked disbelief. Azhferd walked around the table and turned his head to stare at first his knight, then his count.

Borys laid his hand upon Azhferd's shoulder, turning him bodily to face the count and gently forcing him down to a knee.

Hengrek's sword was in his hand. He brought it gently down on first Azhferd's right shoulder, then his left, murmuring words as he did so.

Kozioł couldn't hear what passed between them, but he saw something he doubted anyone else had. It robbed him of the sharpest edge of his joy, replacing it with fear and curiosity.

A light aura surrounded first Hengrek, then his sword, before passing at last to Azhferd. It was as if blackness had been trimmed in silver-grey. No harm seemed to come to either man, and the strange black light, as absurd as such a description was, dissipated almost as swiftly as it had arrived.

Azhferd stood, helped to his feet by his father, who embraced him with undisguised affection. He was then turned and shoved toward Borys, who stopped him.

Borys held up a hand as if reaching to touch the pavilion's high ceiling. "O taaaaaak!" he boomed.

The collective silenced itself almost at once.

Borys brought his hand back down, laying it against Azhferd's black-bearded cheek. "My nephew, I have taught you all that I can, and all that was proper to make you my equal. Now only one thing remains—a tradition held onto from the Black Aerie that once I and my order called home."

Azhferd nodded, stepping back and adopting a resting stance. His hands clasped behind his back, even as his feet spread to shoulder's width apart. The setting sun smote his eyes, brushing his face with the last light of the early winter's day as he waited for what was to come.

"May this be the last blow that you *ever* receive unanswered." With that, and no further warning, Syr Borys, Knight of the Black Griffin, delivered his former squire, his nephew, and the heir to the County Throne, a hellish right cross.

Azhferd staggered, but otherwise kept his feet, and made no sound. His eyes watered, and it was obvious that he was in pain, yet he smiled as he recovered his former stance and position, waiting.

The sounds of shock at this ancient and rarely practiced tradition— one Borys hadn't practiced upon his own son when *he'd* been called to the line days ago—were quickly replaced. Lauding affirmations. Cries of *Aye!* and *Yes!* and *Yeah!* Soon filled the air, building to a final, inarticulate crescendo of joy.

Borys nodded, and after a moment, pulled Azhferd forward into an honest embrace. A moment later and the pavilion was full of such moments as the gathered men, and not a few women and children came forward to offer their congratulations to Syr Azhferd.

-VII-

Venzene Duchy of Kovalun
County Jižní Pochod
Barony of Haluzfeld - Haluz Věže
43 Gerstesykli: 15 Days after the Red Storm at Westsong

Ten minutes after Alojz's death, Eobum and Haiga had finally been able to move again. By then, Fenglem had come up from the rear with what gear they'd scavenged from Alojz's men, several additional horses, and the sadful form of Hrothgian, now dead.

They'd cast about in relative silence for a trail to follow, but found none. It was as Adric had said to Lashjuk—as if they'd simply flown away.

Sulok had been too stunned to react to the news and had stayed in Eranoric's shadow, perhaps a touch closer to him than had become his norm.

Eobum had moved them on in the only direction that held a hope of success. Even if it failed to offer any clues, it would provide shelter before tomorrow came.

Nearly an hour later, the sun was setting. Eobum's sword was in his hand as he led them on toward what he hoped would be a final battle with Ebistian, though, in truth, he'd actually expected it to be the day's final knife wound in his weakening will.

He wasn't finished. He knew that. He would go on and do what he could to pick up Lashjuk's trail with what little information he'd heard from Alojz's last council. But oh, how he longed to find something to vent his rage upon...

They came out of the final wooded trail, at last in sight of Haluz Věže. Eobum heard gasps and moans of frustration and dismay from the others—but he'd expected this. He'd smelled fire and old smoke on the wind, though it had been distant.

The oft-vaunted and oft-mocked Twig Towers were little more than an ominous ruin on their pinnacle. The pocket forest for which the place had been so well known was now a miserable field of burned and stripped cedars—tree trunks burned black where they stood, no sign of green life anywhere.

The township, surprisingly, was almost utterly intact. Rather than an encouraging sign, it gave the place an ill feeling and a haunted look.

Lakkrid came up beside him to his left. He kept some distance between them, though not more than a few feet. Looking up first to Eobum, then to the keep, he spoke in a tone that was respectful and soft, despite the slight, scratched growl that always pervaded it.

"Do you know its name?"

Eobum nodded, gripping his sword's hilt in an effort to calm and quiet his rage. He was rewarded with a touch more control over himself.

"Aye. It's where we were headed before..." He trailed off.

Lakkrid nodded, saying nothing.

Eobum turned, calling the others with his eyes. Eranoric and Adric got them moving. Once they'd gathered round him, he spoke with as little fanfare as he could muster. He wanted his voice even, not the miserable, choked thing it so desperately wanted to be.

"I feared they'd not be waiting here for us. I hoped I was wrong, but this was what I feared. Took us here anyroad because it was our best chance at shelter before the night comes."

They either nodded or stared at him blankly—perhaps numbly.

"I heard them say they were bound for two places, back home to Edmund's encampment, or on to Rosefort, which was our next mission. Rosefort is closer, Edmund's farther by a few days. If we go back to Edmund's, we *might* save him and the rest of the encampment. If we go to Rosefort, we might save *them*, and have an army to come to Edmund's rescue with. We'll find Lashjuk and Maksu—our own, mind—at one or the other of these, and we've no way of knowing which."

"So... where do we go?" This was Eobald, who sounded uncharacteristically somber.

Eobum was glad. He didn't know if he'd have been able to keep from beating the wit out of him if he'd tried to say something smart.

"We pick a place to sleep, and we think. By morning, we'll make a decision and go. All roads seem ill just now. If it weren't so near to nightfall, we'd press on right now. No point risking a trek through the night when we don't know which way's best—most likely—to save our own."

They nodded.

"Eobum... can we... Can we hold a fire? For Hroth?"

Eobum nodded. "Aderano, we can, and we will. He deserves that from us, and more. Once we're as secure as we can be, let's set up a pyre."

They all nodded. Without another word, they made their way into the abandoned, ransacked town.

All choices are ill. All paths are misted over. It's likely I've already lost her—lost them. I should go to Edmund's side and hope for the best, surely. But what if I'm wrong? What if I make that choice and doom the countryside to fall beneath Ebistian's thumb? Lashjuk or not, surely I owe Kovalun something—owe Edmund something...

He looked to Lakkrid, then over to Sulok, now perhaps an orphan.

I owe them something, too—every effort to find Lashjuk. I owe that to her as well... perhaps even to myself.

-VIII-

The Green Lands
43 Gerstesykli: 15 Days after the Red Storm at Westsong

The air was eye-wateringly crisp. Red light hung along the trees amidst the grasses. The sky was a blinding blue, fading to purple, with glowing eyes hung behind each bank of clouds.

Lashjuk saw herself standing beneath a massive willow tree whose limbs were hung with thin tendrils of deep crimson.

"I suggest we move onto the road before they wake," she heard her body say.

She obliged, moving in the direction she saw her own hand point.

There was a muted rustling—so sibilant that it made her eyes water—somewhere behind her in the tall grasses. She resisted the urge to turn and face it, likewise the slightly weaker urge—to run from it as fast as her legs would carry her.

Once they were on the road, she looked about herself. Green lay all around her—a dream of summer, held in unchanging splendor. She turned to regard herself—her body controlled by another as-yet-unnamed entity. She found it hard to meet her own eyes. Looking down, she noted something that caused her heart to stop.

"Something troubles you, Lashjuk?" Her own voice sounded genuinely interested, if not outright concerned.

Yes, something troubled her. She had seen what she now thought might be the truth of her new companion. Lashjuk's body did not cast a shadow of its own. Instead, the immense black bulk of a serpent the size of an oak tree stretched out below her body's feet. At its head was something else entirely—a form she did not at once recognize.

"I... I see you," she said at last.

Her body blinked in confusion, then followed Lashjuk's gaze, and laughed. The laugh was honest and surprised, but not in and of itself a sinister sound.

"I hadn't thought about that," her body said at last. "Come to that, there may be another benefit to being here." She reached out a hand to where the true Lashjuk stood beside her. "Let us see..."

Lashjuk accepted the hand. Odd and unreal as it was to reach for her own body, she made contact with solid flesh, which was something. She wasn't certain if this discovery should make her feel surprise, relief, revulsion, or fear. She didn't have time to consider the matter overmuch.

"Puehv gosek oann cruzeteek gosek. Zul lev zyn diyth puehv ponfehv," she heard herself say.

A warmth passed through her. She felt herself drawn forward, led by the hands—*her* hands—leading her... it was too much. Her mind couldn't make sense of it... not in a way that didn't make her feel whatever the mental equivalent of cross-eyed was.

She felt a familiar sense—one of homecoming and relief she hadn't realized she'd needed. There was a brief light from somewhere out of direct sight—then she was in her own body once more.

Her limbs were sluggish to respond, but at least the awful under-light was no longer threatening to overpower her vision.

To her left, she could sense the presence of her shadow—the *other* that had borrowed her body. She heard rustling but saw nothing more.

"I know you're there. Come out." She was too anxious to find her son and get back to her new family to do more than acknowledge the fear that welled up inside of her. If the creature, whatever it was, had wanted her death, there were certainly easier ways to have accomplished that.

"Are you sssssscertain? You've not given me a form to wear, or be wielded azzzss..."

"Nor will I. I neither know what that means nor how I would go about doing so. Come out. Their trail gets harder to follow with each moment we delay."

"Very well..."

The green trees to her left rustled once more, then were parted as the creature came through them and onto the packed dirt road.

She gaped, then gasped, then just stared. She knew this creature, though it had been far less grand when last she'd seen it—both times she'd seen it, in fact.

It reared up, towering over her by some ten feet, and with a large portion of its black body still along the ground. Yes, it was indeed a massive serpent, as she'd thought, but now she saw the rest of it plain.

Its head was human, or nearly so. If its supple scales were black in color, then how was she to describe its face? It was shaped like one of the darker-skinned men of northern Shesh, but there was no hint of the rich mahogany color or the red or yellow undertones that were common amongst those folk. No, the face was an un-sexed black that seemed at once both shimmering and light-eating.

She had last seen the creature during her visitation with Guuvra, where it swam back into the stone upon which he toiled. Before that, however...

"How did you escape the Vodnik's fate?"

The creature looked surprised but not at all displeased. As it spoke, she found *herself* surprised that its voice was so soft—so dangerously, hypnotically soft.

"I was never his. I'd bound myself to a caster during the last Empty March. My old friend became quite powerful before the Vodnik took him—an acolyte of the..." It trailed off. "This is not the place to discuss such deep matters. When your Eobum broke my old friend's prison, his essence was able to escape at last." The serpent paused, then added, "He was finally able to move on."

She nodded her acceptance of this explanation, though to say she had understood it would be drawing it long, indeed.

"Can we follow them? Can you? For I can barely keep my eyes open."

It regarded her for a moment, then lowered its bulk so that it lay utterly along the ground. "Up-ye, Lashjuk. I will carry you while we hunt. It will be slow going until you wake, yet slow is better than no-going."

She was too tired to be afraid. She did as bidden. The creature's scales were soft and supple. She began to curl up almost instantly, but stopped herself for a moment as she spoke.

"We have to find him... please. I'll give you a name, find you a form, help you take vengeance, only help me save my Maksu."

"Peasssssce, Lashjuk. We are a breath away from bound. *I* will not play you falsssse."

With that, she knew no more. Her dreams were strange, wondrous things wherein she heard whispers of seemingly incalculable import. She knew she would remember none of the secrets they offered upon waking, but that was all right. Those voices didn't matter... not once she'd glimpsed the fire.

VOICES IN THE DARK

-I-

Venzene Duchy of Kamieńalun
County Czarny Wodospad
Village of Auburg
44 Gerstesykli: 16 Days after the Red Storm at Westsong

"I wish you were with … me." Kozioł snapped awake. At first, he had no idea where he was or why it was so damned cold. He'd been… had it been the Green Lands? It'd been stony, somehow—a place of old stone. *Or old bones? Somewhere warmer, at least.* Who'd he been talking to? His shadow? The caster who'd saved him from the hollow ones? He didn't know—couldn't recall. Wherever he'd been, he'd gotten there through dreams, not through the Weave.

He shivered, and all at once, he remembered where he was—Auburg. He lay inside a winter weight canvas tent, wrapped in furs. Azhferd had insisted they sleep thusly for the several nights prior to their departure so as to get everyone used to sleeping relatively raw.

Normally the county arrives a few days early, eats, drinks, and finds trouble to get into, Azhferd had said. *By the time the tournament actually starts, a fair few of ours have to recover their edge—their drive to fight. Camping is a thing to be avoided, other than when it's necessary. It's seen as a hardship. If we camp while we train during the days leading up to travel, the tent won't seem like such a misery. We can train longer, leave later, and not be so beaten down or idle by the time the tournament begins.*

Kozioł wasn't certain about any of that, but when the sun had been shining, he'd thought the idea held a certain romance—a sense of adventure. It was as if they were off on campaign like knights of old.

Or like my father, brothers, and uncle will soon be... are now, come to that, he thought and shuddered.

Now, at some point before dawn, he realized that he both knew a thing and had his doubts about a thing. His doubts were about the romance and sense of adventure that had carried him away when Azhferd had first laid out his plan. It was hard to think about swords, soldiers, and earning a song when your teeth were chattering at speeds a horse might envy.

As for the thing he knew, that was both simpler and more immediate. He needed to make water and knew that while he had to get up to go and see to that, it would mean facing the cold without the meager protection of the furs he was currently wrapped up in.

Well, he thought wryly, *I can brave the cold, or I can be a suffering coward until my bladder lets go. Then I'll be warm, then cold, then sick ... then roundly mocked for pissing myself.* He snorted, causing his breath to smoke. *Well, that settles that. Better to face the cold than to be mocked as a coward ... or a baby.* With that, he threw off the furs, pushed himself to his feet, staggered, and headed into the bitterest watches of the night.

As often happened, by the time he'd sorted himself and turned to make for his tent once more, he was quite a bit warmer than he had been, or at least the cold didn't seem to bother him quite so much.

He stared up at the cloudless, star-shot sky and smiled. All things concerned, he thought, things had gone not merely all right, but better than he'd imagined possible. He had a purpose, a task and responsibility to Azhferd, was discovering a talent he'd never have believed possible, thanks to Yeidil, and the capstone? Azhferd had been called to the line. He was a touch worried about being put in command of the other boys in a few days, but it would be all right... probably. Azhferd was convinced that he was ready, at least, and that was something.

Smiling, he walked back to his tent ... and found his father waiting for him inside.

"Sit," Borys said. He was careful to keep his voice low so as not to wake anyone tented nearby, but the tone didn't fail to carry with it its customary authority.

Kozioł sat. Why not? He'd expected his father would want a word before they rode out. He'd just expected it either last night or perhaps over breakfasts before the count's column headed north. Likely, Borys had seen him up and moving and thought this was as good a time as any.

The man looked at him for a long moment. It was a look Kozioł hadn't suffered under in some years, but one he recalled all too well. When you were beneath that gaze, its weight made it nearly impossible to lie or misdirect. What Kozioł had to lie about he had no idea... then suddenly he did, and his lungs were filled with ice that had nothing to do with the weather.

Borys's face twisted into perhaps the most hideous visage Kozioł had ever seen. It hurt his heart, made him want to cry ... and run. For the first time Kozioł could recall, Borys smiled.

"Zachowałbym swoje sekrety," said he. *(I would keep my secrets.)*

Kozioł blinked, confused by this seemingly obvious sentiment. Of course, he would prefer to keep his secrets. The emphasis suggested he thought Kozioł was at risk of running off to tell someone, either by accident or plan.

"There. Now nobody will hear us as we have our discussion." His voice was soft, delivered through that horrific smile. "We will begin with a simple question." He paused long enough to lock eyes with Kozioł before pressing on. "Which of them has been teaching you?"

"Father, I..."

"Listen to me very carefully, Dargory. Are you listening?" Kozioł nodded, gulping in spite of himself. Parents always held some power over their children, and it was somehow always wrapped up in the use of their full, or at least their proper names. "Do you love Hengrek?"

Kozioł was so startled by this question, he answered without thinking. "Yes. Of course I do."

Borys dipped his chin, then looked up once more. "Do you love your knight?"

Again, Kozioł answered without hesitation. "Yes, Father. Of course I do. Hells, why would you ask such—"

"One of them is working actively to erode your uncle's defenses, Dargory. I've suspected it for some months now, but had no proof. Now I find you learning our ways—our duty and our burden, and in *secret*, no less." Borys's smile died as he uttered that solitary word—secret. "I have my suspicions, but I require confirmation. You will now provide it to me. Now whom, Dargory? Whom is it that has been training you in secret!?"

Kozioł jumped, looking about him as his father's voice thundered. All pretense of secrecy had, at some point, ceased to matter to his fa—But no... no, surely not. Even the crickets still sang.

"You've silenced us?"

Borys nodded, expressions of mingled rage and pride warring in his eyes.

"For how long?"

"Long enough, boy. Now *answer* me."

"She has the same fear—that if we don't do this and keep it secret, she'll lose him utterly..."

Borys drew in a sharp breath through his nose, straightening as if slapped. "Whom?" He drew the word out long and low, making it a predator's growl. "Which one, Dargory? Yeidil or Calpernia?"

Kozioł felt hot tears overspill his eyes and run down his cheeks. His mouth worked as he fought the forces trying to pull him apart... his father on one side, Yeidil on the other, and Azhferd in the middle.

-II-

Venzene Duchy of Kovalun
County Jižní Pochod
Barony of Haluzfeld - Haluz Věže
44 Gerstesykli: 16 Days after the Red Storm at Westsong

The night had grown cold enough to grow claws, though Eobum didn't really mind. He stared at the pyre, watching it writhe and dance over the now unrecognizable form of Hrothgian. The others were, hopefully, curled up within the empty tavern they'd occupied.

He turned his back on the fire and walked a few steps away around the building's side. Looking up, his eyes sought the jewel-bright orange of Sensenglanz—the star at the curved tip of Gerstesykli's chief constellation, the Falx. This time of year, it hung long in the sky, not fading fully from view until the sun was well and truly awake. He drew a mental line between Sensenglanz and the sickle moon, gauging the hour as he'd been taught. *Nearly three—nearly time.*

Walking back to his former perch, he cast about. He was still alone.

He'd drew breath to call Haiga. The agreed-upon call this evening was one of his favorites, the Zimowy Sokół. His brothers and even his son were far better at duplicating its haunting cry as Hrothgian had taught them, but he thought he could manage a passable rendition. Before he'd had the chance to prove that dubious assessment, Haiga appeared at his shoulder.

Eobum gave him as warm a grin as he could muster, given the cold of both the air and his mood. "Was there enough?"

Haiga nodded, though he wore a reluctant expression as he handed over the small glass vial. "Bruu, Ng... erld bruu?" *(Yes, Brother... are you sure?)*

Eobum nodded, snatching the vial more quickly than the question warranted. "Bruu, Haiga. Ed bruu. Ed hrek zak vrekwrin ragshrash gar." *(Yes, Haiga. I'm certain. I will speak with him before he runs home.)*

Eobum knew what was bothering his youngest brother. There had only been enough for one draught, and by rights, it should have gone to Aderano as Hrothgian's closest kin or kith. Aderano, however, had made his mind all too clear on the matter, even through his misery.

Nye, Eobum. I want to. Hells haul me home if I don't, but magic—even old magic... too much o'Venzene's rubbed off on me, sadly—too much fear o'what'd come of it. I'm afraid... afraid I'd go with him...

Movement brought Eobum back to the matter at hand.

Haiga had bowed his head in a gesture of acceptance. "Ed ragbruu de lo ragord erld." *(I will make sure no trouble stalks you.)*

Eobum nodded, looked once more at the pyre, then unstoppered the bottle and drained its meager contents in a single pull. He tried and failed not to pull a face. The flavor... well, calling it a flavor would have been awfully kind. It was like biting into a rotten lemon. Once Haiga had boiled the substance down, then treated it to remove the scent that drew the creatures toward the drinker—something about the sweat it forced the body to produce, he supposed—what was left was anything but sweet.

He ran the back of his hand along his mouth, wiping away the spittle that had been summoned by the vile stuff. His hand came away purple.

He strode to a nearby stone, slightly out of the way of any who opted to pass toward the jakes while he was otherwise occupied. Once there, he arranged his cloak so that it draped around both he and the stone he now sat upon. He thought about pulling up his hood but reminded himself that doing so would only make him more difficult to spot, which would make the whole exercise moot.

Settling in as best he could, he once more commenced staring at the fire—at Hrothgian. He allowed his vision to widen, forced his eyes to drink in the entirety of what lay before him, not merely the spot his gaze happened to fall upon. He felt his body slacken, muscles unknotting, eyes beginning to sting from his refusal to blink.

Slowly, he began to hear noises that did not precisely belong. It wasn't that they were alien things that *couldn't* belong to this pastoral scene, but rather that they seemed source-less. A growling hound sounded at once mere feet away from him, and as if it were expressing its displeasure in a cave or a well. A big-chested horse trumpeted its fear or anger from just beyond the pyre, though again, as if it were held in a stone chamber that Eobum was yet to see or mark.

While he did his best to lose track of time—such direct concentrations were reputed to slow the process rather than speed it up, much like watching any other pot boil, he supposed—he guessed some ten minutes or so had passed this way. The sourceless sounds grew louder, closer, as if they were slowly coming toward the entrances to their invisible caves and stone structures.

A short time later—he refused to guess how long—he saw the first flicker of movement to his right toward the foothills south of town. He resisted the urge, strong though it was, to turn his head in that direction. Haiga was near, he reminded himself, and would keep watch over the area. What he was seeing couldn't harm him ... unless he allowed it to.

As he continued staring at—nearly through—the funeral blaze, trying hard not to blink any more than he absolutely had to, the movement to his right grew closer. He saw a shadowed thing walking through the scant winterberry bushes and scrub pines. When, a moment later, he heard footsteps crunching on the cold grass and rocky scree; he knew it was time.

"Eodenth filth," came a voice. "That they managed to end even *one* of you for what you've done here is sweeter by far just now than any wine that ever was." The voice grew closer, stopping a few scant yards to Eobum— and the pyre's—right. "Never fear, beautiful butcher... I'll stay right here until you wake and enter into this grey place. Sweet savage... I shall design such brave punishments for you—ahhh..."

At first, Eobum feared the voice was speaking to him directly. He was, after all, Eodenth, just as nearly all of his folk were. As the newcomer ended his rant, a thing happened that clarified the situation: a screaming, howling sound that could only have come from a human throat. It grew louder, closer, finally localizing itself on the burning place where Hrothgian's far-too-young corpse was being immolated.

As he watched, it was as if Hrothgian rolled off the platform, hitting the ground on his hands and knees, flesh smoking but otherwise unharmed. His red hair reflected the firelight, almost as if his mane, itself, were still ablaze.

The man to Eobum's right—definitely a man, now, despite its higher tone—spoke up afresh. "Ahhh, here at last. I would have waited longer if I had to, but no matter. It is my decided pleasure to welcome you to the Grey Between. I fear you'll not see whatever your ilk account as hereafter." He paused as Hrothgian tried to regain some sense of his new surroundings. Full of a strangely dark courtesy, the man spoke on. "I shall give you a moment to find your feet before we begin."

Eobum knew that voice. He was certain of it. He rummaged around in the back, sides, and front of his mind but came up with little more than certain familiarity. No matter. He, too, needed Hrothgian to gather himself before he spoke. If he didn't wait, there was a chance the youth would attach himself to Eobum, rather than going on to whatever came next.

Hrothgian shook for a moment longer, then lifted his head, casting about himself as he tried to gain his bearings.

"Where am... Where's Ader?"

"Gone, I've no doubt. Perhaps you owe them for burning you before they left."

"Gone?"

"All of your filthy friends have gone, now, boy." The man sighed theatrically. "They came through whatever bark-boiling sorcery your kinsmen used, sacrificed everyone they could find to their patrons, and moved on to find some other unsuspecting sows ripe for the slaughter."

"I don't..." Hrothgian stood up at last. He started to turn but stopped as he saw... "Eobum! Hells be hid. I was starting to worry! Where are the rest?" Then, as an afterthought, "Who're we burning?"

"He cannot hear you, pup. The fire is yours." The man's voice was almost cheerful as he delivered this pronouncement.

Hrothgian turned to the man, drawing his sword. "I've had more'n enough a'your prattle. Still and silent, else I'll still n'silence'ee."

The man—still mostly in shadow—drew his own sword, laughing. "Oh, yessss. Do, please. Still and silence me, Eodenth filth... horse humper and tree tamer fall too short of the truth, ay? Child-eater, flesh-feaster, death-waker, blood-drinker..."

Hrothgian moved toward him, drawing his sword up and back over his bright shoulder.

As he advanced, Eobum saw the hallmarks of Aderano's training, which in turn bore the hallmarks of Eranoric's. Hrothgian's body language suggested he was full of simple, thoughtless anger. He was selling the fact that his sword was going to either come down in a hammer or lash out in a flat snap. Eobum knew better. Hrothgian's dim-arm bent in as if he would bring both hands to bear...

Suddenly his dim-arm flew out in the arc of a flat snap, but without a sword in its hand. As his foe reacted, leaning back at the waist and bringing his sword to bear in advance of a block he would never need, Hrothgian's true attack began. He fired, bringing his sword down just above the man's knee on his lead leg. The stroke connected and sliced straight through the exposed ... flesh? Could it still rightly be called flesh?

Hroth's foe fell to the ground with a howl of pain that quickly devolved into outright and uproarious laughter.

Stepping back, Hroth froze. His sword moved into a wary guard position across his own body.

Eobum, too, was initially baffled. When, a moment later, the man stood up whole again, laughing still, Eobum thought he understood. As the laughter died, and the man spoke anew, his understanding was proven true.

Hrothgian started to speak, "... How?" He had no further words.

"We shall have such magnificent battles, you and I, my dear demon." He allowed his voice to return to its earlier calm, though with a touch of not-quite friendliness for good measure. "We're dead, you and I. While the world burns around us, we will have time to spar and sprint, trap and torture one another, until we grow tired or the night finally, truly falls over Skolf at last." He allowed his voice to grow soft, almost conciliatory. "None of the living will hear you, boy. Unless you lose yourself to the rage of your ending—becoming a haunt—nobody will hear your laughter ever again, save you and I. We have, I fear, all the time left in the world. We have ... time to kill."

Hrothgian bowed his head, though Eobum was pleased to see he didn't lower his sword.

A light came into being. Like the sounds of earlier, it was source-less but undeniable. Eobum found he could finally see the man facing Hroth. He'd been right. He did know that voice, albeit not well. It was finally time, it seemed. The world of the dead had, at last, become sure, steady, and, most importantly—close.

"You're half right, Excellency. You're both dead, but there are ways—old ways—to say farewell."

Hrothgian spun, utterly forgoing any defense, springing toward Eobum. "You see me! You hear me!"

Eobum nodded, still seated on his stone. "I do. I'm sorry I failed you, Hroth." Hrothgian was mere feet away now, opening his arms to embrace the man he'd called commander. "Stop." Eobum kept his voice flat. "Seeing and hearing's all we can do. If you touch me, it may shake me out of my state. Given the hour, I doubt I'd have time to come back to you tonight, and a good deal can happen to the dead or the living by day."

Hrothgian froze, face falling almost comically. "So it's true? Ader? Alusc, Eranoric? Hells be hid, Eobum, the *boys* were with us! Lakkrid! Sulok!"

"... Are all alive and as well as may be, given your loss."

Hrothgian looked surprised but clearly relieved.

"Turn, now, and look upon your sparring partner." As Hrothgian obliged, Eobum continued. "May I present His Excellency, Baron Vagiaedelt, upon whose lands we now stand."

He saw Hrothgian's body tense, uncertain as to whether he should bow or grow angrier.

Vagiaedelt, on the other hand, merely snorted. "You know the name of the man who you and your fellows were sent to bring low. Is that supposed to—"

"I'd heard you'd grown softer in these last few years," Eobum cut in. "I hadn't thought that extended to your mind as well."

Aedelt blinked, then glared. "How dare you?"

"...Speak the truth of what I see? I've done it most of my life, Excellency. No reason to stop now." He paused, letting the silence deepen before speaking further.

Aedelt looked impassively on, keeping his face a mask.

Eobum released a soft sigh. "We must be nearly at the bell's tolling by now, surely. Look again on my face—on his." He gestured to Hrothgian. "Or have you grown so old you've forgotten how to tell friend from foe? Aye, fine. Your secret sorcery only served your body, not your spirit. Fine, but I and mine did not attack you. Edmund sent us to find you and deliver you a message that... that wouldn't have mattered, in the end. It was based on untruth, and now..." He shook his head, cutting himself off. What more was there to say?

"Eobum... Eobum... *yes*—yes, I *do* recall you." Aedelt snorted, "How could I not after Černé oči? You were lucky Edmund walked in when he did."

Eobum gave a nod. "Gone days, Excellency. Gone days." He turned back to Hrothgian. "I came looking for you, not the baron. I owe you and mean to see that debt paid."

Hrothgian blinked, looking back to his commander. "You owe me nothing, Eobum. You pulled me from the block and gave me—"

"Your ending on the road because I trusted Alojz."

Hrothgian nodded slowly, then moved to sit down a few feet from Eobum's stone seat. "What do I do now? Wait, how in all the Hells... How are you hearing me? How are we speaking?"

Eobum grinned. "There are old rites. Not magic. Not really, at least. You know there are mushrooms, plants, and certain venoms that can make you sick, kill you, or give you vivid dreams."

"Aye." Hrothgian grinned. "Shrooms, spiders, n'serpents, n'no mistake."

Eobum nodded and fought to hold back his grief. This could all be over with a shout of alarm or a sudden storm. He needed to move things along. The problem was, he didn't want to. He didn't want to end their council because it would mean never hearing the voice of one of his own again.

"Well," said he. "There are those that make you dream, even while you're awake. Some that make you feel as if you were drunk or sleep-walking. If you take them in small, pure amounts and at the right hour... at the soul's midnight, when the world grows thin, for instance, well, here we are."

"More and more, I find myself pleased that I let you live, Eobum." Aedelt walked over, grinning sourly. "You're not dazed. You'll recall nearly all of this meeting, won't you?" As Eobum nodded, Aedelt wore a look of triumph, sitting down beside Hrothgian. "Tell me what happened—tell me Edmund's message and why it proved useless. Perhaps I can still put my mind to some wider use before Havoc's Horn knells the true end."

Eobum arched his brows, leaning slowly forward. "I can do that. Hroth, you should hear it, anyway. You should know how this all happened—how and for what you ... died."

Hrothgian winced but nodded. "One last story, then?"

Eobum grinned, if only to stop himself from weeping. "Aye. One last story pays for all." With that, he voyaged on the tale.

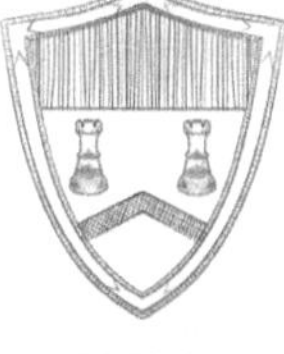

-III-

Venzene Duchy of Kamieńalun
County Czarny Wodospad
Village of Auburg
44 Gerstesykli: 16 Days after the Red Storm at Westsong

"Dargory..." Borys's sigh of disappointed frustration was difficult to listen to. "I cannot force you to tell me... not without actually harming you."

Kozioł tried and failed to hide his relief at this. Borys didn't threaten ... ever. If he laid out a consequence, it was a consequence he not only could but would carry out should you not go his way on a topic.

Borys glowered, which was almost worse than a beating. "Damnit boy..." He sighed this rather than speaking or shouting it. After a moment, he seemed to brighten.

That was another look Kozioł knew well. It was Borys's. *I've thought of a way around this problem* look. He knew he wasn't stupid—knew he wasn't a fool. He also knew that his father towered over him in more ways than one... cunning, for a start. He did his best to become... what, wary-*er*?

"Whichever kinswoman has been filling your head with ancient truths, I presume they've guided you toward making a choice about your path forward, yes?" He paused, then amended, "Miecz lub Tarcza?"

Kozioł didn't think there was much point in denying that. "Aye, sword or shield... Miecz lub Tarcza Clariona."

Borys's nod was perfunctory. "Good enough. Pokaż mi wszystko." *(Show me everything.)*

Kozioł sighed, almost... *happily*. He hadn't meant to, but the blatant way his father was using his magic was both a relief and a source of encouragement. It proved that, if he lived through this encounter, there were times it was permissible—hells, even preferable to use magic openly.

Borys made a soft sound of surprise. "Yet she hasn't forced you to mold your shadow, yet. How badly was it damaged?"

"Not badly." Again, he saw no point in trying to deceive his father outright. Best to answer swiftly and hold on to hope that the honesty would end the interview sooner, not later. "A few miserable wounds, but nothing he couldn't recover from."

"Very well. Have you been given an ultimatum?"

"No, sir."

"Has she explained the duties of each, in turn?"

Kozioł paused, not out of an effort to stall or deny Borys, but rather to try to collect his terrified memories before they ran and hid from him. "Only in brief. It seemed very straightforward. Swords attack, shields defend."

Borys allowed his face to darken for a moment, then shook his head. "Foolish girl, whichever one it was."

"Is... Is that not right?"

"If you take the path of the shield, you will effectively be his armor—a living funnel for his illness, his aches and pains, even his madness. The Weave will be sent after him over and over, as it already has been far too often. It will be largely down to you to detect, deflect, or absorb these threats before they can do any lasting harm. Then there are the physical threats—other knights, ambitious men and women, all who wish to array themselves against him because of who he is, rather than what he is or could become."

Kozioł tried not to gape. This was, without question, a plainer explanation than Yeidil had ever given him regarding magic and his fledgling role in it.

"And the sword?"

"If you become the shield, it will be down to you to be—to become his protector. If you elect the path of the sword, your road will be much darker. You will have to prepare yourself to be and to become his assassin."

Kozioł was on his feet, fists clenched. "You mean to kill Uncle Hengrek!? No! I won't let you! I won't ... continue shouting like a fool, and I've only just realized what you meant." Kozioł sat down rather meekly. "Forgive me, Father."

For his part, Borys seemed content to watch Kozioł play out his little comedy in bemused silence. When they were once more seated across from one another, he spoke up. "Sword, then. I confess to being both surprised and gratified to have witnessed proof of your temperament one way or the other."

"Wouldn't it... I mean, I only meant to def—"

"Defend your Uncle? Hardly. You meant to kill or eliminate the threat to him, not stand there to weather or deflect its damage. You were pro-active, not reactive."

"But I was reacting to what I," he shrugged, blushing as he finished, "thought was a threat..."

Borys laughed. The sound was actually quite warm. "I shall try to explain in simpler terms. The shield is, for example, like unto the count's sergeants. The sword is like unto his knights. The shield stays close and keeps watchful eye and ear out for trouble in all things and at all times. The sword either goes or is sent out into the world to find and encounter, then eliminate threats before they're close enough to require the shield. He or she will fail, eventually. Make no mistake. No defense, no attack is flawless. Someone will get by the sword—will manage to flank him or draw him out. A sword can be used to parry and defend. Of course, it can. It is, however, a tool meant to kill, first and foremost. Do you see?"

Kozioł sat back, trying to absorb the lesson. "I... I think I understand." He lifted his chin, considering. "A sword looks for a target. A shield looks to intercept—seeks to *become* a target in order to save the person he serves."

Borys gave him a look of burning triumph and pride that was so sudden—so alien to the otherwise familiar face that Kozioł fell back from him. This was met with soft laughter. "It's rare enough to see the truth of someone, Dargory, let alone someone you thought you understood." He bowed his head. "I thank you for the instruction. May I learn this lesson well, and may it save me from the Torn Hour when all else has failed, and fear is given form before me."

Kozioł took a moment to pick his jaw up off of his lap. "That was how you knew," he said. "My slip up when speaking to Azhferd."

Borys smirked. "I shouldn't let it worry you. Only one of us would recognize it. It hardly paints *I am a student of the weave* on your forehead."

Kozioł hunched his shoulders, grinning. "I suppose not. Father?"

"Hmm?"

"Why are you telling me all of this?"

"A fair question. Two reasons. My goal isn't to force you to talk. It's forcing you to act—or not to act—as the case may be, in service to the traitor's designs. Truth, as I suspect Azhferd has taught you..."

"... Is the bonfire that drives away all shadow."

Borys made a gesture of agreement. "The second reason is more directly personal. I was unable to save your brothers—save their shadows, that is. Now they both face the world untethered to the weave—unlike you and I. I thought your shadow—your *cień* was as near as no matter to theirs... that it was so wounded as to be denied to you. Finding out that you, at least, have managed to connect with it and begin to walk this road, after all, is a great gift. I would not have you waste that gift ... manipulated by others." He paused, offering a thin smile as he finished. "Not even by your father."

Kozioł closed his eyes, drinking in the man's words. He found he believed him. He recognized that he may be acting naïve, but for now, at least, he believed him.

Opening his eyes once more, he spoke in a soft voice. "Are you tired, Father?"

"Not tremendously so. Why do you ask?"

"Nor am I. I... I was hoping you could tell me more? I know nothing of where it all began, nothing of *the Torn Hour*, nothing of why we—our family is bound up in it."

Borys sat back, considering, then made a *so be it* gesture. "If you like..."

They talked until dawn. It'd been the longest conversation Kozioł could ever recall having had with his father. Borys never again tried to learn who had been instructing him, and Kozioł had never offered it up.

When Borys rode away shortly after breakfast, Kozioł found himself wishing they'd talked sooner. Borys had always been distant. Kozioł had missed having *a* father. He had never really missed *his* father... until now.

-IV-

Venzene Duchy of Kovalun
County Jižní Pochod
Barony of Haluzfeld - Haluz Věže
44 Gerstesykli: 16 Days after the Red Storm at Westsong

Eobum bowed his head, staring at a point between himself and his ghostly audience. Haiga had come close enough to listen, but no closer for fear, Eobum had no doubt, of jarring him from his half-dreaming state.

"You've come far in the, what, decade since Černé oči?" Aedelt sounded genuinely impressed and not altogether pleased at the idea. "Have you left anything out? Any detail might be important, mind you... no matter how insignificant."

Eobum remained silent for a long time, replaying the events on the stage of his mind. At length, he shook his head. "Near as I can tell, Excellency, that's everything."

Hrothgian spoke up for the first time since Eobum had begun his tale. "One thing might or might not matter." He waited long enough to be sure both Aedelt and Eobum were looking at him before saying his piece. "Alojz's men—them that came on me? No noise."

"No footfalls, unsheathed weapons... nothing?" Aedelt looked dubious.

"Nye-nye. No noise from *them*. No words, nye grunts 'r battle cries. They ain't moved like 'ey were trail-crafty 'r cut-purses 'r the like, mind you."

"But no sound of speech. From any of them?"

Hrothgian shook his head.

Aedelt appeared to put that bit of information by stacking it with whatever else he kept in the storehouse of his mind. He looked as if to confirm there wasn't more to say. When Hroth gave his customary one-shouldered shrug, Aedelt nodded and picked up the thread he'd dropped earlier.

"Let us begin with Edmund. If he'd been correct, his plan was a sound enough one. He leapt, however, to a conclusion that we know now was utterly false. The army burning the northeast of Kovalun is not Harn's clever ploy to gain Eoalun."

"Eoden," Hrothgian murmured.

"Hrothgian, is it?" When Hroth nodded, Aedelt went on. "Do try and focus. You and I are dead. Your commander may or may not have much more time with us. If it makes you happy, we two can spar later to determine what name we call your homeland, but for now, hells be hid, fo-cus!"

Hrothgian actually winced, nodding. "Aye, fine."

Aedelt didn't bother acknowledging the response, taking his own advice, and focusing on the matter at hand. "I'd have been more than a trifle impressed had Harn thought of such a ploy, and I must confess, I'm proud of Edmund for coming up with it. You were correct, as Alojz himself proved out. Edmund clearly had no idea where the young Lord had gotten himself to."

Eobum smirked at the idea of Alojz being called young. At thirty-five, Eobum only had the man by a few years.

Aedelt continued. "You were clever to catch him out with his secret society, as well. After we met, you and I, as the last of the rebellion was put down, I was asked to join nearly every such society in Venzene... all the ones that mattered, at any rate. I was, after all, the *architect of Edmund's victories.*" He took no pains to hide his derision at the idea. "They're all steeped in ritual and excess, each more depraved than the last, but they all refer to Emperor Daggryspyd as just that—Emperor. He's called *Keiser*, not Konge."

Eobum lifted his chin, looking thoughtful. "They're looking to supplant him—to pluck or drive the Emperor of Ashes off his throne."

"The *Emperor* of *Ashes*... I like that." Aedelt sounded all but taken with that particular turn of phrase.

Eobum ignored this. "Do you know his servant? His..." He gave a dark chuckle to help the next word along, mainly so he wouldn't choke on it. "*Father*? This ... Shepherd?"

"Ohhhh, yes. Ebistian Konecléta." Aedelt sighed, full of false good humor. "I'd not heard him called Shepherd before, mind you, but he and his works are known to me." As he continued, his voice was full of dark amusement. "A keen eye may have noted that Alojz never had a page or squire of his own... only armsmen, yes?"

Eobum made a gesture of agreement. He'd noticed but not made special note of that fact. Given the number of children in the encampment, he'd simply presumed Alojz hadn't needed a page of his own and hadn't concerned himself with allies outside of Edmund.

Aedelt spoke on. "Ebistian helped to... ahem, *educate* Baron Zikmund. He'd done so from the baron's boyhood until his death. He'd been a fixture of their household for as long as anyone living can recall."

"You don't know him personally, then."

"By rumor and reputation, though, that was enough for my tastes. His proclivities, for want of a better word, have always been questionable, to say the least. All the more so because he's never been seen or reported on, even by the usual rumor mungers, mind you, attending any of the innumerable brothels that would sate his apparent appetites."

Eobum grimaced. "I'd say that fact stands *against* those rumors, normally. Having seen and heard the man, however..."

"It would be a pleasant fiction, would it not? If such things were rumor and rumor alone? Not so, sadly. Ebistian simply prefers his boys to be not only young but of station, or of use to propel his larger plans, whatever they may be."

Hrothgian made no effort to disguise his rage. A brief, blue glow played about him behind his brown eyes, beneath his skin, shimmering along his hair.

Aedelt noticed it and turned to face him fully. "That path leads you away from yourself, boy. Such anger will make you a haunt—a figure of terror who forgets who he is, swallowed by his bitterness..." His voice was both matter-of-fact and oddly gentle.

Hrothgian calmed himself, though it clearly took an effort. When he'd done so, Aedelt spoke again.

"What is it that caused that reaction? You needn't say, but I must ask, for it may or may not be of import."

"You, *Excellency*!"

"What *about* me?"

"You *blithely* go 'long talkin' 'bout how a man like that 'as 'is way with boys—children, mind—as if it 'ere *just* a-nother nobleman's right! You talk of brothels that serve up children like any other meat or wine a' table— as if it's all just... norrrrmal!" He was on his feet now, fists clenched, head looking almost literally on fire with that moon-kissed blue light. "Aye and aye and aye and this monster who looks like a man shoulda just gone to such and sucha place and paid coin to be with a child, oh but it's no worry—just a laugh and lark to know he's toy-en with Baron How-d'ya-do's boys. Now we've somet' to talk 'n mock about! Oh, aye! It's fine! It's *fine*!"

"Idor Adys!" Eobum barked.

Hrothgian's chest hitched. He seemed frozen to the spot.

"I-dor Ad-issss!" Eobum said again.

Hrothgian bowed his head, started to turn away from them both, then seemed to force himself to look back at Eobum. "Aye... Idor Adys, Eobum. I'm with you, still." His voice was low and winded, as if he'd run a footrace. The glow left him, but slowly. When it had gone, Aedelt spoke in a voice that strove to maintain its center.

"I know. Believe me when I tell you, I know."

Hroth looked down at him, eyes wide, then returned to his former seat. He looked back at the baron several more times, then asked the obvious question.

"You as well?"

Aedelt nodded.

"When?"

"I was nine... He was the captain of my father's guard. When my father was slain, and I assumed his lands and authority, the captain became a great many firsts for me—my first tormentor, first fear. A year later, he became my first judgement as a member of the gentry, first order of execution I ever brought to bear."

Hrothgian tried not to gape.

For his part, Eobum didn't trust himself to move or speak. He felt he was intruding on something private but hadn't been given leave to depart or look away.

"The captain was many firsts, as I say, but only one *last*."

After a protracted silence, Hrothgian, apparently, found he couldn't leave the matter there. "What... what d'you mean?"

As he spoke in answer, Aedelt's face bore a smile of such naked satisfaction that it was almost monstrous—the Sheshik cat that ate the songbird. "I killed him. I carried out his execution personally—had my men hold him as I drove first my fists, then iron spikes into him. I made him beg for his life, then beg for death. I left him to hang like a scarecrow from a tree in the garden until he finally slipped sideways and left his body behind."

Hrothgian looked at Aedelt with a mixture of awe and fear.

"He was all of those firsts for me. He was also the last man to make me feel afraid—the last person to make me feel helpless and insignificant. Do you see?"

Hroth did his best not to stare. "Aye," said he. "Well, that's something." It was an empty response—a thing to say while his mind tried to process the scope of it all.

"As for Ebistian Konecléta, scholar-priest of the line of Černooký, well... at court, when things were dull enough to turn to such matters, he was always presumed to be focused on the ambitions of his lord's household. It would seem he had grander and altogether darker ambitions after all."

Eobum allowed the silence to stretch on for as long as he could out of both respect and hope... respect for the men before him and their shared horror, and hope that in the silence Vagiaedelt would prove every inch the strategist he was reputed to be. When he could wait no longer, he, at last, broke the silence.

"This Ebistian has my... well, he has one of mine. Leave it at that. His mother's gone after him, and the lot of them have vanished like an honest man's gold at winter's last market."

"... And you heard their plans to send their forces to both Edmund's encampment, looking to enlist or enslave the good count, and Rosefort in an attempt to do the same to the Kengar lands and their baroness."

Eobum made a "there you have it" gesture.

"Now you want me to tell you where to go. You'll like the answer about as little as I'll enjoy giving it; yet it's the only choice, really."

Eobum waited.

"You make for Rosefort."

Hrothgian spoke up. "What? Why? Edmund—I..." He corrected himself. "Count Edmund needs warning! We still 'ave *folk* there! You'd 'ave us leave 'em be'ind? Leave 'em to rot!?"

Aedelt looked up, tilting his head back to do so. At first, it looked as if he were rolling his eyes in an exaggerated fashion. A moment later, the truth became clear. He was gazing up at the star-shot sky, thinking.

"Aye? Well?"

"Peace... let the man think and answer," said Eobum.

Hrothgian subsided, waiting.

"Hedvika Kengar is your best hope to save Edmund." He snorted as he continued. "I'd say it's your best hope to save the Empire as a whole, but I doubt that would sway you into action. The life of... what was it? The *Emperor of Ashes?*... isn't much of a motivating force for you and those you lead, I presume."

"It is *not*, Excellency." Eobum allowed a dour little grin to play across his face.

Aedelt moved on without comment. "The baroness rules Rosefort in a way that makes her quite unpopular among the nobility. I know Ogden Percoy had hoped to tame her once they married, but I believe he alone thought it an actual possibility. Her place is prosperous because she has made it a priority to spend more on her domain than on her own luxury. She would sooner see her gowns and coach repaired than replaced. What's more, she refused new lands when offered them by His Grace, Harn. She knew she couldn't manage them in the same way she's managed Rosefort."

Hrothgian whistled in surprise. "A rare bloom, that one."

Aedelt nodded, still looking up at the stars. "Her own are loyal to her, as you might imagine. Their force is modest but well-trained."

"How do we know Ebistian will go to Rosefort himself?"

"It doesn't matter."

Eobum warred against the reaction that swelled up in his chest. It most certainly did matter. Lashjuk and Maksu were at the mercy of that monster. Kastan and Edmund would be at the mercy of either that same monster or his minions. Of course it mattered!

"You cannot hope to make it to Edmund in time to warn him. You'd be like a child running ahead of its father as he walks toward the front door—the first to announce that he's arrived. The fort isn't defensible enough against the army Ebistian now commands, in any case—not if it's aligned with the one who broke us here."

"But if we make it to Rosefort, there are stone walls to defend from." Eobum tried to hide his frustration.

"There are, and when you've won through, you'll have an army that will march and gather others as it goes."

"It's an easy thing for you t'say, Excellency. You've no kin there, no—"

"My *son* is there, Hrothgian." Aedelt's voice was full of sudden frost.

"Your—" Hrothgian made a sigh of understanding. "Forgot that brat was yours... begging your pardon."

Aedelt laughed. The sound was honest and full of rue. "He's an ass, but he's my son. If pressed, he'll usually find a clever way around an obstacle. He simply lacks the discipline to take the way before him when that turns out to be what's called for. He'd rather spend three days on working out a way around a project that would have taken him one day to overcome."

"He's not there, Excellency. He left for the War of Counties a few days after we left to come find you."

Aedelt breathed a sigh of relief. "Thank you for that. My advice is unchanged, but thank you for it. News won't save Edmund. An army will. They have numbers and sorcery on their side. Edmund will need—you will need—to counter at least one of those if you hope to win through."

Eobum bowed his head. "I hate the answer, but it's wise counsel. Thank you, Excellency."

After a few more moments of silent consideration, Aedelt nodded and stood. "Commander, I wish you fortune in battle and long, peaceful days at its end." Vagiaedelt bowed formally. "Hrothgian? I shall await you in the next clearing to the south. We've things to discuss that the living needn't trouble themselves with."

Hrothgian gave a nod of thanks. "Fair. Aye. I'll be along."

Eobum felt the sleep trying to overtake him. He fought against it and won, for now. It wouldn't be long, he knew.

"Vagiaedelt?" Eobum caught the man's eye as he moved off, stopping him briefly. "You've served Edmund loyally to the last. For that, and for the good turn you did for I and mine all those years ago... I thank you."

Aedelt smiled, wind blowing through his hair, moving the blond waves to cover his face. "Save who you can, Eobum. I'm glad Edmund stopped me before I had time to kill you. The world is better for it." With that, he walked into the forest and out of Eobum's sight.

"Eobum," Hrothgian began, "I know what you mean to say. You didn't flip a coin or draw a straw. You made a choice over what you heard, saw, and knew. 'S hardly the same thing as being at fault, is it." This wasn't a question, based on his tone.

Eobum made a gesture of acceptance.

"Will you do a thing f' me?"

Looking up, he searched for Hrothgian's brown dreamer's lamps. "Ask."

"Look after Ader. See he goes on, yeah?"

Eobum smiled. "No need to ask me to do *that*, Hroth."

"Aye, like as not, but still... tell him he's not to name his first after me. If he has a second, aye and fine, but not 'is first."

"I can do that." Eobum nodded.

"One more 'fore one or both of us goes."

"Aye, go on."

"A proper message for him?"

Eobum waited.

"Tell Aderano... say to him this. Tu edh tibum—Tu nekt gaeldh ti. Ge ek, ge tivani... en ge oferwlencaþ." *(You are my brother—I can never repay you. Be clever—be your own guardian... be wealthy.)* He grinned at this last, standing up and walking toward Eobum even as he began to first fade, then grow alarmingly solid. "I know it was you who paid for my release. Ader never would've had the coin fer it."

"I..." Eobum's heart was racing. Hrothgian was so very real, suddenly. Eobum swore if he reached out, he could almost touch him. He knew *he* wasn't dead—his heart was not just beating, but thundering.

"Best I be gone. For my life—literally my life, Eobum—for the family I found, or that found me ... thank you." With that, Hrothgian embraced the still seated Eobum.

His hands, his arms were like ice, but Eobum wouldn't have traded it for the wide world. He stood, holding tight to the man—to the first of his to fall, and wept.

The next he knew, the sun was shining on his face. He'd been sleeping with his back to the stone, his body wrapped in his winter cloak. His body would be screaming at him when he moved, but so be it. There was work to be done.

THE PRICE OF AUTHORITY

-I-

County Thorion
The Greenswell
3 Korunasykli: 20 Days after the Red Storm at Westsong

Vilmocz sat on the wagon's peak seat. He'd spent the entire morning staring forward over one horse's ass and thinking about another—the one riding on his right: Sergeant Terrek.

While the Sergeant was older than he by at least two or three years, Vilmocz was fairly certain the man hadn't yet seen thirty harvests. Still, the way he carried himself in both demeanor and physical presence made his true age difficult to pin down.

Then there was Huron, riding to wagon's left. He might barely have seen twenty years on Skolf, and that was being generous. In the right light, his dark flesh tended to match the baked leather color of the armor all three men wore. He was slight of frame, gifted with an unimpressive physique despite the hard labor his kind most often performed in Thorion County.

Vilmocz was fairly certain Huron was a bastard. Either that or his parents were slaves. The hair of the folk from the great desert beyond the last grass was normally an inky black, if the merchants and slave goods he'd seen were any indication. This slender sandblood wore blond on both chin and crown.

I can't figure it. What in hells can Terrek be thinking? He's made Sir Kaith look as if he has no notion of the difference between proper and peculiar! Vilmocz's thoughts spun out in a glower that was nearly palpable, though nobody seemed to notice his dark mood, let alone pay it any mind.

Here we are an hour, perhaps only minutes from journey's end. We may even be able to see Wick when we crest this Hill, and then the outriders or sentries will be able to see us. I should be riding on the left flank, Terrek on the right, and our new lord at the head of our party. His armsmen should be mounted and riding in the van! This is a hireling man's duty! If there are none to be had, or if a lord commands it, it's the sand blood who should be seated on the cart, surely! It's the natural way of things...

The air in the dell was thick and heavy. All around them, there were pockets of fog—their edges like ribbons of dust in the wake of running horses, or flat grey fingers alternately warding off or beckoning on. The general drear made their creaking, crawling upward progress seem endless. In an uncountable sea of similar slopes, this particular hill wasn't incredibly steep. It was, however, wider at the base, adding to the sense of torpor as their horses hauled them to its top.

The narrow, open-backed wagon creaked and swayed. Its freight of goods—several long poles wrapped in tightly furled canvas, various boxes and packs, and a few small casks of both water and wine—were tied down tightly both to the bed of the wagon and to one another making veritably no noise despite the unevenness of the terrain.

Some twenty strides ahead of him, Sir Kaith crested the hill and briefly disappeared.

"Pick up the pace, lads," Terrek said. His voice was as mild as milk, but there was still that ephemeral something that made his commands difficult to ignore, even when they were couched as suggestions or requests.

Vilmocz snapped the leads and clucked side mouth, urging the horse on. Once more, he felt the flash of annoyance at having to do such a menial task, but there was nothing for it, and he'd never shirked a duty in his life. He wasn't about to start now. It would've only made him look petty, and on some level, he knew it.

Still, s'not right—I mean, all right, he spoke up for me to Sir Kaith, and that led to the job, but hells be hid, does that mean he has to lord it over me every time he opens 'is damned mouth?

"Eyes right, Vilmocz," Terrek said. As soon as Vilmocz had acknowledged the order, Terrek, too, sped up and crested the hill, disappearing into the omnipresent fog.

Out of the corner of his left eye, Vilmocz noted Huron falling back, slowing his pace. The annoyance must've shown on his face, for before Vilmocz could open his mouth to utter a word of protest, the sandblood spoke.

"I'll see more trouble coming if you're out in front of me." His voice was both smooth and melodious, even with such simple words to commend to it. "If I can see *anything* coming in this murk."

Vilmocz nodded, grunting his acceptance of these simple truths. The sandblood was right, of course. When there was only one guard, that one guard needed a better view of potential threats. At first, he doubted he would've thought to do it. Almost immediately, he dismissed that conclusion as a product of his overall frustration mixed with the general gloom. He didn't want to admit that Huron had the right of it and was competent. Therefore, he didn't. It was only common sense, he told himself—or perhaps something that the sergeant had recently imparted to the sandblood, possibly over breakfast. It certainly wasn't a matter of overall competence.

Vilmocz was spared continued flailing, buffeted by the whirlwind of his thoughts—which on some level he knew were excuses—when he heard voices up ahead. Through the pockets of mist, and beneath the leaden-grey sky, the direction and distance seemed impossible to fathom.

"...And I have my orders, right and proper. You're welcome to attempt to challenge them, but I don't think you'll much like the result."

The speaker had a harsh, grating voice with mildly exaggerated sibilants making S sounds stray toward SHs. Vilmocz knew the tone instantly. An orc. No doubt part of a raiding party. Bandits, or perhaps something worse. In an instant, he made up his mind, slowed the horse hauling his cart the final yards up the hill, and turned to look over his shoulder, waving his left hand exaggeratedly to gain the sandblood's attention.

Once he'd gotten it, he held up his hand, palm out to instruct the youth to stop. When Huron nodded and did as bidden, Vilmocz sent his dim arm on a wide arc out toward the left, then brought his index and middle finger to his mouth and made as if to whistle. When he'd finished, he raised both of his eyebrows in an expression that asked a simple question, *"Do you understand?"*

Huron cocked his head to the left as if trying to replay the last moments over in his mind, then nodded. He held up one finger briefly, put it down again, then put it to his lips in a shushing motion, raising his own brows in that same question.

Vilmocz nodded, repeating the shushing gesture. As the younger man rode quietly off toward the left of the hill, Vilmocz hoped that all would be well, but time would tell. As his horse had already begun to level off at the hill's top, Vilmocz had no more time to contemplate.

The thin layer of pines and oaks marched northward, fanning out for perhaps a hundred yards. In the distance, he thought he could see a tall structure too wide to be a tree, but the mist made discerning detail impossible. Eminently closer, though almost equally difficult to see with any sort of clarity, five figures sat astride horses facing one another in a rough ring.

Not much of a raiding party, then. Three that we can see, although given the mist...

"I'd watch my tone, were I you." Terrek's voice, and while it was as calm as ever, there was an undercurrent of something that made Vilmocz think the man was about to spring into action, though something held him back.

"Well, you're *not* me. If you were, you be fighting not to roll your eyes at that comment. You don't have what's required to attack me, and we both know it." This was the orc again. He sat slightly in the lead of his two fellows, though they were close at hand.

"And what makes you say that?" Terrek's voice was icy, somehow.

"Because you aren't a dullard or a fool," the orc said. "And your pride isn't such a frail thing that your first thought is to smash whatever offends it." Here, the orc paused for a moment and seemed to sit back in his saddle. "Or have I read you wrong, Sergeant?"

Vilmocz continued riding forward at a slow, steady pace, as if he weren't aware of what was going on in front of him. It wouldn't be long before he was in range. He flexed the fingers of his left hand, preparing to call the sandblood once he knew how many more were waiting in the mist.

"So, you've come to make your demands of me at sword point, as it were, is that right?" Sir Kaith sounded amused.

"Aye, Sir Kaith, and with a sword forged by the countess herself. As I say, you're welcome to challenge them or me..." The orc looked back first over his left then right shoulder, indicating his fellows.

"I'd say that's enough out of you, *tusk*." Vilmocz nearly spat this last word, pulling back on the leads, planting his feet on the footboards before rising to them, and drawing his short sword. "Were I you, I'd take what rabble I had with me and hie f'the hills afore the men of Thorion County water the grass with yer blood." The horse came to a stop, the wagon rolling an extra inch or two as he concluded what, to him, was the sort of speech that made brave men wither and slink away. He was, therefore, utterly flummoxed when his words were met with harsh barks of laughter from the orc.

"Were you me, you would currently be doing everything in your power not to wet yourself from laughter."

Vilmocz blushed, glared, cast about, and saw no movement anywhere around them, nor did he hear any other sources of laughter. Surely that meant no other foes were lurking, cloaked by the mist. So be it. He would show this would-be bandit, or raider, or whatever he was. He drew the first two fingers of his left hand to the corners of his mouth and blew a piercing, ear-shattering whistle. His horse jigged and reared in its traces, whickering in surprise. He managed to keep his balance, loosening the leather strap he held to lessen the horse's need to bolt.

All heads turned. Every eye was on him, which was exactly what he wanted. They didn't see the sandblood racing toward them from off to Vilmocz's left.

Thundering up the hill and through the mist like an outrider from the Coach Devour, Huron charged toward the would-be raiders with a short sword held high and his shield held tightly against his chest.

As Vilmocz felt a smile etch its way across his face, he saw everything unfolding. The raider to the orc's right, nearest to the onrushing charge of Huron, didn't seem to even notice what was about to befall him. This fatal lack of alarm would, Vilmocz had no doubt, mean the man's death.

The orc's reflexes were better. Rather than reaching for a weapon, he snatched up his reins and tried to get his horse to walk backward. The horse didn't appear to be having any of that, however. Instead, it reared high, pawing at the sky and stomping the ground as if it'd seen a snake. To his credit, the orc didn't fall from the saddle, but he was certainly in no position to defend himself.

I have you! I have you! Filthy, ambushing, cozening thing. Not so full of bluster once your head's separated from your neck, I'll wager! Vilmocz's thoughts were a study in triumphant glee. He was utterly bewildered when his own lord spurred his horse forward and brought his shield up to catch the hammer shot Huron threw toward the orc's exposed neck, stopping it just before it would have connected.

"Stand down! Now!" Terrek's voice was a whipcrack.

Huron tried to pull the muscles of his arm at the last moment, even as Sir Kaith's shield was moving to intercept the blow. He turned his mount in time to avoid ramming it into his once-target, or his lord's own horse, slowing and circling back around to face Sir Kaith. Huron's face was obscured by the general gloom, but Vilmocz was certain the youth wore the same confused look he, himself, did.

"Your plan?" Kaith addressed Huron.

Vilmocz was certain the young man would take credit, and perhaps that was all right. Apparently, though it had been executed perfectly, the plan had been a mistake for some damned reason.

"No-my-lord," said Huron, the words strung together luxuriantly, as if gliding down the gentle slope of a rolling hill. "Though, gladly, I will take the blame if I erred."

"Better an aggressive mistake than meekly accepting trouble at sword point." Kaith shook his head. "Your angle of attack was perfect, and," he looked back over his right shoulder at Vilmocz, "the plan was sound. It was also unnecessary, but you haven't traveled with me enough to have even the faintest idea where to draw the line between trust and expectation. Unnecessary, as I say, but well done for all of that."

Vilmocz was beside himself. Absolutely none of this made sense, and he couldn't work out whether he was being praised or disciplined. Moreover, he had no idea why the attack had been called off.

Sir Kaith looked at his sergeant, then at the orc.

Terrek nodded in silent acknowledgement, then turned to address his men, fixing them each with his dead-eyed gaze before speaking.

"This is Olshnak, Sir Kaith's new herald and aid, along with his personal guard." Terrek didn't seem overly pleased, nor was he speaking through gritted teeth. Instead, he wore a thin smile that offered no real glimpse at whatever he was truly feeling. "... By order of Her Excellency, Countess Ylspeth herself."

"Hells, I'm so sorry!" Huron said. As he spoke, he sheathed the short sword and made a gesture of contrition, hand on heart, head bowed first to their lord and then to Olshnak.

"*Sooo* am I," Olshnak said. "A herald, I am not—but as I said, I have my orders right and proper."

Vilmocz still couldn't see the orc's face, but as the creature turned his head, there was the briefest suggestion of his porcine nose and the modest lower tusks jutting from behind his lower lip.

"Form up, then," Kaith spoke with an easy tone of acceptance as he gestured beyond their meeting place. "Wick can't be too far now."

Without so much as a word, Olshnak and his two silent guards fell into step at the back of the line, and they pressed on. Half a bell later, and they were riding through Wick's southern gate.

-II-

Venzene Duchy of Kamieńalun
County Czarny Wodospad
Village of Auburg
3 Korunasykli 20 Days after the Red Storm at Westsong

Kozioł stood as still as he could. It wasn't difficult, for once. Normally, he'd be a ball of nervous energy, knowing he would soon be sparring. This morning, however, his greedy mind's eye was, for the umpteenth time since it'd happened, trying to replay his unexpected lesson with his father. He'd found it impossible to view the world in quite the same fashion, especially when faced with Azhferd or anything he was discussing or planning.

Azhferd, for his part, was currently sat on a strongbox at the foot of his own bed. He was making adjustments to Kozioł's armor, making certain it wasn't pinching or floating as he moved the boy's arms and legs this way and that.

"Are you ready?" Azhferd finally asked. His voice refocused Kozioł's attention.

"I... I *think* so?" His *own* voice—still maddeningly unbroken, much to his frustration—seemed to cast the auditory equivalent of torchlight on his every emotion.

Azhferd's laughter came out easy and soft. He was clearly laughing with, not at, Kozioł's uncertain honesty.

"I'm pleased to hear you're so full of con-fid-ence." He reached over and shook Kozioł by the shoulders with gruff good humor.

The act forced him to smile in spite of himself. He'd never understood why or how, but Azhferd had always managed to jolly him out of whatever ill mood he was in. It was why, partially, at any rate, he'd leapt at the idea of becoming his squire.

He still hadn't told Yeidil about his chat with Borys on the morning they rode north, let alone Azhferd. He'd no idea how he was meant to keep such weighty secrets from either of them for long.

Azhferd spoke again, this time in a more serious and sincere tone. "Kozioł, you know more than any three of them put together. They've trained for single combat. There's no denying that. So have you, if memory serves... or was that some other blond boy I was training?"

Kozioł snorted lightly, then grinned.

"Right then. You do recall *something* of how to fight. You aren't going to simply walk out there and die from a stray *glare*? Excellent." Now Kozioł actually laughed, though Azhferd didn't wait for the sound to die down before getting to his point. "They know a bit about how to fight. Their training in *melee*, on the other hand, has been..." He trailed off, meeting Kozioł's eyes and holding them.

"*Pieśń chłopska*," Kozioł's voice came out soft, as if he spoke in his sleep. The old tongue always had that effect on him. He felt, somehow, as if things were both more grounded in reality and full of an almost religious weight when they were conveyed in that ancient wind. Now, of course, he knew the truth. He'd been closer to the mark than he'd ever dreamed.

"That's right, *mały kuzyn* (little cousin)—*pieśń chłopska* a peasant song. Sweet and honest, and usually overlooked... taken for granted. But we know better, don't we?"

Kozioł's smile was now accompanied by the creeping pink stain of embarrassed delight as he heard the old endearment.

He felt Azhferd's hand slide through his blond mop a single time, letting his other hand fall from Kozioł's shoulder.

"Our shadows are..."

"Long." Kozioł's reply was automatic, holding no fire in it.

Azhferd arched his black brows and quirked a bearded smile. "What? I didn't quite hear that..."

"Long."

"Lawned?"

"Long!" Kozioł's grin was enormous, blue-black eyes dancing now.

The man stood, repeating the mantra, the boy of thirteen answering it in ever-increasing fervor.

"Our shadows are—"

"Long!"

"Our shadows are—"

"Long!"

"Our shadows are—"

"Long!"

Another voice—this one deeper and full of gravel—joined Kozioł's after they'd reached the door that led to the upstairs hall.

He didn't recognize the voice's owner, but he threw open the door just the same, still shouting the answering call.

A man stood a few feet away in a black kontusz, his wooden buttons polished to a dull sheen. His black hair and beard were barely tamed things banded together by careless leather thongs.

The chanting stopped as the men saw one another, Kozioł, between.

"My lord," the newcomer began. His voice was all formal neutrality.

Azhferd shook his head. He strode forward, passing Kozioł, and punched the newcomer squarely in the center of his forehead. The blow was so swift and unexpected that Kozioł literally hadn't seen the movement until his cousin's arm had dropped back down to his side. As for the man who'd been struck, he simply stood there and accepted the blow, staggering back and nearly falling to the ground from its force.

"I did warn you about that," said Azhferd. His voice was cold, but Kozioł sensed something else hid just beneath that chilly tone.

"You..." The black-coated man caught his breath and balance once more before continuing, "You did, but that was years ago... the oath of a boy, not a grown man." He snorted, rubbing his forehead where a goose egg had begun to rise. "Wasn't sure you'd remember, let alone still hold to it." He paused, righting himself fully. "Beyond that, I wasn't sure that you'd learned how to throw a punch worth blocking."

Kozioł stepped back, watching the pair with wary wonder. *What is this?*

"I told you then, and I tell you now. Call me that again, Geri—lower yourself in my presence like that again and so help me..."

"Peace, Azhferd, peace. Your mother won't approve, but I didn't see the county coach outside. You win. Ash it is. The rest be damned between us, outside of more courtly climes. As you say." He chuckled as he rubbed his forehead again. "Your uncle taught you how to throw a hellish right cross."

"*Our* uncle," said he. "*Ours.*" Azhferd would not be shaken, it seemed. "And nobody's called me Ash since I was Kozioł's age." He gestured to the boy with his left hand.

"Good Lord—Kozioł?" He turned his attention to face him. "Yes, of *course* it is! I've not seen you since you were too small to be allowed near the horses—they were all afraid you'd get stepped on!" He laughed delightedly, taking a knee as he stepped toward the boy, the hem of his black kontusz rustling. "You don't have *any* idea who I am, do you." A statement, not a question.

Kozioł knew full-well who the man was, now. He simply didn't know his intent. With a minimal effort born of years of practice under Azhferd's patient hand, Kozioł made his face a mask of even neutrality as he spoke his answer.

"You're Geroslaw, the count's bastard," his voice was plain and free of judgement, neither accusatory nor offensive. "My father thinks highly of you. I was with him when he discovered your name had been added to the Bluemark Guard's ranks."

Both men looked at him, quirking their brows in an unintentional mirroring that made questions of their shared parentage unnecessary.

Kozioł fought hard to stave off the weight of their combined stare. "He keeps watch over any and all mercenary bands that set foot in the county."

"You." Geroslaw paused to shake his head as he looked between his half-brother and his young cousin. "You're Syr Borys's son. No question about that, boy."

Kozioł grinned, flushing with pride for a moment before forcing his face back into a more flat, normal countenance. Until recently, he hadn't thought of himself as even remotely like his father... how things had changed.

Geroslaw looked the boy up, then down—obviously reassessing his worth, then turned to Azhferd.

"Still at it, I see."

"Always." Azhferd allowed a small smile to play across his face.

With a snort, Geroslaw turned back to Kozioł, reaching a hand out to knock on the boy's left leg. His knuckles made a dull *thunking* sound as they came into contact with the armor secreted beneath the boy's trousers, covering his thigh.

Kozioł bore this patiently. The movement was slow and deliberate enough to keep his internal alarm-bells from ringing.

"Hidden cuisses?" Geroslaw grinned as he spoke. "That's a bit arcane, isn't it?"

"No, not so much as you might think," said Azhferd. "He's training the other boys today. Best they not be intimidated or distracted by his armor... seeing him wade into combat with nothing more than a helm and gorget for obvious protection..."

Geroslaw was nodding. "It'll inspire them or intimidate them until they figure it out. Even then, it might distract them—play tricks on their undermind."

"Fighting ... is a dance." Azhferd smirked as he began the proverb—one of Uncle Borys's.

Geroslaw smiled, joining his voice to Azhferd's. "What you wear to that dance goes far to make an impression on friend and foe alike." Here Geri made a gesture that Azhferd should continue.

"You can curry awe, respect..." He gestured to Geroslaw to take up the tale.

"... Fear, or friendship. You may wear your wealth or sell yourself cheaply."

"Your appearance," they said together, "will always direct how others think of you... just another lance in the rack, boy." Both men laughed as their recitation ended.

Kozioł merely stared at them, each in turn. He couldn't recall seeing Azhferd this at ease with anyone, save perhaps Yeidil. He seemed unguarded and... well, Kamień jest szary—*happy*.

As their mirth died, Azhferd turned to Kozioł and met his eyes. "Go—no need to keep them waiting. Remember, focus on Syr Ullan's boys. They've had at least some proper training, and they're quick of both mind and body."

Kozioł nodded solemnly. "Work with those who need it ... send those who catch on first to aid the slowcoaches who seem most hopeless." He repeated Azhferd's earlier admonishments as if he were delivering a message of great import, which he supposed he was.

Azhferd offered a grin and a nod at this. "Just so. You're walking uphill, right?"

"Yes, sir." With a brief glance back toward Geroslaw, he moved quickly down the hall, down the stairs, and out the front door with a mixture of excitement and intimidated anticipation dogging his every step.

-III-

Azhferd grinned and put an arm around the older man, turning to guide him in the direction Kozioł had gone. "Surely, you aren't here just to see if I'd remember to punch you and to mock me for old times, though."

"I'm not." Geroslaw managed a smirk. He allowed himself to be led but kept their pace slow and deliberate. "I came to... Ash, I need..."

Whatever it was, it was obvious that he couldn't bring himself to say it or ask for it. Azhferd stopped him short and turned him, hand still on his shoulder as they faced one another.

"Geri, you're my brother. Your troubles are my troubles. You *know* that. If it isn't within my power now, then we wait. When I'm recognized as Count of Czarny Wodospad—you'll be knighted as a banner with land and title of your own. Have I ever wavered on that?"

"Czarny Wodospad." Geroslaw's laughter was warm incredulity. "Nobody calls it that anymore, Ash. It's Blackfalls, all over Venzene. Hells, they don't even call your family Czarnowieża anymore. It's Black Tower, outside of the Duchy, at least."

"The Old Tongue isn't forgotten, Geri—not here."

"I know." His face and voice softened. "I know. Azhferd, I'm just trying to make my own way. If you follow through with that—with making me a banner knight—you risk being seen as soft, either because you've warmed to a bastard your father denied or because you feared making him an enemy."

"*Our* father, Geri. *Ours.* You let me sort out the politics. It's my worry. I trust you as I always have. You won't bring us low. Neither you nor I would ever let that happen."

He saw Geroslaw's face fall, clearly touched. He bowed his head for a moment, but looked back up to meet Azhferd's eye as he began to explain his need at last.

"I've joined the Bluemark to make a name for myself. If I can do that, I can gain the gold and the glory to earn or outright purchase land and title. If I do that, you won't have to stain your reputation or the house's just to keep your word."

"Geri..."

"No, Ash, listen to me. There's war—and not merely the skirmishes of greedy barons and counts—in the North. Eastern Kovalun's in flames. The Eodenth have organized into a horde and are burning, raping, or reaving whatever they run across. It's the single best time to be a mercenary. I may even be able to take and keep a fastness for myself, and that only expands the family's power when I swear my banner to you down the hourglass."

Azhferd kept his face unreadable as he listened, nodded slowly, then asked the obvious question.

"What do you need from *me*?"

"Gold, if I'm honest. Gold to buy better gear of war, and to throw around to keep the soldiers currently under my personal command—and those I recruit—happy and loyal."

"How much?"

Geroslaw's face fell once more. He was struggling not to choke on the answer to this seemingly simple question.

Azhferd fought back the urge to drag it out of him. His brother needed to ask for what he wanted if he were ever to be a leader at *any* level, let alone a ruler. He tried as firm a push as he dared. "Geri ... ask. If I can, I will. Your plan is sound."

Clearly encouraged by the warmth in his little brother's voice, he finally answered. "Four-hundred vévodové."

Azhferd paused and let his eyes half-close. "Four... four-hundred gold vévodové." That was the combined income of two small thorpes over the course of a year—was, in fact, enough to stand *up* a thorpe, knightly manor and all, with coin to spare. "I'll have to win the purse at Zlaté Pole. Can it wait that long?"

"The festival at Zlaté Pole..." Geroslaw sounded distant suddenly.

"A fortnight," said he. "We ride out two mornings hence. I'm to have the command."

"Father isn't going?" Geroslaw trailed off, his eyes finally landing on the thin white belt of leather that hung around Azhferd's waist—the most obvious trapping of a Knight of the Venzene Empire.

His eyes went as wide as banquet platters. He grabbed Azhferd by both shoulders and shook him. "They called you to the line! Ha!! They called you to the liiiiiine!" He pulled Azhferd in for a tight embrace, laughing delightedly.

Azhferd returned it, laughing in spite of himself. He'd expected his brother to be pleased, but this reaction was a good deal more than genuine warmth. Geroslaw was so obviously proud of and happy for him that Azhferd found he was slightly ashamed. He'd not realized the depth of Geroslaw's feelings—of his love and respect.

After a moment, he gently but firmly pushed the man out to arm's length, giving his shoulders an affectionate squeeze. "Aye, done only a few days ago before father rode off with the old Griffin to war."

Geroslaw's face darkened. "I thought *you* were to have the command for the War of—"

"Kovalun isn't the only place that burns, Geri. The Eodenth have begun to take settlements here as well."

Geroslaw's face grew pale. "Then I'm needed here. The gold is needed here. Ash, never *mind* my childish plans, I—"

Azhferd cut him off with a look. When he spoke, he made a point of enunciating each word clearly, taking care to keep his tone neutral. "Your plan is a good one. I want you to follow through with it. You'll do more good for the family by earning gold and glory abroad. An old friend and ally—Count Edmund of—"

"Hartscross, aye. The Bluemark is contracted to fight on his behalf."

Azhferd nodded, showing neither his annoyance at being interrupted nor his delight at knowing Geri was already tied and bound up with Edmund.

"Go, guard, fight, earn glory. Edmund is a good man. Helping his cause helps our own. Never doubt that."

Geroslaw considered.

"I'm actually guarding his banner for the War of Counties."

So *that* was what Geroslaw hadn't told him yet. "Fair enough. Will you be on the field that day?"

"Maybe? My men are set to guard him and were *originally* meant to fight beneath his banner, but he's recently... *hired on* new men of his own to fight for him. I may be fortunate enough to fight in a tournament or two myself, but I doubt I'll be able to even do that much."

Azhferd considered. "You're content to wait for the gold? Until the War of Counties ends, and its purse is awarded?"

Geroslaw nodded, offering an artless grin of his own. "I can wait that long for the balance. I'd like to begin to outfit myself whilst I'm there if I can..."

Azhferd made a sign of acceptance. "I can give you a hundred today. I simply don't have the rest if I mean to fulfill my promises to my fellows and take the field with them."

"No, that's fine... are you certain you can—"

"Nobody's certain of victory, Geri."

"But if you see victory?"

"The purse is at least six hundred and is rumored to be nearly a thousand this year. I'll give a share to the men, obviously, but yes. If we win the day, my share will more than suffice for our plans. If not, I can look to sell some of my personal effects once we return."

Geroslaw's eyes were shining. He nodded, tried to speak, found he couldn't, and instead embraced his younger brother once more.

After a moment, Azhferd extricated himself, albeit gently. "Let's go see how Kozioł's getting on."

Grinning, Geroslaw nodded and turned toward the stairs. Arm in arm, they moved toward the door and out into the training yard.

-IV-

County Thorion
Wick
3 Korunasykli: 20 Days after the Red Storm at Westsong

Kaith's party processed beneath the gate, beyond the wooden city walls, and along the main thoroughfare. The collective music of their hooves and wagon wheels clattering across the cobbles intermingled with the sounds of men, women, and children bustling about their customary mid-day madness—the sole purview of prosperous places.

Wick... it was said that there was more wealth concentrated in this village-sized settlement than any three townships in the county combined. Aside from cobbled streets, the buildings were nearly all stone—from their foundations to their flattened, shorn river stone roof shingles. The streets were evenly laid out and well ordered, wide enough for two carts to ride abreast with room to walk between them. There was even a sewer system that rivaled the one in Thorionden.

There were very few landowners in Wick. Nearly all arable land was owned by the ruling household. While it had modest tracts of rye, root vegetables, and berries of nearly every color, its chiefest claim to fame was its vast acreage of cotton.

It had long been rumored of every hand that touched the lord's fields, from the simplest laborer to the most educated overseer... supposedly, all folk of Wick, regardless of their class or social standing, consistently received greater pay and security than nearly any other person anywhere else in Thorion County.

Sir Reginald, rest him, had been a generous man, although he certainly wasn't so generous that he didn't turn a tidy profit year after year.

Though there were occasionally persons of shortsighted greed who would attempt to cut costs by shorting the pay of those beneath them, that sort of thing was quickly rooted out, its perpetrators imprisoned, banished, or executed, and the balance restored. Lord Reginald spent the twenty-five years since ascending to the seat of his father, ensuring a level of pride and loyalty from nearly all of the people over whom he ruled.

The sun had finally ripped through the clouds with enough force to call their shadows. Kaith could see those of his party stretching out in front of him. He saw Huron's head-turning this way, and that heard his occasional gasps of impressed surprise and came to the realization that at this moment, Huron was more or less all eyes.

The youth—Kaith now thought of him that way, although not quite three years separated them—had been in Thorionden for most of his life. Wick wasn't impressive by comparison, but the fact that it could be compared to the capital on many levels was reason enough to justify Huron's delighted surprise. Beyond the weathered wooden walls surrounding it, Wick was such a bastion of modernity and wealth, artifice, and achievement that it stood in stark contrast to nearly every other settlement in the County. Even Westsong, with its moat and irrigation system, couldn't hold a—

Candle? Really? Was I about to say it couldn't hold a candle to Wick, just as I pass under the—well... not shadow at this hour. The gaze then? Aye, that'll do... the gaze of the braided tower? Really? Kaith chuckled at himself under his breath. Almost immediately, that chuckle turned into an internal war to keep the sobbing, wailing grief at bay. He won the contest, but it was a near thing.

Terrek seemed to sense something, despite his position behind Kaith and to his right. His shadow stiffened slightly before pointing up and ahead of them.

"...And that, lads," Terrek sounded as if he were picking up the thread of a conversation recently put by, "is the Braided Tower."

Kaith took the opportunity to reign in his mind before his grief could grow fangs. Inwardly, he thanked Terrek for the distraction and reminded himself to make note of those small acts of kindness. It showed the man's character as well as his perceptiveness—two things that should not, he knew, be undervalued in an armsman.

The streets narrowed as they progressed northward toward the residence. The Braided Tower stood atop a modestly steep hill; its structure stretched perhaps five stories in height, with a footprint about the size of the capital's throne room. It was, for all intents and purposes, like any other stone outpost throughout the county, with one exception: its exterior had been masterfully designed with colored stone depicting a knotwork pattern from door to parapet. It looked, from a distance and if the mind were allowed its artistic license, like an enormous candlewick.

Vilmocz laughed with obvious derision.

"Don't care for candles, Vilmocz?" Terrek's voice. It was mild, as ever, though Kaith thought he detected more than a hint of reproach.

"Just thinkin' 'bout how the wealthy tend to build with an eye to the look of a place ... and not the defense of it."

"Some—hells, probably most," Olshnak said. "But not those who built *this* place."

Vilmocz laughed with obvious derision. "Once they get inside the walls, it's over. Raiders would have their runna the place. Not much anyone could do 'bout it. Short order, they'd be able to surround and take that pretty little tower." He spoke with the certainty that only a veteran of many battles could justify. Based on that assessment, however, urban warfare didn't seem to be a specialty of his.

Olshnak snorted. He took no pains to hide it.

"Something amuses you, *tusk*?"

"Aye, your clear skill and knowledge of what happens when stone clashes with sword and shield."

Vilmocz seemed unsure as to whether that were an honest compliment or an insult. Clarity wasn't long in coming.

"D'you know what a *Bor knok* is, boy? Sometimes called an Arabor?" Rather than condescending, Olshnak sounded patient.

Instead of answering the question, Kaith noted, Vilmocz decided to deflect with questions of his own.

"You speak Traeadish? That's Traeadish, ain't it? You one of *them*, are you?"

"I do. It is. I'm not. Now, as to answering *my* question?"

Vilmocz said nothing.

Olshnak sighed, then pressed on.

"A *Koleno Země*?"

"What?"

"Koal-len-no zem-nya," Olshnak said, enunciating each syllable with exaggerated emphasis. "It's the original Kovalunth."

Kaith's brows shot up, and while nobody could see them—he was in the front of the column after all—he could tell by his shadow that Sergeant Terrek was just as surprised by the exchange, and the orc's shift in demeanor, as he'd been.

"Catch!" a high, unbroken voice trilled.

The laughter of children followed close behind this gleeful command. There were perhaps four of them in a yard, two houses down a side street to the party's left. No doubt they were playing with a leather ball or some other such implement of the idle, but Kaith didn't see, hear, or think about any of that. His mind was once again back in Westsong, hearing Lanian.

Catch me!

The leather of the reins creaked in his right fist, digging into his palm. Misery and rage mixed with feelings of failure and grief, trying to force their way to the forefront of his mind. All the while, Lanian's voice kept rolling around in the back of his head. It was as if the boy's ghost were trying to hold him down beneath the surface of a seemingly bottomless lake. Even now, he could almost see it, almost feel the water, the lack of footing beneath... Lanian, all the while, clinging to him, laughing, pulling him down to where there were no fires, no fighting, no—

After a protracted silence, Sergeant Terrek spoke up in a steady, clear voice in answer to the original question. "*Bor knok.*" He rolled the R and drew the O sound so that it rhymed with boat, "is *the crown of the hill* in Traeadish." He paused only for a moment to flick his eyes back toward the cart, then looked back ahead and continued. "When speaking of fortifications, well, look ahead. A fortification on a tall jut of land, like a hill or pinnacle, often with walls of stone or wood—and usually a ditch—surrounding it."

Kaith forced his mind to grab onto Terrek's voice, pulling himself back, *willing* his hands not to shake, his chest not to heave. His efforts were rewarded with the relaxation of his right fist and the slow, steady reclamation of his self-possession. The further he'd gone from home—the closer he'd gotten to Robis's home—the harder he'd had to work to keep his traitor mind in check.

"Almost, Sergeant, almost," Olshnak said. He seemed pleased rather than condescending, offering the correction for the sole purpose of education, as opposed to ego.

Kaith's self-control returned just in time to prevent lasting, irreversible damage within his fledgling retinue.

"*Tusk*, if you don't mind your tongue when addressing—" Vilmocz's threat was cut off abruptly as Terrek called a sudden halt.

Kaith had reigned up, stopping his horse's progress and turning his disappointed gaze toward Terrek. He could see immediately that the Sergeant looked, for perhaps the first time any of them had seen, shamefaced.

Terrek, it's been what? Three days since we spoke about Vilmocz. Did you think I wasn't serious? Did you think it only applied to him addressing Huron? He choked down a long-suffering sigh as it tried to escape his lungs. *Terrek's older than I. He won't see past the sense that I've belittled him. A sigh will lead him to think I see him like a troublesome child.*

"My lord, forgive me. The fault is mine. I'll see to it straight away. You needn't trouble yourself." Kaith's disappointment and anger were somewhat muted by the grief this place had revisited upon him. "No, Sergeant." He did his best to keep his voice neutral and detached. "I think it's time I make some things clear."

"I..." Terrek bowed his head in contrition, no longer meeting Kaith's eyes, "Yes, my lord."

Kaith dismounted and walked back toward the wagon.

"Down," said he, as he met Vilmocz's eyes.

Vilmocz did as he was bidden, but did so with a countenance that was anything but resolute. Rage, confusion, embarrassment, and fear all warred within him, turning his face into a patchwork of blush and pallor. When he spoke, too, that patchwork was evident. His voice was jagged— as if he were close to tears, although whether those tears were a reaction born of indignance or self-preservation was unclear.

"My lord, please..." he began. "I've been silent for too long. Everyone seems to've gone mad. Everyone seems to've forgotten their place in the world, and that'll reflect poorly upon you and the countess herself!" Rather than becoming louder, his voice became more plaintive.

Be the bridge. Greggor's—now Sir Greggor's—voice swam up from the back of Kaith's mind. He was pleased to hear it—pleased he could *still* hear it, and that it came to him in as timely and useful a moment as ever. Moreover, he was pleased to hear any voices in his head beyond those of the dead. He seized on Greggor's lessons as a drowning man seizes the line thrown from the shore.

Everything has to be in service to my ultimate goal. Each step I take, each decision I make has to be a means to that end. So what's my ultimate goal?

He considered that for a moment. It was an important question.

In the short-term, I have to deliver the grim news, offer comfort if and where I can, assess and shore up resources, supply chains, and defenses. The long-term goal—I suppose that would make it the ultimate one—is to unify and prepare for what's to come. I need to do what I can to patch the divisions, bring everyone on side, and have them ready when Marcza calls on them— which is to say when the countess calls on them.

All right, fair enough, but recognizing that was only half of it. The other half was, predictably, communicating it to the men who followed him. Had he done that? Clearly not, given this latest outburst.

I've explained it to the Sergeant, but Terrek hasn't managed to pass it along with enough clarity. He did try, I know, but he apparently wasn't clear enough for Vilmocz to understand the why of it, which means I wasn't clear enough with Terrek. All right, that's something that can be remedied.

"Kneel," said Kaith. He made his voice flat—neither harsh nor cruel. His tone wasn't so much commanding as it was a stone wall—implacable and useless to argue against. It was a trick he'd picked up watching Sir Valad.

Vilmocz spread his feet shoulder-width apart, then dropped to a knee in the position that spoke most clearly of fealty.

"Meet my eyes." Once Vilmocz had obliged, Kaith's voice softened to something slightly more conversational. "I recognize that as you see it, you are," he paused, considering, "defending my name, reputation, and station. I believe you when you say that's your motivation. What this comes down to, Vilmocz, is this: I wasn't clear enough when I explained things to the Sergeant, which didn't arm him to be clear enough to *you.*"

He could almost feel Terrek's eyes on him. As for the others, they were impossible to miss. Huron was trying to look around, up, anywhere but at Kaith and the reprimand going on in the middle of the street.

Olshnak, on the other hand, stared with frank interest, though his expression was difficult to read.

"Your actions, your words, the way you carry and comport yourself actually hinders the mission that I've been given." Kaith paused to allow that to sink in and to let Vilmocz speak. Just before he concluded that the older man wasn't going to, Vilmocz, at last, ventured a response.

"How..." He paused. "How is that possible?"

"I will explain, but not here in the street. Either tonight, as we sit at table, or as my first task in the morning when we break our fast, I will sit with all of you together and explain. For now, I need you to curb your tongue and trust that I do, in fact, fully grasp the way others see me. Understood?"

Vilmocz bowed his head, swallowed hard, and spoke in a soft tone of contrition, "Yes, my lord."

Kaith nodded his acceptance. He made a gesture with his right hand, urging Vilmocz back to his feet. He could see sweat darkening the crown of Vilmocz's light brown hair, as well as his beard.

"Mount up. We're almost at the braided tower, and then you won't have to drive the cart for a goodly while. That should please you." Kaith offered the ghost of a grin.

Vilmocz obeyed. He offered his lord a cautious smile, voice betraying more than a hint of pleasure at the prospect. "Yes, my lord."

With a brief nod, Kaith turned and walked back to his horse. In a single, swift motion, he swung back up into the saddle and resumed their progress northward. A few short minutes later found the party passing through the large, arched wooden gate that led on to the tower grounds.

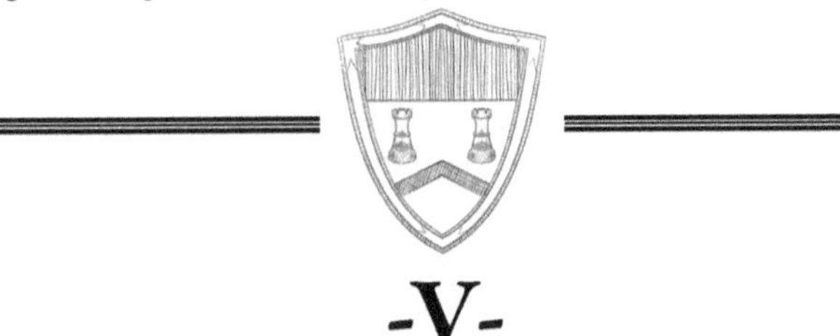

-V-

Venzene Duchy of Kamieńalun
County Czarny Wodospad
Village of Auburg
3 Korunasykli: 20 Days after the Red Storm at Westsong

"All right, line up. Line up! Come on!" Kozioł's voice carried high and clear, but it took a moment for the others to listen and obey. He wasn't the tallest, broadest of shoulder, strongest, nor did he outrank them socially. There was, in other words, no initial reason for them to follow his orders. Still, that was what days like today were about. He would have to put into practice what he'd learned of how to command, or he would have to accept the idea that he was someone who couldn't. Kozioł knew which outcome he wanted but didn't know whether he would be ready or able when the time came.

The sons of the various sergeants and armsmen who were here complied readily enough, but they did so uncertainly. Most of them looked to the young Lords whose household they served—and whom, in the ordinary course, were their regular playmates—before committing to do as they'd been commanded. It was comical to see, actually. In most cases, they would begin to do as they'd been bidden, then stop as if realizing it hadn't been their own lord giving the order. Then they would look sheepish and unclear as to what to do next.

He repeated his order for a third time, trying to keep his frustration at bay.

Quite suddenly, one of the boys got wide-eyed and jumped to obey. One by one, the rest began to follow suit.

Kozioł was initially pleased with himself for having managed to exhort them into action, but then he realized what must've happened. Looking over his shoulder, he confirmed it. His cousin—his lord—had come out of the manor house with his bastard brother in tow.

In one sense, he was relieved. He couldn't think of anything he'd done or said differently this last time. It was some small relief to know the change wasn't utterly random. Still, he was also enraged at his own impotence. If they'd only do as he commanded out of fear of what his cousin would do, then he was failing.

"All right, it took you long enough, but you're finally in position." He tried to make his voice sound mildly annoyed, and no more. In truth, it was all he could do to keep himself from shaking with the storm of fear, frustration, and self-doubt bubbling within him. Fighting, he could do; giving orders to their sergeants, he could do. Hells, *magic* he could do, as impossible as that seemed. This was the first time he was attempting to order his peers around and in front of so many eyes. It was an effort to keep himself from bolting or simply crying under the weight of it all.

He drew a modest breath, held it for a three-count, then forged ahead. "So—every single one of us has been taught how to fight. I've seen most of you fight, and I've been beaten by more than a few of you."

This admission was met with a few chuckles, but it was mostly nervous energy. Encouraged, he continued.

"If we're going to fight in any form of tournament that involves our own personal skill, then I think we're in better shape than most of the other counties. Would you agree?"

There were a few nods, a few smiles, and one or two more expressions and postures that suggested he had specifically been speaking about them and their own prowess. He hadn't, but that was all right. Azhferd had told him to recognize their accomplishments and to begin with that recognition. *Otherwise,* he'd said, *they might question whether or not you're attacking or belittling them when you try to teach them something.*

"The one thing most of you don't know is how to fight in a group. That doesn't mean you won't figure it out quickly, but I know that it isn't something taught by most people these days and has certainly not been taught by your brothers, uncles, and fathers," he paused, "...other than you three."

He gestured to the Ullan triplets, who blushed and grinned back. It was rare that they were singled out for anything positive, and they relished the idea that they had something the other boys didn't when it came to the measure of their noble worth.

"For most of our lives, throughout the tournament circuit, grand melees have been scores of individuals fighting in loose knots of loyalty. That is something we need to change." This was a sentence Azhferd had drilled into his head. He was pleased to have managed to say it as if it'd been his own.

"Why?" This was Eldred, Syr Gazlee's son. He was definitely one of the better fighters among the group, but that hadn't made him distant or self-important. Not to Kozioł, anyway. No, blessedly, Eldred was someone Kozioł accounted as an actual friend.

You were nearly my cousin. Would've been if Yeidil had gotten her way, but never mind. The thought made him grin, taking the sharpest edge off of his nerves. He didn't yet recognize the *power* in that grin. He appeared far more confident than he felt, which in turn lent weight to his words.

This was a question he was prepared for, and he'd been hoping someone would ask it. Still, he adopted an air of thoughtful calm, as if really considering the question before answering it.

"Well," he said as he began to pace, "I'm fairly certain you can defeat me in a one-on-one fight eight times out of ten."

"Six or seven, not eight," Eldred said.

Kozioł didn't think Eldred was simply being polite, just that he was perhaps more humble than he'd given him credit for. As far as that went, it reflected well on Eldred and poorly on Kozioł. He would have to watch that as he made further assessments of people.

"Aye. Fine. Six or seven. Fair enough, though I think you do yourself too little credit." This was met with chuckles and a few appraising looks from the corners of eyes directed at Eldred. "Could you beat both Edmar and me?"

Eldred considered, looking at first Kozioł, then Edmar Ullan—the ringleader of the triplets today—wearing a blue belt around his waist for identification purposes.

"Both at once?" he nodded in a measured, considering way. Probably, but only about half the time."

Kozioł nodded.

"I agree. What if it were just you against the triplets?"

"You're a better shieldman than any of them, so if you're not on the field," Eldred paused, calculating. Looking one final time at the triplets, he finished, "Probably about the same chance. I'd win maybe half the time."

Again, Kozioł nodded. Everyone was paying attention now. All eyes were either on him or the names mentioned thus far. Each boy was weighing out these would-be battles, assessing their likely outcomes for themselves. Most seemed to agree with what'd been said so far.

"And if I enter the fray alongside them?"

Eldred's answer was immediate. He'd seen Kozioł's point and gotten there before the question had been hung in the air. "One, perhaps two in ten. It would be luck, or it would be a mistake that one or more of you made for me to jump on. If there are forests to run into or things to hide behind or climb over, maybe, but even then..." Eldred shook his head. "I'd be lucky to beat you four... once or twice out of every ten engagements."

"And if you had one of your armsmen's sons with you?"

"Depending on which one, my chances may be back up to half the time. Maybe more than that, but either way, I see your point."

Kozioł nodded his encouragement and pushed just a bit harder. "And what *is* my point, Eldred Gazlee? Some here may not have seen it as quickly as you."

Eldred cocked his head to the side for a moment, then grinned. He liked this game. "The point is that when you have people you can trust on the field beside you, you have a better chance of winning even against greater odds."

"Almost."

Eldred blinked, looking at Kozioł in confusion. "Almost?"

"Everything you said is right, but there's a piece missing."

Edmar Ullan spoke up, his unbroken voice tentative at first. "If everybody on the tournament field fights in *loose knots of loyalty...*" As Kozioł nodded and grinned his agreement, Edmar began to sound sly... almost pleased with himself, eyes dancing. "Then a group of people who actually trained to fight beside one another will be damned near unbreakable." He paused for a few beats, then spoke his conclusion in a tone of bright and exuberant understanding. "It means if we put the time in and learn to fight beside one another, to trust one another, we'll win the melees as well as the individual combats at tournament. If we put in the time this year... hells! We may even win next year at Zlaté *Pole*!"

Kozioł nodded and made an *exactly* gesture with both hands.

The reaction to this idea was uncertainty mixed liberally with a ravenous desire to believe. Nearly every boy dreamt of winning glory at tournament, most especially their first. Kozioł had been no exception. If there was something they could hold on to—a plan that they believed could get them to that illustrious and elusive first victory—nearly all of them would embrace it.

"All right," said Kozioł, drawing their attention back to him. "I want two lines. First and foremost, we're going to group together by household. You might as well fight beside the people you already train with. Before days end, though, we're going to mix everyone up. We have to be ready to trust one another and one another's households as well. Let's get as close to even sides as we can. To it!"

While he was surprised at his own confidence, he was even more surprised to see them leap into action at his word.

My men... Azhferd was right. They were my men. I simply needed to give them a reason to follow me.

Smiling to himself, he caught Eldred's eye, then Edmar's. Both gave him a wide grin and an approving nod. He took just a moment to cast an eye back to where his cousin—his knight—took his ease. He was holding court with the elder heirs. Azhferd gave him a brief, encouraging nod. He had, indeed, been watching.

Kozioł allowed himself a moment of self-satisfaction before moving off to inspect *his* men.

-VI-

County Thorion
Wick
3 Korunasykli: 20 Days after the Red Storm at Westsong

Kaith allowed Olshnak into the chamber before him as was proper. If he were to be Kaith's Herald, he would need the opportunity to announce him. The orc stepped in, cast about the chamber, nodded as he cleared his throat, and tilted his head upward to force his voice to carry throughout the room.

As the orc pulled his hood back, preparatory to speaking, Kaith was struck by the realization that he'd seen him before. Once, perhaps twice, in the halls of the county seat, Kaith swore he'd seen the sheet of not grey but silver hair that pooled like water at the back of the orc's neck, resting on his unfurled hood. Normally that color of hair would've denoted someone of great age. The orc *did* carry himself as someone who had a wide breadth of education—a modestly long life, in other words—yet the dark-green-near-black of his flesh was still quite smooth.

Kaith could count the number of orcs he'd personally met on two hands, the number he'd held more than ten words conference with on one—with fingers left over. They seemed to be predominantly green-skinned and black-haired, though there was one he'd glimpsed on the block with blue skin and white hair—very striking.

The realization that he'd seen this particular orc before did its best to take up residence in the forefront of his mind, but as Olshnak announced him, forcing him to take in the room in earnest, he refocused his attention.

Rather than an entry hall, the entire ground floor was one great room. Two stories in height, with a spiral staircase clinging to the curve of the right wall, this massive chamber served as throne room, dining hall, and common area for its residents. A single, massive trestle table stood along the far-left wall. Behind it, high-backed chairs sat like silent judges. Their shadows stretched long in the dim, flickering light.

A pair of waist-high stone braziers stood just inside the door frame. Each held a listless orange flame—casting a wide light that managed to look somehow greasy as it danced.

A quintet of torches were arrayed along the far wall, staining the view with their thin, yellow light. They surrounded the twin banners—the house of Wick's device, a white tower flanked by lit golden candles on a field of red. The high seat sat in pride of place beneath the banners, flanked by two minor mimicries.

They're meant to draw the eye to the banners. The chairs are set up like a chevron beneath the torches. That thought was quickly followed by another. *They look lonely...*

In the center of this grand, round room, sat upon the bare marble floor where no light source directly reached, was Lord Ricgerd. Ricgerd was, Kaith thought, a year his senior, yet he sat as children had since time out of mind, his legs crossed, feet tucked underneath him, knees and shins facing outward. His dark brown hair hung in listless, chin-length curtains to either side of his face. The thick set of his lips was framed by the shag of a dark mustache, which stopped perhaps a finger's width above his jaw. He wore ill-fitting court clothing—well-made, but not well-tailored—rolled up to reveal his massive forearms.

Several bearskins were to his immediate right. Upon these, its head in his lap, lay a sinewy, long-coated hound—red-coated and black-muzzled. It looked miserable and sickly, though that was an aspect more than any obvious outward sign.

"Behold, Lord Ricgerd," the orc spoke in an abraded tone, "may I present Kaith, keeper of Westsong, Knight of Thorion, one of The Nineteen?"

As he concluded, Olshnak stepped aside, making his body perpendicular to the entryway so that Kaith could pass.

Kaith nodded, steeled himself against the storm of emotions that even now threatened to overtake him, and strode forward the requisite few feet.

He drank in the scene as he waited to be acknowledged. For a long moment, no sound came, save the crackling of the fire.

"*Karminove Srdce...*" Olshnak's words were almost inaudible, even to their intended recipient. "A Crimson Heart."

Kaith heard them, but they didn't register for some four or five seconds.

Crimson Heart, Mother's Tears,
a look allays or augers fears,
of safe returns or sorrow-sure,
If heart-kin's heart will beat no more.

Raun, I don't know whether to bless you or curse you for these verses you keep pouring into my skull.

Kaith couldn't decide whether to smile or weep. If this was, indeed, a Crimson Heart, rare though they were, and it had belonged to Sir Reginald or Robis, then Ricgerd already knew. Once they imprinted on someone, choosing them as heart-kin-according to the old stories and songs—the beasts would live till their heart-kin died.

They were magic in the oldest and truest sense of the word—an unknown, unexplainable, yet well-worn truth.

There were more than a few songs and staves wherein a soldier, noble, or even peasant child was away from home and hearth but left their Crimson Heart behind. The joyful ones held verses justifying hope that their loved ones would return, for *the Crimson Heart beats steady still.*

The sadful ones usually held weeping women and children over the graves of their missing family members, ending with *His light is lost, his breath is still, his heart-kin sleeps beneath the hill,* or the like.

Still, the events at Westsong were more than a fortnight ago. Surely the Falx would have come for the hound by now if it were bound to either Robis or his father, wouldn't it?

As if in silent answer, it stirred ever so slightly, rolling one liquid eye to regard Kaith, then closing it again.

Lord Ricgerd continued to look down at the beast, hair shadowing his features. His bright hand softly smoothed down the deep red of its coat, occasionally alternating to slide a single finger in a gentle caress along the shorter black fur that covered its face. After a few moments of silence, Ricgerd looked up, but only briefly, as if he were afraid to look away from the hound for any length of time.

"'Lo, Kaith," said he. His voice came out hollow, as if it hadn't been used in a while. "Come to deliver the grim news, have you?"

I've not seen you since before the Northern Marches tournament, Ricgerd. You demanded I drink with you. We raised health after health to your father—talking through the night, nearly until dawn, speaking of your brother—of the knight he would one day make. He did—he died a hero. Now it falls to me to tell you the tale.

Kaith swallowed, his throat producing an audible click. He drew in a breath, then two, then nodded. *And I cannot even lessen that pain, for you already know—before I can even speak the words, you already know. I failed to save Robis, and I've failed even to offer you the small service of delivering you the ill news myself.*

"I have," he said. "I see there's no need, but yes, I have."

"Who killed them?"

"It's a longer tale—"

"*Who killed them!?*" Ricgerd's voice was sudden thunder filling the chamber.

Kaith had no idea how to answer. How could he tell this man that his father and the brother he'd so loved had died fighting the dead? He could relate that as a story, certainly, but Ricgerd wanted an answer. No, Ricgerd wanted a target. A place, a person, a household, something that he could rally his courage and his sword arm to vanquish. That was what Ricgerd wanted, and it was all he wanted.

"If you want the short answer, I'll give it you, but it won't give you comfort." His voice was cold, as if it'd taken on the aspect of hollow disuse that Lord Ricgerd had cast aside only a moment ago.

Ricgerd again offered another brief glance upward before returning his full attention to the hound. When he spoke, his voice had once again become that hollow, disused thing.

"Go on, then."

"A plague."

For a moment, it was as if the very flames had stopped moving. Time stood still for an agonizing two or three heartbeats before it resumed again. When Ricgerd next spoke, it was in perhaps the bitterest tone Kaith had ever heard.

"A plague..." Ricgerd's left hand clenched into a fist then unclenched again. He repeated the process several more times. "I do not accept that." He spoke this pronouncement in great gusts of sound squeezed through gritted teeth. "I do not accept that there is no one to blame, no one I can... no one I..." His chest hitched, shoulders shaking.

"Your father—"

"Do *not*! Do not speak of my father! Do not come before me spewing sweet words, trying to rob me of my grief, Kaith!"

Now Kaith was shaking, though whether in anger or grief, he, himself, couldn't have said. He overrode Ricgerd, stepping forward and raising his own voice.

"No, I *will* speak, and you *will* hear, Ricgerd!"

Two guards had been stationed to either side of the door, out of sight as Kaith had first entered. As he stepped forward and began to raise his voice in earnest, they moved as well, raising their poleaxes in warning.

Kaith ignored them.

"Your father died a hero trying to save the lives of those who had gone missing. The first to fall to this plague ... and your *brother*? Your brother died saving Sir Lanwreigh of Eastshadow!"

Ricgerd shrieked a full-throated, inarticulate battle cry. The hound raised his head from Ricgerd's lap with what looked like an enormous effort. Ricgerd leapt to his feet and charged Kaith, tackling him to the ground. He began punching him in the head over and over again.

Kaith accepted these blows for a moment, feeling that perhaps he deserved them.

"Sir Kaith!" Terrek's voice?

Kaith didn't know, nor did it matter. It was as if someone had thrown kindling onto a fire. His own grief was suddenly fuel for that fire. It burned so that he had light to see his duty by. He would stand. He would fight.

He retaliated, delivering a punishing headbutt to the bridge of Ricgerd's nose. As the enormous man fell back from him, covering his face, Kaith rolled to his knees and then his feet. He waited for Ricgerd to stand, and when he did, the two squared off anew.

Ricgerd wiped the blood away from his eyes with the back of his left arm, then issued another of those inarticulate battle cries before charging Kaith once again. Rather than ramming him into a wall or trying to knock him down, however, he swung a massive right fist in a hook directly at Kaith's left cheek. Kaith managed to lean back just in time to be out of the way. Ricgerd immediately stopped his momentum and reversed his attack, turning the blow into a backfist.

There was a sudden explosion of pain in Kaith's head. He felt consciousness rushing away from him.

The next thing he knew, he was hearing a deep-throated howling. He was on the floor, being slowly lifted to his feet by both Terrek and Olshnak, the latter of whom had pulled Kaith's right arm over his shoulder for support.

Ricgerd was on his knees before the howling hound.

"No! No! No! Forgive me, please forgive me! I have to find someone, something, some way to avenge Robis... to avenge my father! Please! Please don't! Please don't go!"

The Crimson Heart sat on its haunches, black face pointed toward the ceiling. Blood-red fur seemed to stream down around it in waves as it shuddered with the force of its final cry. As Kaith watched, its chest hitched, and it fell over.

Ricgerd's grief was awful to behold. He shrieked through gritted teeth and wept, even as he caught the beast.

The hound raised its head one final time and licked the blood from Ricgerd's left hand with a single, long caress of its tongue. It held his gaze for one ephemeral moment, shuddering with the effort, and then collapsed.

Now it was Ricgerd's turn to howl, and his howl seemed to shake the tower's very stone.

-VII-

County Thorion
Eastshadow
3 Korunasykli: 20 Days after the Red Storm at Westsong

The day had drained down into a poisonous purple dusk. The insects were tuning up, and the last evening birds were singing their lonely hearts out. Each was underpinned by the wind dancing amidst the tall grasses. The entire affair sounded wet and monstrous, for reasons that weren't immediately obvious. True, *the grass was thin as the cold set in, and the snows drew close upon winter winds*, as the song went. Cold air was always thinner, somehow, as well. Still, that did not account for the sense that the wind was a procession of last gasps, as frightened men finally stepped sideways at journey's end.

"Stop that," Gordan told himself. "Things are grim and darksome enough without my calling down fresh horrors."

He kept his voice low, walking down the long alley of palisades toward Barnic's high seat. He'd been summoned, as had the others, he suspected. Rumor had it that Barnic had received some ill tidings and was anxious to share them, apparently, with his trusted knights.

Gordan resisted the urge to correct the good folk of Eastshadow who'd delivered this summons. They were not, as a matter of record, Barnic's knights. Perhaps they were, for all practical purposes; but they were each considered landed as far as station and the County Rolls were concerned.

He entered the lord's palisade, nodded to those who gave him their grace, as it were, and at last entered the noble's hall.

He ignored the herald, who began to announce him, walking directly toward Barnic and nodding his head in deference rather than formally bowing. If anyone of consequence minded, they kept it to themselves.

He saw Aethen and Raegus sat in wooden chairs to either side of Barnic's not-quite-throne. Two more chairs were arrayed on the outside of this wide wedge. To Aethen's left sat a man Gordan knew as the watch captain, though if he'd learned his name, recent events had driven it beyond his easy reach.

A lone figure stood before the assemblage—a sword on his left hip, no hair atop his head, and an absolutely shredded gambeson—at least as far as his back went

Gordan had never seen him before. Undoubtedly, this man was what all the fuss was about.

After some silent communication with Barnic confirming he was meant to sit in the vacant chair to Raegus's right—he was, apparently—Gordan moved past the standing man and took up his perch, waiting.

"Sir Gordan, this is Padrutt, a warden of the Shivering March," said Barnic. "Go on, Padrutt. Now that Sir Gordan has arrived, we can all listen to your tale at once."

Padrutt nodded, pale face showing a mixture of exhaustion and misery. "Aye, my lord. Where shall I ... Where shall I begin?"

Barnic sat back, considering. "You and yours were patrolling near the river. Best, I think, to begin there."

Padrutt nodded, took a moment to collect himself, then pressed forward. His voice was somehow distant, almost as if he were speaking in his sleep.

"We'd been tracking Nebelblut. They'd been increasing their boldness in the wake of the new realm to the north's defeat of the Shivering Song."

"Nebel...?" Raegus wore his confusion without taking any pains to disguise it.

"Nebelblut, my lord. Goblins're what I mean, sir. Nebelblut's their right name, though."

Raegus made a gesture to indicate Padrutt should go on.

"Aye. Well, as I say, we'd been tracking and tending to them whenever we could. Now the Shivering Song's gone this last year, and the witch-fog with her, the Nebelblut've taken most our time." He paused here, but only for a moment.

He allowed his eyes to focus on one of the torches along the far wall. His breathing calmed—not that it was manic before and grew steady. As he spoke again, his voice had taken on an even plainer mimicry of the man who speaks as he sleeps.

"They tend to make deep, burrowing dens in the softer earth near the river, or in bog-land when they can find it. It was our first patrol since the new season's duty'd begun. We found a new thing. Not merely a freshly dug den, but a deep, underground cave system."

The seated men, Gordan among them, looked at one another in turn, then back to Padrutt. This had all the hallmarks of a tale none of them wanted, but each of them needed to hear.

"Go on." Barnic spoke gently, but with an insistence that Gordan didn't think he could have managed. He could have been either forceful or diplomatic. He'd always marveled at how Barnic managed to do both at once.

"Normally, we'd enter a den, post guards outside of it, and kill the things where we found them. Often we'd find missing stock, sometimes a child they'd taken—that sort of thing, but usually, it was just them in small warbands."

"But not this time?" Raegus sounded anxious. Gordan couldn't much blame him.

"No, my lord. The cave had scores of them and caches of weapons. No Nebelblut cubs, neither. Just those girded for raids. It was a raiding camp. Our Sergeant Gorman had the right of it. There were far too many to take on. We were two dozen, which is enough for our work on any other given day. Against the scores we saw, however..."

Gordan found himself gripping the arms of his chair. He wasn't certain if he were angry or afraid, nor was he certain he wanted to find out. He kept seeing the force that had attacked a few days ago—kept seeing the guardsman, the light going out of his eyes—the single-minded goblin focused on retrieving his arrow, never mind Gordan's sword crashing down upon his head. He fought the urge to shudder.

"What then?" Aethen was leaning forward, his mop of curly brown hair hung in his eyes.

"Aye, well, the sergeant pulled us out before we'd been seen. He made the order to send a triad to Wick, one here to Eastshadow, and another to Rockvale. The rest would keep a watch on the cave, hunt along the river for other ways in or out, and try to seal them off."

"A fair plan," offered the guardsman whose name Gordan hadn't bothered to learn. "Thank you for being swift in your delivery, warden."

"Begging your pardon, but that ain't the end of it."

The guardsman sat back, brows raised, and waited.

"We broke, each to his duty, but didn't make it more than a furlong before we heard screams."

"Goblins don't scream," Gordan heard himself saying.

"No. They do not, sir. Near as I can tell, the rest of my brothers fell before the Nebelblut. I made it, as did Doanne."

"Doanne? The Wardens of the Shivering March have women among their number?"

"Aye, Aethan. Did you think Marcza was the only woman capable of wielding a sword?" Raegus sounded annoyed and defensive.

"Hardly. Just didn't realize the Wardens thought the same way. They're always going on about their brothers, not their brothers *and sisters*. I'm surprised about it, not unhappy."

Barnic held up a hand to silence the byplay. Both men subsided at once. "Go on, Padrutt."

The warden shrugged, looking down briefly. "Not much more to tell, Lord. Never seen 'em like that—crazed and in numbers bigger than any we've ever heard report of. Nebelblut focus on their task. They aren't prone to distraction or much emotion. These were enraged. Lott fell before we knew what was happening. We ran as soon as we'd cut a path through them. Here we be."

Barnic nodded evenly. "Thank you, Padrutt. Please take some wine and food, if you're up to it, and stay while we make our plans. If there are questions, it's best you be here to answer them."

"May I see my sword sister, Lord?"

"As soon as we finish here, Warden."

Padrutt nodded but made no move for refreshment.

Gordan didn't blame him.

"Thoughts? Questions? Suggestions?" Barnic sounded as if he already had a plan, to Gordan's ear, at least. He had that distant look in his eye, as if he were watching a far-off battle play out on the stage of his mind.

"We need to shore up our defenses at once," Aethan said. "We have to be ready!"

"What still needs shoring up?" Raegus had meant it as an honest question, but it'd come out almost chidingly.

"The palisades? The fences? Foodstuffs?" Aethan had grown heated and defensive.

"My lords," the guardsman cut in. "The defenses were shorn up by order of Sir Jastar before he left. We're moving as swiftly as we can. No hand is idle. I can promise you."

"Then we need to train our men. They need to know how best to kill these ... things."

"Same as a man, my lord," said Padrutt. "They take more sword strokes, axe swings, or arrows, but they go down the same way."

Aethan nodded, slightly mollified by this news.

Silence fell upon the room for perhaps a minute. At last, Barnic spoke up. "Gordan, do I read your face wrong, or are you ready to depart come morning?"

Gordan, who had been thinking of no such plan, merely looked at Barnic. "I ... can do that if you think it best."

Barnic nodded at this. "As I see it, we have to send word to Wick, then to Rockvale. We must assume that Padrutt is correct, and they are the only survivors of their force."

Padrutt bowed his head but said nothing.

"Raegus, I'd like you to join Gordan. Ride for Wick. Tell the Lord Ricgerd and his captains what Padrutt's reported, then either ride on to Rockvale or commission one of Ricgerd's men to go."

Raegus blinked, sat back, rubbing his chin for a moment, then nodded. "Aye. I can do that. Why both of us, though? Surely one knight is enough..."

Barnic took a moment to answer. "I'm thinking of the road, and then what lay beyond it. Both of you together are stronger than either one of you alone, of course. You know one another's moods and minds. It may well come to a fight, an ambush-something like that. In that case, you'll fight as one far better than either of you alone, with a small detachment of guards who know you only by name and reputation... True?"

Both men nodded at that.

Barnic spoke on. "When you get to Wick, you may need to hold the line there. Again, two are better than one. If you need to shore up *their* defenses..." He trailed off. Further explanation was unnecessary.

Between the pair of them, they could arrange and order defenses much faster together than alone. A united front made such things far easier to digest—especially when that united front was made up of knights. Especially when dealing with an unbelted lord—a lord who was not yet a knight.

Gordan looked at Raegus and offered a shallow smile. "Shall we sit squire for one another come morning, then?"

Raegus snorted. "Aye, if you like. I'll saddle your horse, and you can see to mine. I promise no burs in your horse's saddle blanket this time."

Gordan was drawing breath to laugh and make some glib reply when Barnic cut them off.

"If there's nothing more, then...?" No one spoke up. "Padrutt, one of my men will escort you to where your sword sister is being cared for."

Padrutt bowed, offering thanks, and swiftly exited the chamber.

"Cadwyd." Barnic looked to the guard captain, solving the riddle of his name for all and sundry.

"My lord?"

"Please see to the defense projects. I should like Sir Aethan to have a status report come morning. Sooner if possible."

"Yes, Lord Eastshadow." Cadwyd stood, bowed, and exited the chamber.

As soon as he did, Barnic spoke up in a stony tone. It so reminded them of Valad that all three men shuddered, in spite of themselves.

"Listen to me, all of you. When in those seats and in this hall, you stand as honored advisors. You represent not me, not Eastshadow, and not yourselves. You represent the Valadin. Save your play for the field, or the feast hall—save it for the jakes or the joust, I care not... but do *not* forget yourselves in those seats again, or I shall bar you from sitting in them." The subtext was plain. He would also bar them from sitting in his councils.

Gordan bowed his head. "Aye. Fair, Barnic." He was about to add that it was all still very new to them, but it was just as new to Barnic. They'd been knighted literal moments apart, after all.

Both Raegus and Aethan made similar statements of contrition.

Barnic had never raised his voice. He hadn't so much as offered them an unkind look. Once more, Gordan admitted to himself that he had been the right choice to rule over Eastshadow.

"If there's nothing more, then?" Barnic's question was perfunctory.

They all shook their heads.

"I expect you each have your own matters to attend to. Gordan? You've had slightly more personal experience with the creatures than Raegus. I'll expect you to take the lead when dealing with this commission to Wick, and hopefully to Rockvale."

Gordan looked at Raegus, then nodded back to Barnic. "All right."

With that, Barnic stood. They followed suit. A moment later and the trio'd left Barnic alone in his hall, each affected by both what they'd seen and heard.

Goblins... on a war footing. Had the countess known or expected this? Was that why they had been sent here together? Or was this merely her overall ability to plan coming into contact with an unexpected foe? Be it good planning, or good fortune, it had clearly been a good decision.

Gordan vowed to himself to not waste what blessings they apparently had. He would warn Wick, shore up their defenses, and ensure Rockvale was alerted, one way or another... he hoped.

"Hope? No," he murmured as he exited Barnic's hall. "My only actual *hope* is that I don't have to fight the devils again... or that Padrutt exaggerated his count. He must've done, surely. How could there be a cave that large undiscovered by the March Wardens so close to the river? New to him, perhaps, but not the more seasoned among his order, surely."

And did he smell something darksome and familiar on the wind? Was there a hint of that most wretched of Goblin heralds faintly fuming out of the east?

"Or is my undermind just finding shadows to jump at again?" Shaking his head, he sped his step and moved toward his chambers to prepare for tomorrow's journey.

COME STAND WITH ME AGAIN

-I-

County Thorion
Wick
4 Korunasykli: 21 Days after the Red Storm at Westsong

The sun was just starting to crest over the Braided Tower's easternmost outer wall. The sky didn't auger much heat today, but it had already been warm enough to banish the ragged fog that had adorned yesterday's travel.

Kaith walked from the tower's entrance, round to its north side, where the stable complex was. He passed several boys working their morning chores with reasonable diligence. Nobody, so far as he knew, particularly *liked* mucking out stalls. That was the price men paid for keeping horses at the ready, rather than perpetually out to pasture.

He found his cart and hopped up to sit upon its gate, legs dangling over the ground. Smirking, he began to eat his horse bread—*Behold Sir Kaith, the Knightly child who wears Westsong wherever he walks.*

He banished that thought almost as soon as it'd arrived. There were other matters to attend to. The ghosts of gone days—even ones so *recently* gone—needed to find other houses to haunt.

He'd just gotten his first full bite of breakfast down and was reaching for the ale pot he'd carried from the kitchens when Terrek's voice called to him. Looking over, Kaith saw the man walking over at a measured pace.

He's giving me time to ward him off. Appreciated, but hardly necessary.

"Sergeant? Morning. Come to break your fast with me?" He tried to keep his tone friendly without forcing either warmth or distance into it and felt he'd succeeded marginally well.

"Aye, my lord, if it pleases you. The lads aren't far behind." He paused, a few feet between them. "You *did* still want to talk to we three this morning, yes?"

Kaith blinked, then nodded. "I did, Terrek, yes. Thank you." He'd actually forgotten. He'd had Ricgerd on his mind. Matters of his armsmen had mounted up and all but hied for the hills while he wasn't thinking about them. And yes, it was just these three he'd meant to speak with. Olshnak didn't need to be involved. He was a herald assigned to him by the countess—a slave who was unlikely to remain on loan for long. No need to involve him in these matters. The idea that it was Olshnak, by the very nature of his presence that had caused the conversation with Vilmocz and the others to be necessary, had only just occurred to him, but never mind.

Kaith slid over to one side, nodding his head for Terrek to sit beside him. That worthy blinked, bowed his head, and took the offered seat.

"You're an oddment, my lord. I mean no offense, mind, but, aye. You're an oddment."

Kaith chuckled. "Go on then. Tell me why."

"Well..." At first, Terrek looked as if he hadn't wanted to continue down the road he, himself, had begun walking on. A moment later, however, it was clear he was formulating the best way to come at his explanation. "It's hard for me to pin down, but I'll do my best. Most leaders—the good ones, at any rate—find a balance between holding their folk close and keepin' them at arm's length, aye."

Kaith nodded, taking a small bite of his bread. "And I don't do that? Haven't found the right balance yet?" He didn't sound angry or affronted—he hoped. Certainly, he didn't *feel* either of these. There was a bemused curiosity he took no pains to hide, however.

"No... you've a balance—a genuine one, mind you. It's just not a *normal* one." He paused, looking down, then meeting Kaith's eyes in earnest. "You've come out to break your fast in just about the humblest spot in Wick, bar the jakes." He smirked dryly. "Though I admit the smell's nearly as bad."

Kaith snorted at that, shrugging a shoulder. "I wanted clean air. The tower's full of the stench of grief and misery. I'll be drenched in that soon enough, I expect. Best get some air whilst I can."

Terrek arched his brows, nodding slowly. "And there. That very observation—it's not the sort of thing most fighting men mark, let alone really take into account."

"Greggor's teaching," said he.

"Nye, my lord. Greggor teaches patience, perception-to employ a sense of the people you're to speak with right enough. Then there's yesterday. You took Vilmocz to task in a way most men would find too soft, yet it wound up affecting him more deeply than if you'd blackened his eye over it. Lord Ricgerd liked to have beaten you senseless yesterday, yet unless I misread you, you've no plan to be revenged for the insult."

Kaith shook his head. "None. He offered no insult."

"Aye, but he did. You forgiving him for it and letting it go don't change that."

"Not so. Insults are intentional things, on the giving end, at least."

"Forgive me, my lord, but no. People accidentally insult one another all the time. That's not what happened yesterday, regardless. Lord Ricgerd liked to beat the blond off of you for a time. That's an insult if ever there was one."

"Not so," Kaith said again. "People take issue, consider a thing an insult all the time. If you call to some peasant or slave in the street, at an inn, or the like, and the man doesn't answer you, you might well take offense, especially if you're not being quiet about it. If it turns out the man's got a stuffy head? Doesn't hear well? He clearly wasn't ignoring you a'purpose. The moment you find that out, continuing to feel insulted is a choice. If you choose to keep holding a grudge, so be it. Don't change the fact that our man did nothing to insult you."

He grinned at Terrek's look of disbelief.

"Aye, but yesterday—"

"Lord Ricgerd was drunk on grief yesterday. He on grief, and for a time—I was drunk on guilt. I'll have to fight, for a time, not to turn to that bitter brew again. Aches are real, but insult? No."

Terrek cocked his head to one side. He looked like a bird sensing movement near at hand, trying to find its source. "We cannot both be right. If I take issue and insult, yet you meant none, which of us is right?"

"Both and neither. The issue's not which of us is right. It's which of us is humble enough to bend."

Terrek bowed his head. "Right—now *that's* Greggor talking."

Kaith grinned. "Aye, every maddening word. He's right, and it makes you want to kick his teeth in some days."

They looked at one another, then burst out laughing.

"Aye and aye and aye to that, my lord."

Huron came out from the stable complex. Apparently, he'd beaten both Kaith and Terrek out of doors this morning—not that it was a contest.

"Huron!" At Kaith's word and the accompanying wave, the dark-skinned youth smiled and walked over. He was naked to the waist, a thin sheen of sweat covering his chest. His upper body was well defined but bore little mass. He bowed as he arrived within easy speaking range.

Kaith wrinkled his nose. "No, Huron. No need for that unless we're in formal places. I'll not have any of you bowing to me as one of us walks to and from the damned jakes."

Huron looked to Terrek, then back to Kaith. He grinned. "All right. If that is what you wish." His voice was, as always, innately musical.

Kaith had only heard him sing a few times when they'd been boys. He found himself wondering if Huron might be able to fill the role of entertainer as well as armsman. Most such men could sing, play a drum or other instrument. Some knights, he knew, insisted each of their armsmen learn a bardic trick, as it was often called. He had no intention of being that firm on the idea, but if such a thing could be fostered, it might make the road less dull and diplomacy less difficult.

"I was tending to our horses. Best I get them used to me, I think."

"Not robbing the stable boys of their work, Huron, are'ee?" Terrek seemed to be chiding the youth, not actually chastising him.

Huron's face split into a sunny grin. "They should be so lucky, Sergeant." He pronounced Terrek's rank in three syllables—Sar-gee-ent.

Kaith was about to make some jibe or other when he heard a small, clear voice singing from within the stables. It was warm and fabulously young, despite the singer's chosen song.

He was fairly certain it was a girl's voice, given how easily it enunciated the words. Had it been a boy, he would have had to be so young and small as to make such clear articulation a feat of utter sorcery.

The trio turned their heads, wearing transported expressions.

There's a gauntleted hand,
Reaching up toward the heavens,
For a sign, for a song, for a sword.
And the ghosts of the gone-sires,
Fear their words were forgotten,
So in silence, they've stood and endured.

Vilmocz came into view, followed by a surly-looking Ricgerd. The former didn't so much as slow his stride, but Ricgerd stopped in his tracks, head snapping toward the stables.

What in hells... Kaith's initial surprise at seeing the pair together faded almost as soon as it'd arrived. *Ricgerd must've caught Vilmocz by the ear on his way out.*

It sounded like the singer had no idea she had an audience. She poured out great gusts of song without a care in the wide world.

There's a sheen on a shield,
Gleaming bright in the morning.
Aye, the sun shines for shieldmen, lone.
And the ghosts of the gone-sires,
Feel their own fire stirring, As it burns them, and beckons them home.

Vilmocz arrived, opened his mouth to speak as he bowed, but a look from Terrek stilled his tongue. He waited, to his credit, in respectful silence.

Ricgerd had begun to move once more, now veritably stalking over to the stables. His face was a thundercloud waiting to burst.

Kaith thrust his remaining bread into Huron's chest, hopped free of the wagon's bed, and strode to intercept the lord before he could enter beyond the stable's gate.

He stepped in front of Ricgerd, blocking his path and shaking his head. Ricgerd's chest expanded as he drew a breath to argue, but something in Kaith's face seemed to give him pause. Ricgerd subsided without fanfare, though his face showed obvious pain.

Kaith understood why as the singer voyaged on the final verse of the song.

There's a hold neath the hill,
Where the sons of dead soldiers,
Do get drawn down the red ruined road.
Where the ghosts of the gone-sires,
Fight and fear they're forgotten,

So at glory, they grasp, not at gold.
So at glory, they grasp, not at gold.

As the final note faded, Kaith put an arm around Ricgerd's shoulders, turning him bodily, leading him over to the cart where his men stood and sat.

"I want that song banned in my lands," Ricgerd murmured. "It's a hateful thing."

"All right..." Whether Kaith had agreed with the man or simply accepted this pronouncement was a thing he'd left deliberately unclear.

As they arrived at the cart, Terrek standing and all three men bowing to Ricgerd, Kaith dropped his arm from around the man's shoulders.

Ricgerd's voice was low and rumbling as he spoke. "Kaith—*Sir* Kaith, forgive me. I owe you ... I owe you an apology and more."

Kaith shook his head but didn't speak. Ricgerd hadn't finished and interrupting would have been not merely rude but cruel. It was clear the man was finding this conversation difficult enough already.

"I do, indeed. You came personally to deliver the news and the weapons of... of both of them to me. You could have passed the duty off to another, I've no doubt. I expect the countess chose you because of... because of the time and effort you spent on my brother... on Robis." He paused, collecting himself. "Any reason's enough. I took my grief out on you, and that was unworthy. You've my apology. I owe you more than words for how I've behaved, and I won't forget that." With that finally out and in the air, Ricgerd bowed his head and awaited whatever judgement or reply he'd earned.

Kaith bowed his own head for a long moment. When he raised it again, he placed a hand on Ricgerd's bright shoulder.

"Robis was... hells, Ricgerd, he was a force to behold. He was everything—every bit the knight you and I talked about." He bowed his head again. "But it wasn't right for me to *make* you hear that... not before you were ready. It was selfish of me."

"Selfish? Hells, how?" Ricgerd laughed bitterly. "You were trying to ease my grief at his loss!"

"No. Not entirely, at least. I was trying to ease my own, as well as my guilt. I couldn't save him—couldn't save Lanwreigh either. They were both with me, and I them. I led them. I led them, and I lost them. It's something I have to carry for the rest of my days."

Ricgerd's jaw worked. His throat's apple rose and fell several times. Finally, he shook his head, unable to trust himself to speak.

Terrek, Vilmocz, and Huron stood by, heads bowed, saying nothing.

"It's so, Ricgerd. There's no denying it, no getting round it. They're gone, and I couldn't save them. But..." He held up a finger on his free hand. "I *can* do something. We both can."

Ricgerd lifted his gaze to first regard the finger, then Kaith's face. He was mesmerized, miserable, and mad for whatever hope Kaith could render. "What...?"

"We can live," said he. "We can make their loss mean something—can live lives that at least try to justify their sacrifices."

"When the Falx finally comes for you..." Ricgerd's voice called to mind shifting stones on a mountainside. "No one can help you."

Kaith nodded, smiling through his tears. He spoke the rest with Ricgerd, their voices intermingling, lending strength to one another. "The best you can hope for is to make your life—make your death mean something."

Ricgerd nodded, mouthing an "Aye" before embracing Kaith as a brother.

The armsmen looked either on or away based on their own sensibilities.

As they separated, Ricgerd was smiling. "Come. Let's set a proper meal before you and yours. Later today, we'll see my brother and father off and inter their weapons with the proper rites. Then we can talk about whatever comes next."

Kaith cast an eye to his men before heading back inside. A moment later, he heard them following.

He thought witnessing that little miracle might have been more instructive than a dozen conversations between he and his men. Once more, he silently gave thanks to Greggor for his many, many lessons.

-II-

Venzene Duchy of Kamieńalun
County Czarny Wodospad
Village of Auburg
5 Korunasykli: 22 Days after the Red Storm at Westsong

Kozioł stood, tightening the girth strap around his borrowed steed. Tellan Ullan, the first of the triplets to finish his own chores—predictably, as he was the most conscientious of them—was seated in the corner of the stall atop an overturned water bucket not long emptied. The other two Ullan boys—Alwin and Edmar—were tending to similar tasks in nearby stalls.

"I barely slept last night," said Tellan. Rather than sounding tired, he sounded damn-near exuberant. "I kept thinking about Zlaté Pole! The games, the food, the people coming from all over Venzene ... and the tournaments, of course."

Kozioł chuckled, albeit briefly. The horse was playing games with its breath, making the tightening of the strap problematic. If he didn't get it sorted, there was a real risk he might find himself sliding, riding on the horse's right or left side ... before he fell off utterly and became the butt of every joke for roughly the next decade.

"How are you *not* excited?" Tellan sounded incredulous. "I know you've been before, but not like this ... not in service to a knight, the commander of the county forces, and all. Hells! You may even get to fight!"

Kozioł reached down and tickled the horse's belly. He felt it breathe as it reacted to the sensation and swiftly hauled on the strap's loose end to tighten it. The horse stomped its foot as if it knew it had been tricked—which, he supposed, it very well might. Horses were often quite a bit smarter than the people who rode them. Certainly, it was so with his *true* horse—his cień.

He turned to Tellan as he tucked the long end of the strap into position. This part he could do without looking at his hands.

"Oh, I'm excited. Never fear. It's all-new for you, though. I was just as ready to burst as you the first time I went. As you say, I've been before.

It's still exciting for me, just not new." He flipped down the stirrup and, stroking the horse's neck absently, stepped back to face Tellan properly. "It's like … it's like being excited that cook's going to make your favorite supper or knowing you're riding, well, here to Auburg. You've done it before, but you loved it."

Tellan rolled his eyes, though he smiled. "You're trying to compare the War of Counties with my father's cook?"

Kozioł started to protest, but then saw the look on the other boy's face. "Yes." He made his voice serious, changing tactic to play along, "Yes, I am."

There was a moment of silence wherein both boys simply stared at one another. Then, at the same time, they burst out laughing.

Geroslaw came into the stables, walking to where his own horse was quartered. Casually, in a good-natured, avuncular tone, he called out, "Laughing won't make the work go faster, boys."

"Work's done," said Kozioł. He made a shushing gesture to Tellan, a twinkle in his blue-black eyes.

"Done, is it? Care to come help *me*, then?"

"No."

Kozioł heard Geroslaw stop short at that, uncertain how to respond to such cheek. He apparently simply decided to ignore it, though Kozioł did hear him sigh in exasperation. Then he heard the stall door open and the skidding of a boot as its owner stopped short.

"…Who's dressed you, ay?" His voice was soft, almost playful. He was clearly talking to his stallion. "Who's dressed you? A fine job, at that." Then, in a louder voice, he said, "Kozioł… did you see who was in with Krwawa Zima?"

"Bits of him, aye."

"Did you see his face?"

Tellan stifled a giggle, covering his mouth with both hands.

"No. Didn't see his face."

Geroslaw sighed. "He doesn't normally let anyone but me dress him."

"He seemed fine—calm as you please."

"You saw him get saddled, then?"

"I did."

"But you've no idea who was doing the work?"

"I know the boy…"

"Does he have a name?"

"…Doesn't everyone?"

Geroslaw groaned softly at the byplay. "Do you *know* the boy's name?"

"I do."

"...Is it Dargory the soon-to-be-dead-boy-who-doesn't-answer-simple-questions?"

Tellan made no further attempt to hide his laughter. He lost all semblance of control and veritably erupted into giggles.

Kozioł's cheeks were beginning to hurt, his smile was so broad. With a voice that held back laughter the way certain smokers held back their breath while speaking, he quipped, "That's an awfully long name..." He heard Geroslaw lunging across the hall toward him, and he began laughing at last. "All right! All right! It was me!"

Kozioł's mount stomped again, giving a nervous whicker for good measure.

Geroslaw poked his head over the stall wall, an open ceramic jar of what looked like winterberries in his bright hand. He grinned darkly, bound black beard and thick black brows adding to the menace he projected. "I'll get even with you for it. When you least expect it, Kozioł... ohhh, yes. I shall have my revenge..." He turned and walked back across the hall.

Tellan blinked, suddenly afraid. "Revenge? But you did him a kindness!"

Kozioł bowed his head, smirking to himself. "Aye, but I also touched what was his, and without permission. Usually isn't an issue when you do something like this, but some people are ... particular about their gear."

Kozioł knew he *might* get into some trouble for doing such a deed without permission, but he doubted it. Besides, the horse was beautiful—otherworldly in its size and splendor. He'd been willing to risk getting into trouble just to be near the beast. There was, for all that, a better-than-average chance that Geroslaw was entirely teasing. None of them really knew the man, though.

He was saved from further thought on the matter as Eldred ran in, headed straight for Kozioł.

"El-dred Gaz-lee..." Tellan spoke each syllable in a slow, descending quartet of notes as if to add *I might have known* at the end.

Eldred skidded to a halt at the stall door. "Tell-an Oo-lan," he began. His voice was dramatic and serious, though he wore a lopsided grin as he spoke. "At last... we meet *just* in time to say ... farewell."

The absurd delivery of this was enough to send Tellan into hysterics once more. His foe defeated, Eldred turned back to Kozioł.

"Come to see us off?" Kozioł began leading his horse toward the stall door, forcing Eldred to step back.

"I have. Wish I were going with you, but my tatuś made it clear. We stay to protect the county. He isn't riding to war, so neither am I."

Tatuś, Kozioł thought, and not for the first time. *It's well you know how to fight, Eldred. You may be the only boy I know who still calls his father that. When the rest of us talk of our sires, it's tata, if not outright ojciec. How've you not outgrown... hells, it's like hearing one of the merchant's or armsmen's sons saying daddy instead of da, dad, or father.*

"Fair enough. Next year, yeah? We'll stand together on the field next year." He led his horse free of the stall and walked him out of the way so Tellan could follow. He was surprised, therefore, when Eldred embraced him.

"Be safe, and if they let you fight—knock them all into the dirt for the rest of us." He pulled back, smiling, though it was a strained thing.

Kozioł accepted the embrace, returning it out of reflex. He wasn't angry or embarrassed, just confused. As Eldred pulled back and Kozioł saw his face, confusion began to melt into alarm. "What's wrong?"

"I... nothing. It's foolish."

"It's *not* nothing, and it's *not* foolish. Tell me." There was something here making his hair stand up. It wasn't fully fledged fear, but it was rapidly approaching that state.

"I had—" Eldred was suddenly red-faced. He leaned forward. "I had a dream. Last night, this was. I thought I heard an old woman singing, or laughing ... or crying, maybe, just outside my window at home."

Kozioł grew pale. "Złodziej Kołyski?"

Eldred looked suddenly sad. "Maybe. They say she walks more often in these last two years than before. I dreamt of more, though. I—"

Geroslaw led his stallion out of his stall, cocked his eyebrow at the boys, then moved toward the exit. "We head out as soon as all the horses are loaded and in the column, Kozioł," said he.

"Aye—won't be a minute. Ullans?!" He raised his voice to ensure he was heard. Three voices answered *aye* in eerie unison. Already he could see Tellan leading his horse out of her stall and toward the entrance.

"I dreamt of the world swallowing me—all vines and dark grasses. I'm being a baby, I know, but I have this horrid feeling I won't... I won't see you again." Eldred's voice was steady, though his eyes were shining.

Kozioł dropped his reigns and pulled his friend in for a proper embrace. "Just a dream, surely," he managed. Talk of vines and dark earth made him think of the hollow ones. "Stay safe, and I'll do the same. If all else fails... if you have another dream, speak to my cousin. Yeidil'll know what to do and won't laugh at you for acting like a child."

Eldred pulled back, nodding, wiping at his eyes. "All right," said he. It was all he could manage.

Deiter appeared at the entrance, casting about for him, like as not.

"I'm here. Just saying goodbye." He put a hand on Eldred's shoulder, then picked up the reins and led his horse out without so much as a glance back.

Whatever Eldred was dreaming of, Yeidil would know what to do. Hopefully, it was nothing but an overactive imagination. He doubted that, but he had hope.

Once he'd cleared the stables, he mounted up and rode to his place in the line, just behind his lord.

Azhferd gave him a grin, looking him up and down, then lifted his chin as he spoke to the assemblage.

"We go to secure a place in the inns and taverns, firesides, and bard songs for years to come! We ride to show them just how long our shadows truly are!" He looked at those who had come out to see them off, bowing his head toward them. When he looked up again, his words came out upon a rush of familiar melody. "Glory forward, home behind. United both in heart and mind. Let them all go run and hide..."

They half-sang, half-shouted their reply. "From the Black Tower, we shall ride!"

For a moment, Kozioł forgot about Eldred Gazlee and his odd dreams. He was caught up in the singularly strange and wonderful moment. His lord was leading the county off to win glory abroad, and he was riding off beside him.

With a heart full of new fire, he urged his horse forward. At last, they were on the move. In five short days, they would finally arrive at Zlaté Pole.

-III-

County Thorion
The Eastkindle
5 Korunasykli: 22 Days after the Red Storm at Westsong

Gordan waited in the saddle. Raegus had stepped off to attend his necessary. While the man was certainly more than capable of squatting against a tree without help or supervision, they both thought it best not to force one another to play catch-up after such a stop.

They'd been traveling for a few days now and without incident. Still, Gordan had felt a watchful presence marking their progress. He'd first marked and then frankly dismissed the sensation before they'd gone their first hour. Since then, it had faded and returned, faded, and returned, and each time it came back, it was somehow stronger than before.

He was fairly certain Raegus felt it, too, though neither of them spoke up about it. His taken brother, if that was the proper term—he had an idea it was but hadn't taken the time to ask the heralds when he'd had the chance—seemed to grow more chatty with each passing hour.

And that's your way, isn't it, Rae? You blather endlessly before a fight... your way of bleeding off your battle sweats, which is fair enough, I suppose.

As if the thought had summoned him, Raegus came tromping out of the willow grove they'd chosen, walking back toward his mount. He eyed Gordan as he approached, but they'd known one another for too many years for Gordan to mislabel that look. It was the simple, straightforward confirmation that all was yet well, and perhaps a sheepish apology for the smell he'd brought into the world.

Gordan gave a nod and a shrug for good measure. What in hells was the point of doing anything else? There'd been no change between the time Raegus had dismounted and the time he'd returned to the saddle, after all. It was bad before and had gotten no worse.

They rode on in silence, each to his own thoughts, for the moment. Gordan had an idea that Raegus would start blathering again within a few short minutes.

The real frustration was that the *sense* of watchful foreboding was just that—a sense. There was no sign, scent, sigil, or seal to point to, nothing that spoke of trouble or an enemy. Even the birds and insects continued singing their vapid, empty songs, blithely going on as if nothing out of the ordinary were afoot. Yet there was this indefinable sense that all was not well.

He'd tried to banish the idea. Of course he had. Given what he'd been through, it was more than reasonable to be paranoid about the unseen enemy, be they dead things rising or death's hand rising as he'd come to think of the goblins—there was ample reason to be on guard.

"We ought to be there by sunset," Raegus said.

Gordan grunted his acceptance of this. It was hardly news. It hadn't been news when Raegus had spoken of it an hour ago, nor three bells before that.

"Give us a song, Gordan, yeah?"

Gordan sighed. A song? He was a fair enough singer, but only Valad had ever asked him to perform. His brothers were polite, but had never seemed overly impressed by his voice.

"Go on," Raegus pressed. "Give us something to drive off the dusk."

Gordan fought the urge to roll his eyes. "It's an hour or more before dusk. Besides, by then, we'll be inside Wick's walls, drinking and eating. Better singers there, too."

Raegus sounded annoyed, insistent, and even more nervous. "Aye, fine. A song to help us gallop past the gloom, then. Just sing something... please?"

Gordan suddenly heard it—or rather stopped hearing it. The birds had stopped singing. No insect sounds rang out, only the soft sighing of the wind through the willows and the waist-high grasses. He saw what he should've seen straight off. Both his and Raegus's horses had their ears nearly straight back against their skulls.

Trouble starts far and wee, Valad used to say. *So much so that you won't always hear it coming. Dogs and horses are wiser than we. They'll hear or sniff a threat more often than we'll see or hear it, most of the time. Feed and care for them well, then mark them and how they react. The warnings they give you only need save your life a single time before you see the value in the bond we share.*

"Make ready to ride hard," he heard himself saying. "For now ... slow up."

"Slow?"

"Do as I *say*, Raegus! Argue later."

They slowed, watching, listening, waiting for the proverbial hammer—or perhaps the literal one—to fall.

The wind dropped away, then shifted, blowing from the northwest. On it came a mingled misery of scents: dung, blood, fear ... and the stomach-clenching stench that heralded death's hand.

"Goblins," Gordan said through tight lips.

Raegus nodded curtly. He tried not to shudder. An instant later, he unslung his shield from where it rested against his back. No sooner had he settled it into position along his dim arm than the tree line broke into open meadow, revealing the source of that noisome perfume.

To the north, they saw a wagon overturned, its horses nowhere in sight. The bodies of the dead were strewn about in various states of gore. Atop a low hillock, perhaps a dozen small figures hunched or squatted low around another, larger one.

Who or whatever they were surrounding, they were holding it down as it writhed, clearly trying to break free.

A muffled, muted howl of fear came from that hilltop. It was the sound of a fully grown man pleading for mercy that surely wouldn't come.

...Unless we bring it. No sooner had Gordan recognized this simple truth than he found himself urging his horse toward the hill, his sword suddenly in his bright hand. *What in all the hells am I doing?* The answer came almost as soon as his mind had grasped the question... *acting worthy of my spurs. That's what I'm doing.*

He heard Raegus behind him, first giggling, then laughing outright. Good. It was enough. They were two, but they were mounted. If they couldn't save the man, they could at least punish those who were tormenting him.

They rode up and over the hill, through the goblin's ring, their swords flashing like summer lightning. Gordan was careful to avoid trampling the prone man—and it *was* a man, to be sure. His horse leapt over the poor fellow, and as Gordan saw him plainly, he heard himself growl in rage and surprise.

From scarred head to sprung boots, rusted chain shirt to empty sword sheath—this man was, without question, either the world's unluckiest, most unsuccessful mercenary or was a brigand who was, perhaps, getting what was coming to him.

Gordan felt his sword connect with a goblin head as he passed back down the hill's other side. To his right, he saw Raegus hauling his sword-arm high, clearing it free of the groping, grasping hands of the goblins even as he spurred his horse down the hill.

Again, they made no noise, though Gordan could see nearly a dozen monstrous faces screaming silently, fangs bared and glistening, many-jointed fingers bending and pointing impossibly.

He turned, maneuvering his horse with his knees, making ready to charge again. It was then that he saw it.

A tall goblin—taller than the rest by perhaps a whole head—was coming out from around the overturned wagon, holding a longsword in one hand and an arrow in the other. That arrow looked *far* too familiar.

His mind was snapped back to his first, and thus far, only other encounter with these otherworldly things. He saw the hands pulling the goblin up over the lip of the palisade, saw it reaching to recover its bone arrow, felt the dull impact of his own sword against the creature's unyielding flesh... he saw its annoyed insistence as it focused on recovering its missile. It had clearly been *frustrated* at his full-force sword strokes, not afraid or angry, let alone in any semblance of pain. Recovering the arrow had been all-important...

Raegus's movement pulled him back into the moment at hand. His brother had ridden past him and was turning his horse to set up another run, moving to flank him on his right.

For his part, Gordan refused to wait. "Thorion!" he cried, charging up the hill, aiming right for that taller goblin-thing. The others were greedy, alien creatures, but the new arrival seemed somehow worse. Looking at it made the hair on the back of his neck stand on end.

At first, he couldn't understand why. As he swung his sword at it and found himself parried almost lazily by the longsword, he suddenly knew. The Goblin wasn't merely larger... it was broader, more well-muscled, and stood perfectly upright, just as any man would. It was, he reckoned, as *tall* as any man in the county, as well.

Gordan could hear Raegus screaming his own battle-cry from somewhere behind him. As he guided his horse back around for yet another run, he was forced to rein up short. "Storms be swift..." It was all he could manage.

The tall goblin had moved to where the bound man was. He'd drawn the arrow in his hand up high, as if it were a dagger, and rammed it home into the man's upper body. A pale light too brief to name or categorize suddenly burst upward along the arrow's shaft. When the Goblin pulled the arrow free... the creature began to change.

It seemed to stretch and shift, growing taller and broader of chest. Its arms and legs were suddenly the size of young tree trunks. The transformation occurred so swiftly that the creature staggered under its own sudden weight. The goblins raised their hands in silent triumph. The creature regained its balance, standing tall... *impossibly* tall. Gordan hazarded it as fully eight feet, and perhaps a bit more.

He thought he'd never been so afraid in his life... and then the thing turned, pointing its now-blue-ish finger directly at him, its face wearing a broad, wicked grin.

"Run. Run!" He did his best to shout this, but was genuinely too afraid to know if he'd seen what he thought he had. Had the thing begun to mouth words... words in the Trade Tongue?

A moment later, he heard hoofbeats thundering alongside him. Neither he nor Raegus looked back as they rode, each fearing to be the one who broke the silence. Each fearing to speak the truth aloud.

Jastar had had the right of it. They were intelligent, clearly. Goblins were cradle-tale monsters rumored to bring with them everything from minor mischief to murder. They'd steal a man's fine buttons, a maid's clothing, coin, or freshly baked pies. In particularly horrid tales, they would thieve cattle, or unattended horses, come to claim their own—disobedient children, or in more vengeance-driven tales—the abused ones, stealing them from neglectful parents. They were the minions of sorcerers and witches, savage pets ready to punish at their master's word.

Yes, indeed. Goblins are cradle-tale monsters. Gordon's undermind refused to let go of the ritual he'd seen—the arrow, the light, the transformation. *The Nebelblut, however, are something else entirely.*

Half a bell later, as the sunset began to paint the sky red, they rode at speed through Wick's gate, demanding they close and bar it... demanding, in Ylspeth's name, that they make ready for battle.

-IV-

County Thorion
Eastshadow
5 Korunasykli: 22 Days after the Red Storm at Westsong

Barnic was lost in thought. He was fully dressed, seated upon his bed, and absently watching the serving girl build up the fire in the hearth.

He was thinking about Westsong, of course. They'd just kept coming. He'd wondered again and again where they'd all been coming from. It had been as if for every once-man or once-woman he'd felled, two more rose up.

It'd been Marcza who'd seen what was happening—that some of them had some form of wretched sorcery at their disposal—and were quite literally summoning reinforcements out of thin, heated air.

"Never mind wounding them, disabling them—never mind fighting duels!" she'd commanded. *"Take their heads, or shove them into the fire—nothing more, nothing less! Thorion!"*

They'd obeyed, of course, but that had been reactive, not a conscious decision. He'd liked—had always respected Marcza, but had never been comfortable with the idea of her being on the battlefield. Not until that moment, at any rate.

Oh, he hadn't begrudged her learning to fight, nor any other thing she chose to do, but he'd had a difficult time thinking of her as a warrior. Women were to be protected, not patronized by encouraging action that could rarely, if ever rightly, be rewarded.

Women weren't knights and soldiers—not if they were still accounted *women*, at least. They could not be genteel—could not be accounted feminine *and* be seen as equal in war. *That* was a *masculine* calling, after all. A woman could certainly prove herself capable at such arts. The price she *paid* for being *recognized* for it was no longer being seen as, well, a woman.

That was what he'd thought—what he'd believed utterly until Westsong. She was no less a woman, no less beautiful in his eyes—yet she had not only fought like Saint Hyrro of Traead walking the world once more, she had *led* them. Through her presence of mind, they had survived long enough for Kaith and the countess to ... to do whatever it was they'd done to end it at last. Marcza's eye and mind were keen, and her sword arm strong, yet she remained, in his eyes at least, the very embodiment of the word *woman*.

"Mi'lord?"

The servant girl's voice slapped him out of his long thoughts. "... Gathering wool. What is it?"

She was a girl of perhaps sixteen or seventeen, he thought. She was pretty, but, to his mind at least, *looked* like a girl, as opposed to a woman. He was forcibly reminded of his final conversation with Jastar the night the goblins had attacked. "The Nebelblut," he murmured.

The girl's eyes grew large. "Mi'lord, ee'mustn't say such 'r ee'll call down a terrible mischief..." Her voice was breathless and horrified. This did nothing to alter his view of her as still a young girl, but he smiled just the same.

"What do they call you?" He did his best to make his voice kindly.

"Kelsey, mi'lord," said she, offering him a child-like curtsey.

Barnic repeated the name, trying to commit it to memory. Judging by her sudden blush and the way she was leaning toward him, he thought she might be misreading his kindness for outright *desire*. He was drawing breath to say something further-he'd no idea what that something might've been-when there came the sound of rapid footfalls approaching in the hall, followed by a hammering upon his door.

"Lord Eastshadow! You must come! Sir Aethan says... He says..."

Barnic stood, walking to the door and yanking it open. "Out with it, man!"

The guardsman who stood there looked as if he'd seen... well, as if he'd seen Westsong. His face was pale, lips white, eyes wide. He was holding to his courage, but it was a near thing. "They've come, Lord. We're surrounded..."

The girl—Kelsey, she'd said—gasped behind him and sat down on the bed. He heard the soft crunch of the fabric as her weight crushed it.

Barnic took a moment to consider, holding up his hand, palm out to the guard. If Aethan had sent for him, and if this man spoke of them being surrounded—besieged—he would need to be seen, be heard, and be calm. He would need, in other words, to be in command. He stepped back a pace, turned, and picked up his sword. It was still in its sheath upon its belt. Pulling it around his waist and knotting it into place, he nodded to the guard and made a gesture for him to lead the way.

"Kelsey..." He looked back over his shoulder.

"Mi'lord?"

"The children will need your strength." He was referring to the pages and young girls who served as fledgling maids and cook's assistants in the lord's residence. He placed a hand on the guardsman's shoulder, slowing him just a touch. "We'll see to the trouble without. I need you to see to the trouble within before it grows out of control. Will'ee do it?" He hadn't meant to drop into her accent on this last question, but it was starting to get into his blood. He'd been here for just under a fortnight, but pronunciations—hells, sometimes whole words seemed to sneak in, like rats finding a way into the cellar.

He felt the guard breathe a sigh of relief—a thing he hadn't expected but certainly welcomed. Kelsey, meanwhile, stood once more, back straighter than before the guard's arrival. "Yes, mi'lord. I'll see to it."

"Thank you." He nodded to her, turned back to the guard, and bade him lead on. A moment later found the hall doors open to the outside. Two things struck him at once. The first was the bite of cold. The temperature had dropped sharply in the hour he'd been indoors. Perhaps it was a normal and reasonable change, but it felt like an ill omen to him.

The second thing that struck him was the miserable, low stench that could only belong to the Nebelblut. Judging by the strength of the smell, there were a job lot of them, indeed.

"Take me to Aethan," he said. He made his voice sharp but not panicked. This wasn't the time for panic ... not yet, at least.

The guardsman murmured his assent and moved quickly through the courtyard of the grand palisade. He bolted up the wooden stairs along the wall, two steps at a go. Given the man was in a shirt of iron chain, this spoke well of his strength, at least.

Barnic followed, marked Aethan's lanky form, made it halfway to the man's side, and stopped short.

He saw a veritable sea of lumpish grey shapes stood tall within the long grasses on one, two, three sides of his palisade. The only side they weren't currently peopling was the one which led from the grand palisade to the other districts of the village—the killing road between the seven wooden gates.

"They're just... just *standing* there!" This was one of the guardsmen near at hand, his bow nocked and at the ready, though not yet drawn back.

Barnic finished his walk to Aethan. He could see the fear in the man's amber eyes. Normally they held a striking warmth when reflecting torchlight. Tonight, however, they were tiny stones that seemed somehow cold and empty.

"Report."

Aethan grinned, though there was no humor in it. "Archers. There'll be at least one in three that are archers. Maybe more."

"Do we have enough—"

"No. Your palisade and one or two others might have enough, but the rest... if they press the attack, which they will—never doubt it—you can expect to lose them."

Barnic thought nodded, then turned to the guard who brought him. "Find me Cadwyd."

"Ee'll be in 'is bed, Lord."

"Which district?"

"First Well, Lord."

"Aethan?" Barnic didn't bother to detail his question. Aethan would understand it without him wasting time spelling it out.

"Southeastern-most—he'll survive once it starts. First Well's as safe as we can hope for."

Barnic nodded. He spoke first to the guardsman. "You're strong. Are you fast?"

The man blinked, then grinned. "Aye, mi'lord. If it's a footrace, I won't disappoint."

"Even in your iron?"

"...Second-skin, Lord." Was that pride he'd heard? He hoped so. Pride would beat back fear, for the moment at least.

"To the gate," said he. "You won't open it wide, just enough for you to slip out on my mark. You're for First Well." He held up a hand. "Aethan? First, second, third, or third, fifth?"

"Second, third," said Aethan.

So the eastern side palisades were numbered one, two, and three from south to north. That made the western side four through six. Presumably, that was the order in which Sir Cedric had created the districts when he became Lord of Eastshadow. Fair enough.

To the guardsman, then, Barnic gave his final word on the matter. "Get Fourth Well evacuated into First with haste, as quietly as you can. Set archers to cover the southern parapet of First, in case the Nebelblut start to flank. If you manage to get, Fourth emptied, or nearly so, move on to empty Fifth into Second. Do you see?"

The guardsman was grinning. "Aye, Lord. If all's well, you'll have wall to wall in the eastern districts, but folk'll be safe." This wasn't the time to argue how safe any of them would be. "Will I 'ave time's the real question."

Barnic turned back to Aethan. "Archers need to focus along the corners—northeast and northwest more than anywhere else ... at least for the first volley. Be prepared to spread out along the walls as needed. Send word to the other district captains. Where's your banner-bearer?"

"He's just there." Aethan waved a pimple-faced youth over. The boy held a banner pole in one hand, its flag still tightly furled, and a massive horn in the other. As he approached, Aethan continued speaking. "You want to make them look north while your man runs south." He grinned, looking a touch more like himself. "Won't work, but it's better than sitting and waiting."

"You're so sure?"

"Not at all, brother." His grin widened as he pointed to nearby archers to get into position. "Remember Valad's talk of how to view the world? Is the mug half full or half empty?"

Barnic nodded, snorting. "Yes, and aye, and I do."

"Well, I always find it easier to be sad I'm through half a measure than happy I've half a measure left." He placed a hand on Barnic's shoulder and spoke a final word before stepping forward to their archery line. "I'd rather think fondly on what I've lost than try and cheer myself with what I've got left. Makes me savor every drop in the mug, rather than pretend everything's just fine."

Barnic turned to regard his runner, but the man was already down the stairs, waiting by the gate. "Fair," said he.

Aethan drew his sword, making ready to give the orders as necessary. "At your word, Lord Eastshadow..."

-V-

County Thorion
Wick
5 Korunasykli: 22 Days after the Red Storm at Westsong

"No, Ricgerd, I swear it to you as sure as Falxes on fall fires—he was trying to get Robis to speak up and volunteer. He reached his foot across, slow and steady beneath the table, found his target, and squeeeeeezed." Kaith leaned forward as he drew out the word, grinning at his host even as he pressed his foot down on the man's booted toes.

They sat at the long trestle table, Ricgerd snorting at its head, Kaith to his right. A few other local would-be courtiers—Ricgerd's childhood friends, or so they accounted themselves, seated with them.

Ricgerd's eyes were wide as he listened to the tale. He grinned, mustache twitching as he looked at Kaith.

A man called either Alec or Aleks—the fellow had been so disinterested in courtesy that Kaith hadn't heard clearly—now stood up, leaning across the table. His mouth worked, his thin face a perfect, pre-tantrum red.

His hair was black—showing Venzene heritage somewhere in his line's history. It was hung fashionably to shoulder length, save a single silver braid that had been either dyed or added as adornment. In the dim candlelight, this affectation looked like some large animal had tried to eat

Alec-Aleks' head but pulled away before the job was done, leaving behind a great runner of drool.

Kaith saw the fellow flare at the nostrils, working himself up to saying whatever was on his mind. Tired of waiting, he met Terrek's eye across the room, then addressed the man whose name he did not precisely know, directly.

"Something ... troubles you, friend?" He kept his voice mild ... foot slowly withdrawing its pressure from Ricgerd's own.

"Aye, *sir*. It's ee. Ee're bovering me. How dare ee speak ill th' dead like 'at?!" His voice was undoubtedly meant to be intimidating. It had a practiced gravel to its otherwise smooth baritone, which gave it an element of danger.

He's spoiling for a fight—one he doesn't actually have to take part in, for the guards would put a stop to it in Ricgerd's hall before it went far. Why? What's he hoping to... Kaith suddenly understood. The man wanted to earn Ricgerd's favor—wanted to be seen as one of his stalwarts. *Well, what of that? Let him, so long as Ricgerd remains aboard the wagon with the rest of us. I've no right to pick his friends for him, have I...*

"How've I spoken ill of anyone, friend?" He did his best to present as little an air of intimidation as possible. Laying both hands on the tabletop, palms down, he met the man's hostile gaze with bemused curiosity.

"Ee know perfectly well 'ow ea have ... sir."

"That's *twice* you've spoken my honorific as if you'd tasted something sour, friend. Best of my knowledge, I've done nothing to call your anger down, and I'm certain you aren't trying to wake my own. Let's come at this a-fresh, ay?" Kaith continued to wear that same expression of bemused curiosity. "I was there and speak only truth of Sir Reginald. He meant to draw the not-yet Sir Robis into offering himself to aid the forester's wife in her time of need. He found my foot instead. No insult, just a thing to laugh at..."

Alec-Aleks slammed his hands on the table-top, beginning to lean forward over Kaith. He'd drawn breath to make an answer when Ricgerd reached up—as casually as if he'd meant to swat a fly—and backhanded his so-called childhood friend. The blow was hard enough to force him back into his seat.

"I'll not have you insult my guest at my table, Aleks Silverson."

"But Ric—mi'lord, this man was speakin' ill of your father!"

Ricgerd stood without a word, walked over to the suddenly terrified Aleks, and grabbed him by his moderately expensive-looking tunic. He hauled him out of the chair, turned him bodily so they faced one another, and brought down a tremendous headbutt somewhere above the man's right eye.

Aleks yelped in pain, which was no wonder. He staggered and would have fallen were it not for Ricgerd's hands holding fast to his shoulders.

"You'll not see a meal in my hall again for a fortnight," said Ricgerd, voice surprisingly low and calm, almost as if he were offering consolation. "At that point, you may be allowed to return to it. For now..." He turned him, shoving him toward the door and the waiting guards. "I want you out of my sight. *No* man insults a guest in my home... *no* man."

Kaith saw Aleks nearly fall twice on his way to the guards, one of whom put an arm around the man's shoulders and escorted him from the tower's main chamber.

Ricgerd looked at the other four men seated at the table, nodded, then retook his place at its head.

"...My lord?" A slightly rotund youth, who'd sat on Kaith's right, spoke up. "Forgive me, but can you explain to me where he offended you?"

Here's one to watch, thought Kaith. *Greggor would either love or hate this one, depending on his real intent. He's a thinker, at least. That's something.*

Ricgerd grabbed his wooden mug, glowering at it as if it had personally offended him. It was to the mug, in fact, that he addressed his reply. "Am I a fool, would you say, Tavin?"

The rotund youth, whose name was apparently Tavin, blanched for a moment, then smiled. "What an absurd question, my lord..."

Kaith noted that the man hadn't answered it—had, in fact, artfully sidestepped it entirely. He was pleased, therefore, when Ricgerd spoke again.

"Aye, it is. I'll have you answer it as well as complimenting it."

"I... my lord, you are a warrior—your strength is the stuff of legend. You are wise enough to surround yourself with those who lack your prowess upon the field, yet add their strength of mind and will to bolster your own."

Ricgerd nodded at this. "Sir Kaith?"

"Ricgerd?"

"Would you agree with Tavin?"

Kaith took a moment to look both men up, then down again. "I would." He caught Tavin's triumphant grin from the corner of his eye—and saw it wink out in shock a moment later. "You aren't a *smart* man. A fool? No, but you're not the man I'd send word to beg aid from if I needed a great mind."

The room fell silent. Almost all faces wore disbelief and shock in nearly equal measure.

Ricgerd, on the other hand, nodded at this, then reached a hand every bit as swift as the one that had bloodied Aleks's lip out to his right. The room winced, but nobody seemed capable of looking away.

They were understandably all but undone when Ricgerd's hand fell on Kaith's shoulder and gave it a companionable squeeze, followed by Ricgerd's nod and heartfelt laughter.

"M—" Tavin started but couldn't find his voice to finish at first. As Kaith's own smile and laughter joined in, however, he at last unearthed it. "My lord, this man has clearly and directly insulted you! He's done it at your table and in front of we, your friends! You cannot expect us to stand by and say or do *nothing*, surely!"

"Truth and honesty, Tavin, are called *truth* and *honesty* for a reason. Insults are something else entirely. It's why they've different names for them. I hope someday you'll learn to tell them apart."

The outer door chose that moment to burst open, heralding the sound of booted footfalls as they raced toward the hall.

"My lord! My *lord*! We are besieged! Two knights have made it inside the gate in just the nick! They sent me to find you!" This breathless burst of information was delivered by a guardsman who looked to be just downstream from his boyhood. His gambeson was pristine—as if he'd taken it from the local armsmaster's stock just this evening.

Ricgerd stood, reaching for his sword from beside the high seat.

Kaith, who was standing as well, lifting his chin to set his men in motion, caught Ricgerd's eye and bowed his head as he spoke. "Terrek, take Vilmocz and head to the town's gate. Huron? Find Olshnak and tell him what we know."

"The orc?" Ricgerd did nothing to hide his confusion. "What do you need a herald for?"

"This one's a siege engineer as well. We'll want him to give your defenses an eye—find what weak spots there may be."

Ricgerd grinned, eyes wide. "Aye, good! With sword in hand and spear behind?"

Kaith belted his own sword on. "Aye, I'll stand with 'ee again. Still angry I missed the northern marches tourney, after all."

Ricgerd's grin was enormous. He laughed, a nearly demonic *ha-ha*! As the pair made their way toward the door and the still fairly breathless guardsman, Kaith asked a question that should have occurred to him sooner.

"Two knights, you say? Did they have arms or give their names?"

"I didn't see their arms, mi'lord. Heard a name, though. Sir ... Gordan?"

Kaith stopped short, considering. "One of my brothers, then. Ill reason to see him, but we'll be glad of his sword arm to be sure."

With that, they moved down the hall, their tablemates forgotten.

-VI-

Venzene Duchy of Kamieńalun
County Czarny Wodospad
5 Korunasykli: 22 Days after the Red Storm at Westsong

Geroslaw leaned over to his right, setting his head close enough to Azhferd's ear to allow their conversation some degree of privacy. "Do you plan..." he paused, rethinking his approach before asking his question anew. "Do you hope or expect to do it?" He grinned. "At Zlaté Pole, I mean."

Azhferd kept his face solemn. It wasn't difficult. The wind had picked up, blowing snow to rest along his black beard, in his eyebrows ... even on the brim of his kolpak hat. His red kontusz alone seemed immune to this dusting.

"Well? You've been called to the line now. You've the right to call others as and when you like. We both know their loyalty to you, and after seeing the way they've taken to your training—as if you were already their knight—it wouldn't be out of the question, would it?"

Azhferd shifted the subject as they rounded the next bend, and their stopping point came into view. Kozioł, the sergeants, and the pages had ridden ahead to find and secure a place to camp. They were to set up tents and a cook-fire in advance of the main force's arrival—the noble heirs and gentry's sons.

"Geri, look," said he, lifting his chin in that direction.

"Aye, the camp. They've done a fair enough job. Certainly, they wasted no time. You've not answered my question, Ash…"

Azhferd shook his head lightly. Keeping his voice neutral, he tried again. "Take another look, Geri. You might see it now."

Geroslaw winced, grinned, and sat more fully upright in his saddle. He saw a modest fire with a large spit already in position above it, a scattering of tents great and small, the wagons, their horse teams, and a dozen other steeds huddled together … and a horse he didn't recognize. It was pale-coated, short-eared, and as sleek as a snow leopard on the hunt. No wonder he'd missed it. It nearly disappeared into the snow-spattered landscape around it.

"Who does that fellow belong to?"

Azhferd shrugged, smiling in a way that turned him into a younger version of their father. "Perhaps we should find out." He paused as Kozioł jogged to the road's edge, ready to meet them. "Perhaps my squire knows."

A moment later, they'd dismounted as Kozioł took both sets of reins.

"A knight," the boy said without prompting. "He says he, or at least his family's, from Biały Klif, but his accent is strange. It's not rich and rolling like the Sheshik, and it isn't Venzene, as far as I could tell. Flat sounding, I'd say."

Geroslaw nodded, blinking down at the boy. He wasn't certain if he was impressed, amused, or disturbed by the report—both its content and its thoroughness.

Azhferd gave no sign of whatever reaction he might have had to Kozioł's tale. He asked two questions, however. "Where is he—or perhaps *they*, if he had armsmen—now?"

"In front of Lord Vonrik's tent, warming himself. It was the first one stood up, as it's the simplest."

"And did you happen to hear what name or line he offered?"

Kozioł rolled his eyes, blushing as he put on a sheepish grin. "I did. Forgive me. His name is Dorean—Syr Dorean of Cedar… hall? That was it. Syr Dorean of Cedarhall. Do either of you know it?"

Azhferd and Geroslaw exchanged a silent consultation, then both shook their heads.

"Anything else, Dargory?" Geroslaw was disappointed to see Kozioł not so much as blink at the use of his given name, but never mind.

"Maybe?" When both men looked at him expectantly, he shook his head as if to clear it. "It was in the way he introduced himself. His title."

Azhferd's voice was conversational, albeit low in volume. "…Syr?"

"No. He pronounced it... he pronounced it *surr,* as in *yes sir*—as if it were a common sign of respect, not an accolade to be earned."

"You *did* say his speech was strange," Geroslaw offered.

Kozioł shook his head. "I did, but when I repeated it to confirm I'd heard him rightly—*Sairr* Dorean—he was swift to correct me." Here he took on an obvious attempt to sound like the man in question. "*Surr,* young squire. *Surr* Dorean... not Syr."

The two men dismounted, Azhferd's hand landing on his squire's shoulder for an affectionate pat. "See to the horses, then get either into the tent or near to the fire." He turned to Geroslaw and arched his brows. "Would you be good enough to act as my herald in this matter?"

Geroslaw snorted. "Am I announcing *you* or distracting *him?*"

"Both, of course. I need to see that all's in readiness in our tent before inviting the man in for a drink and a chat."

Geroslaw began to nod but finished by bowing his head in case they were being observed. "Of course, my Lord... Auburg?"

Azhferd shrugged. "What does it matter? You'll be the one introducing us. If you use a different title, you can use it again when you make introductions."

They parted company.

Ten minutes later found one of the Ullan boys headed over to Geroslaw, who was entertaining the affable Sir Dorean. Kozioł had been right. The man's speech had, indeed, been strange. Still, he was charming, polite, and engaging. *The Ullan*—Geroslaw hadn't so much as a guess which one of the triplets it was, nor did it much matter at present—took on a wide-eyed, formal tone as he announced that Syr Azhferd would like to offer hospitality to both Geroslaw and the newcomer.

Sir Dorean seemed pleased and mildly impressed by the offer and the way it was delivered.

Given Azhferd had invited Geroslaw to share the tent with he and his men while they shared the road, he couldn't help but smile. Furs had been hung on the walls, making the inside both warmer and quieter. It reminded him of the command tent Count Edmund had used, and Lord Alojz before him.

"Lord Azhferd," Geroslaw began. "May I present Sir Dorean, Knight of County Thorion, Lord of Cedarhall. Sir Dorean, may I present Syr Azhferd, Lord of Auburg, commander of the combined forces of County Blackfalls."

Both men bowed, Dorean noticeably more deeply than Azhferd, and then took their seats around the small wooden table that had, apparently, been traveling in one of the carts.

Mulled wine—spiced and blessedly hot—was poured for all by Kozioł. Geroslaw noted he didn't make eye contact, nor did he spill so much as a drop.

After a few minutes of utterly vapid pleasantries, Azhferd spoke up with a touch more seriousness in his soft voice. "I've invited you to share a drink with me because I was told that you were a serious man—a man who has earned the accolade of knighthood and is the master of his own lands. They aren't lands, forgive me, that I have personally heard of, but the world is wide. Nobody can be expected to know everything."

"I thank you, Sir Azhferd," he began, though he mispronounced the honorific, at least from the Venzene perspective. "You've honored me. Clearly, you and your household have not forgotten the edicts of hospitality. Would that all men had such a grasp of the old ways."

Azhferd made a gesture of appreciation that also served to transition to a new topic. Geroslaw found himself both surprised and impressed at how easily he'd managed it—was managing this entire affair, in fact.

"Tell me, sir. What brings you to my county? Are you simply passing through? Do you ... have family nearby?"

"I do have family some days northwest, but I must confess my hope not to be forced to impinge upon their hospitality any longer than necessary. I make for the War of Counties, where I am to meet the rest of my party."

Azhferd nodded, leaving the matter of his family alone for the moment. "You would be welcome to share the road with my company. We, too, are bound for Zlaté Pole."

Dorean smiled broadly. "I'd hoped that would be the case and gladly accept the offer." He paused for a sip of wine, then asked an unexpected question. "Tell me, sir, do you have but one member of the Bluemark in your service?"

Azhferd saluted with his wooden goblet. "Geroslaw was born in Auburg, which is my holding. He isn't strictly in my service ... at present."

"I see..." He made a gesture of consideration, then asked, "May I address him for a moment, sir?"

Azhferd motioned his acceptance.

"Geroslaw, my fellows and I come to Zlaté Pole in hopes of procuring the services of a company such as yours. All is, I fear, not well in Thorion.

I wonder if you would consider arranging a meeting with whomever is appropriate to negotiate contracts on the Bluemark's behalf these days... my dear friend Sir Giles is attempting to secure the Coterie of Bronze, who are rumored to attend this year for single combat and small team events, but I should prefer the Bluemark." He paused for a moment, then grinned as he added, "I began my career serving in their ranks some years ago. Tell me, is Eane still counted among your number?"

Geroslaw brightened. "He is when last seen, yes. He's off on contract with a largish chunk of ours in the south—beyond even Thorion, mind." This small bit of information was of little practical value to anyone. The vague area south of Thorion spanned hundreds of miles of ever-more-frigid forests and marshlands. He may as well have pointed in a direction and said *Eane is that way*, for all the good it would do this man.

Dorean nodded, grinning even more broadly. "When I retired from service, it was due to winning a tournament in Thorion County. Eane was my captain at the time and released me with a simple admonishment. We never forget our own, Dorean, he said to me, so long as they don't forget us." He lifted his wooden goblet to Geroslaw in a small salute, bowing his head.

Geroslaw followed suit, grinning in spite of himself.

"Will you make the necessary introductions, then?" Dorean sounded both wistful and hopeful in equal measure.

He considered for a moment, then gave a nod of agreement, slowly. "I can do that. I may be able to negotiate myself, depending on how things play out at the tournament. In either case, I can make certain you speak to the right person, and gladly."

"Ahhh, excellent... and so, I say to you, Geroslaw... Odvážna krv."

Geroslaw nodded his head and clicked his goblet against Dorean's. "Aye, sir. Odvážna krv, indeed."

Epilogue

-I-

The Green Lands
5 Korunasykli: 22 Days after the Red Storm at Westsong

I can be here ... away.
Ayomth ahn oh.
Ahn oruu, Ahn oruu, Ahn oruu.
I hold my own.
Oh, and I have fire for...
Oh, and I have fire in my heart.
Oh, and I can die in fire...

Lashjuk dozed, *dreaming* of fire. Voices—a chorus of whispers—grasped at her as she floated past them. They spoke of vital things she knew she mustn't forget, and which were gone as soon as that thought had burst upon her.

There were angry, rasping taunts, inarticulate rage that was somehow at once both deadly and impotent, a hunger that would never—could never be sated—yet which burned and roiled as each new meal came near its red, shifty mouth.

Between all of this, surrounding and occasionally overtaking the other sounds, there was the song. The voice was as familiar as her own, though it was certainly not *her* singing. It was sweet and haunting and full of words she didn't recognize.

No, I recognize them. I simply don't understand them.

She hadn't heard the melody before ... had she?

On and on and on, she floated. Every now and again, she thought she heard Maksu laughing uncontrollably, Sulok weeping softly, Eobum speaking to... not to her, but to someone. At one point, she thought he, too, might be weeping, but even in her half-mad slumber, she doubted these phantasms. They may have been true things, and they may have been echoes of her battered heart.

These moments of madness were interspersed with long bouts of utter black silence. She both feared and reveled in these. Oblivion had its allure when all the world made you weary. She knew she didn't want to remain in that state for long, but for minutes, perhaps even hours at a time? That was a gift she would gladly receive.

"Lashjuk? Lashjuk... Lashjuk, you must wake." Was *that* voice familiar? She thought so, but couldn't be certain. Oblivion was calling her back with its beckoning silence. She turned away from the voice, and for a moment, she thought she'd won the contest, earning her the peace of the utter—the soft emptiness—of the black beyond... whatever that was. She found herself wondering where such phrases had come from. She couldn't recall having heard them, let alone said them before.

A new sound came to her. No, that wasn't right. It wasn't a sound. It was a sense, a presence... an aspect moving, expanding, undulating in the utter that surrounded her. Was it whispering? Sending out thought rather than sound? Madness, surely, but then what about her life these last few weeks *hadn't* been tinged with madness? She couldn't hear it in the normal sense of that oh-so-familiar word, but she still somehow received it. It was a distant thing, but too certain, too *real* to be simple fancy.

"I... I hear you. Do I know you?" She felt herself rolling in the grass. The grass? Was she meant to be in the grass? Surely not, yet she was certain she smelled, heard, and felt it as she moved. The presence reached out to her once more. "I... on your back? That makes no..."

Her eyes snapped open in shocked understanding. She saw the deep blue of dusk above her, and yes, she was indeed laying atop the grass beneath that brilliant blue sky.

She sat up, casting about for her... her what? Her friend? Her companion? Her mount? She didn't know how to think of the creature that had aided her. She found it—smaller than a house cat, yet truly and clearly the same creature. It was wriggling around her in a slow circle amidst the grass.

"Gi awka glem, what happened to you?" Hearing the words made her wince. That had been Eobum's favorite expression of disbelief or incredulity. It meant blood and iron in her mother tongue.

"Mother tongue," she murmured. That brought her mind back to where she was and why she was there. It brought her mind back to Maksu.

She scooped the serpent up into her arms, then gave it to lie across the back of her neck, which it did without complaint.

"What? We're *where*?" Once more, she had sensed its meaning but not heard its voice. "Is it you I'm... well, not hearing, but..." She trailed off, considering. "Prove it to me." She paused for a moment, then bowed her head in thought. *How indeed?*

"Wrap yourself about my brow like a noble's circlet. If you do that of your own accord, I'll know it's you, I'm..." She shrugged. "... hearing."

Within seconds, the black serpent with the all-too-human head had, indeed, wrapped itself around her forehead.

She shuddered at the realization. "All right. I believe you. Why have you lost your voice? Why've you become so small a thing?"

The creature moved back down to rest across her shoulders and the back of her neck.

"...Haven't bonded yet... haven't finished the... you've exhausted the power you... Wait, *all* of it? You've no ability to help me find my son? To get us back to Eobum?" She cocked her head to the side as if listening. Nodding, she got to her feet and cast about herself.

Lashjuk stood beneath a green canopy of monstrously large trees. She was in a grove of the alien things, on a hilltop she didn't think she could otherwise have picked out from any of the dozens of others she'd seen in this place.

She sensed the serpent's urging and nodded, walking through the grove to the hill's other side. The trees ignored her. She had no idea why that thought should have bloomed in her mind in the first place, let alone why it should bring her such comfort. Of *course* the trees had ignored her. They were trees, after all. No tree she'd ever seen had ever expressed so much as an opinion in any way she'd ever seen or heard.

As she exited on the hillock's far side, she saw perhaps fifty men on horseback with a similar force on foot. Both of these surrounded a traveling coach that would likely be the envy of any noble who laid eyes upon it. She doubted the Emperor himself had better. It was tall and long, well-built out of dark woods that seemed to shimmer in the pale light of day's end.

"What? All right." She stepped to the left and climbed atop the humped up turves there, giving her a slightly higher vantage from a slightly different perspective. All at once, she understood why she'd been bidden to move.

The magnificent coach had a single blemish to mar the visage its owner wanted to project. The team that drew the vehicle was made up of horses, as one might expect, but any hope of meeting other expectations stopped there. The horses were sun-bleached bone. They weren't bone-white—they were made utterly of bone.

"Not pos—"

She nodded, shuddering. "They look like the bones of draft horses." She paused, shook her head, then nodded it. "Warhorses? Fine, but what does it matter? Who are... Ebistian? My Maksu is..." She began to move.

No sooner had she taken her first steps down the hill than the coach and its escort began to move. Mere feet beyond where they'd stood, they simply winked out of existence.

"No!" She began to run down the hill. She knew she'd never catch them, but standing by and crying off Maksu's rescue never occurred to her.

By the time she'd made it to the bottom of the hill, the coach itself had rolled forward and disappeared.

She screamed ... not knowing what else to do. She clenched and unclenched her fists, reached back to pull an azhkast—in her mind, it was the one that had killed the Vodnik, but she didn't know for certain—and swung the weapon around her head like a quarterstaff.

Finally, she stopped her screaming and fell to her knees, too full of anger to even sob. A moment later, her head snapped up, looking at the air before her.

"You can? Can you get me back?" She paused, eyes growing wide. "What am I to do when I've rescued him?" She rolled her eyes in anger, voice bitter. "Hide? Your *wise council* is that I rescue him and *hide*?" Her face softened somewhat, as did her voice. "How do I perform the... yes, but I know nothing of magic... but if..." She bowed her head.

"You'll send me back to Skolf, and when I recover my boy, I'm to hide. When I feel safe enough to sleep, you'll find me back here, and you'll teach me the rite, yes? Have I heard that rightly?" A sigh escaped her clenched jaw. "Hells, what choice?" She snorted. "Aye, fair. You're right, of course. I didn't come this far to leave him in that demon's hands."

She considered walking toward where the column had disappeared. Fenglem had taught her to mark her surroundings—to mark the terrain in her mind, looking for bolt holes, animal dens, and places to ambush from. She was relieved to find she was doing so now, and without prompting.

"Aye, but are there places to hide back on Skolf? Does the land look ... like this?" She gestured around with the azhkast she still held.

"You can see through to *Skolf*? Gi awka glem, *yes,* I want you to show it to me!"

Her vision underwent a strange redoubling, then she saw the landscape on the other side of whatever vale lay between here and there. The landscape wasn't simply different from her current surroundings. It was all-too-familiar. She was looking at the outskirts of Count Edmund's encampment!

A battle was taking place between several hundred men, women... Hells, were those children on the wall? The attacking force seemed predominantly made up of Eodenth and what were more than likely Eodenth Gnoerks.

And the Bluemark are on the damned walls...

She saw, but could not hear, drums being beaten with large wooden mallets from the back of the enemy line. They played in a strange, shared rhythm, each hand striking in lock with his or her fellows.

"What? Where!" She saw Ebistian exiting his coach, smiling sourly as he surveyed the battle—a battle his own forces were not yet engaged in.

A regal-looking woman in a flowing azure dress rode over to meet him, and they began to speak. Their expressions suggested no love lost between them.

No matter. This was her chance. She moved to the coach's door, then realized she couldn't touch it. As real as it looked, it wasn't here—wherever here truly was.

She cast about, trying to find a place to hide once she arrived, then smiled a triumphant smile.

"Do I need to walk when you send me there?... Some movement. Can I roll? *Yes,* on the ground. Where *else* would I roll?" She nodded, a darksome grin—a predator's grin crawling across her face.

Lashjuk moved to the coach and got down on the ground beside it, her body parallel to its length. She rolled back and forth a few times, testing and readjusting her starting position. At last, she was satisfied.

"At my word, then. You'll work your will, and I'll roll beneath the coach. Are you ready?" She drew in a few shallow breaths as if she were about to jump into cold water. "Vrek... Tok?... Morl!" She rolled right.

The sound that struck her was almost too much to bear. Screams, drums, battle cries, arrow fire, line commands, calls for aid of one sort or another—it was all there, all at once, and all *impossibly* loud.

The drums—hells, the drums! She could feel their vibration strongest of all, hammering past flesh, invading—overriding—merging with the rhythm of her pounding heart. It was all she could do to remember her own *name*, let alone what she was doing there!

Lashjuk's eyes were watering. She somehow managed to reach up and grasp one part of the keel pole that ran the coach's length, hooking her ankles over another. If she was patient for just a moment longer, she would be able to...

Ebistian laughed, high and somewhat madly. "You took Haluzfeld to nearly no purpose! You failed utterly! You weren't able to gain Vagiaedelt. Your position is tenuous at best—another incompetent, small-minded devil serving nothing but its own designs."

A woman's voice came in answer, clearly of Kovalunth high birth. "Do you not recognize the flesh I wear, Shepherd?" She sounded indignant now—affronted, and somehow petty. "I am become Eliška of Haluzfeld! I am enough, for now, until Edmund has been brought to heel! Now be gone! You are of no use to our plans. I demand that you depart this place at once, in the name of Nawen of Vápntagh!"

"Yesss, I'm certain you *do*! Well, T'lendak, fortunately, I answer to only one creature by need and due. Any others must earn my respect themselves, and the Storm Queen hasn't managed to do so in *centuries*. Now ... I suggest you tend to your men before they're overrun."

Eliška met this derision with a throat full of disdainful laughter. "Shepherd, my men have this matter well in hand. We've nothing to fear from Count Edmund's meager defenders, I assure you."

Ebistian sounded as if he were absolutely delighted as he made his reply.

"No, you're *quite* right. You've nothing to fear from Edmund's men... alone. Rikten? Order the attack, please?"

"Yes, Shepherd," came the reply.

"What?! No!" The woman's horrified tones were almost comical to hear.

The man, apparently called Rikten, overrode her, a smug and altogether satisfied note in his voice. "Cut the heathens down! Charge! Charge! Charge!"

Ebistian simply laughed as the horses and most of the footmen charged away toward the encampment.

There won't be a better time... Lashjuk made ready to move.

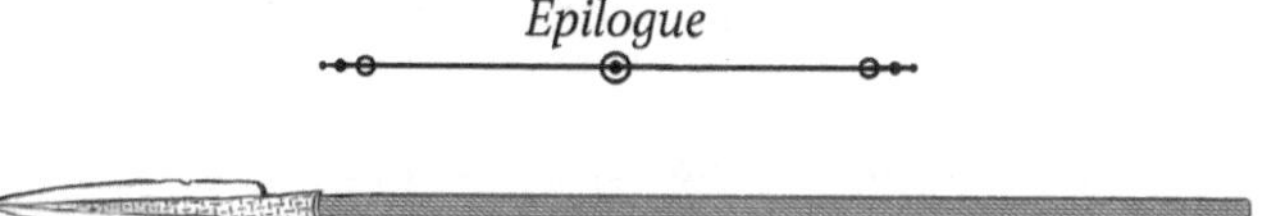

-II-

Venzene Duchy of Kovalun
County Jižní Pochod
Barony of Rosefort
5 Korunasykli: 22 Days after the Red Storm at Westsong

"Do you know their names?" Eobum heard Sulok break the protracted silence, no longer willing simply to crouch there in wonder, staring at the three small army encampments that lay smoking in the twilit valley below. After a moment during which only the wind spoke, he amended, "Or would it be better to ask do you know who they fight for?"

For a long moment, neither of the two men crouched beside him spoke. Just before the silence became fearful, Aderano, at last, spoke up on his left.

"Not I." He leaned back, looking past Sulok to where Eranoric sat. "If you don't, Eobum'll likely have it."

Eranoric grinned thinly. "I don't, and I'd bet you're right."

"It doesn't matter," Sulok said with a touch of sourness.

Eobum winced from the tree line behind the trio. He'd made no noise on his approach, hoping to catch a glimpse of how the younger pair were truly holding up. Sulok's reaction had, unfortunately, been a sting he'd expected.

Aderano put a hand on the boy's shoulder. "Little brother," said he. "There's enough misery n'anger to go 'round. They're both 'ungry beasts, those two. No sense feeding 'em. Otherwise, they'll just keep hanging 'round, getting underfoot..." He raised his dark eyebrows, face betraying a tight smile as he reached his other hand down to grab at Sulok's belly. "They'll start chewing and clawin' at you..." He tickled the boy, albeit briefly. Loud laughter was the last thing they needed, though discord in the unit was nearly as deadly.

Sulok fought against the smile that bullied its way onto his face. He fell back on his rump as he tried to get away from the tickling hand.

That was enough for Aderano. He ceased his efforts, for now at any rate.

"Well?" Eranoric spoke up, sounding mildly impatient.

"Well what?" Aderano and Sulok asked together.

"Not talkin' to you two."

"I know two of them." Eobum resisted the urge to sigh as he spoke up from the darkness behind them. "On the left—the golden stallion on the green field? That's the Percoy banner—Caros and Kastan's household. The three scarlet chevrons with the diving hawk? The white banner, I mean. That's the house of Červenávýška—iron miners. They never seem to run low on luck—their mines never seem to run dry." He paused, stepping forward, at last, to squint down into the valley in earnest, then shook his head. "No. That third banner I've not seen before. Not as proper heraldry, I mean."

"But you've seen it on, what, *improper* heraldry?"

Both Aderano and Sulok snorted at this, the latter briefly letting loose with an actual giggle.

"Something like that. Looks like a noble's banner, right enough, but the chop on it looks... Eodenth."

"Chop?" Sulok sounded as if he hadn't wanted to ask the question, but his curiosity had beaten out his anger.

"The fancy folk call it a *device*," said Aderano. "Just a puffed up waya sayin the thing on a banner or shield—the heraldry."

In this case, the chop was a rampant horse with spears pointing away from it to the north, south, east, and west—all in red—on a field of gold.

Eranoric made a grunt of surprise. "It's... how's it run again? Gar-ee-maned something? The spearman that guards the horses?"

Eobum gave a brief smile. "Getting better," he mused. "Garemand Vani Eosh."

"Gar, what?" Eranoric sounded as if he'd been asked to explain the secrets of how Aldhelm made his stew... to someone who didn't know what fire was. Like so many of his brothers in the unit, Eranoric knew very little of the Eodenth tongue outside of the few line commands Eobum had taught them.

"Garr-eh-mund Vah-nee Yo-sh." Eobum took pains to enunciate slowly. "The spearman who guards the herd—the horses."

"Who's that? Just a shepherd for horses?" Sulok sounded disappointed.

"In the long supposed-dark before Venzene rule, he was either the first or among the first Eodenth gods. Most Eodenth live and die by their horses."

"But not us?"

Eobum arched a brow at Sulok's use of the word *us* but answered nonetheless. "We're scouts. Stealth is our best weapon. We need to know things more than we need to frighten or kill them."

"Aye, my lord," Eranoric put in. "And it's harder than Aderano's head to get a horse to be stealthy. They stomp when they like, whicker when they please, and flick their tails and manes whenever the mood strikes 'em. Hells, even their stench is loud."

Sulok managed another grin at this, but his mood was clearly darkening as the topic lost its hold over him.

"Aderano, go see if Alusc's got supper ready."

Blinking at Eobum, he nodded and rose to do as told.

"We need to speak, Sulok."

"Aye," the boy said, standing and making as if to leave. He stopped when Eobum put a hand on his shoulder.

"You and I, not Eranoric and I."

"...I don't want to speak with you, Ng. I'll do as you say, but..."

Eranoric started at that, beginning to stand.

Eobum forestalled him with a brief shake of the head, then crouched down so he could look Sulok in the eye. "If you'll do as I say, then you'll stay to speak with me."

Sulok glared, then bowed his head. "All right." His head snapped up as he heard the scraping sound of a knife being pulled swiftly from its sheath. His eyes were large and panicky as he saw the blade in Eobum's outstretched hand ... pointed toward its owner.

"You blame me," Eobum said.

"No... yes! Of course I do!" He kept his voice low, hissing and spitting the words, rather than shouting them. "She trusted you! Maksu trusted you! You were supposed to help us, to give us a place to be safe—instead, you tried to take my mother, take my brother as your own!" He was shaking, breathing as if he'd sprinted over rocky ground. "Now she's gone, Maksu's gone... now I'm the only one ... left." He bowed his head, sobbing silently.

Eobum made the knife disappear, bowing his own head. He tried to pull the boy in, in an effort to comfort him. Comfort was so clearly what he needed.

Sulok resisted, finally going so far as to shove Eobum—which really only succeeded in shoving himself back from the man.

"Sulok..."

"No! I hate you! I wish we'd never met you! I wish you were the one my Og'd killed!" Sulok's rage came out in a scratched series of wounded sobs.

Eranoric stood, face cloudy with misery, anger, and frustration.

"Here, then…" Eobum's voice was raw and hollow. He produced the knife once more, offering it to Sulok hilt first.

"I don't *want* a gift, damn you… I want my *life* back."

Eobum shook his head, face grey. "I can't give you that. I can only either give you a new one…" He snatched up Sulok's bright hand and forced the knife's handle into it, pulling it toward his own throat. "…Or I can give you mine." He stopped short of actually touching his flesh with the blade, releasing Sulok's wrist. Eobum's gaze was enough to hold the boy to the spot.

"Wh—what?"

Eranoric spoke, keeping his voice soft. "Sulok, he's offering you a chance at revenge for what you feel he's done."

Eobum readied himself. He doubted the boy would kill him, but there was a chance. More than likely, however, he would cut him, draw blood, and cry off. A dangerous gambit, but a necessary one. *He has to see—to know that he isn't alone and that none of this is his fault. If he blames me, then he needs—deserves the right to hold me to account.*

Sulok stood there, looking into Eobum's wise eyes. Twice he stiffened his arm as if about to stab forward, but both times he subsided. Finally, he dropped the knife, sneering. "You knew I wouldn't do it—knew I was too afraid, too weak to." The voice this was carried on was too black for any child to be forced to listen to, let alone use.

"Is *that* what you think? What you believe *I* think?" Eobum bowed his head, then looked at Sulok a final time. "Gi awka glem… you've proven to be stronger than anyone could've hoped for. To have come through all you've seen and stand here now? When a good many men would be curled up in a corner over *half* of what you've been forced to see?" He shook his head. It didn't matter. How he felt didn't matter. Eobum was the author of all because Eobum was the easiest target—the simplest face to ascribe to the relentless foe that was fate. He drew in a breath, steeled himself, and did what he thought was best, despite the circumstances. "Eranoric?"

"Eobum?"

"You love him? You've claimed him?"

"I do, and I have. He's as much mine as I can make him."

Sulok's eyes went wide, his jaw clenched.

"You'd teach and train him, protect him from harm, take up his causes, fight with and for him when the need arises, and the foe's too great?"

Eranoric nodded solemnly. "Aye and aye, if he'd have me."

Eobum plucked up his knife and replaced it in its sheath before returning his attention to Sulok. "Will you, Sulok? Will you join Eranoric's line and family?"

Sulok's chin quivered. He mouthed two words in response, though no sound came out. "Bruu. Yes."

Eobum nodded, bowing his head, and replaced his hands on the boy's shoulders. This time he met no resistance. "When we find your mother and brother, it will be her part to say aye or nye to it. In her stead, however, and at least until she's here to speak on the matter, I say it's so. You're one of us now and stand as the newest among Eranoric's line. That makes you a part of my line, for Eranoric's my brother as sure as any man living."

Sulok nodded, too full of emotion to speak. He was smiling, weeping, and shaking all at a go.

Eobum turned the boy bodily and gave him a gentle shove into his new captain's arms. As the pair embraced, Eobum stood, met Eranoric's eyes, and nodded before he silently slipped away.

It's like losing her all over again, he thought as he approached their low fire. *Still, it's best. Sulok was pulled to him from that first day's travel together. Now he has a right and proper place among us, and Eranoric has a second son—one that, hopefully, won't be stolen from him this time.*

He approached the ring of logs and stones that served to ring their tiny fire. The night would be reasonably warm, given the heavy clouds overhead, but a touch of fire was good for the mind and heart, not just the body.

He sat down with his back against a large ashwood log and closed his eyes. Three small forces camped below—maybe 'hundred and fifty men, all told? That hardly mattered. They could have been fifty or five thousands, and it would have made little difference to them. They'd no intention of engaging any force they didn't have to.

Alusc knelt to his left, Aderano sat atop a log on the fire's other side. Both men were looking at him furtively, then at one another.

"Your captain'll want a word with you both." Eobum nodded back over his left shoulder toward the place from whence he'd come.

Aderano nodded, standing, but Alusc held him back with a glance before turning to address Eobum. "Didn't mean a word. You have to know he didn't."

Eobum bobbed his head in a distinctly Adric-like nod. "Let it be their news," said he.

Alusc looked at him with more than a touch of concern but nodded, gesturing to the meal he'd prepared as he stood to go. A dry stew, by the smell of it—meats, mushrooms, peppers, and a thin layer of východní cheese to bind it, all heated on a cook-pan, portion by portion, and dropped into a bowl. The entire affair took only a few minutes once the lot of it had been cut up. Together with Aldhelm's seemingly endless supply of spices, Eobum had never met with one that didn't count as delicious and altogether satisfying.

He waved them off. He'd eat soon enough. "We'll reach the baronial keep before noon," he whispered to himself once they'd gone.

"Will we find them there, do you think?" Lakkrid's voice heralded his arrival as he moved to sit next to his father. He leaned in, feet out at an angle. "Or do you think they wound up back home?" Eobum sighed as he draped his arm around his son's shoulders. "I think we can afford to hope."

"Hope's free, they say."

Lakkrid sighed, nodding. "Hope doesn't hunt *for* you, though."

That had been one of Eobum's earliest lessons, not only to his son but to the others as they joined his ranks. "No." He hauled a smile into position on his face. "No, it does not, but it does do something else."

"What's that?"

"Hope gets you up in the morning. It drives you on, even when giving over and crying off tempt you and try to tell you not to bother."

Lakkrid looked up, meeting his eyes.

"What's that look for?" Eobum's smile felt a touch less forced.

"So... hope *does* feed you, then?"

"After a fashion, yes. Hope won't go hunting for you when you're hungry, but it can feed you when everything else around you tastes like poison." Eobum did his best to keep the doubt out of his voice. He didn't think the situation was hopeless, *but* the idea of not seeing Lashjuk again—of never finding Maksu or Kastan, hells, the simple idea of not having a home to go back to was affecting him more than even *he'd* thought possible.

He ran his fingers through his boy's hair, then reached across to grab one of the bowls Alusc had indicated, if only to have something else to concentrate on.

After a moment, Lakkrid uttered a single laugh of triumph. His face wore a grin that did Eobum's heart good.

"What is it?"

"Kastan," said he.

Eobum blinked. "What about her?"

Lakkrid reached to grab the next bowl, then sat back with a relieved—almost contented smile. "If Og and Maksu aren't here in Rosefort, that means they're at home, right?"

"So it seems." Eobum did his best to keep the uncertainty out of his voice.

"Well? Kastan's there! If Og and Kastan find one another, there's not much that could stop them."

Eobum considered, then nodded. "That's true..." He laughed. He kept it low but found he couldn't stop himself. His grin remained even after the sound had faded. He'd found himself surprised—ambushed by hope. As far as ambushes went, he'd certainly lived through worse. The two of them fighting side by side? Yes, he found he could picture that very clearly, and the idea seemed more than just fancy.

Lakkrid giggled before taking a bite of supper. "It *is* true ... even *if* her sword is made of dirt."

Acknowledgements

There are many, many people without whom I could not have written and released this book, all of the books that will follow in The Cycle of Bones and future series.

Jim Trice, Dawn Hart, David Shepherd, Knut Martin Fjelldal, Diane Worden, Ed & Scott Abbot, Sean Dorosinski, Nicholas Ranch, and Jancie Johnson Ter Louw, you made up the foundation upon which I stood. Without your love and support, this book would never have come to pass.

My Beta readers on this project Sean Lewis, Laura Simmons, Doug Miller, Terry Mosterller, and, of course, my editorial staff Joe Mistretta, Laura Simmons, and Gwen Hernandez; your individual and collective help was (as always) invaluable and insightful.

Christopher Murillo—my sound designer and mix-engineer extrordinaire, for your work on the various soundtracks for these books, as well as the "Scions of Skolf" animated series. You know all the things I don't when it comes to audio engineering. I learn something new every time we work on a project. For that, your patience, and your endless enthusiasm, I'll always be grateful.

Simon Vance—the narrator for the *Dawn of Unions*, and the literal embodiment of the voices in my head, at least for Thorion County; you most assuredly did *not* have to offer me your services. I cannot thank you enough. I've learned so much from you. I'll do my level best to carry those lessons over to this and all future works.

Jeff Brown—the man responsible for bringing the faces and places in my head to startling and stunning life; my only complaint is having to wait until the next book is ready for art before I get to work with you again.

My Research team Krista "Brekke" Capps, Thomas Mitchell, Heather Little, Dave Scheidecker, Sayf al-Dawla bin-Arslan al-Rumi, and my translators Knut Martin Fjelldal (Norwegian,) Ben Beyeresdorf (German,) Inga (Polish), Ags—Baroness of Baked Goods (Polish and

Arabic,) Janshuro (Czech), and Lucy (Czech,) thank you for putting up with my endless questions and clarifications.

To my Hastati Gard—it was an honor and one of the great joys of my life to train, stand, and fight at your side. Protego Regnum.

A special and enormous thank you to my Patrons on Patreon. Your love and support make all of this madness possible in more ways than just the obvious financial one.

Lastly, a thank you to Corwyn's Cadre. You've been with me for years as I recorded and toured, fought, and foundered, and you've proven not just willing but excited to walk down this new road at my side. You continue to humble me. I hope to always make you proud.

Thanks for all the Electricity,
JP Corwyn

Book Club Questions

1. We follow several points of view as we begin to see the wider world and how it begins to contend with events similar to what happened at Westsong. Which, in your opinion, would you consider the "main" character or point of view?

2. Edmund and Eobum have very different views on Edmund's plan to effectively seal off Eoden (or Eoalun, if you prefer the Venzene Empire's name for it). Edmund thinks it's more important to save those inside Eoden's borders. Eobum fears reprisals for those "from" Eoden but living elsewhere in the Empire. Where do you stand on the issue?

3. When did you realize that Geroslaw was Azhferd's half-brother and Hengrek's bastard son?

4. Kaith told Terrek that he took no insult from his fight with Ricgerd. Is he a fool/too forgiving, or do you agree with his assessment?

5. Do you feel that Eobum should have given into his baser instincts and slept with Lashjuk?

6. Do you think Yeidil's suspicion of her mother was justified?

7. Do you think Yeidil's bitten off more than she can chew by taking Kozioł as a secret apprentice?

8. Do you think Syr Borys is right to be angry at "whoever" has begun teaching Kozioł?

9. It seems as if Yeidil, Calpernia, and Borys are all mistrustful of one another's motivations, or at least unwilling to tell one another their entire truths. Do you believe one of them is playing the others false? If so, which one? If not, why not?

10. Do you believe that Lord Alojz was being honest with Eobum? Or was he just trying to manipulate events to get the unit on side with his larger plans?

11. Is Gordan right to be angry that he and his squire brothers are being forced to remain in Eastshadow under Barnic? Or is he being short-sighted?

12. Did Jastrab overreact when he killed Steffan's two subordinates? Should he have let Edmund hang them instead?

13. Should Fenglem have faced any punishment for killing members of the Bluemark Guard?

14. Do you feel that Hadwald was making too much of the pressure when speaking with Azhferd that night at Auburg? Or was he right to feel real fear that he'd fail everyone?

15. Were you surprised when Azhferd was called to the line? He certainly was!

16. Was Kaith too soft on Vilmocz when they were riding toward, or even into Wick? Was Terrek?

17. What do you suppose Jastar's "commission" is? What's he being sent to do?

18. Sir Dorean and Sir Giles, it seems, are looking to hire mercenaries to take back to County Thorion—or so Dorean tells Azhferd and Geroslaw. What do you think they mean to do with a company of mercenaries?

19. What do you think Kastan's conflict with her father stems from? (Hint: the truth is in Eobum and Lashjuk's argument on the balcony).

ABOUT THE AUTHOR

What do you see when you close your eyes? Does your mind conjure more than just images? For JP Corwyn, that sense of the click-click-clicking of the world goes far beyond just the visual. Legally blind from birth, Corwyn has made a career out of connecting the words and worlds in his head with the hearts and minds of those around him.

With four studio albums under his belt, Corwyn has graced stages from Florida to New York, west to Mississippi, and abroad.

JP's harbored a dark, secret obsession throughout his musical career. He's spent years building fantasy worlds—entire universes for later use in his other driving force—writing fiction.

"For me, it's more like archeology than creation," Corwyn says. After spending 20+ years unearthing the cultures, languages, histories—all the things that bring a world and its people to life—it was time to embark on his epic fantasy series The Cycle of Bones.

When he's not writing prose, you can usually find Corwyn on stage or in the studio. He's always working on something new, but you might catch him at a coffee shop, a game store, or even a medieval fair.

Find out more about JP
Linktree-
https//linktr.ee/jpcorwyn

Discover more at
4HorsemenPublications.com

10% off using HORSEMEN10